Love Under Fire

Love Under Fire: Second Chance Seduction

JANE GODMAN

CAROL ERICSON

DEBORAH FLETCHER MELLO

MILLS & BOON

First Published in Great Britain 2022
By Mills & Boon, an imprint of HarperCollins*Publishers,* Ltd
1 London Bridge Street, London, SE1 9GF

www.harpercollins.co.uk

HarperCollins*Publishers*
1st Floor, Watermarque Building,
Ringsend Road, Dublin 4, Ireland

LOVE UNDER FIRE: SECOND CHANCE SEDUCTION © 2022 Harlequin Books S.A.

Secret Baby, Second Chance © 2018 Amanda Anders
Sudden Second Chance © 2016 Carol Ericson
Reunited by the Badge © 2019 Deborah Fletcher Mello

ISBN: 978-0-263-30439-8

MIX
Paper from
responsible sources
FSC™ C007454

This book is produced from independently certified FSC™ paper to ensure responsible forest management.

For more information visit: www.harpercollins.co.uk/green

Printed and Bound in Spain using 100% Renewable electricity at CPI Black Print, Barcelona

SECRET BABY, SECOND CHANCE

JANE GODMAN

This book is dedicated to my wider family circle (you know who you are!). They are always there to support me. Thank you!

Chapter 1

"We've found Beth Wade."

Vincente Delaney had been waiting to hear those words for the last twelve months. Waiting and dreading. Now they had finally been spoken, it was as if his mind wasn't sure how to process them and his emotions didn't know how to react. He'd imagined that, as soon as he was told, he would be torn apart by anger and pain. Instead, all he felt was a curious detachment, as though he was viewing the scene as an outsider.

"Why wasn't her body with those of the other women Grant Becker murdered?"

He was pleased to find his voice sounded normal. That he could ask the question without crumbling. He supposed it was because there had been plenty of time to prepare for this moment. Twelve months ago, the police had told him that Beth fitted the profile of those killed by the murderer known as the Red Rose Killer and she was likely to have been one of his victims. Ever since then, this situation had been at the back of his mind. He hadn't thought about it every minute of every day. Not quite that often.

Of course, it had been made worse because the man responsible for the deaths of all those women had been someone Vincente had known most of his life. Grant Becker had been his brother Cameron's best friend. Vincente and Grant had gone hunting and drinking together. To learn that Grant, the sheriff of West County, was not only a serial killer, but that he could have been responsible for killing Beth… Vincente shook his head. He still struggled to come to grips with the reality of what had happened in his hometown. Grant was dead now, but the legacy of his crimes had rocked the city of Stillwater, Wyoming, to its core.

"Oh, dear Lord, Vincente. I'm so sorry. That came out all wrong." Laurie, Cameron's wife, was a detective in the Stillwater police. She moved swiftly across the room to place her hand on his arm. "Beth isn't dead. What I came here to tell you was that we've finally found out where she's been living since she left Stillwater."

The emotion did kick in then, so hard and fast he felt light-headed with it. Relief hit him first. *She's not dead!* The long, anguished months of picturing her murder, of wondering if there was anything he could have done to save her, of thinking about all the might-have-beens… And all that time Beth had been alive.

"Where is she?" His initial relief was followed by something colder and harder. Beth was alive. Questions began to form. Dozens of them. Why had she left? And why so suddenly? What was her life like now? Was she single? Married? In a relationship? Why did those things matter? She had walked out on him without an explanation. If not in the middle of the night, near enough. It wasn't the action of someone who wanted to be with him. Nevertheless, she owed him some explanations.

Laurie shook her head regretfully. "I can't tell you that. If someone disappears the way Beth did, they do it for a reason. They don't do it because they want to be found. We have to respect her privacy." She gathered up her jacket and keys. "I wanted to come and tell you as soon as I found out because I knew what it would mean to you to know that she's alive. I'll be going to see her to question her about the Grant Becker case in the next few days. I'll let you know how she is, but that's all I can do."

Vincente didn't reply. Instead, he watched Laurie go, his body tense and his emotions raging. Beth didn't want to be found. He'd got that message loud and clear sixteen months ago when he tried searching for her. At that time, it looked like Beth had walked out of Stillwater without a backward glance. The clients in the legal practice where she worked as a lawyer had been less than happy at her departure. Her boss didn't have a clue where she'd gone. The landlord of the neat little house she'd rented out on the lake road had been bemused. She'd left most of her belongings and had paid her rent for the next quarter. When Vincente spoke to her friends they appeared genuinely bewildered…either that, or they were putting on a good performance for his benefit.

Then, four months after he had last seen her, the devastating news had emerged that Beth could have been one of Grant Becker's victims. She had the same physical characteristics as the other women Grant had murdered. Beth had dark, wavy hair, blue eyes and the sort of smile that could knock a man sideways. Her looks made her the ideal candidate to attract attention from Grant, to get his token gift of red roses...and then be brutally murdered by him.

Vincente thought back to the last time he had seen her, seeking new clues to her disappearance in light of Laurie's visit today. Beth had turned up at his apartment after more or less ignoring him for a month. The silent treatment had followed one of their fiery clashes. Theirs had always been a stormy relationship, filled with wild fights, frequent breakups and passionate make-ups. Even though sex with Beth had always been explosive, that night had been one to remember. She had barely crossed the doorstep before they were tearing off each other's clothing, dropping T-shirts and jeans on the floor and kicking off boots as they kissed their way to the bedroom.

As he'd tugged her underwear down, his hands had lifted her and her knees gripped his hips. "Why are you here, Beth?" He had managed to gasp the words out as he walked her backward to the bed.

"Because I can't stay away." Her voice had been anguished as she pulled his head down to meet her lips. "No matter how hard I try. That's where the danger lies."

Those strange words were the last thing he remembered her saying to him. They had fallen asleep in each other's arms and when Vincente woke, Beth was gone. Although he had searched for her, it was only when he thought she had been killed that he realized how much the loss of her had torn him apart.

The police investigation had been one of the largest West County had ever seen. The search for women, including Beth, who had gone missing within the time-frame of the murders was wide-ranging and ongoing, but Vincente hadn't been able to leave it at that.

Guilt gnawed at him over those missing four months before the police had begun their inquiries. Sure, he had tried to discover where Beth was before Laurie had told him she could be one of Grant's victims, but had he done enough? If he hadn't simply assumed she'd walked out on him, could he have saved her?

Twelve months ago, as Stillwater was being rocked by the news that one of its sons was a serial killer, Vincente had been trying all over again to discover Beth's whereabouts. He had gone over every conversation, every confidence, every contact they'd ever had, searching for a clue. He'd even driven around the highways of West County late at night, hoping to catch a glimpse of her.

Even though his head had told him repeatedly to prepare for the worst, his heart had insisted on keeping a tiny flare of hope alight.

Now he knew she was alive and he was supposed to leave it at that? His lips tightened and his jaw clenched.

I don't think so.

Beth Wade stared at the stack of papers in front of her with a mingled feeling of tiredness and despair. The deadline to have this paperwork completed was looming, but she'd hardly slept and her brain was refusing to cooperate. She thought briefly of her old job at E. Powell Law in Stillwater. Back then she'd have flown through a routine task like this...

Those days were gone. This was Casper, not Stillwater. She was no longer a rising star in a prestigious law firm, dealing with clients and grappling with difficult cases. She worked from home for an hourly rate and, if she didn't get started, she wouldn't get paid.

The knock on the door shook her out of her weariness. Twisting her hands together in her lap, she turned her head toward the sound. No one ever knocked on her door…

Cautiously, she rose from the kitchen table and walked silently down the hall. Maybe she could ignore it? Whoever it was would assume she was out and go away.

"Ms. Wade? My name is Laurie Delaney." The voice was pleasant and confident and… *Delaney*? "I'm an officer with the Stillwater Police."

With her mind spinning, Beth opened the door.

Her visitor smiled. "I'm also Vincente Delaney's sister-in-law." She said it as if it wasn't an earth-shattering statement. As if, even though Vincente was always at the back of Beth's mind, hearing his name spoken out loud wouldn't make her go weak at the knees.

Beth waved aside the badge Detective Laurie Delaney held out. "I'm not questioning that you are who you say you are. I'm just…"

"Bemused?" Laurie supplied helpfully.

Bemused was an understatement. *Stunned* would be a more accurate summary of how Beth was feeling. The woman standing on her doorstep was a police officer, and she was Vincente's sister-in-law. That was a hell of a chunk of information to assimilate on any day. Midmorning on a Monday, after a sleepless night? It was taking a while to process the information. Realizing they were still standing by the open door, she gestured for Laurie to come into the house.

She had known when she left Stillwater that she

would miss Vincente, but she had never anticipated the depth of her longing for him. The feeling of loss was like a shard of glass lodged permanently in her heart. Even so, she couldn't succumb to her desire to ask Laurie questions about him. Just hearing his name had intensified her craving for him, ratcheting the ever-present pain up to a level where it was almost unbearable.

Beth hadn't left Stillwater to get away from Vincente. She had left because her life was in danger, and, if she'd stayed, she'd risk exposing him to the same harm. The anonymous person who was threatening her had made that clear.

No police. Whoever had sent the photographs and newspaper reports had included that chilling warning in the accompanying letter. But Laurie wasn't here because Beth had contacted her. And no matter how scared she might be of that letter writer, Beth could hardly slam the door in a police officer's face.

Once they were inside the narrow hall, a furry black-and-white shape trundled up to them, almost knocking Laurie off her feet. Beth hauled the wriggling, tail-wagging figure away from her visitor. "Sorry. He still hasn't got the message that he's meant to be a guard dog."

Laurie, who was clearly used to dogs, squatted and clicked her fingers. "He's beautiful. What's his name?"

Beth rolled her eyes. "Melon. He's a border collie. His previous owner named him. He thought it was funny."

"Sorry. I don't get it." Laurie looked confused.

"Melon-collie. Melancholy. They sound alike. It's meant to be a joke." Beth rolled her eyes. "I always have to explain it."

Laurie laughed. "I get it now. Melancholy? He doesn't suit his name."

Since Melon was lying on his back, with his tongue lolling as he waved his paws in the air, he seemed to be doing all he could to prove her statement correct.

"Despite appearances, he actually has a very good sense of who he should let into the house and who he should be wary of. He was trained as a search and rescue dog, but he injured his paw and needed some time out of action. When he was well again, his owner had a new K-9 partner. Luckily, it was around the time I was looking for a guard dog," Beth said. "I decided I needed one, since I'm living on my own with—" she bit her lip, annoyed at the near slipup "—no one else around."

"You can never be too careful," Laurie agreed.

Leading Laurie through to the kitchen at the rear of the house, Beth let Melon out into the yard before holding up the coffeepot. "I was just about to take a break from work."

It wasn't true, of course. Although the kitchen table was littered with papers and her laptop was still open, to say that she had been working would be stretching a point. She had been trying to get her brain in gear before she began to review the client evidence she had been sent.

If she was honest, she might have also been indulging in her regular pastime of daydreaming about Vincente. About what life might have been like if only she hadn't had to leave. About how she was ever going to get rid of the gnawing, yearning ache that came with the knowledge that she would never see or hear from him again.

Laurie didn't need to know the details of her daily struggle. And caffeine might be what Beth needed to help wake her sluggish brain cells.

"Coffee would be good." Laurie took a seat at the table.

"Did Vincente send you?" Even as she asked the question, Beth realized how foolish it was. If Vincente knew where she was, he would never send someone else in his place. He would be here himself, filling this room with his presence. With his dangerous masculinity. The thought sent a thrill of remembered longing down her spine.

"Vincente has no idea I'm here. And I won't tell him where you live." Laurie's tone was reassuring, the words confirming what Beth had just been thinking. "This is actually an official visit, but it's nothing to be concerned about."

Beth carried the coffee over to the table and took a seat opposite Laurie. "Now I'm intrigued."

"It's an intriguing story, and not a pleasant one. You may have heard about it if you've been following the news from Stillwater. Have you heard of the Red Rose Killer?"

"Goodness, yes." Beth had hardly been able to believe what she had been hearing when she had visited the grocery store and overheard a conversation about what had been happening in her hometown. Although Stillwater was a three-hour drive from Casper, the story of the murders had been gruesome and newsworthy. "I don't know all the details, but I knew Grant Becker. Was it true? I couldn't believe it when I heard someone saying he was responsible for killing all those women."

Laurie's expression was grave as she nodded. "I was a newcomer in Stillwater at the time, but I know how it rocked the whole community. I was working undercover on another job when I found out that Carla Bryan, who everyone thought had died in an accident, had actually been murdered. Carla was my cousin. Once I started investigating, it turned out that Grant had killed at least six other women who had the same physical characteristics as Carla. We're saying at least six because the investigation is still ongoing." She took a sip of her coffee. "It's the reason I'm here."

Startled, Beth raised her brows. "It is?"

"You left Stillwater very abruptly, and you have the same physical features as the women Grant Becker killed," Laurie said. "Dark hair, blue eyes, clear skin, slim figure, nice smile." She ticked the characteristics off on her fingers. "This was a huge investigation involving the FBI and the Stillwater Police Department. We couldn't rule out the possibility that you might have been one of Grant Becker's victims."

Beth took a moment to let that information sink in. "So you've been looking for me all this time?"

Laurie nodded. "Almost twelve months. When we didn't find your body with the others, we put out an alert asking you to come forward."

"I didn't see anything." Beth bit her lip. "I don't have much time for TV or newspapers." In a way, it was better that she hadn't known the police were looking for her. Knowing would have been a dilemma of epic proportions. How could she have ignored that? Yet, at the same time, how could she have responded to it? "How did you find me?"

"Even though you've been using an alias, your boss saw your picture in our newspaper advertisement and phoned in."

And there you have it. It was that easy. If the police could find her that way, anyone else could. Vincente

could. Worst of all, *he* could find her. She always thought
of the person who sent the letter and photographs as a
"he", but it could just as easily be a woman.

Her thoughts must have shown on her face because
she became aware of Laurie watching her with concern. Leaning across the table, the other woman clasped
Beth's hand. "This is really not a big deal. Now that we
know you are alive, I can cross you off our list of possible victims. I just came out here today to ask you a few
questions. I hope that's okay. I certainly didn't want to
worry you."

Beth forced her features into a smile. It would be
very easy to confide in this woman. To go upstairs and
get that envelope, lay everything on the table and tell
her the whole story. That way she could hand over her
cares to someone else. But she didn't have that luxury.

It's not just my own safety that's at stake here.

"Ask away."

The searching look in Laurie's eyes was still there as
she flipped open her notepad. "I need to know whether
you left Stillwater to get away from Grant Becker."

Beth shook her head. "Apart from the fact that Grant
was friends with Vincente, he and I barely knew each
other."

"So why did you leave Stillwater so suddenly?" Laurie asked.

At that moment—and with monumentally bad timing—a soft, demanding cry crackled over the baby monitor.

Vincente parked his car in a side street at right angles to the little house. From this vantage point, he could
watch the front door without being too obvious.

Following Laurie around for the last three days had not been easy. Pursuing a seasoned detective in the small town where everyone knew them both? He had set himself an almost impossible task. But Laurie had said she would be questioning Beth about the Grant Becker case in the next few days. She had specifically said she would be "going to see" Beth. Vincente figured that, sooner or later, Laurie would lead him to Beth.

He decided the only way to check on his sister-in-law's whereabouts was to make it look like, by some fluke, they kept bumping into each other. At the end of the second day, Laurie was joking that she'd seen more of her brother-in-law lately than she had of her husband.

Chasing around town, getting in Laurie's way had played hell with Vincente's work schedule. His younger brother, Bryce, who ran Delaney Transportation with him, had sent him an increasingly frantic series of messages demanding to know why he had abandoned his office. Unable to explain that he was stalking Laurie, Vincente had feigned illness.

"You're never ill." Bryce managed to make the statement sound like an accusation.

"First time for everything." Vincente had done his best to sound feeble.

"Steffi was hoping you'd come over for dinner tonight. Cameron and Laurie will be there." Knowing how much Vincente enjoyed evenings spent around the table in his brother's rambling, comfortable home, Bryce had clearly decided to try another approach. Since his recent and blissfully happy marriage, Bryce enjoyed gathering the family together while his wife, Steffi, regaled them with stories of the animal sanctuary she was establishing. They had come a long way from the days when

Bryce had been the local stud, and Steffi was a famous Hollywood actress.

"Maybe next week when I've shaken off this flu." Vincente had turned down the invitation with real regret.

His stalking tactics had proved frustratingly unsuccessful. Until today. Today, his patience, or thinly disguised impatience, had finally paid off. Laurie had left home at her usual time this morning, but instead of going into town and making her way to the police headquarters, she had headed south.

After an hour of following her at a discreet distance, Vincente had gained an inkling about her destination. Beth's parents were dead, and she'd lost touch with most family members over the years. But he remembered that she spoke about friends of her parents who lived nearby in Casper whom she had visited now and then as a child. Although they weren't relatives, she had called them her aunt and uncle and always regretted losing touch with them. Vincente had forgotten all about them back when he had been searching for her, but he supposed it was possible that, when she left Stillwater, she'd gone to a town she knew. He became increasingly convinced he was right. The police wouldn't have known about the connection because the people he was thinking of weren't Beth's family.

Knowing Laurie would recognize his car, Vincente had rented a nondescript black sedan. Subterfuge really wasn't his style, but he was determined to find Beth and ask her the questions that refused to go away. Even in his rental car, he had stayed well behind Laurie. He had a healthy respect for his sister-in-law's powers of observation. The woman who had tracked down the Red

Rose Killer was more than capable of recognizing that she was being followed.

Once he was convinced he knew where she was going, Vincente had overtaken her on the freeway. Pulling in at a gas station on the outskirts of Casper, he had waited, hoping his hunch was correct. When Laurie's car came into view, he had released a long sigh of relief. If he'd been wrong, he wasn't sure what his next move would have been. All he knew for sure was that giving up wasn't an option.

Keeping his distance once more, he had followed Laurie to this quiet neighborhood in Casper. She had pulled up outside a house that was set back slightly from the street. Although he hadn't been able to see too much, he had watched as the door was opened and Laurie went inside. That had been almost an hour ago, and he was going half-crazy with tension, waiting for the opportunity to *do* something. He had been told more than once, by both of his brothers, that patience was not his best quality.

Finally, he saw a movement over at the house. Tilting the old cowboy hat he'd worn as an additional disguise low over his brow, but peering out from under the brim, he slunk down in his seat. Laurie came out of the house alone. No one accompanied her to the door. There could be any number of reasons why the occupant of the house had chosen not to escort her out. From Vincente's point of view, it was frustrating. Once again, he was denied the opportunity to get a glimpse of who lived there.

As Laurie made her way to her car, Vincente considered his options. Follow her back to Stillwater? Or stay here and find out if this really was Beth's hiding place?

He almost laughed aloud that he was even asking him-self the question.

Once Laurie had driven away, he waited a few min-utes to be sure she really had gone before leaving his car and going across to the house she had left. As he approached, he sized up the building. Nothing about it made him think of Beth. It had a slightly neglected air, as if the owner didn't have the time, energy or money to spend on it. He contrasted that with the Stillwater house she had lived in. That had been as neat as wax. Being organized seemed to come effortlessly to Beth, spilling over into how she dressed, her surroundings and how she dealt with other people. Vincente wondered, not for the first time, if the reason she had struggled with their relationship was because she couldn't neatly package up her feelings for him. When they were together there was no controlling what they felt. It had always been raw, primal...and incredible.

The thought spurred his feet up the front step. His heart was pounding so loud it almost drowned out the sound of his knock on the door. Prepared for disappoint-ment, his nerves—already under intense pressure—were ratcheted up to crisis level when he heard a voice call-ing out.

"Did you forget something, Detective?" It wasn't just any voice. It was Beth's voice.

He wondered how she would react if she checked who it was through the peephole in the door. Her words indi-cated she thought Laurie had come back again, and he heard a key turn in the lock immediately after she spoke.

The door swung open and the smile on her lips faded. As she gazed at him in shock, Vincente took a moment to drink in her appearance. Her hair was shorter, just reaching her shoulders now instead of the waist-length mass in which he had loved to bury his hands. It was scraped back into an unflattering ponytail. She looked thinner. And tired, definitely tired. Almost to the point of exhaustion. But maybe the reason for that was sitting on her hip.

The baby wore pink sweatpants and a T-shirt with butterflies embroidered all over. Not quite a toddler, she was a perfect little girl. Her black hair clustered in a halo of curls around her head and she studied Vincente with eyes that were huge, dark and framed by thick, spiky lashes. The hint of olive to her skin and the full ruby lips were additional confirmation of his first suspicion. It was like looking in a mirror.

Vincente almost took a step back in shock as he gazed at his daughter.

Chapter 2

The shock of seeing Vincente on her doorstep robbed Beth of the power to do anything. Thought, speech, movement—those basic functions deserted her just when she needed them most. The only thing she seemed capable of doing with any degree of competence was stare at him. Just stare…and maybe, deep down inside, feel the old longing to throw herself into his arms. But those days were gone. She wasn't that person anymore. She didn't have the luxury of acting on impulse where he was concerned. Where anything was concerned.

"What's her name?" Vincente threw her off balance with the question. *Like I was well-balanced before he asked.*

"Lia." It was surreal. She had pictured seeing him again so many times, but it had never been like this. She had imagined she would be cool and collected. Not that he would take away the ability to think of anything except how wonderful it was to see him again.

"You gave our daughter an Italian name?"

"No, my mother's name was Amelia." Even as she said the words, Beth realized her mistake. Vincente had said "our daughter," and she hadn't denied it. She lifted an impatient shoulder at the thought. Why would she deny it? Lia *was* his daughter. He only had to look at her to know that.

"Can I hold her?" Beth was amazed at the humble note in Vincente's voice. It was something she had never heard before, had never imagined he was capable of.

"She's not great with strangers." She issued the warning just as Lia decided to take matters into her own hands.

Holding her plump little arms up to Vincente, she wriggled her body away from her mother and toward him. Beth was so surprised at this phenomenon that she could only stare in astonishment as she handed Lia over. Vincente gazed into his daughter's big brown eyes with an expression of wonderment. In that instant, something inside Beth's chest lurched.

"Woof," Lia commented solemnly.

"It's her only real word," Beth explained. "She copies the dog."

"Is that good or bad?" Vincente couldn't seem to drag his eyes away from Lia's face. "I don't know anything about these things."

"Well, she's only eleven months, so she makes lots of sounds, but actual words aren't really her thing." For the second time that morning, she became conscious that she was keeping a visitor standing on the doorstep.

But this wasn't just any visitor. It was *Vincente*. "I don't think this is a good idea."

Fire blazed in the dark depths of his eyes. She could see him fighting to keep his anger under control for Lia's sake. When he spoke, his jaw muscles were rigid. "I agree. Finding out I have an eleven-month-old daughter that you didn't have the decency to tell me about is the worst idea I've ever heard of."

Vincente's moods had no gray areas, only extremes, but his anger had never scared Beth. Now, it terrified her. Not because she feared he would hurt her. This was Vincente. She knew he was incapable of doing her any physical harm. It wasn't fear of *him* that had made her flee Stillwater. But his gaze was a knife in her ribs, digging deeper with each passing second. Where once there had been warmth, there was now only contempt.

A fierce longing to tell him the truth swept over her, and she thrust it aside. Annoyance bubbled up in its place, and she hugged that emotion to her. It was typical of Vincente to do it *this* way. To confront her, invade her space, then become judge and jury and deliver his verdict all within the space of a few minutes.

"I've moved on with my life." She tried for a hard tone as she delivered the words. It wasn't true, but she needed to convince Vincente it was.

"Fine." The disdain left his eyes as they moved from Beth's face to Lia's. "Maybe we could continue this inside, since I'm not walking away now I know I have a daughter?"

Inviting him in would make a huge statement. But what would she gain by keeping him standing here? She knew Vincente's stubbornness only too well. When he said he wasn't going anywhere, he meant it. The thunderstorm was coming. Where it took place was irrelevant. She led Vincente into the family room, and he sat on one of the sofas. Lia commenced an exploration of his face, pulling at his neatly trimmed beard and trying to poke him in the eye. Her delighted squeals broke the ice, and Beth found herself smiling at Vincente's efforts to hold on to the squirming little bundle. Conscious of the untidy room, her shirt with its missing button and the stain on the front where Lia had spilled milk that morning at breakfast, Beth made a hurried movement to pick up some of the abandoned toys that littered the floor.

"Why didn't you tell me?" Even though it was the obvious question, it stopped her in her tracks. Since she had no idea where to begin with an answer, the series of increasingly anguished howls that rent the air provided a welcome reprieve.

"What the hell is that?" Vincente looked horrified.

"It's my dog, Melon. He wants to come in." Beth went through to the back of the house and opened the door.

When Melon reached the door of the family room, he paused, his ears flattening and his tail drooping. Beth could almost read the dog's mind. Visitors were a rarity, but Melon was a sociable creature, and, on the whole, he liked them. This one, however, had the audacity to place his hands on Melon's beloved baby. That couldn't be tolerated.

Crouching low, Melon bared his teeth and growled at Vincente. Since aggression toward humans wasn't in his nature, he mitigated the threat by wagging his tail.

"Sit!" Vincente's voice was stern. Beth recalled that he always did have a way with animals.

Melon, clearly realizing the error of his ways, dashed over to him, and attempted to lick his hand. "I said 'sit.'"

To Beth's amazement, Melon sat.

"He doesn't do that for me." She couldn't keep the aggrieved note out of her voice.

"You have to show him who's boss." Vincente snapped his fingers. Melon sidled forward, resting his head on Vincente's knee and gazing up at him with adoring eyes.

Beth took a deep breath. "Look, I'm not trying to avoid this conversation, but I have a huge amount of work to do and the deadline is tomorrow. And I need to get Lia's lunch ready…"

"You look tired." Vincente's eyes probed her face. Although it felt strange to have him here, a comment such as that was oddly comforting. It reminded her how well he knew her. He was the only person who really did. "More than tired. You look done in, Beth."

"You have no idea." She gave a shaky laugh. "Lia is teething, so she's not sleeping too well right now. I'm trying to fit work around her schedule, but since she doesn't really have a schedule—"

"Why don't you get some rest while I look after her?" The blunt words cut across her floundering and the hard look in his eyes had softened slightly, but the tension level between them remained high.

This was classic Vincente. Like a seasoned boxer, he knew how to cause a distraction before delivering the knockout blow. "I thought you wanted to talk?"

There was a razor edge to his smile. "Okay. Go. Tell me why I wasn't even worth a call or a message."

Beth wanted to go to him. To take his face in her hands and tell him how much he meant to her, how much their time together had meant. But although he looked like Vincente, he was a stranger. A hard, cold man who had put up a barrier between them. And she knew that, no matter what she said, it would only push him further behind that barricade.

"There is nothing I can say to make this right."

Even behind the anger, she could see Vincente's pain. In the past, she'd have known how to take the hurt away. This time, she was the cause. The knowledge caused tiny shards of ice to pierce her heart.

"You don't get off that lightly, Beth." She could see his muscles bunched tight beneath his T-shirt as he held his fists clenched. "This isn't like that time you drove my car into the wall and forgot to tell me. Or when I smashed that old china cat."

That was it. Vincente had always known how to get to her. Despite her determination to stay calm, Beth felt anger crashing through her. How dare he bring up past hurts at a time like this?

"You mean the antique figurine my grandmother left me? The one you broke and didn't tell me? The one I found in pieces in the trash?"

"Exactly." There was triumph in his eyes. "This isn't anything so trivial. This is about how we made another person and you didn't even bother to call me."

To her horror, Beth felt tears burn the back of her eyelids. When she tried to speak again, her lips trembled and her voice refused to work. Vincente started to speak again, but she held up a hand.

"No more." The word was little more than a croak and she struggled to get her voice back under control. Pointing to Lia, she shook her head. "Not in front of her." She took a deep breath. "And you're right. I'm tired."

His expression was grim, but she saw a glimmer of understanding in his eyes. "So do what I suggested.

Get some rest." The inflexible note was still there. "Because we are having this conversation, Beth. Whether you want it or not."

Flustered, she tried to hit on a reason to refuse that didn't involve going straight to ordering him out of her house. "She doesn't settle easily with people she doesn't know." Since Lia was curled comfortably into the crook of his arm, that excuse wasn't going to work. "You're not used to children."

"No, I'm not, but you'll only be upstairs. You're dead on your feet, Beth. I'm worried about you." In place of the continuing tempest, the unexpectedly gentle note in his voice shook her equilibrium even further.

She remembered that knack he had of catching her off guard. He was right. She couldn't remember the last time she'd slept for more than an hour or two at a stretch. If she didn't get some rest soon, she would fall down. And what use would she be if she was exhausted? If she didn't meet tomorrow's deadline, she would lose her job. She was already behind with the rent…

The situation was ridiculous. How many times had she pictured meeting Vincente again? Not once had the imaginary conversations she had conducted in her head included him offering to babysit. And behind the concern, she knew—because who knew him better than she did?—that his anger that was still waiting to be unleashed.

"Let me do this, Beth." A persuasive note in his voice, the one she hated because he used it to get her to do just about anything he wanted, made an appearance. "For old times' sake."

"I can't believe you just said that." She rolled her eyes.

He laughed. "Nor can I. The shock must have gone to my head."

"Okay." She had never thought of Vincente Delaney as an angel in disguise—the thought caused her to smile inwardly, since she had occasionally thought of him as a *devil* in disguise—but there had to be a first time for everything.

"All Lia's toys are in the box over there. There is pasta in the fridge for her lunch and she likes banana after it. She'll drink plain water from her own special cup. Oh, and her diapers and wipes are in this bag."

Vincente's calm deserted him slightly at those words. "I can come and get you if we have a diaper situation, right? That's something I'm going to need to do under supervision the first time." First time? The words had a confidence about them that unsettled her.

"Wake me if there's a problem."

She went to the door, turning back to look at him as he bent to talk to Lia. Although seeing Vincente here had tilted her world off course, the effect he was exerting over her pulse was not entirely due to the shock. He always did have the power to knock her sideways with his presence. Even though she had spent a lot of time over the last sixteen months dwelling on her memories of him, she had underestimated his magnetism.

What was she thinking? Every rational thought screamed at her to get him out of here. She had broken all her ties with Stillwater for a reason. A dangerous, life-threatening reason. Leaving had hurt more than she'd believed possible. Leaving Vincente? That had been its own kind of hell. She'd never known if they'd last forever. The longest they'd ever managed was a few months. Not because they didn't care. *We cared too much.* That had always been their problem. Everything between them was too much. Too passionate. Too intense. Too raw. Too hungry. It was like they burned each other up whenever they were together. But Beth had never imagined being with anyone else. Had never imagined her life without Vincente in it, even if it was only in their own, unique, on-off, tempestuous way. Until the letter and the photographs. They had changed everything.

"Get some sleep, Beth." Vincente's dark eyes seemed to read her thoughts. "Then we'll talk some more."

Just this one time, she told herself sternly, *and only because I'm so tired. Then we'll talk some more.*

Those words had an ominous ring to them.

Vincente's mind wanted to dwell on the shock to his system. He was struggling to know what to feel, although anger was making a strong case for being his most powerful emotion. How could Beth keep something like this from him? If Lia was eleven months old, that meant Beth had to have been four months pregnant when she left Stillwater. Vincente thought back to the roller-coaster ride that was their relationship. Yes, four months before Beth left, they'd been right in the middle of one of the most intense "on" times of their on-off periods. Soon after, they'd split up following a fight over something or other. He couldn't recall the reason, but he did remember Beth calling him arrogant and conceited before she slammed out the door.

Anger continued to bubble deep inside him, as hot and destructive as lava. It churned and boiled, desperate for release, and he knew there was a real danger of becoming too much for him to handle. He wanted to find a release. Slam his hand down on a table, kick a door, shout at the person responsible…

Four months and she didn't tell me? She came to my apartment the night she left Stillwater and she didn't mention that she was carrying my child? She left me sleeping and walked out of my life, prepared for me to never know about this person who shares my DNA?

He couldn't reconcile those thoughts with the Beth he knew. They'd always been honest with each other. From the moment they got together that first time they'd known what they had was different. Unique. Mind-blowing. But Beth had always known the truth about Vincente. He couldn't commit to a normal relationship. Hearts, flowers and promises of forever weren't for him. It didn't take much soul-searching to find the reasons why.

Even within his own family, Vincente had always felt like an outsider. The only unpredictable thing his rancher father ever did was fall in love with a beautiful Italian socialite. When Kane Delaney brought Giovanna Alberti home to Stillwater, she had batted her long eye-lashes at him and declared that Wyoming was too boring to be her home. By the time Vincente was born, the marriage was in its death throes.

Even their son's name had been a cause for disagreement. Giovanna had wanted a full-on Italian name, while Kane had held out for something more American. In the end, they had compromised. Instead of the Italian "Vicente" or the American "Vincent," they had named him "Vincente." It was a metaphor for his life. With a foot in each world, he belonged in neither.

The ink was barely dry on the divorce papers before Vincente's mother had reverted to her maiden name and returned to Florence. Although he saw her occasionally, her aristocratic world might as well have been a million miles away from his Stillwater home.

Vincente knew Beth wasn't like his mother. He wasn't naive enough to believe that she would walk out on him and break his heart the way Giovanna had done to Kane. No, he was more afraid that *he* would be the one to hurt *her*. All he knew for sure was, however much he wanted Beth—and Vincente had never wanted anything in his life as much as he'd wanted Beth—there was something missing in his psyche. *Call it the Alberti gene. We don't do long-term.* His mother was on her fifth marriage. He was not going to put Beth through the same sort of torture.

And Beth had understood. She had always accepted him for what he was. Their relationship hadn't been one-sided. It hadn't been about her trying to get a ring on her finger and him resisting. It had always just been them. Doing it their own way.

Of course, a baby would have changed things. How? He couldn't answer that because the knowledge that Lia even existed had only just hit him. Had Beth run out on him because she thought he wouldn't be able to cope with the commitment? A wave of shame washed over him at the thought. She must have known him better than that. Surely, she must. If she thought he would leave her to cope with their child on her own, then she hadn't known him at all.

That brought another emotion to sit alongside the anger. As he looked down at Lia's perfect features, he felt an overwhelming sadness.

He hadn't wanted a child. If anyone had asked him why, he'd have said he'd be the world's worst dad. He

was selfish, impatient, untidy, and he didn't like responsibility. Also, no sleep, no free time, no social life? No,
thank you.

Now, he was in shock as his feelings on the subject
had sharply reversed. Because how could he not want
this beautiful little being? And how much of her life had
he already missed? He hadn't been there when she was
born. Hadn't heard that first cry or seen her first smile.
She was crawling, pulling herself upright and making
noises. Some of them almost sounded like words. She
had a personality all her own...quite a strong one from
what he'd seen so far. *She looks like me. This little person
has been growing up without me.* The mingled feelings
of joy and loss tugged at something deep within him.

Other than telling her Giovanna had left when he was
a baby, he'd never talked to Beth about his mother, but
she must have known there was a twisted branch in the
Delaney family tree. It didn't take much imagination to
work out that Giovanna's abandonment was at the root of
Vincente's issues. The loss of a parent had impacted his
whole life. Yet Beth had repeated the pattern with Lia?

He wanted to storm and rage at Beth for what she'd
done, but he also needed to find out why she'd done it.
This was Beth. Beth, to whom he had been closer than
any other person in his whole life. There had to be a
reason why she had deprived him of almost a year of
his daughter's life. He had to get this right, for all they'd
once been to each other, but also for the innocent child
who was caught up in the middle of this.

The innocent child who was sliding from his knee
with a purposeful glint in her eye. Vincente had never
realized it was possible to move so fast at a crawl. Before he knew it, she had reached a vase of flowers and

toppled it onto the floor. As he stooped to pick them up, she launched herself at the dog, grabbing him by the tail. Melon let out a yowl and ran for the door. That was the moment when Vincente decided it was probably a good idea to postpone the soul-searching and concentrate on the babysitting.

As he watched Lia and tried to keep up with her, some of the negative emotion coursing through him melted away. It was replaced by a new warmth as he felt an immediate connection to his daughter.

She was *his*. As well as the physical similarities, he could see other traits they had in common. When he tried to take something from her, a militant light entered her eye and she thrust out her chin, mirroring his own stubbornness. As he sat with her and tried to help her stack her blocks, she brushed his hand away, determined to try it for herself.

Although he'd been consumed by rage and shock as he'd crossed the threshold of this house, he'd resolved to do his duty. He had a child and he would take care of her. What he hadn't expected was this rush of pure joy he felt every time he looked at her.

Lia might look like him, but her smile was all Beth... or the Beth he'd once known.

He hadn't been exaggerating when he told Beth he was worried about her. Physically, she had barely changed, but there were other differences that became more apparent the longer he was with her. She was wound as tight as a coiled spring, tension apparent in every part of her slender body. The way she held herself taut as though poised for flight, the tilt of her head as if she was listening for a subtle sound and the way those glorious denim-blue eyes refused to settle on one thing.

He had thought at first it was because she was unable to make eye contact with him. Gradually, he realized her gaze was constantly moving, checking her territory, seeking reassurance that everything was normal.

She was exhausted. That had been apparent the moment he set eyes on her. And he had used it to his advantage. By offering to look after Lia while she got some rest, he supposed he had been manipulative, but wasn't he entitled to be devious in the circumstances? He had just come face-to-face with the daughter he didn't know he had. And he hadn't been entirely underhanded. Although, after the initial shock had worn off, his first emotion had been simmering rage, he could sense Beth's turmoil. Offering to look after Lia while she got some rest served a number of purposes. He got the chance to spend precious time with his daughter—*a tiny fraction of the eleven months I've lost*—Beth could recoup some of her strength for what promised to be the ordeal of the conversation they needed to have and Vincente could catch his breath.

He suspected he and Laurie were the only visitors this house had seen in a long time. Lia was immaculately dressed, but, like Beth herself, the house was clean without being exactly cared for. It was far from being a hovel, but her nervousness, together with the way she fussed around, picking up toys and plucking at the stain on her shirt, drew his attention to the details. She was clearly focused on appearances and finding them lacking. What had happened to the happy, sociable woman he'd known in Stillwater? Yes, Beth had a baby now, but would that turn her into a recluse? He didn't know enough about these things. Maybe it would.

But what worried him more than anything was the

feeling he got that all this was about more than being protective of her child. No, it wasn't a feeling. He knew her too well. It was a certainty. Beth was scared. More than scared. She was terrified.

Beth woke abruptly with a rising sense of panic. She was fully dressed, lying on top of the bedclothes. How could she be asleep during the day? What about Lia? Gradually, the events of the morning came back to her and she heaved a sigh of relief. The sensation of contentment soon dissipated when she realized what she had done. *I left Lia with Vincente. Today might be the day I actually took leave of my senses.* She sat up abruptly. After sixteen months in hiding, she had not only opened her door to the man she had decided never to see again, she had blithely handed her daughter over to him.

Our daughter, she reminded herself. Lia would be safe with Vincente; there was no question about that. The problem was, now Vincente knew he had a daughter, there could be no going back. He would want to be involved in her life. That was a conversation that was going to take every ounce of Beth's considerably depleted energy.

Pausing only to run a brush through her hair, drag it back into its ponytail and slip her ballet flats back on, she made her way back down the stairs. When she reached the family room, a scene of total devastation greeted her. Vincente was seated on the floor, half reclining against the sofa. His shirt was pulled out of his jeans and his hair and beard were smeared with something that looked suspiciously like dried banana. Lia was asleep with her head on his shoulder.

"She trashed the place," he whispered. His expression was stunned. "As soon as you left the room, she just went for it."

Every toy Lia owned was scattered across the floor. The wildflowers Beth had picked the day before were shredded into tiny pieces. The vase they had been in lay on its side and water formed a pool on the carpet around it. Cushions and throws had been dragged from the sofas and piled in a heap on the floor. It looked like a whirlwind had been through the room. And it had. Beth knew what Whirlwind Lia at full force could do. Vincente would not have stood a chance.

"I think she wore herself out." Vincente smiled ruefully as he indicated the sleeping figure in his arms.

Although she had only just woken up, Beth felt weariness crowding in on her once more. Stooping, she lifted her slumbering daughter into her arms. "I'll take her upstairs."

As she carried Lia from the room, she was aware of Vincente watching her intently. Once upstairs, she settled the warm, sleeping bundle into her crib, pulling a blanket over her. There was a draft coming through the open window, which she closed before returning to the crib. Bending to kiss Lia's soft cheek, she studied her face for a moment or two. Sleeping or waking, she could watch her forever. Right now, she supposed she should go and get the less attractive task of talking to Vincente over with.

When she reached the den, Vincente had picked up the throws and cushions and placed them back on the sofas. He paused in the act of placing Lia's toys back in their box. "No wonder you look tired."

"Laurie said she wouldn't tell you where I lived."

"She didn't." His expression was half wary, half apologetic. "I followed her without her knowledge." He ran a hand over his face and, feeling the residue of the banana, grimaced. "Is there somewhere I can clean up?"

Beth directed him to the bathroom and went into the kitchen to fix coffee, shaking her head at the normality of the situation. This was *Vincente*. The thought was on a loop inside her head. They didn't do polite conversation. They'd never needed words. The last time she'd seen him, she had kicked his apartment door shut and torn his shirt off. They hadn't exchanged more than a few sentences that night. It had almost killed her to sneak out of his apartment without saying goodbye. She had left his apartment, gotten into the car that was already loaded with her luggage and driven out of Stillwater for good. The ultimate irony had come two weeks later, when she realized that the recurring stomach bug that had been bothering her was actually a four-month pregnancy.

Vincente reappeared with his shirt tucked in and the banana removed. As Beth poured the coffee, she was conscious of those melting dark eyes watching her face. "When were you planning on eating lunch?"

"Don't do this, Vincente." She handed him his coffee and took her own to the table, grimacing as she viewed the paperwork that she still hadn't touched. If she pulled another all-nighter, she might just meet the deadline.

"Do what?" He came to sit opposite her.

"I know these tactics. This is where you soften me up before you go for the kill." She took a deep breath. "I know how angry you are. Just say what you have to say."

He didn't speak for a moment or two and she took in the tight set of his jaw, the glitter in the dark depths of his eyes and the way his clenched fist rested on his muscled thigh. "You think angry comes close to describing what I'm feeling right now? I'm so far beyond that it's not true. But I want to understand why you cheated me out of almost a year of Lia's life. I'm trying to contain my feelings so we can have some sort of rational dialogue for the sake of that little girl upstairs, and because I'm concerned about you—"

"Oh, no." Beth sprang to her feet. "I see where this is going. You think you can walk in here and pull a stunt like that?"

"What the hell are you talking about? What stunt?" Vincente looked up at her, his expression bemused.

"Get some rest, Beth. Let me do this for you, Beth. For old times' sake?" Her voice quivered as she mimicked his concerned tone. "What will you tell the judge when you try to take my daughter away? You turned up here and found I was incapable of looking after her? Depressed? Unstable? An unfit mother?"

Vincente got to his feet, facing her across the width of the table. "Is that what you think?" His voice was harsh. "That I've changed so much I would do that to you?"

"I'm sorry. It's just that losing her…it's my worst nightmare." He didn't know—couldn't know—what she'd been through. The debilitating anxiety and isolation of postpartum depression was something she still found hard to come to terms with, even now she was over the worst of it. At times like this, when she felt under pressure, some of the symptoms resurfaced. She no longer needed medication, but she did occasionally keep in touch with her counselor. Right now, she focused on regulating her breathing. It was one of the techniques she had learned for coping with stress.

"Beth, no matter what I'm feeling, I would never try to take Lia from you."

Beth knew Vincente well enough to sense when she could trust him. He couldn't be trusted to turn up on time to a date. She couldn't trust him to remember birthdays and anniversaries. No matter how many times she told him, trusting him to remember that she hated anchovies on her pizza never worked. But when it came to the big things? She knew he would never lie to her. This was one of those times. There was nothing but truth in those dark eyes.

"I still want an answer to my question. Why did you leave Stillwater without telling me you were pregnant?"

She took her seat again, making an effort to relax the tension in her limbs. Following her lead, Vincente sat down, as well. How could she tell this story without telling him all of it? Vincente wasn't a fool. He was the smartest person she knew. Not only was he the most quick-witted, well-read, articulate person to have made her acquaintance, but he was also the most perceptive. And where Beth was concerned, he was incredibly intuitive. He had always been able to tell when she was lying.

"It wasn't like that." She took a sip of her coffee, buying a little time. "I didn't know I was expecting a baby when I left Stillwater."

"Math is my job, Beth. I've already done the calculations. Lia is eleven months old. That means you must have been four months pregnant when you ran away—" she nodded in confirmation "—yet you didn't know?" His voice said it all. She hadn't been some kid who didn't know her own body. She had been a twenty-seven-year-old attorney with a promising career.

"I had a lot on my mind." God, those words sounded so lame. But it was true. The newspaper report had arrived two months before she left Stillwater. She hadn't known that Lia had already been growing inside her, hadn't noticed the missed periods and the changes in her body. Her whole focus had been on the nagging worry at the back of her mind. The worry that had ratcheted up to a whole new level a month later with the arrival of the letter and the first photograph. By the time the next one turned up in her mailbox a week before she left Stillwater, she had been half-crazy with worry. Any physical symptoms her body had been displaying had come second to the turmoil of her emotions.

Receiving anonymous threats had been bad enough. When those warnings became directed at anyone close to her, she had panicked. Because there was only one person close to her. Whether he liked it or not, Vincente had been the one who meant the most to her. Even though it had broken her heart to leave, even though missing him had been a constant ache ever since, it had seemed like the only way she could protect him.

Now he was here, and she couldn't tell him the truth. *I'll come after the ones you love...* Even the thought of those words made her shiver.

Vincente frowned. Clearly, he wasn't buying her explanation. Beth didn't blame him. She wouldn't herself if she was the one listening to it. *A lot on my mind.* It was a classic fobbing-off phrase. His lips parted in preparation to ask more just as a cry from the baby monitor, for the second time that day, provided an interruption.

This cry was different. This wasn't one of Lia's usual noises. It was a high-pitched scream that brought Beth straight to her feet and had her running for the door.

At the same time, out in the yard, Melon went into a frenzy of barking.

"What is it? What's wrong?" Picking up on her panic, Vincente was right behind her as she dashed up the stairs.

"Someone is in Lia's room."

Chapter 3

Vincente got all the confirmation he needed about Beth's state of mind when she hurtled from the kitchen and charged up the stairs. "Someone is in Lia's room? What the hell do you mean?" How had she reached that conclusion from the noise she had heard Lia make through the baby monitor?

Beth didn't answer. He could hear her breath catching in her throat in a series of gasps as she reached the top of the stairs and burst through a door to her left. To Vincente's relief, Lia was lying on her side in her crib with a pink-and-white blanket pulled up to her chin. Her long lashes shadowed her cheeks and her breathing was rhythmic.

Beth made a sound that was somewhere between a sigh and a sob. She raised a hand to her lips, but it was shaking so wildly she couldn't complete the action and she lowered it back to her side. When she turned to look at Vincente, her eyes were urgent and haunted, their blue depths awash with unshed tears.

"Beth—" *just what was going on with her?* "—she's fine. No one has been in here."

The tears spilled over as she blinked, and she brushed them impatiently away with the back of her hand. "She cried out as if someone had touched her." He could see doubt creeping in now as she turned back to look at Lia. "That's how she cries when a stranger tries to hold her."

She shivered slightly as if a chill had caught her unawares. Turning slowly, she looked at the open window. "No. I closed that when I brought her up here. I know I did."

"Maybe you forgot. It's easily done."

The uncertainty and trembling were gone now. Momentarily, he was looking at the old Beth. "I know I closed the window. I felt a draft and I moved across here to close it before I came downstairs." There was a militant look in her eye. One he remembered well. "I'm not wrong about this, Vincente."

She moved to the window and leaned out. "Look." She pointed. "Someone has placed a ladder up against the side of the house, right below this window. That's how he got in."

Vincente was still skeptical. "In broad daylight? And why didn't that mad dog of yours attack whoever it was that was setting a ladder up against the side of the house and climbing in through one of the windows?"

"Because this room is at the side of the house." Beth was pacing now, wrapping her arms around her waist as though hugging herself. "Melon is in the backyard.

He was barking to warn me, but he couldn't get around to this side."

"So, this person, whoever it was, climbed in, touched Lia and made her cry, climbed out again and ran off?" Vincente said. "Why? What did he, or she, hope to gain from it?"

"He wanted to frighten me. He said if I told anyone… if I involved the police…" She struggled to regulate her breathing. "Now you and Laurie have been here. This is his way of warning me."

Vincente was about to pursue the subject further when Lia stirred and rolled onto her back. The action revealed an item that had been hidden under the blanket. Although Vincente could see it was a photograph, he couldn't make out the detail, and he didn't get a chance to look too closely. His attention was taken up by the remarkable effect the picture had on Beth.

As soon as she saw the photograph, she gave a little cry and ran from the room. Picking up the picture, Vincente straightened the blanket over Lia before following her. When he found Beth, she was on her knees beside a bed. Presumably this was her own bedroom.

As he watched in surprise, she hauled a suitcase out from under the bed and opened it. Pulling open the closet, she began to throw clothes into the suitcase.

"What are you doing?" *Apart from losing your mind?*

"Getting out of here." She brushed past him and, opening a drawer in the dresser, carried an armful of underwear over to the case. "Right now."

Beth's heart was beating so fast it felt like it was going to burst right out of her body. Her chest grew tighter as if her ribs and lungs had expanded beyond their capacity and, with nowhere to go, they were forced to stay inside her. One minute she couldn't inhale. The next, her breath was coming in great, whooping gasps as though she'd just finished running a marathon.

Then her stomach decided to join the party, giving a huge backflip that sent sick bile rising up into her throat, making her gag. And the whole time her mind was playing one thought on a loop, over and over.

Get out.

She raced wildly around her bedroom, scarcely aware of Vincente until he blocked her way, forcing her to stop what she was doing and look at him.

"You have to tell me what this is about."

"No." *Don't tell.* That was what the letter had said. *I'll know if you do.* "I can't."

"Beth." He caught hold of her hands, and his touch slowed some of the madness in her heart. "I am not letting you leave here like this. You may have run from me once, but it's not happening again. I will keep following you until you tell me what is scaring the hell out of you." He lowered his voice, so it became softer and more persuasive. "You have always been able to tell me anything."

She looked into those midnight eyes. He was right. No matter what crazy point they had been at in their relationship—midfight, making up, wildly in love, just friends—Vincente was the one person to whom she could always take a problem. Even when she was mad at him, she used to go to him for advice. *That was before I had a madman on my tail. And now he's after my daughter.*

The thought sent a renewed flare of panic storm-

ing through her and she tried to tug her hands away.
"I can't."

Vincente pointed to the picture he'd placed on the
bed. "That was placed in my daughter's crib. If you won't
tell me what it's about, do I need to take it to the police?"

Beth felt the color, what little there was left of it, drain
from her face. "No. Please don't."

"Then talk to me, Beth." He released one of her hands
and picked up the picture. "We can go to Lia's room, if
you feel more comfortable there."

She nodded. "Give me a minute to get something."

While Vincente returned to the nursery, Beth withdrew the envelope containing the letter, newspaper report, and the other photographs from the drawer in her
bedside table. Was she really going to do this? She had
run from Stillwater because of this. She had left her old
life behind, partly because she had been in danger, but
also because any people to whom she was close had been
in danger. And Vincente had been the closest of all. Oh,
he didn't know that. Or maybe he did…but he would
never admit it. Vincente didn't do close. He was great at
the physical stuff. But emotionally? *No. We never went
there. Every time things strayed close to the L word,
we'd find ourselves breaking up again.*

But this was no longer just about Beth. Someone had
been in Lia's room today, and that someone had already
killed two people. Beth was determined to do all she
could to protect Lia, but maybe she needed help. And
what better person was there to help her than Lia's father?

Even so, this wasn't going to be easy. She'd been
keeping this secret for two long years and it felt like part
of her. Opening up, even to Vincente, was going to be

tough, particularly as there were parts of the story that were so hard to tell.

When she reached Lia's room, she leaned over the crib. The sight of that little figure always restored her equanimity and she smiled as she breathed in that unique Lia-smell. Looking up, she was aware of Vincente's eyes on her. There was only one chair in the room, and he indicated for Beth to take it while he sat on the floor nearby.

Okay, let's do this. She sat down, gripping the envelope tightly. "This started way back when I was eighteen. You know what happened the summer before I went away to college, right?"

They had both lived in Stillwater all their lives, but Vincente was five years older than Beth. She was closer in age to his younger brother, Bryce. As a teenager, she had been increasingly aware of the dark, broodingly handsome oldest Delaney brother, but it was only when she came back after college and started working for a law firm in town that the attraction had ignited between them.

"I remember what you told me, and I saw the news reports. I know people in Stillwater still talk about it now and then. But I was in Italy that summer visiting my mother." His lips twisted into a smile that was both bitter and affectionate. "It was one of her weddings, possibly the fourth. I've lost count. I always thought you told me a shortened version of what happened on the mountain because you couldn't bear to talk about it. Although I know some of the detail, if it's important to this story, tell me about it again."

"You're right. Even though I couldn't forget it, I tried to avoid discussing it. At that time, I loved rock climbing." *At that time.* Those words held a world of memories and meaning. "I belonged to the West County Climbing Club. It was run by a group of experienced climbers, who encouraged those of us who were new to the sport. We traveled all over the state, climbing the Tetons, Ten Sleep and Sinks Canyon. That summer, they organized an expedition to climb the Devil's Peak, the highest point on the Stillwater Trail."

"How many of you went on the climb?"

It still didn't seem real that Vincente was here in Lia's pink-and-white room. He was seated with his back against the closet—the one on which Beth had carefully stenciled teddies and bunnies—with his knees drawn up and his clasped hands resting loosely between them. He looked so big and masculine. That should be reassuring, right? His presence should make her feel safe and protected. Maybe it would…if it wasn't for the contents of the envelope she held in her hands.

"There were two instructors and eight junior climbers. Although we were amateurs, the Devil's Peak is so difficult, we had to have a high level of expertise before we could be included in the team. Although I was only eighteen, and the youngest member of the group, I had been part of the club since I was thirteen. I'd done some tricky climbs and Rick Sterling, the lead instructor, was my mentor. He had partnered me on several tricky climbs and he decided I was qualified enough to join this one." Beth tried out a smile. "I was so excited when he said I could go along. In hindsight, I wish he'd told me to stay at home."

"I don't know much about these things, but I know the Devil's Peak is a beast of a climb," Vincente said.

"I read an article not so long ago rating it one of the top ten hardest in the country."

"It's a killer." Beth winced as she said the words. "Climbing the Peak was always going to involve an overnight stay. We started out hiking through the alpine meadows at the base, then it became like a rocky moonscape before we had to tackle a vertical notch known as the Keyhole. The drop-offs from there were like nothing I'd ever seen. It was vertigo-inducing. We were about halfway up when, without warning, the weather changed. We were caught in a snowstorm. The wind was lashing around us and more snow was whipping off the surrounding peaks. We were completely exposed. Halfway up a dangerous rock face with nowhere to go."

"Surely your instructors had checked the weather conditions before you set off?" Vincente asked.

"They had. This was totally unexpected. And it was one of the recommendations that came out of the inquiry that followed. Now, climbers are warned that the weather on the Devil's Peak can change in minutes and that forecasts are not always accurate. We didn't have the benefit of that warning."

"So you had to choose whether to go up or down?"

"We chose to keep going." There had been no right or wrong choices. The only decision had been to keep moving in one direction or another. Beth recalled the tension as, blinded by the snow in their faces and buffeted by the wind, they had continued with the climb. Rick had reasoned that, once they reached the next plateau, they could set up camp as planned. "Physically, and mentally, it was the most challenging thing I've ever done. Clinging on to the rock while the wind tried to drag me off set every muscle screaming in agony. After a few hours, my arms and legs felt like Jell-O. My brain was mush, I can't remember having a single coherent thought during that time. We were almost at the top when one of the group fell. His name was Cory Taylor and, after the instructors, he was probably the most experienced climber among us. It was at a point when we'd almost reached safety. He *should* have been okay by then."

Beth paused, drawing a breath. It had been so long since she'd talked about it. The horrors of that day hadn't receded in the intervening years, but she'd thought about it less over time. She supposed that was what coming to terms with it meant. It didn't go away, but she learned to live with it. When the letter arrived, it had brought it all flooding back, of course. In the two years since then, it had resurfaced regularly.

"I know his injuries were bad." Vincente's voice was gentle.

"He broke his neck and his back." She spoke bluntly. There was no other way to tell it. "We were roped together in pairs. When Cory fell, it was only the skill of Rick's coleader, Tania Blake, that stopped him and his partner plummeting off the rock face and into oblivion."

She paused, taking a moment to collect her thoughts. Leaning forward, Vincente placed a hand on her knee, and his touch ricocheted through her like a streak of lightning. It was good and bad. Good because it grounded her, reassured her and brought her back to normality. Bad because she felt a resurgence of all the old feelings tingle through her nerve endings...and how wrong was it to feel like that in this situation?

"Between us, we got Cory to the top of the Keyhole. By that time, we were in a full-blown storm. We had no way of getting medical help for Cory. No radio or cell phone signal. Nothing." Beth covered her face with her hands at the memory. "It was awful. He was in so much pain. I can still hear his screams, still hear him pleading with us to let him die. He kept saying it was what he wanted. It was the most awful sound I've ever heard. And we were so helpless. There was nothing we could do. One of the team, Peter Sharp, was a paramedic. He gave Cory painkillers, but they couldn't even touch the pain he was in. We had pod tents that we were able to get up in spite of the snow, and we took turns to sit with him during the night. I was the one who was with Cory when it happened."

"When he died?" Vincente asked.

"When he was murdered."

Lia woke up right at the point when Vincente was going to suggest Beth needed to take a break anyway. Telling the ten-year-old story was clearly taking its toll on her. Although Vincente had heard a watered-down account from Beth herself several years ago, and had endured the town gossips' version of events now and then, hearing the details was harrowing. He still wasn't sure what the "Murder on the Devil's Peak," as it had become known in Stillwater folklore, had to do with Beth's current problems, but he guessed she was leading up to that.

Worry continued to play in a loop as he observed Beth and thought about what she was telling him. Either the incident on the mountainside had some connection to her current state of mind or her problems were out of control. Either way, he was concerned about her.

The story she had told him was worse than he had imagined. He knew she had been on a climb that had ended in danger and the death of one of her companions, but he hadn't paid attention to the details. That hadn't been because he was uncaring. It had been because he had believed Beth wanted to put the whole episode behind her. Now he knew she hadn't done so. He had been shocked by what she'd told him. Beth had lived through a nightmare. Had she ever really recovered from that?

Beth carried Lia down to the kitchen and handed her to Vincente while she fixed her formula. "Although this still feel weird, you have no idea how useful an extra pair of hands is." After the drama of the last few hours, he was pleased to see her make an attempt at a joke.

"Why didn't you get yourself a proper guard dog?" he asked as she opened the door and Melon bundled excitedly into the room.

"Melon *is* a guard dog." Beth seemed offended on behalf of her pet.

Melon brought Vincente a chewed-up tennis ball and dropped it at his feet in an invitation to a game. When Vincente ignored him, the dog pushed the toy closer with his nose. "I hate to be the one to break this to you, but that is not a guard dog."

Beth brought the bottle of milk over, and Lia reached out eager hands for it. "She'll do all the work if you sit down with her," Beth said.

They moved to sit at the table. "Are you ready to tell me the rest of it?" Vincente asked as Lia leaned contentedly back against his arm, making little gulping noises as she drank the milk.

Her weight on his arm felt right and his heart expanded with the strength of his feelings. He wanted to keep her here in his arms, safe and warm, just like this, forever.

"I don't know what happened, if that's what you

mean. I was in Cory's tent with him. The idea was to talk to him, to keep telling him everything was going to be okay. In reality, I'm not sure he even knew there was someone there, let alone that he could understand what we were saying. He was out of his mind with pain. I had my flashlight and my book with me and I was reading to him. Then I felt a blow to my head and I blacked out. Sometime later, the next person came into the tent to sit with Cory. They found I was unconscious with a head wound, and Cory was dead. He had been suffocated. We didn't know that for sure until the inquest. We thought— hoped, even—that he could have died in his sleep."

"Did you have any idea who did it?" Vincente asked. Although he was focused on what Beth was saying, part of his mind was on the warm weight of his little girl against his arm. He had started this day not knowing she existed and now having her there felt like the most natural thing in the world. If Beth was right and someone was threatening her, threatening them both...

What he felt for Lia went way beyond the natural protectiveness any normal adult felt toward a child. Within minutes of meeting her, his hard, outer shell had melted, leaving him with a new vulnerability. He had a family to care for now. The thought of anything, or anyone, harming a hair of his daughter's head had him snarling inside like a tiger. He pressed his cheek against her hair, breathing in the scents of shampoo and baby powder, feeling the hook that connected his heart to hers digging in a little deeper.

He looked up to see Beth watching him. She came within his protective sphere, as well. She always had.

"No. We thought—" she bit her lip as she answered

his question "—this sounds awful, but we thought someone had done it as a sort of kindness."

"A misguided way of ending his misery?" It was a horrible idea, but he understood what she meant.

Beth nodded, tears filling her eyes. "It can't ever be right to take a life, but anyone who heard his cries couldn't fail to be moved. The storm was over by then and Rick found a place to get a signal. He called the Stillwater Ranger Service and they sent an emergency team. Once it was known how Cory had died, there was a police investigation, but no one was ever charged with his murder. It got a lot of press attention."

"Did you bear the brunt of it because you were with him when he died?" Vincente had been out of the country at the time, so he hadn't seen the news reports.

"Some of it was brutal, suggesting that I knew what happened, that I colluded with the person who killed him, even that I did it. The attention died down eventually." Beth bit her lip. "But the memories took a lot longer to fade. I couldn't go rock climbing again after that. I think some of the club members still got together— maybe they do even now—but I couldn't face seeing any of them. Talking about what happened just seemed all wrong. Anyway, it had started to fade naturally into the background. I still thought about it, but less and less often. Then I got this."

She reached for the brown envelope that she'd brought downstairs with her. Opening it, she withdrew an old newspaper cutting. It had been written a day or two after Cory's death. The headline was Climbers' Death Storm Horror. Whoever had sent it to her had taken a red pen and carefully scratched out the words *climber* and *climb-*

ers throughout the text, replacing them instead with the words *murderer* and *murderers*.

"When were you sent this?" Lia had drained her bottle and was struggling to be put down. Vincente dredged up a memory of babies and feeding. "Doesn't she need to be burped or something?"

"No, she's older now. She'll be fine." Lia crawled with surprising agility over to a box of toys. Beth's eyes followed her and remained on her as Lia settled down to play. "About two years ago." She returned to his question.

"Why didn't you tell me at the time?" His earlier anger had given way to a nagging feeling of anxiety. His worries about Beth were growing by the minute, settling in his gut as a physical ache. He had a feeling it wasn't going to shift any time soon.

She withdrew the other items from the envelope and pushed them toward him. "Because of these. The letter, and the first photograph were sent a month after the newspaper article."

There were four photographs, all similar to the one that had been left in Lia's crib, and a short letter. Vincente read the letter first.

Greetings, Murderers,
When you killed Cory Taylor, you took away my life. Now I'll take yours. One by one. You don't know who I'll come for first. You don't know who'll be next. Don't tell. I'll know if you do, and I'll come after the ones you love. Enjoy looking over your shoulder. One day, I'll be there.

"Beth, this is sick, but you can't let it get to you. You should have gone straight to the police." Vincente was outraged to think that she'd been living in fear all this time because of this.

He was shaken to the core at what he was seeing and hearing. Beth had run from her life in Stillwater, from *him*, because of this hateful letter? Part of him wanted to ask why she hadn't trusted him enough to share what she'd been going through, but the haunted look in her eyes told him all he needed to know. Beth hadn't been capable of thinking of anything beyond the sheer terror caused by these threats.

Although his initial reaction was to give in to the rage he felt, Vincente knew he had to deal with this differently. Storming out of the house in search of the person who had written those words wasn't going to help Beth, or protect her and Lia.

Beth was so fragile; any wrong move on his part could tip her over the edge. He had to show her she could trust him. No matter how much he wanted to punch the wall, he had to act with compassion.

"Look at the photographs, Vincente." Beth lined them up in front of him on the table. "This is a group photograph, taken just before we set off on the climb. We all had a copy of it as a memento of the expedition. This was my copy—" She tapped an unmarked version of the picture with one fingertip before moving along to the next photograph. "And this is the one that was sent to me with that letter. It's the same photograph, but in this one there is a red *X* over Cory's face."

Vincente could see the pattern that was emerging along the line of photographs. "A month later, I was sent this picture." Beth pointed to the next photograph. "In this version, there are two red *X*s. As well as Cory's face being crossed out, there is a red *X* over the face of Andy Smith, one of the other climbers." She moved on to the next picture. "I got this picture the day before I left

Stillwater. Three *X*s. This time, the expedition leader, Rick Sterling, has his face crossed out."

Vincente had a feeling he wasn't going to like the answer to his next question. "Did you get in touch with Andy and Rick after you received these pictures?"

She lifted her eyes to his face. "I tried, but they are both dead."

Vincente took a moment to let that information sink in. "What about the police, or anyone else who was on the climb? Did you try to contact them?"

"You saw what the letter says." Her face was ashen. "Once I heard Andy and Rick were dead, I knew it wasn't an idle threat. If I'd tried to speak to anyone, I'd have been putting you in danger. The only thing I could do was leave."

Chapter 4

Vincente envied people who sailed through life on unruffled emotional seas. In comparison, he steered through passionate storms. His feelings swooped from high to low, but rarely seemed to settle in that midrange known as calm. The only times he'd truly found inner peace had been during those times with Beth when their relationship had been stable.

Even so, he'd never known a day like this one. It had him on the emotional ropes and was pounding him into submission. Just how many sensations could a few hours throw at him? The initial anger he'd felt toward Beth for concealing Lia from him was still there. Perversely, amid everything else that was going on, he felt cheated out of the big confrontation he needed. His rage wanted an outlet and it wasn't going to get it.

In the past, there had been a script. Vincente was

good at being mad. Hard, biting comments that provoked a reaction from Beth were his specialty. His anger craved her response. A smile twisted his lips. Beth didn't do submissive. She had always snapped right back at him, giving as good as she got. The air between them would crackle with fire and intensity. The outcome always hung in the balance. Would one of them storm out? Or would they end it by tumbling into bed, finding a resolution that didn't need words?

Okay, nothing as big as a secret child had ever come their way. Anger and hurt this bad had never featured in their lives. Even so, Vincente's initial instinct had been to turn his fury on Beth. When he had gotten over the initial shock, all he wanted to do was incite one of those huge, explosive fights.

Restraint didn't come easily to him. He choked back a laugh. Most days, it didn't come to him at all. But it hadn't taken him long to see he needed to find some of it. Right around the time Lia was trying to hitch a ride around the house attached to Melon's tail, he realized this was a situation that required careful handling. And things had gotten a whole lot stranger since then.

Vincente had to put aside his feelings of anger and hurt about Lia. No matter how cheated he felt that he had been kept out of his daughter's life, he had to rise above it. And, once he had learned about the photographs, part of him could understand Beth's motives.

Now, it was dusk and Vincente had offered to take Melon for a walk while Beth prepared dinner. The dog was bounding wildly in and out of the trees, chasing imaginary prey and occasionally returning to check on Vincente, his tongue lolling and his flanks heaving. Guard dog? Beth had to be kidding. Melon was a likable idiot. At least this activity had given Vincente some thinking time.

He wasn't sure there was a murderer lurking behind the anonymous messages. More likely it was a sick mind, someone who took pleasure from tormenting Beth with evil threats. But whoever it was, whatever their motive, that person had been inside Beth's house today. Inside Lia's room. That strayed beyond idle threats, and into the realms of dangerous. Even if the sender of those letters had no real intention of committing murder, it didn't matter. Beth believed he wanted to kill her, and now Lia. She was terrified by it. So terrified she had run from her home. The thought of what she had been through sent a surge of emotion through him. Beth had been in hiding for all these months, cowering in fear of her nameless tormentor, struggling to bring up their child on her own.

Alongside a renewed feeling of anger, Vincente's chest constricted. The feeling of helplessness was overwhelming. Telling himself he couldn't have done anything because he hadn't known wasn't good enough. Although it was irrational, he couldn't shake the feeling that he *should* have known.

I should have done more to find her.

It was all very well blaming the Red Rose Killer investigation. Had he ever really believed she was dead? A connection like theirs didn't just fizzle out when one person went away. The pain he'd felt when she left had been like nothing he'd ever known before. But he had nothing against which to measure it. Beth had been the only person with whom he'd had any sort of relationship and he'd always known their mini-breakups weren't permanent. That sounded overconfident, but that was how it was between them. They'd had a bond that was different to anything he saw in other couples around him, as unique as it was unbreakable. When Beth had left for good, the closest thing he could compare it to was the grief he'd felt when his father died. But losing Beth had felt more acute. More raw. As if he knew it was something from which he would never recover.

There had been no one he could to talk to about it. Growing up, his relationship with his half brothers had been antagonistic. They had been family in the remotest sense of the word. Vincente had been almost two when Cameron was born, and Bryce had come along two years later. Vincente didn't need any in-depth analysis to tell him that he'd been jealous of his half brothers, even though their mother, Sandy, had done her best to make him feel loved. Their childhood had set the tone for an uneasy distance between them in adult life. It was only recent events that had made the three brothers see they could be a formidable team when they put their minds to it. Taking on a vicious serial killer and then a corrupt, murdering politician had made them realize they were bound together by unbreakable ties of love and loyalty.

Even though he was closer now to Cameron and Bryce, confiding in his brothers about his emotions wasn't an option. Vincente didn't open up to others, and he certainly didn't do feelings.

Among all the other emotions fighting for dominance, there was also a powerful concern for Beth. He could understand the change in her now, but it didn't mean he was any less worried about its impact. He wasn't even sure if she had that spark in her anymore, the one that would fire up and fight back at him if he pushed her. Deep in his chest, the thought triggered a shard of pain. This scared, broken woman wasn't *his* Beth.

His shoulders sagged. The weight of his responsibility felt huge. He had no intention of shirking it, but he needed to get it right. *Had* to get it right. It was too important. He had to take charge. For Lia. For Beth. For all of them.

He stepped back inside the house, releasing the catch on Melon's lead.

"Thank you." Beth's smile hit him right in the center of his chest. "I never seem to find the time to walk him as often as I should."

"I did some thinking while I was walking." He might as well plunge right into this. "And I think you should come back to Stillwater with me."

Beth was pleased at the way she managed to get her shaking hands under control before she placed the dish of pasta in the center of the table. She gestured for Vincente to take a seat and concentrated on serving the food before she spoke.

"I can't go back to Stillwater."

"I know what you're thinking—"

"No, you don't."

No one could possibly know what she was thinking. Because no one had lived through the fear with her. She had been alone when she had experienced that feeling of her heart pounding so hard it felt like it was trying to burst out of her chest. The sensations of her muscles tensing and her breathing coming too hard and fast? They were things she had learned to deal with by herself. Lia wasn't an easy baby to settle. Beth hoped that wasn't because she picked up on her mom's anxiety... her counselor assured her it wasn't. But, each night, having spent hours settling Lia, Beth would then lie awake, her ears straining to hear every tiny sound.

Vincente joked about Melon, but the dog had been Beth's only comfort in the long, sleepless hours. She knew Melon would warn her if there was a problem.

She drew a breath. "Someone wants to kill me, Vincente. There was no mistaking what that letter said. He warned me if I told anyone, he would come after the people close to me. If I come back to Stillwater with you, it will be obvious you know about the letter and the photographs. I would be putting you and Lia in danger." Even though she had to refuse, the temptation to agree had been overwhelming. And she didn't have to look far for the reason. Ever since she had seen Vincente standing on her front step, her emotions had been on a wild rollercoaster ride…but he was *here*. Just being with him again, even for this short time, had eased some of the tightness in her chest. Leaving him had been the hardest thing she'd ever done. Even through the drama of these last few hours, his nearness had been a bittersweet indulgence. She was like an addict who had given in to her cravings. Losing him all over again would be the worst kind of hell.

Even so, she had find the same inner strength that had driven her to leave Stillwater. The thought made her shoulders droop. She wasn't sure she could still summon that kind of fight.

Vincente stopped eating. Reaching across the table, he removed Beth's fork from her hand and placed it on the table. His fingers were warm as he clasped her hand. Even though she knew his intention was comfort, nothing more, the gesture sent a shock wave thrilling from the point of contact along Beth's nerve endings. She was conscious of the way Vincente's fingers filled the spaces between hers. Of how she'd missed them there without knowing it.

"You can't keep dealing with this on your own. And you can't keep running. He found you this time and he'll do it again."

Those words said it all. With them, he summed up her terror and exhaustion. Could he tell how much she wanted to relax her body and place her head on his shoulder? How much she wished she *could* to go back to Stillwater with him? When he'd said those words, an image had come into her mind. Crisp and clear. Like a snapshot of a beloved memory. It was of her hometown on a bright, sunny day.

Stillwater was a beautiful city, cradled in the embrace of some of the most sensational mountain scenery Wyoming had to offer. The Stillwater Trail wound high above the city itself, leading on a wild adventure through pine forests, past the vast, haunting expanse known as Tenderness Lake and up toward the base of the most dramatic point of all. Devil's Peak dominated the whole area, and could be seen from most places in the city.

The residents of Stillwater congratulated themselves that the spirit of the Old West was still there, on their streets and in their hearts.

Beth had never understood the obsession some of her friends had with getting away from Stillwater as they were growing up. Small-town life had stifled them, they said. Stillwater was a place where everyone knew everyone else, where everybody knew a little *too* much about the next person's business. That was part of what Beth loved about it. She liked that there were no strangers. She liked walking down Main Street and greeting people by name, going into the stores and getting the latest news—okay, the latest *gossip*. She still felt a thrill of pleasure each time she entered the memorial hall, the place where Stillwater held its barn dances, rock concerts, bake sales and children's Christmas parties. When she'd gone away to college, she'd enjoyed the contrast of living in a big city, but it had only confirmed what she already knew. She was a small-town girl and Stillwater was her home.

"Come back with me, Beth. Stay with me. I'll keep you safe." Those midnight eyes were magnetic. Vincente's eyes were so beautiful it actually hurt her to look into their depths. They had been the first thing that attracted her to him. Unusually for such dark eyes, Vincente's were expressive, conveying the extent of his emotions. Now, they were telling her she could trust him. And Beth did trust him. She knew he wouldn't let her down. But it wasn't that simple.

"Rick Sterling and Andy Smith are already dead." She pulled her hand away. Saw the flash of fire in his eyes and felt a corresponding pang of regret. "They probably thought they could keep themselves, and those around them, safe."

"We don't even know if they had received letters and photographs from this guy before they died. Maybe that's something we should check out."

"You make it sound so easy." Suddenly everything was easier. From taking a nap in the afternoon to walking Melon, to thinking about a way out of the nightmare that had haunted her for almost two years. Because Vincente was here, her heart felt that little bit lighter.

"It may not be easy, but it has to be done." His expression was resolute. "How did they die?"

Beth gazed down at her untouched plate of food. She didn't want to do this. Didn't want to have a conversation about people in that photograph with crosses through their faces. *Because what if I'm next when he gets his red pen out?* The panic began to rise again, its hateful fingers gripping her throat. There were a dozen excuses she could make to get up from the table and end the discussion. She still had that work to finish. There was a pile of Lia's laundry that needed to be folded. Melon had shredded a newspaper and hidden the pieces under Beth's bed…

But she knew Vincente. Knew that determined look. He wouldn't let this go. It would be unfair to cheat him out of the whole story. And, when she thought it through, what options did she really have, other than to place her trust in him? If she ran again, she had nowhere to go, no money, a car that was held together only by rust, and a baby and a dog to care for. Maybe handing Lia's safety over to her father was the smartest move she could make right now. By involving Vincente, Beth would be instantly doubling up on the people looking out for Lia. That could only be a good thing.

She was worried for his safety if he became involved, but he was already involved. The person who had been in Lia's room earlier in the day had entered the house while Vincente was there. Maybe *because* Vincente was there. The timing of that day's warning could have been a coincidence. Or it could have happened because Laurie and Vincente had found her. Either way, Beth had to accept that she needed help. Most of all, she needed Vincente.

"Rick Sterling died on a climb and Andy Smith was killed when he took an overdose of painkillers." She looked up, a challenge in her eyes. "I know what you're going to say."

"But I'll say it anyway." His voice was surprisingly gentle and un-Vincente-like. "Those deaths could have been accidents. Even suicides."

Beth shook her head so hard her ponytail swung from side to side. "Not when you link them to the photographs."

"Think of it another way. When did they die?"

She blinked. "I don't understand."

"Did Rick die before or after you got the photograph with the red X over his face?" Although his voice remained calm, there was message in Vincente's gaze. He was urging her to see something she could have missed.

Beth raised a hand to her lips. "I didn't check. I don't know when they died."

"If someone with a grudge knew that Rick and Andy were already dead, he could have hatched this plan with the intention of scaring you. If the photographs were sent *after* Rick and Andy passed, then it's possible these were just accidents and the sender of the letters has been exploiting that."

What Vincente was saying made sense. Beth had been so spooked to discover that Rick and Andy were dead, she hadn't considered the timeline of events. She had simply assumed that the photograph showing Rick's face crossed out had been sent before he was killed, and that the same had happened with Andy. Her terrified brain had made the connection that both men had been murdered by the person sending the pictures. But if they died *before* the pictures were sent, then Vincente was right. Their deaths could have been accidents and the sender of the letters and photographs was a nasty opportunist. Someone who had used their deaths as a chance to spread fear and anxiety. It could still be someone close to Cory, of course. A person seeking revenge for his death. But they might not be prepared to go as far as murder.

She hadn't tried to investigate Andy's and Rick's deaths. Fear of what she might find, together with her pregnancy and subsequent post-partum depression, had left her incapable of taking control of the situation. Now Vincente was offering a different approach.

Vincente pointed to the envelope that was still on the table. The photograph that had been placed in Lia's crib was on top of it. Facedown, because Beth couldn't bear to look at it. "Whose face has been crossed out on that one?"

"Danielle Penn." Beth shivered slightly. "She was the closest thing I had to a friend in the group. Although she was about five years older than me, we were the only girls in the team. There was Tania Blake as well, but she was an instructor, so she felt like an authority figure."

"I'll ask Laurie to do some investigating into the deaths of Rick and Andy. At the same time, she can check out Danielle. We may find out she's alive and well and has no idea what this is all about."

"The letter said no police." Vincente was offering her a glimmer of hope, but Beth had been too scared for too long. She didn't know if she could take it.

"Laurie is my sister-in-law. She'll do this in a way that won't draw attention to you."

Vincente was watching her face, waiting for her response. Beth managed a slight smile. Hope. It had been missing for so long, she hardly dared let herself feel it now it had come along.

"Your apartment isn't suitable for a baby and a dog," Beth said. The modern apartment block overlooking both the Ryerson River and Savage Canyon had been the scene of many of their most passionate encounters. It would feel strange to go back there in different circumstances.

"I wasn't thinking of staying there. Remember the Dawson ranch out on the road to Park County? Cameron and Laurie bought the place when they got married. Cameron plans to sell his other house, the place by the lake where he used to live, but he hasn't gotten around to it yet." Vincente cast a glance in Melon's direction. "I take it he can swim?"

Beth pictured the beautiful, designer house perched high among the pine trees above Stillwater Lake. Designed by Carla Bryan, Cameron's late architect girlfriend who had been murdered by the Red Rose Killer, the lake house was the perfect hideaway. With its private beach, encircling cliffs and high-tech security system, it was about the safest place Beth could think of.

Even so, there were still things that worried her. "Once I go back to Stillwater, *he* will know where I am. Even if we're not talking about a murderer, things could get nasty."

"You can be as visible or invisible as you choose. You can show yourself to the people you trust, but you don't have to let anyone know where you are staying. And don't forget—" he took her hand again "—I'll be with you."

She swallowed hard. "I don't have any money. I can't let you keep me until this person is caught, Vincente."

He speared a piece of cold pasta and placed it in his mouth. "You know how hopeless I am at cooking. You can help me out by ensuring that, while we are together, I don't have to survive on takeout pizza and microwavable meals."

While we are together. Beth didn't have to wonder if he picked up on the irony of those words. She caught the flare in the depths of his eyes as he said them.

Together was in the past. She wasn't sure what the future held, but so many things had changed when she'd walked out of Stillwater sixteen months ago. Walking back again wasn't going to magically turn back the clock.

The logistics of getting Beth, Lia, Melon and all their belongings to Stillwater had proved to be more of a headache than Vincente had originally envisaged. Cameron was away at a political conference, but when Vincente called him, he had come through for him on the lake house. It was a relief, even though Vincente hadn't expected anything less from him.

"Of course you can stay there." There had been a note of mild surprise in his brother's voice when Vincente made the call. "Is there a problem with your apartment?"

"Not exactly. But I'll have a few houseguests." He watched as Beth neatly placed Lia's clothes in a suitcase. Each time she turned away, Lia pulled them out again. "Look, I have to go. I'll explain it all when I see you. Can you ask Laurie to call around and see me tonight?"

He scooped Lia up under one arm and she squealed delightedly. "Will your car make it to Stillwater?"

If Beth owned the vehicle he'd seen out in front of the property, it didn't matter what the answer was. That old rust bucket was a death trap and there was no way she and Lia were traveling to the end of the street in it, let alone driving for three hours to get to Stillwater.

The corners of Beth's mouth turned down. "I'm not sure…"

"Here's the deal. We'll transfer Lia's baby seat to my rental car, take the basics with us now and I'll get someone to come out here later to pick up the rest."

Beth pushed her hair back from her face in a familiar gesture that tugged at a specific point just south of his abdomen. *Be honest.* It was *well* south of his abdomen. A delicious, if inappropriate, reminder of the sort of control she once had over his body.

"I'd forgotten how decisive you can be."

He grinned. "Decisive? That's not what you used to call it."

She returned the smile. "Okay. I'd forgotten how *bossy* you can be."

It was a bright moment after the drama and tension of the previous day. A day that had ended with Vincente cramming his long limbs onto one of those small sofas for what had to be the worst night's sleep of his life. Now, he was tired, aching and in need of a shower and a change of clothes. He wanted to get back to Stillwater and get on with this. Beth wouldn't feel safe until she had some answers, and he was determined to provide them.

"These are the essentials?" Vincente regarded the mountain of baggage with a disbelieving eye.

"Welcome to the world of living with a baby." Beth ticked the items off on her fingers. "She needs her crib, her high chair, her bottles and formula, diapers, wipes, changing mat, favorite toys and you have no idea how many outfits she can go through in a day…"

Vincente handed Lia back to her. "I surrender. I'll load this into the car while you get ready."

When Beth emerged from the house with Lia in her arm and Melon's leash in her hand, Vincente held the passenger door open for her. Beth shook her head. "I'll travel in the back with Lia. Melon can sit up front with you."

Melon bounded onto the front seat. "Why is that?" Vincente asked.

"Because Melon likes cars and Lia doesn't," Beth explained.

Her statement became clear as they set off. Lia maintained a high-pitched wail that nothing Beth did could diminish. Beth tried singing, storytelling, pointing out features of interest on the roadside…none of it worked.

"Is she in pain?" Vincente asked. It was the only thing he could think that would explain such anguish.

"No. She doesn't like being strapped in." Beth sounded remarkably serene in the face of so much distress.

Melon, meanwhile, gazed out the front window and sniffed the air coming through the slight gap in the window with evident delight. After about half an hour, the screaming subsided and became snuffling sobs before turning into silence.

"She's asleep." Beth heaved a relieved sigh.

"Does she do that every time you get in the car?" Vincente wasn't sure how Beth coped with that when she was in the driver's seat.

"We don't go out much." He sensed a world of information in that sentence. Vincente glanced in the rearview mirror, but Beth's dark head was bent close to Lia and he couldn't see her face.

They continued the drive in near silence. When they reached Stillwater, Vincente drove along Main Street, secure in the knowledge that the tinted windows would protect Beth from prying eyes. His hometown was doing what it always did. Sarah Milligan was brushing the sidewalk outside her general store. The chalkboard menu outside The Daily Grind invited customers to try a slice of homemade lemon cake with their coffee. In front of Dino's, the restaurant owner, also named Dino, leaned against the door frame, chatting to a passerby…as he did every day. It was all safe and familiar.

As he turned onto Lakeside Drive, with its backdrop of pine trees and mountains on one side and the sparkling expanse of lake on the other, he risked another glance in the mirror. Beth's cheeks were wet with tears.

Chapter 5

The lake house fitted perfectly into its environment. All glass and natural wood, it perched above the rock face, jutting out over the lake so every room seemed to be suspended above the water. The large family room had floor-to-ceiling windows that opened onto the wraparound deck. Furnished in colors reflecting the pine forest outside, it managed to be elegant and comfortable at the same time.

Hauling their belongings from the underground garage hadn't been an easy task, but it was done. Beth was glad she'd brought the baby gate. The house was all on one level, but the deck led to steep steps down to the lake. Having the gate in place meant the door could remain open and they could enjoy the fresh air while keeping Lia safe. Melon had hurtled straight down to the lakeside and could be seen darting back and forth at the water's edge.

Beth had taken in the features of the property when they'd arrived. Its beauty was obvious, but safety was her main concern. The house ticked all the boxes. Turning off Lakeside Drive, Vincente had approached the house along a narrow lane. When he reached the gates, he used an electronic fob to open them and drove directly into the garage. He explained that Cameron had upgraded security following an incident a few months ago when a group of men had broken in and attacked Bryce and Steffi. A camera system on the gate regulated visitor entry. No one could gain admittance unless someone in the house granted them access. Visitors didn't drive into the garage. There was a small courtyard at the front of the house where they left their cars.

"The alarm system also includes cameras on the exterior wall, so you can see who is approaching." Vincente had pointed them out to her. "The only other way to reach the house is from the lake itself."

It was so different to the little house they'd just left. There, she'd felt exposed all the time, as though she had needed three-hundred-and-sixty-degree vision. It felt like staying safe had just gotten a whole lot easier. But maybe that had something to do with the man who was standing next to her as she looked out at the view. Vincente was over six feet of lean, hard muscle and he was dedicating himself to taking care of her and Lia. She'd take that over a sophisticated electronic method any day.

Lia was awake and displaying no ill effects from the trauma of the car journey. Having tested the baby gate and found it wasn't budging, she was crawling around, exploring her new surroundings.

"It doesn't affect her for long," Beth explained. "Like I said, she hates to be strapped in. She wants to roam loose around the car and can't understand why she has to be confined in one place. She's an explorer."

"She must take after you."

Beth smiled. "I seem to have lost my intrepid spirit lately."

Her rock climbing days had ended abruptly with Cory Taylor's death, but she had continued to enjoy other outdoor pursuits. Hiking, kayaking, caving, snowboarding… In the past, anything that allowed her to explore the natural beauty of her home state had appealed to her. It was only since her abrupt flight from Stillwater that her love of adventurous activities had been curtailed. She felt a tiny flicker stir inside her. Maybe it was nostalgia. It could even have been excitement at the thought of new possibilities.

The scent of the lake mingling with pine forest and mountain air—the aromas of home—must be getting to her.

"I put Lia's crib in the master bedroom. You sleep in there. I'll take the guest room."

Was it her imagination, or did something slide quietly away with Vincente's words? But it would be silly to think of it as a missed opportunity. An opportunity for what? To pick up where they left off? To relive the past? Too much had happened for that. She wasn't the same person. She didn't want the same things from life that she had sixteen months ago. *And he wouldn't want me now anyway.*

Her spirits had been tested to the limit in the time they had been apart until she no longer felt like the same person. The impact had been physical as well as emotional. She'd lost weight. Always slender, she knew she looked in the mirror now and saw a woman who was thin and drawn. Why would Vincente, himself so vigorous and full of life, want anything to do with the shadow she had become? The thought made her raise a hand to self-consciously fix her ponytail.

"Why do you do that?" Vincente gestured to her hair. "Why scrape it back that way?"

"Oh." Her hand fluttered in midair, caught in surprise at his words. "It's easier. I don't have time to style it anymore. What with Lia and everything…"

Why was she floundering as she explained her hairstyle choice to him? She sighed. Because it was Vincente. No matter what she tried to tell herself, how he looked at her, how he thought of her, mattered. *He* mattered. They might have both moved on, but he would always have this power over her. The thought caused her breath to catch uncomfortably in her throat. She knew, without a shadow of doubt, that no other man would ever affect her the way Vincente Delaney could. Maybe he picked up on her self-conscious thoughts, because Vincente looked away, releasing her from his probing gaze.

"I need to get a shower and borrow some of the clothes Cameron keeps here." Vincente tugged at the front of his T-shirt with a grimace.

"I'll make coffee." Cameron's kitchen had some basic provisions, and Beth had thrown enough into a bag to feed them for a day or two. After that? She was relying on Vincente's ingenuity.

While Vincente showered, Beth checked the family room for hazards. The decor was minimalist and there wasn't much that could harm Lia. Beth moved a few large chunks of quartz from the coffee table to a higher shelf and secured the screen more firmly in front of the log fire. Lia followed her, babbling contentedly.

Beth swung her daughter up into her arms, carrying her to the window so they could look down at Cameron's private beach. "What do you think?"

Stillwater Lake was a huge body of water. In the far distance, Beth could just make out the sailboats close to the leisure marina. It was a popular place with water-skiers and speedboat enthusiasts. Across the other side was the spot known as Catfish Point. It had been named by the fishing enthusiasts after the most popular activity over on the quietest part of the lake. But where she stood now—on the deserted side—this was the most beautiful view.

Steep cliffs rose on either side of the small bay and behind the house itself, making it impossible for anyone to accidentally access this cove. Melon dashed along the pebbly shore, occasionally darting into the water. His tongue lolled from one corner of his mouth as he patrolled the shoreline, already protecting his new territory.

"Woof," Lia commented, raising her hand to wave in the dog's direction.

There was a warm feeling in the pit of Beth's stomach. Contentment. Security. Confidence. All those words were too soon, too strong. She was going to settle for calling it an improvement on what she'd left behind. Back in Casper, she'd been alone, looking over her shoulder all the time. Now she had Vincente's protection... and she was no longer alone. It almost felt like they were a family, safe and enclosed in their own little world.

When Bryce called for the fourth time that day, Vincente had decided he couldn't postpone the explanations any longer. "I'm out at the lake house. It'll be easier to explain face-to-face. Before you come out here, stop by my apartment and pack a suitcase full of my clothes. And bring lunch…for three-and-a-half."

When he went into the kitchen, Lia crawled over to him and tugged at his pants, demanding to be picked up. Something in his chest gave way each time she did that. He didn't need to do anything to bond with her. He only had to look into those big brown eyes and he fell deeper in love with each passing minute. He lifted her into his arms, and Lia pulled sharply on his beard, giggling delightedly at his exclamation of surprise.

Beth carried their coffee through to the family room, where she had placed Lia's toy box in one corner. Vincente set his daughter down to play, while he explained to Beth that his message was likely to make Bryce drop everything and tear down to the lake house to find out what was going on.

"I'll have to tell him why I can't be in the office. We divide the running of the company between us. Bryce is in charge of operations and I take care of finance and administration. He's going to need to find someone to replace me."

Beth bit her lip. "Is this going to leave your business in a mess?"

He shook his head. "No. It would leave it in more of a mess if I handed the financial side of things over to Bryce. Luckily, he knows his own limitations when it comes to bookkeeping as well as I do. Will you be okay with seeing him?"

"Oh, goodness, yes. There is no way I would distrust either of your brothers." She smiled reminiscently. "It will be good to see Bryce again. Half my friends were in love with him when we were growing up."

"The days when he was known as the Stud of Stillwater are behind him. He's a happily married man."

He couldn't possibly envy the little smile that crossed Beth's lips when she spoke of Bryce, could he? He should be glad to see her smiling, not experiencing this sudden caveman-like desire to growl and beat his chest. Reminding himself that those days were over, he turned his attention to Lia. She was systematically taking each toy out of the box and discarding it. Vincente wondered what Cameron would think if he could see his beautiful family room looking like a…family room.

"Will she be okay with the move?"

"I think so. Where she is doesn't matter. All she really needs is me. And probably Melon, who she loves. Although—" Beth smiled shyly "—she has taken an instant liking to you, which is good. We don't see many people. She's always been wary of strangers." A frown flitted across her brow. "I worry about what the seclusion does to her."

"She's probably too young for it to affect her. But it's another reason to resolve this and do it fast."

Beth was about to respond. Instead, she looked up sharply as a voice rang out. Vincente frowned. He should have warned Bryce not to use his key to get into the house. He got to his feet as Bryce came into view. His wife, Steffi, was with him.

There were shocked looks all around. Beth gazed in amazement at Steffi, the woman who, until she went on the run following an accusation of murder, had been Anya Moretti, one of Hollywood's most famous actresses. Bryce stared at Beth, whom he, along with the rest of Stillwater, believed had been murdered by the Red Rose Killer. Steffi stared at the beautiful baby girl who, having emptied her toy box, was carefully pushing her toys under the sofa.

The silence was broken by Melon, who appeared at the baby gate and launched into a volley of angry barks at the strangers who had invaded his new home.

"When I said it would be easier to explain it face-to-face…" Vincente raised his voice above the onslaught. "I hadn't taken into account the guard dog."

Bryce managed to tear his gaze away from Beth's face. "That's not a guard dog."

The comment provoked a number of reactions. Vincente started to laugh at the way his brother had repeated his own words.

Beth fired up in defense of her pet. "Melon is the *best* guard dog."

Steffi dropped to her knees beside the baby gate and ruffled Melon's ears. "He's a sweetheart." Melon rolled his eyes in delight.

"I think some introductions are needed." Vincente raised his brows at Beth, seeking her permission. She understood what he was asking and nodded in reply. Nothing in his life had ever matched the feeling of pride that swelled his chest as he stooped and picked up Lia. "I'd like you to meet my daughter."

Beth couldn't quite believe that Steffi Delaney was Anya Moretti, and that the woman helping her serve lunch was also the woman who had starred in some of her favorite movies. She seemed so…normal. Pretty, lively and clearly devoted to Bryce, but down-to-earth and fun. She made Beth laugh by comparing Melon to some of the dogs at the animal sanctuary she ran.

"Believe me, I would rather live with my pigs, goats

and horses than the more dangerous animals I knew in Hollywood."

"It sounds like you have an amazing place." For the first time in a long time, Beth was having a conversation with a stranger about something other than groceries or rent. Talking to Steffi was easy. Beth was amazed to find she was relaxing, even starting to enjoy herself.

"You should bring Lia out to visit," Steffi said. "She'd love it."

Beth gave a noncommittal reply. No matter how much she might want to get to know Steffi better, no matter how much she might want to take Lia to see the animals, leaving the lake house might be a dangerous option.

There was a curious atmosphere in the room, as though everyone had a dozen questions to ask, but no one quite knew where to start. When they sat around the kitchen table to eat lunch, it was Vincente who turned the conversation in a serious direction.

"I'm going to take some time away from the business."

Beth sensed an unspoken communication pass between the two brothers. It was almost as though, in that fleeting instant, Bryce was checking that everything was okay with his older half brother. Once he got the reassurance he needed in Vincente's answering look, the tense lines of his body relaxed slightly. Something had clearly changed in the time she had been away. Before she left, Vincente's relationship with both his brothers had been strained. Although the three of them worked together and ran the company well, they didn't get along personally. Beth had known Vincente's feelings were clouded by hurt in his past, and her heart had ached for him. His antagonism toward Bryce had been particularly strong, stormy clashes a regular feature of their encounters.

"How long will you be away?"

"I'm not sure. Which is why I think Trey Reid should step up and take my place while I'm gone." Vincente's eyes seemed to challenge Bryce.

"Isn't he a little new to the company to take on that kind of responsibility?"

"In the time he's been with us, he's demonstrated that he's got flair and he's willing to learn. We don't have anyone else with his brains, initiative and leadership skills," Vincente said. "If I'm going to be out of action for some time, you'll need that sort of support. And I'll keep in touch with him by phone and email."

"Are you able to tell us what's going on?" Steffi's voice was gentle. "I don't want to pry, but we may be able to help."

"Beth has a stalker, someone who has been sending pictures and letters, threatening to kill her. That's why she left Stillwater and went into hiding. I knew the police had found her, so I followed Laurie to Beth's home in Casper. The person who has been trying to intimidate her has also said he will harm those closest to her if she tells anyone or goes to the police." Somehow, the way Vincente told the facts, coldly and calmly, made it sound even worse. "While I was at her house yesterday, he gained access to the property and left another picture in Lia's crib."

Steffi reached out and covered Beth's hand with her own. "How horrible."

Bryce frowned. "But if your intention is to hide from him, you could be here for a very long time."

"The plan is to keep Beth and Lia safe by staying here

at the lake house, but the most important thing is to find out the identity of the stalker and put a stop to what he's doing," Vincente said. "That's why I've asked Laurie to come and see me tonight. Although this person has insisted on no police, Laurie is family. She'll be able to keep her inquiries quiet."

"Before Bryce and I got married, I had a problem— not a stalker, but a dangerous killer who was on my tail—and Laurie helped me out." Steffi's words triggered a vague memory. Even from her hiding place, Beth had caught snippets of headlines and grocery-store gossip about Anya Moretti disappearing and going on the run.

"Ahem." Bryce cleared his throat, raising his brows at his wife. "I seem to recall I helped a little too."

Steffi laughed. "Did you? I don't remember."

He growled. "When I think of how I chased across the country with you…"

Steffi patted his cheek. "You are my hero, and you know it."

Their obvious, glowing happiness brought a sudden, unexpected lump to Beth's throat. She looked up and caught Vincente's eyes on her face. There it was again, that feeling of losing something they never had. *Domestic bliss was never on our horizon, so why am I craving it?* Maybe it was the situation she was in. She felt like a prisoner who had been reprieved. Given a snippet of normality, she wanted more.

The long months of fear, of not feeling safe, of starting at every phone call or knock on the door. That sense of being hunted. She had dreaded having to leave the house. Every time she got in the car, it became a nightmare journey during which she spent more time checking to see if she was being followed than she did concentrating on the road. What if *he* tried to snatch Lia as she lifted her from the vehicle? What if *he* tampered with her car when she parked it outside the bank?

Routine had been her enemy. Never going anywhere at a set time. Appointments she made for herself and Lia were fraught with fear. She remembered in the darkest days of her postpartum depression, begging her doctor not to write anything down, not to keep any records about her. Unable to explain why, she had watched with a feeling of helplessness as he gently overrode her wishes and made his notes anyway. *I am not being irrational.* She had wanted to pluck the pen from his hand and make him listen to her. *Someone wants to kill me.* Instead, she had subsided into tears. The only way she had been able to deal with her fears had been to use the strategies her counselor had given her. Although she didn't share her story, the techniques had helped with both her postpartum depression and her anxiety that the person who had threatened her might find her.

Even inside her little rented house, there had been no escape from fear. Sleep, going online, going into the yard…the uncertainty about who might be watching, waiting to pounce when she least expected it. Those things might not have occupied her mind constantly, but they were always at the back of it.

Her pregnancy had been a lonely one. Nothing had prepared Beth for the feeling she got when she held Lia in her arms for the first time. It had been like reaching into her soul and finding an unbreakable connection between her and this tiny, squawking person. *I made you.* That had been her first thought. Her second had been a brief moment of sadness that Vincente couldn't be there to share it. It was a bond of adoration and protectiveness so perfect it took her breath away. And it never faltered. But bringing up a baby was hard work. Doing it with no adult company was even harder. She hadn't left Stillwater only to put a new set of people in danger.

She decided it was no wonder she was envious of Bryce and Steffi. It wasn't surprising that her thoughts should turn to Vincente and think of what might have been. He was Lia's father. He had turned up on her doorstep like a knight in shining armor. He had been uncharacteristically understanding about what had happened… the anticipated fireworks hadn't happened.

But "might have been" for us was never forever. And now we don't even have that.

If she was going to stay in the same house as him, she might need to give herself regular reminders about that. With difficulty, she tore her gaze away from the melting depths of his dark eyes and forced herself to focus on what Bryce was saying.

Chapter 6

"We can take a picnic." Vincente gestured to the mirror-still lake and the perfect, clear blue skies. "Catfish Point will be quiet. There's no chance that anyone down there will recognize you. They won't look up from their fishing rods and nets long enough to pay us any attention. And even though there's no chance we'll need it, I'll take a gun."

After Vincente and his brothers had been forced to take action against Grant Becker twelve months ago, Cameron kept a locked gun in a cupboard in the house. Knowing he had one of his own licensed weapons close by gave Vincente an added feeling of security.

He could tell Beth was wavering. After a week spent cooped up in the lake house, or on the beach below, she needed to broaden her horizons…and stop living in fear. His words about the dedicated fishermen made her laugh. Despite not going beyond the confines of the house, she had been doing more laughing as the week went on. Could he take credit for that? Hell, he was going to.

"Are you seriously proposing to introduce a baby and a dog into the midst of a quiet sport like fishing? And you think no one will notice us or object?"

"We'll find a place a little way down the bank from the most popular fishing locations." He moved a fraction closer. Close enough that he could feel the warmth of her arm. Not touching, but better than touching. The anticipation of touching was a thrill, a tiny spark of magic in the air between them. He watched Beth's eyes, seeing the moment they darkened as she felt it, too. There had been more of these moments between them over the past day or two. Unspoken exchanges. Maybe it was wrong to read anything into it…but it sure felt right.

They'd never had this. This sweet, slow burn. Their relationship had been a microwave: touch a button and they were horny and all over each other. This was different. This was a slow cooker. The heat was building, simmering, growing hotter all the time.

Was it going anywhere? He had convinced himself it wasn't a good idea to pursue it. But he sure as hell was enjoying the burn. Sixteen months without sex was probably to blame for his overheated imagination. After Beth left, he hadn't wanted anyone else, had not even been able to contemplate the idea of being with another woman. A week of being in close proximity to her and his sex drive was back with a vengeance…along with some very erotic memories. Memories that were keeping him awake at night with the knowledge that there was only a wall between them.

Still not doing anything about it.

He had convinced his mind, but his body seemed to have other plans.

Catfish Point was a spectacularly beautiful location. The jagged peaks in the distance allowed only a glimpse of clear blue sky above, but the day was bright and warm. Summer was fading into fall and the colors of the trees on the shore were a tapestry of green, brown and gold. From this angle, only part of the lake could be seen. It was easy to imagine that Stillwater Lake was smaller and quieter. The boats, water-skiers and swimmers who dominated the other side of the water might not have existed.

Vincente chose a spot farther down the bank from where the serious fishermen would be.

"Although this is not the season for fishing these waters," he explained as Beth placed a blanket on the grass. Lia was asleep and Vincente placed her carefully down. Melon dashed off into the trees to explore. "Anyone coming out here today is unlikely to have much success."

"I forgot you used to come here with…" Beth's voice trailed off.

Vincente knew what she had been about to say. "Yes, I used to fish with Grant Becker."

She grimaced. "I didn't know how comfortable you were with talking about that."

"It still doesn't seem real. I'd known him for most of my life and never suspected anything. Even though we weren't close friends, I still wonder if I should have known he was a killer, if I could have done something."

Beth sat down, and Vincente joined her. "I don't know much about these things, but it seems to me that the reason serial killers are successful is that they are able to hide their crimes for a long time. There is something in their makeup that means they can do that. When they are finally caught, it's always a shock to the people who knew them."

He relaxed, half reclining so he could study her face as he spoke. "It was a horrible time for the town. Grant was born in Stillwater and he was a well-known figure in the county. This city is too small for something like a serial killer in our midst not to rock the community to its core. And it hit our family hard. It made us take a closer look at ourselves."

"It seems to have worked out well." He could see Beth treading cautiously and realized it was because conversations about his family had always been off-limits. He hadn't felt able to open up to her before, even though she'd been closer to him than anyone. "You and Bryce seem to be getting along better than before."

"The three of us had to work together to rescue Laurie from Grant and then again when Bryce and Steffi were in danger. I guess we forgot to be angry and remembered that we loved each other."

"And you thought I was dead." She wasn't looking at him, her eyes were fixed on a point somewhere beyond the lake, but he could sense the tension in her.

"That was the hardest thing of all." Could he explain his emotions during that time to her? Could he explain that feeling of a giant hand ripping apart the fabric of his life and leaving his heart in tatters? "It was bad enough when I thought you'd left. I couldn't understand why you'd gone, and I was hurt and angry. But when Laurie told me you could have been one of Grant's victims—" he drew a breath and tilted his head back at the sky, battling with his emotions "—I didn't want a world without you in it, Beth."

She was silent for a long time. When she turned to look at him again, her eyes shimmered with unshed tears.

"I'm so sorry I hurt you…"

Vincente acted on instinct. To hell with restraint and resolve. He reached out a hand and slid it behind her neck, drawing her face down to his. The instant their lips touched it was as if all those months of being apart had never happened. There was only this. This rightness. The touch, taste and feel of Beth was all that mattered. It was all that would ever matter.

As her lips parted, urgency took over and Vincente moved his hands to her waist, drawing her closer. At the same time, Lia gave a cry and sat up, rubbing her eyes.

Vincente groaned, pressing his forehead to Beth's. They were both breathing a little bit harder, and he liked the familiar blaze of desire he saw in her eyes. "I don't know whether her timing is good or bad, but I do know we have some unfinished business here."

Vincente had been right. A few hours away from the house had done Beth good. The sunshine, fresh air and glorious views had refreshed her. Throwing sticks for Melon, stopping Lia from crawling into the water, laughing with Vincente over memories of other times they had visited the lake…all of those things had done her good. Maybe kissing Vincente had also contributed to the overall feeling of well-being she had as she packed their belongings away. No matter how much she tried to tell herself it had been a mistake, her lips—and other parts of her body—tingled insistently at the memory.

He had said they had unfinished business. She watched him now as he chased Lia toward the water one last time, turning it into a game that made the little girl giggle as she tried to crawl faster than he could run.

We'll always be unfinished business.

The thought sent a shiver down her spine. Beth was scared by the intensity of that brief kiss. It confirmed what she had already suspected. She wanted Vincente as much as ever. The hold he had over her body was stronger than her own will. He only had to touch her and she melted. Nothing had changed, yet everything was different.

She didn't know if she could resist him, but she had to try. Because she was frightened of the consequences if she didn't. The fight back from postpartum depression had been long and hard; she had never discussed the letters and the photographs with her counselor. Beth always wondered whether there might have been contributing factors. She would never know for sure, but she had been in a bad place before Lia's birth. Leaving her hometown, leaving her friends—leaving *Vincente*— and fearing for her life: none of those things had helped make her pregnancy an easy one.

When her counselor had spoken to her of risk factors for depression, two things had resonated with Beth: stressful life events and lack of support. Both of those had been features of her pregnancy. She had been vulnerable after Lia's birth and had succumbed to a very dark time.

I won't go back there.

Vincente had always been honest about his inability to commit to a permanent relationship. In the past, she had been able to accept that. Things were different now. *I'm different now.* She didn't want the free-wheeling lifestyle they'd once had. She needed stability, for herself and Lia. The temptation to give in to what she felt for Vincente was overwhelming, but she knew where it would lead them. And she couldn't risk a mood-lowering breakup. Her name-calling, door-slamming days were over. That had once been part of who they were; it had driven them to greater passion. In a way, it saddened her to let it go.

It's called growing up. And, my God, I've had to do a lot of that in the last sixteen months.

The problem was, she couldn't see anything in Vincente that told her he'd changed in any way. He'd forged a new bond with his brothers, and that was a positive thing, but she couldn't imagine his approach to romantic ties would ever change. The damage went too deep.

As he charged up the riverbank with Lia slung over his shoulder, the laughter in his eyes was infectious. And dangerous.

As he drew closer, he studied her face. "Are you okay?" He'd always had this knack for being able to pick up on her moods.

Beth tried out a bright smile as she took Lia from him. "Fine."

Those dark eyes missed nothing. "You never could lie to me, Beth. I don't know why you try."

She sighed. "Just sad, I guess, at having to leave the open air and go back to a sort of captivity."

His phone buzzed and he reached into the pocket of his jeans to get it, scanning the message quickly. "Good or bad, Laurie has perfect timing. She's coming over this evening."

Beth's heart gave an uncomfortable thud. "Does that mean she's found some information?"

For the past week, Laurie had been making inquiries into the deaths of Rick Sterling and Andy Smith. She had also promised to find out what she could about Danielle Penn. To keep it low-key and not draw attention to the case, she was doing this outside of her working hours. She had explained that the task would take longer than usual. To Beth it felt like forever.

"She didn't say, but it seems likely." He took her hand and every sensible thought about keeping her distance grew wings and flew over the mountaintops. "Look on the bright side, it could be good news."

She felt her lip wobble. "I haven't had many bright sides lately."

Vincente placed a hand over his heart in mock hurt. "I'm not a bright side?"

That made her laugh. "You always were hopeless at flirting."

"That's not true and you know it." He stooped to pick up the rug and picnic basket. "I'm actually very good at it."

"Ah, I must have not been around at the time."

They strolled back toward the car, squabbling light-heartedly about his ability to charm the birds out of the trees. Picking up on the mood, Lia babbled excitedly. An exhausted Melon trotted alongside them. Beth could almost believe it was idyllic. If she discounted the death threats and danger. She knew what Vincente was doing, and was grateful for his thoughtfulness in trying to distract her from the looming meeting with Laurie.

A lone hiker was walking toward them as they neared the car. It was an unusual sight. Stillwater Lake wasn't an easy place for walkers. The shoreline wasn't accessible all the way around. There were sharp cliffs and places where dense pine forest came all the way down to the water's edge. Most hikers preferred to take the Stillwater Trail, which led them to Tenderness Lake, a smaller, prettier body of water, higher in the mountains, the shores of which could be walked around in a day.

As the man drew level with them, he halted, turning his head to look at them.

"Beth?" His voice was familiar, his tone shocked. "Bethany Wade?"

Hours after the encounter, Vincente had run out of curse words to describe the crazy twist of fate that had led them into a chance meeting with Beth's old boss. What the hell had possessed Edgar Powell, who knew the area well, to come out walking at Catfish Point? And why did he have to do it today, of all days? Interpreting one of Lia's lengthy babbled monologues would be a better use of his time than attempting to answer those questions. Ask anyone in Stillwater and they would tell you the same thing. Edgar Powell was a well-respected lawyer, a stand-up citizen, the nicest guy you could ever wish to meet…but he was eccentric.

Fortunately, Beth seemed to take the encounter in stride. Meeting Edgar again, after she'd left her job without giving him any notice or a reason for going, must be difficult, but Vincente wasn't able to detect any resentment on either side. Edgar seemed genuinely delighted to see Beth, and Vincente recalled the affection with which she had always held her boss. Going to work had never been a chore for Beth. She had always loved her job at

E. Powell Law. If Vincente remembered rightly, before she left, there had been talk about her becoming a partner.

They didn't linger. Edgar accepted the excuse that Lia was tired. As he turned away, Beth cast a quick glance at Vincente before hesitantly stepping up to the older man. Placing a hand on his arm, she pressed a quick kiss onto his cheek. "One day, I'll tell you the whole story. In the meantime, would you mind keeping this meeting to yourself? I'd prefer it if no one knew where I was."

Edgar patted her hand. "I always knew you wouldn't have gone the way you did without a very good reason. I only wished you'd come to me so I could help." He fished in his pocket and produced a business card. That was Edgar Powell. The man who took his business cards on a hike. "Call me if you need anything. Or if you want to do some freelance work. The office hasn't been the same without you."

As Beth prepared dinner, the card remained on the counter and Vincente was aware of her casting the occasional glance at it. When they sat down to eat, Lia, fiercely independent, insisted on feeding herself and was soon covered in spaghetti and sauce. She preferred a collaborative style of dining, one that involved a handful of food for herself and then a few morsels dropped on the floor for Melon.

"I'm glad Cameron can't see his pristine kitchen right now," Beth said.

"We may have to do something about her table manners before we take her to Dino's Restaurant."

Beth started to laugh. "I can just picture Dino's expression if she decided to use one of his elegant dishes as face cream."

It occurred to Vincente in that moment that all his

happiest moments had been with this woman. But this one was different. Sitting at the kitchen table, enjoying a family meal, a shared appreciation of the antics of their daughter…there was a new note to his happiness. The laughter froze on his lips as he tried to analyze the feeling. Could it be contentment? How would he know when he'd never experienced it before? He was aware of Beth regarding him with a puzzled look.

That was when Lia decided things would probably be even more amusing if she tipped her bowl upside down and placed it on her head. At the same moment, the buzzer signaled the arrival of Laurie.

When Vincente answered it, he rolled his eyes at Beth. "She's not alone. Cameron *is* going to get a look at his kitchen."

Beth placed her head in her hands. "Do I need to start looking for a new place to stay?"

The visitors paused on the doorstep. A twinkle lit Cameron's eyes as he surveyed the scene. "Bryce told me there was a new addition to the family. Does anyone mind if I don't kiss her right now?"

"You take Lia for her bath." Vincente rescued Beth from her embarrassment. "I'll clean up in here and make coffee."

It turned into a group effort, with Cameron making the coffee while Laurie helped Vincente with the cleanup operation. By the time they'd finished, Beth had brought Lia through from the bathroom. The baby was pink and glowing from her bath and clearly sleepy. Although she regarded the new arrivals with curiosity, she was more interested in her bottle and fell asleep halfway through drinking her milk.

"I'll take her." Vincente held out his arms and Beth

placed the sleeping figure in them. He was aware of Cameron's gaze on his face as he cradled Lia close to his chest. His brother's expression was hard to read. "I'll be back in a minute or two."

After settling Lia in her crib and turning on the baby monitor, Vincente returned to the family room. Cameron was still regarding him with that same fixed expression. It was unnerving, as though his brother was seeing him for the first time.

"Do you have some information for us?" There was a nervous hitch in Beth's voice, and Vincente moved closer to her, hoping to offer her some comfort with his nearness.

"I do." Laurie withdrew a notepad from her shoulder bag. "As you'll already know, Beth, the members of the West County Climbing Club came from right across the county. My investigations would have been easier if the people I was trying to find information about had lived in Stillwater, meaning I would have access to the police records here, but none of them did. I started my inquiries with Andy Smith, who resided in Elmville at the time of his death. I spoke to one of the detectives I know in the Elmville Police Department. I wasn't able to find out a lot more than you already told me. Andy had recently separated from his wife of ten years, had started drinking heavily, was in danger of losing his job. He'd called his wife the day before his death. She said he was drunk. It was a long, rambling call, during which he told her there were reasons for his decline—" Laurie consulted her notes "—forces at work behind the scenes, things he couldn't divulge. Those were his exact words. She thought he sounded paranoid and urged him to get help. The next day, she tried calling him and contacted the police when she got no response. He had taken a lethal cocktail of prescription drugs washed down with alcohol. Although the police believed it was suicide, the coroner returned a verdict of accidental death. There wasn't enough evidence to prove he knew what he was doing."

Beth shook her head in disbelief. "I know a lot can change in ten years, but the man you've just described is so totally different from the person I knew. Andy was the most easygoing guy you could ever meet. He was the joker on our team. We could always rely on him to lift our spirits and make us laugh. And when Cory died, Andy had recently gotten married. He was devoted to his wife."

"The only thing that may be relevant to your problem, Beth, is that, at the time of his death, Andy had been burning old letters and photographs."

"What?" Vincente sat up a little straighter.

Laurie held up her hands in a helpless gesture. "There was very little left of the items. No way of knowing exactly what had been burned."

Vincente was aware that Beth's face had paled. "If Andy Smith had been sent the same letter, newspaper article and photographs as Beth, why would he burn them? Especially if he planned to take his life?"

"He wouldn't." Beth spoke mechanically "But he didn't kill himself. The person who sent the photographs killed Andy and made it look like suicide. Then the murderer got rid of the evidence by burning it."

Chapter 7

Beth decided Laurie must be very good at those parts of her job that required her to reassure members of the public. She had a calm, authoritative manner, but she managed to be approachable at the same time. "There is no way of knowing for sure what happened inside his house on the day Andy Smith died."

"Andy's words were that there were forces at work, things he couldn't divulge. He meant he was being sent the same letter and photographs as me. He couldn't tell her because if he did, she would be in danger."

"That's one possible explanation." Laurie's voice was cautious.

Beth didn't respond. Getting into a discussion about it wasn't going to achieve anything. She *knew*. That was enough. She was aware of Vincente's gaze on her profile. Did he think she was going to fall apart? She had never felt more in control in her life.

"What happened to Rick Sterling?" Beth leaned forward, her eyes on Laurie's notebook.

"He died in a climbing accident." Laurie was searching for the right page.

Beth felt her lip curl in an expression of disbelief. "Rick was the most experienced climber I knew."

"That was pretty much what everyone told the police in Jackson who investigated the incident. Rick had been working as a guide in the Grand Teton National Park for the last five years when he died. On the day it happened, he was taking a small group out on a climb. It was straightforward. There was nothing about it that should have presented a problem, even to the most inexperienced climber. They were almost finished when Rick called to his deputy to take over. He said that one of the group had slipped and was stuck on a ledge. Rick was going to climb down to the rescue. No one saw Rick again."

"His body must have been found, surely?" Vincente said.

Laurie shook her head. "The ledge he climbed down to was above a steep ravine. If he fell from that—and the Grand Teton rangers have no other explanation for what happened to him—Rick would have fallen into a very deep, fast-flowing river. His body was never recovered."

"What about the person who was stuck on the ledge?" Cameron asked. "Did they fall, as well?"

"That was the strange thing. None of the group *had* been stuck. They were all accounted for at the end of the climb, and no one knew what the deputy was talking about when he asked if anyone had needed rescuing from the ledge. There was some speculation that Rick had lost his nerve after the Cory Taylor incident and that maybe—out of guilt because he hadn't been able to save Cory—he'd imagined someone was in trouble this time. Then, as he went to the aid of this nonexistent person, he'd gotten into trouble himself and fallen."

"Oh, don't you see?" Beth couldn't sit still any longer. Getting to her feet, she started to pace the room. "There *was* someone on the ledge. It wasn't one of the group, it was the murderer. When Rick went down to help, he was pushed off the ledge."

Even if it wasn't obvious to the police, it was crystal clear to Beth. She had known Rick Sterling. He had been her friend and mentor. She could picture him now, the most upright, honest, honorable man she had ever known. It wasn't just his muscles that had been powerful. Everything about Rick had been strong, including his character. There was no way the person on that ledge had been conjured up by a disordered mind.

"Did Andy Smith die before or after Beth received the photograph with his picture crossed out?" Vincente asked.

Laurie went back to her notes. He got the feeling she already knew the answer to his question and was buying a little time to give Beth some breathing space. "He died two days after Beth was sent the picture."

"And Rick Sterling?"

Laurie checked her notes again. "Beth was sent the photograph and Rick died four days later."

"So we're not dealing with an opportunist who knew these men were dead and decided to use that as a chance to scare Beth with these photographs." Vincente's expression was grim. "This person sent the photographs to Beth and then killed Andy and Rick."

Laurie nodded. "I'm afraid so, but we can't jump to conclusions."

"You're not going to try and say this was a coincidence?" Vincente's voice was incredulous. "That this guy just got lucky and both times he crossed out a face in those photographs, the people he chose just happened to die a few days later?"

"I'm not saying anything right now." Laurie remained calm in the face of her brother-in-law's skepticism. "I'm going to keep an open mind and I hope you'll do the same."

Beth waited for the terror to hit, the overwhelming darkness that had sapped her strength for so long. This last week had brought some respite from the worst of it. Not because she truly believed that it was all okay, but simply because she was no longer alone. And maybe that was the reason why it didn't come back full force right now. Or why it came back differently. When Vincente came to stand beside her, although the fear was there, her spine straightened and her chin came up and...*oh, my goodness, I feel like* me *again*. From somewhere deep inside, her old fighting spirit surged, just a little, and she welcomed it, seizing it eagerly.

"What happens now?"

Laurie gave her an approving look. "Now you're staying here, you are within the jurisdiction of the Stillwater Police Department and I have informed my colleagues of the situation. There is an alert on this address and on calls from your cell phone number or Vincente's. You've done all the right things so far. You are staying on a very secure property. You're being careful about who you see and where you go. Don't relax that vigilance. If there is any further contact from this person, let me know immediately."

"You're saying you can't do anything unless he harms me, right?" Beth tried to smile, but it became something more like a grimace.

"I'm saying we'll do everything we can to protect you." Laurie's gaze was steady. "I'm getting back to my colleagues in Elmville and Jackson about reopening these cases in the light of the threats against you—"

"But the letter said no police," Beth interrupted. "If you reopen the cases, he'll know I've talked to you."

"Trust me, Beth. Your name won't come into this."

Trust. After everything that had happened, it didn't come easy. Until the sender of the photographs was found, it was all she had. She looked up at Vincente and he smiled, an expression that warmed her in spite of everything. Maybe trust wasn't the only thing she had.

"What about the photograph that was left in Lia's crib last week?" Vincente asked. "This killer found out where Beth was living and got into her house."

"Do you have any idea how he did that, Beth?" Laurie asked.

"No. I thought I was being careful." Beth managed a rueful smile. "But you found me, as well."

"And now the woman in that picture is in danger," Vincente said. "What was her name?"

"Danielle Penn." Beth remembered Danielle from the climbs they had done together. Recalled the pretty, fun-loving woman with a mischievous smile, who loved the outdoor lifestyle and the wide-open spaces as much as Beth did. Did she want to hear that Danielle had killed herself, or died in a so-called accident?

"I was hoping you might be able to give me some

more information about her, Beth. When Cory Taylor died, Danielle lived in Cedar Hills, right at the opposite end of the county from Stillwater. She left soon after, and I haven't been able to trace her," Laurie said.

"Although she'd lived in Wyoming for several years, Danielle was Canadian. Is it possible she went home?" Beth asked. "I think she was from Toronto."

Laurie scribbled a few notes. "That helps. I'll get right on it tomorrow. And, of course, I'll be speaking to Cory Taylor's family to see if I can find out who might be responsible for sending the letter and photographs."

"What about the other surviving members of the West County Climbing Club?" Vincente asked. "If Beth is right and the items that had been burned in Andy's house were the same photographs and letters she's been getting—and the letter is not addressed to Beth, it's general, as if it *has* been sent to more than one person—then it seems likely other people have been sent them, as well."

"I've been thinking about that." Laurie flipped her notebook open to a clean page, as she got ready to take more notes. "The problem is that, if they've been sent the same letter as Beth, containing the same threat, they are going to experience the same reluctance to speak to us. If I turn up at their houses or at the next meeting of the West County Climbing Club and start asking questions, they are going to take to the hills."

Cameron placed a hand on her knee. "That was a really bad pun, my love."

Laurie frowned. "Take to the hills?" Her expression lightened when she realized what she'd said. "Sorry. But you see my dilemma. Ten people went on that climb. Nine of them returned. We know that two more have since died, and I have to tell you that, despite my official line about not jumping to conclusions, I don't like Danielle Penn's chances. If I'm right, and Danielle is dead, that leaves six survivors, including Beth. Those other five people are not going to talk to the police. It's highly likely they won't even admit they've been sent copies of the photographs."

"They might not open up to the police." There was an urgency in Vincente's voice that made Beth turn her head sharply to look at him again. "But I wonder if they would talk about it to each other."

It was late when Cameron and Laurie left. After Beth gave Laurie details of the other surviving climbers, Vincente had opened a bottle of wine and switched the conversation to other matters in an attempt to lighten the mood. Although he wasn't sure he would ever succeed in taking her mind completely away from the murders, Beth had smiled and laughed in the right places.

Laurie's news had hit Vincente like a thunderbolt. He supposed a small part of him had been prepared for Beth to be right and for the person who sent the photographs to be a murderer. But if he was honest, he had convinced himself that they were dealing with a poisonous schemer. Someone who had loved Cory Taylor and who was hurt and suffering. A person who wanted to frighten Beth because she had been with Cory when he died.

When Laurie confirmed they were likely dealing with a killer, Vincente's initial reaction had been shock. Then concern for Beth had kicked in. He had been afraid she might be too fragile to deal with this. Although she had always believed that Rick Sterling and Andy Smith were murdered, a clinical delivery of the facts from a police officer might have been too much for her to cope with.

Instead, she had surprised him. He'd seen a flash of fire in the depths of her eyes. Her voice had been calm and her hands steady. He could tell she was scared, but she wasn't going to let fear pull her under. A fierce sense of pride washed over him. Although she had run from Stillwater when she got the first photographs, she had done it with the best of motives. And she had kept herself and Lia safe in difficult circumstances. She hadn't spoken about that time, but he could tell, more from what she left unsaid, how tough it had been. Now, when the tension had been ratcheted up to a new level, she seemed to have found new reserves of strength. No. They weren't new. He could see elements of the old Beth emerging. She was starting to heal, and he wanted to nurture that. At the same time, he wanted to bring this nightmare to a speedy end.

"You asked if the members of the climbing club would talk to each other." Beth was curled into a corner of the huge, squishy sofa. "What exactly did you mean?"

Vincente had dropped that idea into the conversation and deliberately not elaborated on it. He had just let it sit there, but he had known she would pick up on it. And he knew she had already guessed what he meant.

It was late at night. They were alone together. Lia was asleep. They'd both had a glass or two of wine. The only sound was Melon snoring quietly on the rug and the wind outside stirring the pine trees. Physical contact was probably a bad idea.

To hell with it. Vincente moved closer and took her hand.

"Could you go back to the climbing club?"

Her eyelashes fluttered down, shadowing her cheeks as she looked at their entwined fingers. "I thought that might be what you meant." When she looked back up at him, her eyes appeared bluer that ever. "Honestly? I don't know. I haven't done any climbing since Cory died."

"Maybe we could go on a climb together and see if that helps your confidence?" He rubbed his thumb in a circle around her palm. The way he used to. "I'm not in your league, but I've done a few of the lower peaks on the Stillwater Trail."

"Aren't you forgetting something?" Her mouth curved in amusement. He should focus on what she was saying, not on how much he wanted to press his lips to the point where the corner of her mouth creased when she smiled.

"Hmm?"

"Short, dark, likes Jell-O, hates diaper changes…" Beth jerked a thumb in the direction of the baby monitor.

"We could ask Steffi to babysit."

A look of panic swept over her face. "I've never left her with anyone. I don't know if I could."

"Why don't we start by taking Steffi up on her offer of a visit to the animal sanctuary? We could take Lia out there tomorrow. We'll only ask Steffi to care for her while we do a climb if you feel okay with it."

Beth did that thing he'd noticed a few times. It seemed to be some sort of breathing exercise. "Shouldn't we stay here? At least when we're inside the house we know it's safe."

"Beth, this could take a long time. You heard what Laurie said. At this moment in time, no one else is even treating these deaths as murders, let alone linking them. You can't let him turn you into a prisoner." Even though he didn't want her to stay locked up inside the lake house, he wasn't going to take any chances with her safety. "At Delaney Transportation, we have a number of vehicles in the depot. I'll get Bryce to bring me a car with tinted windows tomorrow morning and swap it for mine. We'll change transport regularly and only go places where you feel safe. I'm not suggesting you walk down Main Street waving and smiling."

Although there was still a hint of reluctance in her manner, she nodded. "You're right. I can't hide away forever. It's just been good to feel safe again." Her grip on his hand tightened. "With you."

Vincente wasn't sure who closed the distance between them first. Perhaps they moved at the same time. All he knew was she was in his arms. His hand cupped her chin, tilting her face up to his. When their lips met, it was as soft and warm as the first sip of hot chocolate. The familiar feeling of Beth's body melting into his was like coming home. He kissed her the way he'd dreamed of doing in the long months when she'd been gone. All his feelings were there as his lips caressed hers and his tongue stroked hers. That kiss was the words he hadn't been able to say. The missing her, believing he'd lost her, aching to hold her one last time: it was all there in the sweet wonder of his mouth on hers. He felt his own emotions reflected in the tremor that ran through Beth's body.

When they broke apart, they were both breathing hard. Wanting hard. Beth got to her feet.

"Good night, Vincente." There was an unspoken question in the words.

He remained seated, a battle going on inside him. His emotions were raging out of control. If he listened to his body, he would go to her now and drag her into his arms. He knew from the look in her eyes how she would respond. Knew her well enough to predict the night of wild sex that would follow. But things had changed between them. No matter how hard and ready his body might be, it was time to start listening to reason. And his rational self was telling him what they'd had in the past—wonderful though it had been—wasn't going to work anymore. That, until he figured out what *was* going to work, he needed to keep his distance.

"Good night, Beth." It cost him every ounce of self-control he possessed to say it.

The animal sanctuary proved to be the perfect antidote to the drama of the previous night. Beth had worn a baseball cap and shades on the drive, and was relieved that the car Bryce had delivered to the lake house had tinted windows. Despite her nervousness, it was good to be out of the house and in a different environment.

"The primary aim of the center is to find new homes for abandoned or abused domestic and farm animals. If we can't find a home for them, they stay here." Steffi swept an arm around her, indicating the acres of land, including stables, kennels and other buildings. In the distance was the large, rambling house where she and Bryce lived. "Oh, and we also take in wild animals if they are injured or suffering."

"It must be quite a change from making movies." Beth was still finding it hard to accept that the woman showing them around had once been famous for the designer outfits in which she'd graced Hollywood's red carpets. Now Steffi wore faded jeans, a sweater in an indeterminate color and galoshes that were splattered with unmentionable sludge.

Steffi brushed her hair back from her face, leaving

a streak of grime on her temple. "I guess so, but I always used the earnings from my movies to fund an animal charity. I just did it anonymously. When I retired from that life, I decided this was what I wanted to do full-time. Now I get to do the fun parts, as well." She laughed. "Bryce complains that he only married me for my money and he doesn't see any of it because it all gets spent on animal feed."

Vincente was showing Lia around the different pens of farm animals, and she was clapping her hands together delightedly as she observed pigs, hens and goats. Steffi cast a sidelong glance in Beth's direction.

"I've never seen that look on Vincente's face."

Beth followed the direction of her gaze. "What look is that?"

Steffi didn't answer immediately. Instead, she leaned over the barrier of one of the pens, watching a group of rabbits enjoying the grass. "When I first came to Stillwater, Vincente was the person who gave me a job. I was scared out of my wits and barely able to think straight, so I hardly noticed him. What I did notice was that he wasn't happy. And as I got to know him better, that impression stayed with me. He was Bryce's brother, and he helped us when we were in a dangerous situation. But I always knew he was sad." She looked back across at Vincente. "He's not sad anymore."

"You think he's happy?" Vincente was smiling as he watched Lia's face. "I suppose it's hard to be miserable when there is a baby around."

"I don't think he's decided what he's feeling."

"That's very cryptic." Beth turned back to look at Steffi.

"You know him better than I do. I'd say Vincente's

feelings are very deep and very powerful. I don't think he'd let them out until he was absolutely sure about them. Bryce once told me that when they were growing up Vincente was the outsider, because he never tried to be anything else. He said Vincente enjoyed being the stereotypical half brother. Although Vincente was the one who displayed all the signs of jealousy, he was the one with all the gifts. Strikingly good-looking, Vincente is the artistic, intellectual one in the family, yet he can still outrun, outshoot and outswim his brothers if he chooses."

"That's the secret to Vincente." Beth smiled. "*If* he chooses. Life on Vincente's terms is never straightforward."

Steffi nodded wisely. "That's another thing Bryce said. He described living with Vincente as like wrestling an eel."

The image struck Beth as so funny that she laughed out loud. When Vincente and Lia joined them, she and Steffi were still chuckling. It felt good. It was a long time since she'd enjoyed the company of a friend and Steffi was easy to get along with.

"I never knew rabbits could be so entertaining." Vincente looked over the barrier.

"You had to be there." Steffi held out her arms to Lia, who studied her solemnly for a moment or two before returning the gesture.

Beth exchanged a glance with Vincente as he handed Lia over to Steffi. "She doesn't often do that."

"Possibly she just guessed that she's going to have a new baby cousin soon and wanted to be the first to congratulate me." Steffi seemed entranced by Lia as the baby tugged on her ear.

"Hey!" Vincente kissed his sister-in-law on the cheek. "That's wonderful news."

Steffi blushed. "I checked with Bryce and he said it was okay to tell you both today, even though he isn't here to share the celebrations."

Beth managed to reach out and give Steffi a congratulatory embrace without trapping Lia between them. She cast a glance in Vincente's direction. She had made up her mind. She would be happy to leave Lia with Steffi while they went climbing. Interpreting her look, he nodded. "If you'd like to get some practice before your own little one arrives, we have a favor to ask you…"

Chapter 8

The next day, they took Lia to Bryce and Steffi's house, then headed straight out to the Stillwater Trail. Leaving the car close to Tenderness Lake high up in the mountains, they followed the winding trail that led to Tarryn Point. Even though he had lived in this area all his life, its wild, dramatic beauty never failed to fill Vincente with awe. Gigantic trees rose on either side of them, crisp, clean air filled their lungs and a sparkling stream tumbled alongside the path.

Beth had chosen Tarryn Point for their introductory climb. They had both scaled it before, and she had decided it would be a good starting point for rebuilding her confidence. It was a popular place with first-timers, and likely to get busy later in the day.

Although Beth hadn't kept any of her equipment, Vincente had borrowed most of what they needed and purchased a few items at the store on Main Street that specialized in outdoor activities. Luckily, Laurie had been able to loan Beth a pair of climbing shoes in the correct size. Between them they carried ropes, harnesses, a bag of chalk, carabiners and quickdraws. Beth wore a woolen hat with her hair tucked up inside, and she had a pair of wraparound shades pushed up on top of her head, ready to be pulled down when they came in sight of other people.

The day was cloudy, with some sunny spells forecast. There was no rain predicted, which was good. As Beth pointed out, they didn't want to end up abandoning this first attempt because the rock was too slippery.

"I haven't worked out in months." There was an added sparkle in Beth's eyes, a spring in her step and a restlessness in her manner that Vincente hadn't seen before. "This could be a disaster if I find out my muscles aren't strong enough."

His smile was teasing. "I've seen ten-year-olds do this. I think you'll be okay."

Beth pulled a face at him and bumped her shoulder against his. The mood was lighthearted, and Vincente was glad. There had been no soul-searching from Beth about coming here today. If anything, she appeared to look forward to it. The only thing he had noticed as they approached Tarryn Point was that way her eyes were drawn beyond it. The peaks of the Stillwater Trail were an impressive sight, gaping out of the earth like jagged teeth from the jaws of a dinosaur, but one towered above the others. The Devil's Peak was a hauntingly beautiful rock spire. Actually part of a series of the three most inaccessible, it soared higher, steeper and sharper than its lesser-known sisters.

Vincente didn't feel any compulsion to climb the high peaks. Although he enjoyed competitive sports, he didn't look at the Devil's Peak and feel a surge of desire to conquer it. But no one could live in Stillwater without knowing its reputation.

Among the rock climbing community, the Devil's Peak was a coveted prize. It was technically difficult and presented even the most experienced climber with a set of unique challenges.

When they reached Tarryn Point, it was still early and there were only a few other climbers at the base of the rock. Beth chose a place several yards away from them. Placing the equipment on the ground, she began checking the length of rope with her fingers.

"The guy I borrowed it from is an experienced climber. He said it's almost new," Vincente said.

Beth pointed to the sheer rock face. "When you're halfway up there, what would you rather trust…his word, or my fingers?"

He held up his hands in a gesture of surrender. "You're the boss."

She wagged a finger at him. "Don't you forget it."

Because they were alone, they faced a choice of who should lead climb the route and who should remain at the base of the rock and belay. Vincente didn't want to push Beth, but to him, the choice was obvious. Beth was the more experienced climber. She should be the one to go up the rock and prepare the way for him. Having studied the rock face in silence for a few minutes, she began to do warm-up stretches. It seemed to Vincente that she had slipped automatically into a well-rehearsed routine.

When she reached for her shoes and harness and chalked her hands, he breathed a sigh of relief. Beth was going to do this. She was going to climb the rock face and put her trust in him to belay the rope for her. The look of steely determination told her what they both already knew…she was getting her life back on track.

With Vincente belaying, Beth started climbing. It was obvious straightaway that she had a grace and fluidity way beyond anything he had ever seen before. Her technique was relaxed, her grip easy, as she moved with her body close to the wall. Totally in control, using tight muscle movements, she climbed all the way to the top. Vincente had watched other people do this, but he'd never seen anyone as fast as Beth. Once there, she attached a quickdraw to a bolt already cemented into the rock, anchoring the rope in place before rappelling down.

"Your turn." She unhooked her carabiner.

"Wait a second." Vincente paused before he changed places with her. "That's it? No applause? No celebration? You just did your first climb in ten years. Doesn't that at least deserve a high five?"

Beth laughed. "High five? I think it deserves a hell-yeah hug."

Vincente gave a whoop of delight. Sweeping her into his arms, he swung her around in a circle.

"It felt amazing," Beth gasped when he set her back on her feet. "Like I'd never been away."

Even though her eyes were smiling, he noticed the way they slid past him again toward the dark, threatening crags. He wondered if it might have been better to go somewhere else. Somewhere where they couldn't see that towering spire that pierced the clouds. But the Devil's Peak dominated the Stillwater landscape. If Beth was hoping to come back to her old life, she would have to get used to seeing it again.

"I swore I'd climb the Devil's Peak again one day." Her voice was slightly dreamy, almost as though she was talking to the mountain, rather than to him. "To prove it hadn't beaten me."

"And will you?"

She lifted her shoulders, and the gesture seemed to break the spell. "No. I have Lia to think of now. Extreme sports and motherhood don't mix." Her smile became mischievous. "Are you going to stand around here distracting me, or are you going to get some actual exercise?"

They did several climbs, moving to a more difficult part of the rock each time. Beth called a halt when they both could feel the strain on their muscles. "We'll be sore anyway tomorrow without pushing ourselves too hard."

Instead of hiking back down the trail immediately, they found a secluded place close to the lake. Leaning against a rock, they downed their energy drinks and ate the cookies Beth had brought.

"This is my favorite part of rock climbing." Vincente leaned back against the stone, closing his eyes as the sun broke through the clouds and warmed his face.

"I can do it, Vincente." Beth's words made him open his eyes again. "I can go back to the West County Climbing Club. On one condition—"

"What's that?"

"I'd need you to come with me."

While she and Vincente were climbing, Beth hadn't had time to worry about Lia. Once they reached the car and set off to collect their daughter, her anxiety levels started to increase.

Steffi had no experience looking after a baby. What

if there had been an accident? What if the murderer had discovered Lia's whereabouts? The what-ifs became a dozen different nightmare scenarios chasing each other around inside her head.

I should never have left her.

By the time they reached the animal sanctuary, Beth's anxiety levels were almost off the scale. Her whole body was rigid with tension; only her hands seemed capable of movement, twisting together in her lap like tormented animals seeking escape. She knew Vincente was occasionally taking his eyes from the road to study her with concern, but she was so wound up, she couldn't speak.

And, of course, when they got there, Lia was fine. Neither she nor Steffi had suffered any ill effects from the time they had spent together. The worst that could be said was that Lia was a little tired and cranky from the excitement of being somewhere new. With a real effort, Beth forced herself not to seize her daughter and hug her so hard it hurt.

By the time they reached the lake house, Beth was calm again. Going through Lia's usual routine—bathing, changing, feeding, reading a story, tucking her into her crib, kissing her cheek—finally restored her equilibrium. Once Lia was asleep, she sat for long, still minutes watching her. Then she made a decision.

After switching on the baby monitor, she went through to the family room.

"I need to talk to you."

Vincente set aside the book he had been reading. "I hoped you would say that."

Beth took a seat at a right angle to him. "After Lia was born, I suffered from severe postpartum depression. I was never a danger to her, or to myself, and I was never hospitalized. I was on medication for several months and I had counseling. Although I don't attend face-to-face therapy anymore, I still occasionally call my counselor." The words had tumbled out faster than she wanted them to, and she paused to catch her breath. "I'm mostly okay now. But I have…flashbacks. I had one today."

Then she did what she had been hoping to avoid. She burst into tears.

Vincente had always been surprisingly good with tears. He wasn't embarrassed or uncomfortable with them. He wrapped his arms around her and held her, letting her lean on his broad shoulder until the worst sobs had subsided. Then he went and found some Kleenex. Using one to dry her tears, he handed her another so she could blow her nose.

"Do you need to call your counselor now?"

"No. I just wanted you to understand that I'm not going crazy. Leaving your child with someone different for the first time is going to be hard for any parent. But it was always going to be worse for me." She scanned his face to see if he could understand what she was saying. "I know what Jenny, my counselor, would say. She would tell me to celebrate today. Even though I got horribly anxious, I did it. I left Lia with Steffi… and look at me. I'm not a hopeless mess." She blew her nose again. "Not totally."

"No, you're not a hopeless mess, Beth."

The look in his eyes sent a spark of something sinful shooting down her spine. The feeling settled farther south. Surely she shouldn't be getting aroused during *this* conversation? *Ah, Vincente. What you do to me.*

"I'm glad you told me. It was very brave."

She gave a watery laugh. "Brave. That's me. I run

away. Hide behind locked doors. Don't climb a mountain for ten years after a bad experience." Could she say the next words? The intensity of those dark eyes made it difficult, but she forced herself onward. "Lie awake each night thinking about you in the next room, wishing we were together, but too scared to do anything…"

He surged toward her, hauling her to her feet. "I swore I wouldn't do this."

"So did I." She breathed the words into his lips. "But you know what, Vincente? This whole mess has taught me that life's too short. Maybe we should stop thinking about this and just have sex."

"Are you sure?" His hands gripped her hips hard. Wonderfully, painfully hard. "That's what you want? Just sex?"

"So much." She nipped his lower lip with her teeth, and he growled.

"I can give you that, Beth." As their lips met, everything crackled. A firestorm started up inside her and burned along her nerve endings. It scorched the air around them, making it hard to breathe. Hard to think. But as Vincente scooped her up into his arms, Beth decided thoughts were overrated.

When he kicked the door of his room shut and placed her on her feet, they were already tearing at each other's clothes. By the time they reached the bed, every garment had been flung to the four corners of the room. How had she lived without this—without him—for so long? The fierce wanting that had been so much a part of who she was powered through her as she wrapped her arms around him.

Vincente's groan was despairing. "No condoms."

"I went on the birth control pill after Lia was born."

His answer was to move his lips to the point where her neck met her shoulder. He knew exactly what he was doing. It was Beth's most sensitive place, and he sucked her skin, driving her instantly wild. Electricity shimmered from her neck, down her shoulders to her arms, and all the way to the tips of her fingers. Vincente kissed his way across to the hollow of her throat, the scratch of his beard a glorious contrast to his soft lips.

He dipped his head to her breasts, his breath scorching her skin.

"Ah, Beth." His voice was hoarse with need. "You'll never know how much I've dreamed of this."

He'd dreamed of it? All those long, lonely nights when the memories of this were all she'd had to drive away the fear… Then his mouth closed around her nipple and she forgot how to do anything except respond to the commands of his mouth. Her back arched, pushing her breasts closer to him. He devoured her, licking and sucking, his teeth grazing the tender bud until her breath was coming in short, ragged bursts. Beth's core was aching, throbbing in time with each movement of his mouth on her nipple. This was what she'd dreamed of. But more. It was so much better than any fantasy.

As he moved down her body, Vincente gazed at her. Beth remembered that look. He had always stared at her that way. As if she was a goddess and he worshipped her. It made her feel incredible.

Vincente took her hand in his, moving it down her body. With Vincente guiding her, Beth could feel her own arousal beneath her fingers. Vincente groaned as he lifted her hand to his lips, sucking her fingers into his mouth one by one. Beth's eyes fluttered closed as sensation after sensation buffeted her body.

"Keep them open," Vincente rasped. "We've both waited too long to miss a second of this."

His dark head moved between her legs. The heat of his mouth was like a brand against the inside of her knee, inching slowly higher. Beth jerked her hips upward just as Vincente's hot, hot breath whispered against her clitoris. The anticipation was too much and Beth writhed, throwing her head back. Then his mouth was on her and her whole world was reduced to the touch of his tongue and his lips. Nothing in her imagination had come close to this. He sucked and licked and flicked. Beth cried out, arching again, trying to press closer to that magical mouth. Shivers rolled over her skin, and her whole body tensed. It had been too long, and she was so close. Pressure was building inside her body, pulling everything taut like a giant elastic band getting ready to snap and launch her into the orgasm she craved.

"Vincente." Her hands clawed wildly at his hair. "I'm going to..."

And then it hit her. So hard and fast that she cried out. She was soaring out of control, falling over the edge of a cliff and swooping down into nothingness. Letting go of everything but that perfect sensual release as a current of pure bliss burst over her.

Vincente's beard grazed her breasts as he moved back up her body. Beth murmured against his lips as his touch sent new tingles over her swollen mouth. Then Vincente was on top of her, spreading her thighs apart with his knees. She pressed impatient kisses along his jaw, his neck, his ear.

When he thrust into her, it was fast and hard. Beth clenched her muscles tight around him as he pulled out, then pumped into her again. Over and over. The feeling of him filling her was so achingly familiar, so perfect, that tears stung the back of her eyelids. Everything in her pulsed in perfect time with him. This was theirs. Their time. Their rhythm. Their lovemaking.

She could feel Vincente's need matching her own. Could hear it in his ragged breathing. Feel it in the bunched muscles of his shoulders as she tightened her arms around him. See it in the blaze of passion in his eyes.

The longing was building inside her again. Her body was tightening, ecstasy building once more. The heat became a flame as Vincente placed his hands beneath her buttocks, lifting her closer to him, driving harder and faster, letting her feel him fully embedded. The furnace sparked, then roared, then exploded.

Her release rushed through her, a crescendo of sensation that just kept coming. Wave after wave crashed over her as she called out Vincente's name. He plunged deep one last time, then gasped out his own completion.

After a minute or two of catching their breath, Vincente pressed his forehead to Beth's. "I am so glad my imagination didn't lie about how great it's always been between us."

She gave a shaky laugh. "It's the one thing we never got wrong."

He moved to lie next to her, drawing her into his arms. They lay like that, in silence for a long time. "I think I'm going to need a repeat performance." She tilted her head in time to catch the wicked smile on his lips. "Maybe more than one. How do you feel about a change of room?"

She nestled closer. This felt good. *Just sex, remember?*

"We can hear Lia from here, and she was used to her

own room in the house in Casper, remember? I don't have a problem with a new roommate." She returned the smile, resting her chin on his chest. "Particularly when the benefits are so enjoyable."

Vincente gave a groan of submission as she kissed her way down his body.

Chapter 9

Vincente woke slowly the next morning, vaguely aware that it was still early and that his arms were full of Beth's soft, warm curves. He lay still, not thinking, just feeling, enjoying the little things he'd missed. The difference in size between her slender arms and his muscular ones. Her pale skin compared to his tan flesh. The smattering of golden freckles across her shoulders. The way she burrowed her head deep into his chest, her hair tickling his chin. The way his heart felt lighter when she was with him.

His emotions were a riot of confusion. The overwhelming need to protect Beth and Lia, to shelter them from harm, was radiated back at him by her nearness. Holding Beth in his arms didn't make every care and stress disappear, but they faded into the background. This moment was so good he never wanted it to end. All he wanted to do was bury his face in her hair and drift away on the scent of heaven.

As he came further awake, he analyzed his choices. He *should* get up, shower and dress, and be ready to call Trey Reid and find out if he needed any help. His temporary replacement at Delaney Transportation was doing a good job, but Vincente still checked in every day to make sure. He *could* obey the promptings of his body and wake Beth with a kiss. Since he was perfectly content, he decided to lie still, feeling her warmth, absorbing her comfort and indulging in the moment.

When his cell phone rang sometime later, Beth murmured a protest. Slipping from the bed, Vincente pulled on his jeans and left the room to take the call. It was Laurie.

"I've got some information about Danielle Penn. Can I come over?"

Vincente scrubbed a hand over his face. "I guess that means it's not good news."

"You guessed right."

He ended the call as Beth emerged from the bedroom wearing the shirt he'd discarded the night before. She looked half-awake and unbearably sexy. The urge to drag her back to bed was almost irresistible. Almost.

As she rose on the tips of her toes to press a kiss on his lips, he caught hold of her waist. Draw her too close and he would be lost. Instead, he returned the kiss lightly.

"You are way too tempting for this time of the morning." His voice was filled with regret. "But Laurie is on her way over."

Her expression changed instantly, becoming wary. Before she could speak, there was a shout from the master bedroom and Lia started rattling the bars of her crib, her usual demand for breakfast.

"You see to her, I'll fix coffee." As she turned to go, Vincente caught hold of her wrist, halting her. "Last night was amazing."

Her smile was pure mischief, chasing away the look of fear. "Which time?"

He groaned. "Go now…or I won't be responsible for the consequences."

By the time Laurie arrived, they had, between them, achieved the remarkable feats of both showering and dressing, eating breakfast and getting Lia ready.

"Even the guard dog has been fed," Vincente said with a note of pride as he buzzed Laurie in. "No one would ever guess we've hardly slept."

"You have your T-shirt on inside out," Beth pointed out as she gulped down her third cup of coffee.

Laurie looked far too alert as she strode into the kitchen with a bright smile. Accepting the offer of a drink, she followed Vincente and Beth through to the family room. Lia, who had developed a newfound confidence, insisted on spending a few minutes on Laurie's knee, examining her badge before crawling away to play with her toys.

Laurie got straight to the point, pulling the familiar notebook out of her shoulder bag. "It's not good news. Danielle Penn died a week ago."

Beth reached for Vincente's hand, the color draining from her face. "How did she die?"

"Initially, it looked like she committed suicide." Laurie delivered the facts in her usual no-nonsense way. "She hanged herself. But even before I explained about Rick Sterling and Andy Smith, and the photographs and letter you'd received, the Toronto Police Service had some doubts. They already suspected it could be murder."

"Why?" Beth leaned forward, her gaze intent.

"Because she died on her wedding day…and she was wearing her bridal gown."

Beth's face paled even more, her fingers tangling tighter with Vincente's. Even though he hadn't known Danielle, he winced at the image of a bride with her head in a noose. "It's a pretty extreme way out, but maybe she just couldn't go through with it?"

"That was how it was meant to look," Laurie said. "But there were some things that didn't add up."

"Such as?" Since Beth seemed incapable of speaking, Vincente continued with the questioning.

"Danielle had fresh scratch marks on her wrists at the time she died. The coroner speculated that she could have been self-harming, but there was no evidence to suggest she'd done that in the past. Nothing was found under her nails to either suggest that the marks were self-inflicted, or that she'd scratched another person. There were no older injuries—no one had ever seen any signs that she had harmed herself previously. The other possibility was that she had been involved in a struggle. Also, the heel had broken off one of her shoes." Laurie shrugged. "We can speculate about how, in a distressed and suicidal state, she damaged the shoes she was going to wear for her wedding. Equally, we can picture a scene where she was wearing them as she fought for her life."

Beth exhaled audibly. "She'd have fought. That's the sort of person she was. But Danielle was tiny…and on her wedding day? When she was already in her gown? Even if she'd been sent the letter and the photographs and been taking care of her safety, she wouldn't have been prepared for *that*."

"Exactly." Laurie nodded. "I told the detectives investigating Danielle's death about the letter and the photographs. They questioned her family and her fiancé, but no one knew anything about them. If she was sent copies, she never told anyone."

"Were there any other reasons to suspect she was murdered?" Vincente asked.

"The other reasons are more feelings than facts. Danielle was just so darned happy to be getting married. It's hard to get inside someone else's head, but everyone who knew them described her and her fiancé as the most loving couple ever. One of the detectives sent me a video clip of the wedding rehearsal dinner that the family released. It gives a flavor of Danielle's mood." Laurie withdrew her cell phone from her jacket pocket. "It's just a couple of minutes, if it's not too painful for you to watch it, Beth?"

"Okay." Beth gave a determined nod.

Vincente took the phone and held it so they could both see the recording. It showed a couple dancing with a group of people around them laughing and clapping. The person filming it had focused on Danielle. Petite, blonde and pretty, she couldn't have smiled more if she'd tried. And she couldn't take her eyes from her husband-to-be. Laurie was right. Danielle's happiness was so infectious it came right out of the screen and grabbed him.

"Stop." It was a sharp demand from Beth.

He pressed Pause and handed the cell phone back to Laurie. He guessed seeing her friend so full of life and knowing how she had died had been too much for Beth. "I'm sorry…"

He turned to her, expecting to see tears. Instead, he saw dawning shock. She held her hand out to Laurie in an impatient demand for the return of the cell phone. Rewinding the recording a few seconds, Beth paused it again.

"Can you enlarge a still of this frame?" She held the phone up so Laurie could see the blurred image.

"I guess so." Laurie's face was bemused. There was nothing much to see. Just a group of people smiling as the camera panned and Danielle twirled in the arms of her fiancé. "Why?"

Beth tapped the screen with one finger, singling out one of the guests. "Because this guy here is Rick Sterling."

The West County Climbing Club was situated in the town of Whitebridge, on the southwestern edge of the county. It was an hour's drive from Stillwater, and Beth spent most of that time explaining to Vincente why she refused to accept that Rick Sterling had killed Danielle. In the end it came down to one simple, unshakable belief.

"Rick is a good guy."

"Things can happen to good guys and turn them into killers." Vincente was driving another of the cars from the Delaney Transportation fleet. Lia was with her aunt Steffi again. Both of them were so delighted at the arrangement that Beth had been able to quell the flurry of nerves she felt when they left. "What happened to Cory Taylor had an impact on all of you. And Rick was in charge. Who knows what effect it had on him?"

Beth turned away to look at the landscape flashing past. The countryside had taken on brighter tones in the past few weeks, changing from the brown-and-green hues of summer to the red-and-orange tones of fall. The cottonwoods had assumed a yellow hue so flashy it looked like the trees had been sprayed with reflective paint. Beside their neon brightness the other trees put on a more dignified show as they prepared to shed their leaves. In the past, this display had never failed to soothe her. Fall was her favorite time of year, bringing thoughts of walks in the cooler weather, hot, sweet drinks, pumpkin pie and cowl-neck sweaters. This year it only made her wonder if her nightmare would still be going on when the first snows of winter came.

Vincente placed a hand on her knee, his grip light but steady. "If Rick is such a good guy, why did he fake his own death? And why was he at Danielle's wedding rehearsal?"

His voice was gentle, but she couldn't ignore those questions. She slumped farther down in her seat, tilting her baseball cap down over her face. There was a killer on her tail, and right now Rick looked guilty as hell. Laurie had passed the information on to the detectives working the case in Toronto. They were enhancing the image from the video clip and interviewing the other guests about Rick. Laurie said Rick would be long gone and Beth suspected she was right.

Even though the climbing club was still located in the same sports center in which the group had rented space ten years ago, it had moved on in other ways. Beth had been able to find details of meeting dates through the website, and the membership appeared to have grown. There was a thriving kids' club and there was now an indoor climbing wall and gym.

"In my day, we ran around the track, then climbed the nearest rock face," Beth said with a touch of envy.

Vincente laughed as he parked the car. "In my day? How old are you again, Grandma?"

She was glad things hadn't gotten awkward between them. The thought almost made her laugh. Awkward? Things had gotten very, very good. This "just sex" thing was working out fine. Better than fine. As distractions went, Vincente was the ultimate way to divert her mind from unpleasant thoughts. The only problem was, she might just be a little bit obsessed with the diversion...

"Vincente is kind of a unique name in West County." Beth emphasized the Italian pronunciation. "It singles you out. If the murderer is here, he could trace us back to Stillwater through your name."

"What do you suggest I call myself?" He leaned against the car, folding his arms across his chest and smiling down at her. Even though she was about to walk back through that door for the first time in ten years, her heart did a double somersault and her mouth watered. All because Vincente Delaney, the man she had woken up with this morning, was giving her *that* look.

"I don't know." She pretended to concentrate on the question instead of on how much she wanted to run her tongue along his lower lip. "You don't look like a Vinnie."

"Vinnie?" The word came out as a growl.

"Maybe just plain Vincent?"

"Honey." He hooked his fingers in the waistband of her jeans, tugging her closer. "I've never been 'plain' anything."

Beth wriggled free. Making out in the parking lot was tempting, but possibly not the wisest thing to do when she was supposed to be lying low. "I'll introduce you as Del. Short for Delaney."

That brief exchange meant she walked toward the climbing club with a slight smile on her face. And she guessed that had been Vincente's intention.

As they neared the club doors, they passed an old Ford Mustang parked in one of the bays. There was a sticker in the rear window announcing in giant letters that *Rock climbers do it up against the wall!*

Vincente rolled his eyes. "If that's a sample of climbing humor, remind me to give the Christmas party a miss."

The first thing Beth noticed when she stepped inside was the smell. It instantly transported her back in time ten years. It was a sporty aroma. Varnished floors, someone's forgotten, unwashed gym clothes and the scent of sweaty bodies. The room the climbing club used also added another layer. Cheap coffee. Beth guessed they were still using the same nose-wrinkling brand.

There was a table set up just inside the door, and a man and a woman were seated at it, taking names. The woman's mouth dropped open in surprise and her pen clattered to the floor as she stared at Beth.

"Bethany Wade! Oh, my Lord. How wonderful to see you after all this time."

She had risen and was coming around the table with the clear intention of embracing Beth. It was only when she got up close that Beth finally recognized her. That was how much Tania Blake had changed since she last saw her.

Ten years ago, Tania had been the coleader with Rick Sterling on the ill-fated Devil's Peak climb. Beth remembered a woman in her thirties. While not exactly beautiful, Tania had been strikingly attractive, with a stunning figure. A strong feature of her personality had been her confidence. Vocal, opinionated and loud, the one thing Tania had never done was conform.

This woman was a shadow of the one Beth had known. It was hard to tell if Tania still had her stunning curves, since her figure was hidden beneath baggy, unflattering clothes. Her brown hair was gray at the temples and cut in an unflattering, uneven style. Her face was drawn, her skin pale and blotchy. The dark circles beneath her eyes added to the impression of ill health. As Tania drew her into a quick, awkward hug, Beth noticed the way the other woman's hands shook.

"This is my friend Del. I hope you don't mind if we sit in on the meeting. I haven't been climbing for a long time, and I'd like to get back into it." Beth didn't have to fake the emotion in her voice. "But it's been hard…"

Tears filled Tania's eyes as she pressed Beth's hand. "I know exactly what you mean. It took me a long time to come back here. There are a few other people from the Devil's Peak climb who are still members. You may see them here tonight."

"Who are they?" Beth scanned the room. There were a number of people occupying the seats that had been set out in rows facing the low-level podium that was used by visiting speakers. Most of them had their backs to her, so it was difficult to judge whether she knew them.

"Peter Sharp is already here." Tania nodded toward a man seated near the front of the room. "And Isaac Harper sometimes stops by. The meeting will be starting soon. Why don't you take a seat, and we can catch up over coffee?"

They moved away and Vincente caught hold of Beth's arm before she could take a seat. "That woman is living on her nerves. Was she like that when you went climbing with her? No way would I trust her as my partner."

"No. She was the coleader with Rick, and she was one of the most capable people you've ever met. Unlike Rick, climbing wasn't her full-time profession. She also had a high-powered job as a computer systems analyst."

"She is definitely not coping now. I wonder if there's a chance her anxiety could be related to the murderer." Vincente cast a glance over his shoulder at Tania, who was fussily tidying the table. Her companion gave a definite eye roll as she knocked a pile of papers to the floor. "She looks like a woman who could be living in fear."

"I'll see what I can find out when I talk to her later." Beth led the way to where Peter Sharp was sitting.

Peter had been the oldest member of the team on the Devil's Peak expedition. He would be a useful person to talk to, having been Cory's climbing partner for many years. He was also the paramedic who had tried to relieve Cory's pain during that nightmare on the Devil's Peak. He was a quiet, modest man; Beth hadn't known much about him except that he and Cory had seemed unlikely friends. Peter was an introvert, while Cory had been such a big personality.

"Peter?" He looked up as she approached. "I don't know if you remember me—"

As soon as he saw her face, Peter flung up a hand as though warding off a possible attack. "Please go away."

"I just wanted to say hi." Beth was shocked at the pain on his features. "It's been a long time."

"I don't want to talk about what happened back then. Not to you. Not to anyone. Not ever."

Vincente placed a hand on her arm. "I think it would be best if we sat somewhere else."

Beth nodded, allowing him to draw her to a seat toward the back of the room. She felt stunned by what had just happened. She had to force her mind off the encounter and onto what was being said as the man who had been at the door with Tania moved to the front of the room and introduced himself.

"For those of you who don't know me, I'm Neil Stone…and yes, I've heard every joke there is about my name and rock climbing." There was a ripple of polite laughter. "I'm the president of the West County Climbing Club, and I'd like to extend a warm welcome to our new members and to our guests."

Stone proceeded to spend the next half hour outlining recent successes and proposing future plans. He had a mind-numbingly dull voice, and Beth was aware of Vincente shifting restlessly in his seat. She turned her head to look at him and encountered one of his scorching looks.

"Are you bored?" She kept her voice low so that only he could hear.

"Not when I can look at you."

"Flirt." She mouthed the word at him.

He shook his head. "Honest."

Aware of someone watching them, Beth glanced around and caught Tania's gaze on them. Feeling like a kid caught passing notes by the teacher, she felt the color flood her cheeks as she hurriedly focused her attention back on Stone.

Chapter 10

When the meeting ended, most people stayed for coffee. Beth noticed Peter didn't hang around. He was sprinting out the door almost as soon as Stone said his last word.

"Why does he come here if it makes him so uncomfortable?" she asked Vincente the words that had been bothering her ever since she had spoken to Peter.

"Was it being here that affected him, or was it seeing you again? He seemed quite composed until you approached him," Vincente said. "It's possible seeing you brought back painful memories."

Beth was unconvinced. "If that's the case, wouldn't he feel the same when he sees Tania? And she said Isaac Harper sometimes comes to meetings."

"Who knows? But you were the one who was with Cory when he died. Maybe that was why he reacted so strangely to you. Since Peter has gone, there isn't much we can do about him right now. Let's concentrate on Tania. You talk to her while I socialize."

Beth went to the table where the coffee was being served. She knew from past experience that the only way to make it palatable was to add plenty of cream and sugar. Having completed this task, she searched the room, seeking out Tania. The other woman had returned to the desk and was sorting through a stack of papers.

"Can I get you a coffee?" Beth's words as she approached made Tania jump. "I'm sorry. I didn't mean to startle you."

"It's okay." Tania let out a long, shaky breath and attempted a smile. "I guess I just startle easily. Coffee would be good."

"Cream and sugar?"

Tania nodded. "Plenty of it."

When Beth returned with the drinks, they went to sit in a corner of the room. Beth noticed Vincente in the middle of a group of people who were having a very animated conversation. She contrasted their laughter to her own companion. Tania's hand shook so badly as she held her cup that some of her coffee slopped onto her jeans. She looked at the stain as if she wanted to cry.

"Here." Beth took a Kleenex from her purse and placed it over the spilled coffee on Tania's knee.

"Oh." Tania stared at the tissue for a moment, then rested her coffee cup on it. "Thank you."

"Is everything okay with you, Tania? You seem… tense." *Tense?* The woman was wound tight as a spring.

Tania's gray eyes lifted to her face. "I haven't seen you for a long time, but it was no secret among the people who knew me. I had a tough time dealing with what happened." Her lip trembled. "With Cory's death."

"We all did." Beth kept her voice gentle. She tried to remember what happened immediately after Cory's death. How had Tania reacted? She couldn't recall. If anything, she'd have said the two coleaders went into a kind of automatic response mode, shutting down feelings and simply moving from one action to the next. But once the immediate aftermath was over, Beth had distanced herself from everyone and everything to do with the climb. She hadn't seen anything more of Tania.

"No. You don't understand." Tania made a gulping noise as she swallowed. "I had a breakdown. Oh, it was a gradual decline, but Cory's death was the trigger. I just couldn't cope with the feelings of guilt."

"Did you get any help?" Beth placed a hand on Tania's other knee, the one that was free of coffee stains.

"They told me later—after I was diagnosed with severe depression—that I left it too late. If I'd asked for help sooner, things wouldn't have gotten so bad." From her own experience, Beth knew it was never too late to get help. It seemed an odd thing for a medical professional to say, but she didn't want to upset Tania further by questioning her. Tears spilled over, but Tania appeared not to notice them. "You know what I was like back then. I thought it was a weakness to admit I couldn't deal with it by myself."

Having suffered from depression herself, Beth knew exactly what she meant. That first cry for help was one of the most difficult parts. For someone like Tania, someone once so assured and confident, it must have been that much harder.

"I've been in the same situation." One thing she had

learned from her own experiences was that taking the stigma away was important. Mental health issues were often seen as something shameful, something that should be hidden away. Tania had been brave enough to open up to her. The least Beth could do was reciprocate. "I suffered from postpartum depression. Our experiences were probably not the same, but I can relate to what you are saying."

For the first time, there was a flash of emotion other than grief in the washed-out depths of Tania's eyes. There was a spark of interest, and something more. Was it gratitude? Beth wasn't able to interpret it.

"I was hospitalized." The words were tumbling out now, as though Beth's own admission had released them. "For a long time. And my life changed. *I* changed. I lost my job, my friends—even my family changed their attitudes toward me..."

"But you came through it. You survived." Although Beth used the encouraging phrase, she wasn't sure it was true. Was she talking to a survivor? She wasn't convinced. Cory was the one who had died on the mountain, but they were all victims to varying degrees. Tania was alive, so in that sense she had come through the experience. But the damage it had caused meant her life had been destroyed.

Although she sympathized with Tania, Beth was here for a reason. If Tania's anxiety had been made worse by threats from the murderer, she had to find a way to approach the subject. She sipped her coffee, grimacing at the oversweet taste and tried to find a way to start. Tania's next words startled her.

"Nine people came down from that mountain alive, and three of them have died in the last year and a half."

Tania's stress levels seemed to have been ratcheted up to crisis point. She was shaking so hard her teeth were chattering. Beth took her coffee cup from her and placed it on the floor.

"Breathe in deep through your nose and out slowly through your mouth." She waited while Tania followed her instructions. After a few minutes of deep breathing Tania appeared calmer. "It's horrible to think of people we knew dying, but we have no reason to believe that Rick's, Andy's and Danielle's deaths were linked." Beth hated to push her when Tania was clearly already so distressed, but both their lives could depend on this. "Do we?"

Tania looked nervously around the room. "Not here." Her voice dropped to a whisper. "I don't want to talk about it here."

Beth's heart gave a thud so loud she wondered if Vincente might be able to hear it all the way across the room. "Why don't we meet for lunch tomorrow?"

Tania nodded. "Give me your number and I'll call you."

Beth drew a piece of paper and a pen from her purse. She might be excited at the prospect of getting information, but she wasn't about to get sloppy. Tania was as frail as a young tree in a thunderstorm, but if the murderer somehow got to her and found Beth's details…

"Why don't I call you?"

"I've decided to speak to Edgar about doing some freelance work."

Vincente had noticed a change in Beth since they had returned from Whitebridge. On the drive back to Stillwater, she had told him about her conversation with

Tania, and her conviction that the other woman, although fearful, wanted to talk about the deaths of their fellow climbers. They had discussed ways she could meet with Tania the next day without exposing herself to danger. Eventually, they had come up with a plan with which Vincente was happy.

Then Beth had lapsed into silence. Vincente, casting occasional glances her way, had been unable to interpret the expression on her face. Something about the visit to the climbing club had triggered this mood of deep intro-spection. She had shaken it off when they collected Lia, laughing as Steffi filled them in on the details of their daughter's stay with her. Now, as they took some post-dinner exercise by strolling along the pebbly shoreline of the private beach beneath the lake house, Beth's ex-pression was determined.

Vincente, who was carrying Lia on his shoulders, paused in his stride. He had wanted Beth to break free of the restraints imposed on her by the murderer. But Dani-elle's death changed things. The video clip of Rick Ster-ling heightened the danger. At the same time, it meant they had a clearer idea of whom they could trust. Not that there had ever been any doubt about Edgar Powell. His concerns were more about logistics.

Beth appeared to be reading his mind. "I'll work from home."

Home. He glanced back at the lake house. The lights were on, casting a golden glow through the protective pine trees and onto the deck. Home was what it had become over the last few weeks. His, Beth's and Lia's. Melon dropped a stick at his feet as if to give him a not-so-subtle reminder. Okay, it was the damn guard dog's home, too.

It occurred to him, in that brief moment of clarity, that nowhere had ever felt like home to him until now. Not properly. His stepmom had done everything she could to make the house he grew up in feel comfortable for him. Sandy Delaney, Cameron and Bryce's mother, had been a big-hearted woman who had included Vincente in every aspect of family life. It wasn't her fault his own mother had already done too much damage. Later, when he left home, he had resided in a series of bland apartments, finally settling in the luxurious downtown riverside complex where he now lived. And that was the point. It was where he *lived*. It wasn't home. Just like his mother's increasingly lavish Italian villas weren't home when he went to visit her.

Because home wasn't about the place. It was about who was there. He could take Beth, Lia—and Melon—to a shack in the mountains and they would make it home. The thought took his breath away.

"Vincente? Are you listening to me?"

No. I am scaring myself senseless.

"Yes." He recovered quickly. "But how will you communicate with Edgar? I mean, I'm assuming the stuff you guys will be dealing with won't exactly be straightforward. Will a phone conversation work?"

Her brow wrinkled. "I thought about that and I don't think it would. I wouldn't be able to go into Edgar's office. Sitting in a busy law office in the middle of Main Street wouldn't exactly be following Laurie's instructions to keep a low profile. Which is why I wondered how you would feel about letting Edgar know where I'm staying. That way, he could bring the work to me and we could have a regular meeting about it here at the lake house."

Vincente considered it, weighing up the different sides of the argument. Laurie had told them to stay vigilant. They needed to remember that now more than ever. Yet he wanted to see that new spark in Beth's eye. The one that said she was ready to move forward. And they were talking about Edgar Powell, one of Stillwater's most well-respected citizens. If they couldn't trust him, they couldn't trust anyone.

But we can't trust anyone...

"Let's ask Laurie. We'll be seeing her tomorrow."

Beth nodded. "Good idea."

They turned back toward the house. "What made you decide this today?"

"I'd been thinking about it ever since Edgar gave me his card, but there seemed to be too many reasons not to do it."

He kept his eyes on Beth's profile, watching the sweep of her lashes and the curve of her lips. She had stopped dragging her hair back into a ponytail and was wearing it loose in the old style he preferred. He didn't flatter himself that it had anything to do with him. It was another statement about how she was getting back to the way she wanted to be.

It was a pleasant evening and Lia's feet were warm and bare in his hands. She tangled her fingers in his hair and made the soft cooing noises that told him she was getting sleepy. He didn't need to analyze the feeling anymore. Vincente was thirty-three years old and he was finally able to recognize contentment.

"Then today, after talking to Tania, I realized how close I'd come to being like her."

Vincente frowned. "You are nothing like her."

"I could have been." She turned her head to look at

him. "We both fought a mental illness. The only difference is in the degree to which it got a hold on us. And, when I looked at her, it just made me more determined than ever not to let *him* control my life. Getting back to work may only be a small thing, but it would be a start."

They reached the wooden stairs that led up to the deck. Beth placed her foot on the first step, turning back to look over her shoulder. "And, Vincente?"

He was swinging Lia down from his shoulders to his arms, ready to carry her into the house, but something in her voice made him pause. "Yes?"

"I'm glad you decided to follow Laurie to Casper that day. Until you came along, I couldn't see a way out of the hopelessness I was feeling. Without your help, I'd have just sunk deeper." She laughed. "Now come on, let's get that sleepy baby inside."

She ran lightly up the steps, and Vincente followed at a slower pace. That had been a perfect moment. Beneath a star-studded sky, gazing into Beth's eyes, he'd been tempted to tell her what the last week or so had meant to him. But how did he put what it had meant into words when he didn't understand it himself? That word, the one that scared him half to death, danced enticingly just out of his reach.

Did he love Beth? Did he even know how to love? He had always believed the part of him that should perform that function was broken. Now, as he watched her trim rear end sway just above him, a tight feeling gripped his chest. He had let that important moment slip away, and the sense of loss was overpowering.

He had no idea what he was feeling, but he was being flung in every direction by the storm of emotions coursing through him. He had always felt more for Beth than for any other person in his life, but there were other layers to their relationship now. Some of them were to do with Lia, but most were simply about *them*. And Vincente didn't know what the hell to do with this newness. His customary decisiveness had deserted him. There were so many unknowns, he didn't know where to begin. Beth had said this was just sex. Was that true? Or had it been her way of getting past his fear of intimacy? Had he used up any chance he had of more? Did he even want more? More importantly, did she?

He was so terrified of screwing this up, he didn't know how to act around her anymore. And that was making him crazy. In the past, Beth had been his best friend as well as his lover. Now she felt like a stranger. Someone whose next move he was constantly trying to analyze.

He wanted to sit her down and talk for hours about his feelings…and hers. But if he didn't know what outcome he wanted, what use would that be? Over the last year, he had seen both his brothers fall in love. Cameron and Bryce were blissfully happy with their wives. But Vincente had long ago convinced himself that long-term wasn't for him. He believed the Delaney capacity for domesticity had bypassed him. When it came to family life, he was an Alberti. He had inherited his mother's destructive genes. For the first time ever, he allowed himself to wonder if he might have been wrong in his assessment of his own genetic code.

And if he was, where the hell did that leave him and Beth now?

Kissing Vincente had always been heavenly. It was everything the fairy tales promised, and more. More, because his kisses hinted at a wickedness and spice those genteel princesses in the storybooks knew nothing about.

The first touch of his lips on hers fanned the flames of passion that had been rising between them all evening. His mood had been hard to interpret. Brooding, but not dark. Introspective, but not low. Every time she looked his way, he was watching her. Almost as if he'd never seen her before. When she finally quirked a questioning brow in his direction, he moved toward her and initiated this scorching kiss.

Beth lost herself in his heat. Vincente's beard was rough against her skin, the familiar sensation delightfully abrasive. His mouth searched hers, his tongue flicking and caressing. Beth moaned at the sensation. Moaned at how much she wanted him. It had always been this way. Ever since that first kiss.

"Do you remember the first time?" She was breathing hard when they broke the kiss. But so was he.

"Of course I do. I was shocked. You came on to me so hard I didn't know what hit me."

"*I* came on to *you*? Your memory is failing you, Delaney. What actually happened is you could barely wait until we were outside Dino's before you slammed me up against the wall and…oh!"

The breath left her body with a combination of surprise and the sudden force of being pinned to the wall with Vincente's big hands holding her shoulders in place. "You mean like this?"

"That's exactly what I mean." Beth ran her fingers over his forearms, moving up to explore the hard muscles of his biceps and shoulders.

"I think my memory might be returning." His dark eyes glittered with desire, exactly the way they had that night. The same shivery feeling tracked its way down her spine. "Remind me what came next."

She looped her hands around the back of his neck brought his head down to hers. "Then I guess things may have gotten a little out of hand."

Beth explored his mouth, sucking and nipping at his lower lip as she arched her body into his. There had been other kisses before Vincente. She'd dated, had boyfriends. But nothing had prepared her for what she would feel when she kissed Vincente. Her whole body reacted, became part of the kiss, was controlled by him. Wanted his domination. She trembled with desire, instantly needed more and knew he felt the same.

Vincente growled against her mouth. "Damn it, Beth." He may have uttered something similar back then.

His erection pressed hard into her belly, and she pushed up onto her toes to press herself more intimately to it. Vincente placed his hands under her buttocks and lifted her even closer. Wrapping her legs around him, she held on tight, not breaking the kiss as he strode down the hall toward the bedroom.

His mouth moved lower, nuzzling a trail of fire as he kissed and licked along her jaw and up to her ear. He kicked the bedroom door closed and set her on her feet, immediately yanking her blouse open. Beth helped him by tugging it the rest of the way off. Her other clothes quickly followed and Vincente's gaze was soon devouring her naked body.

"You're beautiful." He'd said those words that first time in the same hoarse, worshipful tone.

He stripped off his T-shirt and jeans, and molten heat flooded Beth's core at the sight of his erection straining against his black boxer briefs. Vincente moved toward her with a determined look in his eyes, catching hold of her around her waist and almost throwing her down onto the bed. He joined her, straddling her and pinning her arms above her head with one hand holding her wrists. The raw need in his eyes matched her own, and Beth arched her back toward him, offering herself to him. His hold on her hands was light, but she was excited by it, turned on at the thought of him dominating her.

Vincente changed position, moving between Beth's thighs and using his knees to spread her legs wide. As his gaze slid down her exposed body, Beth squirmed, enjoying the sensation of him looking at her. Enjoying her. Vincente raised his eyes to her face, and she moaned, signaling her need to be touched, or licked or sucked. Now.

Vincente's mouth was hot on her breast, his tongue a hungry rasp on her nipple. Her core tightened with pleasure in response. Vincente slid one finger along her center, and she jerked as though he'd applied electrodes to her nerve endings. He swirled his fingertip around her clitoris for one amazing moment, before he plunged two fingers into her, hooking them into a tender spot deep within. Beth bucked and writhed against his hand as his fingers continued their magic while his thumb teased her sensitive nub.

It felt like too much sensation. She was breathing hard and fast, her heart thundering out a drumbeat against her ribs, her entire body pulled taut. Her orgasm was building in every part of her, in her skin, her bones, even in her teeth. Building, pulsing, burning. Demanding to be let out.

Her muscles clenched around Vincente's fingers as he drove her relentlessly on. She cried out as her release finally came, flooding through her in warm, honeyed waves.

"That was…"

"Just the beginning."

Vincente released her hands so he could remove his boxer briefs. Even though she had just come, the sight of him made her mouth water, and she reached out a hand to caress him. Vincente groaned with pleasure at her touch.

Gripping her thighs, he hauled her against him, holding her in place so she could feel him hot and hard at her entrance. Beth licked her lips. "Hold my hands again."

Fire flared in the depths of his eyes as he gripped her wrists. "You like that?" he rasped. "You like it when I'm in charge?"

She squirmed against him, the words firing her hunger up even higher. "Yes, Vincente."

"Then I'm in charge all the way. You don't come until I give you permission. Understand?"

Beth moaned. She felt like he'd just triggered a series of heavenly electric shocks along her nerve endings. This was so far beyond any boundaries they'd pushed before. It was so deliciously wrong…and she loved it.

Vincente pushed against her, then paused. "Understand?"

"Yes, Vincente."

His name turned into a cry on her lips as Vincente thrust himself into her, ramming his erection so deep Beth saw stars. Her tight muscles stretched to accommodate him, and that wonderful aching feeling filled her. Vincente dragged out of her and drove back in, the angle hitting her deep inside at just the right place. Beth rocked her hips up to meet his next thrust. Pressure was already building inside her. She was a geyser threatening to blow, her internal muscles clenching around him.

"Not yet, Beth." Vincente gripped her wrists harder, his dark eyes glittering a warning as he raised his head. "I haven't given you permission."

He pumped harder and faster, and she bit back a sound close to a sob at the delightful torment. She was teetering at the edge of release. So close it was painful. Clamping her muscles tight around his pounding shaft, she managed to delay her orgasm. It was the most perfect torture. She had never felt so alive. Her whole body buzzed with a new awareness. The fluttering inside her vagina was building, spreading throughout every cell in her body.

Vincente fit into her so perfectly, keeping the sensations growing, bonding their bodies together. Beth started to shake uncontrollably. Her spine arched and her toes curled. She needed to grip something, but her hands were restrained.

"Vincente, please." She could barely speak. "I need…"

He released her hands and she grasped his shoulders, her nails piercing his flesh. Burying his fingers in her hair, he gazed into her eyes.

"Now, Beth. With me."

He thrust into her once more, and Beth came. The intensity of her orgasm devastated her. It was as if a ball of fire had traveled from the point where her body connected with Vincente's, up her spine and out through the top of her head. The experience left her boneless and weightless, floating on a cloud of bliss. Her entire body shuddered with wave after wave of aftershocks. Through it all, Vincente's gaze remained locked on hers while his own body tightened with his release.

After what felt like hours locked together in ecstasy, Vincente slowly withdrew from her and moved to lie at her side. Still stunned by the emotional roller coaster, Beth curled into his arms.

Beth wanted to explain what she'd felt. To tell him about the strength of her feelings. What had just happened between them had transcended anything physical. And she knew, when he'd looked into her eyes as they climaxed together, that Vincente had experienced it, too.

She tilted her head back to look at his face. And that was when, through the thin drapes covering the bedroom window, she saw the silhouette of someone standing on the deck.

Chapter 11

The note of horror in Beth's voice as she cried out jerked Vincente out of his post-sex drowsiness. He opened his eyes to find her already scrambling from the bed and diving into her clothes.

"A man. On the deck." She pointed as she ran toward the other bedroom. To Lia.

Vincente bounded up, grabbing his jeans and tugging them on. If there was someone on the deck, why the hell hadn't Melon raised the alarm?

When he thought about the layout of the house, the answer became obvious. There was only one way for an intruder to get onto the deck outside the bedroom window. He, or she, would have to come down the cliff face, onto the roof of the house, and climb down from there. There were no alarm sensors there, because no one ever imagined a trespasser would seriously make the attempt to get in that way. Melon was in his bed in the kitchen, overlooking the lake. That meant he was on the opposite side of the house to the bedroom. As long as the guy had climbed down from the roof stealthily, Melon wouldn't have heard anything.

"Lia is okay." Beth emerged from the bedroom, her face pale, but relieved.

"Stay here. I'll check outside."

"Be careful. And take Melon. He is search-and-rescue trained."

There was a flashlight in one of the kitchen drawers and Vincente took his gun, as well. He took Melon with him on his search as Beth had instructed. His assessment of Melon's capabilities wasn't as high as Beth's, but Melon was a collie. He enjoyed herding things. Livestock, other dogs, people, cars, bikes, crawling babies... if it moved, Melon's instinct was to round it up. He didn't bite, but he was obsessive. If his object didn't cooperate, he would push and poke it into submission. If there was someone hiding on the grounds of the lake house, that person wouldn't escape Melon's sheepdog instincts.

At this time of night, the lake had a different feel to it. The darkness somehow emphasized its size, giving the impression of endlessness and timelessness. The twin disks of the moon, one in the sky and the other shimmering on the lake's surface, were huge and mystical. There was something menacing about its cold, primal beauty.

The house and its surrounding area were an easy place to search. The boundaries were clear. There were cliffs on three sides of the house and the lake on the fourth. The house fitted neatly between them. It was part of the genius of its design. The architect who had planned it was Carla Bryan, Laurie's cousin, one of the victims of the Red Rose Killer. Carla's vision had been for a home that appeared to be part of the cliff face itself. She had succeeded. It also meant the house was protected by its surroundings.

Melon, delighted by this middle-of-the-night game, dashed along the water's edge while Vincente trained his flashlight on the building. Although they walked along the shoreline twice, neither of them found anything to cause them concern.

Which left Vincente with a dilemma. Either Beth had imagined what she saw, or the trespasser had found a way of escaping before Vincente left the house. The most logical conclusion was that Beth's mind had been playing tricks on her. But Vincente was reluctant to accept that, to dismiss what Beth was saying. Because if he did that, he was gambling with Beth's and Lia's lives. And his gut told him Beth had too much control to jump at shadows. He wasn't prepared to take a risk. Which meant he had to go with the unlikely explanation that a trespasser with superhero qualities had paid them a visit in the night.

"Nothing." He returned to the house, locking the door behind him.

Beth wrapped her arms around her. "I know what I saw."

He unloaded the gun and placed it back in the secure cupboard before pulling her into his arms. "I believe you."

She melted against him, resting her head against his chest. "He must have rappelled down the cliff." Her words confirmed what he had already guessed.

"Could he climb back up again on his own?"

She raised her head with a frown. "I'm not sure. Let's go and take a look at it."

They went through to the bedroom, and Vincente unlocked the sliding full-length glass doors that led onto the deck. Melon followed them, clearly having decided this was still part of the fun.

Vincente shone the flashlight onto the cliff face. It rose steep and dramatic as if extending up from the roof of the house itself. Beth studied it for a few minutes.

"It's not easy. But it could be done. And see up there—" she pointed to a deep fissure in the rock face "—I figure an experienced climber could have got to that point really fast. When I shouted out, he could have reached up to that crevice. As long as he knew what he was doing, it would be easy enough for him to climb most of the way inside that cleft. He would have been hidden away inside there while you were searching the beach. Once you came back inside the house, he was safe to come out onto the rock face and finish his ascent to the top."

Vincente gazed up at the cliff; although he was worried for Beth's and Lia's safety, he couldn't help being amazed at the skill and daring it had taken to undertake a stunt like that. His thoughts were interrupted when Melon dropped an item at his feet.

"What the hell...?" Vincente stooped to pick it up, turning the metal object over in his hand. It was a carabiner, a clip that attached onto clothing or equipment to enable climbers to move up and down a rock face.

The next morning, Laurie arrived earlier than they had originally planned, after Vincente called her and explained what had happened during the night.

"How can you be so sure it was a man?" she asked Beth. "All you saw was an outline through the drapes."

"Because of his height and body shape. I've never seen a woman so tall and muscular."

Vincente watched her face for any signs of strain, but she looked remarkably calm under the intensity of Laurie's gaze. It was even more remarkable, considering that she hadn't slept after Melon's discovery of the carabiner. Vincente had left Melon outside overnight, secure in the knowledge that the dog would kick up a rumpus at the slightest sound. Sending Beth back to bed, Vincente had commenced his own all-night vigil. He had spent most of the time in the family room, from which vantage point he could see the front door and the passageway that led to both bedrooms. Every half hour or so, he had walked all around, checking that everything was okay. Each time he had done so, Beth had been awake.

"You really think someone would attempt that climb alone and in the dark?" Laurie looked skeptical. "Even in daylight, that cliff is a killer. In the dark, it would be a hell of a dangerous thing to do."

Beth hunched a dismissive shoulder. "Not if you know what you're doing. I could do it."

Vincente pictured the way she had shimmied up Tarryn Point. "She could," he assured Laurie. "She climbs rock the way a marine climbs rope. I'll call the alarm company and get them out here today to look at an upgrade to the security system. We need sensors on the roof and on the decking." He turned to Laurie. "Do you have any more information on Rick Sterling's whereabouts?"

She shook her head. "Nothing. He seems to have disappeared after he left Toronto. Why?"

"The figure Beth saw was tall and muscular. That describes Rick Sterling. He's certainly capable of rappelling down the cliff and getting onto the roof last night. And I'm guessing he wouldn't think twice about Beth's suggestion that he climbed partway back up the cliff, concealing himself in the crevice so I couldn't see him when I shone my flashlight around."

Laurie turned to Beth. "Wouldn't any member of the West County Climbing Club who was on the Devil's Peak team be capable of this?"

"Yes," Beth said. "We were all experienced. And we'd all be able to do a tricky solo climb at night."

"That means we can't focus on Rick as our only suspect," Laurie warned. "While he may look guilty as hell after being there when Danielle died, we can't rule anyone out."

Her words reminded Vincente of Beth's desire to get back to work. "How would you feel about Beth letting Edgar Powell know where she's living so she can start doing some freelance legal jobs for him?"

Laurie pursed her lips. "We're talking about a serial killer who has threatened you and the people around you, Beth. While I know Edgar Powell and I don't believe he is that killer, we can't risk him slipping up and giving away details of your location."

"What about if we arranged for Beth and Edgar to have a regular meeting in a neutral place?" Vincente asked.

"That could work." Laurie nodded. "Did you have somewhere in mind?"

He thought about it. "My apartment. It's secure, and no one can get in without being admitted through the intercom system. I could take Beth there once a week and wait with her while she meets with Edgar."

Beth laughed. "Just you, me, Edgar and Lia?"

He grinned. "If that's what it takes."

Her eyes were warm on his face. "Thank you." She picked up her purse and jacket. "I'll call Edgar when I get back from Whitebridge."

Laurie got to her feet. "Ready?"

Beth nodded. "I guess it's time to find out what Tania Blake is so scared of."

Tania was already waiting in Sweet Cakes Bakery in Whitebridge when Beth arrived. Laurie entered a few minutes later and took a table at the back of the restaurant, where she could watch them but not be seen by Tania.

Although Beth had called Tania that morning and finalized the details of the meeting, she had half-expected her not to show up. As she slid into the booth, she was struck again by Tania's decline. She had never seen anyone whose nerves were pulled so tight. There was nowhere else for Tania's tension to go; she could only snap. By the way she was trembling, her breaking point wasn't far off.

They ordered sandwiches and coffee, and Beth made light talk while they waited for their orders to come. It was hard to call it conversation, since Tania was barely engaged in it. She responded to Beth's comments about a couple of local news stories with one-word answers.

"I can't do this…" Tania got to her feet, spilling the contents of her large shoulder bag on the floor as she did.

As she got onto the floor to pick up her belongings, Beth knelt beside her. Their hands met on an envelope that was partway open. As Tania snatched at it and Beth released it, she could see part of the contents. The photograph was unmistakable. It was the copy of the group picture…and this one also had Andy Smith's face crossed out in red.

"We need to talk about that." Beth tried to disguise the hammering of her heart by concentrating on keeping her voice level and quiet.

Tania swallowed hard, her eyes shifting warily around the room as she slid the envelope back into her bag. "I don't know if I can." A tear fell onto the back of her hand, and she stared at it as though she didn't know where it had come from.

"I've been sent the same pictures." Beth got to her feet, holding out a hand to help Tania up.

Although the other woman hesitated for only a few seconds, it felt like hours. As she waited with her hand outstretched, Beth was aware of Laurie's gaze on them. She wished there was some way she could communicate what she had just seen to the watching detective. Instead, she concentrated on her breathing. Not any mindful technique. She found she didn't need her usual exercises to stay calm. Just the regular rise and fall of her chest. In and out. Normality.

Slowly, Tania reached up her hand and placed it in Beth's. Together, they returned to their seats. At the same time, their food arrived.

Once the waitress had made sure they had everything they needed and left them alone, Tania spoke in a low voice. "You were sent copies of the photographs?"

"Yes. Did you also get a copy of the newspaper article and a letter?" Tania nodded. "And the last picture you got, was that a couple of weeks ago…the one with Danielle Penn's face crossed out?"

Tania's hand was shaking so hard she had to put her coffee cup down again. A strangled sob issued from her lips. "Yes. I thought it was just me. That he was coming for me. I've been so scared."

Beth took her hand. "Me, too. But now we know two of us were targets, it increases the possibility that all of the Devil's Peak team were. Because the letter threatened the people who were close to us, it's possible we've all been living in our own little hell, too frightened to say anything. What about Peter Sharp and Isaac Harper? You've seen both of them regularly—do they seem scared at all?"

Tania shook her head. "I don't know. I never thought about it. Peter comes along more regularly than Isaac, but that might be because he lives locally. Right here in Whitebridge, in the same house he was brought up in. The one next to the church. Although he might stop coming so often now." Her face took on a new expression. The nervousness dissolving to be replaced by a disapproving frown. "I heard he met someone through one of those internet dating sites."

She was starting to ramble and Beth tried to get her back on track. "You didn't notice a change in either of them around the time you got the first photograph?"

"No, but I was so scared, I probably wasn't concentrating."

Given Tania's reluctance to talk to her, the answer to the next question seemed obvious, but Beth felt obliged to ask it anyway. "Have you spoken to anyone else about this?"

Tanya shook her head. "I couldn't. You saw what the letter said…"

"What about Peter and Isaac? Do you think they discussed it?"

"I don't know" She twisted her hands together on the handle of her bag. "They barely speak to each other, and Peter never wants to talk to anyone. Whenever he come along to meetings, he seems uncomfortable. But who could it be? Who would do such a terrible thing?"

Beth and Laurie had discussed how to handle this on the drive. Beth wasn't going to reveal any information she had about the murders, or about Rick Sterling. "It could be anyone. Did you ever think of going to the police?"

Tania sprang back as though Beth had slapped her. "We can't. The letter said…"

"Don't panic. I'm not suggesting we do it. I just wondered." Beth thought for a moment Tania might be about to bolt out the door. "Who do you think it is?"

Tania shook her head. "It can't be anyone who was on the climb. None of the group would do something like this."

"You sound very sure." Beth wasn't hungry. The drama of the previous night, followed by this meeting, had drained any appetite she might have had. Forcing herself to appear normal and take an occasional bite of her sandwich was hard work.

"I got to know everyone on that climb." Tania seemed calmer now. "And I've given it plenty of thought."

"Do you think the photographs were sent by someone close to Cory who had a grudge against us? Possibly that person thought we didn't do enough to save him?"

There was a flash of anger in Tania's eyes. "We didn't.

Someone killed him." Her newfound fire didn't last. She slumped in her seat. "I did everything I could to help him…" Tears spilled over and flowed unheeded down her cheeks.

"You were the one who saved him. If it wasn't for you, he'd have plunged off the side of the mountain."

Tania's lips seemed to make an attempt at a smile. It wasn't successful. "Looking back, I wonder if it would have been better if I'd let him fall."

Stillwater was a small city, and the Delaney brothers were influential businessmen. While Beth had been in Whitebridge, Vincente had spoken to the owner of the alarm company about upgrading the system.

"He said it will take a few hours and they can do it the day after tomorrow."

The corners of her mouth turned down. "This is not a big house. Where do you want me and Lia to hide while they do the work on the alarm?"

"You can come with me and hide out at Cameron and Laurie's place. We're invited for lunch."

She smiled. "You think of everything."

"I do, and right now I'm thinking of opening a bottle of my favorite Chianti. Join me?"

Beth nodded, rolling her neck and shoulders to relieve tense muscles. "That sounds like heaven. Did you and Lia enjoy yourselves while I was away?"

Although Beth had told Laurie the details of her encounter with Tania on the drive back from Whitebridge, Laurie had come back to the lake house so they could discuss the situation in more detail with Vincente. Once Laurie had gone, Beth had called Edgar to talk about a part-time working arrangement. By the time she had ended the call, they were into the evening routine of dinner, followed by getting Lia ready for bed. This was the first chance they'd had to talk alone.

"We did. We have a new game. I build a tower with her blocks. She knocks it down. One of us shrieks so loudly with laughter it makes Melon run away and hide. We can play it endlessly and never get bored."

Beth laughed as they took their drinks into the family room. "Two years ago, if someone had asked me what you'd be like as a father, I wouldn't have been able to answer. I'd have said it was a stupid question, not worth answering because it was never going to happen."

Vincente remained silent as he drank his wine. She was right. He hadn't wanted children. It had been part of not seeing a long-term relationship in his future. If he didn't do commitment, he sure as hell couldn't do family. If he'd had any regrets about that, he'd buried them long ago. Too selfish. Too busy. Too damaged by his own experiences. They were the reasons—excuses, he could call them any damn thing he wanted—he had used.

Now Lia was here, and he had never known a feeling like it. Every time he looked at her, his heart soared. The little things about being her dad were the most amazing moments of his life. Her hand in his, the way her face lit up when she saw him…even the way she pulled on his beard in excitement. Her laughter could make him forget every bad thing that was going on around them. Lia was his greatest achievement, and she made him believe in himself. No way would he repeat the mistakes his mother had made. There would be no Alberti gene when it came to his daughter. Only Alberti lessons.

Beth placed her hand over his. "I'm sorry, Vincente.

I didn't mean that the way it sounded. You are a wonderful father."

He laughed, lightening the mood. "Tell that to Lia when I don't build her tower fast enough."

They sat in companionable silence for some time. "I don't think the guy on the deck last night was the murderer." Beth's sudden pronouncement startled him.

"What makes you say that?"

"Because we haven't been sent another photograph." She was curled up into the corner of the sofa, and he wondered how she managed to get her limbs into such a small space and still be comfortable. "When he is ready to come after me, he'll send everyone a picture with my face crossed out. I haven't had that and neither has Tania."

Vincente frowned. "Are you saying it was a random intruder who just happened to be proficient at rock climbing?"

"No. There has to be a connection, but I don't think he came here to kill me," Beth said.

"Maybe he came to leave the next photograph, but when you cried out it startled him?"

"There are easier ways to get the photograph to me. If he figured out where I'm living, he could just leave it in the mailbox. Or, if he had it with him last night, he could have left it on the deck before he ran. And as I said, Tania hasn't received the next picture, either." Beth shook her head. "Until we get that, he's not ready for his next murder."

"You're probably right, but we're dealing with a serial killer. I don't know if I want to get inside his head and try to predict his next move."

"No, let's not get complacent. I don't like the idea that

we have a connection to the killer, even if it's only that we know how he works. I suppose it's possible he could change tactics." She shivered. "Something Tania said got me thinking that we could be looking at this all wrong."

"What do you mean?" Her face had always been like an artist's canvas, displaying the range of her emotions. It fascinated him to watch as they changed and deepened. Now, she was intent on her thoughts, lost in the memory of her conversation with Tania.

"She said it maybe would have been better if Cory had died when he fell. At first, I was shocked at the brutality of those words." Beth raised troubled blue eyes to his face. "For Tania, the woman who saved him from plummeting to his death, to say such a thing sounded so cold. But, when you think about it, what she said made a horrible sort of sense. If Cory had died in that way, he wouldn't have suffered such awful pain, and none of these consequences would have followed. The person who killed him would not have felt compelled to take such a dreadful step. Whoever is sending these pictures and committing these murders would not feel they had to avenge his death. When Tania saved Cory, she did it with the best of intentions, but her action set in motion a chain of outcomes no one could have foreseen."

"How does that mean we are looking at it all wrong?" Vincente asked.

"I think we should be trying to find out who killed Cory."

Vincente took a long, slow sip of wine. "Ten years on, that's a very big job. If the police couldn't find out at the time who killed him, what chance do we have now?"

"Probably none, but we have a lot better motivation." He tilted his wineglass her way in acknowledgment.

She had a point. Given recent events, the murder of Cory Taylor should be a higher priority. They would have to talk to Laurie about reopening the case. The police could openly question the remaining members of the Devil's Peak team about the decade-old murder and put some pressure on them to reveal new evidence. In the meantime, maybe Beth, who had known him, could offer some insights that had been missed at the time.

"Tell me about Cory Taylor."

Chapter 12

Beth placed the photograph, the original of the group picture, on the coffee table. She pointed to Cory Taylor with one fingertip. He was standing in the center of the group with one arm around Danielle Penn and the other around Peter Sharp. Beth recalled posing for that photograph. It had been taken the night before they set off on the climb. They had gathered at the sports center to check the equipment and Rick had asked the janitor to take the picture. The mood had been relaxed, but excited. Just before the janitor had taken the shot, Andy Smith had made one of his corny jokes and they'd all laughed. Cory's hundred-watt smile had been captured by the camera, but the flash had dimmed the perfection of his dazzling green eyes.

The photograph had come to mean something else since it had been taken. It had always been a reminder of the ill-fated expedition during which Cory had died. Lately, of course, it had taken on a more sinister meaning. Beth tried to look at it now as it had been on that night. And tried to remember the man at its center. It wasn't difficult. Cory had been very memorable.

"This picture doesn't do him justice. Cory was the most handsome man I had ever seen." She gave Vincente a smile. "Present company excepted, of course. He was also very charming. But he never took those things for granted." She sighed. "I don't know if I can explain what I mean by that. I think some people—men and women—who have both looks and charisma, rely on those things to get them what they want in life. Cory never did. He was just a genuinely nice guy who had time for people. He'd remember the little details of your life. If I told him something, he'd always ask me about it the next time I saw him. But it wasn't just me—Cory did that with everyone."

"It sounds like you were a little bit in love with him."

"Maybe I was." She looked back at the picture and felt the smile touch her lips again. "Maybe we all were. I don't think what I felt for him could be described as romantic. You just couldn't help loving Cory."

"What did he do for a living?" Vincente asked.

"Cory was an artist. A very talented one. When he died, he'd already had a few successful exhibitions. That was another sad aspect to the whole thing, if there weren't enough of them already—his career was really set to take off."

Vincente frowned as though he was chasing a memory. "I think I've seen his work. Did he paint Wyoming mountain scenes?"

"Yes. He said he had traveled around the country getting different perspectives, but the light here was unique and compelling. And there was enough material to last him a lifetime." She gulped down a mouthful of wine. "Turns out he was right, because his life was cut short."

"And you have no idea who killed him?"

Beth closed her eyes, remembering what it had been like inside that tent. It had been difficult to move in her bulky clothing. Having completed the climb, she had piled on the rest of the garments in her backpack, relying on layers for warmth. The interior of the tent had been surprisingly bright, the snow outside providing a natural glow. Although the wind had died down, it still roared wildly, howling around the tents as though testing their strength. Beth had been lying on her side, tucked into her sleeping bag, facing Cory with her back to the entrance flap.

"Let me die…" His voice had been a pathetic croak.

"We'll be able to get help soon." She remembered how hard she had worked to keep the tears out of her voice. "The storm is almost over now."

"…wanted to die so bad…"

She hadn't heard the tent flap open. A slight movement behind her caught her attention. Before she could turn to look, there had been a flash of searing pain in the back of her head. The next thing she'd known, there was blood all over the sleeping bag and Peter Sharp was examining her, while a group of people was gathered around Cory.

"No." She opened her eyes. "Obviously, I thought about it, but I have no idea."

"Who discovered what had happened to you and Cory?"

"It was Mike Bradbury. He was the next person to

come and sit with Cory. He had a flashlight with him and when he saw the blood on my sleeping bag, he raised the alarm." She swallowed hard. "As well as attending to my injuries, Peter Sharp, who was a paramedic, checked on Cory. That was when he found out Cory was dead."

"You said Tania saved Cory and his partner. Who was his partner on the climb?"

"We were paired according to ability. An experienced climber with a less skilled one. I was the least experienced climber, so I was paired with Rick, who was the most proficient member of the team. Cory was quite an expert. He was with Peter, who was by no means a novice, but he'd spent less time on difficult peaks than Cory had. They had been climbing partners, and good friends, for several years."

"So, when we saw Peter Sharp, and he said he didn't want to talk about what happened back then, he probably had more traumatic memories than anyone…except you?" Vincente asked.

Beth had never considered it that way. "You're right. When Cory fell, Peter must have thought he was going to die too. Except—" she frowned, trying to remember "—I don't know how it happened, but Peter *didn't* fall." Her expression was puzzled as she thought back to that day. Her memories were clear, even if she saw them through a blizzard. "He didn't do anything much. It was Tania who started to haul Cory up, then Rick moved across to help her."

"How common is it for a climbing rope to snap or break?"

"It can happen," Beth said. She pointed to the photograph. "But that's what we were doing that night. We were checking the equipment. Every inch of rope had been carefully tested. And there was no mention of a damaged rope, either when we reached the top of the Keyhole and made camp, or later during the police investigation."

"We thought Peter didn't want to talk about what happened on the Devil's Peak because the memories were too painful...

"...but maybe he has another reason why he doesn't want anyone to inquire too closely into what happened."

Edgar Powell had always seemed to be a fixture of the city of Stillwater, as much a part of the scenery as the Devil's Peak or the Ryerson River. Vincente remembered going to the office of E. Powell Law as a child a few times. The attorney didn't seem to have changed since Vincente's father, Kane Delaney, used to do business with him. The office in the center of Main Street looked exactly the same as it always had. Yet there was something at the back of Vincente's mind. He was sure his father had once said Edgar wasn't from Stillwater.

"I don't know." Beth wrinkled her nose when he asked her. "I always thought he was from around here. I've never heard him talk about his family. I'm not sure he has any."

Vincente shrugged. "Maybe I got it wrong."

There had been a time when the downtown area of Stillwater was in danger of dying out. The railway line used to run all the way out to the Hope Valley coal mine, but the established industries of the region had experienced a slump. The railway tracks were rusted over and weeds grew between them. No coal had been mined in Hope Valley for decades and it was now better known as the place where Grant Becker had hidden the bodies of his victims.

Other Wyoming traditions had been hit hard in recent years. Ranches like the one Cameron and Laurie had bought were standing empty, and young people had been leaving the area to find work elsewhere. Cameron and the council had been faced with the huge task of bringing people back to the city. Although there was still work to be done, they had succeeded in promoting the town and the surrounding area as a tourist destination. Hotels, bars, restaurants, coffee shops, craft shops, farmers' markets…these days, anything quaint and Western was thriving. The ranches were reopening as travelers flocked to sample the scenic delights.

As a result, the city had begun to expand beyond its original boundaries in order to make room for the sudden increase in its population. A few years ago, Vincente had moved into a new apartment complex overlooking the river. Ryerson Heights was the sort of development Cameron and his fellow local politicians were keen to encourage, even though some traditionalists sneered at the modernization of their hometown.

When creating this apartment block, the designer had seen the advantages of a unique plot of land. The source of the Ryerson River was high up in the mountains. As it wound its way down toward the town, it had carved out some dramatic geological features. The developers had advertised this building as having not one, but two of the best, but most contrasting, views in Stillwater. At the rear was the stunning but inhospitable gorge known as Savage Canyon. In front, the Ryerson River took a wide meander before it tumbled into the cascade known as Eternal Springs.

As he pulled into the parking lot, Vincente thought how strange it was that this apartment no longer felt like it belonged to him. In such a short space of time, the place he had called his home for several years had become just another building. He had never felt any emotional connection to anywhere he had lived before, but if he was told he would have to walk away from Ryerson Heights right this minute and never see it again, he would be able to do it and not feel a pang.

His apartment was on the second floor, and Beth smiled reminiscently as they entered. "Your bachelor pad."

He grimaced. "Why does it always feel like that's a derogatory term?"

"It wasn't intended that way. I have some fond memories of this place." She laughed. "In fact, I'm more likely to call it your 'den of iniquity.'"

He took Lia from her, placing the baby on the floor. Lia scooted away in search of new adventures and they both followed her, checking for anything that could be a hazard.

When they were sure the place was safe, Vincente gripped Beth by the waist, drawing her to him. "I don't remember you complaining about my den of iniquity."

She caught hold of the front of his shirt. "No. I think we can safely say I never did that." Passion flared between them. Hot and hard as ever. "Not then. Not now." She rose on the tips of her toes, fitting her body to his. "Not ever."

He groaned. "There are two reasons why we have to stop this right now." Beth raised a brow. "One is that

Edgar will be arriving any minute. The other is that Lia is about to eat the TV remote control."

Laughing, she went to rescue the gadget from Lia's plump fingers. Sure enough, the buzzer sounded seconds later. When Vincente answered it, Edgar's slightly pompous voice filled the room.

"Come on up." Vincente pressed the button that would release the door at the front of the building. "Make sure no one else follows you inside, please."

"Naturally."

Even through the intercom, Vincente got a sense of Edgar's outrage that he would suspect him capable of such a transgression. He knew Laurie had visited Edgar and, without telling him the reasons why Beth had been forced into hiding, had impressed upon him the need to protect her privacy and safety. Knowing Edgar, he would follow Laurie's instructions to the very last letter.

The best word to describe Edgar was *round*. He wasn't very tall, and Vincente wondered if his waist and height measurements might be the same. But it would be unfair to suspect that Edgar was unfit. He hiked, cycled and swam. Vincente had no idea how old he was, but the attorney managed to do all of those things with the same vigor and enthusiasm he had put into them twenty years ago.

Edgar's eyes sparkled with pleasure as he folded Beth into a hug, and Vincente noticed again the genuine affection between the two of them.

"I'm so glad you offered to do this. Things have been a little crazy in the office lately. You'll be doing me a real favor."

After a few minutes, they had their heads buried in a pile of paperwork. Vincente left them to it, taking Lia on a tour of the apartment. The views were spectacular, particularly now that fall was here. His home state was always beautiful, but the fall colors added an extra layer of vibrancy. From the front windows, the wide sweep of the river with the snowy mountain peaks in the distance offered a lush, panoramic aspect.

The contrast with the vista at the rear of the building was striking. His apartment had views that were Wyoming in miniature, with the waterway at the front and the wild fissure at the rear.

Savage Canyon didn't get its name by chance. As he gazed out at the dark, brooding view, Vincente noticed with surprise that someone was entering the canyon. He'd never seen anyone go inside the ravine. Locals didn't go there. Stillwater was popular with hikers, climbers and kayakers, but even those who were the most dedicated to outdoor activities steered clear of Savage Canyon's hostile environment. There were plenty of other places to get their adrenaline buzz…ones where there was a better chance of coming out alive.

There was no reason for him to feel uneasy about what he was seeing. The council hadn't issued any specific warnings about Savage Canyon. There was no reason why a lone hiker shouldn't go in there. It just felt… wrong. But with everything that was going on in his life right now, wasn't it possible anything out of the ordinary would feel wrong?

He shrugged the feeling aside, a task that was made easier when Beth called out from the other room to tell him she and Edgar had finished their meeting.

Beth knew the Dawson ranch well, although the property had been empty for several years. Renovating it was an ambitious project, but as Vincente parked the car at the side of the house, she could see exactly why Cameron and Laurie had fallen in love with this place. The view offered everything Wyoming had to offer, with grass and wildflowers in the foreground rising up to meet a pine-topped ridge and snowcapped mountains in the distance.

Laurie stepped down from the porch to meet them. In jeans and a lightweight sweater, and with her hair loose, she appeared more relaxed than in her formal work attire. She linked arms with Beth and led her inside, showing her around the rooms that were already completed, while Vincente took Lia through to the kitchen. Melon was greeted with cautious interest by Cameron's two dogs before the three of them raced off into the distance in a cloud of dust.

"It's stunning." Beth sighed with a touch of envy as she looked out at the mountain views. The furnishings had all been chosen to reflect the colors of the landscape. "I love the lake house, but I can see why you chose to move out here."

"I had other reasons for not wanting to live at the lake house," Laurie said. "It was Cameron and Carla's home. Even if she hadn't been his girlfriend before we met, it would have felt very strange for me to have moved into the home my dead cousin designed."

"Even though we've only been there a short time, I forget it was Cameron's," Beth admitted. "Maybe it's because of the enforced seclusion of the last few weeks, but it's almost like I've never lived anywhere else."

Laurie's gaze was steady, almost as if she was attempting to read her thoughts. Beth decided she really would not want to be on the receiving end of an interrogation from Detective Delaney. Instead of the lengthy speech she was anticipating, Laurie simply said, "Is that so?" Those three words seemed to be loaded with meaning. Unfortunately, Beth had no idea what it was.

"Shall we go and rescue Steffi and Lia from the boy talk?" Laurie's mood changed from serious to smiling in an instant.

When they reached the kitchen, it was immediately obvious that no rescue was necessary. Lia, perched contentedly in the circle of Vincente's arms, was entertaining her captivated uncles while Steffi fixed drinks.

"She's going through her entire repertoire." The pride in Vincente's voice brought a sudden, unexpected lump to Beth's throat.

Lia obliged by giving a repeat performance. Clapping, pointing, waving and covering her eyes with her hands before peeking through her fingers...they were all her favorite actions. Then she turned her head to smile at Vincente. "Dada."

He looked at Beth, his expression stunned. "Did she just...?"

She laughed. "I think she did."

"Say it again, Lia. Say 'dada.'"

Lia's cheeks dimpled as her smile widened. "Woof."

There was general laughter, and Lia clapped her hands delightedly.

"I think your daughter just made her first joke," Cameron said.

"Yeah, she got me." Vincente ruffled Lia's curls.

She nestled her head against his shoulder. "Dada."

Laurie placed a hand over her heart. "Vincente, you used to be the big bad brother. Now you're overloading my kitchen with cuteness."

Beth couldn't figure out the look in Vincente's eyes as he accepted a beer from Steffi and handed Lia over to her. The big bad brother. That was his reputation, and Vincente didn't try to play it down. If anything, he encouraged it. *You may be big, Vincente, but I know you too well. You're not bad.* She watched his face as he smiled at something Bryce was saying. *The problem is, I don't know if you've figured it out yet.*

Sixteen months ago, when she ran out on the life she'd known, Beth would have said she knew everything there was to know about Vincente Delaney. Yet, over the last few weeks, he had surprised her. She thought there was a good chance he had surprised himself, even if he might never admit it. Not all heroes wore capes. Sometimes, they even had to overcome their own fears.

To an outsider, Vincente was the ultimate alpha male. He had worked hard to create that illusion, including the impression that he lived only for himself. Other people were allowed into his world by invitation only. He was dominant. Vincente gave orders, he didn't take them. Even though Cameron was the founder and CEO of Delaney Transportation, Beth had never seen Vincente act like his brother's employee. And Vincente exuded the sort of confidence that bordered on arrogance. His whole attitude said it all. He didn't need anything or anybody.

Oh, he was a proud man. He was strong, reliable and capable. Perhaps it was because she was the only person who had ever looked deep enough into his eyes that she knew what was hidden beneath the commanding surface. She knew the frightened little boy whose mom had run out on him still lived inside Vincente. He was still wondering what he'd done that meant he was no longer worthy of his mother's love. And he was trying desperately to make sure no one could ever break through his barriers and hurt him that way again.

But, ever since she had placed her cares—and her life—in his hands, Beth had seen a difference in Vincente. She had seen his underlying quiet confidence shine through. There was no longer any need for pretense. She had needed him, and he had come through. Coolly, calmly and with the self-esteem that had been so deeply buried it might have been hidden forever. That scared child hadn't gone away, but he was growing up.

As the chatter and the laughter ebbed and flowed around her, Beth finally acknowledged what she had always known. She loved Vincente. She loved the strong, bold, brave man who made her heart sing and her body thrum. But she also loved the insecure person he kept hidden deep inside, the one who had persuaded himself he was unworthy of love. And, having convinced himself of that, he had, with classic Delaney hardheadedness, decided he would never try to find it.

Not even with me. She almost laughed at the thought. It had taken her long enough to acknowledge that they were meant to be together. Would Vincente ever see it? They had a lot of problems to solve before they could focus on themselves. And then?

Who knew what the future held for them? Because Beth had changed, too. A return to their former relationship wasn't going to be enough for her now. She knew exactly what she wanted. She wanted Vincente. And she wanted everything with him. She wanted his heart. She wanted to hear him say "I love you." Wanted the hugs and kisses and touches that went with those words. Wanted to ease his sorrow and share his joy. Wanted to see that same look of pride and wonder on his face when their next child came along…

If they hadn't been thrust into this dangerous situation together, would she ever have understood the depth of her feelings for him? Beth wasn't sure. But she knew it now, and there was no going back.

Yes, I want everything. And if I can't have that? A tiny splinter of despair pierced her heart. *Then I'll have to settle for nothing at all.*

Chapter 13

Although the next few days were calm, the atmosphere was one of anticipation. To Vincente, it felt as though they were waiting for something momentous to happen, like war to break out or the government to fall.

Beth started working part-time for Edgar Powell, undertaking some research to help him with court depositions. Although she said the jobs he gave her barely stretched her brain, Vincente could tell she was glad to be exercising her legal mind again.

Laurie had nothing new to report on the case. They had shared Beth's unsettling memories about Peter Sharp's part in Cory Taylor's death with her. Laurie had persuaded her chief that the new murders provided sufficient cause for the Stillwater Detective Division to reinvestigate Cory's murder. Peter had been the first person she had interviewed.

Although he couldn't refuse to speak to a detective in the same manner he had snubbed Beth, Peter had been reluctant to talk about what had happened on the Devil's Peak ten years ago. Laurie had come away with no new information. In fact, when she compared what Peter had told her with his original statement, they were almost identical. It was as if he was repeating a well-rehearsed speech.

"But that doesn't make him guilty." She had sighed as she left the lake house. "We still haven't found Rick Sterling, and I have four other people to talk to, including Tania."

Lia had come down with a cold and wasn't sleeping well. On the third day, her cheeks were flushed and her temperature was elevated. When she kept covering her right ear with her hand and crying, Beth decided it was more than just a minor ailment.

"She needs to see a doctor." She rocked Lia in her arms, soothing her tears. "But we can't take her into town."

"I'll call Leon Sinclair. We can trust him." Vincente reached for his cell phone.

"This is not a good time for jokes, Vincente." Beth gave him a look of horror at the mention of Leon's name.

Vincente had forgotten that Beth had been away from Stillwater for some time. There wasn't much about the city that had changed in her absence, but one of the most striking things was probably the status of Dr. Leon Sinclair. Leon was one of Bryce's friends. A former army medic, he had been given a medical discharge for mental health reasons, although he had retained his license to practice. Upon leaving the army, Leon had come home to Stillwater and proceeded to raise every kind of hell his inventive mind could devise. He had become known as the only man who had been thrown out of every bar in Stillwater in one night. That would have been his reputation around the time Beth left town.

Since then, Leon had undergone a remarkable transformation. A spell in rehab had followed and, although the fight against his demons had been a long one, he had won the battle. He had redeemed himself so successfully that, when there was a recruitment crisis at the Main Street Clinic, the lead clinician had approached Leon with a job offer. It had started out as a short-term position, but there was no sign of it coming to an end anytime soon. To everyone's surprise, especially his own, Leon was proving to be extremely popular with the residents of Stillwater.

"Trust me on this, Beth. Leon is not the same man he was. He's a respectable doctor now, he'll come straight out when I call him, and he won't tell anyone where you and Lia are living." Vincente could say those things with confidence. There had been a lengthy period during which Bryce was the only person in town who had any faith in Leon. He had encouraged his brothers to share his trust in the troubled medic, with the result that the Delaney brothers had occasionally called upon Leon to help them in times of difficulty. He had never let them down. "Leon is a friend and he is completely sober these days."

Beth huffed out a breath. "Okay. But if there is so much as a suspicion of alcohol on that man's breath, he is not coming within a yard of our daughter."

Leon repaid Vincente's praise by arriving within half an hour. Vincente could tell by Beth's face that she barely recognized the former hell-raiser. Leon was still way too pale and thin, and the stammer that had disappeared while he was drinking was evident as he examined Lia. But it was clear he knew what he was doing and that, as Vincente had promised, he was sober. He was even rewarded with a watered-down version of Lia's chuckle, after which the baby rested her head against Beth's shoulder and closed her eyes, succumbing to the slumber that had eluded her for much of the previous night.

"She has an ear infection," Leon said, having shone a light into Lia's ears. "I'll give you antibiotics and she can take infant pain relief, as well. It should clear up in a day or two, but if it doesn't give me another call."

"Thank you." Vincente could see relief replacing the worry that had gripped Beth's features. Because she had confided in him about her postpartum depression, he could see when the signs appeared. He knew when she was fighting an inner battle. But with each struggle, she seemed to grow stronger. And this time, that inner strength appeared almost immediately.

Leon had placed his medical bag on the kitchen counter, and he retrieved it now. As he closed it, he paused, gazing at the item next to it. It was Beth's photograph of the West County Climbing Club.

"How old is this picture?" Leon's gaze became intent as he looked at it.

Beth frowned. "It's ten years old. Why?"

Leon beckoned her over. "If it's that old, I'm guessing this guy—" he pointed to Cory "—has already gotten treatment for his condition?"

A cold feeling tracked its way down Vincente's spine. He could see the same feelings of dread and fascina-

tion reflected on Beth's face. What new twist was this?
"He's dead."

"What condition did he have?" Vincente asked. "And
how can you possibly diagnose it from a photograph?"

"Retinoblastoma. It's a rare form of eye cancer, usually only affecting babies or young children. It occurs
very occasionally in adults. As far as I know, there are
only a handful of documented cases. See how his eyes
are glowing white and it hasn't happened to anyone else
in the picture? That was caused by the abnormal reflection of the camera flash, a sign of a tumor in the eye…
or, in this guy's case, in both eyes. I'm no expert, but it
appears quite advanced. It's fatal if left untreated." Leon
glanced from Vincente to Beth and back again. "Hey, I
didn't mean to upset you by telling you this. A camera
flash is a commonly used method of detecting retinoblastoma in kids these days. It's so successful that some
organizations run ad campaigns targeted at parents of
young children. There wasn't the same awareness of it
ten years ago."

Vincente gestured to the photograph. "This guy's
name was Cory Taylor. He was the climber who died in
the Devil's Peak incident."

Leon nodded. "I remember that. It happened just before I joined the army."

"Would Cory have been aware of his condition?"

"I can't tell that from this picture," Leon said. "I don't
know enough about the illness, and I don't know enough
about him. Like I said, this appears advanced, but I can't
say that for sure. If it *was* advanced, I'd have expected
him to be in considerable pain and for his vision to have
been affected. If the cancer had been present for some

time but had gone undetected, it's possible it had already spread to other parts of his body."

"So there's a good chance that, when this photograph was taken, Cory Taylor was very ill?" Vincente asked.

Leon nodded. "I'd say there was a strong possibility he was dying."

"She's sleeping soundly, catching up on the hours of rest she missed last night." Vincente returned from checking on Lia. "Maybe you should try to do the same?"

"I don't know if I could sleep. I can't stop thinking about what Leon said." He flopped down into the seat next to her, and she turned to face him, wanting to share the jumble of thoughts that had been worrying her. "If Cory knew he was dying, it changes everything."

"Do you think he would have gone on a climb like that if he was in pain and his eyesight was failing? From what you've told me about him, he doesn't sound like the sort of guy who would put himself and others in danger."

"Who knows how anyone would act if they knew they didn't have long to live?" While he had been checking on Lia, she had been going over and over it in her mind. Her thoughts kept returning to one memory. One tiny phrase that altered her view of what had happened on that stormy mountain peak. It was so simple, yet so awful, it took her breath away. "Hear me out on something?"

Vincente nodded, his eyes on her face. "Of course."

"When I was alone in the tent with Cory, most of the sounds he made were incoherent. Just moans and cries of pain. He only spoke clearly twice. Just fragments of sentences. He said 'Let me die' and 'Wanted to die so bad.'"

"They both sound like the sort of things a man with a broken neck and a broken back might say," Vincente said.

"No." Beth shook her head. "Listen carefully to that second phrase. Cory said '*wanted* to die so bad.' Not '*want* to die so bad.'"

Vincente frowned. "He was talking in the past tense, but does it change the meaning? He was still expressing his wish to die."

Beth drew a breath. "I think the tense really matters. He was telling me what he *had* wanted. Not at that moment, but as we climbed the Keyhole. I don't believe his fall was an accident. I think Cory tried to kill himself."

Vincente whistled softly. "That's a hell of a big conjecture from just a single word. Particularly as the speaker was a man who was out of his mind with pain, both from his injuries and probably, as we've just learned, from cancer."

"I know." Despite Vincente's skepticism, Beth couldn't let go of her growing certainty. "But what if I'm right?"

Vincente leaned his head back, gazing up at the ceiling. He was silent for a long time before he turned to look at her. "If you're right, he planned it. Cory knew when your team set out for the Devil's Peak that he was going to take his life. And that means Peter Sharp must have agreed to help him."

Beth nodded. "If Cory hadn't confided in Peter, his plan wouldn't have worked. You can't throw yourself off a rock face when you are attached to another person. Not unless you want to take your partner with you. But if Cory and Peter had arranged it between them, then it was simple. When Cory was ready, he would give Peter a signal. Cory would fall—or jump—from the rock, and because Peter was prepared for it to happen, he would have been able to make sure he wasn't dragged to his death, as well. They hadn't counted on the storm. We should have been more spread out along the rock face, with no chance of anyone coming to Cory's aid. Peter should have let go of the rope."

"But he hadn't counted on Tania coming to the rescue."

"It was a superhuman effort on her part," Beth said. "Even in the blizzard, she managed to pull Cory part of the way back up before Danielle, her partner, joined in and helped. Then Peter roused himself from what appeared to be shock and got involved. Rick and I moved across from our position to assist, as well."

"I can't picture the woman we saw at the climbing club having the strength to haul an injured man up a cliff face."

"She was very different back then. Tania was strong, both physically and mentally. And don't they say you find reserves of energy you didn't know you had in difficult situations?" Beth asked.

"You should know." Vincente's gaze moved over her face, touching her skin like a caress, warming and soothing. "You've had so much thrown at you, yet you still keep fighting."

Beth felt a blush heat her cheeks. "This murderer hasn't left me much choice."

"If you're right—and it still feels like a huge leap—then we finally know who killed Cory Taylor..."

They said the name together. "Peter Sharp."

Once the antibiotics kicked in, Lia made a remarkable recovery and was soon back to her lively, beard-and-tail-pulling self.

"I think it's time to pay Peter Sharp a visit," Vincente said as they finished breakfast.

"You don't think we should speak to Laurie first?"

He decided Beth was looking outrageously sexy. Since she had just crawled out of bed, there was no particular reason for his conclusion. Her hair was mussed up, her eyes were slightly bleary and she wore one of his shirts and a pair of his socks. And he would never get tired of seeing her that way in the mornings. He would never get tired of *her*...

He forced his mind back to her question. "No, I don't think we should tell Laurie about Cory's illness. Not yet."

She poured milk onto Lia's cereal in response to the increasingly noisy demands from the high chair. "Any particular reason for this decision?"

"Several. But one of the most important ones concerns Cory Taylor's family. What if they didn't know about his cancer?" He poured coffee into two cups and handed one to Beth. "Hell, what if Leon is wrong and it's just a faulty, ten-year-old photograph? I don't want to put Cory's family through any more pain for something that may just be a hunch."

Beth walked past him with Lia's breakfast, pausing to rise on the tips of her toes and plant a kiss on the corner of his mouth. "You, Vincente Delaney, are a very nice man."

He pretended to look startled. "Don't tell anyone. You'll ruin my reputation."

She pulled a chair up next to Lia's high chair and commenced the feeding routine. One spoon for Beth, one for Lia. While Beth scooped cereal into the baby's mouth, Lia splashed in the milk, hammered out a drumbeat with her spoon and rubbed soggy cereal into her hair. She batted milky eyelashes at Vincente and held her spoon out to him.

"Sweetheart, as tempting as that is, I'm going to pass," he said. "How would you like to spend some time with Aunt Steffi today?"

Having called Steffi to agree on a time, they set off a few hours later. Leaving an excited Lia at the animal sanctuary, Vincente took the road toward Whitebridge.

"At least we know from the information Tania let slip where Peter lives. And it's Saturday, so there's a chance of him being at home. But what if he refuses to talk to us like he did last time?" Beth asked.

"Then we use the threat of the police. He has had one visit from Laurie—he won't want another."

"If Peter did help Cory in his suicide attempt and subsequently assisted his death, he isn't going to confess to it. He's gotten away with it for all these years. All he has to do is keep quiet." Beth shifted restlessly in her seat. "We have no proof and he'll know that."

"Did he look like a man who was at peace with himself?" Vincente asked.

"No, but…"

"Maybe he doesn't want to get away with it anymore. Maybe it's time for the secrets of the Devil's Peak to be told."

Beth didn't appear convinced, but she lapsed into silence for the remainder of the journey. She continued to amaze him with her fortitude. There had always been an incredible connection between them, but how she had dealt with this crisis had shown him her true character. She was handling this whole thing with an emotional and mental strength that was beyond anything he would have believed possible. That she was doing it having fought her way back from the debilitating depths of depression only added to his admiration.

Vincente had been reconsidering a lot of things lately. One of them was just how well he had known Beth. He had believed he knew everything about her. Now he wondered how much of that knowledge had been superficial. She had always been the person he wanted to hang out with, the person to whom he could talk for hours; she shared his interests and his sense of humor more than anyone else he knew. And, of course, he wanted to drag her off to bed at every available opportunity.

That last one will never change.

They had been driven into an incredibly tough situation. They were living in close proximity 24/7, constantly looking over their shoulders to see if a serial killer was lurking in the shadows, sharing the care of Lia, and obliged to form new bonds with Vincente's family. Everything had changed, including the way Vincente viewed Beth. There were depths to her he had never considered until now. The things he had known about her before still mattered. She preferred mountains to beaches, romance novels to horror stories, beer to champagne, and pizza to caviar.

Now he also knew that she had a fighting spirit that would put a world championship boxer to shame. She possessed a grace and poise that meant she could present a calm face to the world even when her nerves were worn raw with stress. Even under duress, she had the sort of generosity that meant she could sympathize with the sufferings of Tania Blake and try to reach out by sharing her own experience to help reduce the other woman's pain. Her physical attractiveness was obvious. He had also discovered that her inner beauty was endless.

Just what the hell are you going to do about all these new feelings?

Even with everything else that was going on, it was the question that had been tormenting him for days. The only thing he knew for sure was that doing nothing wasn't an option. He sensed the final confrontation was looming, and, once this nightmare was over, it would signal the end to the intimacy they now shared. Was he prepared to let Beth walk away?

He flicked a sidelong glance in her direction, and his whole body blazed with the force of his feelings. That was what being with her did to him. When he was with Beth, her presence acted like a mute button on the rest of the world. Fear, anger, pain…they all faded away when he looked into her eyes.

And yet you still have to think about this? You have to ask yourself what this is called, and whether it's forever.

He bit back the laugh that almost rose to his lips. He could call himself every kind of fool there was, but he'd wasted enough time already. His biggest problem wasn't sorting out his own head and heart. They were finally aligned and telling him exactly what he needed to do. No. He had more important things to worry about.

Starting with how the hell, in the middle of all this mayhem, he was going to find the time for a conversation that started with persuading Beth he had loved her all along.

Chapter 14

The Whitebridge Episcopal Church was a pretty, traditional building with white wooden walls and green trim. Its spire could be seen from the approach to the town, and Vincente parked the car in the street opposite. Beth had become so used to wearing her disguise of baseball cap and shades that it was second nature to her now. She tilted the brim down low over her face as she followed Vincente toward the church.

"Tania said Peter lived in the house next to the church."

There was only one house matching that description. Nestling within a protective apron of white-barked and gold-topped aspens, the tiny dwelling looked like the sort of home that belonged to a storybook character. It was perfectly maintained, with not a single leaf daring to mar the flawless, emerald lawn. As they drew closer,

Beth was certain they were being watched by someone inside the house. Her suspicions appeared to be confirmed when the door was opened almost as soon as Vincente knocked.

She had been prepared for anger. Even possibly the threat of violence. But the look on Peter's expression made her step back in shock. Not because she was afraid for herself, but because she was frightened for him. Vincente had asked if she thought Peter Sharp was at peace with himself. Looking at him now, there was no doubt about the answer to that question. He was in hell.

Although Beth's face was hidden, Peter must have remembered Vincente from the last time they had met and made the association with her, because he gave a tortured groan. "I told you, I don't want to talk."

As he began to close the door, Beth stepped up close. She would only get one chance at this and she didn't have time for tact or hesitation. "Did Cory try to kill himself?"

The door's forward motion halted. Peter's face crumpled. "How can you ask me that…?" The words lacked heat.

"Because someone is trying to kill us all, and what happened to Cory is the key."

His shoulders slumped in an attitude of defeat. "You'd better come in."

The interior of the house was as new and pin neat as the outside. Peter led them to a small sitting room that overlooked a flower garden and gestured to a sofa. "A police officer came to see me." There was a haunted look in his eyes as he took a seat opposite theirs. "Why is this happening now? After all this time?"

"Because Andy Smith and Danielle Penn are dead,

and it's possible they were murdered." Beth decided not to mention Rick Sterling. "Did you get sent a copy of the newspaper article, and then a letter and the photographs with people's faces crossed out?" Beth asked.

Peter nodded miserably. "That's what I mean. Why now? Whoever is doing this must have felt all this hatred ever since Cory died. Why wait until now to start attacking us?"

"You're right." She turned her head to look at Vincente. "It's an aspect that hadn't occurred to me. Cory died a decade ago, yet the murderer waited eight years before sending the newspaper article, letter and photographs. What was the trigger two years ago that made him want to start killing us?"

"I can't believe this is happening. When I agreed—" Peter broke off, burying his face in his hands.

"So it's true? You agreed to help Cory kill himself?" Beth jumped on the words as proof. Until now, she had only half believed her own theory.

When Peter raised his head, his face was streaked with tears. "Cory was my best friend." He made a sound that could have been a laugh. "Who am I kidding? Cory was my *only* friend. You know what he was like. He had this big personality that wrapped itself around you. For a long time after we became climbing partners, I couldn't understand how someone so popular and with so many gifts would want to be friends with me. He wore me down. We'd hang out sometimes. I'm sure other people looked at us and wondered what the hell the guy with the movie-star looks had in common with the geek."

"Cory had a mind of his own. If he chose you as his friend, it was because he liked you." It was strange how, ten years on, she was getting a glimpse into a friendship she hadn't understood back then. This intensely shy man was clearly uncomfortable talking to them, and yet she sensed a part of him wanted to open up and tell them about Cory.

"That was what he used to say." Peter's expression had taken on a faraway quality, as though he was looking back in time. "When he was diagnosed with eye cancer, he didn't tell anyone except me. Not even his family. He'd left it too late, you see, and it had already spread throughout his body. He'd been ignoring the symptoms, hoping they'd go away. When he told me about it, he was quite calm, but he was already in pain and was losing his sight. He knew the next thing would be complete blindness."

He turned his head and looked at one of the pictures on the wall. The scene was unmistakable. Tenderness Lake was a focal point on the Stillwater Trail. The artist had captured a perfect moment. The mirror-smooth surface of the lake, the majesty of the mountain range, the ribbon of low-hanging clouds, the rounded pebbles peeking through the water's edge in the foreground... the palette was exclusively blue, teasing out every shade and nuance. The visual impact was stunning.

Beth raised a hand to her lips. "Oh, poor Cory! His eyesight was everything to him."

"That was the hardest part. He said he could cope with the pain and the thought of dying, but he couldn't stand to go blind." Peter dragged his gaze away from the picture with an obvious effort. "When he made the decision to take his life, he was quite calm about it. He thought it through carefully. For the sake of his family, he wanted it to look like an accident. He had convinced himself it would be easier that way. He wanted them to remember him as an active person, a person who died doing what he loved, rather than—and these were his words—'the guy who swallowed a bottle of pills rather than facing the end with dignity.'"

"But why did he need to involve you?" Beth asked. "If he was going to make it appear that he had died in a fall, he could have gone out on a solo climb and not come back."

Her thoughts went to Rick Sterling, who, it appeared, had staged his own death in an accident. There were so many twists and turns to this story, it felt like they would never get to the truth.

"Because his eyesight was already failing. If he was alone, he couldn't be sure he wouldn't fall and injure himself badly at a lower height. He risked a horrible impairment that left him in agony, but didn't kill him. The irony was, of course, that it happened anyway." Peter scrubbed a hand over his face as though trying to rub away the memory. "He needed my help to get him to a high point. A place where, once he decided to stage a fall, he couldn't possibly survive."

"And you agreed to help him because he was your friend."

He nodded, the tears beginning to flow again. "At that time, he was my only friend." Beth recalled Tania's words that he had recently found someone with whom he was happy. She was glad. The thought of his loneliness was painful.

"Why don't I make coffee?" Vincente raised his brows at Beth and she nodded gratefully.

While Vincente found the kitchen and could be heard clanking cups, Beth moved across to kneel on the rug beside Peter's chair. Clasping his hand in both of hers, she looked up into his face. Bleak sadness clouded his features.

"I made Cory a promise I would make sure he didn't come back down from that mountain. I had to see it through. When it was my turn to take over and watch him, I decided that would be the time to do it. Killing him was the hardest thing I've ever done. When I held the pillow over his face, he didn't even fight. It was like he knew what was happening and he welcomed it." He gulped back a sob. "Although I don't regret it, there is one thing I'm sorry about… I wish it hadn't been necessary to hit you."

Beth lifted a hand to the back of her head. "I don't think there's even a scar."

"How did you figure out I was the person who killed him?"

"It was something Cory said when we were alone in his tent. He said he wanted to die so bad, and I guessed that he was talking about what happened when he fell," Beth said. "I was the only person who heard him say it, so whoever is sending these pictures still doesn't know that it was you who killed Cory."

"I wonder if he, or she, cares?" Peter drew a perfectly folded handkerchief from his pocket and dried his eyes.

"What do you mean?"

"The letter addressed us all as murderers and said he would come for us one by one. I may have held the pillow over Cory's face, but that rage was directed at all of us. This person blames everyone who took part in that climb." Peter returned the clasp of her hands. "Although I said I have no regrets, I do feel guilty about the effects of what happened. And I've kept silent for too long. I had already decided to tell my story to that superefficient Stillwater detective. My partner persuaded me it would be the right thing to do, but don't count on it stopping this killer."

Beth sat back on her heels, considering his words. "I wonder how he decides on the order of the victims? Is it random, or is there a pattern?"

"What do you mean?" Vincente asked as he returned with the coffee cups.

"Andy, then Rick, then Danielle. That's the order the photographs were sent. If Peter is right, and the killer blames all of us equally for Cory's death, I wonder why he selected the victims in that order? Is it to do with location?" She shook her head. "No, it can't be that. Andy was in Elmville and Danielle in Toronto."

She left Rick out of the conversation. Even though his face had been crossed out of a photograph, she knew he wasn't dead.

"Maybe he is apportioning blame?" Vincente hazarded a guess. "Killing those he considers most guilty first."

"If you use that logic, Peter and I should have been the first people killed." She gave Peter an apologetic smile. "I was with Cory when he died, and Peter was the person who was with him when he fell."

"And I'm next."

Peter's words sent a chill down Beth's spine. "How do you know that?"

"Haven't you received the latest picture?" He got to his feet, moving to a desk that was piled high with books. Reaching into the top drawer, he withdrew a photograph and brought it to Beth.

She didn't want to look at it. Every instinct told her to throw it down on the floor and run. Just like she had wanted to do when they found the picture in Lia's crib back in Casper. Run and keep on running. Instead, she took the picture from Peter and forced herself to look at it. There were five red crosses on this copy. Cory, Andy, Rick, Danielle and now Peter. Bold red lines slashing through their faces. She could feel the killer's rage as he took his pen and marked them off, one by one.

"When did you get this?" Her hand shook as she gave the picture back to Peter.

"What day did you come to the climbing club meeting? It was in my mailbox the next day." He frowned. "I wonder why you didn't get a copy."

"He doesn't know where I live." The words provided a measure of relief from the shock of looking at the picture. Ten people. Five crosses. Half of them should be dead. Peter was the next target…and Rick was still on the run.

Before they could discuss it further, there was a knock on the door. Beth cast a scared look in Vincente's direction, but Peter reassured her. "I'm expecting a delivery. Wait in here."

As he left the room to answer the door, Beth moved closer to Vincente anyway. The house was so small they could hear every sound as Peter drew back the catch on the front door. "Can you carry it through to the kitchen?"

There was the sound of two sets of footsteps walking along the wooden floorboards in the hall. A moment or two of silence followed, then Peter uttered a startled exclamation. "You!"

The gunshot was horribly loud, freezing Vincente and Beth into a moment of immobility. Then, springing into action together, they darted out of the room and into the hall. They were in time to see a black-clad figure dash out of the open front door. They saw nothing of the killer's face, only catching a glimpse of the back of a hooded sweatshirt before the door slammed closed.

In the kitchen, Peter lay in a crumpled heap. The perfect circle of a bullet wound was in the center of his right temple and a puddle of blood was forming on the floor beneath his head. A gun lay close to his right hand, placed to look as if he had dropped it when he fell.

Vincente muttered a curse, and Beth could read his dilemma on his face. The killer was seconds away from them. But if Vincente chased after him and left Beth alone, he exposed her to a possible trap. If he took her with him and they confronted an armed murderer who had already sworn to kill her...

Keeping an arm around Beth and holding her tight against his side, he reached for his cell phone. "Laurie? I need you in Whitebridge right now. You're going to need backup."

Two uniformed police officers from the Whitebridge Police Department arrived five minutes after Vincente called Laurie. Vincente showed them through to the kitchen.

"The caller didn't say anything about a body." One of the officers frowned as they surveyed the scene.

"The caller? Aren't you here because Detective Delaney from the Stillwater Police Department called you?" The feeling that he and Beth were in a shared nightmare was growing stronger.

"Detective who?"

After several minutes of trying to explain the situation, Vincente called Laurie. Although she was already in her car, she was able to speak on her hands-free cell phone and assure the police officers that Vincente had indeed been the person to call in the murder. No one was able to explain the confusion surrounding the call, but Vincente and Beth waited in Peter's sitting room until Laurie finally arrived with a Whitebridge detective.

"Looks like a suicide." One of the Whitebridge police officers studied Peter's body from the kitchen doorway.

It took Laurie about two and a half minutes of relaying cold, hard facts about Andy Smith and Danielle Penn to change his mind.

"Forensics will show that there is no gunshot residue on his clothing and his fingerprints are not on the gun."

She never once used the words *jumping* or *conclusions*, but they were obvious from her attitude. The uniformed officer grew red in the face and shuffled his feet as she spoke.

Laurie then questioned Vincente and Beth about what happened. With her usual relentless focus on detail, she missed nothing. When the forensic team turned up, she told Vincente and Beth to go home and informed them that she would call at the lake house later.

They were silent for most of the drive, the horror of what had happened still sinking in.

"Just before he was shot, Peter said 'you.' That means he knew who it was," Beth said.

It was the first time Vincente had thought of it that way. She was right. When he uttered that single word, Peter signaled that he had recognized his killer. Peter, who had been Cory's friend, could have gotten to know the other man's acquaintances. Would he still be in touch with them after ten years? It wasn't impossible, but that single word made it seem less likely that the killer was a member of Cory's family or one of his friends. It felt more like Peter had recognized the person instantly and been shocked at who it was.

So who are you?

Vincente had been close enough to the killer to reach out a hand and touch him. The frustration that he had let him get away left a sour taste in his mouth.

"Although the murderer placed the gun next to Peter's body, it wasn't going to work as a staged suicide this time." He voiced his thoughts out loud. "Apart from the forensic evidence Laurie talked about, we were in the house. There were witnesses this time. It was only a half-hearted attempt to disguise the killing as something else."

"Why is that?" Beth asked. "Did the killer panic because we were with Peter? Did he think that, between us, we might come up with the truth? Or did he just want to scare me even more by showing how daring he is?"

"Maybe it was both of those things...or neither." Vincente briefly placed a reassuring hand on her knee. "Who knows what's going on inside this person's mind? And possibly it's that simple. The killer could be starting to unravel."

"A violent, unpredictable criminal who is becoming more volatile? That makes me feel a whole lot better."

"I'm here." He tightened his grip on her leg. "He won't get past me."

The easiest way to reach Bryce and Steffi's home on the way back from Whitebridge was to drive through the center of Stillwater, then take the lake road out toward the Stillwater Trail. Their house, with the animal sanctuary located in its rambling grounds, was nestled in the foothills of the mountain range. Vincente had deliberately avoided the route through town the last few times he had driven out to collect Lia. Even though the car he was using had tinted windows, meaning Beth was unlikely to be recognized as they drove through Main Street, he didn't want to take any risks with her safety. It would only take a flat tire in the center of town or another unforeseen holdup, and her cover would be blown.

Just as he was about to drive past the turn that would have taken them along Main Street, Beth cried out, startling him.

"Stop!" The exclamation appeared to have been caused when she saw a man jogging toward them along the edge of the highway.

Vincente braked hard. "What the hell…?"

The jogger ran past them, taking the right turn that led into Stillwater.

"Back up and follow him."

Even though he did as she asked, he issued a warning. "Beth, this is dangerous. We're right on the edge of town here."

"Keep going but slow down." Her voice was urgent as she slewed around in her seat to get another look at the jogger. "Now pull over. Look in the rearview mirror." Vincente did as she instructed. "See this guy running along as though he doesn't have a care in the world?" Her hand was on the door handle as she prepared to jump out of the car. "It's Rick Sterling."

"Wait—" Beth was gone before he finished speaking. There weren't enough curse words in the world to summarize what he was feeling, so Vincente settled for one or two as he slammed the car door and ran after her.

Beth couldn't have chosen a worse place for a confrontation. Up ahead, just a few hundred yards away, was the start of Main Street itself. Vincente could see the

giant, skillet-shaped sign of the Pancake Parlor swinging in the breeze and glimpses of the whiteboards of the
cab company office were just visible through the trees.
In the opposite direction, he could still hear the sounds
of the highway they had just exited. To their right was
the brutal scar that slashed across the landscape, the
knife-sharp fissure known as Savage Canyon. It was
a wilderness packed with forest so dense it was almost
impossible to plow through it.

To their left was the Ryerson River and the Eternal
Springs. At least the local scenic attraction wasn't likely
to be busy with tourists at this time of year.

"Rick?"

As soon as Beth said his name, the guy's head
snapped up and he stopped running. Beth halted as well,
giving Vincente time to catch up to her. Although Vincente had never met Rick Sterling, there was no doubt
in his mind. They had the right man. The wary look on
his face confirmed it. Side by side, Vincente and Beth
faced him across a distance of several feet for a few
seconds. Then Rick turned and ran in the direction of
the waterfall.

Beth didn't hesitate. She took off after him with the
speed of an eagle swooping on its prey. Although Rick
was bigger, Beth had determination on her side and she
was closing on him as he neared the top of the cliff from
which the river took a sharp downward plunge. Vincente muttered another curse. Beth had no idea what
kind of danger she would be in if she caught up to this
guy. Rick had faked his own death, been in Toronto the
day before Danielle Penn died and was likely to have
been the person on their deck in the middle of the night.
Taking those things into account, Vincente decided to

concentrate on running after her instead of swearing or shouting a warning.

When Rick reached the top of the waterfall, he cast a glance over his shoulder at Beth, who was close behind him. Crouching low, he placed his hands on the cliff edge and lowered himself into the water. Vincente blinked as the other man disappeared into the spray. He had a horrible premonition about what was going to happen next.

"Beth, don't—"

It was too late. Beth had already launched herself into the waterfall.

Chapter 15

This was a first. Beth had climbed *up* waterfalls in the past, always using ropes and protective gear. She had never climbed *down* a waterfall. At first, the biggest problem was lack of visibility. She took care of that by moving to one side of the cascade itself. The difference was immediately apparent. Although she was drenched, cold as ice and her hands felt numb, moving out of the fast-flowing water at least allowed her to see. Planning a route down the steep rock face had to be her first priority…after clinging on.

She could see Rick below her, moving swiftly and nimbly as a cat. If she didn't act fast, he would be gone. The thought spurred her on. Probing to find places for her fingers and feet, she began her descent. The conditions were just about as bad as they could get. Ten years ago, she had been experienced at climbing on ice and in winter weather, but this surface was even more un-predictable. As she moved downward, she didn't know whether her next handhold would be rock that was loose, mossy or wet. She quickly discovered that the only certainty was it wouldn't be solid.

Everything seemed to be conspiring against her. The pounding of the falls, the freezing spray, the slippery surface...her descending path was more a scramble and a slide than a climb. About a third of the way down, she risked another glance below her in time to see Rick duck across to an exposed section of rock. Determinedly, she followed his course. There was no way she was letting him get away.

Swinging out over a sharp ledge, she hung on by her fingertips the way she had just seen Rick do, scrabbling wildly for a foothold. *Damn!* By taking the same route as Rick, she had miscalculated. He was at least six inches taller than she was. When he had dangled from this overhang, his feet had found a place to grip the rock. Because she was shorter, she wasn't going to make it. Could she pull herself back up? She seriously doubted it.

A glance down told her how much trouble she was in. Her hands were tiring already. When she dropped, she was going to fall at least forty feet onto solid rock.

Lia. Her daughter's face flashed into her mind and she tried desperately to struggle back up. *I can't die like this. She needs me. And I need a chance to tell that stubborn Italian how much I love him.*

Another glance down kicked her heart rate up another level. Rick had seen her and was climbing back up.

Panic seized her. She was helpless. It was no good telling herself he wasn't ready to kill her because he hadn't sent a photograph with her picture crossed out.

He was a serial killer and he was in charge of how he did this. By following him, she had presented him with the perfect opportunity. He could kill her now simply by releasing the grip her fingers had on the ledge. She would drop onto the rocks below. Vincente would know what had happened. He would tell Laurie, but there would never be any proof. Why the hell had she run after Rick?

The answer was simple. She had pursued Rick because she was tired of being scared. Tired of hiding. Tired of living half a life. She wanted normality. A life in which she could walk along Main Street and say hi to her old friends, reserve a table at Dino's and go there on a date with Vincente, take Lia to the park and push her on the swings, and walk Melon along the riverbank so he could play with the other dogs and attempt to herd the wildfowl.

Rick was a few feet below her now and she bit back the sob that rose to her lips as she aimed a wild kick at his head.

He grunted, ducking out of her way. Seconds later, he was alongside her. No matter how hard she tried to retain her grip on the rock, he was too strong for her, prying her fingers away easily. Instead of allowing her to fall immediately, he placed an arm around her waist, pinning her against him with her arms trapped at her sides.

Beth had no idea what torture he had planned for her, but she didn't intend to submit without a fight. Racing heart. Tight chest. Breathing hard. Light-headed. She was a panic attack checklist. With good reason. She squirmed wildly, trying to get her hands free.

"Keep still." Rick's tone held the same authoritative note he'd used when he ran the climbing club all those years ago. He had been her climbing partner. The man she had trusted with her life. How had they gotten to this point? His voice was so evocative, Beth almost obeyed. Even though she was fighting for her life, the temptation to do as he asked was close to overwhelming.

His strength must be phenomenal. Carrying her with one hand, he used the other to swing down from the ledge. She recalled that Rick had always been superbly fit. Clearly, he had maintained that level of physical ability. A wave of despair washed over her. How the hell was she going to fight a man who could climb down a cliff face one-handed?

After he had descended for a few minutes, Beth felt her feet touch a flat surface. Rick released his hold on her, turning her to face the cliff wall and pressing her hands up against the rocky surface. She trembled in anticipation. Was this it? Was this the moment he was going to push her over the edge and into oblivion? If it was, he was stringing it out, tormenting her with his silence.

After long, anxious seconds had passed and nothing happened, she risked a glance over her shoulder. She was alone on a wide ledge, just about as safe as she could be. Glancing down, she saw Rick almost at the bottom of the falls.

Vincente had never known fear like it. When he saw Beth disappear into the mist of Eternal Springs, he faced a split-second choice: follow her or find another way to track down Rick Sterling. If he went after her and Rick, he would be at a disadvantage. Chasing two experienced climbers down any rock face was going to be tricky enough. Down a waterfall? Vincente could only foresee one outcome…and it wasn't a pretty one.

Leaving Beth as he raced back to the car felt like the ultimate betrayal. Like he was running toward an abyss. Because if he'd gotten this wrong that was what he might as well be doing. As he ran, he experienced everything with perfect clarity. The breeze was so cool it felt like icy needles stinging his exposed skin. The blue of the sky hurt his eyes. Stillwater had its own scent. Sagebrush and pine, with a hint of juniper. It reminded him of licorice and root beer. It was the smell of home, but right now it made Vincente want to retch. Although his limbs seemed heavy, his body felt light, as though it had been hollowed out. But his heart…oh, his heart. That hurt too much to bear. He wanted to rip it out and cast it aside so he could think straight. Because his damn heart wouldn't let him get past one single, awful thought. If anything happened to Beth…

Jumping into the car, he gunned the engine. The falls cascaded into a large plunge pool before the Ryerson River continued its meandering journey toward Elmville. The lake road passed close to the pool. Vincente planned to drive out that way, leave the car and cut through the forest. Depending on how fast Rick and Beth climbed down, he should be able to catch up with them at the bottom of the cliff face.

If he misjudged it and Beth confronted Rick before he got there to back her up… No, he wasn't going to let himself think about that. Wasn't going to picture her alone with the man who might have threatened to kill her. Who might have already killed three people.

Once Vincente was on the highway, he pushed the car to its limit, scorching up the road until he reached the point where he could pull over. The distance from the highway to the plunge pool was short, but it wasn't easy to make his way through the trees and undergrowth that covered the ground between them. By the time he heard the roar of the falls, he felt like he had battled a dozen sharp-clawed monsters. His arms ached from pulling aside heavy branches and the backs of his hands were scratched and bleeding.

When he finally broke through the cover of the trees, the first thing he saw was Rick descending the last few feet of the rock face. Covering the distance between them at a sprint, Vincente was waiting for the other man as he stepped onto level ground. Gripping the collar of his shirt, Vincente swung Rick around. The look of surprise on the other man's face lasted about as long as it took for Vincente's fist to smash into his face. Blood spurted from Rick's nose. The feeling of intense satisfaction didn't quite replace Vincente's fear, but it sure as hell helped.

"Where is she?" Vincente raised his fist in preparation for another blow.

As he swung the second punch, Rick shifted his weight, bringing his leg up and kicking Vincente in the shin. The two men toppled to the ground together, trading blows as they fell.

"Where. Is. She?" Vincente punctuated each word with a jab.

Rick grunted and hit back. The guy had a punch like the kick of a horse. They rolled onto the edge of the plunge pool, and Vincente's head rocked back as Rick's fist connected with his cheekbone. He scrabbled wildly for something to hold on to, felt himself falling backward, grabbed hold of Rick's shirtfront and pulled him over the edge with him as he toppled into the water.

The plunge pool was deep. Vincente already knew

that from summer days spent out here diving into it, trying to reach the bottom. When they were kids, Bryce claimed he'd done it one time, but Vincente hadn't believed him. There was a local legend that the pool was bottomless. It sure as hell felt like it now, as Rick's hands closed around his throat and he sank down and down. The blood pounded in his head and the edges of his vision darkened.

Just as everything began to fade, Rick released his grip. Vincente didn't know why, but he kicked out for the surface. When he broke through, he drew in what felt like several lungs full of air. He spent a few minutes just concentrating on breathing. Yes, he still wanted to kill that bastard Rick Sterling, but first he needed to make sure he wasn't going to die himself.

When he felt his strength had returned sufficiently, Vincente swam to the edge of the pool and hauled himself onto the side. A quick glance around confirmed his worst fears. There was no sign of Rick. How the hell had the guy managed to get away so fast? Slumping forward, Vincente let his head drop between his raised knees. Despair washed over him, sour and dark. What now? Rick was gone and he still had no idea where Beth was.

It took him a moment to register a movement at his side. Turning his head, he looked into Beth's eyes as she knelt and draped an arm around his shoulders.

"How…?" The word rasped over his damaged throat muscles.

She looked up at the cliff face. "I'm not sure you'll believe me when I tell you. I don't know if I believe it myself."

They staggered, shivering and wet, from the plunge pool through the trees to the car. Bryce had already been home when they arrived to collect Lia, and the look of shock on his face and Steffi's had been more effective than a mirror.

"You need a doctor." Bryce helped Vincente to a chair in the big, comfortable kitchen.

"I need a drink." His voice was working again by then. Just about.

They both took hot showers and borrowed clean clothing. Vincente's cheekbone was cut and the eye above had swelled half-shut. A mass of deep red bruises mottled his neck, making it look like a lump of raw hamburger. His whole body felt like it had been pounded with a plastic mallet. Although Bryce and Steffi had tried to persuade them to stay the night, they had wanted to get home. Bryce carried Lia out to the car and Vincente promised to give him a full account of what had happened in a day or two.

It was late when Laurie, having spent most of the day in Whitebridge, had stopped by to let them know what was happening. "I wish you'd told me what you suspected, but I don't believe you could have prevented Peter Sharp's death."

"It was just a hunch," Beth said. "And it felt like a crazy one. No one was more surprised than I was when Peter came right out and confirmed it."

"What makes you think we couldn't have prevented Peter's death by telling you?" It still hurt a little to talk, but Vincente's voice was getting back to normal.

"Because, just like the other killings, this was carefully planned. The murderer wants these deaths to look like accidents or suicides. He's not going to risk getting caught. Not until every single person who was on that mountain ten years ago is dead."

"That's what Peter said. He said it wasn't about the in-dividual who killed Cory. The killer has a grudge against all of us." Beth had reached the point where her whole body was drooping with exhaustion.

"The problem was that, this time, you two got in the way of the plan. I don't believe the killer didn't know you were in the house. That's just too coincidental. I imagine Peter's killing would have been more carefully staged, but possibly the murderer panicked. He didn't know what you were talking about. Even the smallest piece of in-formation could have revealed his identity. Peter had to die immediately." Laurie glanced from Vincente to Beth with a grimace. "You both look like hell."

"You have such a way with words, Detective."

Although Vincente responded with flippancy, he had to acknowledge the truth of what she was saying.

Although Beth hadn't sustained any physical injury from her ordeal, she was aching all over and clearly so tired she could barely move. Steffi had helped them out by preparing dinner for them to bring home. Luckily it had been one of those evenings when Lia, tired out by her day with the animals, had gone straight to sleep.

"None of this business with Rick Sterling makes sense." Just when they didn't have the energy or incli-nation to do any more thinking, Laurie was forcing them into it. "From what you're saying, Beth, he actually res-cued you when you were in difficulties?"

"Yes, he could have got away at that point, or killed me, but he saw I was in danger and he helped me."

"He's a wanted man. So why the hell was he out jog-ging in plain view in the middle of the afternoon?"

Vincente shrugged, wincing as the action caused his

aching muscles to protest. "He was running along the edge of the highway, then he turned into the road."

Laurie drummed her fingers as she considered the matter. "Maybe he had car trouble and was jogging into town to get help?"

"That would be a hell of a coincidence. The guy's car happened break down just outside the town where Beth is staying? The same town he most likely visited a week ago so he could climb down onto our deck in the middle of the night?"

"Another alternative could be that he got a ride as far as Stillwater. The person he was with dropped him on the side of the highway, and Rick was jogging into town when you came by."

Vincente considered Laurie's suggestion. "It still bothers me that he was here in Stillwater. Where Beth is."

"That can't be a fluke. Beth is the only member of the Devil's Peak team who is in Stillwater, even though her location is supposed to be a secret." Laurie shook her head, confusion evident in her expression. "Yet Rick didn't kill you today when he had the chance, Beth. On the contrary. He saved your life."

"Rick is a good guy." They were the words Beth had said when they'd driven out to the West County Climbing Club. She repeated them now as though she was clinging to the lifeline she hadn't had as she went down Eternal Springs.

"We can't rule out his involvement in the other murders, even Peter Sharp's. He had plenty of time to get from Whitebridge to Stillwater today. Which reminds me... I'm sorry to have to do official stuff, but I need a description of the person you saw." Laurie took her faithful notebook out of her bag. "Because of the connection to the Devil's Peak Murder, I'm working with the Whitebridge Police Department on this case. I'll take full statements from you tomorrow, but I find it's better to get a description as soon as possible after the incident."

"I didn't see much." Beth shook her head. "It happened so fast. I barely saw him."

"Me, too," Vincente said. "I saw his back view as he ran out the door."

"Let's start with what he was wearing."

"Black clothing," Beth said. "Sweatpants and a top with the hood pulled up."

Vincente nodded. "And black sneakers."

"Did you notice anything else about the sneakers? The brand? Was there a logo?"

He shook his head. "They could have had a gold flash along the side, but he was moving fast."

"Oh, and he wore gloves," Beth said. "I just remembered that."

"Okay." Laurie scribbled a brief note. "What about his size? Did you get any impression about that?"

Beth hesitated. "I didn't think he was big…"

Vincente thought back to what he'd seen in that brief instant. "Beth's right. He wasn't tall, and he didn't appear muscular, but—" he shook his head "—this is based on what I saw in a split second, you understand? He moved like lightning. That had to take some power."

Laurie wrote some more before returning her notebook and pen to her bag. "From what you're saying, this is not the same person who climbed down the cliff here and onto your deck. Although you've only gained a brief impression of each of them, Beth, you described that man as tall and muscular."

Beth nodded decisively. "They were two different people. The guy at Peter's house was smaller, both in height and width."

"I agree. Having been up close to Rick Sterling today, I can say for sure he was not the person I saw at Peter's house." Vincente lifted a hand to his damaged throat. "Rick may have tried to choke and drown me, but he was fighting for his life after I attacked him first. He wasn't the person who killed Peter...and he did save Beth."

"This is the strangest case I have ever known. Right from the start, no one has been who they seem. Cory Taylor wasn't the carefree charmer everyone thought he was. He was harboring a heartbreaking secret. We thought Rick Sterling was dead, but the person with his hands around your throat in the plunge pool today was very much alive, Vincente. Behind his mild-mannered exterior, Peter Sharp was hiding the fact that he killed his best friend." Laurie got to her feet. "Someone else is hiding something. When we find out what it is, we'll find the killer."

Chapter 16

Vincente checked all the locks and closed all the drapes before coming to sit next to Beth on the sofa.

"It's Lia's birthday next week." She let her head flop onto his shoulder. "We can't let him take that away from her."

"No." He ran a hand down her hair, the touch soothing, both of them too tired for anything more heated. "Lia will have the best celebration we can give her."

His hand spread wider to cup the back of her head and Beth looked up into those midnight eyes. They drew her in exactly the same way as they had done on the first day she saw him. He moved closer and tenderly brushed his lips over hers. She parted her mouth beneath his, needing his taste and warmth. Vincente's tongue caressed hers in a firm sweep. Nothing could have worked as well as this to restore her damaged spirits. His touch was so right, so perfect. When they ended the kiss, Vincente rested his forehead against hers and they stayed like that, breathing each other in.

"I thought I'd lost you today." His voice was hoarse and she didn't know if it was because of his injury, or because of the force of his emotions.

"You won't lose me, Vincente."

There was so much that was unspoken between them, but now wasn't the time. They could say more with their bodies than they could with words. That had always been the way they communicated best.

Beth's hands tugged at his shirt, pulling it free from his jeans. Without bothering to undo the buttons, Vincente pulled it over his shoulders and tossed it onto the floor. Beth ran a hand over his chest and abdomen, tracing the bruises that were already darkening in color.

"Are you sure about this?"

He caught her hand and pressed a kiss into the center of her palm. "Just be gentle with me."

"I can't make you any promises, but I don't think you have too much to worry about. I'm not sure I have it in me to be energetic."

She lifted her sweater over her head as Vincente pulled down her borrowed sweatpants and her underwear at the same time. Getting to his feet, he removed his jeans and boxer briefs and kicked them aside.

Kneeling between her legs, he let his fingers wander over her body. Trails of fire followed in their wake. Beth reached up, cupping the back of his head and pulling him down to her for another kiss.

"I may have lied." Her breathing was coming a little harder. "I can feel my energy returning."

Their tongues joined in a heated dance as his hands

moved lightly down her sides, grazing her breasts and hips. He spread her legs wider as his tongue massaged hers with long, strong strokes. When his hand cupped her sex, Beth moaned softly against his mouth. How had she gone from utter exhaustion to full-on raging desire in the space of a few seconds? The answer was simple. It lay in the magic of Vincente's touch.

Lining his erection up with her entrance, he pressed into her waiting heat, driving his full length in all the way to the hilt. Beth gasped, breaking the kiss as she threw her head back against the cushions. Vincente paused, taking his time, letting her feel every delicious inch. Those wonderful hands continued to stroke and soothe. He traced sweet, tiny kisses along her jaw, her neck and her breasts as her nails dug into his shoulders. When her back arched, he began to move. And then it was as if he couldn't stop. The gentleness was gone as the fire took over, blazing out of control within seconds. As soon as Vincente began to pound into her it was too much, but not enough. Beth craved more, even though her whole body was bowing under the pressure of his demands.

She called out his name, and Vincente increased the pace. Harder. Faster. Slamming into her. Her body jerked up from the sofa in time with his relentless thrusts. Her eyes fluttered closed as the first spasms hit. Waves of pleasure crashed through her as she trembled until she was limp. Vincente lowered his head, pumping short and shallow as his own climax hit. Fatigue hit them both and their bodies grew limp and their breathing became heavy and rhythmic.

They kissed slowly, as if they had all the time in the world. Beth lifted her arms and twisted them around his neck. In that instant, everything felt so perfect. If only they could stay just like that, wrapped in each other's arms, maybe they did have all the time in the world. Maybe it would all be okay.

"I don't recommend hanging from a rock by your arms when you haven't done any serious climbing for years." Beth groaned with each movement. "Edgar is going to think there's something wrong with me when I can't concentrate on our meeting because I keep wincing."

"Call him and postpone." Although Vincente's body was a rainbow of bruises, he appeared to be suffering fewer ill effects from their encounter with Rick the previous day than Beth. His face looked like he'd gone the distance with a world-champion boxer, but he was aching less than he'd expected and the tightness in his throat had eased.

Beth shook her head. "Edgar has put his trust in me, even though I've been unable to let him in on the details of what's going on in my life. He hasn't once asked me why we have to meet in such a cloak-and-dagger way, even though he must wonder what's going on every time he comes to your apartment to hand over my next lot of research for his court depositions. The least I can do in return is remain professional."

Vincente let the subject drop. He knew how much she was enjoying the work she did for Edgar, and guessed that had more to do with her reluctance to cancel than anything else. He understood how important it was to her to keep everything normal. Or to at least create that illusion.

With that in mind, they set off after lunch for the

planned meeting with Edgar. "Why is he here?" Vincente regarded Melon with surprise as the dog bounded onto the passenger seat. "What use will he be in a legal meeting?"

"He hasn't been anywhere different for a long time. I thought, once the meeting was over, we could take him for a walk along the riverbank. I've brought Lia's carrier, as well."

Beth was right. After the drama of the previous day, they needed something ordinary like a walk with a dog and a baby to restore their vigor. It was a perfect day. Sunny and clear with stinging blue skies and hint of chill in the air.

"Why not?" He spoke to Melon as he started the engine. "Just behave yourself in my apartment. I don't want any complaints from the neighbors." Obviously feeling a response was required, Melon wagged his tail and lolled his tongue out of the side of his mouth.

When they arrived at Ryerson Heights and left the car, Melon tried to drag Vincente by the leash toward Savage Canyon.

"That is one place we will never be taking a walk, my friend."

Vincente hauled him away and into the building while Beth carried Lia inside. She also took the carrier Vincente would use to hold Lia on his back when they went for their walk later. They mounted the stairs to the second floor and entered the apartment. Vincente always enjoyed the views from the full-length windows across the river. The raw power of the Wyoming landscape was incredible.

Edgar was due in twenty minutes. Beth prepared by setting up her laptop and papers on the dining table while

Lia crawled around, pulling herself up by the furniture. Melon embarked on a thorough inspection of each room, dashing in and out with his nose pressed to the floor. When Beth called him, he glanced up briefly with the don't-bother-me-now expression of a dog who was far too busy to be distracted by human business before returning to his meandering exploration.

When Vincente's phone buzzed, he expected the caller to be Laurie. Things were happening so fast with the case it seemed impossible nothing dramatic had occurred yet that day. When he glanced at the display, it was Trey Reid. With a pang of guilt, he realized it had been two days since he'd last spoken to his temporary replacement. He signaled to Beth that he needed to take the call, and she nodded her understanding.

"Trey. I'm sorry I haven't been in touch."

"Bryce told me things had been busy at home." Trey sounded apologetic. "And it hasn't been a problem until now. I hate to bother you, but…" Vincente could hear the concern in the other man's voice.

"Go ahead."

"I'm doing the monthly audit and everything was going fine until I ran the final program yesterday. I've made several attempts now, but there seems to be a glitch and the totals are all wrong." Trey's frustrated sigh resonated in Vincente's ear. "I've been in the office all night trying to figure it out."

"I've had that problem myself. Let me check my notes and I'll call you back." Vincente groaned at the prospect of attempting to sort the problem out over the phone.

"What is it?" Detecting his annoyance, Beth glanced up from her paperwork.

"Trey has screwed up the audit program." Vincente

ran a hand through his hair. "Actually, that's unfair. It's a complex system and if you don't know what you're doing, one wrong step can mess the whole process up. If I was in the office with him, I could sort it out in five minutes, but talking him through it in a phone call is going to be a nightmare."

She tapped her pen on the edge of the table. He could tell by the look on her face that half her mind was on her work. "Why don't you go down there?"

He gave an emphatic shake of his head. "Because you come first and there is a maniac on your tail, remember?"

"I'm not likely to forget it. Seriously, your office is five minutes' drive from here. Go and sort out your problem. Lia and I will be fine until you get back."

He hesitated. It would be the perfect solution. But... He thought of what was at stake. Saw Peter Sharp's body lying on his kitchen floor, a thick, dark red puddle forming beneath his head. "No."

Beth got to her feet. Coming around the table, she took his hands. "We can't let him do this to us, Vincente. We can't become prisoners because of him. You chose this apartment for my meetings with Edgar because it's safe. The only people who know we're here are Edgar and Laurie. And I'm meeting *Edgar*. After your family, there is no one more trustworthy."

She was right, of course. He was being paranoid. And it would be so much easier to fix the computer glitch in person. "I would be gone fifteen minutes at the most."

Beth grinned. "Now you're talking sense. Don't forget we have Melon to take care of us."

He rolled his eyes. "Now you're *not* talking sense."

"Don't insult my dog." She pushed him toward the door. "Go."

He kissed her before going out. Closing the door carefully behind him, he ran down the stairs and made his way out to the parking lot. The sooner he sorted this damn program out, the sooner he could get back and they could have their family walk by the river.

Family. The word was warm in his thoughts as he started the car. Not frightening. Not like a steel trap coming down. Not something that he would someday run from, hurting Beth and Lia in the process. It was what they already were. His family. All he had to do was make it official.

He was still smiling as he stepped into the familiar foyer of Delaney Transportation. A flurry of greetings followed him as he made his way down the corridor to his office. Trey looked up from his desktop computer, his expression both relieved and embarrassed when he saw who it was.

"I didn't want to call you in here…"

Vincente dragged a chair over to the desk. "Let's see if we can't sort this out between us." He knew he could solve the problem in minutes, but it seemed insensitive to say that when Trey had spent all night worrying about it.

Five minutes later, he had explained to Trey exactly which combination of figures weren't working together and the other man was pretending to bang his head on the desk at the simplicity of the solution. "It's so straightforward now you've explained it. I feel like an idiot for not seeing it."

"Everything is easy once you know how it works…"

Vincente frowned as his cell phone buzzed. A nasty

little worm of dread began to writhe around in his stomach when he saw Laurie's name on the display.

Not now. Not when I've left them alone.

"Vincente." Laurie didn't give him time to speak. Just the way she said his name, the way she was shaken out of her usual composure, had him on his feet and heading for the door. "I've found out who the other person hiding a secret is. Cory Taylor was Edgar Powell's nephew."

Even though Beth had encouraged Vincente to go, as soon as the door closed behind him, the apartment started to feel like a scary place.

This is crazy. She tried out a laugh and it sounded false. *The reasons you gave Vincente for why it was okay to go still apply.*

She scooped Lia up and carried her over to the window to show her the view. Lia was unimpressed and wriggled to be put down again. Deciding to make coffee while she waited for Edgar, Beth took Lia through to the kitchen with her. Vincente's cupboards were as chaotic as ever, and she smiled at old memories of trying to make sense of where he kept things. Salt next to powdered detergent. Sugar with the beer.

She had just located the coffee when the buzzer sounded. Trust Edgar to be exactly on time. Not a minute too early or too late. Bouncing Lia up and down on her hip, Beth went to the intercom.

"Come on up, Edgar. You must have smelled the coffee."

She pressed the button that would release the door of the building and went through to the hall. Her smile faded as she opened the front door of the apartment.

"Hello, Beth."

Instead of Edgar's familiar, reassuring figure, Tania Blake stepped over the doorstep and closed the door behind her. Her eyes glittered triumphantly and a curious smile twisted her lips.

Beth took a moment to gather her thoughts, but in reality, the situation didn't take much working out. Her eyes were telling her everything she needed to know. Tania was dressed in black clothing. Sweatpants and a hooded top. Her eyes dropped to Tania's feet. Beth recalled what Vincente had said to Laurie last night.

Black sneakers. They could have had a gold flash along the side, but he was moving fast.

Tania was wearing black sneakers with a gold flash along the outside. And gloves. The same gloves Beth had noticed her wearing the day before.

When she killed Peter.

The thought didn't need any confirmation, but Tania provided it anyway. "I have something for you."

She held out a photograph. It was the one Beth had been dreading. Six red crosses. Cory, Andy, Rick, Danielle, Peter…and now Beth.

My turn.

There was no longer any sign of Tania's depressed demeanor. Beth wondered if she had been faking her illness, or if there were two sides to her personality.

Before Beth could move, Melon emerged from the sitting room. Vincente might mock the dog's intuition, but he immediately picked up on Beth's mood. Throwing back his head, he launched into a volley of menacing barks, directing his threats at Tania.

Tania withdrew a gun from the pocket of her sweatpants and leveled it at the dog. "Get rid of it, or I'll shoot it."

Grabbing Melon by his collar while still holding Lia tightly with her other arm, Beth wrestled the dog into the bedroom.

"Not the baby. I have plans for her."

The words sent Beth's nerves into panic mode as she shut the door. Melon's howls sounded like something from a low-budget horror movie, and he started scratching wildly at the bottom of the door.

Tania frowned. "The neighbors will wonder what the hell is going on. Maybe I should shoot it anyway."

"He'll calm down in a minute." Beth tried to keep the pleading note out of her voice. She should probably save that for herself and Lia.

"We won't be here long anyway."

Before Beth could ask what Tania meant by that comment, the buzzer startled her.

"It's my boss. If I don't answer it, he'll call the police." Would Tania swallow the lie? Beth was desperate. She was prepared to try anything.

"Let him in." Tania moved to stand at one side of the apartment door, concealing herself behind it. "But don't try anything."

Beth pressed the button on the intercom. "Beth, I'm sorry to be so late."

She wanted to sob when she heard Edgar's voice. Should she risk calling out to him? Tell him to contact Vincente? Maybe she could wrestle the weapon from Tania? Beth ventured a quick glance at the gun. Her blood ran cold when she saw where it was pointing. Tania wasn't aiming it at her. It was leveled at Lia.

"Come on up, Edgar."

Tears filled her eyes as she opened the door and Edgar stepped into the apartment. His smile was apologetic. "A last-minute crisis at the office—" a frown chased away the smile "—is everything okay?"

His eyes widened as Tania stepped into view. He barely had time to raise a defensive hand before the gun barrel came down on his temple. Edgar's body seemed to fold in on itself as he toppled to the floor.

Beth cried out and made a move toward him, but Tania grabbed her arm.

"Leave him. We're going for a walk." Tania used the gun to gesture toward the door.

"I need to put Lia in the carrier," Beth said. "I hurt my arms yesterday and I can't hold her for long."

It was true, although she didn't know how far they'd be walking. Another reason for wanting her hands free was that, if the possibility presented itself, she would do anything she could to get away from Tania. Having Lia in a carrier on her back would make escape easier than having a baby in her arms.

Tania made a huffing noise, but folded her arms across her chest as Beth got Lia into her coat and then into the carrier. Since being restrained in any way was what her daughter hated more than anything, this action provoked an immediate protest from Lia. The sound of her distress caused Melon to renew his barking. Between them, they were making so much noise that Beth was half hopeful, half fearful that someone might decide to investigate. She hoisted Lia onto her back and secured the carrier in place.

"The gun will be in my pocket. I don't advise you to do anything stupid." Tania gestured for Beth leave the apartment first.

Why hadn't she noticed that Tania was as physically fit as ever?

Because she hid it beneath those baggy clothes. I saw what she wanted me to see. She drew me in and made me believe she was a pitiful figure who couldn't possibly hurt anyone.

Beth had fallen for Tania's illusion and now she and Lia were about to pay the price.

Chapter 17

Vincente and Laurie screeched into the parking lot of Ryerson Heights at the same time. They exited their vehicles in the same instant.

"Edgar?" Vincente was still stunned. "He's worked with Beth for years. He must have known she was part of the Devil's Peak team. If he wanted to harm her, he could have done it anytime he chose. Why would he suddenly start sending letters and photographs two years ago?"

"Edgar's sister was Cory's mother. They had been estranged for many years, but there was a reconciliation just before she died after a lengthy illness. That was two years ago. Who knows what happened? Cory's mother could have been harboring a grudge against the Devil's Peak team and passed that hatred on to Edgar before she died. She may even have asked him to take revenge on her behalf."

"I know the fact he never told Beth he was Cory's uncle makes it likely he's guilty, but I'm still struggling with it," Vincente said as they raced toward the entrance.

"That's Edgar's car." Laurie gestured to the battered old Fiat that was parked close to the front of the building. She was pulling her gun out of her shoulder holster as they dashed up the stairs.

Vincente reached the second floor just ahead of Laurie. His heart plummeted when he saw the door to his apartment was open. He was moving toward it, when Laurie's voice halted him.

"I need to call for backup before we go in there."

It took him about thirty seconds to consider what she was saying. "It's *Beth*. And my daughter."

"Vincente, I understand how you feel. But I can't let you go do this—"

He placed his hand on the door handle. "The only way you're going to stop me is if you shoot me."

"Why do you Delaney men always have to be so damn stubborn?" There was a note of defeat in the question, but he heard her footsteps right behind him as he stepped into the apartment.

The first thing they saw was Edgar crumpled in a heap on the floor. Laurie dropped on one knee beside him.

"He's alive. It looks like someone hit him over the head."

As she spoke, Edgar stirred. He moaned, opening his eyes and blinking at Laurie as though he didn't recognize her. After a few seconds, he attempted to sit up. The effort was too much for him and he collapsed back onto the floor. "Beth... The baby..."

His words were all the confirmation Vincente needed that Edgar was not the killer.

"What happened, Edgar? Can you remember?"

Vincente leaned over him. As he did, he saw a photograph. His whole body went cold as he picked it up and handed it to Laurie. It was proof of what they were dealing with. It was the familiar picture of the Devil's Peak team. In this one, there was a sixth red *X*. Beth's face had been eliminated.

Vincente hadn't believed the pain he was experiencing could get any worse. In that moment when Laurie called him and he realized he had left Beth and Lia in danger, he had experienced pure agony. Every part of his body had been battered by terror. And every second since had felt like he was being beaten with a bag of bricks. But this? Looking at that picture took the feeling one step higher, made it spin further out of control, gripped his spine and tried to draw it out through the top of his body until he was a useless, whimpering mass. For Beth's sake, he forced emotion aside and concentrated on what Edgar was saying.

"A woman...dressed all in black. She was hiding behind the door when I came in. Had a gun on Beth and the baby." His voice shook. "Hit me over the head."

"Do you know where they went?"

"No. I blacked out."

A desperate howl almost drowned out what Edgar was saying. "It's Melon. He must be in one of the bedrooms."

Vincente went to let the dog out. Melon went wild, jumping all over him, licking his hands and whining pitifully. When Vincente tried to go back and finish his conversation with Edgar, Melon circled his legs, trying to herd him out of the apartment.

"He's stressed," he told Laurie as Melon sniffed a path to the door and back again. "If he heard what was going on and couldn't do anything, the poor dog will feel like he wasn't doing his job."

"He definitely wants to take you somewhere," Laurie said.

She was right. Melon wasn't giving up. He kept returning to Vincente, nudging his legs and whining as he attempted to drive him to the door. At the start of their acquaintance, Vincente hadn't rated Melon's intelligence as particularly high. He had revised his opinion of the dog over time, but maintained the joke with Beth, who always got fired up and defended her beloved pet. Now, he realized Melon wasn't stressed. He was trying to tell him something. He wondered if it was possible Melon might be remembering his search-and-rescue training.

"Can you take me to her, Melon?" It was a long shot. If the person who had taken Beth and Lia had forced them into a car, Melon wouldn't be able to follow their scent. But the dog was so damn insistent. "Can you find your mistress?"

Melon gave an excited bark and dashed to the door. Vincente followed him.

"I'll call the paramedics and get them to come out here to you, Edgar." Laurie shouted the words over her shoulder.

"Just find them." Edgar's voice was still weak, but he managed to make himself heard as they ran for the stairs.

They emerged from the apartment building and Vincente wondered just how crazy he had to be to entrust a task of this magnitude to a dog. But he was desperate, and Melon was all he had right now. There was no question that he was following a scent. His nose was down and his plumy tail was waving.

As they followed him across the parking lot, Vincente paused. "That car—" he pointed to the scarred and battered Ford Mustang "—I saw it at the West County Climbing Club."

It was unmistakable. He remembered the sticker in the rear window. *Rock climbers do it up against the wall!* He'd made a lame joke to Beth about not going to the Christmas party if that was the standard of the humor he could expect.

"Edgar said it was a woman who hit him. Tania Blake was at the climbing club when Laurie and I went there. It could be her car."

Laurie was on her cell phone, calling in the license plate and registration as Melon led them to the rear of the building.

"That dog sure seems to know what he's doing." Laurie panted as they ran to keep up.

Vincente nodded. "I agree. But if he does, our problems are getting bigger by the minute."

"What do you mean?"

"He's taking us into Savage Canyon."

"How did you find me?" Beth asked.

Although Tania was urging her to go faster, the ground underfoot was a minefield of deep fissures and lethal tree roots. Savage Canyon was an alien landscape. Growing up in Stillwater, kids were warned never to come to this place. Beth remembered the way it had assumed almost mystical proportions in her mind. If she had a nightmare, it was always set here, home of the boogeyman, witches and hobgoblins; no one in their right mind stepped foot in Savage Canyon.

In reality, it was a place in which, over millions of years of relentless slashing and slicing, the Ryerson River had carved a brutal path through the Wyoming landscape. With its red-rocked, knife-sharp walls, the canyon was so narrow that little light pierced through to river level. As they penetrated deeper into the trees, it grew increasingly primitive. Beth felt as though they were leaving civilization behind them. Twenty-first-century Stillwater felt a million miles away. She wouldn't be surprised if they were the first people to ever walk this path. Boogeyman? She wasn't scared of meeting a creature from her childhood nightmares. But it felt like dinosaurs might still roam this forest.

Not that any of it mattered when a killer with a gun was at her side. Surreptitiously, she loosened Lia's light-weight sneaker. Slipping it off her daughter's little foot, she dropped it on the ground. A bright pink shoe in the middle of the dark vegetation should be a marker for anyone following them. She bit back the harsh sob that rose in her throat. Why would anyone follow them *here*?

"It wasn't easy." Tania seemed to feel she should be congratulated for her ingenuity. "Not once you left Casper. While you were there, it wasn't a problem." She laughed at Beth's look of surprise. "I'm a computer systems analyst. Hacking is child's play for me. I kept track of all of you through your medical records. I needed to give you the photograph of Danielle, so I was watching you the day the detective and the handsome hero turned up."

Beth allowed that information to sink in. She thought back to the time when she'd been scared and asked the doctor not to keep any notes about her. It turned out she'd been right to be fearful. She saw the open window in Lia's bedroom and the ladder up against the wall. All the time she'd believed she was hidden away, Tania had been able to get to her anytime she wanted.

"Once you left Casper, I lost track of you for a while. But you helped me out by coming to the climbing club, and your boyfriend—" she spat the word out with such venom that Beth felt a fresh wave of alarm "—isn't an ordinary-looking guy. Tall, handsome, with that dark, smoldering thing going on…you really hit the jackpot with him, didn't you?" The mocking edge in Tania's voice made Beth shiver more than ever. "I remembered you used to live in Stillwater. So I started here. It's amazing what people will tell you." Her voice took on a different note. Warm and singsong. "Oh, hey, I just love your town. So quaint and Old Western. I had a friend who used to live here. We're going back…let me see, must be ten years now. Beth Wade. You remember her? You don't say. Disappeared? Maybe murdered? Oh, my sweet Lord. Is Vincente an Italian name? Oh, half-Italian. And his brother is the mayor, you say?" Tania switched back to her mocking tone. "Yeah, people can be so dumb."

She appeared to be enjoying herself now. Talking about her achievements had brought a little smile to her lips. "Of course, even when I found out who he was and where he lived, it was obvious you had gone into hiding somewhere. But I'm a patient woman. I checked Vincente's apartment out every few days. Sat in the parking lot with my memories to keep me warm. I figured he'd come along there eventually to get his mail or pick up some clothes, and he'd lead me to you. Today was my lucky day. Your little family showed up, and then—just as I was on my way in to surprise you all—your body-guard left you alone."

My memories to keep me warm. What did that mean? Would Tania tell her all of it? If Beth was going to die, she'd like to know the real reason. "I'm not the person who killed Cory."

"You all killed him." Tania's voice had taken on a dreamy quality. "By not saving him, you ruined my life."

"You loved him." It was obvious from her face and the quality of her voice.

"Yes, I loved him." Tania's lips twisted into a bitter smile. "And he would have loved me, too, you know. If he'd been allowed to live, we'd have had what you have."

"Cory was dying. He had incurable cancer." Beth didn't know if telling her was going to make things better or worse, but she figured the truth was the only weapon she had right now. "His fall wasn't an accident. He wanted to die on Devil's Peak that day."

"No!" It was the wail of a wounded animal. "You're lying."

"He had tumors in both eyes. By the time he found out, it was too late to save his sight and the cancer had already spread throughout his body. Peter knew and had promised to help him commit suicide. When you saved Cory, you did it with the best of intentions, but it wasn't what he wanted." The gun was pointed at the ground and Beth kept her gaze on it, willing it to stay there as she kept her voice calm and gentle. "Peter was the one who killed Cory. He did it because that was the agreement they had made."

Tania started shivering wildly, shaking her head as though she could make the words go away.

Even as she talked, Beth was remembering what Peter

had said. That this whole nightmare was about more than who killed Cory. He had wondered about the order in which the victims were selected. Andy, Rick—even though he wasn't dead—Danielle, Peter and now Beth. *We'd have had what you have.* Those words that Tania had just spoken were the key. That was what she had been searching for with Cory, what she felt had been snatched away from her with his death.

Happiness. Love. Romance. Each of the victims had found a partner with whom they were happy. Tania was killing the people who had what she thought she'd lost.

"Keep moving." Tania seemed to have recovered her composure as she gestured with the gun. "Cory dying of cancer? I've got to hand it to you. That's quite a story."

They stumbled onward, taking a slight upward path. It hadn't worked. Tania was going to believe what she wanted to believe.

"Why did you start with Andy?" Maybe if she got Tania back on the subject of her achievements, she could distract her. Lia had fallen asleep, and Beth was glad. At least her daughter wasn't picking up on any distressing vibes. Carefully, she began to undo Lia's other shoe.

"Because he was always so damn smug." Tania's voice became high-pitched and jeering. "'Oh, I'm so happy. I have such a great relationship. No one could ever be as much in love as me and my wife.'"

"You killed him because he was happy?" As the incline became steeper, Beth dropped Lia's other shoe.

"I killed him because I could. But, yeah, the happiness thing didn't help him. And yet, when I got to him, he wasn't happy at all. He was a drunken mess. And killing him was easy. All I had to do was get him to swallow some pills with his next few drinks. He didn't even notice what was happening." Tania seemed disappointed. "I had to make it look like suicide, or an accident, of course. If there was any chance of it appearing to be murder, I might be caught before I could move on and get the rest of you. One by one, remember. Just like I promised in my letter."

Beth swallowed to try to get rid of the hard lump in her throat. How could she be here, having this conversation? Trying to sound normal as she walked alongside a serial killer? *With my baby asleep in the carrier on my back?*

"If I couldn't have Cory, the people who walked down off that mountain sure as hell weren't going to be happy."

"Why did you wait eight years to decide that?" Beth asked.

"I already told you." Tania sounded impatient. "I had a few problems. They hospitalized me."

When they met at the climbing club, Tania had told Beth she had been diagnosed with severe depression. If Tania's problems had lasted eight years, they had been more complex than she'd revealed and must have included something more serious than depression. Tania had said she was tracking them by hacking their medical records. *She knew I suffered from depression.* Beth felt a flare of anger at the way Tania had callously used that information to provoke sympathy from her.

"And Rick?" Did Tania know he was still alive? Surely, she must be aware if one of her murder victims had gotten away from her. Much as Beth would love to know the story of what had happened to Rick on that ledge in the Grand Teton National Park, she wasn't sure she was going to hear it from Tania. "He always kept his private life quiet. How could you know whether he was happy or not?"

Tania's top lip curled back, showing her teeth in a near snarl. Beth was willing to bet that meant she did know Rick was still alive. Did she know he was in Stillwater? That was an interesting question. Were they working together? She had never considered the possibility until now. "I don't want to talk about him."

"So, you killed Danielle next." She moved on, since it seemed they were skipping over what happened with Rick.

"She wasn't quite as easy as Andy. She tried to fight me, but I was too strong for her." That faraway note was back in Tania's voice, as though she was recalling a pleasant memory. "She begged and pleaded with me as I got her head into the noose. I enjoyed that part." She turned to look at Beth. "I hope you'll beg. I like begging."

Beth choked back a sob. Of course she would beg. She would do anything to protect Lia.

"Peter was right on your doorstep. You saw him all the time at climbing club meetings. Why did you wait until after you'd killed Andy and Danielle to go after him?"

Tania gave a derisive snort. "Because he didn't count. Not at first. He wasn't *happy*. Not until he met her."

Beth remembered her meeting with Tania at Betty's Bakery. How she'd dismissed Tania's rambling speech about Peter's new partner and wondered if Tania might have some sort of prejudice against people who used internet dating sites. But that wasn't what Tania's problem had been. Her scorn had been about Peter's happiness, not how he found it.

"That's how you decided what order you were going to kill us. It was according to how happy we were."

Tania nodded. "You moved right up my list when I saw you gazing into the eyes of your Italian lover when you came to the climbing club. It was like you were waving a flag with the words *me next* at me."

If it hadn't been so awful, it might almost have been funny. Beth had taken such care to protect herself and Lia. Vincente had done everything he could to look after them. But the one thing they had tried so hard to deny had been the thing that had given them away. Tania had seen it in a simple exchange of glances.

We love each other. We hid from everything else, but there was no hiding from that.

They were alongside the top of the trees now. The narrow path they were following was leading out onto the top of the canyon. Beth wasn't sure what the plan was, but she didn't like the way this was going. High up above the cruel fault in the earth's crust, there were too many ways a disturbed mind could make it look like she had tripped or slipped.

"Did Cory know how you felt?" Beth tried a new approach. "Did you ever tell him you loved him?"

Tania swung around so sharply Beth almost lost her footing there and then. "He would have loved me. We just never got the chance to be together."

Beth wasn't so sure, although she had no intention of saying so. She thought back to ten years ago, contrasting Tania's personality with Cory's. They had been steel and silk. Tania had been arrogant and inflexible. Cory had been easygoing and modest. It would have been difficult to find two people more different. She guessed Tania had fallen in love with Cory's looks. Had she known, on some level, that her feelings would not be returned?

I had a few problems. Did Tania's problems start with Cory's murder, or had they been present before he died? Had she developed an obsession with him, one that had been allowed to spiral out of control in an already unstable mind after his death? Looking at Tania's face as they paused on top of the canyon, it was hard to picture a time when reason had been a feature of her personality.

"Ever since I knew about your postpartum depression, I've been planning how I would do this." Tania smiled, turning her face into the breeze as though they were out for a pleasant hike. "I even came and checked this place out. It all got too much for you—that's what they'll believe when they find out you killed yourself and your baby."

"Not her." Beth couldn't keep the sob out of her voice. "Please..."

"But it won't work as well without her." Tania pouted as she drew a slip of paper out of her pocket. "I typed this note for Vincente from you, explaining everything. How sorry you are. How much you loved him. How you just couldn't take the stress anymore." She looked down into the canyon. "There won't be much of you left when they find your bodies, but I hope they'll be able to read the note. I spent so long getting it just right."

Chapter 18

Panic would be his worst enemy. That was what Vincente kept telling himself. He needed a clear head if he was going to get Beth and Lia out of this. He had to keep regulating his breathing, stopping his mind from racing, taking time to place his feet carefully instead of storming ahead and breaking an ankle on a tree root.

Melon dashed on ahead of them, occasionally darting back to either check they were still with him, or to hurry them along.

Laurie had been speaking on her cell phone to her chief, keeping him updated about what was going on, but she muttered an exclamation. "The signal keeps fading."

"I'm not surprised. This is like going back in time to the Jurassic Period."

Waist-high ferns clung damply to his legs and thick ropes of tangled vine hung down to meet them. The scent of loam, pine and wild garlic was thick and cloying. Vincente saw this view every day from his bedroom window. *Never felt tempted to come down here.* Savage Canyon was the sort of place people admired from a distance. It was nature at its most raw and untouchable. Would the killer really bring Beth and Lia into this alien scene? Melon clearly thought so, and the dog's instinct was the only thing keeping Vincente going.

As Melon followed the route of the river, an object lying among the gnarled tree trunks caught Vincente's eye. "Over there."

Melon got to the bright pink item before them. Snatching it up between his teeth, he brought it to Vincente. Wagging his tail with delight, he dropped what he was carrying at Vincente's feet, nudging it closer with his nose.

"It's Lia's shoe." Vincente managed to get the words out, even though his throat felt like it was closing. He squatted, ruffling the fur on Melon's neck. "I take it all back. You are the best damn dog ever. Now, let's go find them."

Melon needed no further encouragement. Uttering a joyful bark, he ran ahead of them again, snuffling in the undergrowth as he picked up the trail he had been following. Although Melon had been right to bring them this way, Vincente didn't feel able to allow any glimmer of hope to shine through his despair. The killer had chosen this hostile environment for a reason, and it wasn't going to be a good one. Somewhere up ahead, Beth and Lia were facing a dangerous ordeal. He had to get to them in time.

Melon was taking them on an upward path, leading them gradually out of the canyon itself and toward the ridge that overlooked it. Vincente judged that when they emerged, they would be in an isolated part of the countryside, outside of town and miles from any dwellings. The murderer had selected a place that was lonely and inhospitable, away from prying eyes and any chance of interruption. There was a reason for that choice.

They found Lia's other shoe as they ascended. "Beth did this deliberately," Vincente said as he tucked the little sneaker into his pocket. "She's letting us know they came this way."

Laurie placed a hand on his arm, her expression softening as she scanned his face. "We'll find them."

"But will we be in time?"

Before Laurie could reply, her cell phone buzzed, the signal kicking back in as they moved out of the canyon. Her face was serious as she answered and listened carefully to what the caller was telling her. It was several minutes later when she returned her cell phone to her pocket.

"That was Chief Wilkinson. The car in the parking lot outside your apartment, the one you saw at the West County Climbing Club? It does belong to Tania Blake."

"So she is the killer?" Vincente shook his head in amazement. "She seemed so harmless."

"Tania is very dangerous. Long before Cory's death, she had a history of obsessive behavior, including stalking. Although she was never convicted, she was ordered by a judge to seek psychiatric help."

"She told Beth she suffered from depression after Cory's death and had been hospitalized," Vincente said.

"That's only partly true. She spent several years in and out of the hospital, but it was due to a psychotic disorder. Her family used the term 'depression' as a cover story," Laurie explained. "When Tania was discharged from the hospital, she was supposed to remain in her parents' home, under their supervision. When her mother died, Tania left home."

"When was that?" Although Vincente asked the question, he suspected he could guess the answer.

"Two years ago," Laurie said. "The chief is coordinating with the West County Sheriff's Department. They're mobilizing a helicopter to search this area."

Melon interrupted them by giving a low growl and pinning his ears back. "What is it, boy?"

Vincente followed the direction of the dog's gaze. On the ridge, high above them, he could see two figures. They were too far away to hear if he called out to them, but he knew who they were. His heart made a wild attempt to escape through his throat. Beth was standing with her back to the canyon. He could tell from her body shape she was wearing the baby carrier. Tania was facing her with her right arm outstretched. He guessed from her stance that she was aiming a gun at Beth.

What neither of the women on the ravine edge could see was something that was clear from Vincente's viewpoint. There was a third figure. A man was stealthily making his way toward them, closing the distance inch by inch. Rick Sterling was doing a good job of creeping up on them unseen.

"If you shoot me, it won't look like suicide or an accident." Beth remained where she was, refusing to do what Tania wanted. Declining to step off the edge of the ravine and into certain death.

"I'm not planning on shooting *you*." Tania's smile was

smug. "The bullet is for the baby. I have it all planned. You shot her and then jumped. It's all in the note."

Tania had stuffed the fake suicide note into the back pocket of Beth's jeans and now she was forcing her closer to the canyon. Beth knew she was running out of time. If she tried to fight Tania, she risked both her and Lia being shot. If she jumped before Tania fired…her eyes skittered to the chasm behind her. How could anyone possibly survive that fall?

Tania took a step closer, raising the gun. "Time to say goodbye."

A movement behind her caught Beth's eye and she blinked, attempting to clear her vision. She must be imagining things. No one knew they were here. There wasn't going to be any last-minute rescue… She froze as Rick moved into view.

Beth desperately needed something on which to pin her hopes. Every fiber of her being wanted this to be a positive development. Wanted Rick to be the hero who had come to her rescue. But how could that be? Just yesterday, he had his hands around Vincente's throat as he tried to kill him. And Rick had been in Toronto when Danielle died.

Wasn't it more likely that these two were somehow in this together? Beth knew from her experience yesterday that Rick was capable of picking her up and throwing her over the edge of the ravine. Her defiance was in tatters, her thoughts scattering in every direction.

Rick saved my life yesterday. Why would he do that only to kill me today?

"No more, Tania."

The cool, calm words acted like bucket of cold water thrown over Tania. She shuddered violently before swinging around to face Rick, her face an almost comical picture of outrage.

Maybe hope wasn't out of Beth's reach. She wished she could run, but there was nowhere to go. And there was still that damn gun to consider.

"You shouldn't be here." Tania's lip trembled. "You were supposed to die."

"I know you planned to kill me right after you murdered Andy," Rick said. His face was a mess. It looked like his nose was broken, but Beth doubted he had sought medical help. "I figured out right from the start it was you. Cory told me you had a thing for him. He didn't know what to do about it, and he wanted my advice. I told him to act normal, continue to treat you like a friend and maybe you'd move on from it. The problem with Cory was he could be too kindhearted sometimes. I wondered if acting normal for him might make you think he returned your feelings."

"He did." Tania's lips were thin and white. "He loved me, too. He just never got a chance to say it because he died." She waved the gun. "Because you killed him. All of you."

Rick shook his head. "You're wrong, and people are dying because of it. When the letter and the photographs came, I knew they must be from you. Then Andy died, and my picture was next. I couldn't prove anything, but I decided it would be safer if I ducked out of sight for a while. You can't kill a man who is already dead."

"You cheated." Tania sounded like a child playing a game.

"You call it cheating, I call it taking care of myself and looking out for my friends…continuing the job I was supposed to do up on that mountain all those years ago. I wanted to try to keep the rest of the team safe." Rick's voice was regretful. "I haven't done a great job so far. Even though I was at Danielle's wedding, I couldn't stop you getting to her."

"No, you couldn't." Tania's expression brightened. "I was too smart for you in Toronto. I was too smart for you when I killed Peter. I'm too smart for you now."

"Give me the gun, Tania." Rick held out his hand. There it was again. That powerful note of authority. On every climb, he had been the person in charge. It didn't matter what the situation was—whether they were deciding when to stop for lunch or to push on to a summit in poor weather conditions—everyone deferred to Rick. His experience, skills and assurance made him a natural leader. Would the conditioning that had been so much a feature of their team kick in now? Would Tania obey him? "It's over."

"You say he didn't love me, but you can't know that. You can't be sure."

"Tania, I can be more sure of that than anyone." Rick's voice was calm, quiet and filled with memories. "We didn't last long, but for one wonderful summer twelve years ago, Cory and I were an item."

It happened so fast Beth didn't have time to react. Tania covered her mouth with her left hand. She was half-turned toward Beth and, as she staggered under the shock of what she had just heard, the gun in her right hand went off. The bullet hit Beth in the left hip and she reeled backward from the impact of the shot. Her feet teetered on the edge of the ravine. Time slowed to a crawl as she stared down at the Ryerson River. From this height, it looked like a silver ribbon, trickling though the canyon. She swung out, high above the trees as her arms flailed wildly and uselessly. This was it. There was nothing to grab on to. She was going to fall.

She thought she must be hallucinating as Vincente appeared. He crested the top of the ravine at a run with Laurie just behind him. With reflexes like lightning, he dashed to her and caught hold of one of the straps of the baby carrier. For an instant, Beth was suspended over the crevice, only Vincente's fingers preventing her and Lia from going into free fall and plummeting to the canyon floor. Then Rick was beside him, grabbing Vincente around the waist and the two men were working together to haul her back to safety. Sobbing, she clung to Vincente, clawing at his chest as though checking he was real.

Lia's screams were the only thing she could hear. The bullet felt like red-hot wire tearing into her hip. Blood, thick and sticky, soaked through her jeans.

"Lia?" She clutched Vincente's hand.

"She's okay." He eased her down onto her right side on the ground, kneeling beside her. "She's not hit, just scared."

"Don't let her watch...you know..." It was getting hard to talk. Everything seemed to be fading. "If anything bad happens to me, I don't want her to see it."

He was undoing the clips of the carrier and lifting Lia free. His face was ashen and his voice shook. "Nothing bad is going to happen." She could tell he was trying to convince himself as much as her.

As darkness swept over her, she felt Melon licking her hand.

"I'll take her." Rick held out his hands for Lia, and Vincente took a moment to consider the offer. Whatever was going on here, Rick had just helped him save Beth's and Lia's lives. He wasn't the bad guy. Dropping a kiss onto Lia's head, he handed her over to Rick, who patted her shoulder awkwardly.

Vincente turned his attention back to Beth, only vaguely aware of what was going on around him. His hearing seemed to be supercharged. Laurie's voice was clear and decisive, cutting across Lia's cries, as she removed the gun from Tania and began to inform her of her rights. Tania was gazing into space, her eyes unblinking.

In the distance, he thought he could also hear the whumping sound of helicopter blades. Maybe that was wishful thinking.

Don't let it get here too late to save Beth.

She had told him not to let Lia see if anything bad happened to her. The thought caused a choking feeling to rip up from Vincente's chest and tighten his throat. That was typical of Beth. *His* Beth. Putting Lia first even when she was…

No. He tried to push the fear away, but it persisted. Beth couldn't be dying. He wouldn't let her. Fate couldn't be cruel enough to show him what his life could be like with Beth at his side, only to take her away from him again.

Her face looked too pale. Like a beautiful waxwork imitation of the real thing. She was still breathing. Short and shallow, her chest rose and fell with a trace of precious movement. When he took her hand, it felt alarmingly cold. He tried to focus on comforting her, not on how much blood there was. Because there was so much blood… Stripping off his shirt, he pressed it against her hip, trying to stanch the flow.

"Hey." He bent to kiss her cheek. "This has to be the worst plan you could have come up with for getting out of a meeting with Edgar."

To his amazement her eyelids fluttered. "Lia." It was barely a whisper.

"Rick has her." He still wasn't quite sure what to do with that piece of information. The guy almost killed him yesterday, although, to be fair, it was in self-defense after Vincente had attacked him first. Today, Vincente was trusting Rick with his daughter. But this was far from a normal situation. Beth came first right now, and whatever Rick was doing, Lia's snuffles were subsiding.

"He saved us." Beth groped for his hand. "When Tania was going to shoot Lia and make me jump, he kept her talking."

Gratitude flooded Vincente's being, replacing every other emotion he had felt toward Rick. Without his intervention, Vincente and Laurie would have gotten here too late and found Beth and Lia had plunged to their deaths. How could he ever thank Rick for something of such magnitude? He had given them a priceless gift. Because of him, they had a future...if only Beth would make it.

The chopping sound of the helicopter blades was unmistakable now. Looking up, Vincente could see the pilot seeking somewhere to land. The terrain here at the top of the ravine was flat and uninterrupted by trees. Before long, the helicopter was touching down nearby, throwing up great clouds of dust.

Vincente spared a quick glance around. Lia's face was tearstained, but she had stopped crying and had rested her head on Rick's shoulder. That meant she felt safe with him. Vincente could leave her for a few more minutes while he stayed with Beth.

Laurie had worked fast. Tania was now sitting on the ground with her hands cuffed behind her. She was still staring into space as though unaware of what was going on. Vincente didn't know what had happened, but she looked like her whole world had been tilted off course. Her gun lay on the ground some distance away from her. The cartridge had been removed.

Laurie hurried over the helicopter, ducking beneath the blades as a passenger jumped down to meet her. Vincente recognized Glen Harvey. Glen had been through a tough time. He was the deputy sheriff of West County when it was discovered that Grant Becker, his boss, was the Red Rose Killer. Glen had been the one to pick up the pieces, pull the Sheriff's Department back together, and restore some pride to the team. He had recently replaced Grant as sheriff and was doing a good job in tough circumstances.

Laurie was gesturing to where Beth lay, and Glen spoke briefly to the pilot before coming over to them.

"Vincente." He tipped his hat, his handsome face concerned. "We're going to get Beth and the baby into the chopper and take them to Elmville District Hospital. They specialize in gunshot wounds there."

"Can I go with her?" The thought of not knowing what was happening to her, even just for the duration of the journey, was unbearable.

"Yes. It's a four-person helicopter." Glen turned to Laurie. "Chief Wilkinson said he has a vehicle on its way here, right?"

She nodded. "I'll wait here and take the suspect and Mr. Sterling back to Stillwater—"

Her words were cut short as Tania struggled to her

feet and staggered to the brink of the ravine. Moving quickly, Rick handed Lia to Laurie.

Edging closer to Tania, he held out a hand toward her. "This isn't the way."

"Cory didn't love me." Her voice was forlorn.

Tania's feet were inches from the rim. Tiny stones slithered under her sneakers and spilled out into the ravine. She bit her lip as she cast a glance over her shoulder.

"We can get you the help you need." Rick risked taking another step.

"Rick, be careful," Vincente warned as he carefully lifted Beth into his arms. "She's dangerous."

Rick got close enough to hook an arm around Tania's waist. A look of pure cunning crossed her features as she smiled up at him. "I'm still smarter."

Leaning backward, she toppled into the ravine, taking Rick with her.

Chapter 19

Vincente hated hospitals. The thought of all those rooms containing people who were suffering in varying degrees made him uncomfortable. Or maybe it was a metaphor for his fear of loneliness? Although why the hell he was indulging in this level of self-analysis when Beth was in surgery was a complete mystery.

Laurie had contacted Bryce and Steffi, who had turned up a few hours ago. Steffi had taken Lia home with her, but Bryce stayed.

"You don't need to do this."

"You stayed with me when I got shot in the leg, remember? Being a brother works both ways."

The words had provoked an emotional reaction so intense Vincente had been unable to speak. Bryce, who seemed to understand, had gripped his shoulder before going off to get coffee and sandwiches. The surgeon had warned them it could be a long night.

Cameron and Laurie arrived in the early hours of the morning.

"We couldn't stand waiting around at home," Laurie said, hugging Vincente then Bryce.

"This is going to sound like a crazy first question given everything else that's happened, but where's Melon? And is he okay?" Throughout this whole nightmare, the occasional fear that the dog may have been left all alone out at Savage Canyon had bothered him.

"He's at our place, and he's fine." She smiled. "There was a slight problem when he insisted on sitting up front in the patrol car."

"Yeah, he does that." He managed a shaky laugh.

"Is there any news on Beth?" Cameron asked.

"They're still operating. They know she has hip and pelvic fractures, but they aren't sure what other damage the bullet may have done." Vincente leaned his head against the back of the plastic seat and gazed up at the fluorescent strip lighting, something he seemed to have done many times over the last few hours. "And she had lost so much blood…"

The image of Beth lying on the ground at the top of Savage Canyon came into his mind. Despite the drama of Tania throwing herself over the edge of the precipice and taking Rick with her, there hadn't been a moment to lose. Their priority had been to get Beth to the hospital fast. He had left Laurie to deal with the repercussions of the latest sensational twist in a story that had begun ten years ago.

Between them, Vincente and Glen Harvey had carried her to the helicopter. Despite the care they had taken not to hurt her, she had lost consciousness as they placed her inside. Lia had sat on Vincente's knee during the journey, and he was pleased that, although she was quiet, she didn't seem unduly distressed. When they arrived at the hospital, a nurse had taken Lia and given her some food while the trauma team got to work on Beth.

"Did you find the bodies?" He turned to Laurie, seeking a distraction from his thoughts.

"Yes. A combined team of police officers and rangers went into the ravine. They took search-and-rescue dogs with them. Both bodies were on the canyon floor a few hundred yards apart." Laurie didn't need to tell him what sort of terrible state Tania and Rick must have been in. The look on her face said it all. "No one could have survived that fall."

That was what Tania had planned for Beth and Lia. Vincente felt physically ill at the thought. When they had lifted her into the helicopter, he had noticed a blood-stained note sticking out of the right-hand back pocket of Beth's jeans. It had his name on it. With a feeling of dread, he had skimmed through it. As he did, something fiercer than rage tore into him. If Tania had been there, she would have felt his fury pierce her soul.

There was no way Beth would have written such helpless pulp. He had thought of her strength, her pride, her dignity and wanted to crush the hateful note in his hand, obliterating the words forever. Instead, he had handed it to Glen. Tania might be dead, but the investigation wasn't. The people she had murdered deserved some answers.

Just don't let Beth be another of her victims. Let her live.

The same thought had been playing over and over in his mind since he had pulled her back from the edge of that precipice. He closed his eyes as the image drained his energy one more time. When he opened them, the surgeon was coming toward them.

As he tried to stand, Vincente wasn't sure if his legs were going to work. Luckily, he found the strength from somewhere to get to his feet. "Is she…?"

He stopped short of saying the word *okay*, because it was such an ineffective way of asking all the things he wanted to know. Would she be able to walk? Would she be able to swing Lia up into her arms? Would she be able to have other children? Would she be the strong, independent woman she had always been?

"Beth is heavily sedated. We've pinned the fractures to her hip and pelvis and, although it's going to take some time, she should make a complete recovery." The doctor smiled when he saw Vincente's look of relief. "I've conducted a surgical examination of her pelvic organs and found no evidence of any lasting damage. She had lost a great deal of blood and needed a transfusion."

"That's it?" Vincente took a moment to process what he was hearing. He'd worked so hard at convincing himself not to hope—because not hoping was what he did, it was what he was good at—that he wasn't prepared for this outcome. "She's going to be okay?"

"She's been through a major trauma and it's going to be a long, painful recovery…but, yes, she's going to be okay."

"Can I see her?" Although he phrased it as a question, there was no way he was taking no for an answer.

"Beth won't come around from the anesthetic for several hours," the doctor said. "She won't know you're there."

Vincente smiled. "She'll know."

* * *

Beth wanted to wake up, but it was too hard. Every time she tried, sleep grabbed her and dragged her back under. *Not sleep*, her mind insisted. There was a reason for this groggy feeling. If she could focus on one thing, maybe this drifting sensation would stop.

There was a warm hand wrapped around hers. She would concentrate on that. She knew that hand. It was strong and capable, slightly callused. There were scratches on the back. She loved that hand...

"Vincente." The word was somewhere between a whisper and a croak. Her throat felt raw, her mouth dry and her lips scratchy.

The grip on her fingers tightened. "I'm here."

"Water."

He held a specially adapted cup with a straw to her lips, and Beth sucked greedily at it. "The nurse said not to give you too much at first."

She murmured a protest when he took the water away. Then another thought drove everything else from her mind. "Where's Lia?"

"She's with Steffi. I spoke to her earlier. She'd tried to force-feed Steffi's cat her own breakfast cereal, so it sounds like she's fine." He took her hand again. "And Melon is at Cameron and Laurie's place."

Snippets of what had happened were starting to come back to her like flashes of a bad dream, half remembered because she'd tried to bury them. *I was shot!* The memory was like another bullet ricocheting through her and she turned her head to gaze at Vincente. He looked exhausted. Even though he smiled, the lines of worry around his eyes were etched deep. *It must be bad.* She couldn't feel any pain. Couldn't feel anything from the waist down.

No matter how scared she was, she had to ask. "My legs?"

"You're going to be fine." The look in his eyes was like a blanket wrapping around her. She felt it warming every part of her. "The bullet shattered bones in your hip and pelvis, but the surgeon was able to pin them back together. You'll be walking on crutches at first, then with a cane, but you'll make a full recovery."

"My pelvis?" That meant the bullet had passed close to her uterus and other vital parts of her body.

"Apart from the damage the bullet caused to your skin and muscles, there were no other injuries." Vincente seemed to read her mind. "Your internal organs weren't harmed."

She lay quietly for a few moments, allowing the words to sink in. The time after she had been shot was a blur of pain, noise and confusion. A horrible blackness had been trying to pull her under and, no matter how hard she tried to fight back, it had been too strong for her. She knew now, of course, that it had been caused by shock and blood loss.

"What happened to Tania?"

"She's dead." There was something in Vincente's face as he said those words. It meant he had something bad he needed to tell her. "She threw herself into the ravine... but she took Rick with her."

Helpless tears rolled down her cheeks, and Vincente shifted closer so he could cradle her head against his shoulder. The doctors must have used some powerful painkillers on her body, but they couldn't touch the hurt in her heart. Rick Sterling had been her idol when she was learning to climb. Other girls her age had crushes on pop stars. Beth didn't have a crush, but she had hero-worshiped Rick. In return, he had been patient, wise, and good-humored, teaching her everything he knew. Then he had come back into her life two days ago in the strangest of circumstances and saved her life. Twice. He had saved Lia's life, too. Now she would never get a chance to thank him.

"He was a hero."

"He was." Vincente found a Kleenex and dried her tears before giving her some more water. "Laurie is investigating how and why he did what he did, but we owe him everything."

"Is Edgar okay? Tania hit him with the butt of her gun and knocked him out."

There was a slight hesitation before Vincente answered, a fleeting sense of him wanting to say more and deciding against it. Beth was too tired to pursue it. "He's fine. I'm sure he'll come to see you and will want to talk to you."

His face was next to hers on the pillow and she examined every beloved feature. Lifting her hand was hard work, but she managed to trace her thumb along his cheekbone. "When that bullet hit me, the first thing I thought was that I'd fall into that ravine and never see you again."

His dark eyes shimmered with unshed tears as he raised her hand to his lips. For a second or two, he struggled to speak. "Three times now, I've faced the prospect of losing you. The first time was when you left Stillwater. Then there was the other day at Eternal Springs. But this—" the words became choked, and he broke off.

"I've already said you won't lose me, Vincente."

"No, I won't." He got his voice back under control. "I won't, because I'm never letting you go again. I love you, Beth. I just wish I'd had the courage to recognize it and say it years ago."

She smiled through her own tears. "Don't be too hard on yourself. I don't think either of us were ready for forever back then. You might have been the one fighting commitment, but I wasn't doing a lot to tie you down. We both enjoyed the craziness we created."

He laughed. "It was fun, wasn't it?"

"It was. But then it got real…and we found out real was even better than fun."

"If we can be together through what life has thrown at us these last few weeks, then bring on the future." His kiss was featherlight on her lips. "I can't wait to share it with you."

"I love you, Vincente. I've been waiting such a long time to say that." She gestured to the cage that covered the lower half of her body. "I promised myself that once this nightmare was over, I'd walk down Main Street holding your hand and carrying Lia. Looks like we may have to postpone."

"We can take our time. We have forever."

It was a few days before Beth was allowed to see anyone other than Vincente and Lia. Just as she was growing increasingly impatient at lying flat on her back, the doctor judged it was time for her to progress to a wheelchair. On the day Bryce, Steffi and Laurie came to visit, she was clearly delighted to be upright and to have a measure of independence.

They brought balloons, cake and presents. It was Lia's first birthday.

"You said she'd have the best day we could give her." Beth clutched Vincente's hand as tears filled her eyes.

"She still has her mom. That's the best gift ever."

Lia clapped her hands delightedly as she opened her presents, scattering paper and ribbon everywhere. Even when Bryce joined her on the floor and tried to engage her interest in her new toys, it was clear she found the wrapping more interesting than the contents.

"You look so well," Steffi said as she studied Beth's face.

"I feel it. Apart from after the physiotherapist comes to see me and tries to get my legs moving. Then I feel like hell." Beth's smile lit up the room. *Or maybe it's just me she affects that way,* Vincente thought. Every time he looked at her, he felt as though he was the one who had been given a gift.

"We have a surprise for you." Laurie indicated the full-length glass doors that opened onto the hospital garden. "Don't worry. Cameron cleared it with the nurses."

She opened the door, and Vincente wheeled Beth's chair to the opening. When she saw Melon coming across the grass on his leash, with Cameron holding on to him, she clapped her hands with delight. Melon noticed Beth and threw back his head, giving a single, high-pitched yowl.

"My hero." Beth buried her face in Melon's coat as he placed his front paws on her shoulder.

"This hero of yours has been teaching our dogs some very dubious tricks." Cameron's face was expressionless.

Beth turned her head to look up at him, a look of resignation on her face. "What has he been doing?"

"Let's just say things may never be the same in our house again. Our dogs have been taught the benefits of sleeping on the furniture, drinking out of the bathrooms and stealing food from the kitchen counters." Cameron's lips twitched. "Oh, and shredding newspapers. They particularly enjoyed that lesson."

"Melon—" Beth caught hold of his collar, giving him a little shake "—have you been disgracing yourself?"

Melon placed his head on her lap, his expression one of complete innocence.

"Take no notice," Laurie said. "If Melon hadn't led us to you, I wouldn't have been able to disarm and hand-cuff Tania. She would have killed you and Lia as well as Rick. Melon deserves an award for bravery. In fact, I think the mayor of Stillwater should organize a special ceremony."

"I can think of a few things that dog deserves, but awards are not top of my list." Although the words were caustic, Cameron was biting back a smile as Melon noticed Lia and wagged his tail delightedly before holding out a paw in her direction.

"If it's a problem, Melon can come and stay with us instead," Steffi offered.

Beth and Vincente exchanged horrified looks. "There's just one problem with that...the herding. He's a collie, so he has all the instincts, but he doesn't know how to do it properly...your animals would be trauma-tized."

"Don't worry." Cameron rubbed Melon's head and the dog rolled his eyes with delight. "It's not as bad as it sounds. I can live with my well-trained hounds being turned into delinquents while Beth recovers."

Although the others visited for only half an hour, Laurie stayed after they had gone. "I wanted to let you know what we had found out about Rick."

Beth was tired after being in her chair for the first time, so Vincente helped her back into bed. Lia curled up contentedly at her side and began to doze. Laurie took her notebook out and began to read from her jottings.

"Rick had been staying in a hostel right here in Stillwater. It's a place that's popular with climbers and hikers, so possibly it's somewhere he stayed in the past when he did climbs on the Stillwater Trail. We found a journal with his possessions. In it, he had kept a detailed account of his own actions after he faked his death, but he was also following what Tania was doing, and, where possible, tracking the movements of the other members of the Devil's Peak team."

"He said he was trying to protect us," Beth said.

"That seems to have been his sole intention. His notes are dated, and right from the start—the first photograph and letter—he was onto Tania. He kept newspaper cuttings about Andy Smith's death, and there was a sense of frustration in his notes that it wasn't seen as suspicious. He appeared to know something about Tania's obsessive behavior in the past. When he got the picture with his own face crossed out, he decided to fake his own death."

"But Tania was killing people who were happy. If she chose Rick for that reason, didn't he leave a partner behind who was devastated by his pretense?" Vincente asked.

"Rick was intensely private. He never spoke about his personal life or his relationships. But he was also very comfortable with who he was. People, including Tania, often mistook that to mean he had found happiness in his private life. In reality, at the time he faked his death, Rick was single.

"When we were on the top of the ravine, he told Tania he and Cory had once been in a relationship," Beth said.

"Rick was gay," Laurie confirmed. "That may be the reason why he was so keen to protect his privacy. We'll never know for sure."

"So, having faked his death, he set about trying to stop Tania from killing the rest of us? Why didn't he go to the police?" Beth asked.

"Rick did make several anonymous calls to the Whitebridge Police Department when Tania sent the first letters and photographs. He told them they might want to talk to her about it. Even told them she had a previous history of stalking. Unfortunately, it looks like he was written off as a crank. There will be some red faces among my Whitebridge colleagues, but hindsight is a wonderful thing."

"If Rick was in hiding, he couldn't know whose face was crossed out in the next picture," Vincente pointed out.

"That's right. But he was keeping track of what was happening with each of the team and when he found out that Danielle was getting married, he thought there was a good chance she would be next. He traveled to Toronto, and, sure enough, Danielle confirmed his worst fears. She had received a photograph with her face crossed out. Rick urged her to go to the police and name Tania as the suspect."

"She would have refused because of the threat to her loved ones." Beth sounded certain.

"That's almost word for word what Rick wrote in his journal. He offered to stay for the wedding to watch over Danielle—" Laurie's expression twisted momentarily out of her businesslike composure "—but the one time he couldn't be with her was when she was dressing in her bridal clothes."

"And that's when Tania got to her." Beth shook her head in sorrow. "She knew how to find a weakness and exploit it."

"You were the person who worried Rick most," Laurie said. "He felt particularly protective toward you, Beth. He even attempted to analyze why he felt that way in his journal. He stated it stemmed back to your partnership on the Devil's Peak and the fact that he had an added responsibility toward you as the youngest member of the team. He also felt you got an unfair amount of attention over Cory's death. But he was frustrated because he couldn't find out where you were living. Until you walked into the West County Climbing Club a few weeks ago."

"How could Rick know that if he was in hiding himself?" Vincente asked.

"He was watching Tania's every move. He couldn't get up close to her, obviously, but he was watching who went in and out of the club that evening. When he saw you and Vincente were...what was the exact phrase he used—" Laurie flipped through her notes "—here it is. *Head over heels in love...*" She looked up with a smile, lightening the mood momentarily. "Funny how a guy looking through a pair of binoculars got that, but you two never noticed."

"We've figured it out now." Vincente flapped a hand, indicating that Laurie could continue. "You can stop matchmaking and keep policing, Detective."

"Rick knew immediately that, by walking into the club and showing Tania you were happy with Vincente, you had moved your name right up her list. He followed you back to Stillwater after the meeting. When he came out to the lake house that night and climbed down the cliff onto the deck, he wasn't intending to harm or threaten you. He was checking out your security. Rick was making sure you were safe. He couldn't approach you and warn you because he was supposed to be dead."

"Even though Rick was doing all he could to keep us safe, it wasn't enough to save Peter," Beth said.

"Like you, Rick didn't know Peter was Tania's next target. He didn't know Peter was in a new relationship and never saw the photograph with Peter's face crossed out. Rick was in Whitebridge the day Peter was killed because he was following you and Vincente. When he saw Tania arrive at Peter's house, he called the police. That was how the Whitebridge officers got there before I did. When he saw you leaving the house, Rick drove back to Stillwater. He even passed you on the highway."

"If that was the case, why did he end up jogging toward us along the edge of the highway?"

"My theory about car trouble was right. He ran out of gas. He was so focused on everything else that was going on, he didn't look at the fuel needle until it was on empty. And he didn't have a gas container in his vehicle. His plan was to jog into Stillwater, buy a container at the gas station, fill it there and jog back to his car. He wrote in his journal that it was just bad timing he encountered you before he reached the turning into Stillwater. A minute later and he'd have missed you."

Vincente lifted a hand to his throat. The bruises had faded, but the memory of those strong hands closing around it lingered. He knew now that Rick had been fighting for his life because Vincente had given him no choice by attacking him, but at the time Vincente had believed he was up against the murderer.

"Why did he run when we confronted him? At that point, he could have told us the whole story," Beth asked.

"He knew his cover was blown, but he was worried you would go to the police and we wouldn't believe him about Tania. If he'd been arrested, she'd have been free to continue killing people and there'd have been no one to protect his friends. With only a split second to make a decision, he wasn't willing to take that chance," Laurie explained. "What Rick hadn't expected was that you would go after him, Beth. When he saw you were in trouble partway down the waterfall, he couldn't leave you, so he turned back to help. Having saved you, he reached the bottom and was tackled by Vincente. Even though he didn't plan on killing you, he had no choice but to fight back."

"You're sure about that?" Vincente touched his throat. "It sure felt like he planned on killing me."

"In his notes, he said he let you go once he knew you were incapacitated. While you were struggling out of the pool, Rick hightailed out of there as fast as he could. He knew if you caught up with him, he wouldn't stand a chance."

"He was right." Vincente remembered his feelings of anger toward Rick on that day. He thought he was dealing with the murderer. If only he'd known the truth.

"After that, Rick was on Tania's tail the whole time. He'd seen her checking out Vincente's apartment block and Savage Canyon. When she led you out of the building, Beth, I guess he was right behind you all the way."

Vincente shook his head. "You and Lia were rescued by a man who should have been dead, and a dog."

Beth gripped his hand tighter. "You rescued us, Vincente, from the moment you found us in Casper to the moment you pulled us back from the edge of that canyon."

"Home." As Vincente carried Beth through the door of the lake house, the word meant so much more to her than ever before. "It's so good to be back here at last."

"Steffi's bringing Lia over later, and Cameron said he'll drop Melon off this evening. Although he'll never admit it, I think he's going to miss him." Vincente set her down on the sofa in the family room and knelt beside her, rearranging cushions and lifting her feet onto a footstool. "We have the place to ourselves for a few hours."

"I don't know what you were planning." She smiled into his eyes. "But I'm not quite ready for any bedroom gymnastics just yet."

"That wasn't what I was planning. Not yet, anyway." Although he returned the smile, she could tell he was nervous. He reached into his pocket. When he withdrew his hand, he was holding a black velvet box. He flipped open the lid, revealing a vintage ring. The single, square-cut diamond was displayed to perfect advantage by a pretty, engraved band. It was the most beautiful ring Beth had ever seen.

"This was my grandmother's engagement ring. My mother doesn't get many things right when it comes to love, but she told me that she shouldn't be trusted with something as precious as this. She gave it to me on one condition. I would only ever give it away if I was sure the hand that wore it would hold mine for the rest of my life." Vincente lifted Beth's left hand and took the ring from the box. "You can choose another ring, or wear this on a different finger, but…"

She shook her head, blinking back tears. "I love it. I can't believe after everything that's happened to us I'm going to cry because I'm so happy."

"Don't cry. Not yet." As he said the words, Vincente's own eyes glistened. "Bethany Wade, you already make me the happiest man in the world. Will you make it official and marry me?"

The tears spilled over then as she started to laugh and cry. "Vincente Delaney, I would love to."

Vincente slid the ring onto her finger. "It's a bit big. We'll take it into town and have it adjusted."

"Can we go tomorrow? And can we stop at The Daily Grind and get coffee and cake?" Vincente came to sit next to her, and Beth held her hand up, twisting and turning it so she could admire the ring from different angles. "Do normal things? Show Lia off?"

"We can do anything you want, as long as you remember the doctors said slow and steady was the way to approach your recovery."

"I feel so much better already just being home."

Vincente placed an arm around her shoulders. "I wanted to talk to you about that." Beth tilted her head up to look at him. "About this house being our home. Cameron will sell it to us if we want it."

"If?" Beth was surprised by the hesitant note in his voice. "I love this house. I thought you did, too. Why wouldn't we want it?"

"It's not very big."

"There's only three of us. We fit perfectly into this space…" His smile told its own story. "Oh!"

He laughed. "Beth, are you blushing?"

"Well, I didn't know you wanted more children."

"Nor did I. But now I think I would." He twined a length of her hair around his finger. "What about you?"

She nodded. "I would love for Lia to have a little brother or sister in a year or two."

"Maybe more than one?" His voice had dropped to a persuasive murmur. "Melon needs a few if he's going to really hone those herding skills."

"My goodness, you've been giving this some thought, haven't you?" Beth regarded him in wonder. "Now I see why you think the house is too small."

"It is, but while you were in the hospital, I consulted an architect. We can't expand outward because of the cliffs and the lake, but there's nothing to stop us going upward."

Beth laughed. "This is turning out to be quite a day. I get an engagement ring and the house of my dreams. Do you have anything else in store for me?"

His face became serious. "I don't, but there is someone else who would like to talk to you. Do you feel strong enough for a visit from Edgar?"

Four months later

"Whose idea was it to put ribbons on the guard dog?" Bryce muttered the words to Cameron as the three Delaney brothers stood at the front of the church.

"Laurie thought it would be sweet if Melon had a bow on his collar to match Lia's bridesmaid's dress," Cameron said.

"Sweet? He's just ripped it off and shredded it all over the lawn outside. Someone will need to clear the mess up before Beth arrives."

"I can't do it." Vincente smiled at his younger brother. "I'm exempt from Melon duty today. I can't see the bride until she arrives at the altar. It's probably one of the best men's responsibilities." He held up a finger before Bryce could speak. "And remember not to swear in church."

Bryce stomped outside, and Cameron choked back a laugh. "This is probably the first wedding I've been to where a dog is likely to be the most troublesome guest."

"I think you're forgetting something." Vincente rolled his eyes. "My mother is here with her latest billionaire. Although I have warned her against any attempts to divert attention away from the bride."

"That hat is a diversion in its own right."

Giovanna was as out of place here in Wyoming as a designer ball gown at a rodeo. She had arrived in Stillwater a few days ago, and had surprised Vincente by taking an instant liking to Beth. The feeling was mutual. Beth regarded Giovanna with the amused tolerance Vincente wished he could cultivate toward his mother. Lia had also helped establish a new family bond, although Giovanna was outraged at the idea that anyone would know she was old enough to be a grandmother.

"You must bring the *bambina* to visit me in Firenze." Giovanna had extended the invitation in her usual vague way, and Vincente had decided they wouldn't be in any hurry to take her up on it. One day they would take Lia to Italy and introduce her to the other part of her heritage. For now, their priority was to enjoy being a family right here in Stillwater.

"They're here." Bryce resumed his place. "I got all the ribbon cleaned up in time."

The music started up. Vincente looked around to watch Lia walk down the aisle holding Steffi's hand.

Even though she had been doing it for a few months, he was still getting used to the idea that his daughter could walk. It seemed so grown-up. Yet watching her now, she looked so tiny. Oblivious to tradition, Lia spotted Vincente and tottered the last few feet toward him.

"Kiss, Dada." She raised her arms. Vincente obediently lifted her up, kissed her cheek and handed her back to Steffi. The maneuver was swift and didn't hold up the process of Beth proceeding down the aisle on Edgar's arm.

Every time Vincente looked at Beth, he thought she was the most beautiful woman in the world. Today, her white lace dress and shy smile only added to his conviction. As she drew level with him they gazed at each other for what felt like an eternity. The sense of peace and perfection that swept over him in that instant was overwhelming.

Edgar placed Beth's hand in Vincente's and moved to one side. Vincente knew how much it meant to him to be here. It had been hard for both him and Beth when he explained why he had kept his relationship to Cory a secret from her.

"I knew you'd been part of the Devil's Peak team, but I didn't speak to my family and you never mentioned what happened back then. It wasn't something I could talk to a junior employee about," Edgar had said. "Then, when I knew you better, the silence had gone on too long. There was never a right time for me to say 'By the way, I'm Cory Taylor's uncle.'"

Beth had understood. Edgar was a reserved man. There had been enough losses because of what happened on that mountain. She wasn't prepared to lose Edgar as well as Rick. Instead, she had asked him if he would escort her down the aisle when she got married. Edgar had remembered her injuries just in time to refrain from embracing her.

Vincente had been determined to remember every second of the ceremony, but suddenly it was over and he was being told he could kiss his bride. Not that he could find any fault with that instruction.

"I think the idea is we have to stop kissing at some point," Beth whispered.

"It's my wedding. I'll do this my way." Vincente kissed her again. "Are you okay with all this standing?"

"I'm fine." She hooked her arm through his as they turned to walk up the aisle. Although there was a slight hesitation in her walk, the limp was barely noticeable now, and it was getting better every day. "More than fine. I'm happy."

"Me, too. And happy is the way we're going to stay."

* * * * *

SUDDEN SECOND CHANCE

CAROL ERICSON

For Chuck, one of the most avid readers I know.

Chapter One

Beth's heart skipped a beat as she ducked onto the path that led through a canopy of trees. The smell of damp earth and moldering mulch invaded her nostrils. She took a deep breath. The odor evoked the cycle of life—birth, death and rebirth. She'd smelled worse.

She gasped as a lacy, green leaf brushed her face. Then she knocked it away. If she freaked out and had a panic attack every time she delved into the forest, she'd have a hard time doing this story—and getting to the truth of her birth.

Straightening her shoulders, she tugged on her down vest and blew out a breath. She stepped over a fallen log, snapping a twig in two beneath her boot. The mist rising from the forest floor caressed her cheek and she raised her face to the moisture swirling around her.

The scent of pine cleared her sinuses and she dragged in a lungful of the fresh air. She'd definitely classify herself as a city girl, but this rustic, outdoor environment seemed to energize her.

Either that or the adrenaline was pumping so hard and fast through her veins, a massive anxiety attack waited right around the corner.

She continued on the path through the dense foliage, feeling stronger and stronger with each step. She could do this. The reward of possibly finding her true identity motivated her, blocking out the anxiety that the forest usually stirred up inside her.

She'd convinced Scott, the producer of *Cold Case Chronicles*, that she needed to come out ahead of her crew to do some initial interviews and footwork. She had her own video camera and could give Joel, her cameraman, a head start. Stoked by the show's ratings from the previous season, Scott had been ready to grant her anything. Of course, she had a lot of work to do on her own before she got her guys up here. She'd have to stall Scott.

The trees rustled around her and she paused, tilting her head to one side. Maybe she should've researched the presence of wild animals out here. Did bears roam the Pacific Northwest? Wolves? She was pretty sure there were no tigers stalking through the forests of Washington. Were there?

As she took another step, leaves crackled behind her, too close for comfort, and she froze again. The hair on the back of her neck stood up and quivered, all her old fears flooding her senses.

She craned her head over her shoulder and released a gusty breath of air. A man walking a bicycle stuttered to a stop, his eyes widening in his gaunt face.

"Ma'am?"

The relief she'd felt a moment ago that it hadn't been a tiger on her trail evaporated as she took in the man's appearance. He had the hard look of a man who'd been in the joint. She recognized it from previous stories she'd done on her TV show, *Cold Case Chronicles*.

"Oh, hello. My husband and I were just taking a walk. He went ahead."

He nodded once, a jerky, disjointed movement. "Come out to look at the kidnapping site, did ya?"

Heat washed into Beth's cheeks. She wanted to make it

clear to this man that she wasn't just some morbid looky-loo, but what did it really matter?

"We were in the area anyway, and it's so pretty out here." She waved a hand toward the path she'd been following. "Is it much farther?"

"Not much." He pushed his bike forward, wheeling around the same fallen log she'd stepped over earlier. "They were lookin' at me for a bit."

"Excuse me?" Beth tucked her hands into the pockets of her vest, her right hand tracing the outline of her pepper spray.

"For the kidnappings." He hunched his scrawny shoulders. "Like I'd snatch a couple of kids."

"Th...that must've been scary." She slipped her index finger onto the spray button in her pocket. "How'd the police get that idea?"

"Because—" he looked to his left and right "—because I'd been in a little trouble before."

Taking one step back, Beth coiled her muscles. She could take him—maybe—especially if she nailed him with the pepper spray first.

"And because I was there the first time."

"What?" She snapped her jaw closed to keep it from hanging open. Did he mean he'd been in Timberline at the time the Timberline Trio was kidnapped? He definitely looked old enough.

"You know." He wiped a hand across his mouth. "The first time when them three kids were snatched twenty years ago."

Twenty-five years ago, she corrected him in her head.

"You were living here during that time?"

"I wasn't the only one. Lots of people still around from that time." His tone got defensive. "It's just 'cause I had that other trouble. That's why they looked at me—and because of the dead dog, only he wasn't dead."

A chill snaked up Beth's spine. She definitely wanted to talk to this man later if he was telling the truth, but not now and not here in the middle of a dense forest with only the tigers to hear her screams.

"Well, I'd better catch up to my husband. A…are you going to the site, too?"

"No, ma'am. I'm just taking the shortcut to my house." He raised one hand.

Then he turned his bike to the right and her shoulders dropped as she released the trigger on her pepper spray.

"Ma'am?"

She stopped, and without turning around, she said, "Yes?"

"Be careful out there. The Quileute swear this forest is haunted."

"I will and I'm…we're not afraid of ghosts—my husband and I."

He emitted a noise, which sounded a lot like a snort, and then he wheeled his bike down another path, leaving the echo of crackling leaves.

Beth brushed her hair from her face and strode forward. He wouldn't be hard to locate later—an ex-con on a bicycle who'd been questioned about the kidnappings. Maybe he'd have some insight into the Timberline Trio.

She tromped farther into the woods but never lost sight of the trail as it had been well used recently. What was wrong with people who wanted to see where three kids and a woman had been held against their will?

If she didn't have a damned good excuse for being out here, she'd be exploring the town or sitting in front of the fireplace at her hotel enjoying a caramel latte with extra foam, reading—okay, she'd probably be reading a murder mystery or a true-crime book about a serial killer. The Pacific Northwest seemed to have those in spades.

A piece of soggy, yellow tape stirring in the breeze

indicated that she'd reached the spot. Law enforcement had drilled orange caution cones into the ground around the mine opening and had boarded over the top. Nobody would be able to use this abandoned mine for any kind of nefarious purpose again.

She nudged one of the cones with the toe of her boot—it didn't budge. Wedging her hands on her hips, she surveyed the area. No recognition pinged in her chest. Her breathing remained calm, too, so nothing here was sending her into overdrive.

Not that she'd really expected it. Wyatt Carson had chosen this place to stash his victims because he'd discovered it or had searched for someplace to hide the children, not because he'd known it from twenty-five years before when he was just a child himself, when his own brother Stevie Carson had been snatched.

But one kidnap story might lead to another. Maybe the Timberline Trio had been held here before…before what? If she really were one of the Timberline Trio, those children obviously weren't dead. So, why had they been kidnapped? Why had *she* been kidnapped?

There was something about this place—Timberline—that struck a chord within her. As soon as she'd seen that stuffed frog in the window of the tourist shop during a TV news story about the Wyatt Carson kidnappings, she'd known she had to come here. She could be Heather Brice, and she had to find out.

Crouching down, she scooted closer to the entrance of the mine. When Carson had found it, the mine had a cover that he'd then blocked with a boulder. All that had been removed and cleared out.

She flattened herself onto her belly and army-crawled between the cones. Someone had already pried back and snapped off a piece of wood covering the entrance.

With her arms at her sides, she placed her forehead

against one slat of wood and peered into the darkness below. She'd like to get down there just to have a look around. Maybe the local sheriff's department would allow it if she promised to get their mugs on TV.

A swishing noise coming up behind her had her digging the toes of her boots into the mushy earth. She'd just put herself into an extremely vulnerable position—an idiotic thing to do with that ex-con roaming the woods. A branch snapped. She slipped her hand inside her pocket and gripped the pepper spray, her finger in position.

A man's voice yelled out. "Hey!"

Then a strong vise clamped around her ankle. This was it. In one fluid motion, she dragged the pepper spray from her pocket, rolled to her back, aimed and fired.

The man released her ankle immediately and staggered back, one arm flung over his face.

Beth jumped to her feet, holding the spray in front of her with a shaky hand, ready to shoot again.

Her attacker cursed and spit.

Beth's eyebrows shot up. The ex-con had gotten bigger…and meaner.

Then he lowered his hands from his face and glared at her through dark eyes streaming with tears. Those eyes widened and he cursed again.

He cleared his throat and coughed. "Beth St. Regis. I should've known it was you."

Beth dropped her pepper spray and clasped her hand over her heart. She'd rather be facing a tiger right now than Duke Harper—the man she'd loved and betrayed.

Chapter Two

Duke's eyes stung and his nose burned, lighting his lungs on fire with every breath he took. Even through his tears, he couldn't mistake the woman standing in front of him, her shoulder-length, strawberry blond hair disheveled and her camera-ready features distorted by surprise and…fear.

She should be afraid—very afraid after the way she'd used him.

He kicked at the pepper spray nestled in the green carpet between them. "Is that the stuff I gave you?"

"I… I think so."

"Then I'll count myself lucky because that's expired. You should've replaced it last year, but if you had, I wouldn't be standing upright forming words." He pulled up the hem of his T-shirt to his face and wiped his tears and his nose.

Miss Perfect would hate that he'd just used his shirt as a handkerchief—and that was fine with him. He peered at her through blurry eyes and she still looked perfect— damn it.

She wrinkled her nose. "I'm sorry. I thought you were an ex-con attacking me."

She must be referring to Gary Binder, unless there were other ex-cons in Timberline who lived out this way. He'd already done his homework on the case but he had no intention of sharing his info with her. Oh, God, she had to be here for the same case he'd been assigned to investigate.

He narrowed his already-narrowed eyes. "You're doing a story for your stupid show on the Timberline Trio, aren't you?"

"That *stupid show*, as you call it, got a point-six rating last year, more than half of those viewers in the prime demographic." She tossed her hair over one shoulder as only Beth St. Regis could.

"Junk TV."

She clapped a hand over her mouth, her eyes wide. "Oh, my God. That's why you're here. You're investigating the Timberline Trio."

"What else would I be doing here?" He lifted one eyebrow and crossed his arms. "Do you think I followed you to Timberline?"

Red flags blazed in her cheeks. "Of course not. Why would I think that? What we had was…"

"Over."

"Yeah, over." She waved her hand in the general direction of his face. "Are you okay? I really did think you were that ex-con coming after me. Why did you grab my leg?"

"I thought you were falling in."

"Through that small space?"

"I couldn't see how big it was."

"I was fine. As soon as I heard you coming, I got ready for the attack. You told me once I needed to be more careful, more aware of my surroundings."

"Good to see you're taking my advice…about something." He ran a hand across his face once more and sniffled. "Where's the rest of your crew, or are you a one-woman show now? I guess Beth St. Regis doesn't need other people—unless she's using them."

Her nostrils flared but she ignored the barb. "I'm doing

some prep work. My cameraman and producer will be coming out later."

"And the circus will ensue."

"If the FBI is involved, there really must be something to investigate."

She brushed off her jeans that fit her a little too closely, so he kept his blurry eyes pinned to her face.

"Isn't that why this case is on your radar? You must've heard about the new information we got during the investigation of the copycat kidnappings." He cocked his head. "Come to think of it, I have a hard time believing the old Timberline Trio case is sexy enough for *Cold Case Chronicles*. Maybe *you* followed *me* out here."

Her sky blue eyes widened for a split second and then she giggled nervously, her hand hovering near her mouth. "I have no idea what happened to you after…that last case, Duke Harper. You dumped me, and it's not like I've been following your career or anything like a stalker."

A thrill of pleasure winged through his body at her lie. So she'd been tracking him. What did that say about him that the thought gave him satisfaction? It also meant she knew about the royal screwup that had resulted in the death of his partner, Tony.

"That's okay. I haven't watched one of your shows, either." The slight lift at the corner of her luscious lips told him she'd picked up on his lie, too.

"I suppose you're not interested in joining forces, are you? Pooling our resources? We're an unbeatable team. We proved that before."

He snorted. She didn't deserve an answer to that one. They'd been an unbeatable team in bed, too, but that hadn't stopped her from playing him.

"What were you doing crawling around on the ground?" He pointed to the cover over the mine.

"Prep work." She sealed her lips. "Where are you staying while you're here?"

"Timberline Hotel."

She raised her hand. "Me, too."

He pasted on his best poker face. "Makes no difference to me."

"Do you have a partner with you or are you working alone?"

A partner? The FBI would have a hard time trying to find someone to partner up with him after Tony. He shoved his hands in his pockets and kicked at a gnarled root coming up from the earth.

"Oh, come on, Duke. Whether or not you're working with a partner is not giving up any classified info."

He shrugged. He had no intention of giving this woman one morsel of information. She should know that working a cold case was like being exiled to Siberia—for him, anyway. This was punishment and he didn't want to discuss his failure with her.

"I guess you'll follow your leads and I'll follow mine." He circled his finger in the air. "How long have you been here?"

"Just a couple of days. I'm trying to get a feel for the place. I even brought my own video cam."

A flock of birds shrieked and rose from a canopy of trees and the hair on the back of Duke's neck stood up. Hunching forward, he crept toward the tree line.

"What are you doing?" Beth's voice sounded like a shout and he put his finger to his lips.

Voices carried in the outdoors and those birds had taken off because something—or someone—had disturbed them. The abandoned mine was in a clearing, but dense forest and heavy underbrush hemmed it in on all sides.

The trail from the road had wound past an abandoned

construction site to the clearing, and it continued on the other side. The birds had come from the other side.

He reached the beginning of the trail and took a few steps onto the path, his head cocked to one side. Leaves rustled and twigs snapped, but that could be animals going about their business. His gaze tracked through the blur of green, but he didn't spot any movement or different colors.

City life had his senses on high alert, but a rural setting could pose just as much danger—of a different kind.

He exhaled slowly and returned to the clearing, where Beth waited for him, hands on her hips.

"What was all that about?"

He pointed to the sky. "Those birds took off like something startled them."

"I told you I saw a rough-looking guy out here on a bike. Maybe it was him."

"Doesn't explain why he was hanging around. I don't know that you should be traipsing around the forest by yourself." He snorted. "You're hardly an outdoor girl."

She kicked a foot out. "I have the boots."

He opened his mouth for a smart-ass reply but someone or something crashed through the bushes and they both jumped this time. Duke reached for the weapon tucked in the shoulder holster beneath his jacket and tensed his muscles.

He dropped his shoulders when three teenage boys came staggering into the clearing, laughing and pushing each other. The roughhousing came to an abrupt halt when they spotted Duke and Beth.

The tallest of the three boys stepped forward, holding a can of beer behind his back. "Is this, uh, official business or something?"

The other two edged back to the tree line, trying to hide their own beers.

"Nope. I was just leaving." Duke leveled his finger at

the boy. "But you'd better not be operating a motor vehicle."

"Driving? No way, sir."

Beth flashed her megawatt smile at the trio of teens. "Do you boys live here? I'm from the TV show *Cold Case Chronicles*, and we're doing a show on the old Timberline Trio case."

"Oh, hey, yeah. My mom watches that show all the time."

One of the other boys, a pimple-faced kid with a shock of black hair, mimicked the tagline of the show in a deep voice. "*Cold Case Chronicles*…justice for all time."

"That's us." Beth nodded. "So, how about it? Any of you know anything about that case? Parents around at the time?"

The one who'd spoken up first said, "Nah, we just moved here a few years ago when my mom got a job with Evergreen Software."

The kid with the acne answered. "Same here."

The dark-haired boy with the mocha skin who'd been quiet up to now ran a hand through his short hair. "My family was here, but they don't talk about it. *We* don't talk about it."

"We?"

Duke rolled his eyes as Beth tilted her head, that one word implying a million questions if the boy wanted to pick one up. The teen had better run now if he wanted to avoid that steam train.

The tall, skinny boy answered for his friend. "Levon is Quileute. They believe in voodoo magic and boogeymen."

Levon punched his friend in the arm and the tall kid dropped his beer where it fizzed out in the dirt. "Hey, man."

All three boys picked up where they'd left off, crashing

back into the woods, cursing at each other and laughing, startling a flock of birds with their raucousness.

"Well, that's interesting." Beth tapped the toe of her boot. "I wonder what that boy meant about the Quileute not talking about the crime. Did law enforcement ever question anyone from the tribe?"

"Not that I know of, but I'll leave that to your superior investigative talents." He jerked his thumb over his shoulder. "It's been real, but I gotta go."

"I guess I'll see you around, Duke. We are in the same hotel, same small town, same case."

"Don't remind me." He waved over his shoulder and hit the trail back to his rented SUV, putting as much space as possible between him and Beth St. Regis, his mind as jumbled as the carpet of mulch he was plowing through.

She looked the same, except for the clothes. Beth had always been a girlie-girl—high heels, dresses, manicured nails, perfect hair and makeup. The jeans, boots and down vest suited her. Hell, a burlap sack would suit Beth. She had the kind of delicate beauty that shifted his libido into overdrive.

He'd fantasized about those girls when he was a teen growing up on the wrong side of the tracks in Philly—the rich girls with the expensive clothes and cars, the kind of girl that wouldn't give him the time of day unless she wanted to tick off her parents by running with a bad boy.

He'd been drawn to Beth like a magnet for all the wrong reasons. You couldn't use a living, breathing person to fix whatever you'd missed in your childhood. But, man, it had felt good trying.

When he'd had Beth in bed, he couldn't get enough of her soft porcelain skin, the way her breast fit neatly into the palm of his hand and the feel of her fine, silky hair running down his body.

The thought of those nights with Beth's slim legs

wrapped around his hips got him hard all over again, and he broke into a jog to work off the steam.

When he got to the car, he collapsed in the driver's seat and downed half a bottle of water. Just his luck to run into the woman of his dreams on this nightmare assignment.

He dug his cell phone from the pocket of his jacket and called his boss, Mickey Tedesco.

"I was just thinking about you, man. All settled in up there? I hear it's some beautiful country."

"Don't try to sell this, Mick. I checked into my hotel and took a walk in the woods to have a look at where the kidnap victims were held a few months ago, not that those kidnappings had anything to do with the Timberline kidnappings, except that the brother of one of the original victims turned out to be the kidnapper." He dragged in a breath. "Why am I doing this? Doesn't the FBI have more urgent cases that need my attention?"

"You know why, Duke." Mick coughed. "It's always a good idea to ease back into work after a…um, situation."

"I'm good to go, Mickey." His hand tensed on the steering wheel. "I don't need to be poking around a twenty-five-year-old kidnapping case based on some slim new evidence, which isn't even evidence."

"I don't know. It may not have started out too promising, but you might be getting more than you bargained for, Duke. You might have yourself a hot one."

A vision of Beth aiming her pepper spray—pepper spray he'd given her—at his face flashed across his mind. "I might be getting more than I bargained for, all right. That bogus *Cold Case Chronicles* show is out here nosing around."

Mick sucked in a breath. "Beth St. Regis is there, in Timberline?"

"Yeah." Mick knew a little about the drama that had gone on between him and Beth…but not all of it.

Mick whistled. "That makes total sense now."

"It does?" Duke clenched his jaw. "Are they promoting the segment already? She doesn't even have her crew out here."

"No. It makes sense that Beth's doing a show about the Timberline Trio because someone sent us an email about her yesterday."

Duke's pulse skipped a beat. "About Beth? What'd it say?"

"The email, untraceable of course, said 'Stop Beth St. Regis.'"

Chapter Three

Beth parked her rental car in the public parking lot on the
main drag of Timberline and flicked the keys in the ignition. Why did Duke Harper have to be here mucking up
her investigation?

She chewed her bottom lip. He'd been sent out on a
cold case because of what had happened in Chicago. She'd
read all about the botched kidnapping negotiation that had
ended in the death of Duke's partner, a fellow FBI agent.
But Duke had rescued the child.

Tears pricked the backs of her eyes. Duke had a thing
about rescuing children…but he couldn't save them all.

She plucked the keys from the ignition and shoved open
the car door. She couldn't get hung up on Duke again. This
story had presented her with the opportunity to get to the
bottom of her identity, and she didn't plan on letting tall,
dark and handsome get in her way.

She locked the car with the key fob and dropped it in
her purse. The chill in the autumn air had her hunching
into her jacket as she walked toward the lit windows lining the main street.

If she recalled from the TV news story on the kidnappings, the tourist shop was located between an ice-cream
place and a real-estate office. She started at the end of the
block and passed a few restaurants just getting ready for
the dinner crowd, a quiet bar and a coffee place emitting a

heavenly aroma of the dark brew she'd sworn off to avoid the caffeine jitters. The Pacific Northwest was probably not the best place to swear off coffee.

A neon ice-cream cone blinking in a window across the street caught her attention. She waited for a car to pass and then headed toward the light as if it were a beacon.

The tourist shop, Timberline Treasures, with the same frog in the window, nestled beside the ice-cream place, and Beth yanked open the door, sending the little warning bell into a frenzy.

A couple studying a rack of Native American dream catchers glanced at her as she entered the store.

"Hello." A clerk popped up from behind the counter. "Looking for something in particular?"

"I am." Beth gripped the strap of her purse, slung across her body, as she scanned the shelves and displays inside the store. "I'm interested in that frog in the window."

"The Pacific Chorus frog." The woman smiled and nodded. "Timberline's mascot."

Beth's gaze tripped across a small display of the frogs in one corner. "There they are."

The clerk came out from behind the counter and smoothed one hand across a stuffed frog, his little miner's hat tilted at a jaunty angle. "They're quite popular and these are originals."

Beth joined her at the display and reached for a frog, her fingers trembling. "Originals?"

"These are handmade by a local resident." She tapped a bucket filled with more stuffed frogs. "These are mass-produced but we still carry the local version."

"Is there a noticeable difference between them?" Beth held the handmade frog to her cheek, the plush fur soft against her skin.

The clerk picked up a frog from the barrel. "The easiest way to tell is the tag on the mass-produced version. It's from a toy company, made in China."

"The color is slightly different, too." Beth turned over the frog in her hand and ran a thumb across his green belly. She hooked a finger in the cloth tag attached to his leg and said the words before she even read the label. "Libby Love."

"That's the other way to tell." The clerk lifted her glasses attached to the chain around her neck. "Every handmade frog has that tag on it."

"What does it mean?" Beth fingered the white tag with the lettering in gold thread. "Libby Love?"

"It's the name of the artist, or at least her mother—Elizabeth Love. Libby's daughter, Vanessa, makes the frogs now."

Beth took a steadying breath. She'd already figured her childhood frog had come from Timberline, but now she had the proof. "When did her mother start making the frogs?"

"Libby started making those frogs over forty years ago when Timberline still had mining." The woman dropped her glasses when the browsing couple approached the counter. "Are you ready?"

While the clerk rang up the tourists' purchases, Beth studied both frogs. Now what? Even if she'd had a frog from Timberline, it hadn't necessarily come from this store. And if it had come from this store, any records from twenty-five years ago would be long gone.

The clerk returned with her head tilted to one side. "Can I help you with anything else? Answer any more questions?"

"So, these frogs—" Beth dangled one in front of her by his leg "—this is the only place to buy them?"

"The Libby Love frogs are available only in Timberline, although Vanessa sells them online now."

"How long has she been selling them online?" Beth held her breath. Surely, not twenty-five years ago.

The woman tapped her chin. "Maybe ten years now?"

"Is this the only store in Timberline that sells the Libby Love frogs?"

"Oh, no. All the tourist shops have them and even a few of the restaurants." The woman narrowed her eyes. "They all sell for the same price."

"Oh, I'll buy one from you." Beth studied the woman's pleasant face with its soft lines and had an urge to confess everything. "I… I had a toy like this frog when I was a child."

"Oh? Did your parents visit Timberline or get it from someone else?"

"I'm not sure." Her adoptive parents could've passed through Timberline and picked up the frog, but their taste in travel didn't include road trips through rural America.

"It's always nice to reconnect with your childhood. Can I ring that up for you now or would you like to continue looking around?" She glanced at her watch. "I do close in a half hour."

Sensing a sale, the clerk didn't want her to walk out of there without that frog tucked under her arm. She didn't have to worry. Beth had no intention of walking out of there without the frog.

"I'll look around for a bit." Who knew what else she'd discover in there? With her heart pounding, she wandered around the store. She felt close to something, on the verge of discovery.

Maybe in a week or two she'd be ready to track down the Brices and present herself to them as their long-lost daughter who had been kidnapped from Timberline twenty-five years ago. It would be a helluva story for the show, too.

She couldn't forget about the show—she never did. Being the host of that show had given her the recognition and attention she'd missed from her parents. How could she have put that into words for Duke two years ago without sounding pathetic?

Stopping in front of a carousel of key chains, she hooked her finger through one and plopped it down on the glass countertop. "I'll take this, too."

As the woman rang up the frog and the key chain, she peered at her through lowered lashes. "Are you here to do a story on the Timberline Trio?"

Beth dropped her credit card. "What?"

The woman retrieved the credit card and ran her finger along the raised lettering. "You are Beth St. Regis of the *Cold Case Chronicles*, aren't you? I recognized you right away. My sister and I love your show."

"Th…thank you." Wasn't that what Beth had always wanted? People recognizing her on the street, praising the show, praising her? Wasn't that why she'd betrayed Duke Harper?

"I…we…"

"Well, I figured it had to be the Timberline Trio case. We don't have any other cold cases around here. Our former sheriff, Cooper Sloane, made sure of that with the kidnappings we just had. Could've knocked me over with a feather when it turned out Wyatt Carson had kidnapped those kids. Why would he do that when his own brother was one of the Timberline Trio?"

"That was…interesting."

The woman put a finger to her lips. "I can keep a secret if you want, but I think most people are going to realize that's why you're here. Timberline is still a small town, despite Evergreen Software. Word will spread."

"It's no secret. I'll be interviewing Timberline residents and visiting all the original locations." Beth signed the credit-card slip. "I'm just doing some preliminary legwork right now and my crew will be joining me later."

Of course, the good people of Timberline would know the purpose of her visit. Word may have already spread, thanks to those boys in the woods. Soon everyone in town would know.

But nobody needed to know her ulterior motive for the story—including Duke Harper.

It would've been something she'd have shared with him two years ago, but now they had too many secrets between them. She'd noticed he hadn't offered up any explanations of why a hotshot FBI agent was wasting his time on a cold case, although she already knew the reason.

Beth hugged the bag to her chest. "Thanks…?"

"Linda. Linda Gundersen."

"You seemed knowledgeable about the stuffed frog. Were you living here when the three children were kidnapped?"

"No. My sister and I took over this shop when we both retired from teaching in Seattle. She'd dated a man from this area for a while, liked it, and suggested it as a place for us to retire." Crossing her arms, she hunched on the counter. "That was fourteen years ago when property was cheap. Turns out it was a good move because things started booming when Evergreen set up shop here."

Beth dug a card out of her purse and slid it across the glass toward Linda. "If you know anyone who'd like to talk to me about the case, have them give me a call."

"I will. My sister, Louise, would love to be on the show."

"Does she know anything about the case?"

"No, but she hired Wyatt Carson to do some plumbing on our house." Linda's voice had risen on a note of hope.

"I'll see if my investigation on the story takes me in that direction. Thanks again."

"Enjoy your frog."

Beth turned at the door and waved, stepping into the crisp night air. Darkness had descended while she'd been in the tourist shop, and her rumbling stomach reminded her that she'd skipped lunch.

Her hotel didn't have a restaurant on the premises and the yellow light spilling out of Sutter's across the street beckoned.

She had no problem eating alone—her job necessitated it half the time she was on the road, and her nonexistent social life dictated it when she was at home.

The plastic bag in her hands crinkled and she decided to make a detour to her car. If she had a bigger purse she'd stuff her frog in there, but her cross-strap bag had no room for her new furry friend and she didn't want to haul the frog into the restaurant. That part of this story she wanted to keep under wraps until she had more proof.

How many adults looking for answers had made the pilgrimage to Timberline, believing they were Stevie, Kayla or Heather? But she had a strong feeling she'd been here before.

She withdrew the frog from the bag and kissed him before stuffing him back in the bag and dropping it on the passenger seat. She'd kissed plenty of frogs in her day, but this one really was going to make all her dreams come true.

She locked up the car and strode back to the restaurant. It had just opened for dinner and a sea of empty tables greeted her—no excuse for the hostess to stick the single diner by the kitchen or the restrooms. She nabbed a prime spot next to the window, ordered a glass of wine and started checking the email on her phone.

Every time Beth looked up from her phone, more and more people filled the room, and she began to notice a few furtive glances coming her way. Linda had been right. News in a small town traveled fast.

If the locals showed an interest in the story, it would make for some good TV. She and her crew never went into these situations with the goal of actually solving the mystery, although a few times they'd gotten lucky. She'd gotten lucky when Duke had shown up during her story two years ago—lucky in more ways than one.

That *Cold Case Chronicles'* investigation had led to the arrest of a child killer who'd been living his life in plain sight of the grieving families. It had been one of her finest hours…and had cost her a budding relationship with Duke.

When the waitress brought her a steaming bowl of soup, Beth looked up just in time to see Duke walk into the restaurant.

She ducked her head behind the waitress and peered around her arm.

The waitress raised her eyebrows. "Everything okay?"

"Just thought I saw someone I knew."

"In Timberline, that's not hard to do even if you are from Hollywood."

"LA."

"You are that host from *Cold Case Chronicles*, aren't you?" The waitress had wedged a hand on her hip as if challenging Beth to disagree with her.

"I am, but I don't live in…" She shrugged. "Yeah, I'm from Hollywood."

"I wasn't here during the first set of kidnappings but—" the waitress looked both ways and cupped a hand around her mouth "—I could tell you a thing or two about Wyatt Carson. I used to date him."

"Really?" Everyone seemed to want to talk about Wyatt, but that case was one for the books. "Did he ever talk much about his brother and what might've happened to him?"

The waitress's eyes gleamed. "A little. I could tell you about it…on camera. I'm Chloe Rayman, by the way."

"We'll talk before we commit anything to video, Chloe." Beth held out her card between two fingers. "If it's something we can use, I'll have my cameraman film you when he gets here."

"Oh, I think it's something you can use." Chloe plucked the card from Beth's fingers and tucked it into the pocket of her apron.

Even if Chloe didn't have anything of importance to add to the story, the waitress would want her fifteen minutes of fame anyway. Beth's challenge on these stories had always been to separate the wannabes from the people with hard facts. Sometimes the two types meshed.

Beth lifted a spoonful of the seafood bisque and blew on the hot liquid.

"Digging in already, huh?"

She'd taken a sip of the soup and choked on it as she looked into the chocolate-brown eyes of Duke Harper. She dabbed a napkin against her mouth. "Dive right in. It's the only way to do it."

"It's the only way you know."

"I'd invite you to sit down—" she waved at the place across from her "—but I'm sure you have important FBI business."

The wooden chair scraped the floor as he pulled it out. "The only important business I have right now is dinner."

She gulped the next spoonful of soup and it burned her throat. What possible reason could Duke have for joining her for dinner? Maybe he wanted to grill *her* for information this time.

"The seafood bisque is good." She drew a circle around her bowl of soup with her spoon.

Chloe returned to the table, practically bursting at the seams. "Are you Beth's cameraman?"

"Would it get me a beer faster if I were?" Duke lifted one eyebrow at Chloe, who turned three different shades of red.

"Of course not. I mean, what kind of beer would you like?"

"Do you sell that local microbrew on tap here?"

"Yes."

"I'll have that and the pork chops with the mashed potatoes, and you might as well bring me some of that soup she's slurping up."

Beth dropped her spoon in the bowl. "Why did you join me if you're going to sit here and insult me?"

"That wasn't an insult. Are you getting overly sensitive out there in LA? You used to be a tough broad, Beth."

Rolling her shoulders, she exhaled out of her nose. Duke liked to needle her. It hadn't bothered her before—when they'd been in love. But now that he hated her? She couldn't take the slightest criticism from him.

"Pile it on, Duke. I can take it." She set her jaw.

"Relax, Beth. Your slurping made the soup sound good. That's all I meant."

Relax? Was that a jab at her anxiety? She squeezed her eyes closed for a second. If she didn't stop looking for innuendos in his conversation, this was gonna be a long dinner.

She scooped up a spoonful and held it out to him with a surprisingly steady hand. "Try it."

He opened his mouth and closed his lips around the spoon. "Mmm."

Heat engulfed her body and a pulse throbbed in her throat. My God, she couldn't be within five feet of the man without feeling that magnetic pull. And he knew it.

She slipped the spoon from his mouth and lined it up on one side of the bowl just as Chloe brought Duke's beer and another bisque.

"Are you done, Beth?"

"Yeah, thanks." She pushed her bowl toward the eager waitress.

When she disappeared into the kitchen, Duke took a swig of beer and asked, "What's up with the waitress? Is she your new best friend or what?"

"She dated Wyatt Carson and thinks that's going to get her camera time."

"You have that effect on people, don't you? They tend to fall all over themselves in your presence."

She stuck out her tongue at him and took a gulp of wine. She needed it to get through this meal.

"Interesting case, Wyatt Carson." Duke flicked his bottle with his finger.

"I know, right?" Beth hunched forward. "Why do you think he did it? Hard to imagine he'd want to put other families through that hell when he'd suffered the loss of his brother."

"One of two things." Duke held up two fingers. "Either he missed the attention and limelight of those days when his brother went missing or he really did just want to play the hero. He kidnapped those kids and then rescued them. Maybe he thought he could get past his survivor's guilt by saving other children when he couldn't save his brother."

"Twisted logic." Beth tapped her head.

"Do you want a slurp, er, sip?" He held his spoon poised over his soup. "I had one of yours."

"No, thanks. I have some fish coming."

"Yeah, yeah. I know the camera adds ten pounds. You still run?"

"There are some great running trails here. Did you bring your running shoes?"

"Of course. Running is the only thing that kept me sane...keeps me sane with the pressures of the job."

"Same here." So the loss of his partner must've weighed heavily on him. Did he suffer from that same survivor's guilt as Wyatt Carson?

"You doing okay with all that—" he circled his finger in the air "—panic stuff?"

"I'm managing." Did he care? He'd acted like he wanted

to strangle her today in the woods. Of course, she'd just nailed him with some expired pepper spray.

"How are your eyes? They still look a little red."

"I'm managing."

Chloe brought their entrées at the same time and hovered for several seconds. "Can I get you anything else?"

"Not for me."

Beth shook her head. "No, thanks."

As Duke sliced off a piece of pork chop and swept it through his potatoes, he glanced around the room. "Does the entire town of Timberline know why you're here?"

"I don't know about the entire town, but everyone in this restaurant has a pretty good idea by now, thanks to Chloe."

"Do you think that's a good idea?" His lips twisted into a frown.

"How else am I going to investigate, to get information?" She squeezed some lemon on her fish and licked the tart juice from her fingers.

Duke shifted his gaze from her fingers to her face and cleared his throat. "I guess that's how you operate. Stir up a bunch of trouble and heartache and move on."

Beth pursed her lips. "None of the original families is even here anymore. Wyatt Carson was the last of Stevie's family in Timberline. Kendall Rush, Kayla's sister, blew through town, got caught up in Wyatt's craziness and then hightailed it out of here. And Heather's family... They moved away from Timberline, to Connecticut, I think."

"You've done your homework."

"I always do, Duke."

"What I can't figure out—" he poked at his potatoes "—is why you were attracted to this cold case. It hardly has all the elements you usually look for."

"And what elements would those be?"

"You know—sex, drugs, grieving families, celebrity." She chewed her fish slowly. Duke hated what she did for a living—had hated it then, hated it now. She didn't have to answer to Special Agent Duke Harper or anyone else.

She drained her wineglass. "I was following the copycat kidnapping story and got interested in the old story, like a lot of people. There seemed to be heightened interest in the Timberline Trio and talk of some new evidence, so I figure I'd capitalize on that. Right up my alley."

"Excuse me, Ms. St. Regis?"

Beth turned and met the faded blue eyes of a grandmotherly woman, linking arms with another woman of about the same age.

"Yes?"

"I'm Gail Fitzsimmons and this is my friend Nancy Heck. We wanted to let you know that we were both living here at the time of the Timberline Trio kidnappings and we'd be happy to talk to you."

"Thank you." Beth reached into her purse for her cards, ignoring Duke's sneer—or what looked pretty close to a sneer. "Here's my card. I'll be doing some preliminary interviews before my crew gets here."

Nancy snatched the card from Beth's fingers. "You mean we aren't going to be on TV?"

Duke coughed and Beth kicked him under the table. "I can't tell yet. We'll see how the interviews go."

When the two ladies shuffled away, their silver heads together, Duke chuckled. "This is going to be a circus."

"And what exactly are you doing to work this cold case?"

"I have all the original case files. I'm starting there." He held up his hands. "Don't even ask. You can do your interviews with Wyatt Carson's ex-girlfriend's ex–dog sitter's second cousin."

"Don't dismiss what I do. I helped the FBI solve the Masters case."

"You helped yourself, Beth."

Chloe approached their table. "Dessert?"

"Not for me." Beth tossed her napkin on the table.

Pulling his wallet out of his pocket, Duke said, "Just the check."

"You paying?" Beth reached for her purse. "I have an expense account."

"And you're using it to pay for your own dinner. I'm using my per diem to pay for mine. I don't want any commingling here."

She lowered her lashes and slid her credit card from her wallet. Was he talking about just their finances?

"Got it." She tapped her card on the table. "No commingling."

A loud voice came from the bar area of the restaurant, and chatter in the dining room hushed to a low level—enough for the bar patron's words to reach them.

"That TV show better not start nosing around. If anyone talks to that host, I'll give 'em the business end of my fist." The man at the bar turned to face the room, knocking over his bar stool in the process.

His buddy next to him put a hand on his shoulder, but the belligerent drunk shook him off.

"Where's she? I'll toss 'er out right now on her fanny. Tarring and feathering. That's what we should do. Who's with me?" He raised his fist in the air.

A few people snickered but most went back to their dinners. Duke didn't do either. He marched across the room toward the bar.

Beth groaned as she scribbled her signature on the credit-card receipt and took off after him. Duke had always been a hothead, and it looked like he hadn't changed.

"What did you say?" He widened his stance in front of the man. "Are you threatening the lady?"

"You with that show, too?" The man looked Duke up and down and hiccuped.

His friend picked up the stool and shoved his friend into

it. "C'mon, Bill. Take it easy. Who knows? Being featured on TV might increase our property values."

The man, his dark hair flecked with gray, shook his head and stuck out his hand. "Sorry about that. My friend's a Realtor and has had a little too much to drink. I'm Jordan Young."

"Duke Harper." Duke gestured toward Beth. "This is Beth St. Regis, the host of *Cold Case Chronicles* and the woman your friend was threatening."

Jordan Young dismissed his drunken friend with a wave of his hand. "It's the booze talking. His sales numbers haven't been great lately, but it has nothing to do with the recent publicity we've been getting. Hell, Kendall Rush's aunt's place sold for top dollar. He's just ticked off that he didn't get that listing."

He took Beth's hand in his and gave it a gentle squeeze. "I'm a big fan of the show, Ms. St. Regis."

"Thanks." She nudged Duke in the back. "Are you a Realtor, too?"

"Me?" He chuckled. "Not really. I'm a developer, and I have a lot more to lose than Bill here if things go south, but that's not going to happen—Evergreen Software will make sure of that."

"You need to tell your friend to keep his mouth shut about Beth."

"Duke." She put her hand on his arm. His stint in Siberia hadn't done anything to temper his combativeness. "I'm sure he's not serious—at least about the tar-and-feathering part."

Young winked. "Good to see you have a sense of humor about it, Ms. St. Regis, but I can understand your…coworker wanting to be protective."

Duke didn't correct him. If the residents of Timberline knew all about *Cold Case Chronicles* looking into the Timberline Trio, they didn't seem to be as knowledgeable about the FBI putting the case back on its radar. Maybe Duke wanted to keep it that way.

"You can call me Beth." Her eyes flicked over his gray-streaked hair and the lines on his face. "Were you here at the time of the initial kidnappings?"

"I was. Sad time for us." He withdrew a silver card case from his suit jacket and flipped it open. "If you're implying you want to interview me, I might be available, although I don't know how much I could contribute."

She took the card and ran her thumb across the gold-embossed letters. "You'd be the first one in town without some special insight."

"Can you blame them?" He spread his hands. "A chance to be on TV and talk to the beautiful host?"

"Thank you." The guy was smooth but almost avuncular. Duke could wipe the scowl from his face, but she didn't mind that another man's attentions to her irritated him.

"You should take care of your buddy here." Duke jerked his thumb at Bill, still resting his head on the bar.

"I'll get him home safely to his wife. Good night, now." Young turned back to the bar. "Serena, can you get Bill a strong cup of coffee? Make it black, sweetheart."

Duke put his hand on her back as he propelled her out of the restaurant—with almost every pair of eyes following them.

As Duke swung the door open for her, Chloe rushed up and patted her apron. "I'll be calling you, Beth. I don't care what Bill Raney says."

"Looking forward to it, Chloe."

When they stepped outside, Duke tilted his head. "Really? You're looking forward to talking to Chloe about Wyatt Carson?"

"You never know what might pop up in a conversation. Maybe Wyatt remembered something about his brother's kidnapping that he never told the cops."

"Why wouldn't he have told the cops?"

Beth zipped up her vest. "Because he turned out to be a nut job."

"Seems to be no scarcity of those in this town." He hunched into his suede coat, rubbing his hands together. "Where are you parked?"

"In the public lot down the block. This is Timberline. You don't have to walk me to my car."

"Just so happens I'm parked there, too." He nudged her with his elbow. "There have been two high-profile kidnapping cases in Timberline. I wouldn't take your safety for granted here. There might be more people here who feel like Bill."

"I'm hardly in danger of getting tarred and feathered... or kidnapped." She stuffed her hands into her pockets and lifted her shoulders to her ears. She may have already been kidnapped from Timberline once. What were the odds of it happening again?

Duke followed her through the parking lot to her car anyway, occasionally bumping her shoulder but never taking her hand. What did she expect? That they would pick up where they'd left off two years ago? Before he'd accused her of using him? Before she'd used him?

As she reached the rental, her boots crunched against the asphalt and she jerked her head up. "Damn. Somebody broke the window of my car."

"Safe Timberline, huh? Maybe Bill did his dirty work before he hit the restaurant." Duke hunched forward to look at the damage to the window on the driver's side. "You didn't have a laptop sitting on the passenger seat, did you?"

"No, but..." Her ears started ringing and she grabbed the handle of the car door and yanked it open.

Someone had taken the bag from the gift shop. Collapsing in the driver's seat, she slammed her hands against the steering wheel. "My frog. They took my frog."

Chapter Four

Duke's eyebrows shot up at the sob in Beth's voice. Some-one had smashed the window of her rental car and she was worried about a frog?

"Beth?" He placed his hand against the nape of her neck and curled his fingers around the soft skin beneath her down vest. "What frog, Beth?"

She sniffled and dragged the back of her hand across her nose. "Some frog I bought in a gift store. I... It's par-ticular to Timberline."

"I'm sure they have more." He released her and braced his hand against the roof of the car. Why was she over-reacting about a frog? She must be driving herself hard again, maybe even succumbing to those panic attacks that had plagued her for years.

Because she didn't even know about the warning the FBI had received about her. He'd debated telling her but didn't want to worry her needlessly about an anonymous email. Who knew? The emailer may have sent the same message to Beth or her production company. Maybe that was why she was breaking down over a frog.

"You can replace the frog. Will your insurance fix the window on the rental car?"

"I'm sure I'm covered for that." She leaned into the pas-senger seat and peeked beneath the seat.

"It's gone?"

"Yep."

He kicked a piece of glass with the toe of his boot. "You're not sitting on glass, are you? The window broke inward, so there's gotta be some on the seat."

"There wasn't." She climbed out of the car and gripped the edge of the door as if to keep herself steady and upright. "He must've brushed it off."

"We're reporting this." Duke pulled his phone from his pocket, scrolled through his contacts and placed a call to the Timberline Sheriff's Department. "We have some vandalism, a broken car window, in the public lot on the corner of Main and River."

He gave them his name and a description of Beth's rental car before ending the call.

"Are they coming?" She cupped the keys to the car in one hand and bounced them in her palm.

"Of course. This isn't LA." He grabbed her hand and held it up, inspecting the dot of blood on the tip of her ring finger. "There *was* some glass in the car. Are you sure you're okay?"

Her wide eyes focused on the blood and she swayed—another overreaction. She seemed to be taking this break-in hard. Maybe she *did* know about the warning against her—and he didn't mean Bill's drunken threats.

Grasping her wrist lightly, he said, "Come with me to my car down the aisle. I have some tissues in there and some water."

By the time they reached his rental, she'd regained a measure of composure. "Idiots. Why would someone go through all the trouble of breaking a window on a rental car to get to a bag of stuff from a tourist shop?"

"Maybe if you hadn't left your bag on the passenger seat in plain view." He unlocked his car and reached into the backseat for a box of tissues, and then grabbed the half-filled bottle of water from his cup holder. "How many times have I told you not to leave things in your car?"

"Let's see." She held out her middle finger. "Must've been a hundred times at least."

"Very funny. It's your ring finger." At least she'd come out of her daze.

"Oops." She held out the correct finger and wiggled it.

He moistened a tissue with some water and held it against the bead of blood. "Apply some pressure to that. Did you get cut anywhere else?"

"Not that I can tell." She tipped her chin toward the cop car rolling into the parking lot. "The deputies are here."

As two deputies got out of the car, Duke whispered in Beth's ear. "That's what I like about Timberline. Two cops come out to investigate a broken window and a missing frog."

She stiffened beside him but a laugh gurgled in her throat.

She'd sure grown attached to that frog in a short span of time...unless there was something else in the bag she didn't want to tell him about. With Beth St. Regis, the possibilities were limitless.

The first deputy approached them, adjusting his equipment belt. "You call in the broken window?"

"And a theft. I had a bag in the car from Timberline Treasures."

The second deputy pointed at Beth. "You're Beth St. Regis from that show."

"Do you watch it?"

"No, just heard you were in town to dig up the old Timberline Trio case."

"I think Wyatt Carson already did that." She jerked her thumb at Duke. "You do know the FBI is looking into the case again, too."

The officer nodded at Duke and stuck out his hand.

"Deputy Stevens. I heard the FBI was sending in a cold-case agent. The sheriff already turned over our files, right?"

"Special Agent Duke Harper." He shook hands with the other man. "And I have the files."

The other officer stepped forward, offering his hand as well. "Deputy Unger. We'll do whatever we can to help you. My mother was good friends with Mrs. Brice at the time of the kidnapping. I was about five years older than Heather when she went missing. That family was never the same after that. Had to leave the area."

Beth was practically buzzing beside him. "Deputy Unger, could I interview you for the show?"

"Ma'am, no disrespect intended, but I'm here to help the FBI. I'm not interested in being a part of sensationalizing the crime. We've had enough of that lately."

"But…"

Duke poked her in the back. "You wanna have a look at the car now?"

"Sure. We'll take a report for the rental-car company and insurance purposes. Probably a kid or one of our local junkies."

Duke asked, "Do you have a drug problem in Timberline?"

"Crystal meth, just like a lot of rural areas." Unger flipped open his notebook and scribbled across the page.

When they finished taking the report, they shook hands with Duke again. "Anything we can do, Agent Harper."

"Well, they weren't very friendly." Beth curled one fist against her hip.

"I thought they were very friendly."

"Yeah, you get the cops and I get Carson's ex-girl-friend's dog walker's cousin."

"Second cousin's ex–dog sitter."

"Right." She tossed her purse onto the passenger seat

of the car and hung on the door. "Thanks for seeing me through the report...and the words of advice."

He was close enough to her that the musky smell of her perfume wafted over him. "Do you want some more advice, Beth?"

She blinked. "If you're dishing it out."

"Find another case for your show. Get off this Timberline Trio gig. Since I'm in the Siberia of cold-case hell anyway, I can even toss a couple of good ones your way."

Her eyes narrowed. "Why would you do that? You must really want me off this case."

"It's not me." Raking a hand through his hair, he blew out a breath. "Someone else wants you off this case."

"What? Who? Bill?"

"We got an anonymous email and I don't think it was from Bill Raney."

"That's crazy. The FBI got an email about little, old me? How did anyone even know I was doing a show on the Timberline Trio?"

"How long have you been in Timberline?"

"Two days."

"We got the email two days ago."

She sucked in her bottom lip. "You think it's someone here?"

"It has to be, unless the station has been doing promo for it."

"Not yet. We wouldn't release anything about a story we haven't even done yet. It might never come off."

"Then it has to be someone here in Timberline or someone related to someone in Timberline. You haven't exactly been shy about your purpose here."

"No point in that. But why contact the FBI?" She snapped her fingers. "It must be someone who knows the FBI is looking into the case, too. Maybe this anonymous emailer figures the FBI will have some pull with me."

Duke snorted. "Mr. Anonymous obviously doesn't know you."

"You know what's strange?"

"Huh?"

"Why didn't this person warn off the FBI? If it's someone who doesn't want me looking into the Timberline Trio, why would this same person be okay with the FBI dredging up the case?"

"I have no idea. Maybe he thinks *Cold Case Chronicles* has a better shot at solving the case than the FBI." He scanned her thoughtful face. "That was a joke."

"It's strange, Duke. I suppose you tried to trace the email."

"With no luck."

"Must be someone who's computer savvy, which isn't hard to find in this town with Evergreen Software in the picture."

He captured a lock of her silky hair and twisted it around his finger. "How about it, Beth? Why don't you back off? I'll find you another case, a better case for your show."

"You don't really think I'm in danger from an anonymous email, do you? I get a lot of anonymous emails, Duke. Some are unrepeatable."

"What about this?" He smacked his palm on the roof of the car. "Someone sends a threat and then someone breaks into your car. Do you think it's a coincidence?"

"Could just be a tweaker like Unger said. Besides, this could be good for you."

"How so?"

"If someone who was involved in the disappearance of the Timberline Trio twenty-five years ago wants me off the case and is willing to harass me about it, you might be able to pick him up and actually solve the case."

"You think I'd use you, put you at risk to solve a twenty-five-year-old case?" He clenched his jaw.

She swallowed, her Adam's apple bobbing in her slender throat. "I…"

"Just because you did it, don't expect the same treatment from me." He backed away from her car. "Drive carefully."

WITH TEARS FLOODING her eyes, which had nothing to do with the cold air coming through the broken window, Beth glanced at Duke's blurry headlights in her rearview mirror.

He hadn't forgiven her, despite his concern for her safety tonight.

Maybe that concern was all a big act. Maybe the anonymous email was a lie. Why would someone want to warn her away from the case but not warn the FBI?

Unless this someone knew her true identity. Did someone suspect her real purpose for highlighting the Timberline case?

She pulled into the parking lot of the Timberline Hotel with Duke right behind her. They even got out of their cars at the same time. He followed her inside, but made no attempt to talk to her.

She dreaded the awkward elevator ride, but he peeled off and headed for the stairwell. Once she stepped into the elevator, she sagged against the wall.

Was the warning to the FBI connected to the break-in? Had the thief grabbed the bag because she'd left it out, or had he wanted to send a message by taking the Libby Love frog? And what was that message?

She slid her card key in the door and leaned into it to shove it open.

She dropped her purse on the single chair in the room and sauntered to the window, arms crossed. Resting her head against the cool glass, she took in the parking lot beneath her.

Did Duke have a better view? If he'd taken the stairs, his room was probably located on the lower floors. The hotel had just five. Who was she kidding? Duke could run up five flights of stairs without breaking a sweat or gasping for breath. The man was a stud, but not the overly muscled kind. He had the long, lean body of a runner.

She banged her head against the window. No point in letting her thoughts stray in that direction. He'd been concerned about her tonight, but that could just be because he wanted her out of the picture.

Little did he know, she had more at stake here than good ratings.

She could tell him, confess everything…well, almost everything. He already knew that she'd been adopted and hadn't been able to locate her birth parents. If she explained to him her suspicions about being Heather Brice, maybe he could help her. Maybe he'd share the case files with her.

She pivoted away from the window. If she told him that now, he'd suspect her of spinning a tale to get her hands on the information he had. She wouldn't go down that road with him again.

Sighing, she swept the remote control from the credenza and aimed it at the TV, turning it on.

With the local TV news blaring in the background, she got ready for bed. Snug in a new pair of flannel pajamas she'd bought for the trip, she perched on the edge of the bed to watch the news. She hadn't made the local news—not yet.

She switched the channel to a sitcom rerun and flipped back the covers on her bed. Her heart slammed against her chest and she jerked back as she stared at the head of the Libby Love frog positioned on the white sheet, his miner's hat at a jaunty angle.

Chapter Five

Beth slammed the frog head on the reception counter, squishing the hat. "Where did it come from?"

The hotel clerk's eyes popped from their sockets. "Ma'am, I'm sorry. I have no idea how it got in your bed. Perhaps it had been washed with the sheets and the maid thought it belonged to you."

"This—" she shook the head at him until some white stuffing fell onto the countertop "—does not look like it's been through an industrial washing machine. It looks brand-new, except for the fact that it's been ripped from its body."

"Ma'am, I don't know. I can talk to the maids in the morning."

"What's going on?"

Beth gulped and swiveled her head to the side. What was Duke doing down here? Might as well get it over with.

"I found this—" she thrust the frog head toward him "—in my bed when I got back to my room."

He held out his hand and she dropped the head into his palm.

"What the hell? Is this the frog you bought earlier that was stolen from your car?"

"Stolen?" The clerk turned another shade of red. "I can assure you, we don't know anything about any theft."

Beth released a long breath. "I don't know if it's the

exact same toy I bought, but it's the same kind. So if the thief who broke into my car didn't put it in my room, it's a helluva coincidence that someone else did."

The hotel clerk reached for the phone. "Should we call the sheriff's department?"

Duke tilted his head back and looked at the ceiling of the lobby. "Do you have security cameras?"

"Just in the parking lot, sir. We can check that footage to see if anyone drove into the lot without coming through the lobby."

"That's a good idea. It would've been within the past ninety minutes. Do you have a security guard on duty…" He glanced at the man's name tag. "…Gregory?"

"This is Timberline. No security guard." Gregory lifted his hands. "Sheriff's department?"

"Will they come out for a stuffed frog head?" Beth crossed her arms over her flannel pj's, recognizing the ridiculousness of that statement. At least she didn't feel as if she were choking as she had from the moment she'd seen that frog in her bed. Duke had that effect on her—a calming, steadying presence.

Too bad she had the opposite effect on him.

He gave her a crooked smile. "You heard Gregory. This is Timberline. They'll come out for a stuffed frog. It's not just the head. It's the fact that someone broke into your room and put it in your bed…and the smashed car window before that. You want to report and document all this."

Gregory picked up the phone. "I'll call it in. We may learn more tomorrow when the housekeeping staff comes in. I'll make sure we question all of them thoroughly. The night crew was here until about an hour ago, so they could've been here when the, uh, frog was put in your room."

"Thanks, Gregory." Beth tucked her messy hair behind

her ears and flashed him one of her TV smiles. "I'm sorry I got in your face earlier. That frog rattled me."

"I understand, ma'am. If you and the…gentleman—" he nodded toward Duke "—want to help yourselves to something from the self-serve concession while you wait for the sheriffs, it's on the house."

"Don't mind if we do. Thanks, Gregory." She crooked her finger at Duke and then charged across the lobby to the small lit fridge and rows of snacks, her rubber flip-flops smacking the tile floor.

She yanked open the fridge door with Duke hovering over her shoulder. "You're still in your pajamas."

Leaning forward, she studied the labels on the little bottles of wine with the screw tops. "Excuse me. I didn't have time for full hair, makeup and wardrobe once I realized someone had been sneaking around my hotel room beheading frogs."

She wrapped her fingers around a chilled bottle of chardonnay and turned on him, almost landing in his arms. She thrust the bottle between them. "What were you doing wandering around the hotel?"

His dark eyes widened. "Are you accusing me of planting the frog? I was with you, remember?"

"Now who's being sensitive? The thought never crossed my mind, but you were headed toward the stairwell the last time I saw you."

"I stepped outside for some air. My room was stuffy and I couldn't sleep." He held up the frog head. "It's a good thing I did. You looked ready to gouge out poor Gregory's eyes."

"I was spooked." She ducked back into the fridge. "Do you want a beer or one of these fine wines?"

"I'll take a beer." He ran his hand down the length of her arm. "Must've freaked you out seeing that frog in your bed."

She handed him a cold beer. "It did. The fact that it was just his head made it worse. Was that some kind of warning?"

"Is this story worth it?" He took the mini wine bottle from her and twisted off the lid. "For whatever reason, someone doesn't want you digging into this case, and this person is willing to put you through hell to get that point across."

"Would you quit if someone started warning you?"

He twisted off his own cap and took a swallow of beer. "It's different. If someone started warning the FBI off a cold case, it would give us reason to believe we were on the right track."

"Maybe I'm on the right track."

"You just got here. It seems to me that some person or persons don't want a story on Timberline. Having the FBI investigate is a different ball game. Maybe these warnings to you are designed to stop you from dragging the town of Timberline through the mud again. You know, reducing the real-estate prices, like Bill said."

She took a sip of wine. "You saw the people at the restaurant. Most were eager to help."

"There could be two factions in town—one group wants the attention and the other doesn't. The ones that don't want the limelight have started a campaign against you—a personal one." He clinked his bottle with hers. "Give it up, Beth. Move on to something else. I told you. I have the cold-case world at my fingertips now and can turn you on to a new, sexy case."

She took another pull straight from her wine bottle and gritted her teeth as she swallowed. "I'm not going to quit, Duke. I want to investigate this case."

"Evening, Ms. St. Regis." Deputy Unger swept his hat from his head. "Gregory told us you had some more trouble tonight."

"It's the stuffed frog stolen from her car." Duke held out the frog head. "Someone planted it in her hotel room."

Unger whistled. "Someone really wants you gone—I mean off this story."

"Can you check the tape from the security camera in the parking lot?" Beth put her wine bottle behind her back just in case Unger thought she was a hysterical drunk. "Gregory said the hotel had cameras out there. Maybe someone will appear on tape who's out of place."

"I spoke to him on the way in. Gregory's getting that ready for us right now. Let's go up to your room and check it out. See if there are any signs of a break-in."

Duke proffered the frog head on the palm of his hand. "The frog's been manhandled by a bunch of people, but maybe you can get some prints from it."

Unger pulled a plastic bag from the duffel over his shoulder and shook it out. "Drop it in. We'll have a look."

They all trooped up to her hotel room and Beth inserted the card with shaky fingers. She didn't know what to expect on the other side of the door.

Nothing.

Everything was the way she'd left it, covers pulled back on the bed and the TV blasting. She grabbed the remote and lowered the volume. "It was there, on the middle of the bed, beneath the covers."

Unger looked up from studying the door. "No signs of forced entry. You're on the fourth floor. Does the window open?"

"No."

He had a fingerprinting kit with him and dusted the door handle and the doorjamb. Once he finished asking a few more questions, he packed up his stuff. "I'll have a look at the footage now. If I find anything, I'll let you know."

Duke stopped him. "One more thing, Deputy Unger.

A Realtor by the name of Bill Raney was making some threats against Beth in Sutter's tonight."

"We'll talk to him. That man's been on a downward slide lately. I can't imagine him out breaking car windows and sneaking into hotel rooms, but you never know what people will do when their backs are against the wall."

Beth sighed. Why did this have to be happening on the most important case of her life? Maybe if she just explained herself publicly. She honestly didn't care who had kidnapped her twenty-five years ago and she wasn't interested in putting Timberline in the spotlight again. She just wanted to confirm her identity. She wanted to go to the Brices with proof. She wanted to go back to a loving home.

She'd already made a mistake. She should've done her sleuthing on the sly. She should've come to Timberline as a tourist, taken up fishing or hiking or boating. She'd just figured she had the best cover. Nobody would have to know her ulterior motive. Nothing would have to get back to the Brices until she was sure.

"Ms. St. Regis?"

She looked up into Deputy Unger's face, creased with concern. "Are you okay? Gregory offered to move you to another room."

"I think that's a great idea." Duke tossed her suitcase onto the bed. "In fact, the room next to mine on the second floor is empty."

Beth's mouth gaped open. Duke must really be worried if he wanted her rooming right next to him. Today in the forest he'd acted like he'd wanted to strangle her.

"That might not be a bad idea—if you're insisting on continuing with this story." Unger slung his bag over his shoulder and walked to the door.

"Deputy Unger, who exactly doesn't want the old case dredged up from the cold-case files?" Holding her breath, she watched his face. *He* didn't. He'd made that clear before.

He shrugged. "People like Bill. People with a lot to lose—think property values, reputations, businesses—those are the people who want to put this all behind us. The executives at Evergreen about had a fit when Wyatt Carson kidnapped those kids and struck fear into the hearts of their employees—the people they'd lured here with a promise of safety and clean living."

"I don't see how a crime that occurred twenty-five years ago can still tarnish the luster of a city." She grabbed her vest from the back of the chair and dropped it next to her bag on the bed.

"C'mon, Beth." Duke scratched his stubble. "You've been doing the show long enough to realize what can happen to a town when all the dirty laundry is hung out for everyone to see."

"Maybe I won't end up doing the story. Maybe I won't even call my crew out here—but it won't be because someone wants to scare me off. It'll be because I decide to call it quits."

"Whatever you say, Ms. St. Regis." Unger pulled open the door. "Just keep calling us, especially if these pranks start to escalate."

"Escalate?" Beth licked her lips. "It's just a story, just a town's rep."

"You'd be surprised how far people will go to protect what's theirs."

She and Duke ended up following Unger back to the reception desk to switch her room to the second floor—next to Duke's.

Unger scanned the footage while they waited and shook his head. "Nothing out of the ordinary. Anyone coming in or out of that parking lot is accounted for as a guest of the hotel."

Gregory slipped her the new card key. "As I said, Ms. St. Regis, I'll question housekeeping tomorrow morning and we'll try to get to the bottom of how someone got into your room. It won't happen again."

"Damn right it won't."

Duke got that fierce look he must've learned on the mean streets of Philly and Beth shivered. It meant a lot to have a man like Duke on your side—if you weren't stupid enough to throw it all away.

Gregory even looked a little worried. "I'll keep you posted, Ms. St. Regis."

Duke took the suitcase handle from her and dragged her bag toward the elevator.

She shuffled after him, yawning. "I am so ready to call it a night."

Duke gave her a sideways glance and stabbed the button for the second floor. The elevator rumbled into action and Beth closed her eyes. The wine had made her sleepy, and she felt the lure of a comfy bed with no surprises in it, although she wouldn't mind one surprise—a prince instead of a frog.

The elevator lurched to a sharp halt and Beth's eyes flew open. "Whoa. This thing needs service."

The elevator had stopped moving but the doors remained shut.

"Oh, God, not another prank—as Unger called it." Her gaze darted to Duke's face, still fierce but set, his jaw hard.

"I'm the one who stopped the elevator."

"What?" She braced her hand against the wall of the car. "Are you crazy? What did you do that for?"

Duke crossed his arms and widened his stance as if she could pull off an escape from the car.

"You're going to tell me what you're really doing in Timberline, and you're going to tell me now or this elevator isn't going anywhere."

Chapter Six

Duke felt a twinge of guilt in his gut as Beth's pale face blanched even more. Was she claustrophobic, too? He knew she had those panic attacks, and if she started down that road he'd cave. He had a weakness for this woman.

"I... I don't know what you're talking about. I'm here to do a *Cold Case Chronicles* episode on the Timberline Trio—come hell or high water."

"Cut it, Beth. That's not your kind of story and we both know it." He leveled a finger at her. "You're up to something. You may have fooled me two years ago, but I'm tuned in to the Beth St. Regis line of baloney now."

Her eye twitched and her tongue darted from her mouth. "It's personal."

He rolled his shoulders. "Now we're getting somewhere. I knew there was more to this story. Start talking."

"If I do, will you help me?"

He tilted his head back and eyed the ceiling. "Just like you to turn the tables. I'm not agreeing to anything. I just want to know the truth—for a change. Don't you think you owe me the truth?"

Tears brightened her eyes, and the tip of her nose turned red.

He scooped in a deep breath. If she shed even one tear, he'd be finished. But that was how she'd gotten around him last time—pushed all his buttons.

"C'mon, Beth. What are you doing here?"

Drawing in a shaky breath, she covered her eyes with one hand. "You're right. It's not just the Timberline Trio case that brings me here, but in a way it is."

"Is this going to be a guessing game?"

"No." She sniffled. "I do owe you the truth, but do we have to do this here, like I'm some suspect you're interrogating?"

He punched the button. "Sorry about that. I just wanted to get your attention. You're not…?"

"Claustrophobic?" Her lips trembled into a smile. "Sort of."

The doors opened onto the second floor and he ushered her out of the car in front of him and then wheeled her suitcase down the hall after her, his gaze taking in the way the soft flannel draped over her derriere. Beth was probably the only woman he knew who could make flannel pajamas look sexy.

She stopped in front of the room next to his and swiped the card key. As she fumbled with the door, he reached around her and pushed it open.

"You want me to check for frogs in the bed?"

"My tormentor doesn't know my new room number, but go ahead anyway."

In three strides he reached the king-size bed and whipped back the covers. "Frog-free."

She climbed onto the bed and crossed her legs beneath her. "You ready?"

Pulling the chair from the desk in the corner, he straddled it. "I'm always ready for the truth."

"You know I'm adopted."

"And you hit the jackpot with a set of rich parents." He held up his hands. "I know they weren't the best parents, but at least they gave you all the creature comforts your teenage mother couldn't give you."

"I didn't have a teenage mother."

"What?" He hunched over the back of the chair. "You told me your birth mother was an unwed teen who gave you up to a wealthy couple for a better life and then disappeared."

"I lied."

He flinched as if she'd thrown a knife at his heart. What didn't she lie about?

"Okay. Who was your mother and what does this all have to do with Timberline?"

"Duke, I don't know who my birth parents are. My adoptive parents, the Kings, never told me."

"Maybe they didn't want you running after some bio parents and getting disappointed."

She snorted. "I doubt that."

"They wouldn't give you any information? The adoption agency? A birth certificate?"

"I… I think my adoption was illegal. My birth certificate is fraudulent. The Kings are listed as my biological parents. The only reason I even knew I was adopted was because I overheard them talking once. When I confronted them about it, they admitted it but refused to give me any more information."

"That's strange, but what does it all have to do with Timber…?" Her implication smacked him on the back of the head. She couldn't be serious.

"That's right." She dragged a pillow into her lap and hugged it. "I think I'm one of the Timberline Trio— Heather Brice."

He pushed up from the chair and took a turn around the room. "How in the hell did you come to that conclusion?"

She launched into a crazy tale of stuffed frogs and repressed memories of forests and news stories of Timberline until his head was swimming.

"Wait." He sank onto the edge of the bed. "Based on

a stuffed frog you had as a child that happens to be Timberline's mascot, you think you were kidnapped and then what? Sold on the black market?"

"Don't pretend that doesn't happen. We both know it does, and the Kings were just the type to be involved in something like that. The rules didn't apply to them. Their riches always gave them a sense of entitlement."

"From what you've told me about your adoptive parents, I agree. But, Beth…" He reached across the bed and tugged on the hem of her pajama bottoms. "Maybe you have that frog because your parents, the Kings, passed through this area and bought it for you."

"I thought of that, not that I could ever see them vacationing in Timberline, but what about the hypnosis?" She waved her arms in a big circle. "I went to a hypnotist in LA, and I saw this place—the lush forest, the greenery—and it scares the hell out of me."

"There are a lot of places in the world that look like Timberline."

"But combined with the frog?"

"Maybe something traumatic happened here when your parents were passing through. Hell, maybe there was a car accident or you wandered away and got lost—God knows, you'd be the kind of kid to do that, and I mean that in a good way."

"The Kings never mentioned anything like that."

"Why would they? You said they were distant, uncommunicative."

"I just feel it, Duke." She pounded her chest with one fist. "From the moment I saw the Wyatt Carson story and the Timberline scenery on TV, I felt it in my bones. There's something about this place. I have a connection to it."

"Have you tried to contact the Brices?"

"No. I don't want to get their hopes up or make them

think this is some cruel joke. I want to do some legwork first."

"I thought you were convinced you were Heather Brice."

"There's being convinced and then there's proving it. I came here to prove it."

"It would be easy to know for sure with a DNA test."

"I can't put those poor people through that if I'm not sure."

"What do you think is going to happen here? You're going to have some revelation? Everything that happened to you at age two is suddenly going to come back to you in perfect recall?"

She stretched her legs out in front of her and tapped her feet together. "I'm not sure. I just know I have to be here, and I have to investigate."

"You can't go to the Brice house anymore. It's been torn down along with its neighbors to make room for a shopping center."

"I know that." She drew her knees up to her chest and clasped her arms around her legs. "Does this mean you're going to help me?"

He jerked back. How'd he get sucked in so quickly? He planted his feet on the carpet. Was she even telling the truth now? Maybe it was all a trick to get him to turn over what he knew about the Timberline Trio so she could film her stupid show and maybe even piggyback on his success like last time.

She saw it in his face—the doubt.

She touched her forehead to her knees and her strawberry blond hair created a veil over her face. Her voice came out muffled and unsteady. "I'm not playing you, Duke."

A sharp pain knifed the back of his head. He was done—for now.

"You've had a crazy day. Get to bed and we'll discuss

it tomorrow." He pushed off the bed and made it to the door. He yanked it open and paused as she rolled off the bed as if to follow him.

He raised one eyebrow.

"I have to brush my teeth again. Thanks for suggesting this room. I know it's just a frog and a broken window, but I feel better being close to you."

"Good night, Beth."

As the door shut behind him, a whisper floated after him. "I always did feel better close to you."

THE FOLLOWING MORNING Beth opened her eyes and stretched, feeling fifty pounds lighter. There had been a moment at the end of the evening when it looked like Duke was ready to bolt, but overall he'd taken her confession well. And he'd believed her.

She hadn't revealed everything to him, but she wasn't ready for that…and neither was he. Maybe she'd feel another fifty pounds lighter once she did.

Sitting up in bed, she reached for her phone and checked her messages. Scott had asked when she needed her cameraman and the rest of the crew. Maybe she'd never need them. If she played it cool and didn't make a big fuss, her tormentor might stop harassing her and she could get down to the business of her real investigation.

The tap on her door made her yank the covers up to her chin.

"Beth, are you up yet? I talked to the cleaning crew, and I think I know how the intruder got into your hotel room."

"I'm awake. Just a minute." She scrambled out of bed, ran her tongue along her teeth and lunged for the door.

"Sleeping in?"

"I was exhausted." She swung the door wide. "Come on in. What did the maids have to say?"

He put a finger to his lips and closed the door. "Let's

not broadcast this. They had a cart on your floor at about the time we figured someone broke into your room. They carry master room keys with them, and Gregory thinks someone walked by and snatched one, letting himself in your room."

"Doesn't say much for their security, does it?"

"What security? But the hotel is going to change its policy, and now each maid will have a single master key—no more leaving them on the carts. I'm not sure they were supposed to be doing that anyway."

"I hope I didn't get anyone in trouble." She ran her fingers through her hair, wishing she'd told Duke to wait until she'd showered and dressed. "Have you had breakfast yet?"

"No. I went for a run and then met with Gregory."

"Wish I'd been able to join you." She glanced at the alarm clock. "Can I buy you breakfast?"

"To continue our discussion from last night?"

"To eat breakfast."

"Pound on the wall when you're ready."

She released a pent-up breath when Duke left. Still testy, but he seemed as if he trusted her a little more after sleeping on her revelation. She'd have to make sure that trust continued to grow. She could use his help…and maybe his protection while unraveling her past.

She showered and dressed for the weather in a pair of jeans, a sweater and the boots she'd been wearing every day since she got here. Before leaving the room, she called the rental-car company to report the broken window.

Instead of banging on the wall, she knocked on Duke's door.

He answered with a file folder in his hand. As he held it up, he said, "You may want to just eat breakfast, but I have to get to work. Yesterday was a wash."

"There's a restaurant a few miles from here that serves

breakfast." She averted her eyes from the folder. If he wanted to share with her, he would.

"We'll take my car. Did you call the rental-car place?"

"I just did. They're swapping out the car for me. Seemed so surprised about the vandalism and theft."

"I guess it is unusual for this town unless you're determined to dwell on its ugly past."

"You know what I was thinking?" She ducked into the stairwell as Duke held the door for her. "I should've come here as a tourist and done my own detective work without the glare of publicity."

"Without bringing the spotlight with you, a lot of those people last night at the restaurant wouldn't have any interest in talking to you about the case. They might've recognized you anyway and had their suspicions. You just didn't realize not everyone would be thrilled with the show coming to town."

"It's not like it hasn't happened before—people unhappy with the show coming to their town." She shoved open the fire door to the lobby. "I'm going to put those pranks out of my mind and concentrate on my goal. Nothing is going to stop me."

She glanced at the front desk on her way out but another clerk had replaced Gregory. When they reached the parking lot, Beth spotted the ex-con she'd run into before, straddling his bike and examining her broken car window.

"That's the guy I saw in the forest." She elbowed Duke and called to the man. "I saw you in the forest."

The man looked up, a green baseball cap low on his forehead. "Is this your car?"

"It's a rental."

"That's a shame." He scratched his chin. "I heard why you were here—from them teenagers drinking in the woods."

"Do you want to get on camera now, too?"

"No, ma'am. Some things are just better off left alone." He got back on his bike and pedaled away.

"Do you know that man was questioned for the Carson kidnappings?"

Duke waved the file at her. "I do. His name is Gary Binder and he's a former junkie and an ex-con."

"Were you going to tell me about him?" She walked to the passenger side and he followed her. "I mentioned him to you yesterday."

As he opened the door, he shrugged. "Would you blame me for keeping my research to myself?"

Before she could answer, he turned and walked back to the driver's side.

By the time Duke got behind the wheel, she'd decided not to push her luck. If Duke wanted to help her in her quest, he'd do it. She wouldn't push him, wouldn't cajole. When she'd started this journey, she'd had no idea that Duke would be here. His presence did give her a sense of comfort, but she was determined to dig into this thing on her own and to discover the truth with or without Duke.

While he drove, she gave him directions to the little café that sat near a creek bed and served breakfast and lunch only. As they entered the restaurant, she pointed to the back. "They have a deck next to a running creek, but it looks like rain."

"I have a feeling it always looks like rain in Timberline, and I don't want my papers floating away."

A waitress shoved through the swinging doors to the kitchen with a row of plates up each arm. "Sit anywhere. I'll be right with you."

They took a corner table and Duke turned his coffee cup upright. "You still drinking decaf tea?"

"You remembered?" For some reason, the fact that he remembered she'd been trying to give up caffeine gave her a warm glow. "I've been to this place already for breakfast and they have a good selection."

The waitress approached with a coffeepot. "Coffee?"

"Just one. Black." Duke inched his cup to the edge of the table.

"I'll have some hot tea, please."

Duke blew the steam rising from his cup. "How much do you know about Heather Brice?"

"She was the youngest kidnap victim at two, and she was snatched from her toddler bed while her babysitter slept on the couch in front of the TV."

"She was also the last of the Timberline Trio."

"The FBI at the time ruled out any connection between the missing children—no babysitters in common, no teachers, no day care, not even any friends, although Kayla Rush and Stevie Carson knew each other."

"You *have* done your homework." He took a sip of coffee as the waitress delivered her hot water and a selection of tea bags.

"One thing I don't know?"

"Yeah?"

"The new evidence. After the Carson kidnap case was resolved, law-enforcement officials mentioned that new evidence about the older case had come to light, but nobody ever mentioned what that evidence was." She tapped the folder on the table between them. "I'm assuming that's what you have here."

"If you're expecting a bombshell, this isn't it. No confessions. No long-lost bloody handprint. No DNA evidence."

"But enough to send an FBI agent out here to take a look at this cold case."

"An FBI agent who doesn't have anything better to do with his career right now."

"I heard about what happened, Duke. I'm sorry you lost your partner."

"But we saved the child. Tony, my partner, wouldn't have wanted it any other way, and I'm not making excuses for our decision. We both went into that warehouse with our eyes wide-open, both knowing the risks. We were willing to take those risks. Believe me, I would've taken that bullet instead of Tony if it meant saving the kid."

"The FBI didn't blame you."

"Not exactly, but look at me now." He spread his arms.

"I'm glad you're here." She dredged her tea bag in the hot water. "Is your boss expecting any results out here?"

"Mick always expects results. The Timberline Trio case has been a black eye for the FBI for twenty-five years."

"Maybe Mickey Tedesco thinks you're the man to repair that."

"Doubt it."

The waitress hovered at the table. "Are you ready to order?"

Duke flipped open the menu. "Haven't even looked."

"I'll go first." Beth poked at the menu. "I'll have the oatmeal with brown sugar, nuts, banana…and do you have any berries?"

"Fresh blueberries."

"That's fine."

Duke ordered some French toast and bacon.

When the waitress left, he wrapped his hands around his coffee cup. "I don't get why you just don't contact the Brices, tell them your story and get a DNA test done."

"You know about the Brices, right?"

"That they're super wealthy? Yeah, I know that."

"Don't you think they'd be suspicious of people popping out of the woodwork claiming to be their long-lost daughter? It's probably happened to them before."

"You're already rich. You don't need their money."

"I'm hardly in the same league as the Brices. Do you

know how much of their wealth my adoptive parents left to charities and foundations, cutting me out?"

"You mentioned that before, but my point is you're not some pauper trying to cash in on the Brices' wealth."

"I couldn't put them through anything like that based on a hunch."

"Now it's a hunch?" He tilted his head. "You were one hundred percent sure last night that you were Heather Brice."

She linked her fingers together. "It just all makes sense. I can't explain it to you. Even if Timberline had never experienced those kidnappings, I would've been drawn to this town. The fact that a little girl went missing twenty-five years ago only adds to my conviction."

"I don't know why I can't reveal the new evidence. It's not top secret." Duke dragged the folder toward him with one finger. "It has to do with drugs—the methamphetamine market, to be exact."

"Drugs?" Her hand jerked and a splash of hot tea sloshed into her saucer. "What would drugs have to do with a trio of kidnappings?"

"That's what I'm here to figure out. At the time of the kidnappings, law enforcement wasn't looking at other illegal activities in the area. The Timberline Sheriff's Department wasn't forthcoming about the drug trade to the FBI. Who knows why not? These petty jealousies between the local law and the FBI always crop up in cases like this—most of the time to the detriment of solving the case."

"So, the FBI discovered that there was a thriving drug trade in Timberline during the investigation of the recent kidnappings."

"Yep, and we got a lot of our information from Binder, the ex-con on the bike."

"It's not hard to imagine he was involved in drugs. Is that what he went away for?"

"He's been in and out of jail—petty stuff mostly, but what he lacked in quality, he made up for in quantity."

She traced a finger around the base of her water glass. "Are you thinking some sort of human trafficking for drugs?"

"It's a possibility."

Beth shivered. "That's horrible. Why those children?"

"Could've been crimes of opportunity. Those kids were unlucky enough to be in the wrong place at the wrong time. A lot of crime is like that."

"Still not much to go on."

"I told you—Siberia." He planted his elbows on the table. "Now tell me what you think you're going to accomplish. How are you going to figure out if you're Heather?"

She paused as the waitress delivered their food. "Anything else for you?"

Duke held up his cup. "Hit me again?"

"I'm a little embarrassed to admit this, but I thought I might just show up here and it would all come back to me." She swirled a spoonful of brown sugar through her oatmeal without looking up and meeting Duke's eyes, although she could feel his dark gaze drilling her.

"I'm sorry, Beth."

She raised her eyes and blinked. "You are?"

"I'm sorry your parents were so cold and distant. I always thought you had it better than I did with your money and private schools and fancy vacations, but you suffered a form of abuse just as surely as I did."

"I would never compare my life of luxury to what you went through with your father, Duke."

"At least my mom loved me, even though I couldn't save her or my sister from that man."

"Your father and mine were two sides of the same coin, weren't they?"

"And now you're driven to find your real family, but what if this journey doesn't end well?"

"You mean what if I'm not Heather Brice, loved and missed by her family?"

"Can you take the disappointment?"

"Of course." She dug into her oatmeal to hide her confusion. She'd been so convinced she was Heather, she hadn't allowed any doubt in her worldview—until now.

"When do you start your interviews? I can probably get Deputy Unger to talk to you. Maybe if his mom's still in town, she can talk to you about Heather's family."

Beth took a sip of tea to melt the lump in her throat. Only yesterday after she'd sprayed Duke in the face with pepper spray and he'd stalked off had she figured she'd get nothing more from him, and yet here he was, offering to save her again.

Despite his hard shell, he had a soft heart. That was why he thought he could save all the kids of the world.

"I thought…well, I figured you were done helping me with cold cases."

"I don't see this as a *Cold Case Chronicles*' investigation. I see this as a Beth St. Regis investigation."

"I figured you'd be done with that, too."

"Maybe I should be." He bit off the end of a piece of bacon.

"Duke, it was never just about the evidence." She hunched forward. "I don't know how you could've believed that after what we had."

"You used me, Beth—straight-up."

"I took the case files from your room when I spent the night with you, but I didn't spend the night with you to get the case files. How could you think that?"

"Easy. We had sex and then you snuck out in the early morning hours, taking my files with you."

She sighed. If he'd let her prove to him that she wanted

him regardless of what he could do to help her, she could convince him in one night.

She dropped her spoon into her bowl as the truth punched her in the gut. She *did* still want Duke Harper, had never stopped wanting him. She just had one more truth to tell him and she didn't know if he'd ever get over that one.

He turned the file toward her. "Do you want to see this or is it just more fun skulking around in my room?"

"I'll take a look."

While Duke polished off the rest of his breakfast, Beth sifted through the pile of papers in the folder. Apparently, Timberline had suffered from a flourishing meth trade as the town's economy tanked. A lot of money exchanged hands and there had been a spike in crime. Could the drug dealers have branched into trafficking? It happened all over the world. Why would a small town in Washington be immune?

She closed the file. "That's some scary stuff."

"You can see it's not a stretch to imagine that druggie bunch might've been into some other serious crimes."

The waitress tucked the bill between the salt and pepper shaker and Beth grabbed it. "I'll use my expense account in exchange for the information. You see? Everything on the up-and-up."

"Sounds fair." Duke stood up and stretched. "I'm going to have a few meetings today with local law enforcement. Are you going to start making calls and setting up interviews with tomorrow's budding TV stars?"

"I suppose I have to start somewhere." She handed her credit card to the waitress. "Who knows? Maybe someone will recognize me as Heather Brice."

She signed the receipt and joined Duke outside. "I hope the rental company replaced my car already."

"I'll drop you off at the hotel." He placed a hand at the

small of her back, propelling her toward the car. "Stay alert. Don't leave stuff in your car and make sure nobody's following you."

"Following me?" She hugged herself. "That's creepy. I hadn't thought of that."

"Just watch it. I'll even replace your pepper spray for you."

He started the car and wheeled out of the gravel parking lot of the restaurant.

They'd traveled just a half mile when traffic slowed down and the revolving lights of some emergency vehicles lit up the gray sky.

"Traffic accident?"

Duke craned his neck out the window. "I don't see any cars except the ones on the road."

Beth powered down her own window and stuck her head out. "It's a bike at the side of the road—a twisted bike."

Then she saw it—a gurney with a sheet covering a body...and a green baseball cap on the ground.

Beth's stomach churned and her nails dug into the seat of the car. "Oh, my God. It's Gary Binder and I... I think he's dead."

Chapter Seven

"What?" Duke slammed on the brakes and the car lurched forward and back. "How can you tell?"

"That's his bike up ahead and there's a body on a gurney with a sheet covering the head."

"How do you know it's Binder? Maybe his bike's there because he stopped to help."

"It's the hat—the green baseball cap. It's on the ground next to the stretcher." Beth covered her mouth. "We were just talking to him. Literally, he could've been hit right after he left the parking lot of the hotel."

"We don't even know if he's been hit. I still don't see any cars stopped except for the emergency vehicles and all of us on the road." He swung the SUV onto the shoulder of the road.

"What are you doing?"

"I'm still an officer of the law, and I'm going to find out what happened."

His tires churned up gravel as he hugged the shoulder, rumbling past the cars stuck on the road.

A deputy stepped up to block his progress, so Duke threw the car into Park and grabbed the door handle. Turning to Beth, he said, "Stay here."

When he slammed his car door, he heard an echo from the other side and saw Beth heading toward the crash scene. Did he expect anything different from her?

He caught her arm and whispered, "Let me do the talking."

"Folks, you need to get back in your car and keep moving."

Duke flashed his badge. "Special Agent Harper. I'm here on FBI business, Deputy, and I think the victim here is—was one of my witnesses."

As the deputy squinted at his badge, he said, "Gary Binder. Is that your man?"

Beth stiffened beside him.

Duke said, "That's him. What happened?"

"Hit and run."

Beth grabbed his arm and squeezed hard. "Any witnesses?"

"Not yet. Follow me." The deputy jerked his thumb toward the ambulance. "Damn shame since the guy was finally getting his life together."

Beth kept a grip on Duke as they walked toward the gurney, draped with a white sheet, the outlines of a body beneath it, a bloodstain near the head.

Duke didn't need to see Binder and Beth really didn't need to see him. "Who called the police?"

"Someone on a cell phone in a car. She noticed the bike first, and when she slowed down, she saw Binder's body just off the road."

"Any evidence? Tire tracks? Brake skid marks?"

"Nothing yet, but we're going to let the accident investigators do their thing." The deputy shook his head. "Timberline seems to be losing its civility ever since Evergreen Software went in—too many city folks bringing the hustle and bustle with 'em."

Duke swallowed hard. Was that what you called a hit and run out here? A lack of civility? "Maybe someone will step forward or the driver will have an attack of conscience."

"Do you need anything else from me, Agent Harper? We can forward the accident report to you once it's complete."

"That would be helpful, thanks." He started heading back to the SUV with Beth attached to his arm. Halfway to the car, he turned. "Deputy? What was Binder doing out here on his bike?"

"Not sure. He'd been working as a handyman, doing odd jobs, but as far as I know, most of his work was in town. He always rode that damned bike. Someone had even given him a truck recently, but he stuck with the bike."

"To the very end."

Duke climbed into the car and glanced at Beth, whose wide eyes took up half her face. "Are you okay?"

"That's so…creepy. We were just talking to him." She knotted her fingers in her lap. "What was he doing at the Timberline Hotel?"

"Riding on his way to work or wherever he was going." He drummed his thumbs against the steering wheel. "Maybe he was doing work at the hotel and that's what brought him out this way."

"If he was at the hotel…"

"You're thinking he was the one who broke into your room and left the frog head?"

She nodded. "But why would he do that?"

"He'd do it if he was the one warning you."

"He doesn't have any real estate to worry about. Why would he want to scare me off this story?"

"Maybe he was involved in the Timberline Trio disappearance more than he let on in his interview." He cranked on the engine. "I'm throwing that out there, but I have a hard time believing Gary Binder would be sending anonymous emails to the FBI."

"Do you think his death—a hit and run—is just coincidental to all this other stuff?"

"Maybe, maybe not, but it doesn't have to be related to his involvement in the kidnappings or to the threats against you. Binder's the one who gave the FBI information about the drug trade at the time of the kidnappings."

Beth clasped her fidgeting hands so tightly her knuckles turned white. "You think someone was trying to shut him up?"

"Could be, even though it's a little late. He already spilled, unless…"

"Unless he had more to spill." Her knees began to bounce.

"Maybe that's why he was at the hotel. He knew you were staying there and wanted to talk to you. He didn't want to open up in front of me, so he pretended to be looking at the broken window. I'm going to have to review his previous interview carefully." He pulled into the line of traffic, crawling past the accident site. "But if he had more information, I don't know why he didn't give it up the first time."

"I don't know, Duke, but there seem to be some real forces of evil at work in Timberline."

As they passed the last emergency vehicle, Duke looked in his rearview mirror just as the ambulance doors closed on Gary Binder's body. A chill touched his spine.

Whatever evil held sway over Timberline, he'd do whatever it took to keep it far away from Beth…even as she ran toward it.

When they got back to the hotel, the rental-car company had dropped off her replacement car. Duke walked around the car, examining it. He ran his hand along the roof. "Don't leave anything out on your seat this time."

"C'mon, Duke. We both know the vandal would've broken into my car with or without that bag on the seat. He was sending me a message."

"Thanks for the reminder. I'm going to get you a fresh container of pepper spray. At least you proved you know how to use it."

"Are you going to take off for your meetings?"

"After I ask the front desk about Binder. You coming?" Maybe he was stalling, but he didn't want to leave Beth alone. Funny how he'd done a complete one-eighty from yesterday—a few threats could do that.

"Sure, I'll come with you. My interviews can wait."

They walked into the lobby together, and Tammy, the receptionist at the check-in counter, looked up from her computer screen and waved. "Hello. Can I get you anything? I heard about your room, Ms. St. Regis, and we want to make your stay here hassle-free from here on out. The maid staff is being extra careful now."

"I appreciate that."

Duke rested his arms on the counter. "Tammy, do you know a local guy, Gary Binder?"

Her mouth formed an O. "I just heard. He's dead—hit-and-run accident. Who could do that? I never liked Gary much, but you don't leave a dog to die in the street without stopping. Am I right?"

News did travel quickly in Timberline. "Absolutely. I hope they catch the bastard and string him up."

Her eyes popped. "Wh…what did you want to know about Gary?"

"Did the hotel ever hire him to do any work around here?"

"Gary? No way. Management knew his reputation, even though Kendall Rush had given him a chance when she was here."

Beth cleared her throat. "Isn't Kendall Rush the sister of one of the Timberline Trio?"

"Twin." The clerk pulled the corners of her mouth down with two fingers. "She was out here to sell her aunt's house and got caught up with all the craziness with Wyatt Carson. But while she was here, she hired Gary to do some work at the house. I guess he did okay, but management here would still never hire him."

"Do you know why he'd have any reason to be at this hotel? In the parking lot?" Duke tipped his head in that direction. "We saw him out there, probably just before he got hit."

"Really?" Tammy's eyes got even bigger. "I don't know why he'd be here, just passing by, I guess." She licked her lips. "Do you think the sheriff's department is going to want to look at our security tapes of the parking lot?"

"Probably. In fact—" Duke slid his badge across the counter "—I wouldn't mind having a look myself."

"Okay. I know you're FBI and all, but can I call my manager first?"

"Sure." He glanced at Beth. "You can take off if you want, set up those interviews."

"I think I'd rather watch this video." She leaned in close, putting her lips next to his ear, and said in a low voice, "Why do you think Kendall Rush hired him?"

"Don't know. Maybe she felt sorry for him."

Tammy got off the phone. "My manager says it's okay."

She invited them behind the counter and into a small room. She hunched over a set of computer monitors and clicked through several files, launching a video. "This is from earlier today. How long ago did you see him?"

"Over two hours ago."

She cued up the tape, and after several minutes, Gary Binder with his green ball cap came into the frame, walking his bike.

Beth jabbed her finger at the display. "Is he talking to someone out of the picture?"

Binder kept looking over his shoulder, but Duke couldn't see his mouth moving.

"I'm not sure. Maybe he's just watching for cars as he comes into the parking lot, but he seems to have a purpose for coming into the lot."

"Yeah, he's looking at my rental."

After checking behind him once more, Binder wheeled up to Beth's rental car and poked his head inside the broken window. A minute later Duke and Beth appeared in the frame.

They watched a bit longer, but Binder never returned to the parking lot after they took off.

Tammy scrunched up her face. "Looks like he just wanted a closer look at your car."

"Why did he keep glancing over his shoulder? There's not that much traffic on the road." Beth stepped back from the monitors and folded her arms. "Because if there had been, someone would've seen the car that hit him."

"Maybe someone did." Duke backed out of the claustrophobic room. "Thanks, Tammy. I'll tell the sheriff's department about seeing Binder in the parking lot here, and they'll probably want to review that tape, too."

Her fingers flew across the keyboard as she closed down the recordings. "I just wish there was something on there. I suppose they told Gary's mom already. She's a tough, old lady, but Gary was her only kid."

"Sounds like the guy couldn't catch a break." He turned to Beth. "Are you taking off now? I'll be at the sheriff's station if you need me."

"And I'll be setting up shop somewhere to do some interviews."

"You could do them here in your hotel room, or maybe the hotel lobby."

"If I've learned anything from the show, it's that people feel more comfortable talking in their homes."

"Just don't go to Bill Raney's home to interview him." He pushed open the hotel door and they stepped outside.

"I'm not going to be interviewing people who don't want to talk to me."

"How do you know if they're being honest?" He aimed the key fob at his car and the horn blipped. "They could pretend and then change their story when they get you alone."

"I'm only going to talk to the ones I gave cards to last night—Chloe the waitress and a few senior citizens. You don't think I have anything to fear from them, do you?"

"Be careful, Beth. If the same person who's warning you is the same person who hit Binder, he's just added murder to his résumé."

She rubbed her arms. "If someone did kill Gary, it's because he knew something. I know nothing."

"Not yet and maybe you should keep it that way."

"I'll be careful, Duke." She got behind the wheel of her new rental and pressed her palm against the glass.

He waved back. He had no choice but to leave her.

When he drove past the accident scene, the ambulance had already left with its sad cargo and one cop car remained, directing traffic.

Was Binder's death really connected to his willingness to speak up about the Timberline drug trade twenty-five years ago? Deputy Unger had mentioned tweakers being responsible for the vandalism of Beth's car. Did that mean the drug culture was alive and well in Timberline today?

He hoped all Beth got today was half-baked stories of Wyatt Carson. She didn't need to be involved in this case any more than she already was.

He'd almost been relieved to hear about her ulterior motive for being in Timberline. Maybe once she found out she wasn't Heather Brice, she'd give up on this story.

And if she *was* Heather Brice? What could be the danger in that? She'd leave Timberline, reconnect with her long-lost family who now resided in Connecticut and live happily ever after...or not.

Duke's cop radar gave him an uneasy feeling about that scenario. What if the Brice family rejected her, too? She talked a tough game, but she had a vulnerable side she tried hard to mask.

He could speed up the entire process by requesting DNA from the Brices as part of this investigation. They wouldn't even have to know about Beth and her suspicions. Once Beth knew the truth—one way or the other—she could stop sleuthing around Timberline.

He pulled up to the sheriff's station and entered the building with a few file folders tucked under his arm. He hadn't met the new sheriff yet, who was probably just getting up to speed.

Deputy Unger greeted him at the desk.

"I'm here to see Sheriff Musgrove."

"The sheriff's expecting you. Go on back, first office on the right."

Duke thanked him and made his way to the sheriff's office. He tapped on the open door and a big man rose from the desk dominating the office.

"Agent Harper? I'm Sheriff Musgrove."

Duke leaned over the desk and shook the sheriff's hand. "Nice to meet you, Sheriff. What do you think of the hit-and-run accident that killed Gary Binder?"

"That's what I like about you fibbies." He smacked his hand against his desk. "Get right to the point. I think Gary Binder was a junkie who was probably riding his bike recklessly on the road, maybe even riding under the influence, if you know what I mean."

Duke studied the man's red face with a sinking feeling in the pit of his stomach. Clearly he had a sheriff on his hands who didn't have the ability to think out of the box. Too bad Sheriff Sloane wasn't still in the position. He'd heard nothing but high praise of Sloane from Agent Maxfield, who'd worked the Wyatt Carson case.

Duke took a deep breath. "You don't find it coincidental that Binder had just given us some information about the Timberline drug trade during the initial kidnappings?"

"The world is filled with coincidences, Harper. I don't find a junkie getting hit by a car all that coincidental."

Duke shoved his hands into his pockets and hunched his shoulders. "By all accounts, Binder was in recovery, hadn't touched drugs in over a year."

"Once a junkie, always a junkie." Musgrove sliced his big hands through the air. "Is that the course you're going to follow on this case, Harper? Are you going to dig up Timberline's sordid past?"

"No town, big or small, is exempt from drugs, Sheriff." Duke narrowed his eyes. "Are you one of the contingents that would rather not have the spotlight on Timberline?"

"Is it a contingent? I'll be damned. I know the town has worked hard to come back from its failures, and we're on the cusp of something great. I plan to work with the mayor and the town fathers to get it there."

Duke's gaze tracked over the sheriff's head to the awards and commendations on the wall, illustrating a career bouncing from agency to agency. He knew law-enforcement types like this guy, scrambling to secure the highest pension with the least amount of work, kissing ass along the way.

He'd have to report back to Mick that Sheriff Musgrove would be more of a hindrance than a help for this cold case.

His eyes dropped to the sheriff's face. "You weren't here during the Carson copycat kidnappings, were you?"

"No, I was over in Spokane. I read about it, though. Crazy SOB. I was hired in after Sheriff Sloane left for Phoenix—took off with that sister of one of the Timberline Trio. Talk about getting wrapped up in the job." He shook his head.

Musgrove would never be one to get too wrapped up in the work. Put in the hours and go home. Duke never understood guys like that.

For him, the work was a calling, a duty. It had been like that for his partner, Tony DeLuca, too. Guys on the other side never got it.

"I understand Sheriff Sloane's daughter was the final kidnap victim."

"Yeah, yeah. Tough break. I guess he couldn't handle it." Musgrove puffed out his chest as if he could handle anything. "Deputy Unger was here for the copycat kidnappings and sat in on the interview with Binder. He's out front if you want to talk to him. Otherwise, you have free rein here, Agent Harper. Our files are your files, and we'll get you that accident report on Binder if you're interested."

"I am. Thanks, Sheriff Musgrove."

They shook hands again and Musgrove sank heavily behind his desk and returned to his computer. Duke didn't have a clue what the man was looking at, but he could guarantee it wasn't work related.

Duke sauntered up front and stopped at Unger's desk. "Can I ask you a few questions about Gary Binder and the whole Wyatt Carson case?"

"Sure." Unger glanced over his shoulder. "Maybe we can do this over coffee."

Duke got the hint.

"Sheriff Musgrove, Agent Harper and I are going out for coffee to discuss the Binder interview."

The sheriff called from his office. "Did you get those reports done yet?"

"Been on your desk for two hours, sir." Unger rolled his eyes at Duke.

The sound of shuffling papers came from the office. "Got 'em. Keep me posted, Deputy."

"I'll do that, sir."

When they stepped out of the station, Unger tilted his head from side to side, as if cracking his neck.

"The guy's a pain, huh?"

"I'm not gonna bad-mouth my superior, but he's no Coop Sloane."

"I heard good things about Sloane from Agent Maxfield."

"That just proves how good he was, since he and Maxfield didn't always see eye to eye."

"That happens a lot between the FBI and local law enforcement. It's a testament to both of them that they were able to work together and nail Carson."

They'd walked half a block and Unger pointed ahead. "Buy you a coffee?"

"Sure."

A couple of people on laptops huddled at tables and an older gentleman looked up from his paperback when they walked in.

Duke and Unger ordered their coffee and sat across from each other at a table by the window.

Duke stretched out his legs and popped the lid off his cup. "What do you think about Binder's death?"

"I think it's damned strange." Unger took a sip from his cup. "I overheard Musgrove and he's just wrong about Binder. Whatever the guy was into in his past life, he was clean and sober in this one."

"Do you think someone targeted him for his revelations about the Timberline drug trade twenty-five years ago?"

"Seems pointless, doesn't it? We already interviewed him and he told us everything he knew. No point in killing him now."

"Unless he didn't tell you everything. Maybe there was

more to come and someone wanted to make sure he kept his mouth shut."

"The thought did cross my mind." Unger tugged on his earlobe. "It's funny that it happened after you showed up and after that TV host came to town."

Duke's pulse jumped. "What do you know about reaction to *Cold Case Chronicles* delving into the Timberline Trio case?"

"It's divided. You have one faction who wants their fifteen minutes of fame and another that's worried about the town's rep and doesn't want this case being rehashed every five years. Most folks want to move on. The families aren't even here anymore."

"Do you think Beth St. Regis is in any danger?"

"Honestly, if she wants my advice, it's not worth it. I don't think the current residents of Timberline are going to be able to give her any juicy new info about the case. She should find herself another one. I've watched that show before, and she can do a lot better than this."

"Yeah, I've been telling her to move on to something else, but the woman is stubborn."

Especially since she thought Timberline was the key to her past. Duke was still considering ordering DNA from the Brices just to settle this thing for Beth one way or the other.

In fact, that idea was sounding better and better.

Because as much as he wanted Beth right here in Timberline by his side, he had a cold dread that something bad was on the horizon.

Chapter Eight

Beth positioned her video camera on the tripod and smiled at Gail and Nancy. "Could you just start by saying your names?"

Gail jabbed a finger toward the camera. "Does this mean we're going to be on TV?"

Beth gritted her teeth behind her smile. "We shoot a lot of footage, Gail. If we can use it for the story, we'll put it on the show."

She patted her gray perm and smiled. "I'm Gail Fitzsimmons."

Leaning into Gail's space, Nancy said, "And I'm Nancy Heck."

"You don't need to lean over, Nancy. The camera is capturing both of you." Beth cleared her throat. "Did you both know the victims' families?"

Gail answered first. "My daughter used to babysit the twins sometimes."

Beth's heart banged against her rib cage. "Did she babysit Heather Brice, too?"

"Heather was too young. My daughter was seventeen at the time and wasn't interested in sitting toddlers or babies. Kayla and Kendall were older—five-year-olds—potty trained, talking."

"She wasn't babysitting them the night Kayla was kidnapped, though."

"Thank God, no. The parents had left the girls with their aunt. I don't know why. Cass was always a little scatter-brained. Don't you think so, Nancy?"

"Oh, yes, scatterbrained." Nancy seemed transfixed by the camera.

"Is Wendy Simons's family still here?" Beth scribbled on the pad of paper in front of her.

"The girl who was babysitting Heather Brice?" Gail cocked her head at Nancy. "I don't think so. Any of the Simons family around, Nancy?"

"They had a lot of children in that family. That's why Wendy would babysit the little ones. She was the second oldest in her family and helped her mother with her younger siblings."

"I know that, but are any of them still around? That's what Beth's asking."

Nancy reddened to the roots of her silver hair. "I… I don't know about that. I don't think so."

"What was the speculation at the time of the kidnap-pings?" Beth directed her question to Gail because she was clearly the ringleader and had probably just fright-ened Nancy into permanent silence.

"With the first one, Kayla, the police actually thought it was the father for a while." Gail affected a stage whis-per. "The parents were having troubles."

"But once Stevie Carson was kidnapped, they realized it was something more…more sinister." Nancy placed both hands over her heart.

Gail rolled her eyes at the camera. "I don't know about you, but a father kidnapping or killing his own child is pretty sinister."

"Gail Fitzsimmons, I didn't say it wasn't. Why do you have to twist my words?"

"I understood what she meant, Gail." Beth waved her

hands. "Were there any troubles in Stevie's family...or Heather's?"

Nancy had regained her composure and some confidence. "There were always problems in Stevie's family. Maybe that's why Wyatt turned out like he did. But Heather's family? Perfect."

Beth's gaze darted to Gail, waiting for her to disagree with her friend.

But she nodded with a smile on her face. "The Brices were a perfect family, weren't they? The parents adored each other and their children. It was lovely to see and so sad...after."

Beth's nose stung. A perfect family who adored their kids—just the kind of family she'd always dreamed of.

"Yoo-hoo, Beth?"

She snapped out of her daydream. "Yes, go on."

"Do you have any more questions? Because we have a lot more where that came from."

The ladies hadn't told her much she didn't already know, but she could sit and listen to stories about the perfect Brice family all day.

She continued with Gail and Nancy for another forty-five minutes. She'd gotten some colorful quotations from them she might be able to use in the story, but their answers hadn't done much to clear up the mystery—or to solidify her belief that she was Heather Brice.

Beth ended the interview and Nancy sent her away with a tin of cookies and an implied promise of more if their faces wound up on TV. She sent Duke a quick text to let him know where she was, since he'd seemed so concerned when she'd left.

She didn't mind one bit.

Munching on a snickerdoodle, Beth drove to her next appointment at Chloe Rayman's apartment in a new development near the Evergreen Software headquarters. She brought the cookies with her to Chloe's door.

Chloe opened at her knock in full makeup, the ruffle at her low neckline fluttering. "Hello. I'm ready for my close-up, as they say."

"Well, then, let's get set up." She stuck out the tin. "Cookie? They're from Nancy Heck."

"Nancy's famous for her snickerdoodles, but I'll pass. I just brushed my teeth."

Probably flossed and whitened while she was at it.

Beth set up the camera on the tripod and sat in a chair across from Chloe on the sofa. "State your name, please."

"Chloe Rayman. Six eighty-two Treeline Boulevard, number five, Timberline, Washington." She clapped a hand over her lipsticked mouth. "Maybe I shouldn't put all of my personal information out there on TV."

"We'll…ah…edit that out." Beth crossed her legs and took a deep breath. This was gonna be a long interview.

For the next half hour Beth allowed Chloe to chatter on about Wyatt Carson. She had very little insight into the man or what made him tick, and he hadn't talked to her about his brother at all. The interview was worthless to the show and worthless to Beth's personal quest.

As she was trying to think of a way to cut things short, a knock on the door had Chloe gasping and jumping from the sofa.

"That's my boyfriend, Jason. He's really jealous, so I don't want him to know I've been talking about Wyatt."

"Of course." Beth turned off the camera. "I think I got everything I needed."

Chloe ran to get the door as Beth collapsed the tripod and shoved her notebook into her bag. She glanced over her shoulder as a compact man swept Chloe into a big hug. She met his gaze across the room and he released his girlfriend.

"Sorry. I didn't know you had company."

Chloe waved her hand toward Beth. "This is Beth St. Regis with that *Cold Case Chronicles* show. When she found out I used to know Wyatt Carson, she practically begged to interview me. Beth, this is my boyfriend, Jason Foster."

Jason tucked his shoulder-length dark hair behind one ear. "Hey, Beth."

"Nice to meet you, Jason. I was just leaving." She held out the tin. "Cookie?"

"Thanks." He took the tin from her and popped the lid. "You interviewed Nancy Heck."

"Her snickerdoodles have quite a reputation."

He took a bite of a cookie and brushed some crumbs from his chin. "You have a lot of people up in arms over this story."

"Are you one of them?"

He shrugged. "Doesn't bother me, but the elders are buzzing."

"Elders?" She hitched her bag over one shoulder.

"Jason's Quileute and they're kind of hinky about the Timberline Trio case."

"I met a teenage boy in the woods who told me the same thing. What is it about the case?"

"You got me." He pointed to the tin he'd placed on Chloe's coffee table. "Can I have another cookie?"

"Sure. I suppose anyone who did know wouldn't be willing to talk to me about it."

"Probably not, at least not the old folks."

"And the young folks, like you, probably don't know why it's a taboo topic."

"I sure as hell don't, but my cousin might have a clue." He brushed his hands together. "She's a shaman for the tribe, so certain customs and beliefs have been handed down to her more than the rest of us."

"Does she live in Timberline?"

"Yeah, and she happens to be in town. She travels a lot for her shows."

"Shows?"

Chloe curled her arm around Jason's waist. "Scarlett's an artist, has art shows all over the world."

"That's impressive." Beth's skin had begun to tingle with excitement. A shaman? Someone who knew about the case? Maybe she could help Beth with her own personal agenda.

"Do you think your cousin…?"

"Scarlett. Scarlett Easton."

"Do you think Scarlett would be willing to talk to me?"

"Probably. Her studio's out past the north side of town. You can tell her I sent you."

"Would you mind giving me her number?"

Jason pulled a wallet from his back pocket. "I think I have one of her cards. She only has a cell phone and reception isn't great out there, but you can give it a try."

He fanned out several cards between his fingers and plucked one from the bunch. "Here it is."

Beth scanned the black card with a reprint of a watercolor nature scene splashed on the front. "If this is her work, it's beautiful."

"Yeah, that's one of her more normal works. She does landscapes and then some freaky modern art—that's the stuff that gets her the shows and some big money. You couldn't pay me to hang some of that stuff in my living room."

"Don't tell Scarlett that." Chloe poked Jason's heavily tattooed arm.

Beth held up the card. "Thanks, Jason. In case I can't reach her by phone, can you give me directions to her place?"

"Chloe, do you have paper and a pen?"

"Will the back of an envelope work?" She took two

steps toward her small kitchen and grabbed an envelope and pen from the counter, which she handed to Jason.

He squatted down next to the coffee table and sketched out a map. "Scarlett got all the artistic talent in our family, but if you head this way off the main road, you'll see an access road next to a mailbox that's all painted. Follow that and you'll run into Scarlett's place."

Looking at the map, Beth wrinkled her nose. "Do I need four-wheel drive to get there?"

"Nah, it's remote but the access road to the cabin is gravel."

Beth tucked the makeshift map in her back pocket. "Do you guys want the cookies or maybe I should bring them to Scarlett?"

"We'll take 'em." Jason grabbed the tin and hugged it to his chest. "Scarlett's a vegan or vegetarian or something and doesn't touch the stuff."

"I think you're exaggerating to get cookies." Chloe rolled her eyes at Beth.

"You can keep them anyway." Beth hitched the tripod beneath her arm. "Thanks for your time, Chloe."

Jason got the door for her. "Can I help you carry anything to your car?"

"I got it, thanks."

Beth loaded up the car and, seated in the driver's seat, pulled out her phone. She tapped in Scarlett's number and it went straight to voice mail.

"Scarlett, my name is Beth St. Regis. I'm the host of *Cold Case Chronicles*, and I'm in town to do a story about the Timberline Trio. Your cousin Jason Foster told me you might be able to give me some insight into the Quileute view of the crime. Would love to talk to you."

Beth left her number and checked her texts. Nothing from Duke. He must still be busy with the sheriff's department.

She'd give Scarlett an hour or so to get back to her and then maybe she'd head out to her place in case Scarlett never got her message.

She decided to try Sutter's again for lunch and brought her laptop into the restaurant with her.

The place buzzed with a lunch crowd from Evergreen Software, by the looks of their khakis, pocket protectors and firm grips on their electronic devices.

Beth flagged down the hostess. "Can I get a table for one?"

"Your best bet is a seat at the bar. We serve a full lunch menu at the bar."

"Perfect." Beth hoisted her laptop case over her shoulder and wended her way through the tables to the bar. Heck, she fit right in with her laptop.

She hopped up on a stool and opened her case. As she pulled out her laptop, the bartender placed a menu to the side of it.

"Are you ordering lunch?"

"Yes, and I'll have a cup of hot tea."

"Coming right up." The bartender ducked beneath the counter and clinked a mug on the mahogany bar. "You know Bill Raney wasn't serious about those threats, right?"

Beth focused on the woman's face and realized she'd been tending bar last night when Duke had confronted the loudmouthed Raney.

"Did I think he really wanted to tar and feather me? No. What's your name?"

"Serena Hopewell. And, no, I wasn't here twenty-five years ago." She poured a stream of hot water into Beth's cup.

"Why are you coming to Bill's defense, Serena?"

She shrugged. "He's been having a tough time lately. He's been drinking at this bar way too much. The cops questioned him about a few things this morning, and he doesn't need any more trouble."

"I didn't accuse Bill of anything, but I had a couple of…incidents and his name came up with the deputies." She dunked her tea bag in the water. "They were probably just following up. I don't think he's suspect number one."

"It was enough to get him in trouble with his wife, but that doesn't take much these days." Serena tapped the menu. "Do you need a few minutes?"

"Yeah." As Beth flipped open the menu, someone nudged her shoulder.

"I thought you were going out to Scarlett's place." Chloe's high-pitched voice carried halfway around the restaurant as several people craned their necks to take in the bar.

Beth gave her a tight smile. "Thought I'd have some lunch first, and I did leave her a message."

"Good luck with that. Scarlett likes to keep to herself when she's in town."

Jason came up behind his girlfriend. "Our table's ready. Oh, hey, Beth. Any luck with my cuz yet?"

"Left her a message, will probably pay her a visit this afternoon."

"That's probably the best way to get her attention." He took Chloe's hand. "C'mon, babe. We got a table in Austin's section."

When Beth looked up from her menu, she met Serena's eyes.

The bartender lifted one eyebrow. "You've been busy."

"It's my job. I'm here to work." She closed the menu and held it out. "I'd like the soup-and-sandwich combo— veggie chili and grilled chicken."

"You got it."

Beth flipped up her laptop and checked email. She answered an inquiry about a previous story, replied to an anxious message from Scott and opened a document to take some notes about the two interviews today.

When her lunch arrived, she checked her phone again. Nothing from Scarlett and nothing from Duke.

She took a bite of her sandwich, her teeth crunching through the grilled sourdough. Ever since Jason had told her about his cousin's extrasensory abilities, Beth's mind had been toying with a plan.

She'd seen a hypnotist a few times to try to uncover buried memories about her past. That was where she'd seen visions of the forest, which had evoked such cold terror. But she'd gotten no further with the hypnotist. Someone like Scarlett Easton might be able to help her uncover even more. She had to try…if Scarlett was willing.

She finished her lunch, and as she was slipping her laptop back into its case, a man took the bar stool next to hers.

"Give me that River IPA, Serena."

Beth slid a gaze to her left and Jordan Young caught her eye.

"Hello there, Ms. St. Regis. How's your story going?"

"It's going."

Serena put the beer in front of Young. "Little early in the day for alcohol, isn't it?"

"Rough morning, sweetheart." He raised the glass to Serena and took a sip. "I feel like I need to make up for my friend Bill's boorish behavior, Ms. St. Regis. I'd be happy to talk to you about the Timberline Trio case sometime. I was here—" he patted the top of his head "—with a little more hair."

"I'd be interested in what you have to say, and you can call me Beth."

"Pretty name. And you can call me Jordan."

"Thanks, Jordan."

She slipped off the stool just as Serena hunched toward Jordan. "What do you think about the hit and run that killed Gary?"

Beth didn't get a chance to hear what Jordan thought about Gary as she headed for the door, anxious to meet with Scarlett now that she'd decided on a plan.

When she got to her rental car, she checked all the doors and windows—nothing today. She loaded her laptop in the trunk and pulled Jason's map from her pocket.

When she sat behind the wheel, she flattened the envelope on her thigh and memorized the first few directions.

She made the turn from the main road and passed several houses and access roads until she reached the one with the mailbox painted with chickens. Why chickens?

She turned her rental onto the access road, her tires crunching the gravel and her car rocking back and forth. She drove into a tunnel of trees, feeling the chill as her world darkened.

Suddenly the road ended, but she did see the peak of a roof beyond the tree line. She would've needed a four-wheel-drive vehicle to get close to Scarlett's cabin, but the road had ended within walking distance and a path cut through the trees.

She got out of the car and slammed the door behind her. She glanced at the trunk, where she'd stashed her laptop. Duke had warned her about leaving her stuff in the car, but at least it was out of sight. Who would be out here in the middle of the woods, anyway?

Tugging on her down vest, she headed toward the cabin, her boots crunching through the underbrush.

She took one big step over a fallen log. As something whizzed past her ear, she heard a crack in the distance. She yelled, "Hey," as she fell to the forest floor on her hands and knees.

That was a gunshot—and she was the target.

Chapter Nine

Duke heard the report of a rifle from his open window. Beth could be out there.

He stepped on the gas pedal of his SUV and the car tore across the road, spewing gravel in its wake.

He almost plowed into the back of Beth's car. He lurched to a stop behind the rental and bolted from the car.

"Beth?"

"I'm here. Be careful. Some idiot is shooting a rifle."

"Are you okay?"

"I'm on the ground about twenty feet in front of my car."

Duke hunched forward in case the hunter—or whoever it was—decided to squeeze off any more shots.

He spotted Beth, still crouched on the ground, her eyes wide and her face pale.

"I yelled when I heard the shot and dropped to the ground. I recognized it right away, of course."

"Did you see anything? A hunter? I know it's hunting season right now."

"What the hell is going on?" A woman's voice floated out from the cabin.

Duke cupped a hand around his mouth. "Someone's taking shots out here."

She called back. "Everyone okay?"

"Yes." Beth started to rise. "Do you think it's safe?"

"Even those idiot hunters should know by now we're humans and not some defenseless beast."

Duke reached Beth's side and helped her to her feet.

She grabbed his arm for support. "What are you doing here?"

"Stopped by Sutter's and Jason told me you were planning to see his cousin this afternoon." With his arm around her, he led her to a small clearing where a woman with long, black hair stood in front of a rustic cabin, her hands wedged on her hips.

"And who the hell are you two?"

"Are you Scarlett Easton?" Beth brushed off the knees of her jeans and pushed her hair from her face.

"Who wants to know?" The woman stood even taller, as if challenging them to take one more step.

"I'm Beth St. Regis. Your cousin Jason gave me your number. I tried calling, and I left a voice mail but Jason said you don't always get reception out here."

The woman tossed back her head, and her mane of black hair flipped over one shoulder. "I'm Scarlett Easton, and I don't know why my cousin seems to think I need company, but since some moron almost shot you on my property, come on in."

They followed Scarlett to a wide, wooden porch, almost a deck, and Duke stomped his boots on the first step. "I'm Duke Harper. Does that happen a lot with hunters? Potshots in the forest?"

As Scarlett pushed open her front door, she tilted her head. "Happens a lot around here."

Duke exchanged a glance with Beth as they followed Scarlett into her place. Did that mean the shot wasn't meant for Beth?

Scarlett Easton didn't seem like good interview material for Beth, and it didn't seem as if she wanted anyone on her property. So why had Beth come here?

Beth pointed to a cell phone on a table that had been carved from a tree stump. "Are you going to call the sheriff's department?"

"Reception isn't good today." Scarlett dipped to pick up her phone. "If I didn't get your call, what makes you think I can get a call out to the cops?"

Duke tried his own phone and received a No Service message. "She's right."

"But if you could tell that idiot Sheriff Musgrove someone was shooting a rifle, too close to the road, I'd appreciate it."

Duke dragged a hand across his mouth, wiping away his smile. She had Musgrove pegged already and he hadn't been on the job even two months.

"Can I get you something? Water? Soda? Stiff shot of whiskey?" Scarlett jerked her chin toward Beth. "You look as white as a sheet."

"Maybe some water." Beth placed her hands on her cheeks. "That bullet flew right past my ear."

"Idiots." Scarlett shook her head and asked Duke, "Anything for you?"

"No, thanks."

Scarlett cranked on the faucet in the kitchen and filled a glass with water. "The stuff from the tap is actually better than the bottled stuff. Ice?"

"Just the water."

Scarlett handed the glass to Beth. "So what brought you to my doorstep? You friends with Jason?"

"I just met Jason today." Beth took a gulp of water, and her gaze darted to Duke's face. "I host a television show called *Cold Case Chronicles*."

"Never heard of it."

Duke scanned the decor of the cabin—a mix of hand-carved furniture, Native American crafts and original artwork—an explosion of colors and textures that overwhelmed the senses. A bookshelf took up one wall and hardback books and paperbacks jockeyed for space on the crammed shelves…but no TV.

Beth took a deep breath. "It's a reality TV show where we investigate cold cases."

"Let me guess." Scarlett raised her eyes to the beamed ceiling. "You're doing a story on the Timberline Trio."

Beth licked her lips. "Jason told me the Quileute are suspicious about the case. He told me you would have some insight into that."

"Jason thought I'd be willing to sit down with a reality TV show and discuss our Quileute heritage?" She snorted, the nostrils of her delicate nose flaring. "He must be smoking the good stuff these days."

Duke watched Beth, uncharacteristically hesitant. She should be halfway to convincing Scarlett an interview would be the best thing that ever happened to her. There had to be something more to this visit to Scarlett.

"I understand that." The glass of water Beth brought to her lips trembled. "That's not really why I'm here."

Duke's eyebrows shot up. "It's not?"

"It's not?" Scarlett echoed him.

"Can we sit down?" Beth hovered near a curved love seat.

"All right." Scarlett grabbed what looked like a hand-painted pillow and dropped into a chair, dragging the pillow into her lap. "Just let me warn you. I'm not doing anything related to some reality TV show, and I'm not exploiting my tribe's traditions and customs."

Normally, Duke would perch on the arm of a chair but didn't want to destroy anything in this room and end up paying thousands of dollars to replace it. He sat on the edge of the love seat, next to Beth.

"What I'm going to ask you has nothing to do with the show. It's about me."

"Let's hear it." Scarlett tapped the pointed toe of her cowboy boot.

Beth squared her shoulders. "I have a mysterious past. I was adopted, but my adoptive parents refused to tell me where I came from, and my birth certificate has their names as my biological parents."

"Go on." Scarlett drew her dark brows over her nose.

"Anyway, I tried hypnosis a few times to try to reveal any memories, but all I got was a cold terror associated with the vision of a forest."

Duke folded his arms over a niggling fear in his chest. Beth wanted Scarlett Easton to perform some ritual mumbo jumbo on her.

Scarlett held up one finger. "Hypnosis can really only work with the memories that are already there. I doubt you have any memories of being a baby."

"That's my problem. Even if I could dig up my earliest memories, they're not going to tell me who I am or where I came from."

"Right. So, what are you doing in Timberline? I'm known as an artist, not a Quileute shaman. You didn't come here for me."

Duke held his breath and tried to catch Beth's eye, but she'd started down a path and there was no turning back.

"I think I'm Heather Brice."

Scarlett whistled. "Are you kidding me?"

"A variety of sources led me to Timberline—that Pacific Chorus frog, the scenery and my response to it, and the missing children. I just feel it."

"Tell me all of it." Scarlett shoved off the chair. "But I need to get comfortable first. Duke, do you want something to drink? A beer? A shot of whiskey?"

"Whiskey? Ah, no, but I'll take a beer. I have a feeling I'm gonna need it."

Scarlett went into the kitchen, her long hair waving

down her back. She returned with a bottle of beer, which she handed to him, and her arm around a bottle of whiskey with her index finger and thumb pinching two shot glasses together. She put them on the tree table, filled each one about halfway with the amber liquid and then gave one to Beth.

"Tell me everything." Scarlett held up her shot glass and Beth touched it with hers.

They both downed the whiskey in one gulp.

Beth launched into her story—the same one she'd told him, except she hadn't mentioned the hypnotherapy.

Scarlett interrupted her here and there to ask a question or inject a comment. She was seriously considering helping Beth.

"You don't still have the original frog, do you?"

"No. I remember having that frog as a child and it's in my earliest pictures, but I don't know what my parents did with it. They probably threw it away."

"Do you have anything else from that time period?"

Beth nodded. "A locket."

Duke jerked his head to the side. That was news to him. She'd never told him about that, but then, their relationship hadn't progressed to the stage where they'd known everything about each other.

He'd broken it off when he discovered he couldn't trust her, but now he was beginning to see why Beth might've found it difficult to be completely open with anyone.

"You're sure the locket is from the time before your adoption?"

"I always had it. It's not the kind of thing you'd give to a toddler and it's not something the Kings, my adoptive parents, would've ever given to me."

"They didn't discuss the locket with you?"

"My mother just told me it was mine and that someone had given it to me when I was a baby."

"Do you have it with you?"

"It's in my hotel room. Is it important?"

"What is it you're asking me to do, Beth?"

"I want you to use your...sensitivity to help me confirm that I'm Heather Brice. Can you do that?"

"There are certain rituals I can perform. It might not be pleasant."

"For me? I can handle it."

"For me." Scarlett tipped another splash of whiskey into her glass and tossed it back. "You're not going to be seeing into your past. *I'm* going to be seeing into your past."

Duke felt Beth stiffen beside him. "I can't ask you to do that, not if it's going to bring any harm to you."

"I didn't say it would hurt me. It's just not the most comfortable feeling in the world."

Duke hunched forward, elbows on his knees. "What do you get out of it? Money?"

Scarlett whipped her head around, dark eyes blazing. "I don't do this for money. Do you think I'm back on the rez doing magic tricks for the white man?"

Duke held up his hands. "Just trying to figure out why you'd put yourself out for a stranger."

Scarlett collected her hair in a ponytail and wrapped it around her hand. "Let's just say I have my own reasons."

"Is it true what Jason said about the Quileute being skittish about this case? I heard it from a teenage boy in the woods, too."

"Yes."

"Can I ask why?"

"There's a Quileute legend about the Dask'iya, or basket lady, who steals children in the middle of the night without a trace—and eats them. After the kidnappings, most of the elders were convinced Dask'iya had come back and was responsible for the kidnappings."

"But none of the kidnapped children were Native American."

"Didn't matter. The thought of Dask'iya's return struck terror in the hearts of the old folks." Scarlett bit the tip of her finger.

"But?" Duke swirled his beer in the bottle. "You think there's more to it?"

"I'm not sure why that fear led to such secretiveness in our community at the time of the kidnappings."

"You think the fear had its basis in something more… earthly?"

"You could say that." Scarlett stretched her arms in front of her. "If we decide to do this, Beth, I'm going to need that locket. By the way, is there anything in the locket? No baby pictures?"

"Hair."

"As in—" Scarlett wrapped a lock of dark hair around her finger "—this?"

"On one side of the locket, there's a lock of blond hair, and on the other side, there's a lock of reddish hair." Beth shook her head so that her strawberry blond hair danced around her shoulders. "Like this."

"Yours and someone else's."

"I guess so. Are you sure you want to do this, Scarlett?"

"Like I said, I have my own reasons, but you can do something for me."

"Name it."

"You and Mr. FBI Agent here can report that gunshot when you go back to town."

One corner of Duke's mouth tilted up. "How'd you know I was FBI?"

"I heard you were coming. I'm not quite the complete recluse that my family thinks I am, and Cody Unger's a friend of mine—you know, Deputy Unger."

"Good man."

"Anyway, I figure the word of an FBI agent might carry more weight than the word of a flaky artist who complains about the hunters all the time."

Beth collected the shot glasses and bottle of whiskey and rose from the love seat. "We would've reported that shot anyway since it almost hit me. Is there anything else we can do?"

"I'll think about it. You think about it, too, Beth. Think about it long and hard... You might not like what you discover."

BY THE TIME they returned to town, reported the shot in the woods and drove into the parking lot of their hotel, a light rain had begun to fall.

Duke unfurled an umbrella he had in his backseat and held it over her head as they dashed for the hotel entrance.

Duke's father may have been an abusive alcoholic, but Duke had learned chivalry from somewhere. Must've been his military training. Beth had been attracted to Duke immediately when she'd met him two years ago. But he'd been a man who'd demanded complete openness and she'd found it increasingly hard to deliver.

Maybe she'd stolen those files from his room to sabotage their relationship and growing closeness. Would she make the same mistake today? Would she even have a chance to make the same mistake?

Duke hadn't changed. Had *she*?

A blaze in the lobby fireplace warmed the room and created a welcoming ambience.

Gregory waved from behind the counter. "We have our complimentary spiced cider tonight—spiked and unspiked."

Beth headed for the cart next to the fireplace, calling over her shoulder, "If I grabbed a spiked cider after that shot of whiskey at Scarlett's, would you peg me as a lush?"

"Absolutely not as long as you don't judge me." Duke nodded at a couple sharing the sofa in front of the fire. "Mind if we join you?"

The man held up his cup. "The cider's good and not too strong."

Beth picked up two cups of cider from the tray and sank into the chair next to Duke's. "Here you go."

He took the cup from her and placed it on the table between them. "Good fishing today?"

The older man on the sofa glanced up. "How'd you know I was a fisherman?"

"You have the look."

"You mean the look of a fanatic?" The man's wife laughed.

"A dedicated sportsman. How about it? A good haul?"

"Decent."

"Do you hunt, also?"

Beth sat up straighter and watched Duke over the rim of her cup. As Scarlett suspected, Sheriff Musgrove had brushed off the shot in the woods. Deputy Unger indicated that it was protocol to post a notice to all hunters to stay in the areas designated for hunting.

"I've done some hunting, but not this trip." He half rose from the sofa and extended his hand to Duke. "Walt Carver, by the way, and this is my wife, Sue."

"I'm Duke Harper and this is Beth St. Regis."

Holding her breath, Beth waved, but neither Walt nor Sue showed a flicker of recognition. Must not be big reality TV fans.

"Why are you asking? Are you a hunter, Duke?"

"No, but my... Beth almost got hit by a stray bullet from a hunter."

Sue covered her mouth. "That's frightening. That's why I'm glad Walt gave it up."

"Some of these people don't follow the rules and accidents happen."

"How common are accidental shootings?" Duke blew on the surface of his cider before taking a sip.

"I don't have any statistics, but it happens." He patted his wife's knee. "I was always very careful, Sue. No need to worry."

Sue yawned. "For some reason, fishing all day makes me tired. I don't even know if I can muster enough energy to go out to dinner."

"We can order in." Walt took Sue's cup and placed them on the tray. "Nice to meet you folks. Will you be here long?"

"Not sure." Beth smiled. That depended on one beautiful shaman with an attitude.

They said good-night to the other couple and Duke moved to the sofa and stared into the fire, now a crackling orange-and-red blaze.

"What are you thinking?" She settled next to him.

"Wondering if that shot was an accident or intended for you."

"Scarlett seemed to think it had something to do with her." She held one hand to the fire, soaking up its warmth. "The sheriff indicated she called a lot to complain about the hunters and has even started a petition to push their hunting grounds farther north. She doesn't like the hunters and they don't like her."

Duke scratched his chin. "There have been other incidents at her place, but I don't like this, Beth."

"I don't like it, either, but I'm so close." She pinched her thumb and forefinger together. "With Scarlett's help I might finally discover who I am, where I came from."

"And like some fairy tale, you think your mother and father are going to be the good king and queen?"

"I'm prepared for anything, Duke."

"Are you?" He tapped his cup. "If someone could tell you tomorrow whether or not you're Heather Brice, would you leave Timberline?"

"If I *was* Heather, I'd contact the Brices immediately and arrange to see them in Connecticut—if they wanted to see me."

"If you're *not* Heather Brice?"

"I... I'd be back to the drawing board and I'd start following a different path." She leaned back against the sofa cushion and propped her feet on the table in front of her. Duke really wanted her to ditch the story, and this time it was for her benefit, not his.

"A different path away from Timberline and this case?"

"My producer, Scott, isn't all that excited about this case anyway. I could dump it and he wouldn't blink an eye. In fact, he'd be happy since he tried to talk me out of the case to begin with. If I dropped the show, it would make him look good in his father's eyes, since his dad owns the production company."

"Seems we all want you to drop the story, don't we?" He drained his cup of cider. "That was good. Do you want another or do you want to get something to eat?"

"I'm with Sue and Walt on this one. Maybe we can just order in. Pizza? Chinese?"

"Let's ask Gregory what he recommends."

Duke held out his hand and pulled her up from the sofa. She didn't want to let go, but he dropped her hand and put their empty cider cups on the tray.

"Gregory, my man. We're going to order in for dinner. Any recommendations?"

"There's a good pizza place down the road. They have pastas and salads, too." He pointed to the right of the reception desk. "There are a couple of menus there."

Beth reached for a red, white and green menu and held it up. "Vincenzo's?"

"That's it."

Duke joined her and hovered over her shoulder to look at the menu. "How come there's no restaurant on the premises?"

"I'm pretty sure Mr. Young made a deal with some of the town's restaurateurs to build the hotel only and not cut into their business."

"Jordan Young?" Beth ran her finger across the extra pizza ingredients.

"Yep. He developed the Timberline Hotel years ago. Bought the old one and renovated and expanded."

"He should update the security and get cameras in the hallways." Duke tapped the menu. "Pizza and salad?"

"That'll work." Beth shoved the menu into his hands. "You pick the pizza toppings and I'll grab a couple of twist-top bottles of wine."

"I have a better idea. I'll get the food and make a stop at a liquor store and pick up a decent bottle of cabernet."

"Sounds perfect. Do you want me to come with you?"

"I can handle it."

Beth tried to give him some cash, which he refused, and then went up to her room—the one right next to Duke's.

Not that she expected to get lucky tonight with that gorgeous man. She had a few things to tell him before they could reach that same level of intimacy they'd had before, which Beth had discovered hadn't been very deep.

Sleeping with a man didn't guarantee instant intimacy. She'd never had that level of intimacy with anyone before, but she'd come close with Duke. So close, the feeling had terrified her and she'd taken the surest route to torpedo the relationship.

She'd lied to Duke, betrayed him. He'd reacted as she'd expected him to—he dumped her. If she wanted him back, there could be no secrets between them.

Maybe tonight was the night—pizza, red wine and confidences.

When Beth returned to the room, she stepped into the shower and put on a pair of soft, worn jeans and the FBI Academy T-shirt Duke had given her two years ago. The shirt gave her confidence.

As soon as she turned on the TV, Duke knocked on the door. "Pizza man."

She peered through the peephole and opened the door. "I hope you got some paper plates and napkins."

"They're in the bag with the salad." He held up a bottle of wine. "Washington vineyard."

"This will be my third alcoholic beverage of the day. Really, this is unusual for me."

He placed the food on the credenza and turned to face her, his hands on his hips. "You don't have to excuse yourself just because my father was an alcoholic, Beth. Hell, you know I drink, too. I don't think a few drinks make you an alcoholic."

"I know that." She pulled the plates and napkins from the bag. "I just don't want you to get the wrong idea about me."

"I think I did have the wrong idea about you."

"I know." She popped open the plastic lid on the salad. "You thought you could trust me and I betrayed that trust."

"That's not it." He held up a corkscrew. "Bought a cheap one at the liquor store."

"What's not it?" She folded her arms across her stomach. Had he discovered something else about her?

"I've had plenty of time to think about what happened between us, and seeing you again and hearing your story has only confirmed what I'd begun to think about that time, about our relationship."

"Maybe I need some wine to hear this." Duke had uncorked the bottle, and Beth poured some of it into a plastic cup Duke had snagged from the cider setup in the lobby.

"It's nothing bad. I just didn't understand at the time that you took those files on purpose to push me away because we'd gotten too close, too fast."

The wine went down her throat the wrong way and she choked. She covered her face with a napkin. "Have you now added psychology to your other talents?"

"Tell me it's not true." He tugged at the napkin.

"It wasn't conscious at the time. I just really, really wanted those files."

"You could've asked me."

"You would've said no."

"Probably." He tore off a piece of pizza and dropped it onto a paper plate. "All this analysis is making me hungry."

She peeked at him over the rim of her plastic cup. "Is that your way of telling me you forgive me for that incredibly stupid act?"

"Hey, that incredibly stupid act did solve the case, didn't it?"

"Only because I didn't reveal that other piece of info to you that I got from my source."

"Are you trying to make yourself look bad?"

"I just want you to see me, warts and all…this time. I… If there is a this time."

Duke took a big bite of pizza instead of answering her and she let it drop.

He had a better handle on discussing this kind of stuff than most men she knew because he'd been through court-mandated therapy as a teen when his father had beaten his mother to death after he'd accidentally killed his younger sister.

Such tragedy and he'd risen from the ashes a strong man, a good man—and she could've had him if she'd been able to recover from her own tragedies.

They watched TV together, she from the edge of the bed and he from a chair he'd pulled up, and ate their salad and pizza. A meal had never tasted better, but she stopped at two cups of wine. She needed the relaxation but also needed a clear head for her confession.

Duke collected her plate and cup and stuffed them into the white plastic bag. "More wine?"

"No, thanks. Save it. I may need it after my session with Scarlett tomorrow."

"Tomorrow?" He checked his phone. "You set it up for tomorrow?"

"Expecting a text?"

"Work." He tossed the phone on the bed. "What time are you seeing Scarlett and when did you arrange this?"

"When you'd gone outside her place to look around. I'm bringing my locket and heading out there at dusk."

"At night? Really?"

"She works during the day and needs the natural light. She suggested it. At least it's not the witching hour."

"I don't think you'd better call Scarlett a witch. She'd go off on you for sure."

"I wasn't calling her a witch." She pointed to the pizza box. "Breakfast tomorrow morning?"

"Works for me."

Beth licked a crumb from the corner of her mouth. Now, if only they could settle the sleeping arrangements for tonight as easily as that. She could always make a suggestion, but she didn't want to push things.

Duke swiped his thumb across his phone again and placed it on the credenza. "I'll take the trash outside. You don't want to be smelling garlic all night."

He grabbed the white bag and left the room.

Beth blew out a breath. He didn't say "*we* don't want to be smelling garlic all night," so maybe he planned to go back to his own room.

She brushed some crumbs from the credenza into her palm just as Duke's phone vibrated. Was this the text he was expecting?

She spun the phone around to face her, touching the screen in the process. The phone was still unlocked from Duke's last usage.

The text message, from Mick Tedesco, sprang to life, and one word jumped out at Beth—*Brice*. Her eyes darted to the door and back to the phone.

She read the message aloud. "'The request to the Brices was sent and approved.'"

Pressing one hand to her heart, she stepped back. What request? Duke hadn't mentioned any request he'd made from the Brices. Did he plan to steal her thunder?

She heard the key at the door and retreated to the bathroom. How could she even ask him about it now without admitting she'd read his private text?

He stepped into the room. "That's better."

She poked her head out of the bathroom. "Would you mind taking the leftover pizza to your room when you leave?"

His step faltered for a second but he recovered quickly. "Sure. You want me to leave the wine here?"

"You can leave the wine." She ducked back into the bathroom and called out, "Don't forget your phone."

"Got it."

A few minutes later he stood at the bathroom door, his boots back on and holding the pizza box in front of him with the cell phone on top.

Holding her breath, her gaze darted to the phone. Had he checked his very important message about the Brices yet?

"I'll see you tomorrow, Beth. And don't even think about going to Scarlett's without me."

"Of course not." She smiled as she unwound about a foot of dental floss. "We're partners in crime, right?"

A small vertical line formed between his eyebrows. "Right. Good night."

"Good night. Thanks for the pizza and wine."

When the door closed behind him, she threw the second bolt into place and marched to the credenza. She uncorked the wine and poured herself another generous glass.

Then she sat cross-legged on the bed and took a big gulp. It was a good thing she hadn't revealed her final secret to Duke…because the man was keeping one of his own.

Chapter Ten

Duke dropped the pizza box in his room and unlocked his phone to read Mick's message. Releasing a breath, he stretched out on the bed and texted him back. Rush order?

A few minutes later Mick confirmed and Duke ate another piece of pizza to celebrate. He'd hoped to celebrate another way tonight, but Beth had made it clear that she'd expected him to spend the night in his own room. Maybe she hadn't bought his forgiveness-and-understanding shtick, even though he'd been dead serious.

He didn't blame her for not trusting him. As recently as two days ago he'd been railing against her for her actions two years ago. That was before he'd discovered her real purpose for being in Timberline.

He finished the pizza and got up to brush his teeth. He leaned forward and studied his face in the mirror.

Maybe Beth had it right. This time they should take things slow and easy and not jump to any conclusions about each other.

He could do that.

Could she?

DUKE SPENT THE next day in meetings with the local FBI office and on the phone with the Drug Enforcement Agency. He'd touched base with Beth a few times and she'd been busy conducting more interviews and visiting relevant sites like the house of Kayla Rush's kidnapping.

He just wanted to make sure she didn't go out to Scarlett Easton's house by herself. He didn't trust those hunters—or anyone else in this town.

He ended his day in the sheriff's station, shooting the breeze with Unger. Musgrove had gone golfing with the mayor and Jordan Young.

"The local hunters don't much care for Scarlett Easton?"

"She complains about them a lot. She just doesn't like hunting."

"They've done things like that before? Shoot close to her property?"

"Sure, but they've never come close to hitting someone, like they did with Ms. St. Regis."

"Yeah." Duke chewed the edge of his fingernail.

"Do you think it was on purpose?"

"I'm not sure. Maybe someone was trying to scare her off, like with the broken window and the frog head, but that's extreme."

"If the guy was a good shot, he wouldn't see it as extreme since he never intended for the bullet to hit its mark."

"Still, that could be attempted murder."

"You and I know that, but someone willing to take that chance in the first place—" Unger shrugged "—that might not occur to him."

"I told Beth I'd ask you about your mom, if she'd be willing to talk to her about the Brices and what happened twenty-five years ago."

"I'd hate for my mom to wind up on TV."

"I understand. What if I could guarantee that her interview wouldn't leave Beth's possession?"

"Then why would Beth want to interview my mother if she didn't plan to use it for the segment?"

Toying with the edge of a folder, Duke said, "Information."

"Is that why Beth was talking to Scarlett Easton? Information? Because I can't imagine Scarlett wanting to get involved with a TV show. I don't think she even watches TV."

"Just a different perspective. These shows collect all kinds of footage and info they never use."

Unger lifted his shoulders. "I'll see what I can do."

"Thanks, man." Duke checked his phone. Did five o'clock qualify as dusk? "I'm outta here. Keep me posted on any new developments in the Gary Binder hit and run."

"Will do."

When Duke pulled into the parking lot of the Timberline Hotel, his shoulders relaxed when he spotted Beth's rental car. He'd had a nagging feeling all day that she'd take off without him.

He waved to Gregory at the front desk, avoided Walt and Sue in the lobby and jogged up the two flights of stairs to Beth's room. As he knocked on the door, he called, "Beth, it's Duke."

She opened the door. "I saw Scarlett in town. We're meeting at seven."

"Do you want to get something to eat on the way?"

"I had a bite to eat in town. I'll knock when I'm ready to go. About thirty minutes?"

"I'll be ready."

She shut the door in his face.

Had she read his mind and his body language last night? He'd wanted to bed her and, up until last night, he'd thought she'd wanted the same thing.

Maybe he wouldn't get a second chance with Beth, but he still planned to make sure nothing happened to her on this wild-goose chase.

He'd had a big lunch with the FBI boys and figured he could skip dinner, anyway. He showered instead and changed out of his suit. He didn't know what to wear to a haunting, but he was pretty sure it wasn't a suit.

At around six forty-five, Beth tapped on his door.

He greeted her by jingling his car keys. "Let's take my SUV. It has four-wheel drive. Her place is remote, even by Timberline standards."

"Okay." She nervously toyed with a chain around her neck.

"Is that the locket?"

"This is it." She held it out from her neck with her thumb, where a gold heart dangled from the delicate chain.

As they hit the stairwell, Duke said, "I've worked with psychics a few times on cases. While they haven't solved anything for us, there's definitely something there."

"I hope Scarlett can tell me something. Even if it's some small connection to the Brices, it might be enough."

"Enough for what?" Duke pushed open the door to the lobby.

"Enough to warrant some communication with them, but like I said before, I don't want to give them any false hope."

"False hope is never good, especially in cases like this."

She tilted her head and shot him a quizzical look from beneath her lashes before she got into the car.

He started the car. "I'm guessing you didn't get to interview Jordan Young today."

"I didn't. How'd you know that?"

"I dropped by the sheriff's station to see Cody—Deputy Unger—and he told me Sheriff Musgrove was out playing golf with Young and the mayor." He snapped his fingers. "Mayor Burton. Have you met him yet?"

"Not yet. I spent my day videotaping different locations…and replacing my frog."

"You bought another?"

"I wanted to ask Linda, the shop owner, if anyone had come into the store after me or had asked about me later."

"Any luck?"

"Nothing suspicious, anyway. A few people chatted with her about the show, but these were people she knew. She was happy to sell me another frog, though."

"Are you going to keep this one under lock and key?" Duke made the turn off the main highway and the sky immediately darkened as the trees grew thicker.

"I'm going to guard him with my life."

He glanced sideways at her, expecting a smile, but Beth's jaw had a hard line that worried the hell out of him. How long had she been obsessed by this? He'd never seen this side to her two years ago.

As much time as they'd spent together, as many times as they'd made love, he'd never really known her.

The SUV bounced over the rough road and Beth clutched the locket against her throat.

"Are you having second thoughts? Because we can turn right around."

"No. Scarlett said it would be tougher on her than me."

"It's probably not going to be any picnic for you, either, especially if you discover something you weren't expecting."

"I have to do this."

"I know you do." He squeezed her thigh beneath the soft denim of her jeans. "And I'm gonna be right there with you."

She gave him a stiff nod.

He parked the car at the edge of the stand of trees circling Scarlett's house. He poked Beth in the arm. "Any more bullets start flying, hit the ground—and I'm only half kidding."

"Do you see me laughing?"

He kept an arm around Beth's shoulders as they approached the house, even though she'd stiffened beneath his touch. This meeting with Scarlett had put her on edge and he feared she'd drop over into the abyss.

As THEY REACHED the porch, Beth shrugged off Duke's arm. She didn't need a protector, especially one who kept important secrets from her. When was he going to tell her what he was doing with the Brices? Had he actually told them about her quest?

The heavy knocker that sported a bear's head gleamed under the porch light. Duke lifted it and tapped it against the plate several times.

Scarlett answered the door in a pair of black yoga pants and an oversize sweater that hung almost to her knees. "Did you bring the locket?"

"Right here." Beth held it out from her neck.

"Come in and have a seat by the fire." Her gaze raked Duke up and down. "Did that worthless sheriff tell you anything about the shot fired on my property yesterday?"

"He had a couple of deputies searching for a shell casing this morning, but that's about as efficient as searching for a needle in a haystack, and he sent a notice out to the hunters."

She tossed her long braid over one shoulder. "That figures. Do you want something to drink before we get started?"

"You girls aren't going to start tossing back whiskeys again, are you?" Duke raised one eyebrow and his mouth quirked into a smile as Scarlett gave a low chuckle.

Beth's gaze darted between Duke and Scarlett and something tightened in her chest. He liked her. What wasn't to like? The woman was gorgeous with her long, dark hair, mocha skin and sumptuous figure. Even the baggy sweater seemed to hug her curves.

The artist had an earth-mother figure, a body made for

childbearing. Beth ran her hands down her own slim hips and a sob caught in her throat.

"I'm drinking a special tea tonight." Scarlett put her hand on Beth's arm. "Can I get you a cup? You look pale."

"That would be nice, thanks."

"You—" Scarlett leveled a finger at Duke "—don't look like a hot-tea kind of guy. Would you like a shot of that whiskey?"

"I don't touch the hard stuff, but I could use a beer."

Scarlett called over her shoulder as she sauntered into the kitchen. "You might need another when this is all over."

Beth sat in a chair near the huge natural-stone fireplace and curled out her fingers to the flame. "Is this okay here?"

"I'm going to sit in front of the fireplace on the floor." She must've already brewed the tea because she came out of the kitchen carrying two steaming cups. "Do you want sugar or milk?"

"No, thanks." She took the mug from Scarlett and sniffed the slightly bitter aroma of the pale brown tea.

Scarlett put her own cup on the broad base of the fireplace and returned to the kitchen for Duke's beer. Then she settled on a rug in front of the fire and took a sip of tea.

"A... Are there some times that are better for you to do this than others?"

"Like a full moon or something?" Scarlett shrugged. "No. You have the gift or you don't."

Beth sucked some tea onto her tongue and wrinkled her nose. Maybe she should've gone with the sugar.

Scarlett studied her over the rim of her mug. "Doesn't taste very good, does it? It's an acquired taste. I make it myself from roots and berries—an old recipe handed down through the generations."

With trembling fingers, Beth reached for the clasp on her locket. "I suppose you want this."

Three tries and she still couldn't unlatch the necklace.

"Let me." Duke crouched beside her and brushed her hair from the back of her neck. His warm fingers against her nape caused a thrill of excitement to race through her body despite the occasion. His touch always caused an immediate reaction in her body.

"Got it." He held out his hand where the chain pooled in his palm. He leaned forward and dumped the necklace into Scarlett's outstretched hand.

"May I?" She paused, her thumbnail against the crease of the locket.

Beth nodded and Scarlett popped open the gold heart. She flattened it open between two fingers. "This could be your hair—this strawberry blond. The blond could even be your hair at another age."

"That'll help, though, won't it? To have some hair as well as the locket?"

"It might." Scarlett crossed her legs beneath her and stretched her arms toward the fire, her dark eyes glittering in the firelight. "There are a few rules we need to cover."

"Rules?" Beth glanced at Duke.

"No matter what happens, do not bring me out of my trance."

"You're going into a trance?"

"What did you expect?" Scarlett's dark eyebrows jumped to her hairline. "Did you think I was going to search for your locket on the internet?"

"But a trance? Is it dangerous?" Beth bit her lip.

"Draining, but not dangerous—unless you yank me out of it." Scarlett tugged on her braid. "No matter what happens, no matter what I say or do, even if it looks like I'm having some kind of seizure."

"Seizure? Oh, my God. I can't let you do this, Scarlett."

"I've already decided I'm doing it. Like I said, I have my own reasons."

Duke sat on the floor next to Beth's chair and curved

his hand around her calf. "Let her continue, Beth. Scarlett knows what she's doing."

"Listen to your man." Scarlett closed her eyes and cradled her mug. She took a long sip and placed it on the stone of the fireplace.

Her eyes opened to slits and she slipped her finger beneath the chain of the necklace and dangled it in front of the fire. The golden locket seemed infused with a flame as it swung from Scarlett's finger.

She curled her hand around the locket and held it in her fist. She exhaled slowly and her lids fell over her eyes.

Scarlett whispered something under her breath, but Beth didn't catch it. She raised her brows at Duke and he shook his head.

The whispers became a silent movement of the lips as Scarlett's knuckles turned white. Her head lolled back, her long braid almost touching the rug beneath her.

Scarlett's eyelids began flickering and her lips twitched.

Beth slid to the floor beside Duke, tucking her hand in the crook of his arm. She touched his ear with her lips. "I hope she's okay."

"I hope so, too."

Scarlett's chin dipped to her chest, her body still.

Beth whispered, "Did she fall asleep? Is this the trance she was talking about?"

Duke curled his arm around her waist and pulled her closer. "Shh. I don't know, Beth. I've never seen anything like this before."

Beth watched Scarlett's still form and it seemed as if the fire was swirling around her. Scarlett's long hair became the flames, dancing and curling around her face.

Beth put two fingers to her throbbing temple.

Duke whispered, "What's wrong?"

"I feel strange." She looked at the dregs floating in her cup. "Do you think that tea was some kind of drug?"

"What do you mean, like peyote or mushrooms?"

"I don't know." Beth ran her tongue along her dry teeth. "I feel funny."

"It is hot in here."

Scarlett gave a sharp cry and her head jerked back. Her lids flew open but her eyes had rolled back in her head.

"Duke!" Beth grabbed his hand. "Do something."

"You heard what she told us. We could actually do more harm than good if we interrupt her."

Scarlett brought one hand to her throat, clutching at it and gasping for breath.

Beth dug her nails into Duke's hand. She couldn't let this go on. What if something happened to Scarlett in this altered state?

Duke's arm tightened around her, as if he could read her thoughts. "Wait."

Scarlett gave another strangled cry and the hand not clutching the locket shot out. She grabbed Beth's upper arm, her grip like a vise. She pulled Beth toward her, toward the fire in the grate.

Duke held on to her, making her a rope in a tug-of-war.

"Let me go, Duke."

He released his hold on her and she allowed Scarlett to drag her beside her on the rug. Scarlett's hand slipped to Beth's and she laced her fingers with hers.

A flash jolted Beth's body. She could hear Duke's voice calling to her a million miles away as she traveled through darkness scattered with pinpoints of light. The heat from the fire had disappeared and a bone-chilling cold gripped her body. The blackness turned to a deep forest green, rushing and rustling past her.

Then it stopped. She jerked to a halt. The rushing sound became voices—loud, yelling, screaming, crying.

She smelled it before she saw it—metallic, pungent—

blood. So much blood, waves of it, slick, wet. A baby crying.

Beth gagged, ripping her hand from Scarlett's.

Scarlett dropped the locket and pressed her palms against either side of her head. "The blood. The blood. So much blood."

Duke lunged forward and hooked his hands beneath Beth's arms, hoisting her up and against his chest. "Are you all right? What the hell was that?"

Beth's eyes felt so heavy she could barely raise them to Duke's face. "Blood."

"Sit." He pushed her into the chair and then hunched over Scarlett. "Are you okay, Scarlett? Should I get you anything?"

"Water, bring us some water." She stretched out on her back, flinging one arm across her eyes.

A few minutes later Duke pressed a glass to Beth's lips. "Drink."

She gulped the water so fast it dribbled down her chin and she didn't even care. After she downed the glass, she looked up, blinking, clearing her vision.

Scarlett's eyes met hers. "You saw it, too, didn't you?"

Beth nodded.

Dragging his hands through his dark hair, Duke paced to the window and back. "What the hell just happened? Did you drag Beth into your vision? Did you drug her?"

"Hold on there, cowboy." Scarlett held up her index finger. "That tea is not a drug. Yes, it does enhance my visions, but I had no idea it would have any effect on Beth. That's never happened before."

"What's never happened before? You giving someone that witch's brew or you dragging someone into your trance?"

Scarlett pressed her lips into a thin line and then she flicked her fingers at Duke. "How are you feeling, Beth?"

"I feel fine, amazing actually. It was like an out-of-body experience."

"Can you please get Beth more water instead of blustering around the room?"

Duke's mouth opened, shut, and then he growled. He took Beth's glass and stormed off to the kitchen.

"You'll be fine, Beth. I'm sorry I grabbed your hand like that. I am telling the truth. I've never done that before, didn't even know it was a possibility."

"Never mind all that. What did we see?"

"You tell me. What did *you* see?"

Beth's lashes fluttered. "I saw… I smelled blood. I heard people yelling and screaming. I heard a child or a baby crying."

"Amazing." Scarlett shook her head. "That's what I got, too. You shared my vision."

"What does it mean, Scarlett?" Beth took the glass from Duke and gave him a small smile. It didn't seem like he liked Scarlett all that much anymore.

"What do you think it means?" Scarlett settled her back against the base of the fireplace.

"If it's connected to the locket I had before my adoption, it has something to do with my past. Could it be the scene of my kidnapping?"

"Whoa, wait a minute." Duke held out one hand. "There was no mention of blood at your kidnapping. There was no blood spilled at any of the kidnappings."

Beth tapped her water glass with one fingernail. "Could it just be a representation of the violence of my kidnapping, Scarlett?"

"I'm not sure about that. I guess so." She stood up and stretched. "Did you recognize the place?"

"The place?"

"The cabin. I'm pretty sure it was a cabin."

"Oh." Beth slumped back in the chair. "I didn't see a place, just the blood, the smells, the sounds."

"That's another problem. Heather Brice was kidnapped from her parents' house, which was not a cabin." Duke jerked his thumb at the necklace still glinting on the rug where Scarlett had dropped it. "How do you know this... vision has anything to do with you? It could be something connected to the previous owner of the locket. Right, Scarlett?"

"I suppose so, but I was compelled to take Beth's hand, to bring her in."

"The facts are you don't have a clue what you're doing here. You drink some herbal tea, you utter some mumbo jumbo, you have some visions and you leave your clients with more questions than answers."

"Clients?" Scarlett widened her stance and tossed her braid over her shoulder. "I'm an artist. The only clients I have are the ones who buy my art and sponsor my shows."

"Duke, Scarlett agreed to do this because I asked her. While frightened by what I saw and heard, I'm satisfied with what we did here tonight."

"Okay." Duke clasped the back of his neck and tipped his head from side to side. "I'm sorry, Scarlett. I just don't see how this helps Beth."

Beth bent down to sweep up her necklace. "What else did you see, Scarlett? Anything more about the cabin? I didn't join your vision until later. You must've experienced more than I did."

"It was a cabin, a nice one, and it had a red door. I can't tell you anything else specific about it—I didn't see the location, any particular furnishings or the people in it."

Duke snorted and Beth shot him a warning glance.

"But I did see two birds."

"Flying around? That's helpful."

Beth jabbed Duke in the ribs for his sarcastic tone, but Scarlett didn't seem to notice.

"There were two birds…over the fireplace? I'm not sure. I just remember two birds—maybe on a painting, maybe they were those hideous stuffed taxidermy things."

"Anything else?"

"The people—there was a man, a woman and a child, wasn't there?"

"I certainly heard voices, but I'm not sure I could distinguish them, and I did hear a baby or a child crying."

"And the hair." Scarlett reached out and lifted a strand of Beth's hair. "The woman had strawberry blond hair."

Chapter Eleven

Beth took another turn around the hotel room. "What do you think it means? A woman with strawberry blond hair?"

"Who knows? Scarlett Easton is not exactly an expert at interpretation, is she?"

"She never claimed to be." Beth wedged her hands on her hips. "Why did you start attacking Scarlett when she was just trying to help me?"

"Help you? By dragging you into her dream state? I thought—" He raked a hand through his hair. "I was worried about you."

Beth gave him a sidelong glance. "I thought you had a thing for her."

"Scarlett's not my type—too artsy, too reclusive, too... weird." Folding his arms, he leaned against the window. "Would you care if I did have a thing for Scarlett?"

Before he'd started keeping secrets from her? Hell, yeah. Now?

She splayed her hands in front of her. "She's a beautiful woman. I could understand the attraction."

Rolling his shoulders, he pushed off the window. "What are you going to do with the information? What does it prove?"

Duke wasn't going to take the bait.

"It proves—" she dropped to the bed "—that I was in a

cabin here as a child, before the Kings adopted me. I plan to locate that cabin."

"And you're going to do that how? By running around Timberline and looking into all the cabins with red doors?"

"It's a start."

"Then what?"

She fell back on the bed and stared at the ceiling. "Why are you trying to discourage me? I thought you were all in. I thought you were going to help me with this."

"That was before someone hit and killed Gary Binder, before someone started taking shots at you in the forest."

"Gary's death doesn't have anything to do with me, and that shot could've been a hunter harassing Scarlett."

"You're doing it again, Beth." The mattress sank as Duke sat on the edge of the bed. "You're so single-mindedly focused on one goal you're not seeing the whole picture."

"I don't care about the whole picture." She puffed out a breath and a strand of hair floated above her face and settled against her lips. "I need to do this. Scarlett has given me the first real lead since I got here and I'm going to follow up on it."

He shifted on the bed and she held her breath. If he took her in his arms right now and kissed her, she'd kiss him back and to hell with the secrets between them—his and hers.

Standing above her, he shook his head. "Stubborn woman. I'll help you."

Bracing her elbows against the bed, she hoisted herself up. "I'll do it with or without you, but thanks."

"Get some sleep." He nudged her foot and stalked to the door, mumbling as if to himself. "What else am I going to do, let you wander around the woods on your own like Little Red Riding Hood?"

The door slammed behind him and Beth narrowed her eyes.

He could start by telling her the truth about what he was doing with the Brices.

BETH USED HER interviews the next day to discreetly ask about cabins in the area. She also scanned her videos to see if any of the cabins she'd captured had red doors—they didn't.

After her third interview of the morning, Beth slumped behind the wheel of her rental and gave Jordan Young's office another call. His assistant answered after the first ring.

"This is Beth St. Regis again. Just checking to see if Mr. Young has some time today for that interview."

"I'm sorry, Ms. St. Regis. Mr. Young is out of town today, but I know he's looking forward to talking to you."

"I know he's busy. Just tell him I called again and I'm available at his convenience."

"Will do."

Beth's stomach growled and she patted it. She'd skipped out on breakfast this morning because she hadn't wanted to share an awkward meal with Duke. The other night he must've thought they were growing closer, putting their bitter past behind them. He'd even apologized for cutting her off, had admitted misunderstanding her.

She could've had it all back with him if she hadn't seen that text from his boss, Mickey Tedesco. She could ask him about it point-blank, get it out in the open. Of course, then she'd have to admit she'd been sneaking around again and delving into his business.

Was that wrong if he really was keeping secrets from her? It was like the cheating spouse. If your spouse was stepping out on you, didn't that sort of excuse your checking his emails and text messages?

She exited her car and turned up her collar against the

wind. A drop of rain spattered against the back of her hand and she hunched forward and made a beeline for the sandwich shop on the corner.

Ducking inside, she brushed droplets of moisture from her hair. The shop was more of a take-out place, but it did boast several wrought-iron tables to one side.

She ordered an Italian sub at the counter, picked out a bag of chips and waited for the self-serve soft-drink machine. The guy at the machine turned suddenly and almost spilled his drink on her.

"Sorry... Ms. St. Regis."

"Deputy Unger, how are you?" Her gaze dipped to his flannel shirt and jeans. "Off duty?"

"Yes." He held up a plastic bag, bulging with food. "Just picking up some lunch for my hunting trip."

"Oh, you hunt, too." She wrinkled her nose. She was with Scarlett on her distaste of the so-called sport.

"Most of us grow up hunting in these parts...and I always eat my game. I go for the turkey—" he pointed at the take-out counter "—probably a lot like your sandwich."

"I admit it. I'm a city girl. I don't understand the sport."

He sealed a plastic lid on his cup and grabbed a straw. "I talked to my mom about your show. She's actually okay with it."

Beth's heart did a somersault in her chest. "That would be great. Thanks so much for talking to her."

Unger pounded his straw against the counter. "I think she would've contacted you on her own. She heard you were in town doing the story."

"I'm sure a few words from her son didn't hurt." And a few words from Duke to Unger on her behalf.

Unger grabbed a napkin and asked the guy behind the counter for a pen. "Here's her number. Feel free to call her anytime. She's a retired schoolteacher and spends her days with knitting groups and book clubs and volunteering at the public library, but I think this is one of her free days if you have an opening."

"I do." She folded the napkin and tucked it in her purse. "I've been trying to set up something with Jordan Young, but he's never available."

"Yeah, Jordan. He's a big wheeler-dealer in town—has been for years. He seems to get the sweetest deals. We all joke that he must have a dossier on every public official."

"Sounds like he knows the town's secrets."

"He's been here for a long time, even though he's not a local. Came out of nowhere, married a local girl and set up shop pretty quickly—successful guy."

"Which is why he's hard to pin down." She patted her purse where she'd stashed his mother's phone number. "Thanks again."

"Save your thanks until after the interview. My mom just might talk your ear off." Taking a sip from his soda, he held up his hand and left the shop.

She filled her cup with ice and root beer and picked up her sandwich from the counter. She'd have to thank Duke for this interview.

As she sat down, Jason Foster walked through the door. He approached her table. "Hey, Beth. How'd it go with my cousin?"

"We, uh, talked."

"She's a trip, huh?"

Trip—yeah, that was exactly the word she'd use.

"I like her."

"Some do, some don't. Did she tell you anything?" He waved to the guy at the counter. "You got my pastrami?"

"She was helpful."

"Dang, that's not a word I'd use for my cuz." He pointed at the counter. "I have to pick up my lunch and get back to work. Glad Scarlett could help."

He paid for his sandwich and left the store.

She didn't know how close Scarlett and Jason were, but she didn't feel comfortable talking about what went on at Scarlett's cabin. Hell, she didn't even know what had happened there.

She finished her lunch with no more interruptions and then pulled out the napkin with Mrs. Unger's telephone number.

Her anticipation was dashed when she heard the woman's voice mail. Beth left a message and got up to refill her soda.

Her phone started ringing and Beth sprinted back to the table and grabbed it. "Hello?"

"Is this Beth St. Regis from the *Cold Case Chronicles* show?"

"Yes. Mrs. Unger?"

"You can call me Dorothy."

"Dorothy, thanks for calling back." Beth pulled out her chair and sat down. "Your son said you'd be willing to talk to me about the Timberline Trio case, specifically about the Brices, since you knew them well."

"Such a sad time." Dorothy clicked her tongue. "I'd be happy to talk to you, Beth. Do you think I'll be on TV?"

Beth's lips twisted into a smile. "I'm not sure. It just depends. From what your son said, I thought you wouldn't be interested."

"Oh, that's Cody talking. Who wouldn't want to be on TV?"

"Can we meet at your house or wherever you're comfortable?"

"You can come by now if you like. I have a knitting circle at three o'clock, but I'm free until then."

"Perfect."

Dorothy gave Beth her address and she punched it into her phone's GPS.

A half an hour later, Beth reached Dorothy's house,

which was located in one of the newer tracks and easy to find.

She pulled into the driveway behind an old but immaculate compact and retrieved her video camera and tripod from the trunk of her rental.

Before she walked up to the front door, she sent a quick text to Duke thanking him for convincing Unger to let her have access to his mother—even if Dorothy would've contacted her on her own.

Hitching the camera case over her shoulder, she walked up the two steps of the porch and rang the doorbell.

A small, neat woman who mirrored the small, neat compact in the driveway answered the door. "Hello, Beth."

"Dorothy. Thanks for talking with me."

"Of course. Come in. Coffee? Water?" She winked. "Something a little stronger?"

What was it with the Washington women and their whiskey? Must be the cold, damp weather.

"No, thank you. I just had lunch."

"Do you need to set up that camera?"

"I do." Beth gestured to the sofa where a magazine had been placed facedown on one of the cushions. "Sit where you're comfortable."

Dorothy sat on the sofa and folded her hands in her lap. "Is this a good place for lighting and all that?"

Beth extended her tripod on the other side of the coffee table in front of the sofa. "I'm no cameraperson. I have someone who does that for me. I'm just here doing some preliminary interviews. Just casual."

"Oh, thank goodness. Then I have nothing to be nervous about."

"Of course not." Beth's fingers trembled as she touched the video camera's display for the settings. She was the nervous one. This woman could've actually known her as a toddler.

Beth started the interview in the usual manner. Dorothy stated her name, address and the current date, and Beth questioned her about what she remembered twenty-five years ago.

It didn't differ much from the other accounts. The suspicions about Kayla Rush's father, and then the shock of Stevie Carson's disappearance, and the sheer terror when the toddler Heather Brice went missing.

"Three children snatched—" Dorothy snapped her fingers "—just like that. Those of us with young kids were terrified. I didn't let my boys out of my sight for one second for months after the kidnappings."

"And you were close with the Brices at the time?"

"We were friendly, socialized. Timberline wasn't as populated in those days. Evergreen Software brought in a lot of new people."

"Do you remember Heather?"

"A sweet little girl."

"She had blond hair, didn't she?" Beth had been twisting her own hair around one finger and dropped it. "I saw some fuzzy newspaper photos of her."

"It was blond, just like her mother's, although Patty had a little help from her hairdresser."

"Blond?" A knot formed in Beth's gut. "Mrs. Brice was a blonde?"

"She had been. Like I said, she lightened her hair. I think her real color was light brown."

Beth fingered the necklace around her neck. Light brown, not strawberry blond? She dropped the locket against her chest. That didn't mean anything. The woman in Scarlett's vision could've been the kidnapper.

"Was there some evidence regarding hair?"

"No, no. I was just thinking about some pictures I saw that were related to the case."

Beth asked more questions about the family, as many as she could without arousing Dorothy's suspicions again.

She ended the interview with a warm feeling in her belly. By all accounts, the Brices were a close and loving family. They would welcome their long-lost daughter with open arms.

As Beth shut off the camera, she asked, "Did Mr. Brice already have his money when he lived here?"

"They were wealthy because Charlie had sold his first patent, but nothing compared to what they are now." Dorothy dragged the magazine into her lap and smoothed her hands over the glossy cover. "If little Heather had been kidnapped first, everyone would've expected a ransom note."

"Did you keep in touch with the family when they left town?"

"Exchanged a few Christmas cards, but I think Patty and Charlie wanted to put this chapter behind them."

"With all their money, did they ever do a private search for Heather?"

"I'm sure they did, but she never told me about it. They moved two years later." Dorothy pushed out of the sofa. "Would you like something now?"

"Water would be great."

Dorothy called from the kitchen. "I think I have a few pictures of Heather with my boys, if you're interested, but I'd have to find them."

Beth's heart thumped in her chest. She'd seen only the old newspaper pictures of Heather Brice. She'd felt no sense of recognition, but that didn't mean anything. Maybe clearer, color photos would reveal more.

"I'd love to see them if you can find them."

Dorothy returned with a glass of water. "I'll look later and give you a call if I have anything useful."

Beth took a few sips of water. "Do you know of any cabins around here that have red doors?"

"Not now, not anymore."

Beth's hand froze, the glass halfway to her lips. "Not anymore? There was one before?"

"There were several. It was a trend."

"How long ago was this, Dorothy?" Beth wiped her mouth with the back of her hand.

"Maybe thirty, thirty-five years ago. Designs follow trends, don't they? Remember the hideous avocado-green appliances? Now everything has to be stainless steel."

"How many cabins had these red doors?"

"Ten or fifteen?" She peered at Beth. "Why? Is this some new evidence, too?"

"I can't say right now. Were these cabins in the same area or scattered around?"

"I can't remember, Beth. They were here and there. Who knew at the time that any of this stuff would be important?"

"Are there any left? Any cabins with red doors?"

"There might be a few. You'd probably want to talk to a Realtor—not that lush Bill Raney, but you could try Rebecca Geist. She's a sharp gal. Just sold Cass Teagan's place."

"Maybe I will. I've seen a few of her open houses around."

"When are you going to make a decision about the story and the footage?"

"I'll submit everything to my producer and he'll make the decision. Then the rest of my crew will come out and we'll put a story together."

"You won't solve it and neither will that handsome young FBI agent who's out here now." Dorothy put her finger to her lips and said in a hushed voice, "I'm beginning to believe it really was that Quileute basket lady who steals children away and eats them."

BETH COLLAPSED IN her car, a range of emotions assaulting her brain. Whose strawberry blond hair was in her locket? Her own? If so, who was the strawberry blonde Scarlett had seen in the vision? Maybe Scarlett had seen her as an adult.

Her mind shifted, another scattered piece of information in her brain taking shape, like a figure in a kaleidoscope.

Was there a way to find all those cabins that had red doors? If she tracked down each one, would she discover the cabin from her trance?

She threw her car into Reverse and backed out of Dorothy's driveway. She needed to touch base with Scarlett again. Had the shaman remembered more from her dream state?

She drove across town and hit the main highway. She took the turnoff, watching for the colorful mailbox that marked Scarlett's private access road.

Duke hadn't wanted her to come out here by herself, but he'd been busy all day and this couldn't wait. She pulled up when she saw the mailbox and tapped Duke's number on her cell phone.

"Where are you? I've been texting you for the past thirty minutes." His voice was gruff.

"I didn't get your texts. I'm on my way to see Scarlett."

"Damn it, Beth. You couldn't wait for me?"

"It's broad daylight."

"It was broad daylight last time. Stay put. I'm on my way."

"I'm at Scarlett's mailbox at the beginning of the access road. I'll just drive up to her place and wait for you. I don't even know if she's home."

"Stay in your car."

"Duke, I think you're overreacting."

"Let me overreact if it keeps you safe."

She ended the call and swung onto the access road leading to Scarlett's cabin. The rough road bounced and jostled her car, and she drove it as far as the road allowed.

She grabbed the handle, cracked the door open and stopped. She'd promised Duke she'd wait in the car until he got there—a ridiculous precaution, but one she'd honor.

Tipping her head back against the headrest, Beth drummed out a rhythm against the steering wheel and then checked the time on her cell phone. Scarlett must not be home if she hadn't heard Beth's car drive up the road.

She swung the car door open the rest of the way and dragged in a deep lungful of the pine-scented air. The mist caressing the copse of trees ringing Scarlett's cabin gave the area a mythical, mystical quality that suited its inhabitant.

A loud wail shattered the peace, sending a river of chills down her spine. She jumped out of the car and hung on the car door. "Hello? Scarlett?"

An animalistic shriek pierced the air and Beth bolted from the car and ran down the small path that wound its way through the trees to Scarlett's cabin. The front porch came into view and Beth charged ahead.

A vise grabbed her ankle with a snap and Beth tumbled forward onto her hands and knees as a sharp pain knifed up her leg. She hit the ground with a cry and rolled to her back to take pressure off her ankle.

Her eyes watering, she glanced at her injured leg and choked. A trap had her in its steely grip.

Chapter Twelve

Duke cursed when he saw Beth's car and the open door. Why didn't it surprise him that she hadn't stayed put like he'd asked? When had Beth St. Regis ever played it safe?

He slammed his car door and stalked to her rental. The open door gave him pause. He poked his head inside the car and swallowed. Why'd she leave her keys in the ignition and phone in the cup holder?

A low moan floated through the trees and he jerked his head up, the blood pounding in his ears. "Beth?"

"Duke? Duke, I'm here. Help me."

He crashed through the trees, and when he saw Beth on the ground, crumpled in pain, he rushed to her side. He dropped next to her, reaching for the cruel trap that had her boot in its teeth.

"Oh, my God. Did the spikes reach your flesh?"

Her chin wobbled. "I can't tell. It's almost numb with pain. I'm afraid to move or I would've crawled to my car to get my phone."

"Where's Scarlett?" He twisted his head over his shoulder.

"I don't know. I haven't seen anyone since I arrived." She ended with a hiss.

"Stretch out your leg. I'm gonna get this thing off of you."

Slowly she extended her leg, the trap clamped onto her ankle.

Duke placed both hands on either side of the trap's jaws and pulled them apart. The spring jumped and the trap snapped open.

The teeth of the trap had mangled Scarlett's boot, but he didn't see any blood. "I don't see any blood, but I'm going to leave it to the medical professionals to remove your boot."

"Thank God I was wearing them. My foot and ankle hurt like hell, but it's just a mass of pain. I can't tell what's injured."

"Let's get you to the hospital." He scooped her up and tromped back the way he'd come, keeping his eyes on the ground for any more surprises.

"Somebody placed that trap there on purpose, Duke, and lured me out of my car."

"How?" His arms tightened around her and he could feel the erratic fluttering of her heart against his chest.

"I heard wailing and a scream. It sounded like a wounded animal, but it could've been human." She tugged on his jacket. "We need to warn Scarlett. There may be more traps set around her cabin."

"I'm calling the sheriff's department." He settled her into the passenger seat and placed a kiss on top of her head, where his lips met beads of dew clinging to the strands of her hair.

"And Scarlett. That trap could've just as well been meant for her."

"Or you." When he got behind the wheel, he pulled his phone from his pocket. At Beth's urging, his first call went to Scarlett.

"Hello?"

"Scarlett, it's Duke Harper. I'm just leaving your place with Beth, who stepped into a trap outside your cabin."

Scarlett sucked in a sharp breath. "What kind of trap?"

"I'm not sure, but it could be a bear trap."

"A trap? You mean a real animal trap?"

"That's what it looks like to me."

"Is she okay?"

"I'm taking her to the hospital emergency room, but be careful. There might be more traps around your cabin."

"The police?"

"I'm calling the sheriff next. Where are you?"

"I'm at my granny's place on the reservation. How the hell did a bear trap get on my property?"

"I was hoping you could tell us."

"Duke, it could've been meant for me. It might not have anything to do with Beth."

"Yeah, except she's the one who was trapped."

He ended the call with Scarlett and tapped his phone for the sheriff's department. He told them about the wounded animal sound Beth had heard and gave them the location of the trap he'd removed from her ankle.

Tossing the phone onto the console, he said, "Scarlett thinks the trap could've been meant for her."

"It could've been meant for either one of us." Beth winced and rubbed her thigh.

"You doing okay? Hang in there." He sped back toward town, taking the bypass road to the new hospital near Evergreen Software.

He pulled up to the emergency room entrance and carried Beth inside. "She needs a wheelchair. She stepped onto a trap and injured her foot or ankle."

An orderly burst through the swinging doors, pushing a wheelchair.

Duke put her into the chair and followed the orderly back to the examination rooms.

The orderly lifted Beth onto an exam table and said, "A nurse will be right with you."

The paper on the exam table crinkled as Beth hoisted herself up onto her elbows. "Who would do that? You know that trap was deliberately set."

"Of course it was, but who was the prey? You or Scarlett?"

She crossed her arms over her chest like a shield. "It's Scarlett's place. No one could know for sure if I'd be back there, but Scarlett would be there, guaranteed."

"Just seems odd that both of these attacks at Scarlett's cabin happened when you were there. Is Scarlett even in an active battle with the hunters right now? I got the impression she hadn't been around much lately."

"Maybe—" Beth peered over his shoulder at the door "—maybe Scarlett was the target, but not for her anti-hunting stance."

"Then what? Her really creepy artwork?"

"The dream state ceremony last night."

Duke's pulse jumped. That would put Beth right back in the crosshairs since she'd participated, too. He rubbed his knuckles across his jaw. "Whoever placed that trap wants both you and Scarlett to stop looking into the Timberline Trio case. Maybe they didn't care who they snared."

"What I don't understand is why me? Why is this person just warning me and not you? The FBI is investigating the Timberline Trio case, too."

"Because targeting the FBI is a bigger deal than scaring off some reporter and an artist playing at being a shaman."

She smacked his arm. "Scarlett's not playing at being a shaman—she is one."

"For all the good it did."

"It did help. You know I spoke to Dorothy Unger today."

"I got your text. Did she take you by the shoulders and proclaim that you looked just like Heather Brice?"

"Shh." Beth glanced at the open exam room door again. "She didn't, but she did tell me that quite a number of cabins in Timberline used to have red doors—seems it was a trend a while back."

"Those doors may no longer be red."

"I figured that, but she also gave me the name of a Realtor who might be able to help me figure out which cabins had the red doors. If I had that information, I could track down each one."

"Provided they're still standing. Not even the Brices' old home is still in existence."

"I know." She fell back against the table.

He hated to keep dashing her hopes, but she needed to get out of this town. The threats against her seemed to be getting more violent.

He smoothed a hand down her leg. Maybe he'd have some news for her shortly that would turn her away from this story and end this quest that seemed to be hazardous to her health.

The nurse bustled into the room. Touching the toe of Beth's mangled boot, she said, "Ruined a nice pair of boots, too. Let's get this off."

The nurse took a scalpel and sliced through the leather of the boot on Beth's calf. She peeled it off and clicked her tongue. "Your ankle is swollen for sure, but I don't see any blood. It doesn't look like the teeth of the trap made it to your flesh."

"I can't even imagine what that would've felt like." Beth shivered.

The nurse peeled off Beth's heavy sock and Beth grunted. "That looks bad."

"Swollen and the start of some massive bruising."

Duke leaned over and inspected Beth's injured ankle. "Is it broken?"

"The doctor will probably order some X-rays." The nurse ran some antiseptic towelettes over Beth's ankle and foot. "How's the pain on a scale from one to ten, ten being childbirth?"

A red tide crested in Beth's cheeks. "I've never experienced childbirth, but I'd put this pain at a six now—definitely a nine when it first happened."

The nurse held out a small cup with two green gel caps in it. "I'm going to give you a few ibuprofens for the pain and the swelling. The doctor may prescribe some stronger painkillers for you."

A doctor poked her head into the room. "I'm Dr. Thallman. There's a sheriff's deputy here to see you, but we're going to take you over to get some X-rays right now."

"I'll talk to the deputy." Duke leaned over and cupped Beth's face with one hand. "I'm not going anywhere."

He watched as they wheeled Beth away and then went to the waiting room, where Deputy Stevens was talking to the woman at the front desk.

"Stevens, Beth's getting some X-rays." He shook the deputy's hand.

"We have a couple of officers scanning the area in front of Scarlett Easton's place. They already found another trap, closer to the cabin."

Duke pinched the bridge of his nose. "What a sick joke. Any way to trace those traps?"

"Probably not." He swept his hat from his head. "But if we find out who's playing games like this, not only will he never get a hunting license in the state of Washington again, but we'll send him to jail."

"Do you think it's related to Scarlett's war with the hunters?" Duke's jaw hardened. If only he could believe that himself.

"Maybe, but we're not going to rule out Beth's mission here in Timberline. There still are a lot of folks here who are uneasy about the Timberline Trio case getting rehashed again—and let's just say Bill Raney is a hunter."

"I thought you cleared him of the other…pranks."

"We're going to start looking at everyone more closely."

Scarlett Easton burst through the emergency room doors. "Where's Beth? Is she okay?"

"Getting X-rays." Duke pointed at Stevens. "Did you hear they found another trap on your property?"

"I did. Maybe one for me and one for her."

Stevens asked, "You don't have anything to do with Beth's Timberline investigation, do you?"

"Me?" Scarlett drove a finger into her chest. "Not a chance."

A nurse poked her head out of the swinging doors leading to the exam rooms. "Beth's doing fine. Dr. Thallman is looking at her X-rays if you want to come back now, Deputy Stevens."

Duke brought up the rear behind Stevens and Scarlett as the nurse led them to the examination room.

Beth looked up from examining the pink wrap on her foot and ankle. "Pretty, isn't it?"

Scarlett tripped into the room and put an arm around Beth. "I'm so sorry."

"It's not your fault, Scarlett."

"My cabin seems to be bad luck for you."

"It could've just as easily been you caught in that trap."

Stevens cleared his throat. "One of those traps—we found another one."

Beth's mouth dropped open. "Oh, my God. If that one hadn't gotten me, the other one could've done the job."

"And the other one was bigger, could've caused more damage."

"It's a good thing I bought those heavy boots for this trip."

Dr. Thallman squeezed into the crowded room. "It is a good thing. Those boots probably saved you from breaking any bones."

"My foot's not broken?"

"Badly bruised and the bone is bruised as well. Keep it wrapped, keep it elevated and I'm prescribing some pain-killers if you need them." The doctor scribbled on a pre-scription pad and ripped it off.

"Is she okay to leave?" Duke took the prescription from the doctor.

"She is."

Stevens dragged a chair next to the examination table. "Before you leave, I'd like to ask you a few questions, Beth."

"We'll let you talk." Duke took Scarlett's arm. "I'll be in the waiting room, Beth."

When they reached the waiting room, Scarlett slouched on a vinyl chair. "I'm not staying in my cabin tonight. I'd been planning on leaving for Seattle tomorrow and then taking a flight to San Francisco for a friend's show. I can't help Beth anymore."

"You've done plenty."

She glanced at him sharply. "I just need to go back to the cabin to pack, and then I'll spend the night with my granny on the rez. Jason's driving me to Seattle."

"If something comes up, we can reach you on the cell phone number you gave Beth?"

"Yeah. Let me know when it's safe to return to my cabin."

Deputy Stevens caught the tail end of their conversation as he walked into the waiting room. "We have a couple of deputies canvassing your place, Scarlett. If we find anything else, we'll let you know."

"And if I remember anything else, I'll let you know, Quentin."

An orderly pushed Beth into the waiting room in a wheelchair.

Duke crouched beside her. "Can you walk on that ankle?"

She tipped her head at the orderly, holding a pair of crutches. "I'll have some crutches to get around at first, but once the swelling subsides a little more I should be fine."

The orderly handed the crutches to Duke and disappeared behind the swinging doors.

"We'll let you know if we discover anything else, too, Beth." Stevens clapped his hat onto his head. "Good night, all."

"Stevens? Scarlett's going back to her place to pack. Maybe it's a good idea if the deputies stay there until she leaves."

"I'll tell them."

When he left, Scarlett turned to Beth. "What did you want to see me about, anyway?"

"Oh, my God, I almost forgot." Beth pressed three fingers against her forehead. "The woman you saw with the strawberry blond hair in the vision—could she have been me as an adult, as I am now?"

"I don't know. Like Duke said, I'm not great at interpretation. I didn't get the impression that she was you. Why do you ask?"

"I spoke with someone who knew the Brices, and Patty Brice never had strawberry blond hair."

"I never said the woman was Patty Brice. I just don't know. I'm sorry, Beth. I can't help you anymore." Scarlett caught her bottom lip between her teeth. "What I haven't said yet to you or to Quentin Stevens is that the trap could've been a warning from my own people."

"The Quileute? Why?" Beth's eyes widened.

"They wouldn't want me talking about Dask'iya or the Timberline Trio case. I told you that before. The tribe doesn't discuss it."

"Would they really go that far to warn you?" Duke asked.

"It's a possibility. I just know I need to get away." She grabbed Beth's hand. "And you should, too."

"Thank you. I've been telling her that for a few days now."

"That's two to one, Beth. Find yourself another story. The Timberline kidnappings have been nothing but tragedy for everyone involved for as long as I can remember."

Beth squeezed Scarlett's hand. "Thanks for your concern, and thanks for all your help. I'm trying to reach a Realtor right now who can help me track down the red doors."

Scarlett rolled her eyes at Duke. "She's not going to listen, is she?"

"Don't worry. I plan to keep working on her. Are you okay if we leave now?"

"Yeah. You heard Quentin. The cops will probably still be wandering around my property when I get home."

Beth snapped her fingers. "My rental car is still at your place."

"You can't drive with that foot all wrapped up."

"Don't worry about it." Scarlett held up her hand. "I'll have Jason drive the car to your hotel and leave the keys at the front desk."

Duke dragged Beth's keys from his pocket and handed them to Scarlett. "Have a good trip."

They went to their separate cars, Beth awkwardly negotiating the crutches.

As he helped her into the SUV, he asked, "Did I hear you say you called the Realtor already?"

"Called her after my X-rays and left her a voice mail. If she's free for dinner, do you want to join us?"

"How could I possibly miss the discussion about cabins with red doors? Of course. And you're going to need some guidance before you get used to those crutches."

The drive back to the hotel was a quiet one. He was done trying to convince her to give up on this story. He knew one surefire way to do it, and if Mick would ever get back to him, it would be a done deal.

As he pulled into a parking spot, Beth's phone rang. She answered and he exited the car and leaned against the hood to wait.

When she got out, she held up her phone. "Dinner with Rebecca Geist at Sutter's tonight at seven. You in?"

"I'll be there." As she joined him, he took her by the shoulders before they entered the hotel. "I almost lost it when I saw you on the ground, that trap biting into your foot."

Her frame trembled beneath his hands. "It was…terrifying. The sound it made… Ugh. I'm going to hear that sound in my nightmares."

"What's it gonna take for you, Beth?"

"To leave Timberline? The truth. I'm going to leave Timberline when I discover the truth about my identity. Otherwise, what do I have?"

"You have me." He sealed his lips over hers and drew her close, burying one hand in her silky hair.

She melted against him for a moment, her mouth pliant against his. But then she broke away and stepped back.

"I just don't think you understand what this means to me, Duke. It's a lifetime of questions and doubts coming to a head in one corner of the world—right here. All my questions have led me here."

"You don't know, Beth. It's based on feelings and suppositions and red doors and frogs."

"And that's a start."

He closed his eyes and took a deep breath. He didn't want to take that all away from her—the hope, but he'd snatch it all away in a heartbeat to keep her safe.

"Okay. We have at least an hour before we have to leave

for dinner. I'm going to take a shower. I'll stop by your room at around six forty-five."

She grabbed the front of his shirt. "Thanks for not pushing it, Duke."

Did she mean the topic of her identity or the kiss? Because he'd wanted to push both—especially the kiss.

AN HOUR LATER they drove into town and got a table for three at Sutter's. Beth had interviewed almost everyone she'd contacted, except for Jordan Young and a few others. As Beth had limped to their table, a few patrons glanced at her quickly, glanced away and then whispered among each other. Her reception in the dining room had cooled off compared to that first night.

Had the pranks and threats that had dogged her made the rounds and turned people off?

His gaze shifted to Beth studying the menu and his stomach sank. She didn't care how chilly the reception. She had a goal and to hell with anything and anyone who stood in her way—including him.

A flashy blonde entered the restaurant and made a beeline to their table. "Beth St. Regis? I'd recognize you anywhere."

Duke stood up and pulled out her chair as Beth made the introductions. "Nice to meet you, Rebecca. This is Special Agent Duke Harper."

She shook his hand before taking a seat. "Now, aren't you the gentleman? These lumberjack types out here could learn a thing or two from a city boy like you."

Chloe was their waitress again and practically skipped to their table. "Jason told me someone had set some bear traps outside Scarlett's cabin and you stepped on one."

"Yeah, that happened." Beth lifted her wrapped foot in the air.

"That's crazy. Scarlett needs to stop ticking off those hunters."

"Did Scarlett get off to Seattle okay?"

Chloe nodded. "They're on their way. Jason texted me about an hour ago when they left. Can I get you guys some drinks?"

Rebecca ordered a glass of merlot while Beth got some hot tea. "I just took a couple of painkillers. If I mixed those with alcohol, I'd probably fall asleep at the table."

"I'll have that local brew on tap."

When Chloe walked away, Rebecca planted her elbows on the table and turned to Beth. "So, tell me everything. What secrets are you discovering about our little town?"

"Unfortunately the secrets seem to be piling up, and I don't have a clue."

"I heard what happened in here the other night between you and Bill Raney."

"His name keeps coming up, but since that initial threat from him, I haven't seen him at all." Beth glanced at the bar. "I don't think he's the only one who doesn't want me poking around."

Rebecca waved her manicured fingers. "Believe me, honey, the Timberline Trio case is the least of Bill's problems." She winked. "I'm his biggest problem right now."

Duke put his phone on vibrate and tucked it into the front pocket of his shirt. "You're taking away his business?"

"There was nothing to take away. I'm earning business and he's not—maybe if he'd lay off the booze."

"I heard from Dorothy Unger that you were the best, and that's why I called you."

Chloe stopped by with their drinks and they ordered their food while they had her attention.

"I helped Dot get out of her old house when her husband

passed away and got her into a newer, smaller place." She folded her hands. "So, tell me how I can help you."

"Dorothy mentioned that there was a trend toward red doors for Timberline cabins a long time ago. Would you know which cabins had the red doors?"

Rebecca blinked her false lashes. "Red doors. Red doors. Not many of those cabins left."

"Are there some left?" Beth hunched forward, rattling her teacup.

"There are a couple, but I'm not sure if they're the original red-door cabins or if they're newly painted. I'm going to have to do a little research. I have a lot of archive photos of the cabins in Timberline. I'm sure I can find some of them."

"That would be great, Rebecca, and if you point me in the right direction, I can help you do the research."

Duke's phone buzzed in his pocket. He slipped it out and cupped it in his hand. When he saw that Mick had sent him a text, a muscle jumped in his jaw.

"Is that work?"

"Yeah. I'm just going to step outside for a minute, if you ladies will excuse me."

Rebecca patted Beth's arm. "True gentleman, that one."

Duke pushed back from the table and tried not to run out of the restaurant. When he got to the sidewalk, he was panting like he'd just run a marathon.

He entered his code to unlock his phone and swiped his finger across the display. The blood rushed to his head when he read Mick's text and he braced one hand against the wall of the building to steady himself.

He placed a call to Mick. When Mick picked up, Duke said, "You're sure?"

"DNA doesn't lie, my brother, even on a rush job like this one. Is it going to help solve the case?"

"I think so."

"I have to get off the phone. It's late here and I'm helping my son with his math homework."

"Just wanted to verify. Thanks, buddy."

Duke strolled back into the restaurant. He didn't know how he was going to get through the rest of this meal.

When he got to the table, Rebecca was telling Beth all about her wedding plans.

She tapped her head. "Of course, it's all up here right now since my fiancé hasn't actually committed to a date yet."

"Nothing wrong with a long engagement, really get to know someone."

"What about you two?" Rebecca flicked her finger back and forth between him and Beth. "Any wedding plans?"

Beth's cup clattered into her saucer. "Oh, we're not… we're not together."

"Oops." Rebecca put two fingers to her lips. "I'm usually pretty good at things like that."

Duke grabbed Beth's hand. "We were together—once."

"You see? I knew it. I can always tell."

Beth tilted her head at him, a half smile on her lips.

Hadn't he made it clear he'd like to pick up where they'd left off? She'd been the one pushing him away. The night he'd told her he'd made a mistake two years ago had been the night she'd cooled down toward him. If a relationship came too easily for Beth, she'd probably dismiss it as unworthy of her efforts. She liked the struggle. It was what she knew.

Their dinner arrived and Rebecca did her part to keep the conversation going between bites of food. Thank God for talkative real-estate agents.

As they were finishing up, Bill Raney came into the restaurant with a few buddies, including Jordan Young, and bellied up to the bar.

Rebecca narrowed her eyes. "Honestly, Bill wouldn't

have the guts to go sneaking through the forest laying bear traps for unsuspecting women. I wouldn't worry too much about him."

Duke asked, "I gather he's not your biggest fan. Has he ever bothered you?"

"You know, come to think of it…" Rebecca tapped her long nails together. "Someone sabotaged a couple of my open houses last month."

"Bill the Prankster strikes again?" Beth turned her head to take in the group at the bar.

Jordan Young waved her over.

She smiled and stuck out her bandaged foot. "At least Jordan won't think I'm too chicken to go up to Raney."

Young pushed away from the bar and drew up the fourth chair at the table. "Do you mind?"

Rebecca waved her finger at him. "As long as you give me a shot at your next listing, Jordan."

"I'm loyal to my friends, Rebecca, but I admire your success from afar." He tapped the table in front of Beth. "What happened to your foot?"

"I'm shocked you haven't heard yet."

"I've been fishing most of the day. What did I miss?"

"Someone set some bear traps in front of Scarlett Easton's place and I got stuck in one."

"Damn. Did you break it?"

"Just bruised it."

"Scarlett okay?"

"She's fine. Left town for a few weeks."

Jordan tsked. "That's no way to solve a disagreement over hunting. I'll talk to the mayor about cracking down."

"I'm sure Scarlett would appreciate that."

"How about you, Agent Harper? Any luck cracking the cold case?"

"We're investigating a few leads. They're not called 'cold cases' for nothing."

"And you're involved how, Rebecca?"

"I'll never tell. Maybe Beth just wants to buy some property after experiencing the beauty and serenity of the area."

Duke smothered his snort. Timberline had been anything but serene for Beth.

"Well, she's consulting the best." He rapped his knuckles on the table. "You folks enjoy your evening. And, Beth, I should be around for the next few days if you are."

"I'll be here. I'll try calling your office again to schedule something."

He took a card from his card case and called to Chloe. "Do you have a pen, sweetheart?"

She smacked a pen on the table and spun away.

Young scribbled something on one of his cards. "Here's my direct line, Beth. Give me a call when you're ready to interview me."

"Thanks, Jordan."

He sauntered back to his friends at the bar and a hard stare from Raney.

Maybe Bill Raney wasn't the hapless drunk everyone thought he was.

Chloe returned to the table with the check. "Sorry for the delay. I wasn't coming back with Mr. Young here. He can get handsy, if you know what I mean."

"Honey, at my age handsy isn't necessarily a bad thing." Rebecca laughed as she tried to grab the check from Chloe.

Beth was faster. "This is a tax-deductible dinner expense for me. You're going to help me find those red-door cabins, aren't you?"

"I'm going to do my damnedest. Now, if you don't mind, I'm going to scoot out of here and get back to the office to wrap up a few things."

When she left the restaurant after flitting to about five

tables on her way out, Duke wiped the back of his hand across his forehead. "Whew. She's a dynamo."

"And efficient. I have complete faith in her to find those red doors."

Duke stroked her arm. "Let me get you back to the hotel and tuck you into bed. Maybe you can pop a few more of those painkillers and get a good night's sleep."

"You're being awfully...handsy tonight."

"I just want to take care of you, Beth." He laced his fingers with hers. "Do you believe me?"

"I believe you, and do you believe me when I say I just want the truth?"

"I can help you with that, too, Beth." He tugged on her hand. "Let's get out of here."

She leaned on him while she adjusted her crutches beneath her arms, and with a nod to Jordan, she navigated through the tables while Duke ran interference.

When they got back to the hotel, he followed her into her room. "I meant that about tucking you in. Do you want me to run you a bath?"

"I'd probably fall asleep in the tub and drown, but if you want to wait in here while I get ready for bed in case I topple over in the bathroom, that would be great."

"I'm your man in case of toppling." He stretched out on the bed and grabbed the remote control to the TV.

She gathered a few items and retreated to the bathroom.

While she ran the water and banged around in there, he ran a few lines through his head. He could put everything to rest tonight.

She emerged from the bathroom in her flannel pajamas and hopping without her crutches.

He jumped from the bed to help her. "Don't put any pressure on that foot yet."

She dropped some clothes in her suitcase. "I'm fine."

He pulled back the covers and helped her into bed. He wanted to crawl right in after her, but first things first.

She plumped up her pillows and eased back against them. "Aaah, this feels good."

"Do you need any more meds?"

"Not until after midnight. If the pain wakes me up, I'll take a few more."

He filled a glass with water from the tap and put her pill bottle on the nightstand. "For midnight."

"Thanks, Duke. You've been a big help."

"I'm going to be an even bigger help, Beth. I have something important to tell you."

Her face grew still. "What is it?"

He sat next to her on the bed and took both of her hands in his. "You're not Heather Brice."

Chapter Thirteen

She jerked away from Duke, banging her head on the head-board. His touch felt heavy, oppressive, and she snatched her hands away from his. "Why are you saying that? Why are you trying to discourage me?"

"It's more than that, Beth." He tried to take her hand again but she folded her arms and tucked her hands beneath her elbows. "I have proof."

Her tongue felt like sandpaper as she licked her lips. "How could you have proof? What did you do?"

"I requested a sample of the Brices' DNA through the FBI labs."

She clamped her hands over her ears as if that could stop the truth coming from Duke's lips. Bending at the waist, she touched her forehead to her knees. The pieces of her carefully constructed future began crashing down around her—the happy reunion, the loving family, her place in the world.

Duke's hand on her back felt like a lead weight, but she didn't have the energy to shrug him off. A black hole had sucked her into its vortex and she was spinning and spinning with no sense of time or place, no anchor.

"I'm sorry, Beth. I couldn't stand to see you twisting yourself into knots over this, putting yourself into needless danger." He swept aside the curtain of hair shielding her face. "I didn't cause the Brices any anguish. I didn't tell them about your suspicions. I let them know the FBI was working the cold case and needed their DNA. I ran it against yours from some strands of your hair and...no match."

A tear ran down her cheek and she let it drop off the edge of her chin. She managed a hoarse whisper from her tight throat. "Why did you do that? Why didn't you tell me?"

"The bigger question, Beth, is why didn't you ask me to do that? Your excuse for not going straight to the Brices was that you wanted to spare their feelings in case nothing came of your claim, but you always knew the FBI could request their DNA without arousing any suspicions. The fact that we'd taken this case out of mothballs made it easy."

She raised her head and another tear slipped down her face. "You know why."

"You were afraid of the answer. You were afraid of the truth." Duke caught her next tear on the pad of his thumb. "I get that. It's why I didn't tell you I was ordering the DNA."

"I knew." She rubbed her nose against the sheet covering her knees. "I saw a text from Mickey the other night about the Brices. I knew you were up to something. I just couldn't figure out why you wouldn't tell me what."

"Ah, that was it." He ran a hand down her leg and traced the edge of the heavy wrap around her ankle. "Maybe I should've told you, but then you would've been on pins and needles waiting for the results and if the results had been different..."

Falling back against the pillows, she said, "You're glad they're not different. You're relieved I'm not Heather Brice."

"I want you to be happy, Beth." He shoved a hand through his thick hair and left it there, holding the side of his head. "I knew you'd been building up this perfect life with the Brices, envisioning them as the all-American family, a place for you to fit in at last. God, I want that for you, Beth, but you can have that with me. We can have it together. I'm looking for my perfect family, too."

A sob racked her body and she covered her face with her hands. "You can't have that with me. I can't help you create that perfect family because I'm broken. I'm damaged."

The mattress sank as Duke climbed next to her on the bed. He wrapped one arm around her shoulders and pulled her against his chest. "Don't say that. You're the most perfect woman I know—the girl of my adolescent fantasies come to life in living, strawberry blond color."

Taking a long, shuddering breath, she squirmed out of his hold. She grabbed handfuls of his shirt and pulled him close. "You don't know. I've already destroyed any family we could have together."

He touched his forehead to hers and smoothed the hair from her damp face. "I told you, Beth. I understand why you deceived me two years ago. I understand you."

"You don't know me."

"I didn't know you before. I saw you as the untouchable girl of my dreams, perfect in every way. Now I see the human woman that you are, with all your flaws and insecurities, and I still love you. I love you more."

She squeezed her eyes shut and ran her fingers across his rough beard. She'd been waiting so long to hear those words from him…and now she'd have to fling them back in his face.

"I don't deserve your love. I tricked you again. I deceived you." She pulled away from him so she could look into his dark eyes and see the love fade away. "I had a miscarriage. I lost your baby, Duke."

His eyes widened for a split second and grew darker as his pupils dilated. "When?"

"I found out I was pregnant when I got back to LA from Chicago—about three weeks after."

"What happened?"

"This is what happened." She slammed a fist against her gut. "Me. I happened. Unfit for a family."

"Stop it." His fingers pinched into her shoulders. "Tell me what happened to our baby, Beth."

"I don't know. I had the miscarriage just a few weeks after I discovered the pregnancy. It all came and went so fast, it felt like a dream."

She gritted her teeth and braced herself for Duke's anger, for his accusations. She welcomed them. Deserved them.

His hold on her shoulders melted into a caress and he dragged her back into his arms again, tucking her head against the curve of his neck. "I'm sorry you were alone when it happened. I should've been there for you."

"Don't you get it, Duke?" She sniffled. "I didn't even tell you about the pregnancy. I probably never would've told you about the baby."

"I don't believe that for a minute." He rubbed a circle on her back. "You would've told me. You never would've allowed our baby to grow up without knowing his or her father. Whatever your feelings for me were at the time, you would've recognized the value of giving our child a father. I know that about you...now."

"But it's over. I lost the baby."

"Did the doctor indicate that you'd have problems in the future? Was there a reason why you miscarried?"

His heart pounded beneath her cheek and she smoothed her hand over his chest. "No problems. He said it's something that happens in the first trimester sometimes."

"Then it wasn't your fault and you can get pregnant again." He kissed her temple. "You can have that family,

Beth. You don't need the Brices. You don't need the Kings. All you need is me. And I sure as hell need you."

He wedged his thumb beneath her chin and tilted up her head. He traced the tracks of her tears with his fingertip until he'd dried them all, and then he kissed her lips. They throbbed beneath the gentle pressure of his mouth.

Between the kisses he planted along the line of her jaw, he whispered, "I. Want. You. More. Than. Anything."

"Duke, is this coming from pity?" She cupped his jaw in her hand, the stubble of his beard tickling her palm. "Because I'm okay now. I'm sorry I broke down. In fact, I—"

"Shh." He put a finger against her lips. Then he took her hand and guided it between his legs. "Does this feel like pity to you?"

She stroked his erection through the denim of his jeans. It felt like a visit to the candy store and a two-point rating share all rolled up into one big treat.

He growled and unbuttoned his fly. She took the obvious hint and peeled back his jeans while shoving her hand beneath the waistband of his black briefs.

The growl turned into a groan as she teased his flesh with her fingernails and kissed his mouth. He deepened the kiss and tugged at her pajama top, pulling it over her head.

He cupped one bare breast with his hand, dragging his thumb across her peaked nipple. She gasped against his lips and he shifted his mouth to the top of her breast. He kissed a circle around her nipple before sucking it into his mouth.

She arched her back, giving him more, her hips rocking forward, her hand stroking his hard-on.

She unbuttoned his shirt and rolled up his T-shirt, exposing his tight abs. She ran the flat of her hand along the ridges and then ducked her head and pressed a kiss in the middle, his skin warm against her lips.

Yanking on the edge of the shirt, she said, "That's the problem with cold weather—too many clothes."

"Sort of heightens the anticipation, don't you think?" He slipped off her pajama bottoms with one fluid motion.

"Says the man who has just a flimsy pair of pajamas to dispense with."

"There's still these." He ran a finger along the elastic of her bikini underwear clinging to her hips.

"What are you waiting for?"

He pulled down the panties and the silky material skimmed over her thighs. "This is a little more difficult. I'll try to be careful."

He inched the underwear over her knees and gently tugged them past her bandage. His gaze swept across her body, leaving tingles in its wake.

"Nothing but a pink bandage—incredibly sexy."

She wiggled her toes and rolled to her side. "You can get naked now."

He shed the rest of his clothing in record time and stretched out beside her again. He pressed his body against hers, along every line, and she let his warmth seep into her skin.

For a moment she let everything slip away—all the heartache and disappointment. She had her man by her side again and there were no secrets between them.

He followed her spine with one knuckle and caressed her derriere, fitting her against his body, his erection prodding between her thighs.

He traced over the rest of her body, as if drawing it from scratch. Could he recreate her? Make her whole?

His touch gave her goose bumps, made her believe anything was possible. He finished his exercise with a kiss on her mouth. Then he pressed her back against the pillows.

"I'm going to make you feel better than any painkiller in the entire pharmacy." He knelt between her legs and flattened his hands against the insides of her thighs. Lifting her injured leg, he rested it on his shoulder. "The doc said to keep it elevated, right?"

"That's one way to do it."

When his lips brushed her sensitive flesh, her eyes fluttered closed and her fingers burrowed into his hair. He circled with his tongue and then plunged it inside her.

She let out a long sigh, but then the tension began to build like a hot coil in her belly. Her fingernails dug into his scalp as he teased her higher and higher.

Her climax broke her apart into a million little pieces. All the anxiety and fear that had been building up since she'd started this quest shattered. She wouldn't let it take hold of her again.

Duke slid her leg from his shoulder. "Okay?"

"Mmm, more than okay and ready for you. Really ready for you this time, Duke. No more games."

"Nothing between us." He rose to his knees and she wrapped her fingers around his erection.

"Like one."

Bracing his hands on either side of her head, he drove inside her. A spasm of pleasure flashed across his face.

She clawed at the hard muscle of his buttocks, hooking her good leg around his hips, urging him deeper.

His rhythm was erratic, as if the tumult of his senses had overwhelmed him and he'd forgotten for a moment how a man loved a woman.

She touched his face. Their eyes met. He shivered and slowed his pace, plunging into her deeply and pulling out just enough to make it feel like coming home when he returned to her.

As his thrusts grew bolder and faster, she pressed her lips against his warm flesh, baring her teeth against his collarbone.

He moaned, a sound of such pure pleasure it made her

toes curl. On the very next thrust, he exploded inside her. He sank to his forearms and took possession of her mouth. The motion of his kiss mimicked the waves of his orgasm and he didn't stop kissing her until he was spent inside her.

He hoisted himself off her body. "How's your foot?"

Her lips curled into a smile. "My foot had nothing to do with any of that."

"Is it feeling left out?" He slid to the bottom of the bed and kissed each of her toes sticking out of the bandage.

"Did you develop a foot fetish when we were apart?"

"I have a fetish for every part of your body. Don't you know that? I could worship your elbow and count myself lucky."

She crooked her index finger. "I have to admit I'm partial to one part of your body in particular."

"My brain, right?" He settled beside her again and scooped her into a hug, rubbing the gooseflesh from her arms.

"That's it." She kissed his chiseled jawline. "And that didn't feel like pity sex at all."

"As a man, that's the best way I know how to offer comfort. But pity? I don't pity you. So, you're not Heather Brice with the perfect family waiting for you at the end of the rainbow. I knew my family, knew where I came from—and it wasn't perfect. Maybe the Brices aren't perfect, either. You'll weather the storm."

"You're right. The news about the Brices' DNA was just a hiccup."

"I meant what I said, Beth." He massaged the back of her neck. "As long as I'm stuck in cold-case hell, I can turn you on to a few good stories."

"That would be great once I'm done here."

"Not that I won't miss you, but I can drive you to Seattle and you can get on the next plane to LA. I'll have to stay here, of course, but I'm sure Mick won't mind if I take a few weekends off and head to LA."

"I'm not leaving right away, Duke."

"You don't need to pretend with anyone. I'll make sure word gets out that your producer cut the story or you felt you didn't have enough to create a compelling enough episode of *Cold Case Chronicles*."

"I mean—" she pulled the sheet up to her chin, her heart thumping "—I'm not giving up here."

The massage stopped. "What does that mean? You don't have anything on the Timberline Trio. There's no story for you here."

She sat up, adjusting the pillow behind her back. "I don't care about the Timberline Trio case, especially now that I'm not involved in it at all."

His dark brows collided over his nose. "I don't understand. What is there for you in Timberline?"

"What was always here—my true identity. I may not be Heather Brice or Kayla Rush, but the secret to my origin is here in Timberline. And I'm going to stay here until I discover it."

Chapter Fourteen

A chill stole over Duke's flesh, still damp with the exertion of making love. He rolled away from Beth and planted his feet on the carpet. "You can't be serious."

"*You* can't be serious to believe I'd give up now that I'm so close."

"Close to what? For whatever reason, a person or persons unknown to you does not want you poking around Timberline, and as long as you continue to do so, your life is in danger."

"I don't give a damn what the people of Timberline want. I know my past lies here and I'm going to solve the mystery of my identity if it's the last thing I do."

"It just might be."

She flicked her fingers in the air. "There have been some warnings, but nothing life-threatening."

He smacked his forehead. "Someone shot at you."

"He missed. Do you really think an experienced hunter would miss his prey?"

"We don't know that the person shooting at you is an experienced hunter, and I'm sure hunters miss all the time." He fell back on the bed so that his head was in her lap. "Beth, it's not worth it. You don't know what you're looking for."

"I'm looking for a cabin with a red door and two birds somewhere. If I can trace the property records for that cabin, maybe I can find out who had it twenty-five years ago and discover what happened there."

"I'm in awe of your…"

"Brilliance?" She combed her fingers through his hair.

"Stubbornness." He captured her fingers. "What if you do discover your true family? They may not be the loving family the Brices were. The Brices had their child stolen from them. Your family gave you away and didn't want to be traced. I'm not gonna stand by and watch you get devastated by the discovery."

"I… I'm not going to be devastated. It is what it is. I just want to know at this point. Wouldn't you?"

"I would." He pressed a kiss against the center of her palm. "I just don't want to see you hurt—physically or emotionally. You're back in my life now, Beth, and I don't want to lose you again."

"Stand by me. Stay with me. If you're going to be my family, then that's what it takes." She leaned forward and kissed his forehead. "I'm tired of secrets, Duke. I want a fresh start with you, a clean slate before we…do whatever it is we're going to do."

"If you're going to stay here in Timberline, I'll be with you. I'm not going to let you run off looking for red doors by yourself."

"I was hoping you'd say that because I don't think I can do this by myself. I'm better with you, Duke."

"I just hope you don't get hurt."

"If I do, I know you'll have my back."

"Count on it." He slid off the bed and swept her card key from the nightstand. "I'm going to my own room to brush my teeth, but I'll be back."

She snuggled against the pillow and closed her eyes. "I'll be waiting."

When Duke returned to his room he punched a pillow. He hadn't been happy when the Brices' DNA didn't match

Beth's, but he'd been relieved. He'd figured she'd give up on Timberline and go back to LA, but she felt some connection to this place. He had to trust her instincts.

He brushed his teeth and splashed some water on his face. He pulled on a pair of running shorts and returned to Beth's room.

The TV flickered in the darkness and he crept over to her bed. She'd fallen asleep on her back with her foot propped up on pillows beneath the covers.

He dropped his shorts and slid between the sheets, next to her. She hadn't bothered putting her pajamas back on and he rolled to his side to press his body against her nakedness.

She murmured something through parted lips and he kissed the corner of her mouth. Beth had no intention of giving up her search, and whatever happened, he'd be there for the fallout.

THE NEXT MORNING after breakfast, he and Beth joined Rebecca in her office. She led them to a conference room and flipped open her laptop. She eyed Duke over the top of her computer. "This isn't part of the FBI investigation, is it?"

He held up his hands. "I'm off duty today. Would it make a difference?"

"I just don't want to get subpoenaed or have our records called into evidence."

"This is for the show only. You don't even have to be on camera if you don't want to be."

"Well, I wouldn't mind that as long as you get a shot of my sign out front. Unless—" she powered up her computer "—the story ends up driving potential buyers away from Timberline."

Beth shrugged off her down vest. "The case was twenty-five years ago. I don't see how that's going to affect Timberline's reputation. If anything, Wyatt Carson already did that by trying to play the hero."

As she typed on her keyboard, Rebecca gave an exaggerated shiver. "That was creepy, but I still managed to get a good price for Kendall Rush's house."

Duke cleared his throat. "What are you going to look up this morning?"

"I have access to all of Timberline's old housing records, along with some pictures. With any luck, I should be able to identify several of the homes with the red doors."

"Let's get started." Beth scooted her chair closer to the table and leaned over Rebecca's arm.

Rebecca's fingers flew over the keyboard. "Let's see. Twenty years ago, twenty-five, not much construction during that period. Thirty, thirty-five. Now we're getting somewhere."

Beth leaned forward, poking at the screen. "This is new construction for that time period?"

"Yes. I can click on the photos for this bunch."

A cabin filled the computer screen, but it didn't have a red door.

Beth slumped back in her chair. "That's not one."

"Let me click through these photos." Each time Rebecca tapped her keyboard, a new cabin popped up on the screen. None had red doors.

"There's another grouping. I'm going to close out this bunch." She launched another set of photos and Beth sucked in a breath when the first one appeared.

"This is it." Beth practically bounced in her chair. "These are the cabins."

Rebecca brought up the cabins one by one and each cabin sported a red front door.

Duke counted the red-door cabins aloud until she came to the end. "That's eight cabins with red doors. Do you recognize any of them, Rebecca?"

"I thought I recognized a couple." She minimized the window and brought up another application. "I'm going to copy and paste the cabin addresses in here to get their locations and to see if they still exist."

An hour later Rebecca printed out a list of five red-door cabins that were still standing. The other three had been demolished.

"You are the best." Beth plucked the pages from the printer. "If I ever know of anyone moving to this area, I will send them your way."

"Just give me a plug on your show." She squinted at her laptop. "I have to get ready for my open house. Have fun investigating, and if you annoy anyone by poking around, don't tell them I sent you."

When they got into Duke's SUV, Beth smoothed out the paper on her lap. "GPS?"

"Plug in all of them and we'll try to hit them in order of location."

Beth tapped in the address of each of the cabins on the list and they designed a route so they wouldn't be back-tracking.

Duke turned the key in the ignition and glanced at Beth. "What's your plan? Are you going to invite yourself into someone's home, stand in the middle of the room and tell them you're waiting for a psychic experience?"

"I'm not sure yet. I'll figure it out when I get there."

"Okay, it's your rodeo. I'm just the technical adviser… and the bodyguard."

She squeezed his bicep. "I like the sound of that."

They drove out to the first two cabins, which resided on the same street. Civilization had encroached on the wilderness in this area as a wide, paved road cut through the forest, giving the houses on this street manicured back-yards bordering the forest edge.

Duke parked his car on the street in front of the first cabin and looked at Beth. "What now?"

"I... I'm going to get out and walk around. Maybe I'll knock on the front door and pretend I'm looking for someone."

"Yeah, because you're not totally recognizable in this town by now."

"I could use that to my advantage." She unbuckled her seat belt and reached into his backseat. "I'll take my video camera. I was filming areas before."

"Let's do it."

He went around to the passenger side to get Beth's door. She looked up from the camera in her lap. "Might as well start filming now. In fact, this is a good way to get a record of each cabin."

He helped her out of the car. "Are you going to be able to hold the camera and navigate with your crutch?"

"I don't think so. Can you play cameraman for me?"

"Yeah, just don't tell Adam." He took the camera from her. "Where is your crew, anyway? Are they getting antsy?"

"They're working on something else right now. I already indicated to Scott that this segment might not be a go and to hold off sending them."

"All right, then." He held the camera in front of him and framed the cabin in the viewfinder. "Cabin number one in the red-door cabin follies."

Beth poked him with her crutch and then appeared in his frame. "I'm going to knock on the door."

He followed her to the porch and then the door swung open and a boy cannoned down the front porch, leaving the door standing wide behind him. He tripped to a stop when he saw them.

"Hi there. Do you live here?"

"Mom!"

"Tanner, close the door." A petite woman appeared at the doorway. She put a hand to her chest. "Oh, you scared me."

"Sorry." Beth flashed her pearly whites. "I'm doing a little filming in the area. Do you mind?"

"Oh, I know who you are."

"Mom, can I go to Joe's house now?"

"Go ahead." She crossed her arms and propped up the doorjamb with her shoulder. "This area doesn't have much to do with the Timberline Trio, and I didn't even live here then."

"I know that, but a few of these cabins were standing twenty-five years ago. I'm just getting a sense of the area back then."

"You can film outside the house if you want, but I don't have time to talk to you and if the dog starts barking you're going to have to leave."

"I understand. Thank you."

But the woman had slammed the door on Beth's thanks.

Duke shifted the camera to the side. "Ouch. She's not too interested in appearing on TV, is she?"

"No, but I'm not getting anything from this house anyway."

"Like, recognition?"

"Like, any kind of vibe."

"You're not Scarlett." He snapped the viewfinder closed. "You felt those things with her because she let you into her vision."

"She told me I had a particular sensitivity. That's why this landscape in Timberline, the forest, the greenery, sets me off. It always has."

He wasn't going to argue with her or convince her otherwise. He had a support role today and he planned to fulfill that role to the best of his ability. "On to cabin number two, then."

Cabin number two was similar to one—more like a house and inhabited with residents, none too eager to speak with Beth. Duke filmed the exterior for her, but this cabin didn't speak to her, either.

They had more luck with cabin number three. As they drove up to the front of it, Beth sat up. "This looks spooky, doesn't it?"

"It looks abandoned."

"I'm getting the chills already." Beth stretched her arms out in front of her.

Duke cut the engine and hoisted the strap of the camera over his shoulder.

He filmed the front of the cabin as Beth hobbled up to the porch without her crutches. "Hello?"

Duke tried the door, but the rotting wood held firm. He picked at a chip of paint with his fingernail. "I think this still has the original red paint on the door."

"Seems to be locked up tight." Beth stepped off the porch steps. "I'm going to look around the side."

"Hang on." He put the camera down. "The landscaping, if you can call it that, is overgrown with weeds. Grab my arm."

Taking his arm, she leaned against him. He navigated a path through the tangled shrubs and turned the corner of the cabin. The wild brush of the forest grew close to the exterior cabin wall.

Beth tugged on his hand. "The window's broken."

They crept up to the shattered window and Duke dug for his phone. Poking his head inside the window, he turned on the phone's light and scanned the room.

"Do you see anything?"

"It's a big mess. Looks like animals, kids, transients or all three have been in here."

She yanked on the back of his shirt. "Let me have a look."

He backed away from the window and handed her the phone. "It's too high for you to see inside, especially without cutting yourself on the jagged glass."

He scanned the ground and spotted a stump of wood. "This'll work."

He dragged the wood under the window and helped Beth stand on it, holding her around the waist. "Do you see anything that grabs you?"

"No, but it's creepy. I'd like to find out more about it."

"I'm sure Rebecca can help with that."

Duke filmed more of the cabin before they got back in the car. "Three down, two to go."

Beth checked her phone. "They're in the same general area, farther out in the boonies."

"Let's go and you can review my awesomely professional video later."

He swung off the main highway, down one of the many roads that branched into the forest. Cabins and small houses dotted the road. "I wonder when housing for the Evergreen employees is going to creep out this way."

"I think there's something about the zoning that doesn't permit certain types of housing."

"I'm sure Jordan Young is working on an angle for that right now."

"And he'll probably give all the work to his worthless buddy, Bill." She tapped her phone. "Oops. I think the GPS lost its way."

"We don't have too many choices here until we plunge into the forest." He pointed to a marker up ahead on the side of the road. "There's an access road there." When they reached the marker, he made the turn.

Beth's knees bounced and she wedged her hands beneath her thighs. "Reminds me of Scarlett's area."

"Remote and rugged. These must be hunting and fishing cabins."

Beth scooted forward in her seat, her back stiff.

"Are you okay?"

Her lips parted and her chest rose and fell rapidly.

"Beth? What's wrong?"

She cupped her hands around her nose and mouth and huffed out a breath. "Feeling a little anxious. I'll be fine."

The trees crowded in on them, shutting out the light of the afternoon. Mist clung to the windshield and he flipped on the wipers. "We can stop right here, turn around."

Shaking her head, she hugged herself. "It's that feeling, Duke. The forest is closing in on me, suffocating me."

"I'm turning around."

"No!" She grabbed the steering wheel. "I can do this. I can get through it."

They came across a path leading from the access road. "My guess is the first cabin's back there."

"Then we'd better take a look."

He parked and helped her from the car. "How about one crutch?"

"I'll try it." She tucked it under one arm and he held her other arm.

The cabin arose from a clearing. A walkway paved with natural stone cut a path through a neat garden.

"It looks inhabited." He squeezed her hand. "Still getting the feeling?"

The door burst open and a man stepped out onto the porch with a shotgun.

Beth stumbled and Duke caught her.

"You lost?"

"Can you put the gun down?" Duke curled his arm around Beth's body and felt a tremble roll through her frame.

"Oh, this?" He lowered the shotgun. "Just came out here to clean it. Didn't know anyone was here. Got myself a turkey this morning."

Beth found her voice. "Do you own this cabin?"

"No, ma'am. My name's Doug Johnson, if you want to check it out. I rent the cabin once a year to do some hunting—turkey mostly. The wife likes it if I can bring one home for the Thanksgiving dinner." He tugged on his hat. "Are you looking for the owner?"

"Who is it?" Duke asked.

"I rent it from some management company—Raney Realty."

Beth pinched his side. "Bill Raney?"

"Might be, but I deal with a woman." He jerked his thumb over his shoulder. "I think I have a card, if you want me to get it."

Duke waved. "That's okay. We can look them up in town. There another cabin out this way?"

"About a mile up the road."

"Is that one for rent, too?"

"I think it is, but there's nobody there now. It's not as nice as this one."

"Raney Realty have that one?"

"I think so. I keep coming back to this place, so I'm not sure."

"Thanks. Sorry to disturb you." Beth dug her crutch into the ground. "Four down, one to go."

When they got back in the car, Duke touched her icy cheek. "Are you sure you're okay?"

"Do you find it coincidental that the cabin giving me the heebie-jeebies is managed by Bill Raney?"

"Yep." Beth had regained her focus and he didn't even bother asking if she wanted to check out the last cabin. She was like a dog with a bone at this point.

He drove almost a mile up the road until he spied another path with a mailbox at its entrance.

He pulled off the road as far as he could and met Beth

at the passenger door. Her pale face and shallow breathing indicated another panic attack was on the horizon.

"Can I get you something, Beth? We don't have to do this now, or you can wait in the car and I'll take the camera."

"It's so strong, Duke. I wish I had Scarlett with me."

"I'm with you." He handed her the crutch. "Let's go face this thing head-on."

He adjusted his gait to hers, his head swiveling from side to side, his body tense.

Beth fell against him with a cry as she pointed to the mailbox. "Look, two birds. Just like Scarlett said—two birds. This is the place."

Chapter Fifteen

Beth swayed, but Duke kept her steady. The uneasy feelings had been building in her gut as soon as Duke had turned down the access road. Now, standing in front of the mailbox, they overwhelmed her.

Breaking away from Duke, she staggered toward the mailbox and grabbed it. She traced her finger along the edges of the two birds that had been carved at the top of the mailbox. "This is what Scarlett saw."

He placed a hand against her back. "Are you ready to have a look?"

"You're not going to try to talk me out of it again?"

"You've come this far. There's no turning back."

Dragging in a breath, she leaned on her crutch. "Let's go."

A path wended its way toward the cabin, which was a duplicate of the one down the road. The hunter had been right. His rental was in better shape, but this one hadn't been abandoned.

They approached the front door, which was no longer red, and Duke took the two steps in one long stride. He banged on the solid wood door. "Hello? Anyone here?"

"I suppose we won't find any broken windows in this cabin." Beth hobbled around to the side.

The brush had been cleared away from the structure, creating a neat perimeter. Beth followed the outer wall of the cabin, the adrenaline pumping through her body. She pressed her forehead against one of the windows, but someone had tugged a pair of neat curtains across the glass.

She jumped as Duke put a hand on her shoulder. "Can't see inside this one, but this is it—the cabin of my nightmares. I'm sure of it, and the formerly red door and the two birds on the mailbox line up with Scarlett's vision."

"I doubt the owner of the cabin, especially if it's managed by Bill Raney, is going to allow us to just walk in and search around."

"Probably not. What if we rent the place?"

"Wouldn't that seem strange since you've been staying in the hotel all this time? And if Raney doesn't want you snooping around, I'm sure he could come up with a million reasons for the owner not to rent to you."

She traced a finger across the smooth glass. "I wonder who owns it. I really want to get inside."

"Can you get any reception out here? If you text Rebecca, she'll have the answer for you in a matter of minutes."

She pulled her phone from her pocket and tapped it. "No reception. That info is going to have to wait."

"But the rest doesn't have to wait." He brushed aside her hair and kissed the nape of her neck. "I'll be right back."

He headed to the back of the cabin and disappeared around the corner.

A wave of panic engulfed her again and she closed her eyes and pressed her hand against the rough wood of the cabin wall. "Duke?"

"Right here."

Her lids flew open to find him beside her. "What did you find?"

"Whaddya know? Someone left the back door open."

"You broke in?"

"Shh. We're not going to steal anything. We're just looking around to see if it's suitable for renting."

"I'm gonna end up getting you fired over this."

He took her hand. "If I'm going to get fired, we might as well get something out of it."

The forest edged up pretty closely to the back of the cabin, but the place did have a patio with a table, a couple of chairs and a barbecue pit.

Duke pulled the sleeve of his jacket over his hand and pushed open the back door. She didn't notice any broken glass or splintered wood, so he must've picked the lock. The less she knew, the better.

She stepped through the door into a small room off the kitchen with a compact washer and dryer in the corner. Her breath coming in short spurts, she edged into the kitchen as Duke closed the door.

She hesitated at the entrance to the living room where a large stone fireplace took up half the wall.

"Maybe they don't get many renters here because it's not completely furnished or ready." Duke hovered at her shoulder. "Do you want to have a look?"

Beth had to peel her tongue from the roof of her mouth to talk. "I… I'm scared. This room… There's something evil here. Do you feel it?"

Duke stepped around her into the dark living room and ran a hand along the mantel of the fireplace. "It's eerie, but I might be getting that vibe from you."

Beth took one shaky step after him. Curling her fingers around the gold locket at her throat, she closed her eyes. She could use some of Scarlett's magical tea about now.

She shuffled farther into the room, as if being drawn forward by some guiding force.

"Beth?"

Duke's voice seemed far away. Beth battled to get through the fear and revulsion to make her way toward a softer, more benevolent place at the end of this tunnel. The greenery of the Washington peninsula that had always caused her such anxiety rushed past her in a whirlwind. The blood-drenched terror that she'd faced in her shared vision with Scarlett swirled around her, but she kept her focus. There was something more, something sweet and precious, and she had to stay this course to get to it.

"Beth? Beth?"

The wood floor creaked beneath her and she fell to her knees. "I'm here. I'm back. I'll help you."

"Beth, my God."

Duke crouched beside her, his arm circling her waist. "Beth, are you okay? What's wrong with you?"

Twisting around to face him, she grabbed his jacket. "It's here, Duke. There's something here. Something led me here."

He stroked her hair. "I know, babe—the hypnosis, the visions, the red door and the birds have all led you here, but it's not enough. Even if we find out who owns the cabin, it might not be enough."

She pounded the floor through the Native American rug that covered it. "No, I mean it's here. There's something right here."

He dropped his gaze to the floor and ran his hand along the blanket, his brows creating a V between his eyes.

Just like that, he believed her.

"I don't see anything, Beth. It's just a rug." He flipped up one corner of the rug, exposing the original wood floor of the cabin, scarred and scratched. He pressed his hands against the slats of wood and one rocked beneath his hands.

"It's loose." His eyes flew to her face.

She breathed out the words. "It's here. I heard the wood creak beneath my feet. There's something here, Duke."

He reached into his pocket for his knife and flipped it

open. He jimmied it between the loose slat and its neighbor. It lifted a half an inch.

"There's a cavity here."

Beth grabbed the knife, but Duke put his hand over hers. "Easy. We don't want anyone to know we've been here."

He took over and worked the blade back and forth until the wood came up from the floor. When he could get under the slat, he angled the knife and pumped it higher.

He eased up the slat and removed it. "Hand me your phone."

She knew what he wanted, and she turned her phone's light on before dropping it into his hand.

He aimed it into the space beneath the floor. "There's a box in there. Looks like a small fisherman's tackle box. It's too big to fit through this opening. I'm going to have to remove a couple more pieces of flooring."

While Beth held the phone, Duke worked on two more slats until the opening was wide enough to accommodate the box.

"You do the honors."

With trembling hands, Beth reached into the cavity and pulled out the tin box. She didn't know what she expected—her real birth certificate? Adoption papers? A letter from her bio parents?

When she flung open the lid, she gasped and fell back on her heels. Whatever she'd expected to find, it didn't include this.

Duke grabbed a handful of the photos in the box and held them to the light. "What the hell? Nudie pictures?"

Beth studied the pictures fanned out in Duke's hand and gasped.

As she opened her mouth, an explosion rocked the cabin.

Chapter Sixteen

Duke's ears were ringing with the sound of the explosion. He reached for Beth, whose mouth was hanging open in shock. "Are you okay?"

She managed a nod.

His nostrils flared as he sniffed the air. A window in the front had shattered, but the cabin was intact, and he couldn't smell fire.

"The cabin's fine. The explosion came from outside."

He gathered all the photos from the box and shoved them into the camera case. "We need to get out of here."

Beth reached for the wood slats and slid the first one into place. They put the floor back the way it was and Beth covered it with the rug.

Duke slung the camera case across his body and hoisted Beth to her feet.

With the crutch snug beneath her arm, Beth moved as fast as she could for the kitchen.

Once outside, Duke could see black smoke rising from the front of the cabin. He turned and shut the door, clicking the lock back into place with his knife.

"Let's get in the car and call 9-1-1 when we can. We were just driving by when we heard an explosion, right?"

She licked her lips. "Got it."

They got to the front of the cabin and started down the path to the road when Beth gasped. "It's a tire."

With a sinking feeling in the pit of his stomach, Duke pushed through the gate to the road, stepping over twisted metal.

He swore when he saw the shell of his rented SUV twisted, blackened and still on fire.

Beth tried her phone. "Still no reception. I suppose we're going to have to admit to being out here unless you can think of a way to move that burning hulk and all its pieces somewhere else."

"We were walking up to the cabin to do research for your show and heard the explosion."

"We're going to have a chance to try out that story real soon." She cocked her head. "Sirens."

"Doug must've called it in."

She hooked her fingers in his back pocket. "What do you think happened to your car, other than the obvious?"

"Since dynamiting a rental car seems too suspect, even for Sheriff Musgrove, my guess is that it was an expertly placed shot to the gas tank."

"Easily explained away by an errant bullet or teenage prank."

"Or another rogue hunter, but now that Scarlett Easton has left town, who's the target this time?"

"Someone knew we were here, Duke." She rested her forehead against his back. "Someone didn't want us to find those pictures."

"That's going a little far to protect a few naked photos, don't you think. As far as I could tell, they were all grown women."

"It's more than that."

A fire truck roared down the access road, followed by a squad car and an ambulance.

"Hold that thought, Beth. We have some explaining to do."

OVER TWO HOURS LATER, after being dropped off by a deputy, they collapsed in Beth's hotel room.

Duke downed half a bottle of water in one gulp. "That went smoother than I expected. We were the victims, so the deputies didn't seem to care what we were doing at the cabin."

"At least they think it was a threat directed at me this time and not related to Scarlett's feud with the hunters."

"Yeah, but their solution was to tell you to leave town."

"It wasn't too long ago that your solution was the same."

He ran a hand down her back. "Because I wanted to protect you, not because I didn't want to deal with solving a crime. Sheriff Musgrove is a piece of work."

"At least the explosion got him off the golf course."

"You realize it's going to take about two minutes before the entire town of Timberline knows we were at that cabin."

"Who cares?" She patted the camera case. "We found the stash of pictures."

"I'm not sure what good they're going to do us unless you want to start a girlie magazine."

"That's because you didn't look at the pictures." She opened the camera case. "I did."

His pulse ticked up. "Something incriminating."

"Not exactly, but something very, very interesting." She pulled a handful of the pictures from the case and dropped them on the credenza, fanning them out. "Look at this picture and tell me what you think."

"First time I've ever had a woman ask me to look at provocative photos." He picked up the photo of a woman posing in the nude, tame by today's standards, and studied it. He dropped the picture as if it burned his fingers. "That looks like you."

"Exactly, and I can assure you I've never posed nude for anyone here in Timberline before."

He let that pass and picked up the picture again by the corner. He squinted at the pretty woman in the photo with the strawberry blond hair. Then he swallowed hard.

"Beth?"

She looked up from thumbing through the other photos. "Uh-huh?"

"Did you notice what this woman has around her neck?"

"No. An explosion interrupted my examination of the pictures."

He waved the photo in front of her face. "It looks like a necklace of some kind. I can't make out whether or not it's a locket, but I'm hazarding a guess it is."

Gasping, she snatched the photo from his hand. "You're right. A woman with strawberry blond hair wearing a necklace like mine."

Her bottom lip wobbled. "D-do you think this could be my mother?"

Duke plucked the photo from her hand and placed his thumb beneath the subject's chin, studying her face. He couldn't tell the color of her eyes, but the catlike shape matched Beth's, along with her wide cheekbones.

"You could be related, no doubt." Feeling like a voyeur, he turned the picture over. "What does it mean? Someone took risqué pictures of your mother and other women and then hid them under the floorboards of that cabin."

Beth lunged for her phone. "We need to find out who owns that cabin. All the deputy knew was that Raney Realty had the rental listing."

Beth tapped in Rebecca's number and left a message. "She's probably still busy with her open house."

Duke threw himself across the bed and rubbed his eyes. "I'm exhausted."

Beth stretched out beside him, propping up her head with her hand. "The strangest thing happened to me in that cabin. I felt like I was channeling Scarlett. Maybe some of her sensitivity rubbed off on me."

Duke's phone buzzed in his pocket and he pulled it out. "Mickey's calling. Hey, Mickey, this is my day off."

"How'd your meeting with the DEA go the other day? You never got back to me."

Duke's head rolled to the side and he watched Beth's eyelashes flutter closed. Had that meeting been before Beth's foot got caught in a bear trap or after someone had taken a shot at her?

"They're pulling all the files for me regarding drug activity in the area at the time of the kidnappings. Is someone getting anxious?"

"I'll tell you who's getting anxious—Stanley Gerber, that's who."

"Stan the man? The director of our division?"

"We had a situation, top secret. It all worked out, but Gerber wanted to know why you weren't on the case."

"And you told him I was in cold-case Siberia?"

"I did, and he wanted to know on whose orders."

"I guess Vasquez, his second in command, doesn't keep him up to date."

"I'm guessing he's having a few words with Vasquez right about now."

"Do you think he's going to pull me off the Timberline Trio case?"

Beth opened her eyes and nudged him with the heel of her hand.

"Maybe, but I'd like you to follow up with the drug connection first so we can show something for our efforts there."

"I'll see what I can do as soon as those files come through from the DEA." Duke sat up and swung his legs over the side of the bed. "What, no homework duty tonight?"

"It's Saturday. I've been coaching soccer all day."

"Father of the year, Mickey."

"I'm glad someone thinks so. Keep me posted on the drug angle and I'll put in a few hundred good words for you with Gerber."

When he ended the call Beth shot up next to him. "Are you getting yanked off this case?"

"Maybe, but not before I wrap up some loose ends."

She tapped her chest. "I'm your loose end. We need to discover what these pictures mean."

"Let's get some dinner while you wait for Rebecca's callback."

"I can't face going into town tonight. After hearing about that explosion, the townspeople just might come after me with pitchforks."

"There's that new development near Evergreen with a couple of chain restaurants."

"I could use a bland chain restaurant about now, but I need a shower after crawling around that cabin floor."

"Meet you back here in thirty minutes?"

"I think I can manage that."

He went back to his own room, his mind in turmoil. He and Beth had figured someone had to have been tracking them to know their whereabouts this afternoon—unless Rebecca had told someone.

If someone had put a tracking device on his rental car, he'd never know now that the car had been destroyed. The rental company had already towed it away.

Why wouldn't someone want them to find some old pictures? Unless that cabin had something to do with the Timberline Trio case, these threats against Beth made no sense at all.

He'd been concerned when she'd decided to stay in town because he'd figured the people threatening her would assume she was still on the Timberline Trio case, but maybe the attacks had nothing to do with the Timberline Trio.

Maybe someone had objected to Beth's personal quest all along. But why? Why should one woman's journey to find her beginnings cause anyone to feel uneasy?

Showered and changed, Duke returned to Beth's room.

She opened the door, her face alight with excitement. "Rebecca called me back and she's going to look into that property as soon as she gets the chance. She's having dinner with her fiancé, but he's flying back to New York later and she's going to return to her office for some work."

"Then let's enjoy our dinner with some endless breadsticks and all-you-can-eat salad."

She paced in front of him. "I don't think I even need my crutches anymore."

They drove across town in Beth's rental to the newer area that owed its existence to Evergreen Software. When they walked into the restaurant, they barely warranted a glance from anyone.

These were the newer residents of Timberline and, except for that glitch with Wyatt Carson, they were far removed from the Timberline Trio tragedy.

Over dinner, Duke ran his new theory past Beth. "I was thinking in the shower."

"That's where I do all my best thinking." She bit off the end of a breadstick and grinned. That interlude in the cabin had transformed Beth from the scared creature of this afternoon. He'd expected her to be wrung dry from the experience and the discovery, but she'd been energized by it—vindicated.

"Beth, it occurred to me that the threats against you may not have anything to do with the Timberline Trio case. It could be that someone here doesn't want you to discover your identity. Maybe someone discovered your true purpose and has been doing everything he can to drive you away from that purpose."

She stabbed a tomato with her fork. "I thought of that, too. What if…? What if my birth parents don't want me?"

He dropped his fork and interlaced his fingers with hers. "Are you prepared for that?"

"I came out here to find the truth. I can handle it."

"Beth." He squeezed her fingers. "You came out here because you thought you were Heather Brice and you expected to be reunited with your long-lost, loving family. It's not going to be that way."

"I know." She gave him a misty smile. "But the fact that you stayed with me, helped me, didn't turn away from me when I told you about the miscarriage…well, that means more to me than ten loving families."

He brought her fingers to his lips and kissed the tips. "I'll ride this out with you until the end."

After dinner, they closed the place down over a shared dessert and coffee for him, decaf tea for her.

As they got in the car, Beth's phone rang.

"Hi, Rebecca. I'm with Duke. I'm putting you on speakerphone. Do you have anything for us?"

"I have the owner of that cabin for you. You know Serena Hopewell, the bartender at Sutter's?"

"Serena owns the cabin?"

"She's owned it for over twenty years."

"Does she live there?"

"Doesn't look like she ever lived there. It's been a rental, under Raney Realty, for quite some time."

Duke leaned toward Beth's phone. "Inherited property?"

"I don't think so."

"Who'd she buy it from?"

"Some management company—LRS Corp. Never heard of it. Hey!"

"What's wrong?"

"My lights just flickered."

Duke grabbed the phone from Beth. "Rebecca, are you in the office alone?"

"Of course I am. Who else would be nutty enough to be working on Saturday night?" She cursed. "The lights just went out in my office completely. Is it raining?"

Duke and Beth exchanged a glance and Beth asked, "Are your doors locked?"

"Of course. What's wrong with you two?"

"Rebecca." Duke kept his tone calm. "Your life is in danger."

As he uttered his last syllable, the line went dead.

"Rebecca? Rebecca?"

He tossed his phone to Beth as he tried Rebecca's number. "Call 9-1-1."

Rebecca's phone rang until it rolled over to voice mail.

Beth jerked her head toward Duke and covered the phone. "The operator is asking me what the emergency is. What should I say?"

He snapped his fingers and she handed the phone to him. "A woman I was speaking to on the phone thought she had an intruder and then her phone went dead. I can't reach her now."

"Name and address?"

"Rebecca Geist with Peninsula Realty." He gave the operator the address of Rebecca's office and his name, and then he ended the call. "A deputy's on the way, but so are we."

Beth had retrieved her phone from the console and had been trying Rebecca's number.

"Any luck?"

"Keeps going straight to voice mail." Beth hugged herself, bunching her hands against her arms. "I'm worried. Someone must've known she was doing all this research for us. We should've warned her against going back to her office alone."

"She was going back to do some work, not just for us. Anyone who knows Rebecca must know she burns the midnight oil at the office."

"Especially someone like Bill Raney."

As he hit the accelerator, Duke drummed his thumbs on the steering wheel. "She said some corporation had sold the property to Serena. Do you remember the name?"

"It was three letters. L something, but I'm not sure."

"Why harm Rebecca over information like that? She's not the only one who has access to those records. That's public information."

"I hope that's you thinking out loud because I have no idea."

"Unless it's just to further intimidate you, drive you away."

"Yeah, like that's going to happen."

"Beth—" he put a hand on her bouncing knee "—we can research that corporation and Bill Raney and Serena Hopewell from any place. Maybe you should spread it around that you're leaving, there's no story and you're tired of the pranks against you."

"And then actually leave?"

"Yes, leave. We can continue looking into all of it— the identities of those women, the history of that cabin."

"I'll think about it." She pointed out the window. "Look! It's a squad car in front of Rebecca's office."

"Good."

As he pulled in behind the police vehicle, an ambulance came up the road, sirens wailing.

"Duke." Beth grabbed his arm.

He threw the car into Park and shot out of the driver's side just as another squad car squealed to a stop.

His gut knotted as he charged up to the front of the building.

Deputy Stevens stepped in front of him. "Oh, it's you. You called it in, right?"

"What happened? Where's Rebecca Geist?"

Stevens gestured him inside and Beth grabbed the back of his jacket, limping behind him.

Holding up a hand, Stevens said, "Beth, you might not want to go in there."

"The hell I won't."

The revolving lights of the emergency vehicles lit up a hellish scene inside the offices of Peninsula Realty. Papers littered the floor, file cabinets lay on their sides, spilling their guts, computer equipment had been smashed and in the center of it all, Rebecca Geist broken and bloodied.

Chapter Seventeen

Beth cried out and staggered toward Rebecca. She dropped to the floor beside her. "She's still breathing. She's still alive."

"We know that, Beth. The EMTs are here—make way."

Duke touched her shoulder. "Let them do their work, Beth."

She covered her face with her arm as Duke helped her to her feet. "Oh, my God. It looks bad."

"She took a bad beating, but maybe we saved her life. There's nothing we can do for her now." Duke led Beth outside, where they spoke to the deputies.

They explained how Rebecca had been doing research for them on some cabins and how she'd complained of the office lights going out while she was on the phone with them.

Stevens asked, "Did she say anything else after that?"

"Her phone went dead and that's when we called 9-1-1."

"I was the one who responded first and I think I scared the guy off."

"Did he leave any footprints? A weapon? If he beat her with his fists, you're going to be looking for someone with some battered hands."

"I think he may have used a hole-punch."

"A hole-punch?"

"You know. One of those heavy, three-hole punchers?

There was one next to the body. I'm sorry—next to Rebecca." Stevens wiped his brow beneath his hat despite the chill in the damp air. "She was conscious when I got here and her pulse was strong. I think she has a good chance of making it."

"Her fiancé." Beth folded her hands across her stomach. "She'd just had dinner with him and he was on his way to New York."

"Her coworkers will know how to reach him. From what I understand, he's loaded, flies a private jet into Timberline." Stevens waved the other deputy into the office. "What kind of research was she doing for you? Was it for the show?"

"There's not going to be any show on the Timberline Trio for *Cold Case Chronicles*." Duke curled his arm around her hip and pinched her. "Rebecca didn't come up with anything new, and Beth's decided there's not enough for a whole episode on the case."

"I'm sure quite a few people will be relieved to hear that. It's a little different when you have the FBI working on something behind the scenes and not splashing it all over TV."

"I may be wrapping up here soon, too."

"Well, maybe those kids were snatched by that Quileute creature."

"Not even the Quileute believe that, Sheriff." Beth's lips formed a thin line.

They said good-night to the sheriff and Duke caught Stevens's arm. "You'll let us know how it goes with Rebecca, right?"

Stevens shot a sidelong glance at Musgrove shouting orders and nodded. "I'll let you know as soon as I hear anything."

Beth collapsed in the passenger seat. "I hope she's going to make it."

"I hope so, too. She had a lot of head wounds and those bleed profusely. It might look worse than it is."

She pushed her hair from her face and pinned her shoulders against the seat back. "Before I do leave, Duke, I'm going to talk to Serena about her cabin."

"Are you going to ask her who sold it to her? Because I can't remember what Rebecca told us."

"That's one question."

"You might want to ask her how she could afford to buy a cabin like that on a waitress's salary—be more discreet than that, but you know what I mean. Don't you think that's weird?"

"That and the fact that she doesn't even live in it and Doug told us it's not rented out much."

"Be careful, Beth. Let people know you're done with the story, that you're leaving town."

"I will. I don't want to get anyone else involved. I've put Scarlett in danger and now Rebecca."

"And maybe Gary Binder."

"Do you think he knew something about that cabin? Do you think he was at the hotel to talk to me?"

"Maybe, or it could be his drug connection." He tapped his phone. "I got an automated email from the DEA tonight indicating the files I requested are ready for viewing, so I'm going to work on that tomorrow. And you're going to work on getting a flight out of Seattle. I can drive you to Sea-Tac anytime."

That night they made love again and she held on to Duke for dear life. If she had to give up her search in Timberline, he might be the only family she ever had.

THE NEXT MORNING DUKE, already dressed in running clothes, woke her up with a kiss. "Wish you could come with me."

She held up her foot. "As soon as this heals, I'll be right there with you."

"Do you want to have brunch at that River Café when I get back?"

"Okay, and then I'm going to find Serena and that'll be it for me."

"Which means you'll be on your laptop this morning looking into flights from Seattle to LA and on the phone with Scott to tell him the story's off."

"Yes, sir." She saluted. "Scott's going to be so happy this fell through. He warned his father it was a bad story."

"So, you get to keep your life and pump up Scott's ego in the process. It's a win-win."

Two hours later they parted ways after brunch. Duke's rental-car agency had replaced his SUV. Luckily for them, they had used different rental companies or one company would be left wondering just what the hell was going on in Timberline.

That was exactly what she wanted to know.

She drove into town, wishing she hadn't eaten so much at brunch. When she sat down at the bar at Sutter's she didn't want Serena to think she was there just for her.

A call to Chloe had already confirmed that Serena was working today. When didn't she work the bar at Sutter's? Maybe that was how she could afford the upkeep on that cabin.

All eyes seem riveted to her when she walked into the restaurant. If someone wanted her out of Timberline, it could be any one of these people.

She hobbled to the bar on one crutch and hopped up on a stool.

Serena placed a cocktail napkin in front of her. "What can I get you?"

"I'm just going to have lunch again, if that's okay."

"Fine with me." Serena dropped a menu on the bar and got a beer for another customer.

Beth made a show of studying the menu and then closed it and folded her hands on top of it.

Serena returned. "Ready?"

"I'll have a ginger ale and a bowl of lentil soup."

Serena shot the ginger ale into a glass from a nozzle. "Not too popular around here anymore, are you?"

"No, and I can't do a show when the residents have turned against me. I'm calling it quits on this story."

"You can't blame people for getting cold feet. A lot of weird stuff has gone down since you've been here."

"Yeah, like someone shooting the gas tank of Agent Harper's rental car and blowing it up."

"Shows how desperate some of these people are. You don't mess with the FBI."

"That explosion—" Beth toyed with her straw "—happened outside of your cabin."

Serena's eyes narrowed.

"I mean, you own that cabin, right?"

"I do. Excuse me." Serena moved to the other end of the bar to take an order. She didn't return to Beth until she brought the soup.

"One lentil soup."

"Did you inherit that cabin?"

"Who, me? My folks never had any money, didn't even come from this area."

"So, you bought it?"

"I bought it after the Timberline kidnappings. Prices dropped off then. The lumber company had already pulled up roots. I got a good deal from an anxious seller."

"That person must've regretted it once Evergreen Software moved in here and prices went up again."

"Actually, it wasn't a person, just some big corporation that owned other properties. I got lucky."

"Is the corporation still around? What was the name of it?"

"Why do you care?"

Damn, she'd come across as too nosy. She took out her phone and feigned interest in her text messages. "I don't, really. Just curious—occupational hazard."

"I don't remember the name of the company. I'd have to look it up in my paperwork, wherever that stuff is now. Oh, hello, Jordan. Can I get you something?"

Smiling at Beth, he pointed to her soup. "I'll have some of that and a cup of coffee, if you've got some fresh."

"Coming right up."

Jordan swiveled on his stool to face her. "I heard you're not going to do the story."

"Word travels fast." She placed her phone on the bar.

"Small town." He lifted a shoulder. "Too bad."

"Are you one of those who was pro-story? I would've thought you'd be against it because of the business interests you have here."

"Thanks, sweetheart." He dumped some cream into the coffee Serena had brought him. "I'm a forward-thinking person. I think any publicity is good publicity. That whole mess with Carson kidnapping those kids and playing the hero didn't hurt business or our reputation. Some people are too sensitive."

"Like your friend Bill Raney."

"Bill has a lot to be sensitive about. He's a failure. People like me and that little firecracker, Rebecca Geist...we have nothing to fear."

"Did you hear what happened to Rebecca last night?"

"Damned shame, but then, you tend to attract unwanted attention when you're successful. Like you." He sipped his coffee and met her gaze over the rim. "Do you really want to give up?"

"I don't consider it giving up. There's just not enough here to produce a compelling story."

He winked. "You haven't talked to me yet."

"That's not from a lack of effort. You're a busy man, Mr. Young."

"Jordan, and I've got some time right now. Maybe what I have to show you will make you reconsider your decision."

Her heart thumped. Jordan had been around for a while. He just might know more of Timberline's secrets than anyone else since he also seemed to be tight with the town's movers and shakers.

"That depends on what you've got for me."

"You know that cabin you wanted to see out on Raven Road? The one where the agent's car exploded?" He hunched forward and cupped a hand around his mouth. "I can get you inside."

Beth's gaze darted to Serena counting money at the register. "It belongs to Serena."

"Yes and no. Let's just say it's more complicated than that."

"How can you get into the cabin?" She couldn't exactly admit to Jordan that she'd already been inside. She didn't want to get Duke into any trouble, especially if it turned out that Jordan knew the real owner.

"Let's just say I'm like this—" he crossed his fingers "—with the management company."

"H…he doesn't have to be there, does he?"

"He doesn't even have to know. It'll be our secret." He put his finger over his lips and glanced at Serena.

"Okay. What time?"

"How about right now? I don't have any meetings until later this afternoon." He rubbed his hands together when Serena put his soup in front of him. "Thanks."

When she walked away, he dropped his spoon. "I'll tell

you what. You're staying at one of my hotels, the Timberline, right?"

"Yeah, the one that needs cameras."

"I have a little business to attend to there. Why don't you head back to the hotel, let me finish my lunch, and I'll meet you there and we can go over to the Ravens together."

"The Ravens?"

"That's what the cabin's called. Most of the owners of these cabins, especially the ones outside of town, named their places."

"I didn't even know that road was called Raven Road." Beth's hands grew clammy just thinking about the Ravens and she grabbed a napkin and crumpled it in her fist. Her breath started coming in shallow gusts, and she slid from the stool. "Can you excuse me for a minute?"

She made a beeline for the ladies' room and hunched over the sink, breathing in and out. Just talking about the cabin was causing her to freak out. How would she handle another visit there? But Jordan was offering her another opportunity to take a look at the place and she couldn't refuse.

She splashed water on her face and gave herself a pep talk in the mirror. Pasting a smile on her face, she returned to the bar.

"Sorry about that. So, the Ravens is on Raven Road."

Jordan studied her face for a second. "It's a local name, not on the maps. Ravens are important to Quileute legends, so I guess that's where it came from. Does that sound like a plan? You can wait for me in the parking lot of the hotel. I won't be long, and then you can decide if you really want to give up on this story."

"Okay. I'd love to see inside that cabin…for my own reasons."

"Excellent." He took a spoonful of soup into his mouth.

"Anything else?" Serena picked up Beth's bowl and dropped the check.

"No, thanks." Beth left some cash on the bar, swept her phone into her palm and nodded to Jordan.

Beth took her time getting back to the hotel, since Jordan had to finish his lunch anyway. She stopped by the market and picked up some water and a bottle of wine. If this was going to be her last night in Timberline with Duke, she might as well make it special.

She pulled her phone out of her pocket to leave him a text message. She tapped her screen, but her phone wouldn't wake up. She powered it down and tried again. The battery must've died.

Jordan had said he had meetings in the afternoon, so they'd be done at the Ravens before Duke finished working on the DEA files anyway.

When she pulled into the hotel's parking lot, Jordan was just walking out of the hotel.

She grabbed her crutch and scrambled from the car. "That was fast."

"It was just soup. What took you so long?"

She held up the plastic bag with one hand. "Stopped for a few things."

"Perishable?"

"No."

"Why don't you leave them in your car?" He looked at his watch. "My meeting was earlier than I thought, and I'm going to have to make this fast."

"Oh, okay." Leaning back into the car, Beth placed the bag on the passenger seat.

She used her crutch to navigate to his black sedan and the open passenger door.

"How's that foot of yours?"

"It's getting better. In a few days I think I can put more pressure on it and get around without using a crutch."

He helped her into the car and slammed the door.

On the way to the cabin he asked about her theories of the kidnappings.

She stared out the window at the passing scenery before answering. She really hadn't given the Timberline Trio much thought, especially once she'd found out she wasn't one of them.

"I'm not sure, maybe child trafficking, as awful as that sounds. Maybe those kids were just in the wrong place at the wrong time."

"It was a strange and scary time, especially for those with children."

"You didn't have children to worry about?"

"My wife and I were never fortunate in that regard."

"And then you lost your wife… I'm sorry. People do talk in a small town."

"Lorna drowned."

"I'm so sorry."

She'd changed the mood in the car by mentioning his wife. He seemed thoughtful as he gazed over the steering wheel.

He never remarried, so Lorna must've been the love of his life.

When he made the turn onto Raven Road, her fingers curled into the leather on either side of the seat and her pulse rate quickened. She'd thought getting into the cabin and finding the picture of the woman with the locket had dispelled her fears, but the anxiety still hovered at the edges of her mind.

Jordan dragged a hand across his face. "Did you call Agent Harper? I know he was interested in the cabin, too."

"My phone's battery died. He's working, anyway."

"On a Sunday?"

"He works when he gets the call."

"I have to admit I'm a little relieved."

She tilted her head. "Why is that?"

"He's an officer of the law and, technically, I'm entering the cabin without the owner's knowledge."

She smirked. If Jordan only knew Duke had been breaking and entering just yesterday. "I don't think he'd report you. So, do you think the Ravens is connected to the Timberline Trio kidnappings?"

"Could be. Back in the day, it was used for some illicit activities."

"Really?" Like prostitution? Her stomach felt sick at the thought of the pretty strawberry blonde involved in anything sordid.

"I don't know that much about it, but the Ravens had a reputation around that time. I thought that's why you were out here yesterday."

"I think Duke, Agent Harper, may have gotten some hint about something like that, but we barely got to the front door when the car exploded."

"Makes you wonder if some of those old characters are still hanging around, like what happened to Binder. Coincidental that he died in a hit-and-run accident right after telling the FBI a little about Timberline's drug culture."

A chill swept across Beth's body and she hunched her shoulders. She dug her phone out of her pocket and tried waking it up again.

"Still dead?"

"Yeah." She dropped it back in her pocket.

"Reception is bad out this way, anyway."

He swung around the yellow tape tied to a tree where Duke's car had been parked and rolled up the pathway to the cabin.

"Stay right there, Beth. I'll help you out."

He appeared at the passenger door and jingled a set of keys as he gave her his arm for support. "We can get inside the right way this time."

"This time?"

"Well, you didn't get in at all yesterday, did you?"

"N...no."

Her uneasiness still nibbled at the edges of her brain, but it differed from the sheer terror she felt yesterday.

He held her arm as they walked up the two steps to the front door. He used the key to unlock two locks on the door and pushed it open.

The front door opened right onto the sitting room where she and Duke had removed the floorboards and found the pictures.

"After you."

She hesitated, and Jordan put a hand on the small of her back. "We're not going to get caught."

As soon as Beth entered the room, beads of sweat broke out on her forehead. Her dry mouth made it hard to swallow. The room closed around her and she hung on to her crutch as the room began to spin.

"You feel it, don't you, Beth? She led you here, didn't she? Your mother led you to the place where she was murdered."

Chapter Eighteen

Duke pushed back from the desk in the conference room at the sheriff's station and stretched. If the Bureau pulled him off this case, at least he could leave with a good report regarding the drug trade in Timberline and who was behind it. A biker gang called the Lords of Chaos controlled the drug trade on the peninsula. They also ran women and weapons. A thorough investigation of that gang might lead to additional information about the kidnappings.

He checked his phone. Nothing from Beth. He texted her, but the message didn't show as Delivered. He tried calling and his call went straight to voice mail.

Maybe she was getting something from Serena.

Unger tapped on the open door. "Thought you'd want to know. Rebecca Geist is out of surgery. It looks like she's going to pull through, but they're keeping her in an induced coma until the swelling on her brain goes down."

"Thank God. Did her fiancé make it out here?"

"He's on a flight back right now. Do you need anything in here?"

"No. I skipped lunch, so I might take a break in a few minutes and pick up something."

"I can recommend the sandwich place two doors down."

"Thanks." When Unger left, Duke rubbed his eyes and went back to the Lords of Chaos and their dirty deeds.

As he scanned a bulleted list, a name jumped out at

him—LRS Corporation. That was the name Rebecca had mentioned before she'd been attacked. He ran his finger beneath the text on the screen. The Lords of Chaos had rented several properties from LRS and used some of them for their illegal activities, including cooking meth.

Duke switched to a search engine and entered *LRS Corporation, Timberline, Washington*. He skimmed through the relevant hits.

LRS stood for and was owned by Lawrence Richard Strathmore, who'd passed away about twenty years ago. He'd been around during the time of the kidnappings.

He clicked through a couple of biographies. The man and the corporation had owned a lot of property in Timberline at one time. His wife had passed before he did and they had one daughter.

Duke whistled through his teeth. Strathmore's daughter, Lorna, had married Jordan Young.

Duke jumped up from his chair and stuck his head out the door. "Unger?"

"Yeah?"

"Need to ask you a few questions."

Unger walked around the corner with a sandwich in his hand. "Sorry, man. I would've gotten you something when I went over there earlier if I'd known you were gonna be holed up in here all morning."

"That's okay." Duke waved him to the chair as he perched on the edge of the conference table. "Jordan Young is a widower, right?"

"Yeah, his wife died about ten years ago—drowned."

"His wife was Lorna? Lorna Strathmore?"

"Not sure about her maiden name, but Lorna's right."

"Wasn't she loaded?"

"I heard something like that. Young got his money the old-fashioned way—he married it."

"You ever heard of LRS Corporation?"

"I've seen the name on a few things. Why?"

"That was the name of Young's father-in-law's company—owned a lot of property in Timberline."

"Now Young owns a lot of property in Timberline. Why are you asking?"

"Just a curious connection between him and something Beth was looking into." Duke rubbed his chin. "You know much about him?"

"Between me and you?" Duke poked his head out the door and then closed it. "He likes the ladies, and I think he shares that with my boss."

"Is the sheriff married? I don't see a problem for Young since he's widowed."

"I guess I'm being too discreet for the big-city boy, huh? What I mean is Young is into hookers, and I think Sheriff Musgrove is, too, which is a problem for both of them, as far as I can tell."

"Wow, you need to get rid of that guy. He's going to bring the department a world of hurt otherwise."

"Tell me about it." He swung open the door. "Anyway, that's about all I know about Young, about all I want to know about him."

"Thanks, Unger."

Duke tapped his thumbs on the edge of his keyboard. Jordan Young sold that cabin to Serena Hopewell. Why? Was he the one who'd stashed those pictures under the floorboards? Were those women hookers? Was the one who had Beth's locket a hooker?

He needed to reach Beth, tell her everything. He tried her phone again, and again it went to voice mail. This time he left her a detailed message about Jordan Young.

Had she even seen Serena today? Maybe Serena had already given Beth the same info about Young.

He shut down the computer and stacked his files. Then he locked the conference room door behind him.

"Unger, I'm going to Sutter's for some lunch."

"All right, but the sandwiches down the street are just as good."

"I need something else at Sutter's."

The Evergreen lunch hour must've ended because Duke walked into a mostly empty restaurant. He noted Serena working behind the bar and wove his way through the dining room tables to get there.

"You just missed your girlfriend, the TV reporter."

"Did she talk to you about the cabin?" Duke hunched forward on the bar.

Serena's eyes widened. "Why are you two so interested in my cabin? It's just a cabin like any other on the outskirts of town, and it has no relation to the Timberline Trio case."

"That you know of."

"Do you want something to drink or are you just here to harass me?"

"Who sold you that cabin, Serena?"

"Oh, for God's sake. I don't remember—some corporation."

"Why are you lying? The LRS Corporation sold you that cabin—LRS, as in Lawrence Richard Strathmore, as in Jordan Young's father-in-law. Only, Young had control of the corporation when he sold the cabin to you. Why'd he sell it to you? Why'd he give you such a sweet deal?"

Serena backed up to the register, her arms across her chest. "What do you want from me?"

"Let's start with the truth. What was Young using that cabin for and why'd he want to get rid of it?"

He lunged over the bar and grabbed her arm. "And what's this tattoo on your wrist? Does that *LC* stand for the Lords of Chaos?"

She jerked away from him. "You want answers? Talk to Jordan Young."

"Is there a problem?" A restaurant employee wearing

a shirt and tie approached them with his phone out. "Do I need to call the police?"

Duke released Serena and pulled out his badge. "I just have a few questions for Ms. Hopewell."

"It's all right, Randy." Serena flicked her fingers.

When the manager walked away, Duke asked, "Where can I find Young?"

"I'm not sure." Serena rubbed the tattoo on her wrist. "But he was in here the same time your friend was here when she was asking me questions about the cabin, sat right next to her. Maybe even did something to her phone."

Duke's blood ran cold. "What?"

"She went to the ladies', left her phone on the bar, and it looked like Jordan picked it up."

"Did they leave together?" Duke's heart was thundering in his chest.

"No, but..."

"But what?" Duke's hands fisted on the bar. "I'm sure the FBI can find something on you, Serena, from your years running with the Lords of Chaos."

Her jaw hardened. "But she left and then he left not long after they were having a hushed conversation—like he didn't want me to hear what they were saying."

"And did you hear anything they were saying?"

"I heard him mention the Ravens."

"The Ravens? What's that?"

"That's the name of my cabin—you know, the one you broke into before someone blew up your car."

BETH DROPPED TO the nearest chair, her crutch falling to the ground. "My mother was murdered? Here?"

"I'm afraid so, Beth." Jordan pulled a gun from his pocket and aimed it at her.

"The picture." Beth put a hand to her temple where her

pulse throbbed. "The woman with the strawberry blond hair... Was that her?"

"I knew you'd found those pictures. I knew you and Agent Harper were out here, and I thought I could stop you by shooting out the gas tank on his car, but I was too late." He smoothed the pad of his thumb over his eyebrow. "I knew she'd led you to those pictures. How else could you have found them?"

Beth folded her hands in her lap, trying to hold it all together even though she felt amazingly relaxed—maybe because she'd reached the moment of truth.

"You don't seem surprised or skeptical that a dead woman could've led someone to a bunch of pictures."

He sat on the arm of the chair across from her. "That's because your mother was Quileute and so are you."

Scarlett reaching out to her and bringing her along in her dream quest made sense now, but with that hair color, her mother probably wasn't full-blooded Quileute.

Beth trapped her hands between her knees. Jordan Young most likely murdered her mother for reasons she didn't know yet, but she wasn't ready to go there with him. He still might let her go.

"Why did you take me here? Why are you telling me all this?"

"You want to know your identity, don't you?" He spread his hands. "That's why you concocted the story that you were here for the Timberline Trio, although you thought you were Heather Brice for a while, didn't you? I would've been content if you had continued along that path. Why didn't you?"

"Duke—Agent Harper—requested DNA from the Brices and ran a cross-check with mine." She plucked her useless phone from her pocket. "I've called him, you know. I told him I was on my way here."

"That would be hard to do with a phone without a battery." He dipped into his front pocket and held up a battery pinched between his thumb and forefinger.

Beth's stomach rolled. "Are you going to tell me about my mother? Her name? Why she was murdered?"

"Your mother." He stroked his chin. "Angie was lovely, delicate, so much more refined than Lorna, even though my wife was the one with the money."

"Your wife died. You said she drowned." Beth clenched her bottom lip between her teeth to keep it from trembling. Had he killed his wife, too?

"That was later." He ran a hand through his salt-and-pepper hair. "When Angie got pregnant, I realized it was my wife's fault we couldn't have a baby."

The knots in Beth's gut tightened, almost cutting off her breath.

Jordan Young was her father.

His blue eyes, the precise shade of her own, lit up. "That's right, Beth. I'm your father."

She gripped the arms of the chair and vaulted out of it, but her legs wouldn't support her and she stumbled backward, falling onto the chair's cushion.

"Why? Why did you kill her? Because she got pregnant and had your child?"

His brows collided over his nose. "If she had gone away quietly, like she did at first, it wouldn't have been a problem. But she decided to come back. I was married to a very wealthy woman and had a father-in-law who thought the world of me. How do you think he would've felt after discovering I'd gotten some Indian pregnant?"

Beth flinched. "But I must've been two years old. She'd kept the secret that long."

"You weren't two at the time. Your adoptive parents changed your age and birth certificate to mask your true identity. You were a baby, barely one year old. Angie left when you were first born, but then she returned. She shouldn't have come back, Beth."

"You murdered my mother to keep her quiet? To get rid of a messy problem?"

"It was more of an accident, to tell you the truth. She knew I was never going to leave Lorna, and she knew I wanted her to keep quiet." He clucked his tongue. "Your mother wasn't as sweet and innocent as she appeared. You have the pictures to prove that. She tried to extort money out of me."

"Maybe she just wanted child support for me."

"Whatever you want to call it. She also found the pictures of the other women—silly bitch to think she was the only one."

Beth's nose stung. How could she be related to this monster? Duke had been right. It would've been better to stay in the dark.

"Did you shoot at me? Set the bear traps? Beat Rebecca?"

"Bill was more than happy to help with Rebecca. I was just trying to scare you away, but you wouldn't go away— just like your mother. As soon as I heard Beth St. Regis of *Cold Case Chronicles* was in town, I knew there was a problem."

"Y…you knew who I was all this time?"

"Of course. When I offered you up to the market, I insisted on having some say in where you went."

"So, I have you to thank for my cold, unfeeling parents."

He shrugged. "What do you expect from a couple who would take a child off the black market? But I was your father, Beth. I followed your career with great pride—until you came here."

A movement beyond Jordan's shoulder caught her eye. Something had flickered at the window of the back door.

"What led you here?" Jordan glanced at the fireplace.

"Did she speak to you from beyond? I knew she had the gift, not as strong as Scarlett Easton's, but I always feared it."

Was that Duke at the back door? She coughed. "It started with the Pacific Chorus frog. It was a toy I'd had from my earliest years. I finally tracked it down to Timberline because of the Wyatt Carson story on TV. And it was the visions and nightmares I'd always had of a lush forest filled with terror."

A glimmer of light flashed from the laundry room for a second and Beth held her breath as Jordan cocked his head.

She rushed on. "Why would I feel such fear? Was I here in the cabin at one point?"

"You were here when I murdered her."

Beth bent over at the waist, bitter bile rising in her throat. "You killed her in front of her child?"

"It wasn't planned. It was an accident. She just wouldn't shut up about what I owed her and how she was going to get it out of me." He waved the gun in her face and for the first time she really believed he'd kill her.

"I'm not like my mother. I don't want anything out of you. I was going to leave Timberline anyway. I'll never come back here."

"We're alike, you and I." He wagged a finger at her. "I could see that when I watched your show. A hard charger. I admire that, Beth."

"I am like you. I understand why you did what you did. You were only protecting your position."

"I murdered Lorna, too, you know."

Beth covered her ears. "I don't want to know what you did. I don't care."

"I saved you that day, Beth. As I stabbed your mother and rivers of blood soaked your body, I saved you."

Beth choked and covered her mouth.

"But I don't think I can save you this time. If you'd

just stopped digging. If you hadn't gone to Scarlett. If you hadn't asked Rebecca for help. If you hadn't been part Quileute and your mother's daughter."

"Where is she? What did you do with my mother's body after you stabbed her to death?"

Jordan rose from the arm of the chair and placed his hand against the wall above the mantel. "I left her here."

Beth cried out and staggered to her feet. "You bastard!"

The gun dangled at his side and she lunged for it.

Jordan raised his arm, but she was close to him and bumped his forearm.

"Drop it, Young." Duke burst into the living room, his weapon trained on Jordan.

Jordan grabbed her around the waist, gripping the gun in the other hand.

A shot rang out and Beth screamed over the ringing in her ears.

Jordan slumped against her, his blood pumping out of the wound in his chest, covering her body.

She'd returned to where she began.

Epilogue

Safe in the crook of Duke's arm, Beth watched the demolition crew enter the Ravens, followed by a hazmat team from the FBI and Deputy Unger.

"You don't need to be here, Beth."

"I do. My mother led me back here and I owe it to her to witness her release."

He rubbed her back. "He didn't admit to anything involving Gary Binder, did he?"

"No, everything else was him and Bill Raney."

"The sheriff's department has already arrested Raney for assault and attempted murder. They're going to try to determine how much he knew about Young's activities."

"Serena, too?"

"She's left town."

"I guess there's your answer."

"Maybe, or she's protecting herself against questions about the biker gang, the Lords of Chaos, she used to run with."

"Rebecca's doing better. I visited her this morning. Her fiancé is going to take her to Hawaii on a sort of a convalescence-slash-vacation in a week."

"You talked to Scarlett?"

"She's still in San Francisco and is heading for New York after." Beth rested her head against Duke's shoulder. "She wasn't too surprised when she found out about my mother's heritage."

"She didn't know Angie?"

"Her grandmother had known my grandmother, but they didn't live on the reservation and Angie was a free spirit. When she came back to the rez twenty-five years ago, pregnant, she'd talked about a rich fiancé who was going to take her around the world."

"And she never left Timberline." Duke shook his head. "Did Jordan talk much about the black market he used to...place you?"

"No. Do you think it's related to the disappearance of the Timberline Trio?"

"I do, and I think they're both related to the Lords of Chaos. I was at least able to give the Bureau a thorough report of the gang's activities in this area."

"Where to next for you?"

"Wherever you are." He kissed the side of her head.

"I'm sure the FBI is going to have a thing or two to say about that."

"After I tag along with you to LA, I think I'm headed back to Chicago, but not before we make some serious plans."

"I like the sound of that." She fluffed his hair back from his face.

"Are you going to do a segment on finding your mother? It definitely qualifies as a cold case, and the ratings would be sky-high."

She tightened her hold on his arm as the door of the cabin swung wide. "I don't care about the ratings, Duke. Some things are not for the public's consumption."

The hazmat crew navigated the porch steps, wheeling a gurney with a black bag on top of it.

Beth sucked in a breath and Duke pushed off the stone planter and helped Beth to her feet.

As the gurney made its way down the path, a surge of people, Quileute in their native ceremonial dress, gathered on either side of the procession.

A low chant rose and puffs of incense scented the air around them.

One of the elders approached Beth and bowed her head. "You have family now, Beth St. Regis, a whole nation behind you."

With tears in her eyes, Beth nodded and touched the old woman's silver hair.

When law enforcement, the emergency vehicles and the procession of Quileute had cleared out, Duke took her in his arms. "I'm sorry, Beth, for all of it."

"I'm glad I found out. Now I can get to know my mother for the person she was. All the doubts and fears are gone."

He stroked her hair. "It's time to rewrite the past for both of us now. I want to create what we both missed out on—a family. If that's just us or ten kids or one, it doesn't matter. Are you ready for that, Beth?"

She curled her arms around his waist and pressed her cheek against the steady beat of his heart. "I'm ready for all of it, and as long as you're by my side, I know I'm home. Duke Harper, you're the man of my dreams."

* * * * *

REUNITED BY THE BADGE

DEBORAH FLETCHER MELLO

To all my Jewels in The Reading Room

Know that you are much loved and valued!

You all make my heart sing!

Chapter 1

Dr. Paul Reilly stood in front of his business-class seat, waiting anxiously to disembark the airplane. He'd been traveling for some thirty-plus hours, having started with an Air France flight from Accra, Ghana, to Paris, France, and ending with a Delta flight into Chicago. He was past the point of exhaustion and all he wanted was to be on firm ground, and home.

The cell phone in his hand began to beep and vibrate, an influx of incoming messages finally getting through after he'd taken the device out of airplane mode. He stole a quick glance at the lengthy list to determine the urgency of his responding, or not, and then he dropped the unit into the inner breast pocket of his blazer.

The line out of the aircraft began to move slowly. When he spied his first opportunity to make an exit, Paul stepped into the aisle. He reached for his carry-on bag out of the upper storage compartment and pushed forward, beating a woman who was whining about the heat and a couple with four unruly kids out the door. He moved swiftly down the Jetway to the terminal, exhaling a sigh of relief as he shifted out of the crowd toward the baggage reclaim area.

As he waited for the airlines to engage the luggage carousel, he pulled his cell back into his hands and dialed one of the first numbers in his call list. His brother Oliver answered on the second ring.

"Where are you?" Oliver questioned, a hint of stress in his tone.

Paul took a deep breath. "The airport. I just landed."

"Did you get my text message?"

"I got a few dozen. I haven't had an opportunity to read any of them since I left Ghana."

"I sent you the lab results for those tissue samples you gave me. I haven't had a chance to start testing the drug samples yet."

"And?"

"And, something is definitely not right. But you have a bigger problem."

"What's that?"

"The samples have disappeared. All of them. The tissue samples and the drug products."

"What do you mean, *disappeared*?"

"I mean someone took them and now they're gone."

"But you have the results?"

"No. *You* have the only results. I emailed them to you first thing, before I even looked at them. Once I did read them, I needed to do some additional testing, but before that could happen it all vanished. Including the original first round of test results!"

"So, they got both shipments?"

"Both? You sent more than one shipment of samples?"

"Yeah. I mailed one to your office and I mailed the other to the house in Windsor, since I knew you had plans to be there."

"The Windsor shipment might be waiting for me, as long as no one knew you were sending it there."

Paul blew a soft sigh, his mind racing as he tried to make sense of what his brother was telling him. Dr. Oliver Reilly worked for the federal government. He was a cancer research scientist reporting to the Centers for Disease Control and Prevention. Like his brother, Paul had a medical degree, but specialized in emergency care and family practice. He'd chosen to be a public health practitioner over private practice.

Paul trusted Oliver, one of only a few people he knew who would have his back, whatever the situation. "Did you discuss this with anyone?"

"No. Not a soul. Which is also why I didn't file a police report. Whoever knew the samples were here, also knew you sent them. Whoever took them has access to the government labs because there isn't an ounce of evidence to point toward a break-in. Now, I'm not one for conspiracy theories, but something's going on."

Paul took another deep breath. The carousel had just begun to spin, the passengers from his international flight crowding around like a herd of cattle waiting for something to happen. As the first bags appeared out of a hole in the rear wall, the group drew closer, preparing to snatch their possessions as quickly as they could.

Oliver called his name. "Paul! You still there?"

"Sorry, yeah. Just trying to think."

"Look, I'm here to help any way I can. But, this feels like it might be more than either one of us can handle. Have *you* talked to anyone? The police? An attorney, maybe?"

Paul shook his head, oblivious to the fact his brother couldn't see him through the telephone line. His eyes were skating over the crowd, a sense of unease beginning to swell in his midsection. He was suddenly feeling slightly paranoid, like he needed to be looking over his shoulder. "I've got to run. I'll call you as soon as I get to the house."

"Be careful, please," Oliver admonished as the line disconnected in his ear.

Minutes later, Paul sat in the back of an Uber. His

preferred driver, a grandmother from the island of Haiti, was chatting him up about his trip. The older woman had been driving him back and forth for the last year, her wide smile always a welcome sight whether he was coming or going.

"You need a wife," she said, the comment coming out of left field.

Paul laughed. "Why would I want to do something like that?"

"God didn't make man to live his life alone. That's why he gave Eve to Adam. Someone to be your helpmate. A partner to help carry some of the burden and provide comfort when you need it. It's why you need a wife. God has ordained it!" she professed with an air of finality that suddenly had Paul considering the possibilities.

He thought about the women in his life—one woman in particular—then shook his head. "I don't foresee that in my immediate future, Mrs. Pippin."

"What about that beauty queen you were dating? Was she not wifey material?"

"No!" he exclaimed, his head waving from side to side. "She was *definitely* not wife material." For a moment he thought about the Miss Illinois contestant he'd met in the hospital waiting room. She had captured his attention and then all focus had been lost two weeks later when she accused him of cheating because he hadn't answered her call or returned it in a timely manner. She had keyed his car, stolen his phone and had poisoned his fish tank with bleach. He discovered later that he had fared better than her last boyfriend. That poor guy had suffered immeasurable damage when she'd superglued his junk to his leg after discovering he'd slept with her friend. Any man willing to make her his wife would have to sleep with both eyes open at night.

Mrs. Pippin interrupted his moment of reverie. "Your heart is still with that lawyer woman. The one you talk about, but don't talk to," she concluded, grunting slightly as she gave him a look through the rearview mirror.

The faintest hint of a smile lifted across Paul's face. "She broke my heart, Mrs. Pippin. And she left it in a million pieces."

The old woman grunted a second time. "She is still under your skin. She never leaves you. Like a bad juju. That is why all the other beauties you date don't stand a chance. You should call her."

Paul suddenly found himself pondering her suggestion, smiling at the thought of any woman being some kind of mystical charm that could sway him from other relationships. Maybe Mrs. Pippin was right, and he had himself a case of bad juju. He remembered how smitten he'd been, so possessed that he couldn't begin to imagine his life without the beauty who'd felt like home in his small world.

That woman she referred to was Simone Black, daughter of Chicago's illustrious police superintendent Jerome Black and his wife, federal court judge Judith Harmon Black. The last time he had spoken with Simone, their conversation had been tense, and he'd felt battered by the end of it. There had been an ultimatum, or two, and the predictable battle of wills when the two disagreed. Their communication had failed, and both had shut down.

He could barely remember who had started that fight or what they'd even fought about, just that it had been the end for their relationship and months of conflict between them. They had agreed to part ways, choosing to let go of each other, instead of battling for a happily-ever-after that could have lasted a lifetime.

A mission trip to Northern Thailand to treat the in-

digenous people of the Akha tribe, high in the Chiang
Rai mountains, had kept him from falling into a fit of
depression and crying into his cornflakes for months.
Being able to provide medical treatment to patient populations that included local migrant workers, as well as
refugee populations from bordering Myanmar, had kept
him sane and balanced and unconcerned with whether
the woman he had loved was moving on without him. He
had regained focus and come back with a renewed sense
of purpose. The spiritual journey that had been so much
about expanding his horizon and answering a calling,
had become a much needed balm, a bandage of sorts on
an open wound. There had been five more mission trips
since and no wailing over the loss of his woman.

Now, thinking about her was adding to the frustration
he was already feeling. But calling Simone, a prominent
lawyer with the state's attorney's office, suddenly made
more sense than not. Despite their problems, he trusted
her and right then, he needed counsel from someone he
could trust.

Mrs. Pippin was rambling, sharing a story about one
of her many grandchildren. Paul listened with half an ear
as he considered his options. He needed help and Simone
might be willing to point him in the right direction. She
also had connections who might prove to be beneficial
in helping him solve his problem. He knew he'd fare better with her than without her, if only to get a hint or two
of advice.

Paul shifted forward in his seat. "Mrs. Pippin, change
of plans. I need to grab a bite to eat. Do you mind taking me to West Bryn Mawr, please? Down near North
Clark Street."

"No problem at all. Just change the destination in the
app for me."

"Yes, ma'am."

Minutes later she'd turned the burgundy Avalon he was riding in about and headed toward the North Side of town. He pushed the speed dial for the first number in his phone contacts and waited for it to be answered.

Simone Black answered just as he was about to hang up. "Why are you calling me, Paul?" Her tone was wary as she said hello.

Hearing her voice sent both a rumble of anxiety into the pit of his stomach and a blanket of calm across his back and shoulders. The conflicting emotions caused him to struggle to stay focused. He took a deep breath before he spoke. "It's important, Simone. I really need your help."

There was an awkward pause as the woman on the other end took time to ponder his comment. When she finally responded her voice was thick with attitude. "This better be good, Paul Reilly. Do not waste my time!"

"Can you meet me, please?"

"Now? Do you know what time it is?"

"I know it's late, Simone, but I wouldn't ask if it weren't important. And I mean life-and-death important. I really need to talk to you."

There was another lengthy pause before she answered. "If it's that important, I guess I can make the time. But you'd better not be playing games with me!"

He blew a soft sigh of relief. "I'm headed over to our place now. I should be there in ten minutes."

"We have a place?" she replied sarcastically.

Paul shook his head. "I'll be waiting, Simone. I'll see you when you get there."

As he disconnected the line, Paul noted the look Mrs. Pippin was giving him. The old woman eyed him with raised brows. Bemusement furrowed her forehead and there was a hint of hubris in her eyes. He was sure something snarky teased the tip of her tongue, but she bit back the quip, giving him an easy smile instead.

Paul chuckled. He hated admitting when the old woman was right and in the short time he'd known her, her instincts had often been spot-on. This time was no different. Because Simone Black did have his heart on lock. Even with the distance between them, and the young woman's sometimes contentious demeanor that had him wanting to pull his hair out, Paul still loved Simone more than he had ever loved any other woman in his life.

Simone Black had needed to park her car around the corner from their favorite local restaurant. Walking the length of the block in high heels was proving to be quite the chore and she was kicking herself for choosing cute over comfort. But it had been quite some time since she and Paul had been in a room together and she was determined that he saw cute when they next met.

Just hearing his voice over the telephone had sent shivers of excitement down her spine. She hadn't wanted to admit just how much she missed him, because admitting she missed him meant admitting she might have been wrong about breaking up with him. Simone had lost count of the number of times she'd kicked herself for that decision.

Since their separation almost one year ago and him leaving the country, Simone often claimed she'd been abandoned, left pining after a man who had loved his career more than he had loved her. She conveniently left out the fact that Paul had begged her to leave with him, wanting her to follow his dreams as they worked together to fulfill her own. She had always admired his humanitarian spirit but had been ill-prepared the day he announced he wanted to serve patients overseas in developing countries. It had been a calling on his heart that she'd found admirable, but she hadn't been able to see how she might fit in the life he imagined.

But Paul had wanted a future together that included whatever they both needed, and Simone had just been too scared to commit, not wanting to admit that at that time, she didn't have a clue what she had wanted or needed.

She and Paul had met in college, becoming fast friends in a few short weeks. He could make her laugh with little effort and his energy was infectious. Paul's enthusiasm for life had brought out the best traits in Simone and where she was often snarky and difficult with others, with Paul Reilly she was like the easiest breeze on a summer day.

They had absolutely nothing in common, not even a shared interest in the same foods. He was altruistic, and she was often self-centered, thinking only about herself. He believed in a higher power and she proclaimed herself an agnostic. Where he was willing to venture through life all willy-nilly, she was more restrained and guarded and not a risk taker. Paul had treated her with kindness in a way no other man had before. And there had been other men. Casual acquaintances who never quite measured up to the father and brothers she compared them with. The male members of Simone's family had set a standard others had found insurmountable. Paul had surpassed the challenge.

Paul had never tried to control her, allowing her the freedom to find her own way as it suited her. He was nonjudgmental, even tempered and compassionate to a fault. The friendship that had evolved between them had taken on a life of its own. Their intense physical attraction to each other and a willingness to simply trust the process had created a bond that even they didn't understand. It worked, even when it shouldn't have.

Paul leaving after weeks of begging her to join him had been devastating. It had left a hollow void in her life that she'd been unable to fill. She'd regretted the decision more times than she cared to count, and she had never told him, hating to admit that she had simply been too scared to step outside of her comfort zone. Her pride had been the biggest wall standing between them. Now, here she was, racing to see him, and trying to be cute when she got there.

Her heel caught in a crack in the concrete sidewalk and she almost tripped, barely stopping herself from falling forward. She came to an abrupt halt, pausing to take a deep breath to calm her nerves as she steadied herself. The air was crisp, evening temperatures predicting snow in a forecast that was warm one day and practically cataclysmic the next. She sucked in oxygen like her life depended on it.

The two men entering Little Bad Wolf caught her attention. They wore matching black suits and when one shoved his hands into his pants pockets, she spied a holster beneath his jacket. They had an odd, *Men in Black* vibe that felt strangely unnatural. The duo gave her reason to pause, something about them feeling out of sync with the neighborhood. Each tossed a look over his shoulder before moving through the entrance, which made her uneasy. She wanted to dismiss the emotion, her nerves already on overdrive as she thought about Paul and his telephone call and her excitement about meeting him. But there was something that suddenly had her imagining terrorist attacks, hostage situations or something else bringing harm to a host of innocent bystanders.

She would wonder why later, but instinct moved her to

reach for her cell phone and dial the number to the local police station. Two rings and an officer Simone didn't recognize answered the phone.

"Good evening. Is Captain Black available, please? It's his sister calling."

Parker Black answered the line a few seconds later. "Hello?"

"Hey, it's me, Simone."

"What's wrong, Simone?"

"It might not be anything, but can you roll a patrol car out to Little Bad Wolf? I feel like they need to do a safety check of the area."

"Because…?"

"I'm here to meet Paul and two really shady-looking guys just went into the place. One's carrying a gun under his jacket. I'm not sure about the other. But they're not regulars and they don't look like they're visiting Chicago for our pleasant tourist sights. It's just a feeling I get. Something's just not right about them." She didn't bother to tell her brother that Paul had said his problem was a matter of life and death and that something in his voice had been concerning. She doubted the two had anything to do with each other, but she would rather be safe than sorry.

"So, you're meeting Paul the doctor? Your ex-boyfriend Paul? I heard he was back. So, are you two reconciling or is this just a late-night booty call?"

"Just send a car, please?"

"He's a good guy, Simone. Go easy on the brother."

"Thank you, Parker!" she answered, her singsong tone belying her anxiety.

Her brother persisted. "It wasn't cool how you ended things. You're lucky…"

Simone disconnected the call, not even bothering to

say goodbye. She took another deep breath and moved through the door into the space.

Little Bad Wolf was a neighborhood favorite. The gastropub was often packed, a lengthy line waiting to get inside during prime dinner hours. She and Paul had been regulars, eating there at least three, sometimes four times, per week.

The young man who greeted her at the door looked discombobulated, although he tried nicely to mask his distress. He smiled, recognition washing over his expression. "Attorney Black, long time no see!" he exclaimed as he leaned in to give her a warm hug.

Simone hugged him back. "Jacob, hey! Is everything okay?"

The man named Jacob nodded, but there was something about the twitch over his eye that said so much more. "I'm good. Really good," he said as he tossed a look over his shoulder.

Simone smiled. "I've missed this place," she said casually.

"Dr. Reilly is in the back," Jacob said as he grabbed a menu and turned, gesturing for her to follow. "He's been waiting for you."

Simone's gaze skated around the room, eyeing the patrons who sat in conversation, laughter ringing warmly through the space. It was a nice crowd for a late hour.

The boys in black were seated at the oversize bar. The bartender was trying to make conversation, but neither was interested. One sat with his broad back to the polished, wooden structure, staring toward the other end of the room. Simone shifted to see where he was staring, her eyes finding Paul seated at their usual spot in the rear. The sight of him triggered a host of alarms she hadn't been expecting.

Simone gasped slightly, the man lifting her lips in the sweetest smile. He was still a beautiful specimen of manhood with his hazel eyes, warm beige complexion and meticulously trimmed beard and mustache. He had always been fastidious with his grooming and lifted weights regularly to maintain a fit physique. He wore a formfitting gray sweater that looked molded to his muscles and denim jeans. He was as dashing as she remembered, her heart skipping a beat, or two, as she gawked.

His briefcase rested on the seat beside him, a pile of papers on the table that he was shifting awkwardly back and forth. His brow was furrowed, and he seemed completely lost in thought, oblivious to his surroundings. She glanced back toward the two men, shifting to put herself between them and their view of Paul. She bumped Jacob's shoulder, her voice dropping to a low whisper. "Do you know the two men at the bar?" she questioned.

"You mean the two *brutes* at the bar?" He shook his head. "No, and they feel like they might be a problem. You won't believe how they pushed their way in!" he said, squarely in his feelings about their interaction at the door.

Simone gave him a nod. "I thought so, too. It's why I called my brother and asked for a patrol car to come by and do a safety check. When the cops get here, point them in my direction. If those two do anything before they get here, just dial nine-one-one."

"Thank you," Jacob said, relief flooding his face.

They came to a stop at the edge of the table. Paul looked up, startled out of the trance he'd fallen into. He tossed Jacob a polite glance, then settled his gaze on Simone. His eyes widened, and joy shimmered in the light orbs.

"Simone, hey," he said, standing abruptly. He moved to wrap his arms around her, pulling her against him in a warm hug. He pressed his lips to her cheek, allowing them to linger there a second longer than necessary. His hold tightened, his arms like a cashmere blanket in a vise-like grip around her torso.

Simone felt her whole body welcoming him home as she hugged him back. "Hey," she answered, her voice a loud whisper.

Jacob dropped her menu to the table. "Thank you, again," he said before hurrying back to the front of the restaurant.

Paul finally let her go, a warm smile filling his face. "I appreciate you coming," he said.

"You said it was important."

Paul nodded as he gestured for her to take a seat. Sitting down, Simone stole another quick glance toward the bar. The two strangers were both staring blatantly, not bothering to hide their interest in the two of them.

Simone rested an elbow on the tabletop, turning flirtatiously toward Paul. "Do you know Tom and Jerry over there?" she asked softly. She reached a hand out, trailing her fingers against his arm.

Her touch proved just distracting enough to him that Paul didn't turn abruptly to stare back, drawing even more attention in their direction. His focus shifted slowly from her toward the duo at the bar. He eyed them briefly before turning his attention back to Simone. He shook his head. "Should I?"

"It might be nothing, but they seem very interested in you."

Paul's gaze danced back in their direction and he took a swift inhale of air. One of the men was on a cell phone and both were still eyeing him intently.

"We need to leave," he said, suddenly anxious. He began to gather his papers.

"What's going on, Paul?"

"I don't think we're safe, Simone."

"What do you mean we're not safe?" she snapped, her teeth clenched tightly. "Why are we not safe?"

"I'll explain, but I think we really need to leave."

Simone took a deep breath and held it, watching as he repacked his belongings into his briefcase.

"We're not going anywhere until you explain," she started and then a commotion at the door pulled at her attention. She turned to see two of her brothers, Parker and Armstrong, and two uniformed police officers standing at the entrance talking with Jacob. Their chatter carried through the room, the conversation casual. They all appeared to be old acquaintances greeting each other warmly.

The two strangers suddenly began eyeing each other nervously. Their earlier bravado seemed to be momentarily eliminated. Simone shot Paul a look but said nothing. They continued watching and another quick minute passed before the duo finally rose from where they sat at the bar and moved toward the exit door. Sighs of relief seemed to billow throughout the whole room.

The Black brothers were slowly moving toward their table, both eyeing the other two men as they passed each other. Parker acknowledged them with a nod of his head but there was no response. As the two men exited the building, the uniformed cops followed behind them.

Detective Armstrong Black greeted them with a wide grin. "Well, well, well. Isn't this a pleasant surprise!" he said. He extended his hand in greeting and the two men bumped shoulders. "How's it going, Paul?"

"It's good to see you, Armstrong."

Armstrong winked an eye at his baby sister. "Simone."

"Armstrong."

Parker shook his head as he leaned to kiss Simone's cheek. He and Paul shook hands. "Everyone okay?"

Simone nodded. "You two didn't need to come. You could have just sent a patrol car."

"We just wanted to make sure everything was good."

"You two just wanted to be nosey."

"That, too!" Parker said with a chuckle. His phone rang, pulling his attention as he stepped away to answer the call.

Armstrong took a seat at the table with them. "So, one of you want to tell me what's going on? Why the concern?"

Simone turned toward Paul, folding her arms over her chest. Raising her brows, she gave him a questioning look.

He heaved a deep sigh, closing his eyes for a split second. "I made a mistake. I should never have called Simone. I just…well…" He paused. Then shrugged, as if unable to find the worlds to answer the question being posed.

Simone rolled her eyes skyward. "It's nothing," she said. "Those two just looked sketchy and I didn't like how pushy they were being. I was worried that something might jump off and figured we were better safe than sorry."

Armstrong looked from one to the other, perhaps sensing a half-truth and a blatant lie being told. Before he could question them further, Parker rejoined the conversation.

"My guys ran their license plate. It's a rental car that came back to a man named Thomas Donald. That ring any bells?"

Paul and Simone both shook their heads.

Parker continued. "We didn't get a hit on anyone named Thomas Donald and we don't have any reason to hold either of them."

"What about the gun I saw?"

"He had a valid FOID."

"What's that?" Paul questioned. "FOID?"

"Firearm Owners Identification card. It makes it legal for him to carry a concealed weapon," Simone answered.

Parker nodded. "They're gone now, so I wouldn't be overly concerned. I think you may have just overreacted."

"Simone? Overreact? Not my little sister!" Armstrong said facetiously as he pressed his palm to his broad chest. "My little sister *never* overreacts!"

"Don't you two have someplace to be?" Simone said, annoyance painting her expression.

Armstrong shook his head. "Nope. We're officially off duty!"

Paul chuckled, a moment of amusement washing over him. It passed quickly but Simone was the only one who noticed. She met his eyes and held the gaze a second longer than necessary before turning back to her brothers.

"You're intruding on my date."

"So, it is a date?" Parker asked, his grin widening.

"Mom will be very excited. I can't wait to tell her," Armstrong added.

Paul laughed out loud. "How is your mom?"

Simone tossed him another look. "Please don't entertain them. If you talk to them, they won't go away. And they need to go away!" She looked from one brother to the other.

"My feelings are hurt, Simone!" Armstrong said. He pushed his full lips out in a full pout.

"Mine, too, but the hint is taken," Parker said. He rose from his seat, adjusting the jacket of his navy-blue suit.

"I need to get home anyway," Armstrong added. "I have a wife waiting for me!" He grinned smugly as he waved his ring finger, like they needed to be reminded that he was a newlywed, having recently married another detective on the Chicago police team.

Parker laughed. "I have someone waiting for me, too, but she's not a wife."

"Not yours anyway," Simone quipped.

Laughter rang around the table.

"It was good to see you guys again," Paul said, the trio shaking hands one last time.

"Good luck," Armstrong said, his voice dropping to a loud whisper. "She's still mean as hell!"

"I heard that!" Simone exclaimed, her eyes rolling skyward.

The brothers grinned, both leaning to kiss their sister's cheek one last time.

"Stay out of trouble, Simone," Parker said.

"Please," Armstrong echoed.

The couple watched as the two men strolled back toward the door, pausing briefly to chat with an elderly couple who sat near the front of the room.

"I see things haven't changed much," Paul said casually.

"You don't get to do that," Simone snapped. "You don't get to pretend nothing's wrong when clearly something's not right. Now spill it! Why did you call me? Why are we not safe, and who were those two men?"

Contrition furrowed Paul's brow. "I shouldn't have called you, Simone."

"But you did, so tell me why. What's going on, Paul?"

Jacob interrupted the conversation, dropping two drinks onto the table. "Courtesy of Captain Black," he said, smiling brightly.

Simone shook her head. "What is this?" The beverage was a beautiful shade of pink, topped with a fluff of cotton candy and skewered raspberries.

"We call it the Honeymoon Special."

Paul laughed again, relieving the tension between them. "Your brothers have a keen sense of humor."

"They really are not funny," Simone responded, though she felt the slightest smile pulling at her mouth.

"Are you ready to order?" Jacob asked.

"I think we're going to have to take it to go, Jacob," Paul said. "I hope that's not a problem."

"Not at all, Dr. Reilly. Your usual?"

"Yes, sir. The Bad Burger with a side of fries, please."

"I'll take the mac and cheese," Simone said. "Also to go."

"Yes, ma'am. I'll put that order in for you. And I'd like to throw in a dessert on the house. We have a spectacular carrot cake tonight. I'd also highly recommend the vanilla brownie."

"The carrot cake sounds good," Simone said. "Thank you, Jacob."

"And for you, Dr. Reilly?"

"Whatever the lady is having sounds good to me," Paul said.

"Two slices of carrot cake to go. I'll be back shortly with your food," Jacob said as he backed away from the table and headed toward the kitchen.

A pregnant pause bloomed full and thick between them. Simone stared, the look she was giving him so intense that Paul felt his stomach flip as the air was sucked from his lungs. She was even more stunning than he remembered, and he remembered everything about Simone.

Her hair had been freshly cut, her lush curls cropped short in a style that flattered her exquisite face. Chocolate-chip freckles danced across her nose and cheeks, complementing her warm copper complexion. Her dark eyes were large and bright and light shimmered in her stare. And she had the most perfect mouth, her full, luscious lips like plush pillows begging to be kissed. It took every ounce of fortitude he possessed not to lean over and capture her lips with his own. He took a deep breath and held it, hoping to stall the emotion that had swelled between them.

If anyone had asked, Paul would have had to admit to falling in love with Simone at first sight. She'd been the most beautiful woman he had ever seen as she had skipped across the university's quad. He'd stepped into her path and had introduced himself, asking for directions he hadn't needed. Simone had walked him to the destination, talking a mile a minute, which she later admitted had been to calm her nerves about a class that had her concerned. Their friendship had been like spun sugar: threads deeply entwined, intensely sweet and delicately fragile. Simone treaded cautiously, wherein he was always ready to take risks.

After spending a decade together, he had never imagined life without her until the day she'd told him to leave, unwilling to follow where he needed to go. He was still in shock, still hurt by the loss, still hoping for a reconciliation, even if he never said the words aloud. There was just something about the two of them together that worked, making it feel like all was well in the world, even when they were off-balance with each other.

He finally spoke, Simone still waiting patiently for him to say something. "I think Lender Pharmaceuticals is poisoning patients who are taking their drugs."

Simone blinked, her lashes fluttering as she processed the comment. "That's a serious accusation, Paul," she said finally.

He nodded. "I know, and I don't make it lightly, but I

believe that I have irrefutable proof that Lender Pharmaceuticals is purposely providing contaminated medications to doctors and medical facilities here in the United States and abroad."

Paul continued to explain. "I've been working in a clinic in Ghana. In Accra. It's not a large facility but it supports the local orphanages in the area and has been a refuge for the community. I have patients that I had treated for a measles-related virus on a previous trip who should have been well by now, but they're either still symptomatic, showing rapid deterioration or have succumbed to the illness. And not one or two patients, but dozens! The disease is spreading too quickly in communities that should be thriving when you consider the preventive and curative medications that Lender Pharmaceuticals has been providing. On this last trip I think I may have poked a bear by throwing accusing questions at them that the company wasn't expecting."

"What's the drug we're talking about?"

"It's a synthetic drug called Halphedrone-B, which is being used worldwide to treat patients with autoimmune diseases, most especially in impoverished communities, because allegedly Lender is practically selling it at cost. But I think it's the drug that's killing them."

"What kind of proof do you have?"

"The drugs. The patients. The fact that since I called BS on their products, I feel like someone wants to stop me from going public with the information."

"How? What's happened that you haven't told me?"

Paul took a deep breath. He hadn't given the series of mishaps while he'd been abroad any thought until he'd spoken with his brother. He'd experienced several minor accidents that could have been potentially devastating. There had been a car traveling too fast that had just missed hitting him, and a fire, the cause unknown and devastating the hut he'd been sleeping in. Lastly, the close encounter at the airport in Africa with a stranger he'd dismissed as mentally ill, a man swinging a machete haphazardly in his direction until security had taken him down. Considering all of it together, and now the two strangers who'd clearly had him in their sights, had him concerned.

When he finished detailing the incidents, Simone shook her head, the gesture slow and methodic. "What else?"

Paul took a deep breath and blew it past his full lips. "I overnighted blood and tissue samples, and drug samples to my brother. I asked him to run some tests for me. The samples have disappeared."

"Define *disappeared*."

"Someone took them. They knew he had them and they stole them right out of his lab."

"Do you think that someone is tracking you?"

"I don't know what to think, Simone. Hell, I'm not even sure what to do with what I do know."

"So, you called me?"

"I trust you."

There was a moment that passed between them as Simone remembered what that trust meant to them both. How important it had been to protect and nurture each other. To have complete and total faith in what they shared. She suddenly resisted the urge to wrap her arms around him, wanting to pull him close to tell him everything was going to be okay. To say it, even if she wasn't certain that it would.

"You probably shouldn't go back to your apartment. Not until we're sure it's safe. You can stay with me while we figure it out," she said instead.

"I need to go to the hospital. I need to follow up on patients I have here."

She started to argue and then she didn't. "I need to do some research. I also have a sorority sister at the FDA. I'll call her tomorrow to see if they have any open investigations against Lender. I hope you're wrong, Paul, but if you're not, I'll do whatever I can to help you take them down."

Paul reached for her hand, his palm sliding warmly against hers as he entwined her fingers between his own. For as much as he trusted her, he knew Simone trusted him, too. He'd spent most of his adult life assuring her that he would never walk her into trouble he couldn't get her out of, and until now, he'd been certain that he could do that. Now he had doubts and that uncertainty felt like a sledgehammer to his abdomen. "Thank you, but I don't want to drag you into this. Especially if it looks like it might get ugly."

"You should have thought about that *before* you called me."

"I honestly didn't think you'd come."

"You knew I'd come."

Paul held the look she was giving him. He didn't bother to acknowledge that she was right. Nor did he admit that he hadn't really thought it through. He knew he didn't need to tell her that he was suddenly feeling like he was out of his element, or that he was scared. But with her by his side, he had faith it would all work out. He didn't need to say it because Simone knew. She knew him better than anyone.

Minutes later he had paid for their meals and they were walking back up the block toward her car. Neither had spoken, nothing else needing to be said. Both had fallen into their own thoughts, planning what needed to come next, or not. Paul carried the bags of food and Simone had looped her arm through his, lightly clutching his elbow as she steadied herself on her high heels.

The car lock disengaged when Simone pressed her hand to the door latch. Paul opened her side door, closing it after she was settled in the driver's seat. He moved around the back of the vehicle to the passenger side, pausing to rest their dinners on the back seat. He had just opened his door when a gunshot rang loudly through the late-night air. The windowpane in the storefront behind him shattered, glass sounding like breaking chimes against the concrete sidewalk. The building's alarm rang loudly, the harsh tones loud enough to wake the dead. A second shot shattered the car's back window.

Panic hit Paul broadside, rising fear holding him hostage where he stood. He was discombobulated, but he ducked, his gaze sweeping the landscape for an explanation. Simone shouted, the words incoherent as she shifted the car into Reverse. Paul jumped awkwardly into the passenger seat as she pulled forward, grazing the bumper of the car parked in front of her. A few quick turns and they were driving seventy miles per hour on Highway 41 until both were certain they weren't being followed. When she finally slowed to the speed limit, Paul cussed, the profanity moving Simone to toss him a quick look.

"What now?" she asked.

"Whatever it takes," Paul answered, still trying to catch his breath. "We'll do whatever it takes to shut these bastards down.

Simone nodded. "Let's not get killed trying to do it."

Paul took a deep breath into his lungs and held it. His mind was racing, his thoughts a mishmash of questions with no answers. Confusion had settled deep into every crevice in his head; it felt like sludge was weighing down his thought process. "We should find somewhere to lay low," he said. "Until we can figure it all out."

"We can go back to my house..." Simone started.

"No. Now that they've seen us together, I don't trust that they won't find us there."

"Then we should go to the police station."

"Let's just get a hotel room. I don't think we should involve the police just yet."

"Someone shot at us, Paul! We need to file a report! My brothers need to know!"

"I know that, Simone! But I need to think this through. Please, just give me a minute to think!"

"We might not have a minute, Paul!" Simone's voice rose an octave and the tension between them suddenly increased ten-fold. Before either could blink, the conversation took a sharp left turn and they were yelling back and forth, each determined to prove a point when there was none. It was Bickering 101 and reminiscent of when their relationship had gone all kinds of wrong.

Chapter 2

The no-tell motel they'd found by the highway was fetid, reeking of debauchery and sin. The smell of cigarettes, marijuana, sex and body odor was pungent through the late-night air. Simone distorted her face with displeasure as Paul closed the door to room thirty-eight and tossed the key card on the laminated dresser. He sat down on the foot of the mattress beside her and exhaled his first sigh of relief since leaving the restaurant. Simone had finally stopped shaking and Paul felt like he could breathe normally again.

Neither spoke. Both were still reeling from the fight they'd had in the car. Simone had wanted them to drive straight to the police station. Paul had refused, insisting that it would only make things worse. He was adamant that they needed additional proof to substantiate his claims and the only way to get that was if no one knew where they were or what they were after. Simone knew her family wouldn't take them disappearing lightly and she trusted her brothers would look for them. They still hadn't come to an agreement. The argument had been contentious, the intensity of their emotions palpable.

"It doesn't make any sense," Simone finally said, breaking the silence. "No one we know would think our not going to the police is a smart thing to do." There was still an air of hostility in her tone.

And a hint of defiance in his as he responded. "No

one knows what we're up against. Even we don't know yet, Simone."

"Which is why going to the police would make sense. I know my brothers would back us up."

"I don't agree. All that's going to happen is that the police will dismiss my concerns because the proof I have is shaky at best. The preliminary test results Oliver sent me still need to be analyzed and there's more testing that needs to be done. Lender will be tipped off that we're on to them and we won't be able to prove what they're doing or stop them."

"In the movies when people don't go to the police, they die. They fall off cliffs, demons get them, all kinds of horrors," Simone said facetiously.

"In the movies I've seen the police get it, too."

"You're watching the wrong movies."

"You watch too many."

Simone tossed up her hands in frustration. "I'm an officer of the court, Paul! I have a responsibility to uphold the law. I have a damn badge, for heaven's sake!"

Paul cut his gaze in her direction, a smile pulling at his mouth. "Why do they issue you a badge anyway? You're a prosecutor."

Simone shifted her body, turning to stare at him. "Are you making fun of my badge?"

"I just asked the question!"

Her tone was laced with attitude. "It makes me official. It says that I represent the courts of the state and that I took the Attorney's Oath and I've promised to honor its tenets. Don't you dare make light of what I do, Paul Reilly. It's as important to me as the Hippocratic Oath that you doctors take."

"I'm not, Simone. I was just curious about the badge. They don't give us doctors one."

"No, they give you those white jackets with your names embroidered over the breast pockets. Same thing, different medium."

"I cannot believe we're sitting here arguing over a tin emblem." He lay backward on the bed, pulling his arms over his head.

"We're arguing about involving the police. Don't change the subject."

Paul blew a soft sigh as another wave of silence swept between them. Both sat listening instead to the noise in the room. An alarm clocked ticked loudly from the nightstand next to the bed and water leaked from the faucet in the bathroom. There was a steady rhythm of clicks and plops, both just loud enough to be annoying. Minutes passed before he spoke again. "I'll do whatever you think is best, Simone."

"You will?"

"Yeah," he mumbled as he folded an arm over his eyes.

She nodded. "I'll call my brother. We need to at least tell him that we're safe. We can also tell him what we know in an unofficial capacity. If they can help work it from their end, it can't hurt. Until we figure out what the hell we're doing, we can use all the help we can get."

"Okay."

"Okay? Really?"

"Yeah, baby, okay."

A noise outside the door pulled Simone upright. "Did you hear that?"

Paul mumbled, "No. I didn't hear anything."

Simone stood and moved to the window to peer through the blinds. Outside, three working women were gathered in the parking lot changing their clothes. Bare asses and boobs were on full display and no one seemed to be concerned. Laughter rang through the late-night air, their good time fueled by the bottle of booze being passed between them. Simone exhaled, turning back toward the bed. "I don't know if I can stay here..." she started.

The rest of her comment stalled in midair, warm breath the slightest whistle past her lips. Paul had fallen into a deep sleep, jet lag and exhaustion fully claiming him. He snored softly and for a quick moment Simone realized just how much she missed hearing him beside her at night.

Shaking the thought, she grabbed her cell phone from her purse and her food from the meal bag. She took a seat on a cushioned chair in front of the small desk and dialed Parker's number. As she waited for someone to answer, she took the first bite of her macaroni and cheese.

"Where are you?" Parker questioned. "I'm sending a patrol car."

"We're fine, big brother. You just needed to know what happened. I also took the bumper off some guy's car, I think. You'll handle that for me, too, right?"

"If they knew Paul was at that restaurant, they're probably tracking his cell phone. They may even be tracking yours."

"We thought that, too, so we tossed the sim card in his phone and powered it off. I'm using my other phone. The one that's in mom's name. My primary phone was dead, so I left it at the house on the charger."

"You need to come in, Simone. Until we figure out who shot at you, we can't trust that either of you is safe."

"We can't, Parker. Paul truly believes this company is killing patients and he's determined to stop them. If we come in, we might lose our window of opportunity to prove his theory."

"I wasn't asking, Simone. That was an order."

"I stopped taking orders from you when I was ten."

"Then I'm calling Mom and Dad."

"Don't you dare! I just need you to trust me."

Parker yelled, "You don't know what the hell you're doing! Neither of you has a clue what you've gotten yourselves into! Now, where are you?"

Simone sighed. "I love you. And I'll be okay. I promise."

"Don't you dare hang…"

Simone disconnected the call abruptly. She took another bite of macaroni and sat in reflection as she polished off the last of her meal. She didn't have the words to explain to her brother what she was feeling or why they were suddenly acting like fugitives. She honestly wasn't sure what the hell they were doing. But they were together and she instinctively wanted to do whatever necessary to support Paul. He needed her and it had been forever since she'd felt like she added value to his life. Wanting each other had never been the problem between them. Needing each other, and admitting to it, had been a whole other animal neither had been willing to claim. But now necessity had put them together, if for nothing more than to hold on to each other for emotional support, and Simone had no intentions of failing him.

Paul was now snoring loudly, and she instinctively knew that it had been days since he'd last rested well. She was reminded of those days after medical school, during his residency, when his shifts at the hospital seemed to last for days before he was able to come home and fall out from exhaustion.

She dropped her fork and empty container back into the bag. After reaching for her phone she dialed again.

Her brother Mingus Black answered on the second ring. "What's wrong, Simone? And why is Parker texting me to ask where you are?"

"I need you. I'm at the Karavan Motel on Cicero Avenue."

"Karavan? On the South Side? What the hell are you doing there?"

"Someone tried to kill us tonight," she said, explaining all that had happened since Paul Reilly had called her.

"So, you two check into the city's seediest motel?"

"We're not planning to stay, and they take cash," she continued, hoping to rationalize why the no-tell motel had been a good idea and why Paul felt going to the police was not. Even after saying it out loud Simone knew it sounded like she and Paul had lost their collective minds. And she definitely couldn't tell any of them that she just needed to be with Paul because she had missed him terribly.

Mingus listened, taking it all in. A private detective by profession, he heard his sister's dilemma with a different ear than their police officer brother. He didn't yell or give her orders he knew she wouldn't heed like Parker did. Instead, when she was done talking, Mingus said, "Sit tight. I need to put some things in place. I'll be there before breakfast tomorrow. Are you carrying?"

"Yes," she said, taking a moment to check the weapon in her handbag. The Glock 43 had been a gift from her father, the patriarch ensuring she and her sister both knew how to handle a firearm just as well as their brothers. Regular visits to the gun range kept her shooting and safety skills honed.

"Keep it close, and if you need to use it, don't hesitate to pull the trigger. You can always ask questions later."

"What are you going to tell Parker?"

"That I didn't put your leash on you this morning. That he should check with whoever did."

"Thank you," Simone responded, chuckling softly.

"Get some rest. I'm sure you're going to need it," Mingus concluded.

After disconnecting the call, Simone moved back to the bed and kicked off her heels. Laying her body beside Paul's, she eased an arm around his waist and shifted herself close against him. She nuzzled her nose against his back, inhaling the scent of his cologne. The familiar fragrance reminded her of their last trip together, a two-week excursion on the island of Jamaica. They had walked hand in hand along the beaches of Negril, had swum beneath the cascading waters of Gully Falls, and had danced under a full moon in Montego Bay. They'd fallen asleep in each other's arms and woken each morning making love. It had been as magical as any holiday getaway could possibly be. Weeks later, they were no longer a couple, barely talking to each other about the weather.

Taking deep breaths to calm her nerves, Simone closed her eyes and settled into his body heat. She couldn't begin to know what he had gotten her into and despite trusting that Paul would have never purposely put her in harm's way, running from gunfire added a whole other dynamic to his situation. The nearness of him only put her slightly at ease, not enough that she could fully relax.

Sleep didn't come as quickly for Simone as she lay listening to the occasional sound outside the door and the steady rhythm of Paul's heavy snores. Simone hated showing any vulnerability, but she was scared. This was bad and had the potential to get worse.

Her mind continued to race as she thought about what she might need to do to help her friend. Thinking how much she had missed him when he'd been gone and being grateful to have him back, even under the dire circumstances they found themselves trapped in. Wondering if she should heed Parker's advice and run for the security of the police department and shelter with her law-abiding family. Her father was, after all, Jerome Black, the Superintendent of Police, leading the entire Chicago Police Department. Her mother, Judith Harmon Black, was a federal court judge, and both were well respected in Chicago's judicial system. With two brothers on the police force, another who was an attorney in private practice, the baby boy in the family a city alderman, her favorite sibling a private investigator, and her only sister front and center in state politics, law-abiding protection was a given.

Despite her best efforts she couldn't turn her brain off. For another two hours she lay pressed against his back, not wanting to disturb his rest and needing him near, even if they weren't a couple anymore. Thinking about the past and the present, Simone's thoughts ran the gamut from sane to senseless until sleep finally slipped in and delivered her from her misery.

Chapter 3

Outside, the morning sun was just beginning to rise. Paul stood at the foot of the bed staring down at Simone's sleeping form. Fully clothed, she was curled in a fetal position around a pillow. Her mouth was open, low gasps expelled from her lush lips. Her freckles were like stardust across her nose and her skin shimmered under a layer of light perspiration. Simone was a beautiful woman, but there was something about her when she slumbered, where she seemed most angelic and at peace. In those moments her beauty was extraordinary, leaving him to wonder what he had done to get so lucky.

In that moment though, he was wondering what he needed to do to ensure she was protected. How to get her, and himself, out of the mess he'd pulled them into. He sighed, feeling as if things might implode if he didn't tread cautiously. But he had neither the time or the wherewithal to play nice with Lender Pharmaceuticals.

The knock on the door pulled him from his reverie and startled Simone out of a deep sleep. She sat upright, clutching at the well-worn spread atop the bed. Bewilderment furrowed her brow. Rubbing the sleep from her eyes, she threw her legs off the side of the bed as Paul moved to look out the window. He heaved a deep sigh as he sidestepped to the door and opened it, greeting Simone's brother Mingus. The two men embraced like old friends, an exchange of shoulders bumping and chests grazing.

"You two good?" Mingus questioned as he entered the room, carrying two large duffel bags over his shoulder and a tray of coffees from Starbucks.

"No," Simone muttered as she flipped her hand at him. "I need to pee, and I want a shower."

Mingus and Paul exchanged a look, both smirking slightly. Her brother shook his head at her as he extended the duffel bag in her direction.

"Well, I brought you some things from your house. Clothes, your toothbrush…"

"My toothbrush!" she exclaimed, jumping up and down like a four-year-old. "I love you, big brother!"

Mingus laughed. "Until you see what I packed for you. Knowing you, I'm sure it's all wrong."

"As long as you brought me clean panties, I'll be a very happy woman."

"Panties? Ohhh…well… I didn't…"

Simone's eyes widened, a hint of saline suddenly pressing against her thick lashes. "Please, don't tell me you didn't get me any clean underwear. How could you not think to pack me clean underwear? I can't believe you…"

Mingus held up his hand to stall the rant he knew was coming. He winked an eye at her. "Vaughan packed clothes for you. I'm sure you're good."

Relief flooded Simone's expression. "You talked to my sister?"

"She had the spare key to your town house."

Simone nodded. "Excuse me, please, while I go freshen up."

Mingus dropped to the chair, his clasped hands resting in his lap as he gave Paul a look. "Don't rush," he said.

Simone looked from one man to the other and back, then rolled her eyes skyward. "Don't hurt him, Mingus."

Mingus narrowed his gaze and pushed his shoulders skyward. "No promises."

Paul chuckled, dropping his large frame to the bedside. He clasped his own hands together in front of his face as he rested his elbows on his thighs.

She gave them both another look, then moved into the bathroom, shutting the door behind her. "You two work it out," she muttered under her breath. "Not my problem." The pipes rattled loudly as the shower was turned on in the other room. When the rain of water sounded steadily on the other side of the door, both men shifted forward to stare at each other.

"I talked to your brother. He packed that other bag for you. He said to tell you he's headed north to lie low for a few days. That you would know where to find him. He doesn't like how folks are looking at him. He also said he has enough equipment there if you need it. He said you knew what that meant, too."

Paul nodded. "Did he tell you where *north* was?"

"No, and I don't want to know. And, if that's where you're planning to go, you don't need to tell Simone until after you get there."

"I don't know if I can keep her safe, Mingus."

"You better," the other man said with conviction. "She's already a target. They know she's connected to you. If they can't get to you through regular channels, they'll get to you through her. I know I would."

Like all the members of the Black family, Mingus was just as dedicated to the municipality. But he usually worked alone, sometimes in the dregs of the community, beneath the cover of darkness, getting his hands dirty. He sometimes did what others weren't willing to do and he did it exceptionally well. Paul had no doubts he knew what he was talking about.

"I need to go to the hospital. I have patients there I need to check on. I also need to get my hands on some of my files and maybe a new sample or two."

"I don't think that's a good idea."

"I don't have a choice. I have to go, but I'm not taking Simone with me. She can stay here until I get back."

"*If* you get back."

"Such faith!"

"In my line of business, we deal in facts, not faith. And the fact is someone is gunning for you. And maybe it's because you know something about that pharmaceutical company that they don't want you to know. Or maybe not. For all I know, it could be a spurned lover out for revenge."

"Your sister had an alibi. She was with me, so she didn't have a reason to try and kill me."

Mingus chuckled. "Touché!"

Paul sighed. "I need to print the emails my brother sent me so I can study the results from the tests he was able to run. I'll swing by a FedEx office first and then head over to the hospital. I'll be in and out in thirty minutes. Forty-five max. Then Simone and I'll get on the road."

"The print shop is going to want a credit card. Go here," Mingus said, jotting an address down on the hotel notepad that rested on the desk. "Ask for Liza. Tell her I sent you. She'll print whatever you need. You can also use her computers. She can back-door you into any system you need to get into. Tell her what you need, and she'll find it for you."

"And she can be trusted?"

Mingus shot him a narrowed look but didn't bother to answer. Instead, he passed him a set of keys. "I'll take Simone's car," he said. "There's a black BMW parked outside beside it. The registration won't come back to either of you. If you get stopped, the car belongs to Black

Investigative Services. Tell them to call and I'll confirm you're authorized to be driving it. But don't get stopped. I did a little digging last night and the men at the restaurant were a professional team. They didn't miss by accident. They wanted to scare you, not kill you. But if they had wanted you dead, you would be."

The sound of the shower suddenly came to an abrupt halt, Simone cursing loudly about there being no more hot water. The two men exchanged a look and shook their heads.

Mingus continued, "Lender Pharmaceuticals has deep pockets. They can afford to pay well to silence you. If you keep digging and they get pissed off enough, whomever comes next might not miss."

Paul rose from his seat and Mingus stood with him. Both stole glances at their wristwatches.

"One hour," Mingus said. "Go to the hospital. Get in, get what you need and get out. Simone and I'll meet you at that address I gave you in one hour. Then you two need to put some distance between you and Chicago."

Paul nodded and the two men shook hands. "Thank you," he said. "I really appreciate your help."

Mingus chuckled. "Don't thank me. Thank the nuisance in there. If she didn't love you, I'd kick your ass for getting her in this mess. I still might. No telling about me!"

Paul hesitated as he pondered Mingus's comment, wondering if it were possible that Simone did still love him. If they might be more than old friends. If when all of this was finished, Simone would still find favor with him. He suddenly wanted it more than he'd ever admitted to himself previously. He felt a mist of saline press hard against his lashes and he swiped at his eyes with the back of his hand.

Paul gave Mingus a wry smile and then he turned to leave, his hand on the doorknob. For a split second he thought about telling Simone goodbye. Just in case they didn't make it back to each other. Then he reasoned there was no point in tempting fate.

He turned back to face Simone's brother. "I really love your sister. I hope you know that. I never meant for any of this to happen," he said.

"Yeah, I know," Mingus replied. "We all do."

Paul spun back toward the exit, then he stepped out into the early morning chill, closing the door behind him.

Chapter 4

It was the new day shift change, the hospital employees focused on updates about patients and not on him. Paul managed to enter the building and make his way to his office with only two nods of his head and one *good morning* to an elderly man rolling his way down the corridor in a wheelchair. Paul stole a quick glance out the glass partition before closing the blinds.

There were manila folders resting on the center of his desk and a boatload of pink message slips. He didn't bother to look at either pile, instead reaching to unlock the bottom drawer with the smallest key on his key ring. At first glance, it appeared that the drawer held indexed files and nothing more. What Paul was after was duct-taped to the underside of the inner drawer. He pulled the flash drive from its hiding spot and slid it into the back pocket of his denim jeans.

Just as he relocked the drawer, after pausing to grab his calendar from the desktop and sliding it into his briefcase, there was a knock on the door. Paul froze, his eyes skating from side to side. There was a second knock, someone calling his name. He took a deep breath and held it as he considered his options.

Paul secured the zipper on the briefcase and rested it in the seat of the chair. He moved from behind the desk to the door and pulled it open. The voice that greeted him was overly exuberant for such an early morning hour.

"Dr. Reilly! You're back!" The nurse standing before him looked relieved. "Kelly said she thought someone was in here, but she wasn't sure. I wanted to make sure we didn't have another intruder."

"Good morning, Grace. *Another* intruder?"

She nodded. "Someone was in here yesterday, rifling through the files on top of your desk. We called security but by the time they got here, the men were gone."

"Men? There were more than one?"

"There were two men actually. Both white, dark hair, wearing dark suits," she said.

Paul nodded his head slowly. "Do you know what they were looking for?"

"No, sir. I checked everything afterward and nothing was missing. All the files there for you were exactly as you left them. They made a mess, but they didn't take anything. At least I don't think they did."

Paul paused in reflection. He had a good idea who'd been there and what they were after. He also knew that the flash drive was now in his possession and he needed to ensure it stayed with him. He gave his nurse a slight smile. "Well, I'm glad it wasn't more serious, and I appreciate you looking out for me, Grace. Actually, I was just headed out the door. I only stopped in to check on a few of my patients. I'm not officially back for another week."

"Well, we can't wait to have you back with us."

"How are you doing?"

"I'm good. It's been busy around here. We've been short staffed, so you've really been missed. You're one of the only doctors who'll roll up his sleeves to pitch in and help out."

Paul smiled. "I appreciate that."

Grace took a deep inhale of air. "Did you hear about the Lukas kid?"

"David Lukas?"

She nodded. "Poor little thing died last week. We were all heartbroken. Parents brought him into the emergency room suffering from seizures. He didn't recover."

There was a moment of pause as Paul took a deep breath and held it, his eyes closed as he recalled the youngster who had touched the hearts of everyone who knew him. The child had been six years old when he'd first been admitted. His symptoms had mimicked those of influenza, hepatitis and yellow fever. Weeks of testing hadn't been able to find a cause for his symptoms until Paul and his medical team discovered the child had been away on a tropical holiday twelve months earlier. Paul had ordered another round of tests and little David had been diagnosed with malaria. The rashes, high fevers, anemia and subsequent seizures had been consistent with the disease, but the parasites had been missed in the initial testing due to malaria's rarity in the United States.

The treatment plan and prescribed drugs Paul had ordered should have had him back to climbing trees and playing games with his little friends. Learning that the child had died felt like a punch to his gut. The antimalarial drugs sold by Lender Pharmaceuticals were used worldwide and Paul had been confident about their capabilities before he'd learned of Lender's duplicity. Now, that baby was dead, and the guilt was suddenly consuming. Paul no longer had any confidence in any product with the Lender name attached to it.

He opened his eyes and took a second breath. "Did they do an autopsy?"

"The official ruling was complications from pneumonia. I can get you a copy of the autopsy report if you'd like me to."

"I'd really appreciate that. He was doing better when I left. I need to know what happened."

"I understand completely. Dr. Hayes was attending when he was admitted. He may be able to answer some of your questions, as well. Would you like me to see if he's in yet?"

Paul shook his head. "Don't worry yourself. I'll run down to the morgue and see what I can find out myself. I appreciate your help, though."

The iPhone that rested on the woman's hip suddenly chimed. "Duty calls," she said as she reached for the device.

Paul smiled. "Don't let me keep you from your rounds."

"It was good to see you, Dr. Reilly," she said as she exited the room to answer the call.

"It was good to see you, too, Grace."

Paul moved back to the desk to claim his briefcase. He exited the office, locked it behind him and headed down the corridor. Grace had been called into a patient's room and she waved one last time as he passed by the door.

As he neared the nurses' station Paul saw them before they saw him. The two men from the night before stood with a hospital administrator, questioning one of the staff members. He made an abrupt turn as he heard them speak his name, asking about his whereabouts. As he made it to the opposite end of the hallway and turned toward the stairs, they spied him, the administrator pointing in his direction.

Without giving it an ounce of thought, Paul took off running, descending three flights of stairs and tearing out a side door, through the emergency room bay, to the car parked in the back lot. As he pulled the vehicle onto the main road, the two men stood outside the hospital building, spinning in circles as they tried to figure out where he'd disappeared to. Paul kept driving, not bothering to give a second look behind him.

Simone stepped out of the bathroom. She was drying her damp hair with a thin white towel. Her brother was on his phone, texting intently as he sat waiting for her.

"Where's Paul?" she questioned as she moved to the window. She pushed the drapes aside to peer out at the parking lot.

"Hospital," Mingus answered, never lifting his eyes from his cell phone screen.

She blinked. "Why didn't you stop him?"

"Why didn't you?"

She winced, her hands falling to her hips. "If I'd known he planned to leave, I would have."

Her brother shrugged his broad shoulders, his gaze still focused on his phone. "He said he had patients to see."

"And you didn't think that might be a problem?"

"Should it be?"

"Uhhh, maybe? Or did you forget someone was shooting at us last night?" she quipped.

Mingus finally lifted his eyes to give her a quick look. "It's doubtful anyone will take a shot at him in broad daylight," he said.

"And you know this how?"

"I don't really. It's just a hunch," Mingus said as he slid his cell phone into the inside pocket of his leather jacket. He changed the subject. "You need to finish getting dressed. We need to meet your boyfriend in forty-five minutes."

"Meet him where?"

"You sure do ask a lot of questions, Simone! Can you just get ready to leave, please?"

"I ask questions because I need answers and you're not telling me anything."

Mingus blew air past his full lips. "You two need to get out of Chicago. I don't know where you're going, and it's best no one knows, but I trust Paul is going to keep you safe. Now, let's get moving, please. You need to call your job so they're not looking for you. And, you need to call our mother. Tell her Paul is taking you away for a few days to reconcile. I'm sure she'll be very excited! Throw something in there about grandbabies and she won't worry about you for at least a month!"

A wave of panic hit Simone like a gut punch to her midsection. She and Paul were leaving Chicago and the uncertainty of what lay ahead for them suddenly felt daunting. She had a lengthy list of what-ifs and no sustainable answers about the future filling her head and she knew it showed in the angst-filled expression on her face. Her brother picking at her didn't help the situation.

"Talk about planning a wedding and that might buy you two months of freedom from parental interference," Mingus was saying.

Simone's lips twisted and turned, her face burning hot with annoyance. She shook her index finger at her brother. "I really don't like you," she said as she shuffled back in the direction of the bathroom.

Mingus laughed. "I love you, too, Simone. You're the best little sister in the whole wide world."

"And don't you forget it," Simone muttered as she slammed the bathroom door closed after her.

Paul's mind was racing as he searched out a parking space in the West Loop neighborhood. His anxiety level was at an all-time high and he took two deep breaths to calm his nerves. After shutting down the engine of the luxury vehicle, he checked and then double-checked the address Mingus had given him before stepping out of the car.

Paul paused at the chain-link fence that bordered the property. He looked left and then right, assessing his surroundings before he stepped through the latched gate, then reclosed it behind him. He took the steps two at a time and depressed the doorbell. As he waited, he paced, his eyes darting back and forth across the landscape.

The elderly woman who answered the door eyed him with reservation. "What'cha want, baby?"

"Good morning, ma'am. I'm here to see Liza? My name's Paul Reilly. Mingus Black sent me."

The woman didn't respond, still staring at him intently. She was petite in stature, wearing a floral housecoat and a full-length apron that stopped below her knees. There was a dishcloth in her hand and a light brush of white flour dusting her chubby cheek. Her gaze swept over him, running the length of his body from head to toe. After sizing him up she finally unlocked the door and pushed it open to allow him entry.

"Come on in, baby. I'm Pearl Hill but e'erybody calls me Mama. You want somethin' to eat? I got a pan of biscuits 'bout to come out the oven. I got some fatback and bacon, too, but Liza don't eat no meat. You ain't one of them vegans, too, are you?" she asked, her words laced with a Southern drawl and coming in what sounded like one long, drawn-out sentence before she took another breath.

Paul smiled. "No, thank you, ma'am. I'm good."

She sized him up a second time. "You know you hungry," she said with an air of finality. "I'm gon' make you a plate." She pointed down a flight of stairs. "Liza's down in the basement. She's expecting you."

Paul nodded as she continued toward the back of the home and the kitchen. The stately greystone, an architectural staple in Chicago since the 1890s, was built from Bedford limestone and named for its color. It was oversize, the craftsmanship evident in the exterior detail. The interior of the duplex featured wide-plank oak flooring, high ceilings and an abundance of natural light. Moving down the steps Paul discovered the lower-level bonus room with walls of computer screens and a young woman who looked like a bag of Skittles candy had exploded over her.

Liza was very young. Much younger than he'd expected, and he hadn't known what he might have been walking into. Her royal blue hair had a streak of white in the front that was swept across her brow and was pulled into a high ponytail adorned with a barrette of yellow flowers. She wore an orange, yellow and pink tie-dyed sweat suit with red Converse sneakers. She was the Rainbow Brite character on steroids, and she made Paul smile.

"Hey! Mingus didn't come with you?" she said, her hands coming to an abrupt halt atop the keyboard she was typing on.

Paul shook his head. He couldn't help but wonder what she did for Mingus and how they knew each other. "No," he answered, "but I think he's coming."

She shrugged and resumed her typing. "Mama Hill's going to be pissed. She's up there cooking bacon for him right now and she knows how much I hate the smell of pig cooking in the kitchen. He better come."

"He...well...it's..."

"No worries. We'll see him when we see him. Until then though, you'll have to eat the bacon."

Paul took two steps forward. "Is Mama Hill your grandmother?"

Liza shot him a look. "She's everyone's grandmother. So, what do you need?"

"I just have messages on my phone that I need to print out."

Liza gestured for him to take a seat beside her. "What's your email address?" she asked.

Paul reached for his phone, stopping when she asked him again.

"I just need your email address, not your phone." She pushed a pad of paper and an ink pen toward him.

After writing down his personal email address, Paul pushed the pad back to her. "I just need any messages that might have come in the last three days," he said softly.

A few short minutes later paper was spewing from a Xerox multifunction printer in the corner of the room. Liza gestured with her head, pointing him toward the ream of documents filling the output tray.

"So, you're a hacker," Paul said as he began sorting through the papers for those he needed and the ones he didn't.

"I prefer 'skilled computer expert.'"

"You just look so young."

Her brows raised but she didn't look in his direction, studying the screen before her instead. "I'm older than you think," she muttered.

"Can you get into anyone's computer system?"

"What do you need?"

"Everything you can get on a company called Lender Pharmaceuticals and what they have on a drug called Halphedrone-B. Not sure where you'd look, but maybe start in their research and development department? Maybe any communications about the drug between their management team?"

Liza typed, her head shifting from side to side as data

filled the two screens on the desktop and then more information began to cover the larger screens on the walls. Liza stopped typing and stared from one screen to another, deciphering code that looked like a foreign language to Paul.

He was impressed with Liza's expertise as he watched pages of emails and reports begin to fill the computer screens and he wasn't sure why because what they were doing was highly illegal. If he didn't already have enough problems, this might top his list and send him straight to prison. But curiosity had gotten the better of him. And Simone wasn't there to play devil's advocate and make him change his mind about asking for the information. He knew Simone would not be pleased, and he was sure she'd have his head when she found out. He took a deep breath as he imagined the choice words she would spew.

"This may take a minute," Liza said finally, pulling at his attention. "They have some serious firewalls up to keep people like me out."

"But you can get in without them knowing?"

She gave him a look, her expression twisted with evident annoyance at his question. "Go eat some bacon. I'll call you if I need you." She reached for a remote that rested on the table and music suddenly filled the room. It was something classical, a poetic blend of flutes, violins and a piano. She threw him one last glance as she turned the volume up high, then she resumed typing, her blue hair swaying with the music.

Upstairs, Mama Hill had set the kitchen table with five places. A feast for twenty sat table center. There was a platter of hot biscuits, crispy bacon, buttered grits, blueberry muffins, scrambled eggs, a bowl of sliced fruit and a pitcher of freshly squeezed orange juice.

The old woman winked an eye at him as he entered

the room and pointed him to the chair. She stood at the stove, stirring something in a large cast-iron pot. The aroma wafting around the room was mouthwatering and a hunger pang rippled through his midsection. Paul stole a quick glance toward his wristwatch, noting the time he was quickly running out of. Wondering if Simone was on her way, or if perhaps she'd changed her mind.

"Sit!" Mama Hill snapped, seeming to read his mind. Her dark eyes narrowed slightly. "You need to eat!" She stopped stirring the pot she was standing over. "Answer the door first, though. Make yourself useful."

Paul hesitated for a moment, then turned on his heel. He hadn't heard the doorbell, but the look the old woman threw in his direction had him thinking there might be a problem if he protested. He made his way back to the front of the home and pulled open the door. Simone and Mingus stood on the front porch. As Mingus brushed past him, entering the living space, he rolled his eyes skyward. Paul instinctively knew Simone was not a happy camper. He didn't know if he should be scared or not, but the sight of her instantly calmed his nerves.

"Hey," he said, greeting her softly.

When Simone didn't respond, instead giving him a dirty look before she followed her brother, Paul figured it probably wasn't a good time to tell her about the two strangers being at the hospital. Laughter suddenly rang loudly from the kitchen, the matriarch in high spirits as she greeted Mingus. Paul blew a soft sigh. He closed and locked the door and moved back toward the kitchen.

Mingus was making introductions. "Mama Hill, this is my baby sister Simone. Simone, this is Mrs. Pearl Hill, but everyone calls her Mama. Mama has helped me out with a few cases in the past."

Mama Hill pulled Simone into a warm hug. "Any family of Mingus's is family here. Y'all sit down. We was just 'bout to have us some breakfast." She pointed them toward the table.

"It smells good, Mama. And you made your special candied bacon!" Mingus chimed as he pulled out a chair at the head of the table and sat down.

The older woman grinned, her toothy smile gleaming under the morning light. "Made it just for you. I know how much you like my bacon."

Simone looked all kinds of confused as she sat down next to her brother. She clearly had questions, but she sensed she needed to wait before asking. She was also tense, her nerves feeling like she might explode. She was angry at Paul and relieved and all she wanted was to throw herself into his arms and then slap his face for making her worry.

For the briefest moment she stared in Paul's direction, then snatched her eyes away when he sat down and stared back. There was a hint of relief in her gaze and then that sliver of anger revved back up to full throttle. Paul smiled, vaguely amused by the wealth of emotion she was struggling to contain. Mama Hill suddenly tapped him against the back of his head, snapping him back to attention.

"Ouch!" he exclaimed as he reached to rub the offending bruise.

Simone and Mingus both laughed.

"Mama was asking you a question," Mingus said.

"Sorry," Paul responded. "I wasn't paying attention, Mama Hill. What were you saying?"

The old woman chuckled, her head shaking from side to side. "Liza is calling for you. She needs you to come downstairs."

"Who's Liza?" Simone suddenly questioned, giving him another look.

Mingus grinned, eyeing him with a raised brow.

Paul shook his head, looking slightly flustered by the sliver of jealousy that blew over her spirit. "She's a friend of your brother's. She's helping us out."

Mama Hill looked from him to Simone and back. "Take Simone downstairs with you and introduce her. Then the three of you come back up dem stairs and get you some breakfast. Tell Liza Mingus is here."

Paul nodded. "Yes, ma'am."

Simone sat for a second too long before the older woman admonished them both. "Y'all ain't got all day now!"

Mingus laughed, a deep belly guffaw that made Simone shift her annoyance in his direction as she stood and followed Paul to the basement.

Chapter 5

"Dude! Did you know that the pharmaceutical industry raised prices on thousands of drugs this year? Including medications to treat arthritis, high blood pressure and diabetes? Some of these guys hauled in over $25 billion in profits last year. That's some serious price gouging!" Liza looked astonished as Paul and Simone went downstairs.

Paul nodded. "Americans routinely pay more for prescription drugs that are just a fraction of the cost in other countries. The bigger question is why we're the only industrialized nation that allows pharmaceutical executives to raise prices with zero consideration for public health."

Liza pointed her index finger at him. "This really is some shysty mess!" She shifted her gaze toward Simone. "Who are you?"

Paul tossed a look over his shoulder. "Liza, this is Simone. Simone, this is Liza, Mingus's friend." He emphasized the word *friend* so there was no doubt in Simone's mind about his association with the young woman.

"You a friend of Mingus's, too?" Liza questioned.

"Mingus is my brother. He's upstairs, by the way. He got distracted by the food."

Liza's excitement shimmered across her face. "Cool beans! It's nice to meet you."

"It's nice to meet you, too," Simone said, her eyes sweeping the room and taking in all the technology in the space.

Paul could see the questions that caused her brow to furrow. "Liza is trying to find some information for me."

"I see. And how many laws are we breaking right now?"

"You really don't want to know," Liza answered, shooting her another look.

"Were you able to find anything?" Paul asked.

Liza pointed to the printer. "You know none of this is admissible in a court of law, right?"

Paul nodded, moving swiftly to the stack of paper spilling out of the machine.

Liza stood. "The CEO of Lender Pharmaceuticals is a freak, too. He has all kinds of porn on his computer."

"Porn?" Simone questioned. "What kind of porn?"

"Golden showers seem to be his perversion of choice. Some real nasty stuff. But his emails make for interesting reading." She suddenly jumped up excitedly. "And do you know that if he leaves the company his severance package will pay him over eighty million dollars? How crazy is that mess!"

Paul was shifting through the printed documents, having barely heard Liza's last comments. His focus was singular, his attention distracted. He was surprised by the volume of information Liza had managed to obtain and a lab report had him crunching data in his head.

Liza shrugged her shoulders and headed for the stairs. Simone started to follow but Paul suddenly called her name, looking up abruptly from the documents he was reading. She turned around to see what he needed.

Paul was staring at her intently, emotion flooding his face as he struggled with how to make things right between them. How to assuage her anger and get her to understand how much he appreciated her help. He was searching for the right words and struggled with finding them. How best to give her an out before they were both too deep in the midst of it to find their way out.

"Yes?"

"I would understand if this is too much for you to handle. If you didn't want to see this through with me."

Simone bit down against her bottom lip, twisting her hands together anxiously. "Does that mean you don't want me to help?"

"It means I understand if you think it's too much for you to handle."

She gave him a nod and turned, her hand on the railing. He called after her a second time.

"Simone?"

She took a deep breath before turning back a second time, her brow raised ever so slightly. Her tone was soft, just a hint above a whisper. "Yes, Paul?"

"I still love you. I never stopped. I don't know what may happen, but I needed you to know that."

When Paul admitted his love for her, time seemed to come to an abrupt halt, the minute hand on every clock stalling. Words caught in Simone's chest, a wealth of emotion smothering her thoughts. They stood staring at each other, something shifting in their relationship that clearly neither had anticipated. Unable to find the words to respond, Simone could only give him a nod of her head and then she turned, almost running back up the stairs.

Hearing his declaration had been everything Simone had wanted. He still loved her. He had never stopped. Despite the time that had separated them, they had slid back into sync with each other and all she needed to do was say the words back. He needed to know she felt the same way, and she needed to ensure she didn't screw it up like the last time.

When Paul finally joined them at the breakfast table, Simone was regaling the two women with a story about Mingus and one of his many exploits as a child. Mama Hill and Liza were both laughing heartily. The matriarch gave him a stern look as she passed him the plate of bacon.

"Sorry, Mama. I didn't mean to take so long."

The old woman tossed Mingus a look and he was grinning like a Cheshire cat. "I like this one," she said, nodding eagerly. "Yes, I do. I like him a lot." She shifted her gaze toward Simone. "He's a keeper. Not that you asked my opinion, but if I were you, I'd hold on to him. Hell, if I were a few years younger I'd give you a run for your money!"

"No, we're...just..." Simone started, suddenly unsure how to identify the two of them. There was still so much they needed to figure out and even more that needed to be said. Telling people she'd barely known for a hour that Paul was the love of her life had her feeling completely out of sorts.

"Friends. We're just friends," Paul concluded.

Simone gave him a quick look, then dropped her eyes down to her plate.

Mama Hill looked from one to the other and then she burst out laughing, her head waving from side to side. "Friends my ass!" she said. "You young people kill me! Even a blind man can see the kind of *friends* you two are!"

As soon as the meal was finished Paul headed back to the basement with Liza and Mingus. Simone hesitated just long enough for Mama Hill to point her toward the sink and the pile of dirty dishes. Her eyes widened and for a moment she almost balked, catching herself when the old woman pressed a wrinkled hand against her cheek.

"Why are you so sad?" she asked, eyeing Simone intently. "You know that young man has deep feelings for you."

Simone felt a tear slip past her lengthy lashes and Mama Hill brushed it away with a calloused thumb. She nodded. "I do. He's a great guy, but it will never work out. We're too different."

Simone hated saying those words the minute they left her mouth. Hated that she'd even had the thought and had given it life. Every ounce of doubt and fear she had about their relationship manifested in those words, already rationalizing why them being together was destined to fail. Instead of thinking how to tell Paul she loved him back, Simone was reasoning why they shouldn't be together.

Mama Hill fanned a dismissive hand. "Girl, please! If you want it badly enough, you make it work. My late husband and I were like oil and water. That man worked my good nerve on a regular basis, but I loved everything about him. I fought hard for our marriage. Giving up would have been easy but the fight was so much sweeter."

"So how long were you two married?"

"Thirty-eight years. He passed on back nine years ago. Was sitting right here in this kitchen fussing at me when he had a heart attack and never woke up."

"I'm so sorry."

Mama Hill passed Simone a dry towel and then she turned toward the sink. "We was good as gold while we lasted, even with the challenges we faced. I missed him something awful. Wasn't sure I was going to make it when I happened upon Liza. She was just a little bitty thing and smart as a whip. Her mama was lost out here in these streets and her daddy was incarcerated. I became her foster mother and she's been here raising hell ever since." The woman chuckled, joy shining in her eyes.

She continued. "I fostered a few other strays over the years. Then last year they said I was too old. So, now it's just me and Liza and I can't get her away from them computers long enough to meet a man. I keep telling her I want to see some grandbabies around here before I die." She laughed as she rinsed suds from a dinner plate.

Simone smiled. "My mother says the same thing. My brothers will probably give her grandkids before I or my sister do."

"How long have you and that pretty doctor been playing games with each other?"

"Games?"

"Yes. Loving on each other one day, then mad about absolutely nothing the next day."

Simone blew a soft sigh. "Since we were in college together. It's been off and on over ten years now."

Mama Hill shook her head. "Like my Douglas use to say, that's enough time to piss or get off the pot. What are you waiting for?"

Simone pondered the question, dropping the dishrag in her hand down to her side. She had often asked herself that question. When Paul had been overseas the answer had seemed obvious. Now he was back, proclaiming to still be in love with her, and she had no answer that would make an ounce of sense to anyone else.

If Paul had been solely responsible for their future, they would have been married with a dozen kids. He had always been open about wanting marriage and a family to balance his medical career. Simone hadn't needed either and earnestly believed she would be happier without the picket-fence fantasy. She had routinely stalled his quest to move their relationship forward, convinced she didn't need a piece of paper to validate her commitment to him. She had fought him at every turn and he had still loved her. She was feeling pretty crappy about the whole thing as she brushed a fall of moisture from her cheek.

She lifted her eyes to find Mama Hill staring at her. Simone shrugged, forcing a smile to her face. She couldn't find the words to answer, struggling once again not to cry.

Mama Hill clasped a hand to her hip, the look she gave Simone scolding. "Let me give you another bit of advice you didn't ask for," she said. "Love ain't easy. In fact, it's damn hard work! But as long as that love isn't toxic, it's worth every ounce of effort you can give it. You love him and he loves you. Stop fighting it and just let yourself enjoy whatever it has for you."

Mama Hill untied the apron from around her waist. She crossed to the other side of the room to hang it on a hook near the door that led out to a rear deck. "I think I'm going to go watch me some Dr. Phil. I may fall asleep and if I do, don't y'all wake me up. Whatever trouble you two done found yourselves in will work itself out. Just trust your instincts and hold tight to each other and everything will be okay."

"Thank you, Mama," Simone said softly. "Thank you for everything."

The matriarch laughed. "Baby, thank the Lord! Pay me—advice ain't never been cheap!"

Simone laughed with her and when she disappeared behind a closed door at the end of the hallway, Simone turned toward the basement.

"How do you not test a drug? Federal regulations demand they test any product they put on the market. There have to be test results and research data somewhere besides the damn brochure!" Paul snapped, irritation blessing his words.

He was sorting pages into individual piles and then

slipping them into manila folders. With a permanent marker he jotted notes on the front of each, his scribblings only making sense to him. He met Simone's stare as she eased her way to his side, her expression questioning as she peered down at the papers in his hand. He gave her a slight smile as he turned his attention back to Liza.

Liza tossed her hands up in frustration. "I've looked in every file I could get into. There's nothing there before it hit the market."

"And you looked everywhere?"

"Everywhere I could without setting off any alarms that would let their IT department know I was there snooping. I ain't interested in going to jail!"

Paul closed his eyes, falling into thought. Clearly, what he had fathomed was turning out to be true. But there were still questions that needed to be answered. Things that didn't make sense and he wasn't sure if he was even asking the right questions or searching for the correct answers. Mostly, he needed to understand why.

Mingus cleared his throat. "You two need to get a move on it," he said. "It's starting to get too hot for you to hang around here much longer. The police superintendent wants to see you both for questioning."

Simone gasped. "Daddy called you?"

"Not yet. Parker messaged me so it's just a matter of time."

"Where should we go?" Simone asked, a wave of anxiety washing over her.

Her brother tossed Paul a look. "I'm told it's handled. Just send me a text when you get there to let me know you're safe."

Paul had opened his eyes, looking from Simone to Mingus and back. "You can still stay here with your brother," he said. "I'd understand. It might actually be the best thing for everybody."

"That's not an option," she snapped.

Silence rose full and thick between them. Paul finally nodded. "We'll be okay," he said, throwing Mingus one last look. Despite his uncertainty about what might come next, he was happy to know he hadn't run her off and Simone was as determined to be with him as he was determined to be with her.

He changed the subject. "Liza, can you give me all the info they have on the drugs they've manufactured over the last ten years?"

Liza nodded. "That's a lot of paper but if you want it, I can get it for you."

"Please," he said. "I would really appreciate it."

"You know I can put it on a flash drive."

"I know. I'm going to need hard copy. And this, too, please." He reached into his back pocket for the storage device he'd taken from the hospital. "If you can print out everything on here and then give it to Mingus for safe-keeping."

"What's on it?" Mingus asked, eyeing them both with a raised brow.

Paul took a deep inhale of air. "Proof. Data I've been collecting since I first suspected something wasn't right."

An hour later Simone moved to the opposite end of the large work table. She leaned in to her brother's side, wrapping her arms around his waist as she hugged him goodbye. Mingus was on his phone with their mother, purposely avoiding answering questions about her and Paul. He wrapped an arm around her shoulders and hugged her back before pressing a light kiss to the top of her head, then pausing to push the mute button on his phone. "Take this," he said, pulling a roll of one-hundred-dollar bills from his pocket and slipping it into the pocket of her jacket. "Do not, under any circumstances, use your credit cards," he said. "If you need more, you call me."

Simone nodded, her fingers wrapping tightly around the wad of cash.

"I mean it, Simone! If you use your cards anyone looking for you will find you."

"I get it," she replied. Tears suddenly misted her eyes and she blinked to stall them from falling.

Mingus turned his attention toward Paul. "Keep her safe," he said, as they punched fists.

"With my life," Paul answered.

Liza jumped from her seat, moving to hug them both. "I'll keep digging. If I come up with anything, I'll message you," she said.

"Thank you," Paul responded.

"Give Mama a hug for us," Simone said.

"Mama is not the hugging type, but I'll tell her you said goodbye," Liza said with a hearty laugh.

After the couple went outside and settled down in the car, Paul told her, "You know you don't have to do this, Simone." He was giving her one last chance to change her mind and back out.

"Do what?"

"You don't have to come with me. Especially since we don't know what's going to happen."

"I know that. Do you want me to drive?" Her eyes were wide and she gave him a bright smile. Without saying it aloud she was committed to running away with him, determined to make the best of a bad situation. Because being with Paul was the best of anything she could possibly imagine.

Paul shook his head, a slight smile pulling at his full

lips. "No, I'm good," he said. He buckled his seat belt and started the engine. Shifting the car into gear, he pulled out of the parking space and into traffic.

"So where are we going?" she asked.

Paul cut an eye in her direction. "Canada," he answered.

"Canada?"

"Yeah. My brother and I have a cabin there."

"Since when?"

"Since our mother willed it to us. It was her family home. We invested a little money to restore it and now Oliver spends more time there than I do."

Simone stared as he pulled the car onto Interstate 94 east, headed toward Detroit. She suddenly had questions but figured she'd wait until there was too much distance between them and Chicago for him to consider turning around to bring her back. Because she had no intentions of coming back if he wasn't coming with her.

Simone had thought she knew everything there was to know about Paul. But this was the first time hearing he owned a cabin in Canada. When Paul's mother died his second year in medical school, he'd been devastated, the loss unexpected. After the funeral his brother had handled the estate and Paul had thrown himself back into his studies, leaving himself no time to mourn. There had been moments when Simone had been concerned. He'd been moody: zealously happy one minute and bitterly sullen the next. She had suggested counseling, passing him the telephone number of a therapist her mother had recommended. Weeks later he seemed to find a new normal and life had gone on without skipping another beat.

Now there were things between them that she didn't know. Experiences they hadn't shared. A lifetime lived without each other. Thinking about it made Simone all kinds of sad.

Simone reached for the radio and pushed buttons until she found the satellite station. Beyoncé was lecturing in perfect pitch, the lyrics harmonizing with a decadent Caribbean beat. Paul had gone quiet, falling into his own thoughts. Simone eyed him a second time, sensing that he was working through something in his head. She knew this mood and also knew she needed to give him space. She would ask her questions later, when he was ready for conversation. Reclining the seat slightly, Simone settled in for the ride.

Chapter 6

Paul slowed the car as he met a line of traffic on the Michigan freeway. Simone had been snoring softly and she woke with a start. Her eyes were wide as she sat upright and looked around.

"Where are we?" she asked, stretching her arms in front of her.

"Just outside Battle Creek, Michigan. We're a little more than two hours from Detroit."

Simone looked down at her watch. "You've been driving for over three hours. You need a break."

"I'm good, actually. It's given me some time to think. Do you need me to stop, though?"

"I could use the bathroom. And you really do need to stretch your legs, Dr. Reilly. Didn't you lecture me once about preventing blood clots?"

Paul chuckled. "I don't lecture." His laugh was light and easy, making him feel like old times.

Laughing with him, Simone rolled her eyes skyward. "Not much you don't!" she muttered.

Traffic was still crawling slowly. Paul shifted his buttocks against the seat to ease the tension tightening in his limbs. Simone reached for her phone, searching for restaurants near their location.

"There's a travel plaza right off the next exit. They have a diner and a McDonald's and we can fill up the car."

"That'll work. I really want to cross the border before

it gets dark. By the way, you do still carry your passport with you, don't you?"

Simone nodded. "You know I do. But it's a little late to be asking, isn't it? What if I didn't have it?"

"I'd have to leave you in Detroit," Paul said matter-of-factly.

"You would not leave me."

He cut an eye at her, but he didn't respond, and the moment gave them both pause.

Simone took a deep breath. "I was wrong," she suddenly said, her eyes fixed on the roadway in front of them. "I should have gone with you to Africa."

The comment surprised him, and Paul tried not to let it show on his face. Simone saying she was wrong was life-changing, and he wasn't sure if he should send up a flare to celebrate or find shelter and wait for an impending lightning strike. He took a deep breath, blowing it out slowly as he responded. "You did what you thought you needed to do, Simone. There wasn't anything wrong with that."

"I was scared. I was afraid that in chasing you and your dreams I would lose myself."

"I wouldn't have let that happen."

"You don't know that."

"I knew that I loved you enough to want to make sure that your joy was as bright as my own. I still do. But you never trusted that. What kind of man would I be if I didn't do everything I could for you to love me and live in your purpose, too? You always felt like you had to choose one or the other and you didn't."

Simone shifted her gaze to look at him, meeting the glance he was giving her. "I did trust it, Paul. But I let my own insecurities and fears get in the way. I made the biggest mistake of my life. Because I did love you. I still love you, too."

Paul reached for her hand and tangled his fingers with hers. His palm was heated, and his touch was comforting. Simone exhaled loudly, the sound of it like music to his ears. Relief washed over him, and Paul knew that no matter what happened from that moment forward, he and Simone would be better than okay. He trusted that more than he ever had before.

Once they pulled into the Te-Khi Travel Court, Paul found an empty spot, parked the car and shut down the engine.

"So, what now?" Simone asked.

"You and I have a lot to talk about," Paul said finally. The list in his head was lengthy, including wanting to hear what *she* wanted for their future. But the past few hours had begun to wear on him. He was tired and they still had a ways to go before they could rest and she could feel completely safe. Because he desperately needed her to feel that things would be okay. "But I need the men's room first and then we need to grab something to eat so we can get back on the road."

Stepping out of the vehicle, they both cast their gazes around the landscape. Despite the distance between them and Chicago, they were still on edge about being followed. Paul had been reluctant to share what had happened at the hospital, not wanting to alarm Simone any more. He was worried for her. He wanted only the best for them both. Loving Simone fueled his actions and insuring she was protected was foremost in his mind. Protected and happy. At the moment though, that was far from their reality. Simone wasn't content or cheery and she couldn't be until he could get them out of harm's way. He still had his own questions that needed to be answered, so he could only imagine the mayhem spinning in her head trying to make sense of it all.

The truck stop was old but established. It was average at best and the convenience store supplied basic staples. After using the restroom, Paul headed over to the diner and ordered them two daily specials to go. By the time he returned Simone was at the register paying cash for chips, water, a chocolate bar for him and her favorite gummy bears.

He stepped in behind her, dropping his hands against her shoulders. His fingers slid down the length of her upper arms, up and then across her back. He noted the tension beneath his palms. Simone leaned against his chest as she waited for the clerk to bag her items and count out her change.

"Junk food, Simone?"

"Road-trip food. How do you travel?"

Paul grinned. "Fried chicken and French fries, baby," he said, pointing toward the diner. "With two slices of homemade chocolate cake to go. Our food should be ready for us as soon as we're done here."

"They do make the best cake!" the young woman behind the counter interjected.

Simone laughed. "Please, don't encourage him."

The other woman laughed with her. "You two are so cute together. Is he your husband?"

Simone shot a quick glance over her shoulder. Paul was gently kneading the stress out of her shoulders. "Something like that," she said, blushing slightly.

Paul leaned forward and pressed a kiss to the top of her head. The familiar scent of her perfume and the airy aroma of her jasmine-scented shampoo teased his nostrils. As he savored the sweetness that reminded him of so many beautiful moments between them, he felt conflicted.

Wanting to relish the joy they shared despite knowing the challenges they still faced. But he had missed those moments, when the nearness of her gave him pause and everything felt right in their small world. He kissed her a second time before releasing the hold on her shoulders. He said nothing as Simone thanked the woman for her help and then they turned toward the door.

An hour later their stomachs were full, and Simone was trying not to speed. Paul sat in the passenger seat flipping through the papers in one of the many files he'd brought with him. Between intermittent admonishments for her to slow down, he kept his attention focused on the documents in his hands.

"What are you reading?" Simone questioned, giving him a curious glance.

"Trying to make sense out of the drug data Liza pulled off the Lender computer. There's a definite trail with some of their drugs. Research studies, FDA approvals, sales. With Halphedrone-B, there's no data before the sales data. And I mean nothing. There's an amended FDA approval and sales, nothing about the research prior to that."

"Any other drugs follow that pattern or seem skewed?"

"There are three that don't show ever going into mass production or having ever been sold to the public. Not sure why, though. And dozens are still in various phases of testing."

"You probably need to focus on the drugs that don't have a clear data pattern of production and sales history. That might help you figure out what you're looking for."

"When we get to the house, I need you to call your friend at the FDA, please."

"I will. And if I can get to a computer, I can do some research, as well. If we know where they do most of their business, I can search the state court records to see any current or previous lawsuits against them."

"That might be a bit of a problem."

Simone shot him a quick look. "A problem?"

"It's complicated."

"How complicated can it be?"

"The last time I was up here, there was no electricity. Oliver has wanted to keep it rustic and isolated, with no outside distractions. That's why I asked Liza to print everything. Just in case."

"No electricity?"

"We'll be deep in the woods. There's a generator but it's used sparingly."

"So, you're taking me deep into the woods with no electricity?" Her gaze narrowed. Rustic with a hint of luxury she could handle, Simone thought. Rustic with archaic accommodations was not her idea of a good time.

"And spotty cell phone service. There's a house phone, though."

"No electricity, no cell phone service, no internet and your reclusive brother?"

"Oliver's not a recluse. And don't get there picking on my brother. I don't want to hear you two bickering the whole time we're there."

"Is there indoor plumbing at least?"

"It's not totally primitive, Simone."

Simone rolled her eyes skyward. She bit back the snarky comment that was on the tip of her tongue. In the past she would have picked an argument, but she really didn't want to fight. Things were good with them and she wanted to keep it that way, even if she wasn't happy about the potential conditions she was about to be tossed in. "So, no more luxury accommodations, like last night's motel?" she asked instead.

Paul chuckled. "I promise—it won't be that bad. In fact, I think you'll actually like the place."

"I was slightly surprised that I didn't know about it," she said, finally getting that off her chest.

He pondered the statement for a moment before responding. "We weren't in a good place with each other when my brother finalized my mother's estate. I wasn't trying to keep it from you, Simone, but we weren't talking. Not the way we should have been. And, I really wasn't interested in the house and just figured I'd eventually sign my half over to Oliver. But he convinced me to come up for a visit and I've been two or three times since. It's turned out to be a great getaway."

"And now it's a perfect hideout?"

Paul smiled, and nodded. "Until they find us," he said matter-of-factly.

Their light banter continued for the rest of the ride, both catching up with each other. Much time had passed since the big clash that had severed their ties. Despite the level of comfort they'd been able to reignite with each other, there was much they'd missed.

Paul discovered Simone was being courted by one of the top law firms in the state of Illinois, which offered a lucrative seven-figure salary, substantial perks and a potential partnership on the table. He knew it was the next step in what she hoped would eventually be a stellar political career.

Simone was surprised to learn that he had purchased a home in Morocco, the northwest African destination enabling him to do more mission work abroad while affording him a respite from the transcontinental travel. Learning he had considered making the move permanent felt like a punch to her gut.

"So, you're seriously thinking about moving?"

"I've left the option open, yes."

"What about your job at the hospital? You're highly regarded there. Enough that they accommodate your mission trips, so why leave?"

He nodded. "My mission trips help the hospital look good. The board appreciates being able to say that their doctors have international experience and exploiting our humanitarian endeavors. If I decide to leave, I'll be able to maintain my privileges when and if I come back to Chicago.

Simone paused, unsure how she felt or what to say. "I can't move to Morocco, Paul," she finally muttered.

Paul gave her the slightest smile. "I would never ask you to move, Simone," he said. "I did that once and you broke my heart. Remember?"

Before she could respond he pointed toward the exit, motioning for her to bear right toward the Detroit-Windsor Tunnel. She merged onto the toll road, her eyes skating back and forth between her mirrors and the road as she eased slowly forward with the line of traffic. When they reached the inspection plaza they were greeted by an Immigration and Customs official.

It was Simone's first time traveling to Canada and she hadn't expected the hustle and bustle of the big city that greeted them. Actually, she hadn't known what to expect but the tall buildings surprised her.

Paul seemed to read her mind. "Windsor is known as the 'Automotive Capital of Canada.' The town has a diverse industrial and manufacturing history. My father used to work for the Ford Motor Company engine plant which is here. Now it also has a well-established tourism industry and one of the largest casinos in Canada."

"It seems like a great city. I'd love to explore it some, one day," she said softly as she imagined the two of them exploring the city together. Hand in hand. A wave of sadness washed over her as she thought about all she had missed out on with him.

Something in her tone moved Paul to turn and stare. He pointed. "Pull into that parking lot up there. I'll take us the rest of the way. That way you can sightsee while I drive."

"Are we far from your house?"

He shook his head. "No, about another forty-five minutes if the traffic is good."

Pulling into the parking lot of a fast-food restaurant, they took a few minutes to stretch and change places. When they were back in the car, Paul settled behind the driver's seat, Simone drifted off in reflection. She was still reeling from his comment about never asking her to move to the other side of the world to be with him. She was suddenly heartbroken to think that he might not want to resume their relationship. That maybe he didn't see a future for the two of them, no matter where in the world he might find himself. The lyrics to Tina Turner's "What's Love Got to Do with It" suddenly came to mind. Her feelings were hurt but she couldn't muster up the wherewithal to tell him.

The silence was suddenly daunting, and an awkward tension filled the space like helium in an oversize balloon. Simone tried to focus on the city and the multitude of left and right turns Paul was making toward their destination. But her stomach was in knots and suddenly all she wanted to do was cry.

In the Black family, Simone was renowned for her emotional rants. Any slight could send her into overload and have her railing against every sin, real or imagined. Paul could feel the tension rising over her like a thick mist.

She was biting down on her bottom lip as she stared out the window, her brain surely spinning a mile per minute.

For reasons Paul couldn't begin to explain things between them suddenly felt like they did just before they had ended their relationship. Back then it had been easier to say nothing, to ask no questions and simply walk away from each fight. Communication had not been either of their strong suits.

But nothing they had done before had worked for them and he knew for things to be different this time, that they needed to make different choices. Changing their patterns of behavior was an absolute necessity if they hoped for a new outcome. So, this time, he asked.

"What's wrong, Simone? And, please, don't tell me it's nothing because I know there is something bothering you."

Simone shifted in her seat, turning slightly. She took a deep breath and held it briefly before she spoke. "Will you and I always be at odds over what we want in life? Is there ever going to be a time when we want the same thing?"

"I don't understand, Simone."

"I just...well..." she stammered, words failing her for the first time in a very long while. She couldn't begin to explain that it felt like everything was always stacked against them and nothing she could say or do would change that. The old Simone would have waged a verbal war to make that point, fear and anger clinging to every word. The new Simone was determined to not make the same mistakes.

"I'm sorry. Can we please shelve this conversation for now? I want to discuss it when I have a better handle on my feelings."

Paul's brows lifted slightly. "That's fine," he responded. "Whenever you're ready you let me know."

"Thank you," she whispered, still fighting not to break out into an ugly cry that would have her looking foolish.

Paul suddenly took a sharp right turn, pulling onto a dirt road lined with tall trees that quickly became an island of forest surrounding them. About two miles down the single-lane roadway a large log home loomed in the distance. It was a breathtaking sight to behold and not at all the simple cabin Simone had imagined from Paul's description.

The two brothers had expanded the original footprint of the home to add additional living space. With classic hand-hewn logs, a covered wraparound porch, the scenic setting and its familial history, Simone could understand the appeal. As Paul pulled the car into the parking area next to an old Dodge sedan, Oliver Reilly stepped out the front door to welcome them.

Simone stood back as the men greeted each other. The brothers hugged, hanging on like family do when they've been worried. Oliver was tapping Paul against his back and relief hit Simone like a tidal wave. She swiped at a tear that had rolled down her cheek.

"Simone, hey!" Oliver called out as he stepped toward her and pulled her into a big bear hug. "Am I glad to see you! Your brother told me what happened to the two of you."

"You talked to Mingus?"

"Yeah. He needed to get into Paul's place to get him some clothes. Told me you two were hiding out. That's when I figured it might be a good idea for me to come north until we can all figure out what's going on."

She smiled. "Well, it's good to see you, too, Oliver. And I'm really glad to be here. I'm also glad you got that electricity problem resolved," she said as she noted the lights radiating from every window.

Oliver laughed. "That was only a temporary problem! But we sometimes lose power still, depending on the weather. Come on inside. I was just about to put some dinner on. I wasn't sure if you were coming in today or tomorrow. Paul was concerned after seeing those guys at the hospital this morning."

Simone shot Paul a look. She pointed her index finger at him. "You and I really need to work on communicating better with each other!" she snapped.

Paul and his brother exchanged a look.

"Oops!" Oliver quipped. "I just figured…"

Paul chuckled. "I was looking for the right time to bring it up."

"I swear, Paul Reilly…" Simone muttered as she moved to the trunk of the car for her bags.

Chapter 7

Simone had needed some time to herself and she sensed the two brothers wanted their own moment. The home was divided into two separate wings that filtered off a central common area. There was a sizable kitchen and expansive back deck. Paul had led her down one wing to a spare bedroom. As he dropped her bag atop the mattress he pointed across the hallway.

"My room is there. Oliver is down at the other end of the house."

"Thank you," she'd said. "I just need to freshen up."

He had nodded, then he leaned and had pressed a kiss to her cheek.

Simone could still feel the warmth of his lips against her skin. Despite everything else between them, there was no denying their chemistry. Even when they had been at odds over something, their intimate connection always brought them back around, centered, focused and wanting to make things between them well.

Her fingers tapped gently at the spot, her eyes closed. Suddenly everything she had trusted and believed in shifted. She found herself reassessing what she wanted: most important, she realized she needed to be happy. She imagined herself following him to Morocco. Because being with Paul brought her the most immense joy. Falling asleep in his bed, waking to him beside her. Those intimate moments when it was just the two of them and they could shut the world out, nothing and no one intruding on those moments, that made her happy. And then she imagined if she didn't, the very thought of what would follow bringing her to tears. Minutes later, Simone was sleeping soundly.

Oliver moved inside from the rear patio. Smoke billowed from the freshly lit grill. Racks of spare ribs lay marinating in an oversize metal pan as he began to prep the evening meal. Paul looked up from the papers he was studying. The second package of samples had arrived safely, and Oliver had already begun to run the necessary tests.

"The drugs are contaminated," he said, locking gazes with his brother.

Oliver nodded. "It's the bacterium Burkholderia cepacia."

"How did they get this past the FDA?"

"That I can't answer, but I do know that all the samples you sent me tested positive for the same strain of B. cepacia."

"Unbelievable," Paul muttered.

"Look, you and I both know the multitude of ethical issues with the pharmaceutical industry, starting with questionable accountability. Between lack of healthcare reform, price gouging and greed, product contamination is just another blip on an already overloaded radar."

"They can't be doing this on purpose, can they?"

"Highly unlikely, but they are just as accountable for their negligence. But bottom line for them, is their bottom line. They're making money and that's all they care about. Now, it's highly possible this is a fluke. Maybe they aren't aware, but you asked questions that should have raised a red flag for them to do some testing. It doesn't look like they're interested in doing that."

Paul cussed, throwing the pages in his hand across the dining room table. He knew he wore his frustration like bad makeup, everything in his heart filled with horror and pain. He knew the system was broken but never imagined that he would be personally touched by the jagged edges. That patients he'd sworn to help heal would suffer instead because someone else didn't give a damn.

Oliver moved to his side and took a seat. "You been out to the barn yet?"

Paul shook his head. "No. Why?"

"I've been working on a few things that you might be interested in. Why don't you take a walk while I get our dinner ready?"

He blew a heavy sigh. "I should probably go check on Simone."

"How are things with you two?"

Paul shrugged, not sure he had an answer. "We have a lot to work through and this bull isn't helping," he said.

"Maybe the two of you working on a common goal is what you need to pull you back together."

"I actually don't know that we can ever resolve our issues. Simone is married to staying here in the United States with her family and I don't know if I can commit to that. My work is important to me."

"More important than Simone?"

The two locked gazes as Paul pondered his brother's question. Nothing was more important to him than her, not even the work he felt destined to do. He loved Simone. Loved Simone with everything he had in him. But he realized love might not be enough for either of them.

He pushed himself from the table, not bothering to

reply to his brother's question. "I think I'll take a walk and go check out the barn."

Oliver chuckled. "You do that. I'll call you when the food's ready."

Simone was startled out of a sound sleep. The room was dark, except for a small night-light plugged into a socket beneath the end table. She sat upright, clenched fists rubbing at her eyes, then rolled to the edge of the bed before she threw her legs off the side. She hadn't meant to fall asleep and she hadn't intended to sleep for almost three hours, she thought after she stole a quick glance at her watch.

She moved from the bed to the bathroom. Minutes later she felt refreshed, her teeth brushed, face washed and bladder emptied. She took one last look at her reflection in the mirror and pulled her hands through the short length of her hair.

Exiting the bathroom, she gathered her phone from the dresser and headed out the door down the length of hallway to the family room. Oliver stood at the counter in the kitchen. A small television rested in the corner, the station he was watching tuned to a repeat episode of *Family Feud*. He was laughing intently as he sliced vegetables into a bowl.

"Hey!" Simone said, tossing her hand up in a slight wave.

Oliver looked up and smiled. "Hi! You're just in time. I was just about to take the ribs off the grill. Everything else is ready, so we can eat. I hope you're hungry."

"I am and it smells really good."

"It'll taste even better. I promise!"

"Where's your brother?"

"Out in the barn. He needed to blow off some steam," he said as he gestured toward the dining room.

The table was littered from one end to the other with the documents that Liza had printed for him. Folders were piled together and a few pages were scattered across the floor. A notepad and pen sat at one seat, two-thirds of the page scribbled with notes. Clearly, Paul had been busy since she'd last seen him.

"I'd offer to neaten that up, but I wouldn't want to disturb anything. I know how your brother is about something he's working on."

"No, I wouldn't mess with it. We can eat here at the kitchen table. There's plenty of room and we can watch the snow come down while we eat."

"It's snowing?"

Oliver nodded. "We're supposed to get an inch or two. I think it'll just be a light dusting if anything at all. It just felt a little too warm out today, so I don't think the ground is cold enough for any precipitation to stick."

Simone moved to the back door to peer outside. It was pitch-dark out, only a spattering of stars and a quarter moon lighting the sky. Behind the house was a freestanding barn, a light from inside shining to the outside. And snowflakes were falling like dust from the sky.

"It's so pretty," she said, the comment more for herself than anyone else.

Behind her Oliver chuckled. "It's all right!"

Simone turned, her arms folded across her chest. "Can I help with anything?"

"Actually, I'm glad you asked. Would you mind setting the table for me?"

"Not at all," she answered.

He pointed to an upper cabinet. "Plates are up there,

and you'll find the silverware in the drawer below it. Glasses are in the top cabinet on the other side of the sink."

Simone moved into the kitchen and grabbed what she needed. There was a small breakfast table in the alcove that looked out the bay window. She grabbed three place-mats from the corner of the counter and began to set to the table. As she moved to gather three glasses, Oliver cleared his throat.

"It's not my business, but I'm putting my money on the two of you getting back together."

He moved to the table and filled two of those glasses with red wine, then gestured for her to take a seat with him. They both took a sip from their drinks before Oliver continued.

"And I say that not because I'm a gambling man, but because I see how Paul is without you. He's been missing you like crazy. You two are good for each other."

Oliver's comment was chilling, despite the warmth of his delivery. She and Paul were both close to their families and their siblings had a vested interest in what happened in their lives. Simone imagined the two brothers had discussed her more times than she could count. She knew how often she had cried on her sister's shoulder about Paul. That Oliver believed there was hope for them was endearing. She, however, wasn't as confident.

"I think your brother and I might be too broken to make things work."

"Apart, yeah. But you two are like two pieces of a larger puzzle. The last two pieces necessary to finish the perfect picture. You need each other, even when you think you don't."

Simone took another sip of her beverage. There was a moment of pause until she set her glass back onto the table. "So, how's your love life doing? The last time we saw each other you were dating that pastry chef? Right?"

"He owned a bakery. You know, that one down in Humboldt Park."

"The one that specializes in pies? That one?"

Oliver nodded. "They have the best pies! He would make me a different pie every Sunday morning. The chocolate velvet was to die for!"

"He's not making pies anymore?"

Oliver sighed. "Not on Sundays and not for me."

"I'm sorry. You were always so happy when I saw you together."

"He said I worked too much. He needed someone who wasn't always at the office."

"And you don't think you two can work things out?"

"I think when it's right, you know. With us, even when it felt good there was always a lot of doubt. Mostly because he was still very closeted. Being in public with me made him uncomfortable."

Simone pushed out her bottom lip in an exaggerated pout.

Oliver waved a dismissive hand. "It's all good. Haven't you heard? I'm a very eligible bachelor. Men are falling all over themselves to date me! Someone new will be making me pie in no time!"

"There's an attorney in my office who's single. I'd love to introduce you two. He's a really nice guy."

"Nope! Because if things go south, you'll be in the middle feeling bad about it."

"It can be a casual introduction. Like you both show up at the same cocktail party and just happen to cross paths as you're mingling. I'll point him out and you can take it from there. No pressure."

"And who'll be throwing this cocktail party?"

"I will, of course! You know I throw a mean party!"

"Maybe it'll be an engagement party?"

Simone laughed. "Now you're pushing it."

Oliver laughed with her. "I missed you."

"I missed you, too, my friend."

"You and my brother really need to figure it out. You can't keep playing with my heart the way you two do." He winked his eye, then chugged the rest of the wine. "Now, if you'll please grab one of my jackets there on that hook by the door and go to the barn and tell Paul Michael that his dinner is about to get cold, I would appreciate it."

She laughed. "This is serious. You used his full name."

"And I expect you to do the same. Otherwise he'll be out there for the rest of the night."

Her eyes narrowed. "What's so special about the barn?"

"That, my darling, you'll have to see for yourself," he said as he pointed her toward the door. "Now, hurry up. Two more minutes and I'll be taking the corn bread out of the oven."

"You made corn bread?"

"And your favorite macaroni and cheese!"

Simone jumped from her seat and threw her arms around the man's neck. She kissed his cheek. "Thank goodness someone still loves me!"

Oliver laughed. "Woman, no one could ever stop loving you!"

"Paul Michael and I will be right back," Simone said with a wide grin. "Even if I have to drag him kicking and screaming!"

"Tell him dinner is on the table," Oliver said as he rose from his seat to peer in the oven. "And I *will* start without you two!"

Simone stood in the doorway of the backyard structure, her eyes sweeping around the room. What had originally been a barn had been transformed into a laboratory. Oliver had clearly gone to great lengths and much expense to build a space that rivaled some medical facilities. The pristine space boasted fully equipped workstations and state-of-the-art laboratory equipment that included clean benches, biosafety cabinets, ductless enclosures and more. It was impressive and Simone didn't have a clue about most of it.

Paul sat at a table, staring into a microscope. He was completely engaged, his focus distracted from his surroundings. He didn't hear when Simone opened the door and let herself inside. It was only when he paused to jot down some notes that he seemed to realize she was there.

"Hey! You're awake!"

"Hi! I didn't mean to sleep so long."

"You needed the rest. I'm glad you were comfortable."

Simone moved to his side. "This is amazing," she said.

"Oliver's put in some serious work since I was last here. But he wants to move here to Canada and make this his home base. His job at the CDC will allow him plenty of leeway with this setup. Having the lab will enable him to continue his cancer research from home. He has full safety certification and all his Declarations of Conformity. He's ready to rock and roll."

"So, what are you working on out here?"

"Just trying to make sense of the data. I mailed a second box of samples here that made it, and Oliver's been running tests on them. We think that Halphedrone-B is contaminated with a bacterium called Burkholderia cepacia. It's an unscrupulous human pathogen that causes pneumonia in immunocompromised individuals with underlying lung disease."

Simone squinted, looking confused.

Paul continued. "Basically, it attacks systems in the

human body that are already compromised. Then it shuts down organs and eventually causes death."

"Does the drug company know?"

"I can't imagine them not knowing. Why else would they send people after us if they didn't know?"

"But we need to find out for certain, Paul. Right now, it's all just theory. We need to make sure the evidence is irrefutable."

Paul nodded. "I need to run some additional tests, but I also have to get my hands on more samples of the drug. What I sent to Oliver in Chicago originally is gone. Those samples were from a batch lot that had been shipped to my clinic in West Africa and tissue samples from infected patients. What we've been able to test thus far—the stuff that made it here—is a whole other drug lot. We just need to be sure that it's not just unique to one single production lot."

"We'll get it," Simone said. She pressed her fingers to his back and gently caressed the length of the broad area.

He suddenly looked exhausted, closing his eyes as he settled back against her touch. He took a deep breath, blowing it out slowly.

"I think you're the one who needs to get some rest now. Your brother said to tell you the food is ready. Why don't we go eat and get back to this with fresh eyes in the morning? Oliver made corn bread, and macaroni and cheese to go with the ribs!"

Paul laughed. "You're a little obsessed with the food, aren't you?"

"I like to eat, and your brother is a great cook. It's very easy to be obsessed."

"Just give me five more…" he started.

Simone shook her head. "Now, Paul Michael Reilly. Before Oliver comes out here to get us both."

He laughed again. "Damn! My full name? Really, Simone. That's some mess Oliver would pull!"

"He's a great influence," she answered. "So, let's go, 'cause I'm hungry!"

The laughter around the dinner table felt good. The food was delicious, and the company made everything feel right with the world. After filling their bellies, Paul and Simone relaxed, feeling completely at ease. They were safe, and in that moment, safe was home with family and each other. Nina Simone was playing out of the speakers, Oliver's comedic homage to his guest's name. But the soft tones of Nina's *Pastel Blues* album were appropriate for the mood, easing them all into a subtle trance.

Oliver rose from the table first, wishing them both a good night. "I'll let you two do the dishes," he said. "I have to fly to Atlanta in the morning for a meeting at the CDC. While I'm there I'll see if I can find out anything that might help you."

"Just please be careful," Paul admonished. "We don't know who you can trust."

"Not to worry."

"When will you be back?" Simone asked.

"I actually need to go back to Chicago after I leave Atlanta. It may be a few weeks before I get back up here. You two will have the house all to yourselves. I trust you'll take good care of each other." He rounded the table, hugged them both, and then he disappeared to his side of the home.

There was something calming about him and her doing dishes side by side. As Paul had cleared the table, Simone had loaded the dishwasher. Then he had washed the pots and pans as she dried them.

"Do you want to sit and talk?" Paul questioned, "Or are you ready to head to bed."

She smiled. "I had a long nap, remember? I'll probably be up for another few hours."

"More wine? Or my special hot chocolate?"

"That cinnamon hot chocolate you make would be very nice," she answered.

He moved to the cupboard and pulled two mugs from inside. "Hot chocolate coming right up."

Simone moved into the family room and settled herself down on the sofa. It was still snowing, and a fire burned in the fireplace. She watched him as he warmed milk on the stove and added cocoa powder, sugar, cinnamon and cloves. Every so often he would look up at her and smile, the gesture making her heart sing. Paul always knew what she needed, and he was diligent about taking care of her. Too often she hadn't shown him enough appreciation. She made a mental note to do better going forward.

When the cocoa mixture was just warm enough, he added a teaspoonful of vanilla extract and a shot of bourbon, then mixed it with an immersion blender until it was just the right amount of frothy. Nina was still singing softly in the background.

Paul joined her on the sofa, a hint of steam billowing off two oversize mugs. He had topped both with a swirl of whipped cream and a Pirouline dark-chocolate wafer cookie. Simone wrapped both hands around the mug to warm them.

"This smells divine!" Simone said as she inhaled the sweet aroma. "I've missed your hot chocolate."

"More than you missed me?"

Simone lifted her eyes to meet his. Amusement danced in his gaze as he stared at her. Her lips parted slightly and curled into the faintest smile. "I don't think I need to quantify how much I missed you, although it probably isn't nearly as much as you missed me."

Paul chuckled. "So, are you ready to tell me what was bothering you earlier?"

Simone sighed, a low gust of warm breath blowing past her lips. "Where do I start? The fact that so much has happened with you since we broke up that I feel like I've missed out? Or that if you decide to move to Morocco you wouldn't ask me to go with you? Because everything has had me in my feelings and despite my best efforts not to let it get to me, it got to me."

"I get it. I was feeling the same way. Here you are considering a major employment change and I haven't been there to help you make the decision and might not be there to celebrate with you when you do."

"Are we doomed to fail, Paul? Is our loving each other just not enough?"

"We are doomed to fail if neither of us is willing to compromise. I can't have everything I want if you don't get everything you want. It just won't work if we aren't each willing to give up as much as we give. If we're not willing to sacrifice as much as we gain."

"You make it sound so pragmatic."

"Not at all. I just know relationships don't work when they're one-sided."

"Are you saying I'm to blame for our not working? Because I wasn't willing to compromise?"

"I'm saying we're both to blame. Let's be honest, Simone…" He leaned forward and dropped his mug on the coffee table. "You are spoiled, sometimes mean, and convinced the sun should rise and set on your timetable."

She laughed. "I am not that bad!"

"Yes, you are! But I am equally as stubborn, occasionally self-absorbed, and too dismissive of the important things. Neither of us was willing to bend and it broke us. If we decide to try this again, we both have to make changes."

"So, you won't go to Morocco?"

"Or you'll go with me."

Simone shifted in her seat, adding her cup to the table with his. She turned her body until she was leaning against him, nuzzling her back to his chest, Paul wrapping his arms tightly around her torso. He kicked off his shoes and swung his legs up onto the sofa, reclining back against the pillows. The move pulled her alongside him, the duo stretching out until she lay comfortably in his arms. He pulled her closer with one hand and reached for a wool blanket with the other. They snuggled close together beneath the covering, staring into the fire to watch the flames dance.

Simone suddenly clutched the hem of his sweatshirt with a tight fist. She shifted and turned to nuzzle her face against his chest and took a deep breath to inhale his rugged scent.

"I want us to work," Simone whispered, tightening the grip she had on his shirt. "I *need* us to work, Paul."

Paul nodded. He slid a firm hand beneath her chin and lifted her face till she was staring up at him. There was a tear clinging to his eyelash and it rolled down his face, landing on his shirt. "So do I, Simone. Because I love you, and not that I need to quantify it, but I love you as much as I know you love me. Maybe even more!" His smile pulled full and wide across his face.

Simone's eyes skated back and forth across his face, as she felt her own smile become as magnanimous as his. She lifted herself up until her mouth met his in the sweetest kiss, flesh gliding like silk across satin. His hand slid into her hair, pressing against the back of her head.

Their connection deepened as the kiss became frenzied. Heat surged like a firestorm between them, tongues darting past parted lips. The moment was surreal as both allowed themselves to fall into the beauty of it. Outside, snow dusted the landscape, oblivious to the flames that continued to tango inside, embers doing a delicate two-step in raging shades of red and orange.

Chapter 8

Paul reached across the bed to pull Simone against him but came up empty-handed. He opened one eye and found her side of the bed vacant. A loud groan echoed around the room. His morning erection pressed against the mattress for attention then deflated rapidly. He turned and reached across the nightstand for his wristwatch. With no idea of the time, he jumped when he realized he'd slept past his eight-o'clock alarm.

They'd made love for hours, moving from the living room sofa to the bedroom. The fire had died down and the temperature in the room had cooled substantially. But neither had noticed, the heat between them so intense he thought they might combust. Her kiss had been like a lit match, igniting the fervor that had been simmering between them. His hands against her warm skin had been a fantasy come true and when she'd parted her legs and welcomed him home, he'd been no more good.

Pulling himself upright he threw his legs off the side of the bed, his feet brushing against the carpeted floor. He wiped a hand across his face, then stretched his arms upward. He called Simone's name, but she didn't answer. Rising from the bedside, he moved into the bathroom to relieve himself. After a quick shower and shave, he dressed, then went searching for her.

Simone sat at the dining room table, poring through the documents he'd piled against the hardwood top. She was re-sorting each pile, seeming determined to make sense of it all. The sight of her sent a shiver of energy coursing up the length of Paul's spine. Her determination gleamed across her face and he was happy to have her on his side. She looked up, greeting him warmly as he moved to her side and kissed her lips.

"Good morning! The muffins just came out of the oven and the coffee is still hot. Do you want eggs and bacon? Oliver left the kitchen fully stocked."

Paul shook his head. "Coffee's good for now. How long have you been up?"

"Since that darn alarm of yours went off. Then I couldn't get back to sleep. Figured I'd come work on our problem."

Paul moved to the kitchen to fill a mug with morning brew. "Have you found anything?" he asked as he stirred cream and sugar into his cup. He moved back to the formal dining room and sat down in the seat beside her. He took one sip and then another, allowing the first effects of caffeine to take hold.

"I have, actually. I had a very enlightening conversation with my soror."

"Which one?"

"Jillian Tanner."

"Isn't her father head of Tanner Insurance?"

"Yes, as a matter of fact, he is, and Jillian works for the FDA. What do you know about a drug called Phenyl-zeranol?"

Paul took another sip of his beverage as he paused in reflection. "I don't think I've ever heard of it."

"That might be because it was one of Lender's first products, but it was banned here in the United States by the FDA. Since then Lender has had twenty-seven other drugs banned by the government. According to what I discovered, the Food and Drug Administration had sent Lender numerous letters condemning their unsafe manufacturing protocols. They were warned that Phenylzeranol put patients at serious risk for harm."

"Do you know what it was prescribed for?"

"High blood pressure. But it was found to cause liver and blood cell damage, as well as damage to other internal organs."

"And this was how long ago?"

"Just over fifteen years ago. Apparently, a separate investigation found that there were significant violations at their manufacturing plants in India. Several drugs were found to be contaminated with cardboard and other multiple foreign particles. Lender was then taken to task for failing to respond appropriately to the incidents."

Simone took a sip from her own coffee cup, then continued. "They claimed they launched an investigation but then they closed the inquiry without fully reviewing the extent of the problem or taking any further action."

"So, they didn't do anything at all?"

"Well, evidently after a lot of pressure, they eventually recalled the entire lot of contaminated drugs, but that was almost eight months after receiving the initial complaint."

"So, did they destroy them?"

"No. They shipped them overseas and sold them through a distributor that's not bound by FDA regulations."

Paul stared at the document Simone handed him. "What's this?"

"Remember the three drugs you said never made it to sales and distribution?"

He shifted forward in his seat. "Yes. What about them?"

"All three failed FDA standards and were banned.

Their lab tests showed a blatant pattern of disregard, where technicians were regularly deleting any negative test results, then retesting them without bothering to identify how and why the original contamination occurred. There were even problems with drugs the FDA did approve, but because their inspectors don't do any additional tests for purity once those drugs come into the US, they weren't caught until a complaint had been lodged."

"So, Halphedrone-B slipped past the inspectors?"

"I think so. And between what I learned from Jillian and what I've been able to make sense from the documents Liza printed for you, I think Halphedrone-B may actually be one of the same drugs that was previously banned."

"How can that...."

"I don't know," Simone said, "but if I'm right, Lender has been purposely acting with malicious intent, with full knowledge of their wrongdoing. Jillian explained that the FDA is supposed to inspect all factories, foreign and domestic, that produce drugs for the US market. But there are literally thousands of documents, from inspection records to lawsuits, detailing the ways poorly manufactured or contaminated drugs reach consumers. How inspectors miss serious hazards, or drug makers fail to meet standards even after the FDA has taken enforcement action. She said there are hundreds of plants that haven't been inspected for years, if ever. And many inspections are stage-managed so that factories ensure they pass on the day of their review appointments but fall back into disarray the minute the inspectors leave."

"So, more times than not, any bacteria is detected *only* after an outbreak of disease."

"Or when people like you start asking questions and digging for answers."

"Medical sleuthing for dummies."

Simone laughed. "And Lender has a list of infractions that's miles long!"

"So, what now? Because I know I can make the case that their drug has poisoned patients."

"Which is a big question. Can you?"

Paul reached for a folder from inside the briefcase that rested on the floor. He passed it to Simone, who eyed it curiously. "That is a list of patients I've treated in the past five years who have died on my watch. The numbers abroad are almost triple that of the numbers here. More than seventy percent of my patients in Africa had been prescribed Halphedrone-B. I've only prescribed it to seven patients in the past year in Chicago. The last one died last week while I was still abroad. He had just turned seven years old. The autopsy shows he died from pneumonia. They've all died from pneumonia-related issues."

Paul took a deep breath and seemed to hold it as his comment settled between them. Simone could see the frustration in his gaze. He was conflicted at not having been able to do more and feeling whole-heartedly responsible. The hurt on his face fractured a sliver of her heart.

"Pneumonia caused by the bacteria in the medication that was supposed to make them better."

"I'd bet my life on it. I've been tracking the stats for a while now trying to make sense of what was happening and the only common denominator in all my cases was Halphedrone-B."

"So, we continue to connect the dots by detailing what we know and then we hit them where it's going to hurt the most. We go after their profits with a class-action lawsuit."

"That may take forever."

"The lawsuit, yes, but once we file, we also file a formal complaint with the FDA and go public with what we can prove and if nothing else, get the drugs off the market. We'll need to work out the details, but it's a start."

Paul leaned to kiss her again. "Did I tell you how much I love you?"

"Tell me again."

"I love you, Simone Black," he repeated, kissing her a second time.

"I love you, too. Now where can a girl find a computer around here?"

For the next three days, Paul lost hours of time, locked in the lab with the samples he'd been studying since he got there. He'd been running the same tests over, and over again, hoping against all odds that the results might be different, and he might be wrong. He didn't want to admit it, but he was having a hard time accepting that anyone would purposely hurt sick patients just for the sake of a profit.

When he thought of his patients in the rural communities where he volunteered, he became enraged. They were already facing enough challenges without adding distrust of the medical professionals who were supposed to help.

Before he'd gotten lost in the research, he had spent a few good hours on the phone with one of his colleagues in Ghana, telling her what to test for in the patients who were still suffering and prescribing alternate medications to treat them. He had also asked her to ship him samples of the drugs they had on hand and she'd promised to get them in the mail as promptly as possible. He hoped, against all odds, that they would make it to him.

When his stomach grumbled for attention he sat back in his chair. He hadn't heard a peep from Simone since their morning conversation over coffee. Morning coffee had become a ritual, a few quiet minutes before their focus shifted from each other to something else. She, too, had become obsessed with making his problem go away. He couldn't begin to express how much he appreciated her efforts. He had no doubts that if Simone wasn't there to fight the good fight with him, he'd be completely lost. She challenged him, helped him to take the emotion out of the facts and pushed him to consider every possible aspect of the case. She centered him and he whispered a prayer of thanks daily for her being in his life.

Rising, he put the equipment away and began to clean, making sure to maintain the integrity and safety of the lab environment. When he was finished, he tossed his rubber gloves, slid off his glasses, pulled on his jacket and headed back to the house. The temperature was starting to drop, the air chilling quickly. The sun had been lost behind a host of clouds for most of the day and the sky was just beginning to darken.

As he walked through the door, the home phone suddenly rang and he turned to stare at the device that hung on the kitchen wall. It was the ninth or tenth call that day. Simone had answered the first and the second and there had been no one on the other end. By calls four, five, and six, he had turned the ringer to low and they let them go to the answering machine, no one leaving a message. It was concerning and neither thought it accidental. It didn't leave them that they were there because someone had shot at them just a week or so earlier. In the back of their minds both were acutely aware that there was danger still very present in their lives. Whether or not it had found them was still debatable. What they agreed on was pushing past the fear and not allowing it to cripple them. He took a deep inhale and moved toward the dining room.

Inside, Simone was still working, having commandeered a corner of the dining room table and his laptop. There were pages of documents taped to one wall and the floor was littered with balls of crumbled paper. She was alternately typing and scrolling through her cell phone. There was a look of determination across her face and her cheeks were flushed. She bit down against her bottom lip as her eyes darted back and forth across her work. Watching her made him smile. She suddenly looked up, slightly surprised to see him standing there eyeing her.

"Hey! Everything okay?"

Paul smiled. "I was just thinking how beautiful you are."

Simone felt herself blush ever so slightly, her cheeks warming with color. "Thank you," she said, her voice dropping an octave.

"Why don't we take a break? I think we need a change of scenery and I'm tired of baloney sandwiches. I'm starving and I thought we could go get something to eat. There's a wonderful Italian restaurant not far from here that I think you'll like. They have the best Bolognese sauce that I've ever tasted."

Simone pursed her lips, her eyes widening. "You're talking my language now! You silver-tongued devil, you!"

Paul eased slowly to her side. "Rigatoni in vodka sauce, fettucine Alfredo, manicotti." His voice was a loud whisper, low and seductive, his words coming as if he was doing the voice-over for a commercial.

Simone gasped. "Yes! Oh, yes!" She began to pant in jest, her head rolling back as she clutched the front of her sweater. "Talk dirty to me, Daddy!"

Paul burst out laughing. "Really, Simone?"

She laughed with him. "Too much?"

"It's a bit over the top!" He nodded as he leaned to kiss her cheek. "Let's get ready and I'll talk dirty to you later."

Simone reached for him, pulling him to her as she captured his lips with her own. She kissed him passionately, her tongue darting past the line of his teeth. "Why don't we get ready together?" she said, her voice dropping seductively.

Paul kissed her again. "I like that idea! Last one in the shower gets to be on top."

Simone giggled. "I like being on top."

"I know," he said as he winked his eye at her, turned, then was heading for the bathroom and leaving a trail of clothes down the length of the hallway.

Simone watched Paul walk away, his self-assured swagger moving her to laugh heartily. He was a beautiful specimen of manhood, with perfectly sculpted butt cheeks that his briefs clung to like a second skin. He'd been immensely blessed, packing in the front and the back. As he turned once to face her, beckoning her to join him, his bulge strained against the fabric and then he pulled them off, and twirled the garment around his index finger as he did a little jig through the door of the master bedroom. He was such a tease, Simone thought as she giggled softly.

Taking a quick minute to save the file she'd been working on, Simone shut the laptop down, closed her notebook and silenced her phone. She moved swiftly to the master bath, entering just as Paul turned on the water and stepped inside. The room had begun to heat nicely, a gentle mist rising to fill the air. Paul leaned into the spray of water, tilting his face toward the showerhead as it rained over his back and down his chest. Simone marveled at the perfection, thinking she could stare at him all day. Everything about him took her breath away.

As he began to lather soap across his bare skin, she did

a slow strip tease out of her own clothes. She discarded her sweater, then unbuttoned her white blouse, pausing after each button until it blew open. Pushing the garment off one shoulder and then the other, she exposed inch after inch of bare skin to his hungry gaze, until she was standing in nothing but her bra and panties.

Simone pressed a palm to her abdomen, her breathing heavy as she continued to watch him, and he continued to eye her. Her other hand skated over her breasts, her fingertips grazing one nipple and then the other. He held himself in the palm of his hand, stroking the length of male flesh that had taken on a life of its own. It twitched and pulsed beneath his touch, seeming to beg for her attention.

She stepped out of her lace garments and into the glass enclosure, before reaching both hands out and pressing them against his broad chest. She felt his body quiver in appreciation and a surge of heat coursed up and down her spine.

"What took you so long?" he whispered, his breath catching in his chest.

"Better late than never," Simone answered, her own voice husky with desire.

Paul dropped his hands against the round of her shoulders and caressed her gently. His touch was iron strong and when he applied the barest amount of pressure she sank slowly to her knees in understanding. Simone worshipped his chiseled body slowly, damp kisses trailing against his skin as she made her way down to suck the very essence out of him.

No woman ever moved Paul the way Simone did. No one knew his idiosyncrasies or could manipulate him like her. And she was the only female who could leave him quaking with such pleasure that it brought tears to his eyes. After their shower, he lay sprawled atop the mattress, his hips pressing upward as Simone sat straddled over his lap.

She leaned over him for a kiss, the connection deep and hard and making him moan. When the contact broke, she nuzzled her cheek with his, then trailed her tongue along his jawline to his ear and nibbled at the lobe. That gesture always made him crazy and he felt his muscles spasm in response. He tightened the grip he had on her hips, pulling her body back to his. He muttered her name over and over again, each breathless utterance like a divine chant.

As she slid up and down his member, warm and very familiar sensations flooded his body. She worked herself into a frenzy and it had the effect on him that he needed. The pleasure was unbelievable as she slammed her pelvis hard against his, alternatingly hard and fast and slow and easy. He felt himself go deeper and deeper with each of her strokes, knowing that he wouldn't last much longer.

"Oh, sweet baby, I've missed you so much…" he groaned as he met her stroke for stroke.

"…so clo…close…" Simone murmured, and then her whole body exploded.

The moist, satin lining of her inner walls tightened around him like a vise, sending him skyrocketing over the edge. Paul spewed like a volcano, his orgasm blending beautifully with hers as they both dropped into a state of sheer bliss.

Simone collapsed on top of him. She laid her head down on his chest and shoulder, as he wrapped his arms around her. Completely satiated, he drifted off to sleep as she held tightly to him. They both woke up about an hour later.

"I'm starved," Simone said as she rolled down beside him. "And you promised me Italian."

Paul laughed. "You were the one who suggested dessert first."

"I like my goodies," she said as she lifted herself from the bed and headed back to the shower.

Paul propped himself up on his elbow to stare after her. "I like your goodies, too," he said, as she disappeared into the other room. He heard the shower running and Simone singing to herself, completely off-key. Lying back against the mattress, he took a couple of deep breaths and allowed himself the joy of feeling completely relaxed and happy.

Spago Trattoria E Pizzeria quickly became one of Simone's top-five favorite dinner spots. It was everything she loved about Italy, reminding her of the holiday excursion her father had taken her on for her twenty-first birthday.

They were greeted with bruschetta, a basket of warm focaccia bread, a bulb of roasted garlic and a bowl of fresh tomatoes tossed with garlic and olive oil. As she studied the menu, Paul ordered a bottle of Chianti and a traditional antipasto of mild *capicola*, salami, provolone cheese, roasted red peppers and eggplant for them to share.

For their entrées, Simone ordered the Italian risotto tossed with calamari and clams. Paul enjoyed the homemade manicotti filled with ricotta cheese and spinach, served with a meat sauce. They shared a slice of tiramisu for dessert. It was beyond decadent and by the time they finished both were stuffed.

"I just knew you'd need a take-home box," Paul said teasingly.

"No, you didn't."

He laughed. "I forgot just how much you love to eat."

She rolled her eyes, a slight smirk pulling at her lips.

"It really was good," she said. "Better than good! Thank you."

He leaned forward in his seat. "So, are you interested in a field trip?" he asked.

Simone leaned forward to meet him, the gesture feeling conspiratorial. "What did you have in mind?"

"I need to get my hands on samples of Halphedrone-B. Ideally from a different production lot than what we've already tested."

"How do you propose to do that?"

"I have a friend at Henry Ford Hospital in Detroit. I'm going to call him. I think he'll be willing to help if I ask."

"So, you want to go back over the border? And just hope your friend is just going to give you samples from their facility?"

Paul nodded. "Baby, I have a plan."

Chapter 9

It had been well over one month since they'd arrived in Canada. Most of their time was spent in their respective corners focused on their individual tasks. And when they weren't knee-deep in research, they were focused solidly on each other, reinvigorating their connection and rekindling the passion that had always been a cornerstone of their relationship. On this particular day, Paul had been on the phone most of the morning. International calls had occupied most of his time. He'd been hoping against all odds to convince the medical teams on the ground in the African countries to change the medication regime for patients he had treated who were still doing poorly. A few found his reasoning questionable and others wanted proof that he didn't have to give. Considering costs and availability, the alternative treatments he offered were met with trepidation and he felt as if he were banging his head against a brick wall. His frustration was palpable.

Simone had begun to outline the legal brief she intended to file. She'd been acting as her own law clerk, coordinating the data they knew with what they didn't as well as researching the legal precedents she would need to help make her case. Her frustration was equal to his, both challenged by the limitations and resources they had to work with.

Simone paced the floor, her mind racing. Every few moments she would pause to jot something down in the lengthy list of notes she'd been taking. With nothing else that he could do in the lab, Paul was cooking popcorn as he chatted on the phone with his brother. His tone was hushed, and she imagined whatever they were whispering about probably had more to do with her and him than their problem with the pharmaceutical company.

When her cell phone rang, she jumped, startled that anyone would be calling her. Her mother's face appeared on the screen, and Simone took a deep breath before answering. "Hi, Mom!" she said, sounding as cheery as she could manage.

"Where are you, Simone?" Judith Harmon Black asked, not bothering with hello.

Simone took another breath. "With Paul. Out of town."

"Out of town where, Simone?"

"What's wrong, Mom? Why are you interrogating me?"

"They've issued a warrant for Paul's arrest."

"For Paul's arrest?" she said, knowing she sounded like a parrot. "For what?"

"They want him to come in for questioning. Something about the three patients at the hospital and his involvement in their deaths."

"That's ridiculous! Paul would never hurt a soul. He's dedicated his entire life to helping others." A knot tightened through her abdomen and she suddenly felt sick to her stomach. She hadn't believed things could go from bad to worse, but clearly she'd underestimated karma.

"What's going on, Simone? Your father and I are worried sick about you."

"I'm fine. I'm safe," Simone said and then she explained to her mother what they were dealing with. "Now, with what you're telling me, we also need to prove Paul didn't murder anyone."

"You need to come home. Let Paul turn himself in and trust the judicial system to work."

"I can't, Mom. I'm sorry."

There was a thick pause that billowed heavily through the telephone lines. Simone imagined the look on her mother's face, the matriarch not at all happy with her, or with him. Paul had moved to her side, trailing a warm hand down the length of her back. His touch stalled the rise of anxiety that had threatened to consume her, and his presence was instantly calming. He'd been listening to her conversation after disconnecting his own.

Judith blew a gust of air into the phone line. "Let me speak to Paul," she commanded.

"Mom, don't…"

"Now," the older woman snapped.

Simone blew her own heavy sigh as she passed Paul the phone. "It's my mother," she said as she moved to the sofa and dropped down against the cushions.

Paul pulled the phone to his ear. "Yes, ma'am… No… I understand… Yes… Yes… I will… I promise."

There was another lengthy pause and Simone bristled at the lecture she imagined her mother was giving. Judge Black was a force to be reckoned with and she didn't take kindly to anyone messing with her kids or to her children disobeying a direct order. Simone and her siblings had been raised to be obedient and respectful and even as adults walked a fine line where their parents were concerned. Simone knew telling her mother no would not be taken lightly.

But if anyone understood why it was so important to Simone to be there for Paul, she knew her mother would. Her parents had the most solid relationship of any duo she'd ever known, and no one could ever say that Judith Harmon Black didn't always have her husband's back.

Most especially when it came to the law and seeking justice for those being exploited. As a power couple, they were undefeated and Simone wanted that for herself, no matter what it took.

"Would you like to speak to Simone again?" Paul was asking.

Simone shifted forward to the edge of the seat, expecting to hear her own lecture, but he disconnected the call instead, laying her phone onto the table.

"So, she told you about the arrest warrant?"

Simone nodded. "Yeah, but it doesn't make sense. Why would they blame you?"

"I had three patients at Northwestern Memorial that I personally treated with Halphedrone-B who've died. I stole their medical files from the hospital. Now they're saying they think someone purposely caused their deaths. I don't have all the details, so I don't know how they've come to that conclusion. Clearly, someone is trying to hem me up because they can't get to me. Oliver says they served a search warrant on my apartment this morning."

"Is that what you two were whispering about?"

He nodded. "I didn't want to upset you."

"Well, I'm not upset. I'm pissed! So, now we've got criminals trying to shoot at us, and the law looking to arrest us."

"They just want to arrest me."

"Trust and believe they'll handcuff and take me in too for aiding and abetting your criminal activity if they get the opportunity. And that's just the short list of the crimes I've committed." Simone tossed up her hands.

Paul shrugged. "My list is probably a little longer."

"I wouldn't brag about that if I were you."

"So, what do you want to do?" he asked, his eyes wide as he studied her intently.

"What did my mother say to you?" she said, answering his question with a question of her own.

"She told me to keep you safe."

"That's all?"

"Basically. She said she didn't think it was a good idea for us to try and deal with this on our own but that she would trust our judgment."

"She wasn't mad?" Simone asked, looking shocked.

"Oh, she was mad! She was fuming!"

Simone dropped her face into the palms of her hands, swiping at her eyes. She pulled her knees to her chest and wrapped her arms around her legs. She suddenly felt like they had the weight of the world bearing down on their shoulders. She thought they'd been steadily digging their way out and now it felt as if the sides of the hole had caved in, burying them back under. She couldn't help but wonder if they were ever going to catch a break.

Paul dropped down onto the seat beside her. He slid an arm around her torso and pulled her against him, kissing the top of her head.

"Do you want the good news?" he asked.

"There's good news?"

He nodded. "Tomorrow morning the sales rep for Lender will be meeting with my doctor friend. He'll get the samples we need."

"I'd like to ask her a few questions."

"I'd rather we stay as inconspicuous as possible."

"You realize if we don't get stopped at the border going back into the United States, depending on how far that arrest warrant has already extended, that we probably won't be able to cross back into Canada, right?"

"That is very possible," he answered. "But it's a risk we're going to have to take."

"Okay," Simone said, reaching for the bowl of freshly

popped popcorn that he'd drizzled with truffle butter, and sprinkled with cracked pepper and Parmesan cheese. "As long as we're on the same page."

The customs agent who welcomed them back into the United States barely gave them a second look. Once the car was inspected and their documents verified, he waved them on through. They arrived at Henry Ford Hospital some thirty minutes before the scheduled appointment with Paul's friend, Dr. Stephen Alexander, a pediatric resident who'd gone to medical school with him. For ten of those thirty minutes they strategized where to park in case they needed to make a quick run for it.

"Are you sure about this?" Simone questioned, her nerves beginning to get to her.

Paul shot her a quick look. "Right now, no one knows I'm a wanted man. At least I don't think so. So as far as anyone is concerned, I'm just meeting my friend the doctor who's helping me with a problem. I'll go in, make nice and come right back out. But you do not have to do this with me, Simone. I don't want you to be uneasy."

"I don't want you to get arrested. I just want to make sure you're sure about this! So just say you're sure!"

He gave her smile and nodded. "I have to do this, Simone."

"Then I have to do it with you. We're in this together."

The light in his eyes dimmed ever so slightly. He turned in his seat to face her. "Before we go in, there's something I need to tell you."

Simone's nerves suddenly shifted into another gear. Her palms began to sweat and she swiped them against the leg of her black pants. "Why are you giving me anxiety?"

"I don't mean to, baby, but it's important I'm totally honest with you."

"About what?"

"The sales rep for Lender is a woman named Vivian Lincoln."

Simone bristled, crossing her arms over her chest, her jaw tightening. "And?"

"Vivian and I dated for a minute after you and I broke up. It wasn't serious and didn't go anywhere but I wanted you to know."

"Define 'dated.'"

"We went out a time or two. Dinner mostly and to the theater once."

"The theater? What show?" The question came with significant attitude. Simone was simmering on a low burn, Paul's admission hitting her broadside. Despite the length of time they'd been apart she had never considered he might date someone else. She was squarely in her feelings and unable to contain her displeasure. Jealousy grabbed her by the seat of her pants and was hanging on with all fangs.

"Why does it matter what show?"

"What show, Paul?"

"*Hamilton*. We went to see *Hamilton*."

"*Hamilton*? On Broadway? In New York?"

He nodded. "Yes."

"And you slept with her?"

He shook his head vehemently. "No, we've never slept together."

"You went to New York with her to see *Hamilton* and you didn't stay in a hotel room together?" Simone found herself imagining the worst and it broke her heart to even think that Paul had been able to spend time with any woman that wasn't her. She knew she was being irrational, but she didn't care.

"I flew into New York and met her on one of my layovers to Europe. We had time for dinner and the show, then I went back to the airport to catch my plane. I don't know where she went after that."

"Do you like her?"

"I enjoy talking with her, but she's not a woman I would be romantically interested in."

"But you took her to see *Hamilton*?"

"Actually, she invited me."

"What's wrong with her?"

"She's not you," Paul said matter-of-factly.

Simone sat for a moment, pondering his comment. "For the record," she finally said. "I never dated anyone when we were apart. Not even a date for coffee."

He smiled. "I appreciate that."

"Absolutely no one! And trust me, I had more than my fair share of invitations."

Paul laughed. "You're mad."

"I am not mad."

"Yes, you are. But I swear, it was nothing!" He stole a quick glance down to his wristwatch. "We should probably get inside," he concluded.

She rolled her eyes. "You know we're not done with this conversation, right? I have more questions."

Paul shook his head. "No, we're done. There's nothing else to discuss and you are not going to drive me crazy being jealous over a woman who is irrelevant in the scheme of our future. That's not going to happen."

"Who said anything about being jealous?"

He shrugged, eyeing her with a raised brow.

Simone narrowed her gaze slightly. There was a lengthy pause as they sat studying each other. "Okay," she said finally.

"I mean it, Simone."

"I said okay!" There was still a hint of attitude in her tone.

Paul continued to consider her, apparently trying to read the expression on her face. He leaned forward and gave her a kiss on her lips. "I love you, Simone. I don't love anyone else."

Simone smiled, then she pushed open the door and exited the car. The tidal wave of emotion was passing slowly and she was determined not to let it get the best of her. She believed Paul. And she trusted him, having no doubts about any other woman in his life. But Old Simone was trying to rear her ugly head and make his admission more than it needed to be. It was taking everything in her for New Simone to put those feelings in a headlock and send them away.

Paul jumped out of the driver's side as she moved to the sidewalk, turning as she waited for him to join her. She extended her hand, reaching to hold his hand. Their fingers intertwined and he gave her a slight squeeze.

"We good?" Paul questioned as they headed for the hospital's entrance.

"She better be ugly, that's all I'm going to say," Simone answered. "And I mean butt-ugly."

Paul laughed. "There's not a woman around that can hold a candle to you, Simone Black!"

"And don't you forget it!"

Dr. Stephen Alexander reminded Simone of a young Jeff Goldblum. Before Jeff Goldblum had matured into the sexy version of himself that he was now, she thought. He had a beautiful smile that gleamed from his eyes and Spock-like ears that didn't go unnoticed. His chestnut-blond hair was cut a half inch too short and his glasses were too large for his face.

She stood back as the two men greeted each other

with a weird fist-bump-and-hand-tap thing and a deep bear hug.

Paul grabbed her hand and pulled her forward. "Stephen, this is Simone Black. Simone, this is Dr. Stephen Alexander. Stephen and I go way back."

"It's nice to meet you, Dr. Alexander. I've heard a lot about you," she said, as he took her hand and kissed the backs of her fingers.

"The pleasure is all mine. But Paul didn't tell me anything about you!"

Paul laughed as the two shot him a look. "I'm no fool. Stephen's quite the ladies' man and back in the day the women wouldn't even look in my direction if he was around. I couldn't risk the chance of him stealing you from me."

Stephen laughed. "I definitely would have tried," he said as he winked an eye at Simone.

Paul smirked as he wrapped his arm around her shoulder protectively and hugged her to him. "We really appreciate your help."

"I wish I could do more. You know how I feel about Big Pharma. I don't trust the whole lot of 'em."

"Stephen believes in a more holistic approach to patient care," Paul said, directing his comment toward Simone.

"I don't believe physicians serve their patients well when all they're doing is prescribing meds unnecessarily. Unfortunately, the pharmaceutical business has played on people's greed. Incentivizing doctors to market their products and prescribe medications in exchange for payments is just wrong on many levels."

"Criminal enterprise happens in all forms," Simone said.

Stephen smiled. "So, Ms. Lincoln is actually here. She's

down in our cafeteria, waiting for me to join her for a cup of coffee. You didn't tell me she was so attractive."

"If you like that type," Paul muttered. He shot Simone a look, noting the look she gave him back. Her jaw had tightened, and she clenched her teeth. He changed the subject. "Did she leave you any product?" Paul questioned.

Stephen nodded, pointing to a clear cellophane bag filled with samples that rested on his desk. "She's pushing a new blood pressure medication, but I did ask for the Halphedrone-B. She said she only had a few samples left but she tossed them in there, too. Take all of it."

"Thank you. I owe you," Paul said.

"If it will save lives, my friend, you can always rely on me. But I need to run right now. I have a patient I need to check on and then I have a coffee date to discuss homeopathic medicine with Ms. Lincoln. You two be safe out there."

The two men bumped shoulders one last time and Simone gave the man a warm hug. Paul didn't miss the squeeze the good doctor gave her, or that his hands rested just shy of her backside. He bit back his comment, knowing it would only escalate an unnecessary argument and expose the tinge of jealousy that had teased his spirit.

Simone grabbed the samples bag and shoved it into the leather tote over her shoulder. "What now?" she asked.

"We can try to cross back into Canada, or we head back to Chicago. Your choice."

"No, it's your choice. I can't make that decision, Paul."

"I really want to test these samples and Oliver is flying back tomorrow."

"Then we take our chances and hope they haven't put you in the system yet. But I'm thinking the sooner we go, the better."

Paul nodded. "Let's get on the road!"

Exiting the office, they headed in the direction of the elevator. Simone spied a rest room just as Paul pushed the button to go down to the main lobby.

"Wait for me. I need to use the bathroom," she said as she hurried toward the women's room door.

"I'll be right here," Paul replied.

He stepped back out of the walkway and leaned against the wall to wait for her. Surprise flowed through him when the elevator door opened and Lender's drug representative, Vivian Lincoln, stepped out.

"Vivian!"

"Paul! Oh, my goodness! What are you doing here?"

"Visiting a friend," he said. "What are you up to?"

"Business." She gestured to the leather carry bag she was rolling behind her.

"I didn't realize your territory extended this far east."

She smiled. "It does." She changed the subject. "You never called me."

"I was in Ghana longer than I anticipated. I've only been back for a few days."

The woman named Vivian nodded. She took a step forward, pressing a hand against his chest. "If you're not busy, maybe we can grab lunch after I'm finished with my appointment. I think we need to talk."

"About?"

"I heard you might be having some issues with one of our products. I was hoping to alleviate your concerns and maybe answer any questions you might have. I also want to catch up. I've missed you." She gave him a bright smile, her lashes batting at him as she tapped her manicured fingertips against the buttons of his shirt.

Paul hesitated for a split second and then he returned her smile. "I'd love to. I can meet you downstairs?"

"Wonderful! Let me swing by and let the doctor know I can't wait and then we can get out of here."

Paul gave her another bend of his lips, showcasing his picture-perfect teeth. "I'll be in the lobby waiting," he said as he pushed the down button for the elevator to return.

Vivian headed down the hallway, tossing one last look over her shoulder. As Paul stepped into the conveyor, he pulled his phone into his hands to send Simone a text.

Simone was washing her hands when the other woman walked into the bathroom. Waif thin, she was supermodel tall with hair the color of corn silk cascading down her back. Her features were delicate, like fine porcelain. The suit she wore was perfectly tailored and expensive, as were her red-bottomed high-heeled shoes.

She was dialing her phone and she looked slightly discombobulated. She gave Simone a dismissive glance, then turned her back as she waited for the party she called to answer on the other end.

Simone reached for a paper towel to dry her hands. She turned back to the mirror, leaning forward to inspect her face. She was as dismissive of the stranger as the stranger was of her. Until the woman began speaking and recognition settled over her. The stranger had to be Vivian Lincoln!

Simone struggled not to stare. And not to stare so that the other woman noticed. Eyeing her own reflection in the mirror, she suddenly felt frumpish, having thrown on a pair of jeans, running shoe, and her favorite sweatshirt. Her makeup was sparse, just a hint of eyeliner and some lip gloss. She pulled her hands through her hair, hoping to give the curly strands a hint of volume. She didn't look bad, but she didn't look like she'd just stepped off the cover of *Glamour* magazine. Simone suddenly understood why Paul had even considered dating the woman. She was overly attractive and clearly confident. Simone's insecurities suddenly tied a knot in her midsection. She swallowed hard, biting back the feelings that had snuck in to ambush her.

The other woman was tapping her foot anxiously before whispering loudly into her phone. "He's here… I don't know why… I just ran into him in the hallway… What do you want me to do?" There was a lengthy pause as she seemed to be listening to instructions.

She still had her back to Simone as she began to speak again. "We just made plans for lunch… Okay… Okay… I'll do that… I'm staying at the Hyatt, room twenty twelve… Trust me. I'll get him there… Just tell them to hurry… We can't afford for them to miss this time… If I have to, I'll call the police and scream bloody murder as a last resort… I won't… I said I won't…"

When she disconnected the call, inhaling a deep breath of air, Simone was pulling a brush through her hair. She didn't bother to look in Simone's direction as she stepped to the sink to rinse her hands.

Simone smiled as they exchanged tentative gazes in the mirror. "Love those shoes," she said, her eyes dropping to the woman's feet.

The blonde looked where she stared. "Thank you," she said, her tone indifferent.

"Are you a doctor?" Simone asked. "You look like you might be a doctor."

The woman shot her another quick look. "No, I'm a sales rep. I represent a drug company."

"Interesting. It must pay well for you to afford those shoes. Or are they knockoffs?"

"They are very real," the woman said, clearly offended

by the insinuation. She turned toward an empty stall, dragging her medical case behind her.

Simone shrugged. "Good luck with that sales job," she said as she moved to the door and exited the space. She hurried to the elevator. As she waited for it to return to the floor, she read the text message Paul had sent her. Car. Now! Hurry!

Chapter 10

"I can't believe you dated that woman. How did you know she was trying to set you up?" Simone asked Paul once she returned to the car.

"She's a sales rep. There was no reason for anyone in Africa to call a US sales rep about me questioning their international representative. And I haven't spoken to her since before my last mission trip."

"Why did she think she'd be able to get you to her hotel room?" There was something accusing in her tone, her words laced with attitude. Clearly, Vivian Lincoln had reason to think Paul would actually have lunch with her, Simone thought. She was suddenly curious about the time they'd spent together. What else had they shared? How much did Vivian know about her? Did Vivian know anything at all about her? About them and their relationship? And what about Paul? Had seeing her again reawakened feelings he hadn't yet shared with her?

Paul cut his gaze in her direction. "Simone, please, don't do that. You know me better than that."

Simone shrugged. "It was just a question. Don't get an attitude with me."

Paul reached for her hand and kissed the back of it. He'd been sitting in the car with the engine running when Simone came racing back. She'd been beside herself with rage, detailing her encounter with Vivian. Then her emotions had gotten the best of her, her frustrations becoming irrational. Jealousy had always been a character flaw with Simone, even as she asserted with much conviction that she wasn't jealous. It was equally frustrating for him to argue about things that were not relevant in their lives and gut-wrenching to see her put herself through such turmoil. It also annoyed the hell out of him that Simone continually insisted it wasn't him she didn't trust, but the other women who sometimes set their sights on his attention. Vivian was now her latest source of outrage. Her ranting had taken on a life of its own as they navigated back to the Detroit-Windsor Tunnel.

"What happens if they run your information and the warrant comes up?" Simone questioned, changing the subject.

Paul took a deep breath and exhaled. "I'll need you to take the samples back to the house for Oliver. Then I want you to go back home to Chicago. I'm going to need an attorney and you can't represent me from Canada."

"I still work for the prosecutor's office. I can't represent you at all."

"Have you decided against the job offer?"

"No. Not really. In fact, I was thinking that my bringing the case against Lender to the table would probably score me some points."

"So, you'll have two cases to bring to them, because I didn't kill anyone. Not through any fault of my own," he said, his voice dropping an octave.

Simone squeezed his hand as he pulled up to the toll station. The customs inspector asked for their passports and the car's registration. Neither wanted to admit it, but they were both scared. Simone closed her eyes, sending a prayer skyward. A few minutes passed before the agent returned their documents.

"Welcome to Canada," the man said, giving them both a nod. He gestured for them to proceed forward.

The couple held their breath until they passed the toll station on the Canadian side and were five miles away from the border.

Simone suddenly burst out laughing, tears streaming down her cheeks. "Boy, did we get lucky." She held her hand out, palm side down, the appendage still shaking.

Paul exhaled the breath he'd been holding. He'd been scared and couldn't begin to tell Simone just how frightened he'd been. Jail definitely wasn't on his bucket list of things to experience. He also wasn't prepared to be derailed when there was still so much they needed to do to prove their case. He blew out another deep breath. "God was definitely on our side!"

Simone nodded. "I've lost count of the laws we've broken. It'll be a miracle if I can keep my law license after all of this." She swiped at her face with the backs of her hands.

Paul bristled, her expression pulling at his heartstrings. She hadn't asked for any of this and he couldn't begin to know how to make things right and get her out of the mess he'd managed to drag her into. "I'm really sorry, Simone," Paul said. "I never meant for you to get caught up in any of this mess."

"I know. I'm here because I chose to be. I could have walked away before we left Chicago and I didn't. I didn't know what might happen and I didn't want you to be alone. I wanted to be here if you needed me. I failed you once. I couldn't live with myself if I failed you again."

"But Simone, baby, you've never failed me. You had a right to feel the way you did. I never held that against you. I've always just wanted you to be happy."

"I'll be really happy when I can put my foot up Vivian's…"

Paul laughed. "Dial it back a notch," he said stalling the expletive he knew was coming. "She'll get hers. But we need to stay focused."

"I am focused. Clearly, she's knee-deep in this and the fact that she was willing to throw you under a bus doesn't sit well with me. She's not going to get away with it."

"Let it go, Simone. Please!"

"Do not tell me you're going to give that woman a pass?"

"Of course not! She'll get what's coming to her, I'm sure. But since we don't know how she's involved we can't jump to any conclusions."

"You're actually going to defend that witch?"

"That's not what I'm doing. Why are you getting so heated over this?"

The look she was giving him was classic Simone, attitude-filled and unhappy about something. The mood between them suddenly did a nosedive. His frustration level increased tenfold. It was moments like this, going back and forth with her, that made him question what they were doing with each other. Doubt trickled like water from a leaky faucet and suddenly he found himself questioning if they'd ever get past the issues that had torn them apart previously.

Paul's defenses kicked into second gear. "I am not going to fight with you, Simone. I do not have the energy to do that song and dance you like to do when you're feeling insecure about something."

"Insecure?" Her voice had risen a few octaves.

Paul's voice rose to match hers. "Yes, insecure. You get in your feelings and then you lash out. It's Simone 101— if you can't control it, it's a fight. If you feel threatened, it's a fight. Hell, even when it should make you happy, you make it a fight! And I don't want to fight with you!"

Simone sat with clenched fists, every muscle in her body hardened with ire. Her breathing grew labored. "You need to get back into the lab," Simone snapped, her mind clearly spinning in a hundred different directions.

There was an awkward pause that rose like a morning mist. Paul pulled onto the lengthy driveway, stopping when they reached the house. He shifted the car into Park and cut off the engine. Simone was staring out the window, her eyes narrowed, her jaw tight.

"Simone? What are you thinking?" Paul questioned, reading her mood.

"Nothing," she muttered.

"Simone?"

"What?" She met the look he was giving her with one of her own, something like defiance spinning in her gaze.

"Tell me what's going through your head, Simone. You need to talk to me."

"Nothing! Why are you badgering me?"

"Badgering? Really? I'm trying to figure out why you suddenly have attitude."

Simone rolled her eyes skyward. "I need to get back to work," she snapped as she opened the car door and exited the vehicle.

Paul watched her stomp to the door, her arms folded across her chest as she waited for him to come unlock it. Despite his own annoyance, a slight smile pulled across his face. Some things clearly hadn't changed, and Simone's short fuse was still short.

Hours later Simone poured salt-and-vinegar potato chips into a large glass bowl and white wine into a glass. The light was still on in the barn and she knew Paul had thrown himself into his research. She had pushed his buttons and then she had shut down, leaving him annoyed and anxious. It was a typical play out of their relationship handbook and once again Simone felt like she was dooming them both to fail. She stuffed a chip into her mouth as she headed down the hallway to lock herself back in the bedroom.

Simone was feeling slightly foolish and she wasn't quite ready to face Paul and apologize. She didn't have any reason to be angry at him, yet she'd thrown every ounce of her frustration in his direction. It never made any sense before and it didn't now. She needed to do better, yet she seemed unable to get past the bad behavior that had always been her downfall.

The only time emotion didn't rule her life was when she was in a courtroom. In front of a judge, Simone was always calm and collected, the epitome of professionalism. But once she stepped out the courthouse doors she was a simmering volcano and it took little for her to erupt. In her head, being quick to put others in their place, rage against the status quo, and just being a general pain in the ass masked what she was truly going on in her head. Being brash, aggressive, and keeping others an arm's length away kept them from seeing her vulnerabilities and her weaknesses.

She couldn't begin to explain to Paul or anyone else how she sometimes felt inadequate and unworthy. Everyone loved to tell her what a great guy Paul Reilly was, and she was always questioning why someone like him would want her. She could be a handful most days: snarky, ill-tempered and contentious. She wasn't sugar and spice and all the nice things the fairy tales said little girls were made of. She always felt like she wasn't doing enough or being great enough, always falling short on an imaginary scale of her own making. Despite a public perception of her being attractive, intelligent and accomplished, and her parents constantly hammering how wonderful she was, she felt like an imposter in her own body.

Living up to her parent's expectations left little room for failure. She had big shoes to fill and with siblings who'd made it successfully to the finish line with few missteps, she couldn't afford to be a disappointment. To them, or the man willing to take her on and love her. No amount of rationalizing every good thing she brought to their relationship stopped her from doubting her worth and when doubt set in, Simone lashed out and usually at Paul.

After resting her popcorn and wine on the nightstand, she threw her body across the bed and reached for her cell phone. She dialed her sister's number, taking a quick sip of her drink as she waited for the woman to answer her phone.

"Hello?"

"Vaughan, hey!"

"My little sister the fugitive! How are you?"

"That's not funny, Vaughan."

"Actually, it's hilarious! What's not funny is that our parents are on the verge of divorce, arguing about what to do about you. Our father is ready to call in the cavalry."

"Would you please tell them I'm fine?"

"Did Mom tell you there's a warrant out for Paul's arrest?"

"Yes. She said they think he may have killed three of his patients."

"She exaggerated that a bit. A lot, actually. The hospital filed a report that they suspected he was in possession of files for three of his patients and they've not been able to reach him to question why. Plus, they're concerned, because some FBI types in suits with badges have been there asking questions about him. But Parker did a little digging and the suits aren't associated with law enforcement and their badges are fake. Then, when Daddy found out someone took a shot at you both, he issued a city-wide alert to bring Paul in for his own protection and to get you home."

"Does he always have to manipulate everything?"

"Do you not remember who your father is? The superintendent for the entire Chicago Police Department, appointed by His Honor, the mayor, thinks his baby daughter might be in serious trouble. He's going to manipulate everything he can personally control and some things he can't. He's even threatening to issue a warrant for *your* arrest. We've all been given explicit instructions to call him if you reach out to any of us. He tore Mingus a new orifice when he found out our brother helped you go off the grid."

Simone's heavy sigh was tempered with a sudden case of the hiccups as she choked back tears. She was suddenly feeling very emotional and she couldn't begin to explain why. Her family was worried about her, Paul loved her, and she was kicking herself for being ugly about a woman who didn't matter one iota in the grand scheme of things. Everything that had happened since Paul had called her suddenly flooded her spirit and twisted her insides into tight knots. The deluge of emotion was overwhelming.

"What's wrong?" Vaughan asked, as if sensing her sister's distress.

"Mom and Dad really just need to chill," Simone muttered. "I'm fine."

"Are you sure? Because you don't sound like you're fine."

"I picked a fight with Paul for no reason."

"That's sounds like par for the course with you, Simone. Self-sabotage has always been your specialty."

"I didn't call for you to be mean to me, Vaughan."

"Honesty is not mean, little sister."

"Whatever! He told me the other day that I was spoiled. And mean. And he dated this other woman while we were separated."

"Ohhh, so now we're getting to the real reason for your call. Give me all the juicy details. But wait, let me pour myself a glass of wine first because this sounds like it's going to be good."

Simone listened as her sister dropped her phone, still talking as she moved around her kitchen.

"I'm coming… Hold on… Do not hang up… Okay, I'm back. Who is this woman Paul dated? Are they still together?"

"Her name is Vivian Lincoln and she's a medical sales rep for the drug company we're investigating."

"Was it serious? Or just a casual fling?"

"They went to see *Hamilton* together."

"*Hamilton*?"

"Yes!"

"The musical? In New York?"

"Yes! And I met her and she's this horrible person and just because I had a little attitude about it, Paul had the audacity to call me insecure." Simone's voice rose an octave. "There is nothing *insecure* about me!" she insisted.

Vaughan didn't bother to respond, complete silence coming from her end of the telephone line. The quiet was suddenly deafening, and for the briefest moment, Simone thought the cell service had dropped the call.

"Hello? Vaughan? Hello?"

"I'm still here."

"Why didn't you say anything?"

"Oh, I'm sorry. I was waiting for you to say something I could agree with."

"I am *not* insecure!"

"You have moments, Simone. Especially when it comes to Paul! So, why did you get all in your feelings about him dating this woman? You did dump him, remember?"

Simone blew the faintest sigh, her voice dropping to a loud whisper. "You didn't see her."

"Paul loves you, Simone. I can't for the life of me figure out why you have never trusted that."

"He said the same thing."

"Well, you really need to think about it. And you need to think about why you're always so bitchy toward him. Because most men would have been done with you by now. In fact, I'm starting to question why he puts up with you and your bad behavior."

"Paul Reilly loves me."

"Ding, ding, ding!"

Simone laughed. "Okay! I get it."

"He deserves better from you, Simone. He's one of the good guys and there is a long line of women who are chomping at the bit to take your place so stop playing games with him."

"I just can't seem to get out of my own head."

"Well, only you can figure out what is holding you back. We can all tell you how great you are. How great Paul is. Paul can tell you over and over again what you mean to him. But ultimately, if you don't believe it, then why should anyone else care?"

Simone paused to reflect on her sister's comment. Since they'd been little girls, her big sister had been her voice of reason. Vaughan had never hesitated to point out the error of Simone's ways or to turn her around when she was headed off track. When Simone felt like a dim light in a room full of bright bulbs, Vaughan would push her to shine. The bond between them was irrefutable and even when Simone felt off-balance or completely lost, just talking to her sister brought her back to an even keel.

"I need you to do me a favor," Simone said.

"Anything. You know that."

"Ask Mingus to find out everything he can on Vivian Lincoln. She works for Lender Pharmaceuticals but I'm not sure where she's based out of."

"Will this help with the problem you two are trying to resolve? Or is this for your own personal vendetta?"

"It's not personal," Simone said, sharing the details of her bathroom encounter with the woman. "I need to figure out who she's connected to and why she's gunning for Paul."

"What do you want me to tell Mom and Dad?"

"I'll call Dad when we're headed back that way but until then, ask them to please call off the dogs."

"I'll see what I can do. Just stay safe, please."

"I love you, sissy!"

"I love you, too!"

Disconnecting the call, Simone tossed the phone onto the nightstand and fell back against the pillows, debating whether she wanted to analyze her own shortcomings or ponder dryer lint while she waited for Paul to finish what he was working on and come back inside.

Paul paused in the back door that same night, listening to a playlist of love songs Simone had programmed into the sound system. He knew her better than she knew herself sometimes, and he knew she was feeling contrite about her mood swing and the tension that had bloomed like a brick wall between them.

Her tantrums remained a bone of contention between

them and he had come to acquiesce that he'd have to accept her moodiness if they were going to move forward. If he weighed her positive attributes against the negatives, her moments were well worth the heated arguments that always led them back to what was most important to them. Each other.

Simone was a powerhouse and highly accomplished. She'd graduated magna cum laude from Western Illinois University and then summa cum laude from Harvard Law School. As a state prosecutor she was known to be a shark in Jimmy Choo stilettos and pristinely tailored designer suits. She served on multiple corporate boards, volunteered at the Boys and Girls Clubs of Chicago and was well-known in the community for her philanthropy, most especially where it served the issues and rights for women and girls. She was bold, sometimes brash and always brilliant.

Success oozed from Simone's fingertips. Everything she touched was gold. So, it completely baffled him that she was sometimes so doubtful about their relationship and her own self-worth. She could frequently be jealous and too often quick to try to blow them up. They had argued about it often and Paul was willing to wager that her problems had nothing at all to do with Simone fearing failure and everything to do with her fear of being a disappointment to everyone she loved, particularly her parents.

Simone came from a family of high achievers and her parents' expectations were monumental. When the two of them had discussed marriage, Simone had held her mother and father's union up as the example she intended to emulate. They were ride or die for each other, but neither had ever given up on their own dreams. She and her siblings had been raised that relationships weren't to be taken lightly and marriage was sacred. She wasn't willing to take the risk if she believed the union could have major problems. She only intended to be married once and divorce wasn't an option she ever wanted to consider if things went left. Road bumps in the dating stage were red flags she wasn't willing to ignore. Her theories about relationships in general, and theirs in particular, had driven him crazy. Because their biggest challenge had always been getting Simone to simply trust the process, his intentions, and to let their love be what fate intended for it to be. And Simone could never trust what she could not control and manipulate.

He moved to the kitchen. A plate sat table center covered in aluminum foil. A sticky note rested against an empty glass. Simone had drawn a simple heart and signed it with a lipstick kiss. Again, classic Simone, an apology that was everything but an actual apology. But it was heartfelt, and he knew she truly was remorseful about their fight.

Paul pushed the foil aside to expose a baked chicken breast, canned string beans and cheesy potatoes au gratin. He had to smile because Simone didn't typically cook, so the effort must be genuine. He moved to the microwave, set the timer for two minutes and poured himself a glass of wine as he waited for the food to warm.

Minutes later he realized how hungry he was as he wolfed the meal down, barely chewing before he swallowed. It was tasty and quickly stalled the pangs of discomfort that had cramped his stomach. He only wished she had been there to share dinner with him, but he realized it was well after midnight and Simone was probably sound asleep.

After washing the dirty dishes and straightening the kitchen Paul poured himself a glass of bourbon and moved to the living room sofa. Sam Smith echoed out of the speakers, singing some sad, slow song questioning why he was so emotional. Paul sat sipping his drink as the last embers of a fire died down in the fireplace. With everything Paul had on his mind he couldn't focus. All he could think of was Simone, wondering if a time would come when all he needed to worry about was making her happy.

Simone thought she was still in a dream as she rolled onto her back. It was warm and she was comfortable, her body temperature rising sweetly. Feathers, she thought, as the gentlest touch passed against her bare skin. It felt like feathers doing an erotic dance around her knees and up her inner thighs. It tickled, but it didn't, just feeling heated and teasing. She heard someone moan and the slightest smile pulled across her face. And then that touch became a nibble and she gasped loudly, realizing that it was her who was moaning.

Simone took a deep inhale of air and her eyes fluttered open and then closed and then open. The room was dark, just the faintest rays of moonlight shining through the windows. She didn't know what time it was, only that Paul had finally come to bed.

She felt Paul's hands trailing a lazy path down the length of her legs, his mouth fluttering damp kisses against her flesh. He had her body on fire, all her synapses firing with electricity. It felt like the Fourth of July fireworks from her head down to her toes. She murmured his name, a soft chant blowing through the air like a prayer. Then she parted her legs in invitation.

Simone was in agony with desire, the pain like a deep craving that was intoxicating and addictive. When he blew warm breath against her most private space, she pushed herself toward him, the need having grown more than she had ever imagined. She pushed forward again, wanting his touch to quell the rising heat. But he teased again, in no hurry to rush his ministrations. He blew softly against her again, then gently nipped at her inner thigh until he reached the apex of her parting.

He tugged first at her outer lips, then the inner, using his mouth to send waves of pleasure through her, and then his tongue prodded her clitoris and his fingers slipped into her damp, moist cavity. Simone grabbed the bedclothes with both hands and her back arched. She bit down against her bottom lip, fighting not to scream.

Giving in to the frenzy of feelings, Simone felt her body swirl and spin. It was a rollercoaster ride of sheer gratification and she savored the decadent sensations that were suddenly consuming. Her eyes rolled and her muscles clenched and then just like that her world exploded, the sensation like a tsunami rushing through space. It was a staggering tide of pleasure, with rolling waves convulsing through her body. She rode the crest for what seemed like an eternity, slowly slipping back to the sound of Paul's voice murmuring endearments as he kissed a slow trail up the length of her torso, until he was nuzzling his face into her neck. She opened her eyes and he was smiling down at her.

"You good?" he asked, kissing her neck, along her jawline and then her cheeks.

Simone nodded. "Better than good," she whispered back. "Do you forgive me?"

Paul nodded. "I always do. I love you."

Simone nodded her own head a second time and then she widened her parted legs even more as he nestled the entirety of his body against her. As he slid himself into her, she wrapped one leg and then the other around his back, her arms tightening around his torso as she clung to him with complete abandon. He loved her, and he whispered it repeatedly like the sweetest mantra, and Simone loved him back as fiercely.

Chapter 11

The next morning, Paul was already back in the lab when Simone finally crawled out of bed and made it to the kitchen. He'd left freshly cooked bacon and croissants on the table. A clean frying pan rested on the stove and eggs sat in a bowl on the counter beside a softened stick of butter.

Simone wasn't feeling one-hundred-percent and hoped the coffee would give her the push she needed to get her day started. Despite what had turned out to be an incredible night, she was feeling like her body was failing her. She had her fingers crossed that she wasn't coming down with a cold, or worse, the flu.

With her coffee mug in one hand and a croissant in the other she moved into the dining room. Standing before the notes she'd pasted to the wall, she studied the line of data that was known to them with the data that wasn't.

Paul and Oliver had identified the contaminant and had established a pattern of exposure. How the contaminant had been created was still questionable, although Paul had a few theories that he hoped the additional testing would help answer. Nor did they know for certain that Lender even knew about the contaminant and if they did, why they were ignoring it. Simone was discovering that drug manufacturing was far more complicated than she originally realized and companies that routinely outsourced their manufacturing processes and acquired their active ingredients from global marketplaces were subject to all manner of catastrophes.

The hard facts they could prove, they planned to present to the FDA and demand further investigation and a recall of the product. She also planned to file a civil lawsuit, hopeful that litigation would motivate Lender to remove the drug voluntarily and do what was right by the patients affected by their flawed business practices. It wasn't going to be a cheap endeavor and neither one of them necessarily had the personal resources to fight Lender on their own and that meant finding additional legal help, preferably a law firm with deep pockets and a solid reputation. In theory, it all sounded like a solid plan. In reality, Simone knew there was a lot of hard work ahead of them and no guarantee there would be any return on their investment.

She dropped down onto one of the cushioned seats and took a sip of her coffee to wash down the bite of pastry that seemed stuck in her chest, feeling too heavy to swallow. Her stomach flipped and for the briefest second, she thought her breakfast might not stay with her through lunch. The sensation passed just as quickly as it had bubbled her tummy.

She suddenly felt overwhelmed and she knew it might take making a decision Paul would not agree with to get the job done. She closed her eyes and let herself sit in the quiet, her mind racing as she pondered what her next steps would be and if her steps and his led them in the same direction.

"Simone? You okay?"

Paul was standing before her, eyeing her with concern. He was wearing her favorite gray sweatshirt, the one she'd given him for his last birthday. They had gone skiing in

Aspen for an extended weekend and had spent most of their time in their cabin, snuggled against each other. It had been his birthday, but he had made that whole weekend about her, making her feel like the luckiest woman in the world. The memory still made her tingle with joy.

She reached out her hand to press it against his abdomen, relishing the feel of the soft cotton blend. She tugged at him gently, pulling him toward her until his lips met hers in the sweetest kiss.

"I'm good. Good morning."

"Good morning. How long have you been up?"

Her eyes skated from side to side. "What time is it?"

"Just after twelve."

"After twelve? It wasn't quite ten o'clock when I sat down!"

Paul laughed. "You didn't get a whole lot of rest last night."

"I got enough that I shouldn't be falling asleep in a chair!"

His smile was consoling. "It happens."

"Not to me it doesn't. I think I'm catching something. I didn't feel well when I got up."

Paul pressed his palm to her forehead. "You don't feel like you're running a fever, but we don't want to take any chances. Any other symptoms I should be aware of?"

She shook her head. "I was slightly nauseous this morning, but I think it was just because I drank coffee on an empty stomach and got a slight caffeine rush."

"But you always drink coffee on an empty stomach, don't you?"

"Usually. I can't think of anything else it might be."

"Well, just to be on the safe side, I'm going to make you a cup of tea and some chicken noodle soup for lunch.

And I want you to take a dose of vitamin C for me. I think you might just need to take a break today."

"I have way too much work to do. And I'm sure it's not that serious," she said.

"Well, we're going to relax together. I've done all I can do, and Oliver doesn't get in until later tonight. So, we can watch Netflix movies and chill all afternoon."

Simone pursed her lips. She started to balk but changed her mind. She still felt funky and lying around watching movies with Paul wouldn't be that bad. She nodded. "If you insist."

Paul gave her a wink of his eye. "I do. And even though you don't feel warm, I want to get your temperature. Let me grab the thermometer."

That day, they felt like they were on vacation and not trying to save the world, Simone thought as she snuggled against Paul. His idea of chilling was to alternate between watching a documentary and reading some scientific study on his iPad. Simone had been dozing off and on for most of the afternoon, convinced the cold weather was trying to throw her off-balance. She couldn't afford to be sick, as every time she thought about the case her to-do list lengthened substantially.

The sounds of the door opening and closing pulled them both from the reverie. Oliver's booming voice filled the space and lifted the mood from serene to serendipitous. He was in rowdy spirits, delighted to be home and fretful about a storm purported to be racing toward them. He rushed in, greeted them both with hugs and then disappeared down to his side of the home.

Paul laughed. "Well, so much for peace and quiet."

"Your brother's exuberance is in a league of its own."

"I just hope he plans to use some of that energy to cook."

Simone laughed with him. "Me, too!"

As if on cue Oliver barreled back into the room. "I stopped by the market before I came in. Wasn't sure what you two had left in the fridge and I picked up the most stunning red salmon. It's so gorgeous I had to get it for dinner. One of you come help me with the grocery bags. I hope you two are hungry. I thought we'd have Thai black rice salad with honey-glazed salmon, and I picked up a wonderful sponge cake from the bakery for dessert."

Simone and Paul gave each other a look. "Thai black rice salad," they both mouthed in unison before bursting out laughing again.

Oliver halted in the doorway, turning to give them a narrowed look. "Peel yourself off that beautiful woman, little brother, and come help me please!"

"I swear, Oliver," Simone said as she spooned the last of her dinner into her mouth. "You are in the wrong profession."

She slid a finger across her empty plate and into her mouth, licking the last taste of the meal away. It was the first full meal she'd been able to eat since being nauseous earlier that morning. She was feeling much better and she was grateful she hadn't had to cook it. That salad had been a delectable melding of black rice, mango and bell pepper tossed in a vinaigrette of soy sauce, vinegar, honey, sriracha and mint. Combined with the glazed salmon that had been cooked to sheer perfection, it was almost orgasmic.

Paul nodded in agreement. "You should seriously consider opening a restaurant. Everything you cook is good, but this is amazing!" he added.

Oliver laughed. "Y'all can butter me up all you want, you're still washing dishes," he said.

"We will gladly do dishes if you promise to make this at least once per month for us," Simone said. "It was excellent!"

"For you, doll, I'd make it twice per month."

Simone grinned foolishly. She held up her plate. "Can we taste the dessert now?"

Oliver had risen from the table and stood at the counter. He turned back toward her holding a slice of layered orange sponge cake with a decadent cream icing sprinkled with pecans. Simone's eyes widened with joy and she started bobbing up and down in her seat with glee.

Paul shook his head. "You're killing me, Simone! Your sweet tooth is ridiculous. Just go slow though, in case it upsets your stomach, please!"

"My sweet tooth ensures my sanity," she replied as she took her first bite and swooned. "Oh, my goodness! This is pure…" she started, then she purred, her whole body shivering with excitement.

"Okay," Paul muttered. "This is really some delicious stuff!"

Oliver nodded excitedly. "And the bakery is owned by this little cutie from Ireland. His name's Dermot." He grinned widely.

Paul laughed as he swallowed his second bite. "What's with you and bakers?"

Oliver shrugged and rolled his eyes skyward. "Just can't help myself!"

Two slices of cake later and the trio sat planning what they wanted to do next.

"I need a good night's sleep," Oliver said, "but I'll be in the lab first thing in the morning. I'm anxious to get my hands on the new samples."

"Preliminary tests don't look promising."

"That's not good."

"No, it isn't," Paul said, shaking his head.

Simone pushed her dessert plate to the center of the table. "Since we're on the subject, I think we need to go public sooner than later."

Paul leaned back in his chair, crossing his arms over his chest. "What are you proposing?"

"A news conference to announce the pending lawsuit. I think if we call them out publicly, and focus a national spotlight on their practices, it might force their hand."

"That, or they'll tie us up in litigation so quick, neither one of us will ever work in our selected fields again."

"There's always that restaurant," Oliver muttered as he swept the dirty dishes from the table. "You two would look good bussing tables."

Paul gave his brother a smirk, his eyes rolling skyward.

Simone shrugged. "We still have more questions than we do answers. We're never going to be able to fix this by ourselves, and to get the help we require and stop children from dying we really need to do something drastic."

"What kind of danger does that put you two in, though?" Oliver asked. "If Lender sent people to shoot at you, I doubt they're going to sit by and let you just tell the world how bad they are."

"That's what I'm worried about," Paul said.

"Well, we have to do something. We can't just sit up here playing with the data and running tests. We also can't be the only ones looking at these meds. We need to involve the FDA, maybe the FBI, and we haven't even begun to consider the international implications. Do we need to reach out to the World Health Organization as well?"

"She makes a good point," Oliver interjected.

Paul nodded.

"We're in over our heads," Simone observed. "Now we need to figure out how to get out from under and then get ahead of this. It's been almost six, seven weeks now since we left Chicago. We need to think about going home."

"But we don't have any guarantee going public or trying to go public isn't going to get us killed."

"No, we don't, but we knew we were putting ourselves at risk the minute we ran."

Paul took a deep breath. He stood, moving to the sink to rinse the dirty dishes and rest them in the dishwasher.

"I think I'm going to bed," Oliver said. "Let me know what you decide in the morning."

"Thank you for a wonderful meal," Simone said, her smile shining in her eyes.

Oliver winked his eye at her. "I left you another piece of cake on the counter."

She blew him a kiss and giggled like a five-year-old.

Paul shook his head, his own smile pulling across his face. She looked happy and he didn't want to risk anything sweeping that joy from her. "Let's table the conversation until tomorrow. Let me think about it and we can decide what we want to do after Oliver and I finish testing these last samples."

Simone nodded. "That's fine, but we need to make a decision, Paul." She had moved to his side and stood with a dish towel in her hand.

Paul leaned to kiss her cheek. "Are you feeling any better?" he asked.

She shrugged. "I think I ate too much cake."

He laughed. "Why don't you head to bed? If you are trying to catch something your body needs to get as much rest as it can. I'll finish up the dishes and be there in a few minutes."

Simone leaned her head on his shoulder. "I am tired," she said. "Thank you."

Paul wrapped his arms around Simone's torso and hugged her close. He kissed her forehead and then her lips. As she ambled across the family room, he found himself suddenly feeling panicked. What if he couldn't keep her safe?

Concern twisted his insides and the stress tightened the muscles across his shoulders and back. Paul couldn't help but think about what could happen if things went wrong, despite their best efforts. What impact their actions would have on both their careers, most especially Simone. She was only there because she believed in him. What if they went through all of this and found themselves still at odds over their future? The uncertainty was stifling, a lengthy list of questions he had no answers to. No scenario that was playing out in his head guaranteed a successful outcome or that he and Simone would get their happily ever after. That fact haunted him the most.

When Simone woke the next morning, she was feeling shaky again. Not worse than the day before, but not better. Just not one-hundred-percent yet. After a quick shower and change she headed to the kitchen. A note rested on the table. Paul and his brother had gone out to run an errand. She'd been left to fend for herself and she had no interest in the bacon and eggs in the refrigerator. Instead, she made herself a cup of coffee and settled on a bowl of fruit salad Oliver had left for her.

Paul hadn't come to bed, instead sleeping in the room across from hers. She knew it had everything to do with her suggestion about going public. He had doubts and was worried, although he would never say so out loud. But she had seen the concern on his face when she'd left him finishing the dishes. He had probably tossed and turned most of the night, not wanting to disturb her rest. She knew he was still on the fence about what their next step should be and though she understood why, she also knew it was time to do more than just rewrite their plan to do something. She stood by her suggestion to press forward and expose what they knew.

As the coffee kicked in, she felt much better, the fog seeming to lift from her skull. She moved to the dining room and the beginnings of the legal brief she intended to file. It was a good start. Not great, and nowhere close to being the perfection she needed it to be. She needed access to a law library and a paralegal team to help her research legal precedents. She needed more than being there could afford her. She took another quick sip of her coffee. Reaching for her cell phone, she dialed.

Mingus answered on the third ring. "You okay?"

"Yeah. Did you find out anything about that woman?"

"Give me a sec," Mingus said, the sound of papers being shuffled in the background.

He continued. "Vivian Lincoln, age twenty-nine, born in Michigan, was the wife of the late John Thomas Lender, the son of CEO and founder John *Mitchell* Lender. She's been with the company since before her marriage to John Thomas. After his death in an automobile accident two years ago, she inherited thirty-five percent of the company. Rumor has it, she and her father-in-law have been consoling each other in a nonfamilial manner over the past year. Some refer to her as John Mitchell's beck-and-call girl."

"Eww! Her dead husband's father? That's just nasty!"

"Hey, you can't make this stuff up!"

"So, why is she still doing sales if she owns stock in the business?"

"Why does anyone do what they do? From what I could learn, it looks like Daddy-in-Law is grooming her to take over all the business. She spent a month overseas recently learning their distribution business."

"Overseas?"

"Yeah, she was in Africa for a few weeks. Morocco, I think. Then she went to Thailand and China before returning here to the US."

A sudden shiver went up Simone's spine, and questions had her pacing the floor. Questions she couldn't ask her brother.

"So, it's reasonable to think she was talking to her father-in-law when I ran into her in the restroom the other day?"

"Liza hacked her cell records and she did indeed place a number of calls to his corporate office after seeing you two."

Simone nodded into the receiver. "Okay. I appreciate the info."

"And because I know you so well, little sister. She's only called Paul twice. On the day he returned from Africa and on the day you two saw her at the hospital. He has never called her. So, I doubt highly they're having some illicit affair you need to be concerned about."

Simone didn't know if she should thank her brother or cuss him out. She wanted to be angry, but he knew her too well. He knew she wanted to know but would never have asked him outright. Mingus was good like that and she loved him immensely for it."

"You need anything else?" he asked.

"I don't think so."

"What are you two planning?"

"Not sure yet."

"Just be safe, Simone. Please."

Simone disconnected the call, not bothering to respond. She was still trying to make sense of Vivian being in Morocco the same time Paul had been, and her possible connection to his sudden interest in moving there. Had he not been totally forthcoming with Simone? Was there something he was hiding? Had he lied outright? Did he even know she'd been there?

She shook her head, all of it suddenly unsettling. Before she could catch her breath and figure out what added up and what didn't, her stomach pitched, a demon sweeping through her insides. Tossing the phone to the table Simone rushed toward the bathroom, making it just in time to spew her breakfast into the commode.

Paul was surprised to find Simone on the bathroom floor, a damp towel pressed to her forehead. Her knees were pulled up to her chest as she leaned against the tub, her complexion two shades of green.

"I've caught some crud," she said, meeting his stare.

"Yeah, you're not looking good," he said. He instinctively shifted into doctor mode, his mind considering a potential diagnosis as he moved into the space and leaned down to swoop her up in his arms.

"What are you doing?" Simone questioned, starting to protest.

"Putting you to bed. Then I'm going to examine you."

"I'm fine. I'll be fine."

"Is that why you had your head in the commode?"

"Did you know Vivian was in Morocco when you were there?"

Paul's eyes widened. "No, I didn't. Who told you that? And I wasn't in Morocco on my last visit."

"But you want to move there? Isn't that why you bought a house there?"

"It's one of a few places I'm considering, and the house was an investment. It may just turn out to be a vacation spot. I'm not sure yet. What's your point, Simone?"

Simone shook her head. "I was just asking."

"Well, it sounds like you were about to go off on a jealous tirade and I'm not sure why."

Simone didn't bother to answer as he laid her on the bed. He pressed his palm to her forehead and then to her cheeks. He also gazed into one eye and then the other, gently lifting the lids with the pad of his thumb.

"What did you eat?" he questioned.

"Coffee. And a spoonful of fruit."

Paul pressed two fingers to her wrist to feel her pulse. "Have you been feeling bad all morning?"

"I was sluggish when I first got up. It's like my usual energy levels aren't there but I thought I was doing better until I suddenly wasn't."

Oliver suddenly interjected from the doorway. "You're flushed, too. It's not that time of the month, is it?"

Simone shot the man a glare. "Really?" She suddenly paused, counting days in her head as she thought about her cycle.

"You couldn't possibly be pregnant, could you?" Oliver asked, his brows raised.

"That's ridiculous! You need to focus on your culinary skills and leave the doctoring to your brother." Annoyance washed over her face.

Paul was staring at her intently. "Simone, are you still on your birth control?"

"Now you? Paul, I am not pregnant."

"What are you using for birth control, Simone, because we haven't been very responsible since we've been back together."

"I…well…it's…" She was suddenly stammering. "Damn

it," she finally cussed, because with everything that had been going on, she hadn't thought about protection. And she had stopped taking her birth control pills the week she and Paul had called it quits. Panic suddenly swept in and consumed her. She was suddenly petrified because a baby had not been on her short list. She hadn't even considered motherhood! But there was no way possible she could be pregnant and definitely no way she'd be feeling the symptoms of it so soon!

Paul tossed his brother a look. "Will you please run to the lab and grab a venipuncture kit? I need to get a blood sample."

"For what?" Simone asked, eyeing him curiously as Oliver dashed out of the room.

"A pregnancy test, why else?"

"But it's barely been seven weeks since we've been back together. If I am pregnant, which I'm *not*," she emphasized, "it's too soon for any test."

"It's been more than ten days since the first time we were together. If you conceived then, a blood pregnancy test will let us know."

"We can go to the pharmacy and get one of the sticks I can pee on, but it's going to be negative."

"A blood pregnancy test will be more accurate. It can detect the presence of HCG as early as six days after the egg implants."

"HCG? What's that?"

"It's a hormone produced by the placenta in pregnancy. We'll take a sample of your blood and then get a measurement of the hormone in your body."

"And if there isn't any?"

"Then you're probably not pregnant."

Oliver raced back into the room, passing his brother

the medical supplies he needed. "This is so exciting!" he gushed, his excitement palpable.

The duo shot him chilly glares in reply.

"I'll just give you two some privacy," Oliver said as he backed his way out of the room, still grinning like a Cheshire cat.

"I'm not doing this. It's a waste of time," Simone snapped. "Just because I'm a little nauseous doesn't mean I'm pregnant. Besides, don't you get morning sickness, like, in the second trimester?"

"Most women experience morning sickness in their first trimester and it typically starts around week six and stops around week twelve. It's caused by the increased hormones in a woman's body and it might be the first indication of pregnancy. But you know women who have had morning sickness throughout their entire pregnancy and women who never had morning sickness. Every woman is different. Your body is unique, and you may be one of the lucky few who don't follow what others consider to be medical norms."

Simone's jaw tightened. "I still think this is crazy and I'm not doing it," she muttered.

"Yes, you are," Paul replied firmly. He moved to the bathroom and washed his hands. When he returned, he laid out the supplies he needed on the nightstand and slipped on a pair of white rubber gloves. "Extend your arm for me," he said, laying a white towel down for her to rest her arm against.

"You can't make me." She snatched her arm from his reach.

"Take the test, Simone!" Paul's voice had risen slightly as he held up a cotton swab saturated with alcohol.

"I'm not taking that test."

"Take the damn test, Simone," he said, louder.

She flung her arm toward him. "Fine! But you're going to feel really stupid when you find out it's just a stomach bug or some bronchial infection thing." Because she couldn't be pregnant, she thought. There was no way in hell life would play such a cruel trick on her. She wasn't ready and the mere thought left her panic-stricken.

Paul inspected her arm with the pads of his fingers, looking for a sizable vein to draw blood from. He disinfected the site, swabbing her inner elbow. He tied a tourniquet on the upper part of her arm to apply some pressure to make the vein enlarge with blood.

"Make a fist for me," he said. "Now open and close your hand a few times." He pushed against her skin with his finger then inserted a needle gently into her vein. He attached a small vial for the venipuncture and as it began to fill, he untied the tourniquet. The process took a few quick minutes and then it was over.

"Now what?" Simone snapped as she folded her arm upright, her finger pressing down on a gauze pad to stop the bleeding.

Paul leaned in and pressed his face to hers, his cheek gently settling against her cheek. He whispered into her ear, his breath warm against her skin, "No matter what happens, Simone, it's all going to be okay. I promise." He gently kissed the side of her face. Gathering the vial and the remnants from the medical supplies, he headed out of the room.

Despite the gesture, Simone knew that for all his calm, this had thrown Paul for a loop even more so than it had thrown her. And truth be told she couldn't begin to fathom what would come next if the test came back positive. They had once talked about marriage and children, both deciding that such was light years down the road for them. Then they broke up, their relationship disintegrating, and they'd been grateful there was nothing for them to divvy up or fight over for custody. Neither she nor Paul were prepared for parenthood. They could barely hold their relationship together. Tossing a child into the mix would be like throwing lighter fluid onto a raging fire. No kid deserved that.

Simone took a deep breath. She felt a thousand times better. Her stomach no longer seemed like a rollercoaster gone awry and she felt halfway whole again. There was simply no way she could be pregnant. Not when everything seemed to finally be falling into step for her and Paul.

Rising from the bed she moved to the bathroom to brush her teeth and wash her face. When she felt completely refreshed, she headed to the kitchen for that last slice of orange sponge cake.

Oliver had changed into a lab coat and had taken the blood sample. Paul stood off to the side and watched as his brother prepped the specimen.

"Do you want to know my methodology?" Oliver questioned.

"I know the process," Paul answered. And he did. He could recite verbatim the technical steps from start to finish. The science spun in his head because that was all he wanted to focus on and it would be a few hours before they knew for certain. But he wasn't prepared to think about what he would do if Simone were pregnant. Just the prospect of such a thing being possible had him in knots, fear settling in too comfortably. One more concern to add to his worry list.

"What are you going to do if the test is positive?"

"I'll do whatever I need to do."

"My little brother is going to be a father!"

"Foreshadowing, are you?"

"Wishful thinking. You and Simone will make beautiful babies and I can't wait to be an uncle."

"I don't know if I'm ready for fatherhood." He began to pace the floor, then sat back down staring as his brother worked. His nerves were frayed and he was anxious. He was also conflicted, not quite sure how he honestly felt about the situation. But mostly he was terrified that Simone would break under the pressure, almost guaranteed to not take the news well. Deep down he knew it would break his heart if Simone didn't want to mother his children.

"Hell, I don't think anybody is *ready* for it until it happens."

Paul shrugged. "Probably not. How long before we know?"

"You know how this goes. I'm going to test, retest, then retest again. You'll know before the day is done. So, why don't you go check on Simone. Make yourself some lunch. Take a walk. When I know, you will." Oliver tossed him a look over his shoulder, his expression smug. "Maybe even go buy you some cigars to celebrate."

"You already think you know, don't you? You are so not funny!"

Oliver grinned. "Congratulations, Dad!"

Chapter 12

When Paul entered the kitchen, he looked like death warmed over. They had successfully avoided each other for most of the day, and outside the sun was beginning to set. Simone stopped eating in midbite, her fork hovering above the last of her cake, finally getting around to that sliver Oliver had saved for her. She knew before he could begin to tell her. That cake was suddenly doing flips in her midsection and something like genuine fear pierced her spirit.

Paul slid his fingers into the short length of her hair as he leaned to press a kiss to the top of her head. "As soon as we get back to Chicago, you need to make an appointment with your ob-gyn. They may want to run the test again, as well as give you an ultrasound. It's still very early. I'm thinking we probably conceived that first night we were back together."

Simone dropped her fork to the plate, the silver rattling awkwardly against the china. "This can't be happening! There has to be some kind of mistake. There's no way I'm pregnant. We haven't been back together long enough! I remember sex education," she quipped.

"Then you remember it only takes one time!" Paul snapped back.

"But it takes weeks for that damn egg to implant. It has to! So the test is wrong," she said, pouting profusely.

Paul sighed. "Clearly, you *failed* sex ed. Implantation

doesn't take weeks." He shook his head as he continued. "Oliver will run the test again, but he's very thorough."

Simone pulled her knees to her chest, wrapping her arms around her legs. She dropped her forehead against her thighs. She felt like she'd been slapped with a sledge-hammer. This was not supposed to happen. She had always imagined the point in her life when she would share with a partner that they were expecting a baby, romanticizing the moment. But there was nothing romantic about her current situation. It actually felt instead like the two of them were being punished for something horrific they had done. Because a baby clearly wasn't what either needed. They weren't at that place in their personal relationship, barely holding what they shared together by a thin thread. They had made mistakes they were still trying to atone for. Were still struggling to get it right. Tossing a baby into the fray was just wrong on many fronts.

She suddenly thought about the adage her father often invoked. That if you wanted to make God laugh, tell Him your plans. She imagined the good Lord was having Himself quite a snicker.

Paul dropped to his knees beside her, reaching to wrap his arms around her body. He hugged her tightly, then slid his hand beneath her chin and lifted her head so that he could stare into her eyes.

"I know it's a shock, and not at all what we were expecting, but I don't want you to have any doubts about how much I love you. We have plenty of time to think about this and decide what we want to do. I'm sure you need to get used to the idea, just like I do. But no matter what, Simone, you and I are going to be fine. I hope that you trust that."

Simone leaned forward and pressed her lips to his. In that moment, she wished she had half of his confidence.

But truth be told, she was scared, and she didn't know if she even wanted to proceed with this pregnancy.

"So, you want this baby?" she questioned, the words coming before she could stall them.

"Why wouldn't I, Simone? This baby was conceived in love. Our love. Of course, I do!"

She nodded her head slowly. Uncertainty and doubt rushed through her like a tidal wave through a calm ocean. Her confidence had taken a hit and she was feeling so completely lost, most especially when Paul was standing rock solid in support. Because she wasn't feeling as convinced about this pregnancy as he was.

She kissed him again. "Why don't we table this conversation until later? I need to make a few phone calls and get some work accomplished before the day's done."

Paul stared at her intently. A moment passed between them and both knew the dynamics of their relationship had taken another shift. He nodded. "Whenever you're ready," he said. "Oliver and I still have some work to do in the lab, so I'm going to run back to the barn and see what I can get accomplished, as well. And I would really like it if you took it easy. You need to put your feet up and relax." He kissed her one last time, then disappeared out the back door.

Everything about the rest of the evening felt awkward at best. Simone was grateful that most of the work Paul needed to do kept him out of the house and that most of the work she needed to do kept her focused on everything except her situation.

She was pregnant and having Paul's baby. And wasn't having Paul's baby ultimately what she wanted more than anything else in the world? Wasn't that part of her ten-year plan? She had already determined that Paul was her future, so having his children was a part of that plan, as well. Right? So why was she feeling like her whole world was coming to an end? And why was she feeling like Paul felt the same way but was desperately trying to put on a positive face to keep her from having a nervous breakdown? She knew she needed to talk to him, but she was afraid of saying the wrong thing and making a bad situation worse. Why couldn't she find the words to say what she was feeling? And why wasn't she happy? She suddenly had more questions than answers.

By the time the men finally made their way back into the home, Simone was in bed, pretending to be asleep. She didn't want to face Oliver's excitement or have Paul look at her with any reservation of his own. And she didn't want to let her mood sour the evening. She was grateful that neither man tried to engage her. They let her be, understanding that she just really needed time alone.

It was hours later when Paul crawled into bed beside her, curling his body around hers, his hand pressing warmly against her stomach. He placed a damp kiss against the back of her neck and minutes later began to snore softly. In that moment, Simone knew only one thing with certainty: she wouldn't be there when he awoke.

The next day, the sun outside was shining brightly. Paul woke slowly, reaching out an arm to pull Simone to him. He was only half-surprised to find the bed empty, his hands brushing against a sheet of paper instead. He lifted himself up enough to read the note she'd written. The words *I'm sorry, I love you* had been printed in dark ink against the stark white paper.

Paul crumpled the paper in his hand and rolled onto his back pulling both arms up and over his head. He didn't need to check to know that Simone was gone. The last time he woke to a note on the pillow had been when Simone had broken off their relationship, only saying she was sorry. Those two words to apologize for not following him on his mission journey had been all she'd left him with. Two words to say she didn't love him enough to want to stay in the fight. Two words that had haunted him for months. In that note she hadn't even bothered to say she loved him. Now, once again, Simone was apologizing, and he didn't know if it was for a pregnancy neither had expected or leaving him high and dry without the courtesy of a conversation.

He stared at the ceiling. He wanted to be angry, but he didn't have the energy to invest in being mad. His heart hurt, a physical ache that made him want to yank the organ from his chest. He felt abandoned and hated that his adult self was even remotely considering that Simone might be gone for good. But he had more questions than answers and once again, she had left him hanging.

Oliver was sitting in the kitchen savoring his morning cup of coffee when Paul finally made his way there. The two men locked gazes before he rose from his seat and poured his brother a cup of brew. "I'd say good morning, but you don't look like there's anything good about it."

Paul shrugged his shoulders. "Were you awake when she left?"

Oliver nodded. "I tried to get her to stay, but she said she really needed to go back to Chicago. She said she left you a note."

"Well, you know Simone. She's not one for a lot of conversation."

"She said to tell you she'll call once she's home and settled and that she'll see us in a few days when we get back. She also took all of the data with her."

Paul shifted forward in his seat, his coffee mug locked tight between his palms. "What do you mean, she took *all* of the data?"

His anxiety level suddenly quadrupled. That data made Simone a target and he couldn't begin to reason why she would put herself at risk, especially now that she was pregnant. Had she not even considered her own safety? Their child's? He had no doubts that the men who'd been after him would go after her so he couldn't begin to imagine what she had to have been thinking.

Distress flooded his eyes with tears, his gaze shifting frantically back and forth as he considered everything that could possibly go wrong. Trying to decide the best course of action to insure she was safe and well. Deciding if he should go after her and if he did, if she would want him there.

"She took everything she was working on as well as the test results that we had finished."

"Did she say anything else?"

Oliver shook his head. "No, just that she needed to do this. And that everything would be okay."

The drive back to Chicago took Simone three hours longer than the first trip to Windsor had. And only because Simone had taken her time debating whether or not she should turn around and go back. Because she had wanted to go back to Paul. Just like she hadn't wanted to leave him, even though she knew it was for the best.

This pregnancy had thrown them off course, becoming a distraction from what they should have been focused on. She heard it in Paul's voice. From the moment he confirmed her pregnancy, he'd become concerned only with protecting her. They'd lost a whole day and would have lost many more had she stayed. Days overthinking and overanalyzing their relationship and her condition. Days concentrating on everything but what they needed to focus on. It was way too much for her to handle and if she had stayed it would have been a battle of wills that neither would have won.

Her cell phone rang again for the umpteenth time, and again, Simone pushed the button to cancel the call. She wasn't ready to speak to Paul yet. He'd be mad for a few days, she thought. But eventually, he'd get over it.

As she pulled into the assigned parking space, Mingus exited his car. Her brother was like clockwork, coming whenever she called. He opened the driver's door and greeted her.

"Please don't tell me you two had a fight?"

"No, nothing like that. And hello to you, too!"

"Your boyfriend has called me a half-dozen times wanting to know if you'd made it back. He said you're not answering his calls."

"I will. I just needed some time to think and I couldn't focus."

Her phone suddenly rang again. She and her brother both stared as she turned it over in the palm of her hand, looking at Paul's reflection on the screen. Mingus snatched it from her and answered the call.

"Paul, hey… Yeah, she just pulled in… She's fine… I know… I'll tell her… Later…"

Mingus disconnected the call. "He said to tell you he loves you."

Simone nodded. "Thanks." She blew a soft sigh as she and Mingus exchanged a look.

The loud screech of car tires at the end of the road suddenly pulled at their attention and shifted the mood. A car was careening in their direction, seeming out of place for the evening hour. Simone could feel her brother tense as he suddenly drew his weapon and stepped gruffly in front of her. With a soft shove he pushed her back into the vehicle and as she fell back onto the seat, her own anxiety rose substantially.

The car sped past, the driver seemingly oblivious to the two of them standing there. As he lurched through the stop sign at the other end of the road, rounding the corner out of sight, Mingus secured his weapon, putting it back into the holster beneath his jacket.

It wasn't until the vehicle was out of sight that Simone realized she'd been holding her breath. She took a swift inhale of air, her pulse racing, and then she cussed, profanity spewing out of her mouth.

"You okay?" Mingus asked as he extended his hand in her direction.

Simone nodded. "Only slightly bruised."

"I didn't push you that hard."

"Like when I was five and you didn't give me a concussion?"

"That was not my fault."

"Says you!" She wrapped her arms around his waist and gave him a tight hug.

"I'm not comfortable with you being out in the open like this. Let's get you inside," Mingus said, his gaze sweeping back and forth over the landscape.

Simone nodded, her own comfort level suddenly diminished. It had taken a split second to be reminded that home might not be safe and running from one problem had probably landed her squarely in the center of another.

She reached into the back seat of her car and passed a large box into her brother's hands. "Can you get this for me?"

As he took the container, his gaze narrowed. "You

okay? You seriously don't look good. You actually look a little green!"

Simone shook her head. For a split second she thought about telling him the truth, but she wasn't quite ready for that conversation. Of all her siblings she knew Mingus would understand and forgive her for a little white lie. "I think I might be coming down with something. It's all good, though."

"So, do you want to tell me what's going on with you and Paul?"

She engaged the lock on her car and headed in the direction of her home. "No. I'm tired and I need to get some rest. I have an appointment tomorrow."

"What kind of an appointment?"

"A job interview, of sorts. Two actually."

Her brother's brows lifted curiously. "You're thinking about leaving the prosecutor's office?"

She nodded as she pushed her key into the lock and opened the door of her home. It was a stunning property in the heart of Bronzeville, one of Chicago's most sought-after neighborhoods. The luxury, two-story residence was nestled amid historic architecture. As she'd moved into the space, Simone was reminded why she loved the place as much as she did. The spacious rooms with distinctive, massive windows, ten-foot ceilings, and contemporary finishes epitomized the lifestyle she enjoyed. And she had really missed her stuff!

For just a second Simone suddenly imagined a baby crawling across those polished, hardwood floors and her breath caught in her chest. Imagining all she would have to do to baby proof the structure suddenly had her heart racing. Her eyes swept from the glass-topped tables to the bookshelves lined with books and knickknacks from her travels. It all felt very daunting. Her stomach flipped as she pressed her palm to her belly. Shaking the sensation that suddenly had her feeling ill at ease, she turned her attention back to her brother.

"What about Paul's problem?" Mingus was asking, eyeing her curiously.

"It's why I'm leaving the prosecutor's office. Private practice will afford me a better opportunity to help him fight this."

"Cool! Make yourself a target, why don't you!"

"I can't *not* do this, Mingus."

"Have you even considered the danger you might be putting yourself in? Corporations like Lender, with deep political connections and ties to dirty money, don't necessarily play nice when they feel attacked."

"What do you know that you haven't told me? What political connections and whose dirty money?"

"A couple of its board members don't have stellar reputations. There's a disgraced politician or two, that Bernie Madoff mentee who avoided prison by the skin of his teeth, and your father's old buddy Alexander Balducci. Rumor has it he's criminally connected to the mob and they've killed people for lesser offenses. But you already know those stories. You've prosecuted a few, if I recall."

Simone shook her head. "And you have all that information for me, right?"

Mingus pointed to a file folder resting on her dining room table. "Every dirty detail I've discovered since you've been gone." He suddenly broke out into song, riffing off his comment with the lyrics of the old Kelly Clarkson song *"Since U Been Gone."*

"You are so stupid," Simone laughed, the moment of levity a welcome reprieve.

Mingus shrugged, the smirk across his face endearing. "I've been called worse!"

"I appreciate your help," she said as she turned on the lights in the living room. "I'm sure you have better things to do with the rest of your night."

"You really don't think I'm leaving you here alone tonight, do you?" Mingus double checked the lock on the front door.

"I'm sure I'll be fine, Mingus."

"I know you will," he replied. "Because I'm not leaving. You got anything to eat up in here or do I need to order us a pizza?"

She blew a soft sigh and Mingus stared, waiting for her to answer. When it became obvious that he had no intentions of leaving, or arguing with her, she asked, "Is Pizano's still open?"

"For another hour, I think. You want deep-dish?"

"No, thin crust with pepperoni and sausage."

As her brother dropped the box onto her dining room table and his large frame down onto her sofa, Simone disappeared into her bedroom. Closing the door, she sat against the edge of the bed and took a deep breath. Paul had said he loved her and for the moment, that was all she wanted to focus on because nothing else mattered.

Paul was still wide awake when his cell phone rang. Awake and angry. For a split second he thought about not answering the call, but he had a lot on his mind that he needed to say. When he answered, there was a lengthy pause before Simone finally spoke.

"I know you don't understand, but I had to leave. I needed to think, and I knew I wouldn't be able to focus if our attention was consumed by this pregnancy."

"You ran, Simone. We promised each other that we would talk things out and instead you ran."

"I didn't run, Paul."

"Did my saying I wanted our baby scare you?"

"You're damn right it did! Most especially because I don't know what I want, and I didn't want to say that and have you think I'm this horrible person."

"You didn't trust me."

"I didn't trust me, Paul! No matter what has happened between us, you've always been this rock. Consistent, predictable, and sometimes stubborn. You, I trust. I knew when you said you wanted this baby that you meant it with every fiber of your being. Just like I trust you when you say you love me."

"But you still ran." The annoyance in his tone was thick. "You took off like you always do when things get hard. This isn't how we fix our relationship, Simone. I need to be able to trust you when things get difficult. Most especially now!"

"But I'm not as confident as you are. Because all of this scares the hell out of me. Because you want to move to Morocco, and you can see this incredible life where our loving each other is enough to make it work. I was just getting comfortable with that idea, even knowing that there were things we still needed to work on. That I needed to work on for myself. Now suddenly, there's this whole other little person who'll be dependent on me to get it right and I'm petrified that I will fail you both. I'm not prepared to fail, Paul!"

Simone was sobbing and it was gut-wrenching. Paul wanted to reach through the telephone line to take her into his arms and hold her. But Simone didn't want to be held. She didn't want to be seen as vulnerable, or weak. She had known he would want to make everything better and she had done what she needed to do to stand on her own. To fix what she needed to fix to be an even better version of herself. She had left, hoping he would understand, despite knowing it would infuriate him.

Paul blew the softest sigh, a weight lifting from his spirit as his anger began to dissipate. Despite his frustrations he understood her. He knew her better than she knew herself sometimes. And he knew she had something to prove. Maybe even more so now that she was pregnant. But it still grated against his last good nerve that she was still quick to act impulsively, still quick to make assumptions, and always challenging the status quo when she didn't need to. But she was also the light of his life and the grasp she had on his heart was insurmountable. "I love you, Simone and whatever you want, I'll support your decision," he said begrudgingly. "If you're not ready to have this baby, I'll understand."

"I would never make a decision like that without you, Paul. Because I love you, too, and no matter what happens, it has to be what's best for us both. I just needed time to myself to figure it all out."

Silence filled the space between the phone lines. Both needed a moment to sit in the other's truth. Taking it all in was both cathartic and repressive, a wealth of emotion flowing between them.

"You should get some rest," Paul said. "You've had a long day."

"Mingus ordered pizza."

"Thin crust from Pizano's?"

"With pepperoni and sausage."

Paul chuckled and Simone felt herself smile.

"You need to come home," she said. "I have a plan."

"Do I even want to ask?"

"No. It will only start another fight."

"It'll probably take us another two, maybe three days

to finish testing the rest of the samples we have here. My box from Ghana arrived today."

"That's fine. It'll be more ammunition for us to work with and I still need to put some things here in place. Just come when you can, please. I miss you."

"I miss you, too, baby. I'll see you soon."

Chapter 13

When Simone exited the offices of Thurman, Brown and Taylor, she was ready to be done and finished for the remainder of the day. The prestigious law firm had made her a substantial offer weeks earlier and initially she'd been excited to accept, the prospect intriguing. Unfortunately, she had to respectfully turn them down. She had hoped to offer them the case, but at the last minute had chosen not to mention it. So now she needed a plan B and another law firm that was capable and interested in supporting the litigation she hoped to bring against Lender. But she was exhausted and in need of a serious nap and she had to wonder if this was going to last her entire pregnancy.

She was grateful for Mingus, who stood leaning against the car waiting for her. His arms were crossed over his chest and the dark shades on his face made him look only slightly menacing. But just the sight of her family lifted her spirits.

"You still here?" she questioned.

"I'm not going anywhere, Simone. Besides, we both know if you really wanted to ditch me, you would."

She gave him a slight smile. "Actually, I like having a personal chauffeur. You've come in handy."

"I may have found my calling. So, where to next, mademoiselle?"

"The law offices of Black, Turner and Hayes, please. Do you need the address?"

Amusement crossed Mingus's face. "Nah, I think I got that one," he said as he opened the passenger door.

Simone tapped her hand against his chest before she slid into the passenger seat. "See, you are good for something," she said teasingly.

Her brother laughed as he slid across the car's hood and into the passenger seat. "So, what's up? Why are we going to see your brother Ellington?"

"I have an interview with his law firm."

"When did that happen?"

"It hasn't yet, actually. He doesn't know I'm coming."

Mingus laughed. "And you call me impulsive!"

"I wish I could explain it, but I can't. Not yet. Let's see if Ellington will let us in first."

"Hey," Mingus said, as he maneuvered the car toward LaSalle Street. "It's whatever. You don't ever have to tell me anything and I'll be good."

Simone laughed. "I appreciate that. Thank you."

He reached for her hand and gave it a light squeeze. "Whatever you need, you know that, right?"

She felt herself getting emotional, so she nodded, then changed the subject. "How's Joanna? I need to call her, but with everything going on…"

"She's pulling her hair out! She's in Atlanta with her mother. Her aunt had to have surgery, so they went down to take care of her. She'll be back next week."

"She'll be bald next week. Her mother has that kind of effect on people," Simone said with a slight chuckle.

"Damn! I was just getting attached to her hair!"

"You're so stupid!" She tossed her brother a look. Mingus and her best friend, Joanna Barnes, had been together in a relationship for a few months. Ever since he'd been hired to investigate false charges that had almost gotten the history teacher incarcerated. He'd fallen head over heels for the woman and loved her almost as much as Simone loved the two of them together. Everyone in the family was ready for them to be married but her brother was taking his sweet time asking the beauty to be his wife. The couple had only been together a few short months and Simone knew they didn't feel they had any reason to rush. "So, when do you plan to make my bestie an honest woman?"

Mingus grinned. "When are you going to say yes and marry Paul?"

"Now you're hitting below the belt!"

"Turnabout is fair play. So, you tell me when you plan to get married and I'll let you know when I do!"

"That might be sooner than you think. You never know!"

"Oh, I know," her brother responded with a deep laugh.

Simone shifted against the leather seats, turning to stare out the window. The weather was questionable, the temperatures almost too warm for the time of year. It wasn't spring yet, but winter still had a hold on the season. The month before, there had been snow on the ground and now the trees looked like they were thinking about blooming.

Three turns and ten short minutes later, Mingus pulled the car into a parking spot in front of the law office of Black, Turner and Hayes. The glass-and-steel skyscraper was located in the three hundred block of LaSalle Street, with the offices occupying the sixty-fourth floor of the massive building.

After feeding the parking meter, Simone led the way into the building, which boasted floor-to-ceiling windows in the exterior offices, expensive contemporary decor and a library and conference room reminiscent of an old English library with polished wood-paneled walls, hardwood floors and three walls of leather-bound law books lined meticulously on shelves.

The two siblings stood together patiently as the young receptionist engaged the intercom and announced their arrival. There was no missing the surprise in their brother's voice when he repeated their names for verification.

"Yes, sir. They don't have an appointment but would like a moment of your time if it's possible."

Simone and Mingus shot each other a look, fighting not to laugh out loud.

A few minutes passed before Ellington Black came down the hall to greet them.

"This can't be good," he said as he shook his brother's hand before pulling Simone into a deep bear hug. "Where have you been? You've had the old people losing their minds."

"I didn't mean to," Simone said. "I told them not to worry."

"That's like telling them not to breathe," Ellington replied. He gestured for them to follow him to his office. "So, to what do I owe this honor?"

Mingus shrugged. "I'm playing bodyguard. Garnering favor from the parents being a good big brother. Until further notice, I go where she goes."

Ellington laughed. "They've got the fox watching the henhouse!" He pointed them toward two wingback chairs as he closed the office door. "So, what's up?" he asked, looking from one to the other.

Simone reached into her briefcase and pulled out a file folder. "I have a case I'd like for your firm to consider. And I want you to hire me to litigate it."

Ellington eyed her with a raised brow as he opened the

file and began to read. He shifted forward in his leather executive's chair as he slowly flipped through the pages. "How many patients do you believe have been affected?"

"There are thousands overseas and maybe a few hundred here in the United States."

"Have you filed your complaint yet with the FDA?"

"I'm just waiting for the results for the last tests Paul and his brother are doing now."

Ellington dropped the folder to the desk and tapped it with the palm of his hand. "What happened with John Thurman's firm? I understand they were certain you were going to sign with them. I'd think you would want to put this in their hands."

"We couldn't come to terms that we were both in agreement with. There was no point in even mentioning this to them."

Ellington folded her hands together, his elbows resting atop the desk. "What if I can't meet your terms?"

"You will have more invested in my demands than they ever will."

"So that begs the question, what do you want that they wouldn't agree to?"

Simone shot her two brothers a look and took a deep breath. "I'm pregnant and if I have this baby, I'll need some flexibility with my schedule because my baby's father is thinking about moving to Morocco. I'm fully committed to whatever my responsibilities will be, but I'll also need time to figure out this motherhood thing and a possible transcontinental relationship. I'll need you to work with me. Thurman wasn't interested."

The two brothers exchanged a look, shock and awe blessing their expressions.

Ellington sat back in his seat, turning his gaze to stare

at his sister. He cleared his throat, still allowing the news to sink in. "You said *if I have this baby…*"

"I can't wrap my head around it right now. I'm not even sure it's real," she said, taking a moment to tell her brothers about her last forty-eight hours.

"Damn, Simone! How do you just leave that man hanging like that?" Ellington exclaimed. "That would hurt my feelings!"

"Paul understands me," Simone said, sinking into a slight pout.

"That brother *loves* you. Anyone else would have left you ages ago! I know I would have!" Mingus interjected.

"Which is why I would never date either of you! It's a good thing we're related."

The trio laughed.

"Seriously," Ellington said, "you know we'll support you however you need us to. But I still don't know if I can give you a job."

Simone nodded. "I know, and I'm willing to bet that I can convince you to hire me."

Ellington gestured toward his brother. "Can you excuse us, please? We have some negotiating to do and knowing our sister it might get heated. Maybe come back in an hour?"

"Or two," Simone chimed. "I doubt he'll give in that easily."

Mingus nodded. "I'll be in the lobby! You two do your thing," he said. Rising from his seat, he leaned to kiss her cheek, pointed his index finger at his brother and disappeared out the door.

Simone shifted in her seat, she and Ellington locking gazes. "I want to be a partner," she said, "with a corner office."

Ellington laughed. "And so it begins!"

* * *

Almost three hours later Simone exited Ellington's law office and rode the elevator down to the first floor. Mingus was outside chomping on the last bite of a hot dog. He swiped at a dab of mustard that had fallen on his shirt as he balled up the foil wrapper and shot it into a wastebasket on the sidewalk.

"Y'all done?"

Simone nodded. "Done and finished. I'm ready to go home now."

Mingus nodded. "Must mean you've got a job!"

She laughed. "And a corner office!"

"Ahhh, the beauty of nepotism."

"Nepotism has nothing to do with it. I'm more than qualified and Ellington's been trying to get me to come work with him since I got my law degree. Now's just the right time. Of course, he still has to run it by his partners and there are two I will need to sit down and formally interview with, but I'm thinking what I bring to the table will help seal the deal."

"Okay."

"Why'd you say it like that?" Simone asked.

"I just said 'Okay.'"

Her eyes rolled skyward, a scowl pulling across her face. "You play too much. Take me home."

"Aren't you moody? Them pregnancy hormones done kicked in big-time!"

"Leave me alone, Mingus," she said as she slid into the passenger seat.

Mingus chuckled as he closed her door and rounded the car to the other side.

The ride was quiet, and it was obvious she was exhausted. She leaned her head against the window and closed her eyes. When she next opened them, Mingus was parked in the heart of Chicago's Gold Coast neighborhood in front of the Black family home. Situated on the large corner lot, the stone-and-brick architecture was a timeless reminder of a whole other era.

"Why are we here?" she asked, her head snapping in her brother's direction. "I said to take me home!"

"You need to have a conversation with your parents."

"Why the hell do I need to do that? I'm not ready to talk to them yet." Annoyance flushed her face.

Mingus passed her his phone, a text message filling the screen. Because your other brother doesn't know how to keep a secret and once he tells, it's probably a matter of minutes before Ma and Pa Black find out.

Her eyes narrowed as she began to read the message from Ellington, a mass text addressed to all her siblings.

I have news about Simone! Meet me for drinks at 7 if you want the details. And, it's good gossip, Vaughan! You pick the spot!

"I'm going to kill him!" Simone muttered between clenched teeth. She began to type furiously, responding to the message Ellington had conveniently forgotten to include her in. Mingus snatched his phone from her hands, a wide grin filling his face.

"Go tell them. Let them lay eyes on you so they can stop worrying about you being gone and go back to worrying about your screwing up your life. Then we can go cuss out our brother at seven o'clock. It'll be good for you to let us all love on you. We missed you!"

Simone lifted her eyes to meet her brother's gaze. She knew he was right, but she wasn't sure she was at all ready for the confrontation. She took a deep breath and watched as Mingus exited the car, moving to open the door for her.

"I don't know..."

"Yes, you do. But take a minute to think about what you plan to say. We've got time."

The solid wood-and-glass front door with its ornate iron details was rarely locked and the siblings entered without knocking. Stepping inside felt like entering the comfort and quiet of a family retreat. There was a quiet that was not typical, but the calm felt immensely welcoming.

Mingus called out. "Hey! It's just us! Who's here?"

Their mother's voice echoed down from the second floor. "Mingus? I'm in my office, son!"

Mingus gave his sister a nod and gestured up the marble staircase. "I'll let you take it from here. I'm going to go see what there is to eat in the kitchen."

"Didn't you just eat?" Simone questioned.

Her brother shrugged. "Stop stalling," he said as he moved toward the kitchen at the back of the home. "I'm looking for dessert!"

Simone shook her head and turned toward the stairwell. She moved through the home, past the walls papered in silk, the sparkling chandeliers, ornate wood moldings and fireplaces meticulously carved in stone. The windows were draped in sumptuous fabrics, and every detail, from the coffered ceilings to the highly polished hardwood floors reflected her parents' refined taste.

Her mother was in her office, seated behind her large glass-topped desk. When Simone walked into the room the matriarch looked up in surprise, uttering a loud gasp at the sight of her.

The Honorable Judith Harmon Black was a tall woman, nearly as tall as her sons. She towered above Simone, who hadn't gotten her height from either of her parents.

The judge had picture-perfect features: high cheekbones, black eyes like dark ice and a buttermilk complexion that needed little if any makeup. She was dressed casually, which was a rarity, but still donned her requisite pearls. A hint of blush to her cheeks complemented her fair skin and her lush silver-gray hair fell in thick waves past her shoulders. The sight of her mother suddenly had tears welling in Simone's eyes. Judith's smile leaped across the desktop to wrap Simone in a deep embrace.

Judith stood. "Simone!" she said as she moved around the desk and wrapped her youngest daughter in a warm hug. "Thank God! You're home!"

Simone suddenly felt as if a cloud burst, tears raining down her cheeks. She stood in her mother's arms and clung to her for a good few minutes. Her mother held her and allowed her to cry until she didn't have any tears left.

Judith cupped her hand beneath her daughter's face and lifted her chin. She wiped Simone's tears with her thumb, then reached for a tissue from a box on her desk, pressing it into the palm of Simone's hand.

"What's going on?" Judith asked. "This isn't like you. You were never a crybaby, so what's with all the boo-hoo-hooing?"

Simone shook her head. "I'm pregnant," she blurted, the words racing past her lips before she could catch them.

Judith's eyes widened as she pointed Simone into a cushioned seat. She moved back to her own chair and sat down. "When did this happen? How far along are you?"

"Paul says it's just a few weeks, but I have an appointment with Dr. Seymour tomorrow to confirm his test results."

"And how does Paul feel about this?"

Simone shrugged. "You know Paul. He's always ready to step up and do the right thing. It's why I love him. He's a standup guy! I don't know if I would want to do this without him."

"You don't need a man to do the right thing for you, Simone. You know full well how to be self-sufficient. Your father and I didn't raise any of you—most especially you and your sister—to have to depend on someone else for your own needs or happiness."

Simone held up a palm to stall the lecture she felt coming. "We wanted to try and work things out. We were making plans. Then this just happened and well, I'm not handling it as well as Paul is. I honestly don't know if I'm ready to be anyone's mother." Her voice dropped to a loud whisper. "I'm scared, Mom. I don't think I've ever been this scared of anything. But this has me petrified! I'm a hot mess on a good day. I don't want to screw up my child!"

Judith leaned back in her chair, twisting a silver ink pen between her fingers. A slight smile pulled across her face. For a brief moment she seemed to drift into thought as Simone sat staring. Simone suddenly felt like she was six years old again when she had poured bleach into the family fish tank wanting to clean the water. She'd been devastated when all the goldfish were suddenly floating on top and her siblings were screaming bloody murder at her. She'd sobbed like a baby then, too, ankle socks and patent-leather shoes swinging as she'd sat with her mother waiting to be told what a horrible person she was. But her mother hadn't called her horrible. In fact, she'd commended her for trying to do what she thought was right. Then she'd told her that learning about her fish and how to care for them would ensure future accidents didn't happen. "Educate yourself," Judith had admonished. "Be smart about everything you do."

Now all she could think was if she could kill her pet

fish what chance did a baby have in her hands? She didn't get a do-over if a well-meaning act went awry! Even if she did read every parenting book imaginable.

Judith seemed to read her mind. "I think you'll be an amazing mother, Simone," she said softly. "And together you and Paul will be incredible parents, whether you are in a relationship with each other or not. And I trust this because I know you will always put your child first and do whatever you need to do to protect her."

"Her?"

Her mother grinned. "A grandmother can dream, can't she?"

Simone laughed, shaking her head. Her mood seemed to lift, if only for a moment. "Paul wants to move to Morocco. He bought a house there."

"Why Morocco?"

"It's central to those places where he's established his medical missionary programs."

"I do admire his philanthropic spirit. He's a good soul."

"He's a little irritated with me at the moment," Simone said, explaining how she'd left him high and dry in Canada without so much as a warning.

Her mother shook her head. "I can't reiterate it enough, Simone—a relationship will not work if you don't communicate with your partner. Your father and I work because we've learned how to have the hard conversations. You can't run just because you don't like what Paul has to say. You need to sit in his truth and own yours. And you both have to be committed to doing that together."

"I know, but I needed to focus, and I couldn't do that. It was just easier to leave."

"No one said your relationship would ever be easy and you can forget about marriage being easy. It's hard, and it requires an investment of your time and energy and your commitment to work hard through the challenges when they come."

Her mother took a deep breath before continuing. "And what you did wasn't fair to Paul. Even if you decided to leave, he had a right to express how he felt about that, and you needed to hear it."

"I know," Simone said sighing softly. "And I'm working on doing better. I really am. Paul loves me, and I love him. But I don't think I can move to Morocco. Especially now with a baby coming."

"Then don't. But instead of looking at things so narrowly, allow yourself the luxury of being open to whatever the future holds. I'm sure Paul will help you figure it out. If being with him is what you want, then let him help."

"You'd be okay if I took your first grandchild to Africa?"

"It would mean your father and I would be doing much more international travel. We would make it work."

"Please don't tell Daddy about the baby yet. I think it's something Paul will probably want to have a conversation with him about first."

"I can respect that," her mother said with a nod. "So, what about the case you and Paul were working on? How's that going?"

"I'll be leaving the prosecutor's office to work the case in private practice."

Judith's brow lifted slightly. "You're planning to open your own firm?"

"No, ma'am!" Simone said with a shake of her head. "I'm joining Ellington's law firm as a junior partner. There, I'll have the full weight of the firm behind me when I file the class-action lawsuit."

"Well, you're just full of good news today, aren't you, baby girl?"

"Do you think Daddy will be mad at me and Paul? That we didn't get married before getting pregnant?"

Judith shrugged. "Your father wants you to be happy no matter what. I'm sure he'll hiss and scream at first, but probably not for long. His bark has always been harder than his bite. I have no doubts though that if he hears it from Paul first, Paul will get the brunt of it before your father gets to you."

Simone sighed. She stole a quick glance to her watch. "Then I need to run and go swear your other children to secrecy."

Judith laughed. "Who'd you tell?"

"Mingus and Ellington."

"You know Ellington can't keep anything secret!"

The two women chatted for a few minutes longer before heading down to the kitchen to check on Mingus.

Her brother was dozing in a recliner in the family room.

Their mother shook her head as she tapped him gently. "Are you okay, son?"

Mingus opened his eyes slowly, looking from his mother to his sister and back. "I'm good." He yawned, stretching his limbs up and out. "How about you two?" he questioned, looking toward Simone.

His sister smiled and nodded, her eyes shifting to his. The conversation between them was quick and silent, no words necessary. Because Simone did feel better, like the weight of the world had been lifted from her shoulders. She knew her baby would be fine because even if she screwed up, there was family supporting them. They would make sure her baby would be okay. Her whole face lifted in a smile. Her baby! She and Paul were having a baby! Suddenly the prospect of that didn't feel so daunting.

He reached into the breast pocket of his leather jacket and passed his mother an envelope. "That information you were looking for," he said. "Let me know if you need anything else from me."

The two exchanged a look and Simone could feel the energy between them shift as the moment became awkward. Her gaze swung from one to the other, but it was obvious it was not a conversation she was privy to. Her curiosity waved and she wanted to ask about their exchange but she knew better than to intrude. Mingus might share if she asked him when they were alone, but she knew her mother would not take kindly to her being nosy in business that was not hers.

Her mother slipped the envelope into the back pocket of her slacks. "Thank you," she said before changing the conversation. "Simone, do you want something to eat?"

"No, thanks. I'm headed to dinner to go kill Ellington and then I'm going home. It's been a long day."

Her mother laughed. "Tell your brothers and sister I expect them all here for Sunday dinner. It's important. And call your father, please, so he at least knows you are home." She wrapped Simone in one last hug.

"Thank you, Mom," Simone whispered.

Her mother kissed her cheek. "Trust your instincts, Simone. They will never lead you wrong. And please don't hurt your brother too badly. I like Ellington."

Mingus laughed. "You like us all!"

Simone giggled. "Nope, they *love* us all. Mom and Dad only like some of us. Me especially!"

"Glad I'm special, too!" her brother said as the two headed out the door, their mother smiling as she watched them exit the home.

Chapter 14

There was no denying the family resemblance as the Black siblings gathered for dinner at Thithi's Restaurant, one of their all-time favorite spots for Thai food. They were a pretty family with distinguished features and warm complexions indicative of their biracial heritage. Even seated, it was easy to tell that the brothers were all tall, with athletic frames, much like their father. The sisters had both gotten their mother's high cheekbones and dark eyes. They had inherited the best genetic material from their parents, and each wore it well, along with their jazz-musician names that spoke to their parents' aesthetic. Armstrong, Davis, Ellington, Parker, and Vaughan were laughing heartily amongst themselves. Ellington was sitting with a smug expression on his face that quickly bottomed out when he caught sight of them. "Hey, we weren't expecting you," he exclaimed as the hostess pulled up two additional chairs to the table.

"I'm sure you weren't," Simone said, her gaze narrowing. "It's hard to gossip about me when I'm here, right?"

Ellington laughed. "It wasn't like that, Simone!"

"Yes, it was," Vaughan said as she jumped from her seat to give Simone a hug, the two women holding tightly to each other. "I'm so pissed at you," Vaughan exclaimed when she finally pulled away. "Why didn't you call someone to let us know you were okay?"

"Because I *was* okay! Y'all don't call every day to check in with anyone."

"We didn't have people shooting and trying to kill us a few weeks ago, either," Parker said as Simone moved around the table to give them each a hug and kiss.

"When did you get back?" Armstrong asked.

"Last night."

Davis stood and hugged her, as well. "Missed you, sis!"

"Where's Paul?" Vaughan questioned, throwing a quick look toward the door.

"He's still...well...he..." Simone stammered. She wasn't ready to tell them that she had left Paul in Windsor. She wasn't in the mood for the judgment she knew would come from her brothers. She also wasn't ready to announce her pregnancy or explain plans she hadn't yet made. She shook her head. "I'm sure we'll all see him in a day or two."

Vaughan punched Ellington's shoulder. "So, this is the news you had? You could have just told us in a text that Simone was finally back home."

"He had more news than that," Mingus said, tossing in two cents as he reached for a menu.

Simone shot her brother a look.

"I did have more news," Ellington said, that smug look returning. "I am pleased to announce that attorney extraordinaire Simone Black has officially joined the law firm of Black, Turner and Hayes, eventually to be Black, Turner, Hayes and Black. After a quick discussion with the other partners and a vote in favor of meeting all her demands, she now reports to me! Once all the appropriate contracts are signed, of course."

There was a round of cheers as they all congratulated her, the warmth of it moving Simone to tears. She suddenly wished Paul was there to share in the joy with her.

"I guess I need to give the prosecutor's office my official resignation," she said, batting back the moisture in her eyes.

Ellington laughed. "Yeah, you need to do that. You can't stay on leave with them and work for me."

Parker leaned forward in his seat. "What's going on with that problem of Paul's? You two have any resolution yet?"

"It's why I'm back. I need to put some things in motion."

"And the two men that shot at you?"

"They didn't find us, so..." Simone shrugged.

"Which suggests you might not be safe," Armstrong snapped, their siblings nodding in agreement.

"You still need to come down to the station to give us a statement," Parker admonished. "And I mean it, Simone."

"I will! When Paul gets back, we'll both come right down to see you."

"No, Paul can give us his statement when he gets back. I expect to see you first thing in the morning."

"Really, Parker?"

"I mean it."

"I'll make sure she gets there," Mingus interjected.

Parker shot him a look as the others laughed.

"I mean it," Mingus said as he gestured for the waitress and ordered himself a drink. "I'll have her there bright and early. Won't I, Simone?"

"Yeah, whatever," Simone muttered, her focus on the menu and the chicken pad thai she wanted to order.

"Anything else you want to share with us?" Ellington suddenly questioned.

"Yeah," Mingus added. "Anything?"

The two brothers exchanged a look, Mingus clearly

fighting not to laugh out loud. The others were trying to figure out what was going on.

"What are these two fools talking about, Simone? What else aren't you telling us?" Vaughan asked.

Simon shot them a glare, swiping the smirks from her brothers' faces. "I have more news, but I can't share it until I've had a chance to talk to Daddy *first*," she snapped. "I hope all of you," she paused, glaring a second time at Mingus and Ellington, "will respect that."

"You and Paul got married!" Vaughan exclaimed. "You eloped!"

"You better not have," Parker interjected. "I can't speak for Paul, but I know you are not that crazy!"

"I know that's right," Davis added. "Pops would kill you and I don't even want to think what he'd do to Paul!"

"He'd bury Paul," Armstrong laughed.

"She's gonna wish she and Paul had eloped," Mingus mumbled under his breath.

Simone glared. "Y'all keep guessing. Have your little fun. I'm not paying you an ounce of attention. When I have something I want y'all to know, I'll tell you."

Ellington held up his hands as if he was surrendering. He leaned to kiss her cheek as he changed the subject. "Since we're all here, there's something that's been bothering me."

"What's that?" Parker asked.

"Is something going on between Mom and Dad that all of us don't know about?" Ellington asked, looking toward Vaughan. "Or a few of us don't know about?"

"I was wondering the same thing," Armstrong said. "Mom hasn't been herself lately."

Simone's gaze swept around the table. "I hadn't noticed anything. Did my being away cause a lot of friction between them?"

"It definitely didn't help," Mingus quipped.

"Something's going on," Vaughan answered. "But I don't know what it is. Any of you talk to Daddy lately?"

"I had lunch with him yesterday," Parker noted. "But he didn't say anything, and he seemed fine."

"Well, they're not fine together," Vaughan said. "They barely spoke to each other this past Sunday. And when they did, they bickered about everything."

They suddenly all turned toward Mingus, eyebrows raised as they eyed him questioningly.

"Either of them say anything to you, Mingus?" Parker asked.

"No," he answered, but there was a moment of pause just long enough for the rest of the brood to question how truthful he was being.

"You know something," Vaughan finally quipped. "What's going on?"

Mingus reached for his glass and took a sip. He didn't bother to give her an answer but the look he shot around the table spoke volumes. His silence was suddenly deafening and they all instinctively knew not to push the issue with him.

"Mom said to tell everyone that she expects us all to be at the house for Sunday dinner. Maybe we can figure out what's going on then," Simone interjected, genuine concern washing through her.

"Y'all need to stay out of it," Davis said. "It's not our business unless they want it to be."

Simone suddenly thought about her conversation with her mother. If something was going on with their parents, she trusted the two would talk it out and make it work. Because everything her mother and father preached, they lived whole-heartedly, and she was desperate to have that with Paul.

"Davis is right," Armstrong interjected. "Mom and Dad will work out whatever is wrong. *If* there is anything wrong at all."

A wave of silence draped the table as their server delivered the plates of food that had been ordered earlier. Simone reached for her sister's hand on one side of her and Mingus's hand on the other. Both squeezed her fingers, nothing needing to be said as Parker led the family in prayer, blessing the food and their good fortune. She was home, with family, and all was right in the world. For the first time in a good long minute she felt like things were beginning to look up. Now all she needed was for Paul to return to make it even more perfect.

Paul and Oliver had spent the better part of the day analyzing and testing the last drug samples they'd received. After recording the last results, he had secured the data and forwarded results data to Simone. They were finishing up in the lab when Paul's phone rang. He was about to answer the call when Oliver stopped short in the doorway and pulled his index finger to his lips to shush him. He shut off all the lights and they were suddenly standing in darkness, just the faintest hint of light shining through the door.

Paul felt the hairs on the back of his neck stand at attention. He silenced his phone instead of answering it and moved to Oliver's side, using the light from outside to peer around the open door. "What's wrong?" he whispered.

Oliver pointed to the house and a shadow moving past the family room window. "I think there are two of them," he said as he slowly closed the lab door and locked it. He engaged the flashlight on his cell phone. "They can't see inside here," he said, "but I didn't want them to see any light reflecting under the door. Who do you think it is?"

Paul shrugged, trying not to let the fear show on his face. His heart was suddenly racing, and he broke out into a cold sweat. "Whoever it is, I don't think they mean us any good."

"What do you want to do?"

"Well, we're not going down without a fight!"

Oliver nodded his agreement. He took a deep breath and moved across the room to one of the locked cupboards. Taking a key from his pocket and then opening the door, he pulled out two hunting rifles and passed one to Paul. "This place is a fortress, but if they breach that door, shoot."

Paul released the weapon's magazine and opened the chamber. "You keep them loaded?" he said, his voice a loud whisper.

"You're damn right I do! I live in the woods and most times I'm here by my lonesome."

"Is there a reason why you didn't put any windows in this space?" Paul questioned.

"Yeah, I didn't want anyone being nosy to see in."

"Makes good sense to me. But now we can't look out!"

Oliver shrugged. "What now?"

"If it's the men Lender hired and they're after me, there's nothing in the house for them to get their hands on. Simone took all the data. If this is some random robbery, they might walk off with that big-screen television of yours. Either way, I'm not going to go ask them what it is they want. We need to get to the car and get back across the border." He suddenly thought about Simone, grateful that she hadn't been there, inside, alone, when they'd intruded on the space. He couldn't begin to image what he would do if she were in harm's way.

"My passport's in the house. I'm also thinking they're probably parked down the road since we didn't hear a car pull up. That might be a problem if there's more than one of them."

Paul cussed, suddenly feeling trapped. "We need our passports."

"We need to live to tell this story to my niece or nephew," Oliver quipped.

Paul rested the rifle he was holding on the table and pulled his phone from his pocket. A missed call from Simone lit up his screen. Ignoring it, he dialed 911 and took a deep breath.

"What is your emergency?"

"Yes, ma'am. My name is Dr. Oliver Reilly," Paul answered, giving his brother's name and the home's address. "My brother and I just returned from a walk and there are intruders in our home. Can you please send someone?"

"Do you know how many there are, Dr. Reilly?" the operator questioned.

"We think there are two, maybe three men and it looks like they might be armed," he continued.

"I have a patrol unit in route, sir. Please do not engage with the men. Our officers will be there any minute now. Are you in a safe location?"

"Yes, yes we are. We're hiding in the barn behind the house," he concluded. "And we definitely won't engage them."

When he disconnected the call, Oliver shot him a look, his eyes rolling skyward.

"It was just a little white lie," Paul said, seeming to read his brother's mind. "But if they ask where we walked to, you'll have to answer. Make up whatever lie you need to."

"Like I've ever gone walking in the dark around here! We're both going straight to hell!" Oliver said. He turned and pulled the door open just a fraction to peek out. He noted the footprints in the light sprinkling of snow that covered the ground. They stopped just short of the barn and turned, heading back toward the other side of the house. He quickly closed the door and relocked it.

"Did you see anything?" Paul whispered.

Oliver shook his head. "No. Nothing good at least."

The next few minutes felt like an eternity. At the sound of sirens careening toward them, Oliver returned both rifles to the cupboard and relocked the cabinet. He and Paul moved back to peek out the door. Three patrol cars from the Windsor Police Service pulled into the parking area behind the home and several officers exited with their weapons drawn. As one officer moved toward the barn, a second on his heels, the others entered the house through the rear door.

Paul slowly pulled the barn door open, he and Oliver both exiting with their hands raised. He announced them both. "I'm Dr. Paul Reilly, and this is my brother, Dr. Oliver Reilly."

The officer recognized Oliver and greeted him with a nod. "Dr. Reilly, it's Liam Trembley, sir. Are the intruders still inside the house?" he questioned.

Dropping his arms, Oliver shook his head. "Officer Trembley! I'm sorry I didn't recognize you. We're not sure, but we didn't see them leave. Once we saw them walking through the house, we locked ourselves here inside my office. Then we called you."

The officer moved through the door and into the space. Oliver turned on the lights to give him full view of the room.

"This is some setup you have here, sir. What do you do?" Trembley asked, his gaze sweeping around the room.

"I'm a research scientist. Currently, I'm studying the impact of cancer cells on diseased tissue."

"You a scientist, too?" the officer named Liam asked, directing his question toward Paul.

Paul shook his head, folding his arms over his chest as he tucked his hands beneath his armpits. "No, I'm a physician. I practice medicine in the United States. I'm here visiting my brother for the week." Paul shot Oliver a look, beginning to sway nervously back and forth as he remembered the warrant with his name on it.

Another officer stepped out of the home and called out to them. "All clear! The house is empty."

Officer Trembley gave them a nod as he moved back to the entrance. "Why don't you go see if anything was taken? Officer Poole and I will take a look around out here."

The two brothers both blew a sigh of relief, but the emotion was tentative. They couldn't help but wonder if the two men were gone, where were they now and how long before they'd come back?

Paul knew what they'd been looking for and he couldn't help but be concerned that maybe this time it hadn't been their plan to let him survive. What would have happened if he and Oliver had been ambushed? Even thinking that things could have gone very wrong and he wouldn't have been able to get back to Simone and their baby had him feeling some kind of way.

Nothing inside was out of place. The televisions were still intact, and Oliver's gold watch rested on the counter. The police quickly eliminated theft as a motive for anyone to enter the home without permission. The brothers did as well, sensing the men Lender Pharmaceuticals had sent had invaded their space more interested in doing them harm than anything else. Paul had no doubt the drug company was still trying to shut him down.

"Is that your car parked down at the end of the road?" one of the officers questioned.

"No," Oliver said. "We saw it when we came in but figured someone had just broken down and left it there."

"One of my officers got the license plate and if we can't reach the owner, we'll have it towed to impound," he said.

"And you said you'd been out walking?" another officer asked, looking from Oliver to Paul.

Oliver nodded. "We just wanted some air, so we walked down to the main road and over to that lot that's for sale across the way. We're thinking about buying it. We were out longer than we anticipated because Paul thought he saw a coyote. I thought it was a dog, but we wanted to wait until it went on its way just to be safe."

"I'm pretty sure it was a coyote!" Paul muttered.

The two officers exchanged a look but said nothing. Officer Trembley stepped inside the home. "There are fresh footprints headed into the back woods, but they turn back around to the front of the house and cross through the yard. It looks like there were two people but there's no sign of them and the car that was parked at the edge of your driveway is now gone. One of my men is going to dust for fingerprints and I'll post a car at the end of the road tonight just to be safe."

Paul nodded. "We're actually headed back to the States tonight. I need to be back in Chicago tomorrow."

"And I'm flying to Atlanta after I drop him home," Oliver said. "I won't be back until next week."

"Just stay in touch with us," Officer Trembley said. "And, if we have more questions, we'll give you a call. There's no sign of forced entry and with nothing missing I'm not sure we know what's going on yet."

Paul shot his brother a quick look. "I think I might

have left the door unlocked. Do you think it could have been someone just being nosey?"

"That's possible. We still want to err on the side of caution, though."

"I appreciate that," Oliver said, extending his hand to shake the other man's.

Officer Trembley gave them both a slight smile. "My guys should be finished in about an hour, then we'll get out of your way."

"Take your time," Oliver responded. "Can I get anyone coffee?"

The officers all shook their heads no and continued about their business. The two brothers stared at each other.

"I'm going to go pack," Oliver finally said. "Let me know if they come up with anything."

Paul nodded, his anxiety level at an all-time high. All he wanted in that moment was to get back to Simone. To get Lender out of their lives, and finally be done with the mess. He wanted to trust that whatever she had planned had to be far better than what they were currently going through.

His voice dropped to a low whisper. "You do that, big brother. Because as soon as they're done, we're getting the hell out of Dodge!"

Chapter 15

Paul wasn't answering his cell phone and Simone didn't know whether to be angry with him or worried for him. She'd left a half-dozen messages and he hadn't bothered to respond to any of her calls. She'd even left a message for Oliver and that, too, had gone unanswered. It left an unsettled feeling in the pit of her abdomen, but she didn't know whether to attribute that to nerves or morning sickness.

Dinner with her family had lasted longer than she'd planned but it had felt good to be back in the presence of her siblings. They kept each other grounded and she trusted that if she needed them, they would be there for her. Even Mingus and Ellington trying to instigate trouble was done in love and the back-and-forth banter that kept them laughing was everything.

She'd been tossing and turning for hours, unable to drift off to sleep. Despite her exhaustion and the long day ahead of her she knew she wouldn't rest well until she heard Paul's voice and knew he was safe. She blew a soft sigh. Tossing her legs off the side of the bed and then standing up, she wrapped a flannel bathrobe around the T-shirt and shorts she was wearing and slid her feet into a pair of plush slippers.

Moving to the living room she found Mingus wide awake, reading a novel under the light of his Kindle, and sipping on a glass of bourbon. His bare feet were propped against her coffee table. He'd made himself at home and looked very comfortable.

"You can't sleep either?" she asked.

Mingus shrugged. "I wanted to finish this book," he said, gesturing with the paperback in his hand. "You not feeling well?"

Simone shrugged as she dropped down onto the sofa beside her brother. "I can't reach Paul. I don't know if I should be worried or not."

"Paul can handle himself if something comes up. That brother's gone into war zones to administer medical care to refugees. There's not a lot that can shake him. He's tough. He'll be all right."

Simone leaned her head against her brother's shoulder and extended her legs beside his. "I miss him."

"I'm sure he misses you."

Mingus reached for his glass and took a sip of his beverage. "Can I get you anything?" he asked.

She shook her head. "I just want to sit here for a minute."

He nodded and returned to his book, his sister settling against him to calm her nerves.

Mingus had left the window blinds open, the patio door reflecting the view from outside. There was a full moon and Simone stared out at the late-night sky spattered with stars. Her brother was right. Paul was one of the most resourceful men she knew. He'd be fine and she trusted they'd be back in each other's arms before she knew it.

She was just about to head back to her bed when there was a sharp knock on her front door. She sat up abruptly, shooting Mingus a quick look. Her brother gestured for her to stay put as he stood, pulling a large revolver from the waistband of his pants. He eased his way to the door and peered out the peephole. With a shake of his head, he secured his weapon and pulled open the door.

Paul stood anxiously on the other side. Simone jumped to her feet, excitement bubbling up as she threw herself into his arms. Her arms locked around his neck as he lifted her off the floor, her legs sliding around his waist and latching behind his lower back. The kiss was deep and intense, their two bodies so entwined that it was almost impossible for Simone to tell where hers began and his ended.

"I was worried about you," Simone gasped when she finally pulled herself from him. "Why didn't you return my calls?"

"Oliver and I ran into a little trouble. We had some unwanted company at the house."

"That's not good," Mingus interjected.

Paul shook his head. "No, it's not good. I don't know how they found the house, but we got lucky." He took a seat on the sofa and gave them a quick play-by-play of everything that had happened since she'd left Windsor.

Simone felt concerned. "Where's Oliver now? Is he safe?"

Paul nodded. "He should be landing in Atlanta as we speak. I dropped him off at Detroit Metro and made sure he got on a plane before I came here."

"He's not going to his house there, is he?" Mingus asked.

"No. He's going to stay with a friend."

"I'm going to put security on him until this is over," Mingus said as he began tapping a message into his cell phone. "When he calls, you tell him a man named Porter will contact him and will stay with him until I tell him otherwise."

"That's not..." Paul started before being interrupted.

"Yes. It is," Simone said firmly. "It's very necessary." She hugged him again, feeling immensely blessed to have him back with her. She had missed him, but until he had walked through the door, she hadn't realized just how much not having him there had actually hurt.

Mingus rolled his eyes skyward. "Well, on that note, I'm going to bed."

"You're staying?" Simone asked. "Now that Paul's here…" She paused, though seeing her brother's expression stalled her words.

"Until this is over, I am your personal bodyguard," Mingus answered. "And that goes for you, too, Paul. I'm the third wheel until further notice. And if you need to strike out on your own, someone from my team will be with you."

Paul extended his arm, the two men shaking hands. "Thank you," Paul said.

Mingus nodded. "She's got a full day tomorrow. You might want to make sure she gets some sleep." His comment was more of a demand than a casual statement.

"I swear!" Simone exclaimed. "You're not the boss of me, Mingus!" she yelled at her brother's back as he exited the room and disappeared down the hallway.

Paul laughed as he pulled her back into his arms and hugged her close.

"He's like having another father!" Simone quipped. "Even my dad's not that annoying!"

"Your brother is a great guy. I appreciate him being here to support us."

Simone shrugged. "Whatever!" She stepped out of his arms and took a step back. "Are you hungry? Do you want me to make you something to eat?"

Paul shook his head. "No, thank you. I'm exhausted. All I want is a shower and a bed."

Simone gave him a slight smile. "That I can make happen," she said as she moved to check the door lock one last time. "And I plan to personally tuck you in and kiss you good-night," she said, her voice dropping to a seductive tone.

As Paul smiled back, she grabbed his hand and pulled him along behind her to the master bedroom.

Hours later Simone's stomach was doing flips and her whole body convulsed with pleasure as Paul lay between her parted legs, his mouth pressed possessively to her most private place. His touch was determined, his tongue lapping at her greedily. Her body arched and then dipped as heat swarmed through her nerve endings and electricity fired through each sinewy muscle. His touch was wanton and intoxicating and Simone gasped for air at the intensity of it.

A shower had been reinvigorating for them both. Simone had joined him beneath the flow of warm water, needing to feel his body pressed closely to hers. She had dropped to her knees to worship at the fountain of his maleness until she had him unsteady on his feet, his whole body shuddering with gratification. Their need for each other had been volatile, something decadent and explosive rising with a vengeance between them. It was unexplainable and left them both drunk with wanting until they could barely see straight, and rational thought seemed virtually impossible.

She struggled not to cry out, the bedclothes clutched so tightly in her fists that her nails were digging deep into her flesh. Her back arched again and all her muscles vibrated like strings pinged on a violin. His name rolled past her lips, the sweetness of it melting like chocolate against her tongue. Her body exploded, her orgasm hitting with an intensity that had her shaking. Her temperature rose exponentially, perspiration bubbling against her skin. It was sheer bliss.

Paul crawled slowly up her body, a line of damp kisses teasing her flesh. He licked her belly button, one nipple, then nuzzled his face in the fold of her neck. The aftershocks still had her quivering and he helped her ride out the last waves of her orgasm before rolling onto his side to lie beside her. He adjusted a pillow beneath his head.

Simone muttered something, her words incoherent. She laughed, her back twisting against the mattress as she stretched her limbs. The lilt in her voice bounced sweetly off the walls.

Paul chuckled. "You okay?" he asked, his eyes lifting to stare over at her. He dropped his hand to her tummy and allowed his palm to rest gently against her.

"I'm better than okay," Simone finally answered. She shifted closer to him, needing to experience as much skin-to-skin contact as she could muster. She felt almost desperate for his body heat and the feel of his flesh against her own. Between missing him and worrying about him, her nerves had been frayed and she felt relieved to have him so close. "How about you?"

"I have no complaints," Paul said with just the slightest nod of his head.

He curled himself around her body, cradling Simone in his arms. His eyes were closed, and she could tell he was slowly slipping into that warm space between wake and slumber. His breathing began to slow, air coming in low, even gusts past his lips.

Simone settled into the comfort of each exhale, the sound not quite a purr as Paul began to snore softly. Just as she felt herself slipping into sleep with him, his deep voice vibrated through the late-night air.

"I need to speak with your father."

Simone nodded. "Okay."

"Okay, but before I do, now that you've had some time to think, I need to know what you want. Where are we going from here, Simone?"

Simone heaved a deep sigh, the conversation coming sooner than she'd anticipated. But she owed Paul answers and she couldn't continue to keep him hanging. He deserved better from her. Especially now that she was carrying his child.

"I owe you an apology," she said, her voice a loud whisper in the late night air. "Although I knew you'd understand why I left the way I did, I should have discussed it with you first. I know that you and I can't move forward if I'm not honest when things are off balance. And I was off balance. I was petrified and I didn't want you to see me be weak."

Silence filled the space between Paul reflected on her comment. He took a deep breath before he spoke. "Well, I didn't understand. I thought we were well past that point with each other. Don't you know that I don't see you as weak? Even when you're struggling with something? And even if you do experience a moment of weakness, I'm here to help you get through it! I'm not passing judgment."

"I'm flawed, Paul Reilly! Immeasurably flawed."

"You're dramatic, Simone. Overly dramatic!"

"I'm getting better. And, I'm committed to doing better. Because I want to be a great mother and a great wife. I want you to be proud of me. And I need you to trust that I will be everything our children need me to be."

"Children?"

"We need to plan at least one pregnancy. Like normal people do. Maybe when Junior here is five or six years old. That is, of course, as long as we don't have another accident when this kid is two or three."

"You can't run out on me again, Simone. If you do, I can't promise I'll chase after you. And you definitely can't run out on this baby if it gets hard. I can't promise what will happen if you do."

Simone swallowed, the emotion catching deep in her chest. Tears suddenly misted her eyes. "I swear, Paul. I will never make this mistake again! I love you! And I love our baby and I want us to be together, no matter where in the world it takes us."

Another moment of silence filled the air until Paul suddenly spoke again. "You know I love you, right?"

Simone shifted her buttocks against his pelvis. "Of course, I do. Why would you ask me that?"

"Just in case your father kills me after our conversation and I'm never able to tell you that again."

Simone giggled. "He won't kill you."

"You sure about that?"

"You're giving him his first grandchild. You'll be good as gold."

Paul's fingers danced warmly over the surface of her stomach, his thumb occasionally tapping against her belly button. Energy quivered with life beneath his touch. "We should go to sleep. We have to be up in a couple of hours," he finally whispered.

They both drifted back into the quiet, trading easy caresses as sleep began to consume them. Without anything else needing to be said, the decision had been made. They were having a baby, planning a future, and only needed to get past the problem that was conveniently being ignored.

"I'm filing the formal complaint with the FDA this afternoon and tomorrow we're holding the press conference to announce that we're bringing a civil lawsuit against Lender Pharmaceuticals." Simone made the pronouncement the next day over a bowl of yogurt and granola and a cup of morning coffee.

Paul was about to take a drink from his own cup of coffee when he paused midsip, suddenly feeling uneasy about the next steps. He knew they were opening a big can of worms and he was fearful the tactic might come back to bite them. It was one of the only times the unknown felt like it might be a challenge he wasn't equipped to beat.

"So, what can go wrong?" he asked. "Because I'm thinking something might go wrong."

Simone placed her cup onto the table, pushing it from her. "Nothing is perfectly fail-safe. We're not going to know what will happen until we take action. But we have the full support of my brother's law firm and that's going to bode well for us. Ellington has even agreed to personally sit second chair."

Paul nodded. "And you're good with working for your brother? I know how excited you were about the other law firm."

"I was excited, but when I reasoned what would be in the best interest of the case, and our family, joining Ellington's firm made more sense."

She took a breath before she continued. "Announcing the lawsuit will draw attention to Lender that I'm sure they're not going to be happy with. But I fully intend to shine a very bright spotlight on what they've done. I'm also going to shine a light on you."

"On me? Why me?"

"Because if you're the face of the complaint and the lawsuit, Lender is less likely to continue to try and come after you. How would it look if you publicly call them out for their wrongdoing and then something happens to you? That's not the kind of publicity they want. Trust me. That's also why we're holding the press conference at the hospital. I've already made the arrangements. I have every intention of doing whatever it takes for this to make national news and inevitably go viral and get international attention."

"The hospital has probably fired me by now."

"No, you're still very much employed. In fact, you're about to be their local hero. The crown prince of everything that should be right with medical care in today's environment. You'll need to present your studies to the board before we talk to the press, but that's just about giving them the facts of the case. You'll take a stand, defend the science, and our lives will go back to being normally dysfunctional."

Paul blew a heavy sigh, staring intently at Simone. She seemed unfazed, totally focused on a plan she was certain would put things right. She swallowed the last bite of her yogurt and stood up from the table, clearing away their dirty dishes.

"I need to get dressed," she said. "I have my doctor's appointment and then we need to get that arrest warrant lifted."

"That won't happen until Daddy lays eyes on you," Mingus interjected, moving into the room. "Good morning."

Paul shook his head. "Good morning."

"Parker can lift it, can't he?"

"Nope! The superintendent filed it. Only the superintendent can unfile it. There's also the option of an overly eager rookie pulling you over and taking you in. You might even get tased if you're lucky," Mingus said sarcastically.

"So, after we leave the doctor's, we need to go see your

father," Paul said, rising from his own seat. "I can't afford to get arrested."

"Well, we also have an appointment with the hospital administrator this afternoon and I need to run by my new office so I can start delegating the workload so we can prepare for tomorrow's press conference."

Simone took an inhale of air, holding it deep in her lungs. She already felt taxed from everything that needed to be accomplished before the day ended. She anticipated the next day would be equally exhausting. Despite her body functioning with a mind of its own, Simone was determined to push though and do what she needed to do. She couldn't afford to fail. Everything Paul held near and dear depended on her succeeding.

Paul moved to her side, seeming to read her mind. "Everything's going to be fine. We'll get through it and if it becomes too much for you, you need to let me know." He leaned and kissed her cheek.

Simone tapped her fingers against his chest. "I'm going to get dressed. You need to practice."

Paul looked confused. "Practice?"

"Begging. I'm sure my father won't accept anything less."

Mingus and Simone laughed heartily.

Paul nodded. "Yeah," he said, joining in with the laughter. "Today is going to be a very long day!"

Simone and Paul left the doctor's office with a prescription for prenatal vitamins, a lengthy list of follow-up appointments and well wishes from her favorite physician and his staff. Once his diagnosis had been confirmed, Paul sat with his chest pushed forward, gloating like it was his greatest accomplishment in the whole wide world. Simone was equally excited but determined not to let it show. Just in case. Nothing was certain in life and if the past few weeks were an indication of what might lie ahead of them, she didn't want to tempt fate and be disappointed.

Mingus drove them from the medical center to their brother's law offices and waited while the two went upstairs to see Simone's new space and meet her staff. Paul stood back, pride painting his expression as she threw herself right into the fray, giving orders. It took no time at all for everyone to know that she was living up to her reputation. She was known for being a fierce litigator: well-prepared, fair-minded and tough as nails. She expected one-hundred-percent from anyone working for her because she always gave that and much more. She was impressive, and watching her, Paul understood how passionate she was about the work she did. She loved her job as much as he loved his. As she settled in, he excused himself, taking the elevator back down to the lobby.

Mingus was leaning against the car, his arms crossed over his chest. Paul joined him. Standing side by side, the two looked like perfection sculpted from clay. It didn't escape Paul's attention that passersby were taking notice of them, some staring blatantly. He was acutely aware that a few women gawked, and they were drawing attention that neither had anticipated.

"Well, now," Paul said, as a young woman wearing skin-tight leggings, wedge sneakers and a bomber jacket stopped to press her telephone number into the palm of Mingus's hand.

Mingus winked his eye at her and when she rounded the corner out of sight, he tore the sliver of paper into tiny pieces and dropped them to the ground. "These women will get you hurt out here," he muttered.

Paul laughed. "I don't typically have problems like that."

"Give it time. I bet as soon as you're in the park pushing little junior around in his stroller, the women will be all over you."

Paul laughed. "And Simone will definitely hurt someone."

"Starting with you," her brother added.

A moment passed before Mingus spoke again. "You know, if you were anyone else, I'd kick your ass for knocking up my sister. But since she loves you, and the rest of us actually like you, I'm going to give you a pass."

Paul chuckled. "Do you think your father will give me a pass?"

"Oh, hell no! You're a dead man walking."

Paul stole a quick glance down to the cell phone in his hand for the time. It wasn't quite the lunch hour and he anticipated Simone wouldn't be finished anytime soon. He sent her a quick text message, advising her to stay put until he returned. When she replied, asking where he was going, he told her a little white lie, not wanting her to worry. Knowing that she was already stressed had shifted him into protective mode, wanting to ensure he did nothing to add to her anxiety. There was a quick back-and-forth exchange before she seemed to be content with his answers.

He turned his attention to Mingus. "Do you know where I can find your father right now?"

Mingus nodded. "Yeah, why?"

"I think I need to speak with him without Simone. She said she'd like to work until we have to meet the hospital administrator and I could use a ride."

Mingus reached for his own cell phone, shooting Ellington and Simone both a message. He suddenly gestured toward two men parked in a car on the other side of the street. The passenger nodded, then exited the vehicle and crossed over to where they stood.

"If she tries to leave, send me a message," Mingus said.

The man nodded, shooting Paul a quick look before moving into the building to take up space in the lobby.

"They work for you?" Paul questioned.

"Yeah. Backup. Just in case. You have a target on your back, remember?" He rounded the car to the driver's side and opened the door.

Paul shot a look over his shoulder as he slid into the passenger seat. "It's hard to forget," he muttered.

Minutes later they pulled into a parking space on Forty-Seventh and King Drive. As they stepped out of the car, both men stole glances around the block, looking up one side of the street and down the other. Mingus pointed toward the entrance to Peach's Restaurant.

Paul shot his friend a look. "You're really making me interrupt your father's lunch?"

Mingus shrugged, his grin a mile wide. "You asked me where he was, and this is where he is. Every other Thursday from eleven thirty until two. Meeting with the other Southside Heavies."

Paul's gaze narrowed. "Southside Heavies?"

"You'll see," he said as he moved toward the restaurant's entrance and pulled open the door.

The two men stepped inside, and Mingus pointed Paul toward the back of the room and a table surrounded by eight men in deep conversation. Paul recognized Simone's father, Jerome Black, and Pastor Randolph Hinton from Mount Episcopal Baptist Church, one of Chicago's most renowned megachurches. The others looked equally prestigious and intimidating.

"The man seated next to my father is Darryl 'T-Dog' Rockman. He's a lieutenant with the Disciple Kings. Beside him is Alderman Lincoln Haynes and next to him is real estate mogul Maxton Price. He owns a good third of the property on the south side of the city."

"I recognize Pastor Hinton and the man beside him looks familiar, but I can't place where I know him from."

"That's Illinois House Speaker Mike Zell. And on his left is Floyd Mac of Mac's Barbershop, and last, but not least, Dr. Gregory Graves, founder and director of The Graves Boys Academy."

Understanding fell against Paul's shoulders. The men around that table were renowned for their activism in the community, each impacting the lives of its citizens in ways that weren't always visible to the public. They were highly respected by their core base and carried significant weight in what did, and more important, what *didn't* happen on the South Side of Chicago. It was a truce of major proportions to have them all seated around a table breaking bread together.

Paul nodded, slightly awe-struck. The magnitude of what was going on was not lost on him. The men around that table were iconic, superheroes to the Chicago masses. He aspired to accomplish a third of what most of them in the room had already accomplished in their lifetimes. He found himself hoping that his work to right the wrongs of Lender Pharmaceuticals would have as significant an impact to those who had trusted him with their health. "Southside Heavies!"

Mingus grinned. "You know Miss Nanette, don't you?"

"Yes," Paul said. Nanette was a fixture in her Chicago neighborhood, a community mother of sorts. Everybody on the South Side who knew her, loved her. She was known to feed the neighborhood to help pay her mortgage, selling plates of her home-cooked offerings. Her home was considered neutral ground for the gangs, and at any given time the lowest of the city's downtrodden and Chicago's most elite could be found dining together at her table.

"Miss Nanette coined the phrase. In fact, she instigated the first meeting of the Southside Heavies. Periodically, the faces change. Members drop or are added but they all come to the table with the same mission. To do what's best for the residents they serve."

A pretty woman with a satin-smooth complexion suddenly stepped forward to greet them warmly. "Table for two, gentlemen?"

Paul shook his head. "We just need Superintendent Black's attention for a quick minute."

She threw a glance toward the table of men and then turned back toward him. "They really don't like to be disturbed."

"It'll be fine," Mingus said as he pushed past the woman and headed in his father's direction.

Paul grinned sheepishly. "Sorry about that," he said, "but it won't be a problem. I promise."

The woman's eyes were wide as saucers as her gaze floated after them. Jerome Black looked up, only slightly surprised as the two men stopped at his table. "Mingus! I wasn't..." he started just as Mingus side-stepped and Paul slid front and center. The patriarch sat back in his seat, eyeing Paul intently. "Dr. Reilly."

"Good afternoon, sir," Paul said, acutely aware that every eye was suddenly focused on him. His nerves felt fried and his knees were shaking as he struggled not to let his anxiety show.

There was a moment of hesitation and then the Simone's father introduced them. "Gentlemen, I'm sure you all know my son Mingus."

There was a round of nods and greetings, Mingus

shaking hands with the pastor and dapping fists with the gang leader.

"And this is Dr. Paul Reilly."

"Good afternoon," Paul responded, moving to shake hands as each man introduced himself. He turned his attention back to Simone's father. "I apologize for the interruption," Paul said, "but I was hoping to have a quick word with you, sir. Or if I might schedule some time to speak with you later?"

"No. We need to talk now!" Superintendent Black snapped. He stood up, excusing himself from the table. He gestured for Paul to follow behind him. As the two men disappeared toward the restaurant's kitchen, Mingus slid into the seat his father had just vacated.

Laughter rang out warmly behind them as the two men sauntered through the kitchen area and out the back door to the alley in the rear. Jerome turned, both hands clutching his sides. The patriarch was a distinguished man with salt-and-pepper hair, a rich, chocolate-brown complexion and a full beard and mustache. He was tall and the two men stood eye to eye evenly. His expression was stoic, and Paul knew he was in a mood, and clearly not happy. For a split second Paul would have preferred going hand-to-hand in combat with the two men from Lender than the conversation he was about to have with Simone's father.

"Where is my daughter?"

"She's safe, sir. At the moment, she's at Ellington's law office, working."

Jerome gave him a slight nod, seeming to file that bit of information away. "How dare you put my child in harm's way? Have you completely lost your mind?"

"No, sir, and I did everything I could possibly do to ensure Simone was safe."

He shouted, "You should have never left the state with

her! You should have turned yourselves in to the police so that we could have protected you both. That's what you should have done!"

Paul didn't respond as the man continued to rant. There was nothing he could say to defend his actions, or Simone's. They had worried her parents, and her father was spewing that back at him. Paul understood his fear because he had also felt it, unable to shake the emotion, even when he and Simone had been going through it together. Most especially after discovering she was pregnant, their unborn child inadvertently in danger as well. There was nothing he could do but apologize.

"I'm very sorry, sir. It was never my intention to put Simone in harm's way. We were just reacting to the situation to the best of our ability. The decisions we made were done with no ill will intended, sir."

Jerome snapped, "I expected you, of all people, to have an ounce of sense more than Simone. I know how impulsive my daughter can sometimes be. I expected you would be able to keep her in line. I was depending on you!" He swiped a hand across his brow as he turned, inhaling deep, swift breaths to calm his nerves.

"Again, sir, I regret how things happened. We never meant to worry you or Judge Black. But Simone is safe and well." He took a breath as Simone's father turned back around to stare at him. His eyes were narrowed, and his brow was furrowed. Paul imagined that if looks could kill he might actually be standing there dead. He persisted.

"Superintendent, I love Simone. Your daughter is my entire world and I would give my own life to protect hers."

Jerome grunted, his eyes rolling skyward.

Paul continued, "I know that there is nothing I can say right now that will help you to understand why we did what we did, so I'm not going to try. But I need you to believe me when I tell you how much Simone means to me. I hope to make her my wife and for that to happen, sir, we both need your blessing. Simone would never have me if she didn't have your permission. She respects your opinion, sir, and it would not sit well with her if you didn't approve of me, or our being together.'

Jerome took another deep breath, but he didn't say anything. The muscles in his face, though, had relaxed significantly and the vein that had been pulsing with a vengeance just minutes earlier had calmed significantly. Paul took that as a good sign. He continued to talk.

"Simone wanted to be here when I spoke to you, but I knew I needed to speak with you first. Man to man. Because I love Simone as much as I do, sir—it's just as important to me that you support our being together. Not just for Simone, but because I don't ever want you to doubt that I have your daughter's best interests at heart. Or that I won't do whatever it takes to protect and take care of her."

Jerome stared at him intently, his head bobbing in a slow nod. "I guess she could do worse," he finally muttered, a hint of levity returning to his tone.

Paul smiled, feeling his mouth lift in an easy bend. "Let's just hope she can't do any better!" he said.

Jerome laughed heartily. "I'm still pissed," he said after the moment of flippancy passed.

Paul took another deep breath. "Then I should probably share our other news with you now."

"Do I even want to hear this?"

There was just the briefest moment of hesitation and then Paul said, "Simone and I are pregnant. We're expecting a baby. I'm excited about it, but she still has some reservations. She needs your support now more than ever. I need your support because Simone and that baby are my family and I don't want to lose them."

The silence grew full and thick as Jerome just continued to stare Paul down. Paul sensed that the levity that had risen between them had been quickly extinguished. He suddenly wished he could find a hole to crawl into, something like fear piercing his midsection. He watched the patriarch's jaw tighten as he ground his teeth together and that vein was pulsing like it was trying to sync with a marching band.

Jerome suddenly snapped, "I swear! I should just lock your ass up and throw away the damn key!" He did an about-face, moving back through the door into the kitchen, the fixture slamming harshly behind him.

Paul hesitated before he followed, thinking he might have pricked the man's last good nerve. Wondering if he had just overshared before the patriarch had been ready. He clearly wasn't happy or excited by the news and Paul wondered if he was rethinking whether or not he approved of Paul being with his daughter. He blew a heavy sigh, his hands clutching his sides. He leaned his head back, his eyes closed as he whispered a quick prayer skyward.

Minutes later Paul reentered the dining room, moving back to the table, and Mingus, who stood at his father's side. The superintendent had retaken his seat. The others around the table all turned to stare, giving him a harsh look. Paul was suddenly very uncomfortable and then just like that, they broke out in laughter. Simone's father was shaking his head from side to side.

The two men said their goodbyes and exited the restaurant. As they made their way to the car, Mingus slapped him against the back. "Dad said to tell you he expects you at Sunday dinner. He also said I should kick your ass if you even think about not showing up."

Paul blew a sigh of relief and grinned. "Trust and believe, my brother, that won't be a problem. By the way, did he by chance mention whether or not he's lifted that warrant he issued for my arrest?"

When Paul walked into Simone's law office, she was on the phone being harangued by her father. Jerome had gotten to her, reiterating his displeasure with the two of them. Simone was listening, unable to get in a word as her father bellowed over the phone line, as Paul dropped down onto the small sofa that decorated the space, empathy painting his expression.

Simone shot him a look, her eyes rolling skyward. Annoyance flooded through her, compounded by frustration as her to-do list played in rotation in her head. She didn't have the time or the energy for her father's tantrum, but she also knew she needed to let him vent because he was really pissed with her and Paul.

She nodded into the receiver. "Yes, sir… No, sir… but… I didn't…yes, sir…we were planning…" Simone sighed and pulled the phone from her ear. She cupped her palm over the mouthpiece. "Did he scream at you, too?"

Paul nodded. "He ripped me a new one! My ass still hurts!"

With a slow shake of her head, Simone pulled the phone back to her ear. "Yes, Daddy… I promise…we will… I can't…okay…okay…yes, sir…yes… I love you, too, Daddy!"

After disconnecting the line, Simone tossed her phone to the desktop and joined Paul on the sofa. For a brief moment they sat staring at each other and then both laughed.

"That was rough," Paul said. "I really thought he was going to lock me up and forget where he put the key."

"He still might. He hasn't yelled at me like that since I was in high school. I felt like I was six years old all over again." It hadn't been often that her father had yelled when she'd been a child, but Simone had always dreaded those moments. As she'd gotten older, she realized his bark was worse than his bite and if she simply sat and listened, those moments would pass quickly and she'd be his favorite baby girl again.

"I think he still likes me, though," Paul said.

Simone laughed. "I know he likes you. You've been summoned to Sunday dinner. He likes you a lot." She lifted her face to kiss his lips.

"That's good, because I really wasn't planning to go anywhere," Paul said as he kissed her back. "So, how has the rest of your day been?"

"Busy, but I think we're ready for tomorrow. You and I need to go through the data one last time. Then we'll send our formal complaint to the FDA with copies of all our documents. When we leave here, we'll go sit down with the hospital administrator and their legal team, present our case so that they are aware of what you are doing and why, then I just want to go home and put my feet up."

Paul nodded. "If you're up to it, I'd like to make one more stop. I'd like to run by our friend Liza's to see if she can look something up for us. There is something that's been bothering me."

Simone laughed. "She's a hacker, Paul, not a library!"

He shrugged. "She's good at what she does and if she finds what I think she can find, it will further support our case."

"Then we run by there. Are you looking for something in particular?"

"I need the FDA test data for those three Lender drugs that were banned."

"Is any of that public data?"

"I'm not sure. I can call and ask first, but I'm thinking it probably isn't. But I need to see the numbers and compare them to the results Oliver and I got from some of our tests. Your theory that maybe those drugs and Halphedrone-B are actually one and the same has been gnawing at me. If those drugs are contaminated and the contaminant is the same, it may be enough to prove they simply changed the name and knowingly repackaged a tainted product."

"I was just throwing it out there as a what-if."

"I know, but if you're right…" His voice trailed off as he considered the possibility.

Simone finished the thought for him. "If we're right, then Lender purposely poisoned patients and sheer greed was their motivation. Bottom line, if they knowingly sold drugs that had been previously banned, that's criminal and I want to do whatever we can to shutter their doors."

"I honestly find it unfathomable that no one in that company would have found this to be wrong on every level imaginable."

Simone gave him a nod. "Well, let's go see what we can find out. Let me send my brother a text so he can warn Liza that we're coming," she said as she rose from her seat and moved to reclaim her telephone.

"If Ellington doesn't mind, I'd like to borrow an empty office," Paul said. "I need to place some calls to my colleagues overseas. They need to be aware of what's going on. I think if I tell them that we've gone forward with filing the complaint and that we're announcing our intent to sue the drug company the doctors will be more inclined to pull the drugs voluntarily instead of waiting for an official recall."

"Follow me," Simone said. "I'll find you some space. I actually have a little juice in this joint."

Paul laughed. "Simone, please don't get yourself fired. It's only your very first day!"

* * *

The office receptionist waved for Simone's attention as she and Paul were headed out the door. Excitement bubbled from the young woman's cheery spirit, her exuberance a refreshing greeting to clients. Her name was Candace, and like Simone, she was new to the firm.

"Attorney Black, there's a package here for you. It was just delivered." Candace pushed a white container across the marble counter toward Simone. It was the size of a large shoe box and nondescript, with no identifiable markings.

"For me?" Simone's eyes widened in surprise, the delivery unexpected. "Do you know who it's from?"

"One of the local delivery services dropped it off, but there was no card attached to the outside."

"Did you have to sign for it?"

Candace suddenly looked nervous that maybe she'd done something wrong. "No, ma'am. He just said he had a package for you and then he turned around and left."

"Were you expecting something?" Paul questioned, suddenly on guard. He stepped between Simone and the box, the gesture instinctively protective.

Simone shook her head. "No. Unless someone in the family sent it. Maybe a welcome gift? Parker and Armstrong had flowers delivered earlier today to say congratulations."

"Text everyone and ask," Paul said as he lifted the box from the counter and moved swiftly to the conference room, setting it in the center of the table.

Within minutes of Simone pushing Send on the text message, Mingus and one of his associates stepped off the elevator, both moving swiftly to where they stood in the conference room door. "Did you try to open it?"

her brother questioned, looking from them to Candace and back.

Simone shook her head. "Paul just carried it from the reception desk to there."

"I shook it," Candance interjected, her voice a loud whisper as she stood twisting her hands together nervously. "I don't know if that's important."

Mingus nodded, then moved to the table, spinning the box in a slow circle.

"Be careful," Simone admonished. "Maybe we should call Parker and have him send over a bomb team?"

Paul shot her a look. "You need to stand back, please."

"You both need to stand back," she snapped back.

The man with Mingus pushed past the couple and closed the door, leaving them standing on the outside of the room.

Paul inhaled a deep breath. "We're not doing this. This is ridiculous," he said, turning to face Simone. "We can't live like this. You and the baby are my life. If anything happened to either of you…" The words caught in his chest as he choked back hot tears that threatened to fall from his eyes.

Simone was crying, her anxiety level having finally spilled over. She stepped into his arms, grabbing at the front of his shirt as he pulled her against him.

The door to the conference room suddenly flew open, Mingus's associate moving swiftly past them back toward the elevator. Mingus stood in the corner of the room on his cell phone. His expression was stone, no hint of emotion across his face.

They moved into the room, their gazes questioning as he disconnected the call.

"What is it?" Simone asked.

"Where do you two need to go from here?" Mingus asked.

Paul answered. "The hospital for a meeting and then I wanted to swing by and see Liza."

Simone asked again. "What's in the damn box?"

Mingus shook his head. "Parker's on his way to get the box. He wants to dust it for prints. I doubt he'll find anything, though. My guy is headed to see if he can track down that delivery man."

"Is it something bad?" Simone persisted.

"I need to put a few more of my people in place and then we'll leave," he responded, ignoring her question.

Simone shook her head, moving closer to the table. "Why won't you tell me..." she started.

"Leave it alone, Simone," Mingus said.

"Is it bad?" Paul asked, his anxiety level still rippling with a vengeance.

Simone flipped her hand at her brother as she moved to the box. The top was askew and she pushed it off to peer inside, pulling the box toward her.

The cry that echoed around the room was gut-wrenching. It was a dull wail that sounded like pain and fear twisted in a tight knot. It pierced the quiet in the room with such turmoil that Paul and Mingus both rushed to Simone's side.

"Damn, Simone!" Mingus admonished.

Paul reached for her, trying to pull her close, but Simone pitched forward back toward the door and dropped to her knees, vomiting into the trash can in the corner. Tears streamed down her face and she was shaking.

The two men exchanged a look as Paul turned to see what Simone had seen. A small kitten lay inside the container, its little head severed from its tiny body and its white fur matted with dried blood. Paul closed his eyes, fighting the urge to rage. The cruelty of the act was beyond reason. He turned and moved to where Simone sat sobbing. He pressed his hands to her shoulders and pulled her from the floor.

"I need to take her home," he said to Mingus. "I'm canceling the meeting."

"No," Simone said, swiping at her eyes as she fought to regain her composure.

"Simone, you're not safe. They were clearly sending us a message. So, we're finished. We're not doing this."

"Yes, we are," she said, sniffling loudly. "We have to, Paul. We can't let them scare us off."

"Well, I am scared. I'm scared to death that something will happen to you and the baby. I would never survive that, Simone."

Simone wrapped her arms around his neck and kissed his cheek. She pressed her palm to his chest and tapped gently. "I'm going to the restroom to freshen up my face. Then we need to leave or we're going to be late for our appointment. We didn't come this far to quit," she said.

"Besides, we have a whole police department behind us," Simone continued as she pointed toward the lobby and the officers who were headed in their direction.

Paul and Mingus locked gazes. "Can you talk some sense into her?" he asked.

Mingus shrugged. "Not my fight, bro! I'm just here to protect and serve."

As Paul watched her walk away, disappearing down the length of corridor to the restrooms a wave of despair washed over him. Simone wanted to push forward, and he knew nothing he could say would deter her. She would get her way. But this message had been way too close for comfort and he had to make sure he stopped the threat to their safety in its tracks. He just wasn't sure how.

Chapter 16

When Simone woke the next morning, Paul was still poring over the documents Liza had found for him the previous day. Piles of paper were strewn around her living room and he sat at the kitchen table entering data into a program on his computer. He hadn't gotten an ounce of sleep and he was clearly singularly focused on finding an answer to questions that hadn't been asked yet.

He looked up as she moved into the room, heading to the kitchen for a cup of coffee. A bright smile pulled across his face. "Good morning, beautiful!"

"Good morning! Did you come to bed at all?"

Paul shook his head. "No. I had to weed through this information. Plus, after that delivery yesterday, I had a lot on my mind."

Simone nodded her understanding because she hadn't rested well, either. "Did you find anything?" she asked, gesturing toward the papers in his hand. She inserted a decaffeinated K-Cup coffee pod into her Keurig coffee maker and pushed the start button.

"As a matter of fact, I did," Paul said, a smug smile crossing his face. "I compared the lab results from those products that were rejected to the products we studied, and the similarities are undeniable. The contamination is even worse in some cases. I think we can prove Lender renamed and relabeled contaminated products and has been selling them as Halphedrone-B. Looking back over some of their financial records, the costs for the initial production of the drug cut deep into their bottom line. I think they stopped production after the second year and replaced it with merchandise that had been previously rejected. Product that's been stockpiled in a warehouse in Mumbai because if they had destroyed that excess drug it would have crippled their profit margins. They'd already gotten Halphedrone-B approved and no one was looking hard at subsequent product. I believe we can make the case and connect many of the dots."

Simone sat down at the table, bringing two freshly brewed cups of coffee. She passed one to Paul who took it eagerly, his excitement abundant. He obviously felt like he'd struck gold and the joy was written all over his face.

"So," she said, her mind beginning to race. "I now have to figure out how we introduce stolen evidence. Because we're not supposed to have this data, so we can't just say *look at this* without them questioning how we came into the information."

Paul took a large sip of his coffee. "You'll figure it out. I believe in you! And if not, maybe they can give us side-by-side prison cells."

Simone smiled. "I may have to call in a few favors because I don't look good in convict stripes."

Paul laughed as he took a second sip of brew. "What time is the press conference?"

"Three thirty. We need to be at the hospital before then, though. I have a few loose ends to tie up and obviously I need to figure out how to include or not include this new information. I should probably run it by Ellington when I get into the office."

"Please, do that. Please!"

Simone rolled her eyes. "What are you going to do between now and then?"

"I need to get a few hours of sleep, then I'm heading over to the hospital. I need to get updated on a few patients and hopefully start to get back to work. I should already be there in plenty enough time for the press conference."

"Just don't be late."

"I won't be late, Simone."

"Just to be sure I'll send Mingus back to get you."

"I can drive. I know he'll have one of his guys tailing me, but he definitely doesn't have to go out of his way," Paul said.

"Yes, he does. It's necessary. Just to be safe."

"Just to make sure I show up?" he shot back.

"I know how much you hate public events."

"I hate giving speeches and I definitely don't plan to speak this afternoon, so do not put me on the spot."

"Would I do that?" she asked.

"I mean it, Simone!"

She giggled. "No worries, baby! I got you!"

Paul shook his head, his look skeptical. "I need a shower and then I need to lie down. How soon before you leave?"

"I'm going to finish my coffee, then get dressed. I'll leave right after that. If you're asleep, I won't wake you. But make sure you set your alarm."

Paul stood up and shuffled his papers into a neat pile. He leaned to kiss her cheek. There was just a moment of hesitation, his lips lingering against her skin, as if a question on the tip of his tongue, as if he suddenly felt uncertain about asking it.

Simone sensed his trepidation as she pressed her palm to the side of his face, leaning back to stare into his eyes. "We've got this," she answered. "Everything's going to be fine. I promise."

As Paul headed toward the bedroom, Simone sat back

in her chair, dropping into reflection. They were going through the motions, pretending all was well, even as doubt and uncertainty kept rearing its head. What had happened in the office had left her battered. And angry. She hated being threatened and she didn't take the warning lightly, but she refused to let it beat her. Because for as much as she needed Paul and his strength to forge ahead, he needed her to be equally as strong. They were both on emotional overload and her hormones were spinning her in a hundred different directions. But she was determined to be the rock he needed, an immovable boulder barreling against anything that threatened their future.

Despite concerns about his safety and that of his patients, Paul had finished his rounds at the hospital and was going through patient charts when Nurse Grace knocked on his door. She poked her head inside to see if he was busy.

"I'm sorry. I didn't mean to disturb you, but you have a visitor."

Paul looked up from the lab results he was reading. "A visitor?"

"Vivian Lincoln would like a minute to speak with you. And I apologize, I don't remember which drug firm she's with."

"Is she alone?"

Grace nodded. "She is. If this isn't a good time, I can send her away. I already told her you have an appointment with Dr. Cartwright, so you won't have much time for her," she said, referring to the hospital administrator.

After a moment of consideration Paul nodded. "That's fine. You can send her in," he said. With Mingus's men positioned outside the door and in strategic locations on the hospital floor, Paul doubted highly that he needed to be worried about Vivian trying anything. He had to wonder, though, what she wanted and why she was there. He closed the files he'd been reviewing and placed them on the credenza that sat behind him.

He reached for his phone, debating if he should text Simone. He decided to wait until he saw her and could answer the mountain of questions he anticipated would be coming.

There was a second knock on the door. "Come in," Paul called out as he moved onto his feet and rounded the desk to stand in front of it.

Vivian moved through the entrance, closing the door behind herself. "Dr. Reilly."

Paul nodded, noting the formality in her tone. He responded likewise. "Ms. Lincoln. What brings you here?"

Her gaze swept the length of his body, shifting from his head to the floor and back. "May I sit down?"

Paul gestured toward a seat with his hand. "Please."

"Thank you."

Paul returned to his own seat, still eyeing her cautiously. An air of tension had risen in the room, feeling like thick mud weighing him down. "So, to what do I owe the honor?"

"Let's not play games, Paul. You need to call off this witch hunt. There is absolutely nothing wrong with our product and your lies will only serve to discredit you."

"Excuse me?"

She continued, "We have people at the FDA, so we're fully aware of the complaint you lodged this afternoon. And I understand you have questions and concerns, but you're blowing this well out of proportion. Lender is in the business of saving lives and you're trying to criminalize our efforts."

Paul bristled, indignation rising with a vengeance. The

audacity of her statement was laughable. That she honestly thought he'd file a complaint without proof would have been insulting if he had cared about her opinion.

"I have people at the FDA as well, and I trust there will be a thorough investigation into any and all claims I may have. I'm trying to hold Lender accountable for their actions. If everything is as copasetic as you claim, then you shouldn't have anything to worry about."

"You really don't want to do this. If you know what's good for you…" Her eyebrows lifted, her head tilting slightly as she glared at him.

"Is that a threat?"

Vivian stood back up, her high heels clicking against the tiled floor. Her lips were pursed as if she'd sucked on something sour. "We don't make threats, Dr. Reilly. But I assure you, this will not go the way you think it will."

Paul smiled, narrowing his gaze. Clearly, he had struck a nerve and he found it interesting that Vivian Lincoln, of all people, was trying to strongarm him. "I consider myself warned."

She moved to the door, pausing to stare back at him. "By the way, I don't take kindly to being stood up."

"Well, I don't take kindly to being *set* up," Paul quipped.

Still looking like she'd swallowed spoiled milk, Vivian hesitated in the entrance, as if there was one last thing she needed to say, but she didn't, instead, slamming the door closed as she made her exit.

Paul felt his heart racing and he released the breath of air that he'd swallowed. He wasn't sure whether to be concerned or not, but he knew it was too late for them to retract their complaint or to withdraw the lawsuit Simone had filed during her lunch break.

He thought about the children and families still suffering because of Lender and he didn't care what Vivian, or her company, thought about what they were doing. He was determined to stop them, no matter what it took.

The alarm on his Apple watch vibrated against his wrist. The hospital Powers That Be were waiting for him. Although they would remain neutral with relation to his legal actions, they stated at their meeting the previous evening that the administration and the hospital's board had vowed to stand behind him in support. Paul knew it had less to do with him and much to do with reducing their liability to the patients impacted by the drugs that had been prescribed by their staff. After the cat incident it had been welcome news, and as Simone had succinctly pointed out, they were better served standing on the side of what was right than supporting what was very wrong.

Hanging his white coat on a hook in the closet, Paul changed into his suit jacket. With one quick adjustment of his necktie, he took a deep breath to calm his nerves and headed to the conference room on the top floor of the medical facility.

An hour later, after a brief meeting, Paul followed the hospital's board members and legal team out to the south side of the building. The warm temperatures felt more like early fall than the last of winter; the sun was still shining brightly in a clear blue sky, and Paul imagined it was very much a seasonal calm before an unexpected storm.

The meeting had been brief, and most of their time had been spent waiting for everyone to arrive. The discussion had been to reiterate the hospital's position and to ensure everyone was on the same page when the press asked questions. He hadn't had much to say, still mulling over his conversation with Vivian. He also still had doubts that this was the right route to go, but there was no turning back from the decision.

He was surprised by the crowd that stood on the hospital's steps. Simone must have gotten the attention of every news affiliate that reported on the city of Chicago. Reporters, podcasters and journalists stood closely together. A few were doing sound bites to lead into the story. Others were jotting notes into well-worn composition books or dictating into handheld recorders.

There was also a very visible police presence. Uniformed officers were maintaining crowd control. The superintendent himself stood toward the back of the crowd, his wife standing by his side to show their daughter support.

Simone stood at the podium, Ellington by her side. The two looked cucumber cool, unfazed by the flurry of activity around them. There were last-minute microphone checks and one of the paralegals was passing out envelopes of information that included the press release and an assortment of supporting documents.

At one point Simone turned, searching him out, and when their gazes connected, she gave him the sweetest smile and a nod of her head. For reasons he knew he would never be able to verbalize, he was taken aback by the confidence she exuded. She wore it like a badge of honor that complemented the winter-white suit draped around her body. It was paired with an emerald-green satin tank and green suede pumps, and she was stunning. In his heart he saw a warrior woman: fierce, determined and a force to be reckoned with. It was Simone at her very best; the woman he had always known was there even when she herself hadn't been sure. Just the sight of her calmed every ounce of his nervous anxiety.

Simone gestured for him and his colleagues to come

stand on the step directly behind her. He took a deep breath, knowing that they were minutes away from sharing what he had been haunted by for close to a year. It was a moment of reckoning and he could only pray that fate would serve them well as he walked to Simone.

Paul had just reached her side, Simone placing a hand on his forearm as she reached to whisper in his ear, when he heard gunshots ring out. The harsh explosions rattled the calm, the too familiar *bang, bang, bang* sounding loudly through the afternoon air.

Paul was unprepared for the chaos that suddenly ensued, most in the crowd taking flight. He looked left and then right as he grabbed Simone by the shoulders and threw himself around her, pushing her down to the ground. The protective gesture was second nature, her safety his only concern. Beside him, Ellington was shouting but the words were undiscernible, nothing resonating in Paul's ears but the echo of gunfire and the loud screams of panic.

Out of the corner of his eye he saw Mingus racing in their direction, his gun drawn. Other officers were also rushing toward the danger, searching for whomever had fired the shots. It was then that Paul felt the warm flow of blood pouring over his hand, the offending ooze spreading like a Rorschach inkblot across Simone's white blazer. Her body had gone limp and as he turned her in his arms, he realized Simone had been shot; bullets presumably meant for him had struck her instead. Shock wafted through his spirit, holding hands with panic like he'd never known before. He gasped loudly, then screamed her name.

He swept Simone up into his arms and raced toward the hospital's entrance. Muscle memory kicked into action as Paul shifted into doctor mode, screaming out triage instructions. As he reached the doors he called for a gurney and medical supplies, his hands pressed against Simone's two bullet wounds to help stall the bleeding. For Paul the doctor, the moment should have been no different than any other experience he'd had in various war zones. But this was Simone and their unborn baby! This was everything he valued in life. That moment would forever haunt him if he got it wrong and he was determined to get it right, calling on every ounce of medical training he had ever had.

It took less than three minutes before Simone was being rushed into an emergency room bay, a nurse cutting away her new suit so that they could inspect her injuries.

Minutes later, after conducting an assessment of her vital signs and getting an IV started, Paul was still shouting out instructions as another doctor, the surgeon on call, pushed him out of the way and took charge. For a split second Paul lashed out, refusing to relinquish control. Desperation was fueling his efforts, his need to bring Simone back from the brink exponential. Adrenaline coursed through his blood stream and he stood toe to toe with the other man, shaking with rage in his leather shoes.

"Dr. Reilly, we need you out of the way, please. We'll take good care of your wife," he said.

Paul nodded, seeing no need to correct the man. Simone wasn't his wife, but she would be. It might not have been official, but she was his, heart and soul. She was the air he breathed, the water he drank, the sweetest dreams when he slept, the lifeline that kept him standing. She was so much more, and he didn't have the words to tell the other man so. Then suddenly he did.

"She's pregnant," he advised. "Approximately six weeks or so along. We're having a baby. You need to save them both!"

The other doctor nodded as he issued an additional list of instructions as they were pushing Simone out of the emergency room toward the surgical wing.

It was all too surreal. Paul stood still as stone. He was shaking and he held out his blood-streaked hands, fighting to stall the quiver of adrenaline that had consumed him. He wasn't quite sure where next to turn.

"Dr. Reilly? Dr. Reilly?"

Paul did an about-face toward the emergency room nurse calling his name. "I'm sorry, do you need me?"

"The family is gathered in the waiting room, wanting an update. I didn't know if you wanted to give that to them yourself or if you'd prefer Dr. Kennedy do it."

Paul took a deep breath, shaking himself from the trance he'd fallen into. His emotions were raw, and he had no sense of time and place. He only wanted to be in the operating room. He wanted to trade places with Simone, to move her far from the hurt that had rendered her helpless. He needed to be useful and he was feeling everything but. He suddenly couldn't get enough air into his lungs and he bent forward, hands pressed against his thighs as he sucked in oxygen. He felt broken and he had to dig deep to find the strength he knew Simone needed from him.

"Are you okay, Dr. Reilly?" the woman asked, moving swiftly to his side.

He nodded. "I just need a minute to clean myself up," he said to the nurse who was still standing there, staring at him. "Get me an update from the surgical team and then I'll go speak with the family."

"Yes, sir," she said as she turned and exited the room.

Paul moved to a supply closet and found a clean set of hospital scrubs to change into. He didn't want Simone's mother to see his suit covered in her daughter's blood. Quickly discarding his clothes on the floor, he washed his hands and face, then moved back to the nursing station and the nurse he'd spoken to just moments earlier. She held out the telephone for him to speak with the operating room, the words barely registering as he listened to the surgical resident on the other end give him an update on Simone's status.

"Thank you," he said finally as he disconnected the call. He took two deep breaths still trying to calm his nerves.

"Can I get you anything, Dr. Reilly?" another nurse questioned.

Paul shook his head. "Thank you. No. I'm good."

The two women exchanged quick looks. "The family was moved to the private waiting room outside the surgical area. They're waiting for you there," the first nurse said.

Paul nodded and turned, moving swiftly in that direction.

The Black family were all sitting anxiously. Simone's father was pacing the floor, Parker trying to get him to calm down and sit.

The patriarch snapped. "I'll sit when I know what's going on with my daughter," he was saying as Paul moved into the room.

At the sight of him, they all jumped to their feet, throwing questions in his direction faster than he could catch them. He held up a hand to stall the comments and gestured for them to all take a seat. He moved to the empty chair beside Simone's mother and took the woman's hand, squeezing it gently.

"Simone is still in surgery," he started, pausing as he felt the emotion bubble in his throat and tears burn hot behind his eyelids. He took a swift inhale to regain his composure. "She was shot twice in the back. One bullet lodged centimeters from her heart and the other exited out of her abdominal area. There is a lot of internal damage. She has a wonderful team supporting her but it's going to be a while before we know anything. Dr. Dayton is the premier cardiothoracic surgeon here at the hospital and he is working with Dr. Kennedy, who heads our surgical department. I trust them both with my own life, so she's in the best hands. They're doing everything they can to save Simone. Right now, she's stable, but her condition is…is critical," he said, his voice breaking.

Judith pressed her free hand against the back of his and squeezed his fingers. Paul lifted his gaze to meet hers evenly. "What about the baby?" she asked.

"Baby? What baby?" Vaughan snapped, taking a step forward. She shot a look around the room, then glanced back toward Paul.

Paul looked from one face to the other, as well. Simone had planned to tell the rest of her siblings about the pregnancy at Sunday dinner. She'd been excited about sharing her news and had only hoped Ellington and Mingus— mostly Ellington—wouldn't spoil the moment for her.

"Simone is pregnant," he said. "We were planning on telling you all this weekend. But we won't know anything for a while. She's lost a lot of blood and with her injuries and the stress on her body, they're not sure she'll be able to maintain the pregnancy." His voice cracked a second time, hot tears burning against the back of his eyelids. Even as the words had left his mouth, Paul couldn't begin to fathom what he would do if anything happened to either of them. But he knew it would break them both if they lost the baby.

"That baby comes from good stock," Jerome said. "He's a fighter. He'll be fine."

Paul smiled ever so slightly. Simone had already declared their child a girl so he could just imagine what she would have to say about her father's proclamation. He welcomed Jerome's optimism, no matter what the baby's sex.

"How long do they think the surgery's going to take?" Mingus asked.

Paul shook his head. "It might be a few hours. We just don't know."

Silence filled the space and Paul realized he was struggling not to cry. He suddenly felt a hand on his shoulder and looked up to see Simone's father fighting back his own tears.

"We gotcha, son. You can trust that. There's not a soul here in this room, in this family, who isn't here to support you. But Simone is going to need you more than she is ever going to need any of us, so have your moment, then pull yourself together. I have never trusted my baby girl with anyone before but I'm trusting her with you. Don't make me regret that!"

"Thank you, sir," Paul said softly. He swiped at his eyes with the back of his hand.

Parker stepped forward. "Can you give me a statement, Paul? It won't take long," he said. gesturing toward the door with his head.

Paul nodded, rising from his seat. He followed Parker, Mingus, Armstrong and their father into the hallway.

Parker paused for a moment as a family of three strolled past, then he turned his attention back to Paul. "What do you remember? We have a few witnesses who say they think the shooter was a woman. The hospital's security cameras caught a glimpse of the car, but everything happened so quickly, we don't have many leads."

Paul thought back to that moment and what he could recall. He'd been singularly focused on Simone, her hand pressed against his arm, her smile bright. Just the nearness of her had calmed his nerves and then all hell broke loose.

But he did remember the car that had careened off, a late-model Jaguar, and only because he had looked up just as it sped toward the highway spinning rubber along the way. He hadn't seen the driver, but he knew enough to give Simone's brother a name.

"Vivian Lincoln," he said. "I'd bet my last dollar that if she didn't pull the trigger, she knows who did," he added, filling them in on all that had happened just an hour earlier.

"Find her and bring her in for questioning," Jerome commanded, "and call Judge Preen for a warrant to do a search of every place she's shown her face in the last forty-eight hours. Make it as broad as you think you need it to be to get the job done."

Parker nodded. "Yes, sir. The media is also looking for a statement. What do you want me to tell them?"

"We have no official comment at the moment. I am personally focused on my daughter's recovery," Jerome said. He turned toward Mingus, his voice dropping to a harsh whisper. "Call your reporter friend. Leak whatever you think will help us get the most traction about this Lincoln woman and that damn drug company. Put the word out that if they had anything to do with this, I will be coming for them."

Mingus gave his father a nod and turned on his heel, disappearing toward the end of the hallway.

"I need to stay with your mother, but I want you on this," the patriarch said to his sons. "We'll call you as soon as your sister gets out of surgery. Until then, you find who did this. Use whatever resources you need."

Armstrong and Parker nodded, both men exchang

ing a look. Each one extended his hand toward Paul, then bumped shoulders in a one-armed embrace. As he watched them disappear behind Mingus, Paul realized he was suddenly privy to the inner workings of the Chicago police force that few others were privileged to see.

He recalled a previous conversation with Simone once, when the media and local politicians were in an uproar about their newly minted superintendent. People were in a furor about her father's stance on police tactics. In a community with a historic distrust of law enforcement, he followed the law as long as the law allowed him to do his job to the best of his ability.

When necessary, Jerome and company didn't hesitate to walk a very fine line and the family didn't always follow the rules of protocol to get the job done. For them, the ends justified the means. And unapologetically, they were determined to do whatever was needed to get justice for Simone. Paul was grateful for them because in that moment all he could focus on was Simone's recovery.

Jerome gave Paul a look. "My wife's a strong woman but she's having a hard time with this. She feels helpless and she just wants to do something to help Simone get past this. I should be out there looking for the shooter, but I need to stay close. Just in case," he said.

Paul nodded his understanding. "I know how she feels," he said as they moved back through the door.

Inside the waiting room, Judith sat with her legs crossed, her top one bouncing with nervous energy. "One of the nurses brought us coffee," she said. pointing to a half-dozen paper cups filled with French roast. "If either of you is hungry, she said someone would gladly go get us something to eat."

"I don't have much of an appetite," Jerome said.

"None of us do, Daddy," Vaughan interjected. She rose

from her seat to give her father, and then Paul, a hug. "Are you okay?" she questioned, eyeing Paul with visible concern.

Paul gave her a look. He wasn't okay. He was nowhere near being okay. He felt lost, and broken, struggling with being on the outside when he wanted to be by Simone's side, ensuring everyone else was doing their job and doing it well. He shrugged his shoulders. "I'll be better when your sister is back in my arms, safe and sound."

Vaughan gave him a smile. "I have faith that will happen sooner than you realize."

Paul moved to the seat beside the matriarch. "Is there anything I can do for you, Judge Black?"

"You can start by calling me Judith. We're family and family doesn't stand on formality." She gently tapped the back of his hand with her palm.

"Yes, ma'am."

The Blacks chatted casually together, everyone clearly trying to mask their concerns and frustration. Paul appreciated being able to catch up with Simone's siblings, their discussions giving him something else to focus on. And even with the company to distract him, he still found himself wondering what might happen if surgery didn't go well. The mere thought of losing Simone kept him on edge and barely able to function.

It was almost five hours later when the two surgeons, the head of the obstetrical department and the hospital administrator came to speak with them. Everyone's anxiety rose tenfold, the air so thick in the room it could have been cut with a knife.

Paul jumped from his seat first, moving forward to meet them. His gaze shifted from one to the other trying to read their expressions. His heart raced, his blood pressure sky high. "How did it go?" he questioned anxiously.

"How's my daughter?" Judith asked at the same time, her hands wringing nervously together.

Paul reached for the matriarch's hand, tangling his fingers with hers. Judith gave him a slight squeeze, a gesture meant to calm them both. Jerome moved to his wife's other side, an arm sliding around her waist as they all stood holding each other up.

"If you don't mind, why don't we all take a seat?" Dr. Dayton said. "We've been on our feet for a good little while. Now, are you all related to Simone?"

"We're her parents," Jerome answered. "Dr. Reilly is the father of our daughter's baby and these three are her siblings." He pointed toward Vaughan, Ellington and Davis who hovered behind them.

Paul seemed to read the man's mind. "You can speak freely. I'm sure Simone's mother, Judge Judith Harmon Black, will confirm they have Simone's healthcare proxy. And I'll personally attest that Simone would want you to disclose her information to her family.

The hospital's administrator nodded in agreement. "It's fine," Dr. Clarke said. "I know them personally and the Black family have been long time supporters of the hospital."

As the family moved to sit back down, Dr. Kennedy picked up the conversation. "Simone came through the surgery nicely. She's still in recovery and we plan to keep her there a little longer before we move her to ICU. There was significant internal damage and bleeding but luckily the bullet in her abdomen didn't hit any vital organs."

"The bullet lodged near her heart was trickier," Dr. Dayton said. "It was just a millimeter away from puncturing the left chamber. We also didn't realize until we got in there that she had a third bullet lodged just an inch from her aorta," he continued. "We successfully removed them both and don't anticipate any residual complications."

"What about the pregnancy?" Paul questioned, his gaze turning to the third physician in the room. Anxiety flooded through him, the nervous energy spilling out of him.

Dr. Mabel Tripodi smiled, the gesture consoling. "Only time will tell. But you've got a strong little guy there and his mother is even stronger. We are going to treat her pregnancy as a high risk for now. You need to understand that Simone's body has been through major trauma. And it's also still very early in this pregnancy. Right now, I'm concerned about her blood pressure. It's been a little sketchy and that doesn't help. If it becomes too much on Simone and the baby, with everything they've both been through, there is always the risk her body will spontaneously abort, and she'll miscarry."

There was a collective gasp as that news settled in. Paul took a deep breath, his knees beginning to shake and the muscles across his back tightening. The news wasn't anything he hadn't expected, but hearing it stated out loud wreaked havoc on his already shaky nerves and he struggled to maintain his composure. He had questions, many of them, but he wanted to be respectful of her parents and the concerns he knew they had.

"When can we see her?" Jerome questioned.

"It'll probably be at least another hour and only two of you at a time for a few short minutes. The ICU nurses are a tough bunch, so don't be offended if they throw you out at any time," Dr. Kennedy said.

Dr. Clarke interjected. "Superintendent Black, Judge Black, I want you to know that your daughter is receiving the best medical care. I'm sure Dr. Reilly will attest to the fact that she has the best team rooting for her recovery. And if there is anything at all that I or my office can do for you, please do not hesitate to contact me. We hate that this happened. And Superintendent, I'm sure you know better than any of us how much we all wish we could do more to combat the tragic shootings that occur daily here in Chicago."

Jerome nodded. "I appreciate you and your staff cooperating with my men. We definitely want to get as many guns off our streets as we can."

Paul stood up, about to burst out of his skin. "I'd like to check on Simone, please."

"She's still in recovery," Dr. Dayton said. "That's really not…"

"I know the protocols," Paul replied firmly.

Simone's physicians exchanged a quick look with the administrator.

"That should be fine," Dr. Clarke said. "As long as you have no objections, Superintendent? Judge Black?"

"None at all," Judith answered. "Dr. Reilly is the father of our daughter's baby and one of her emergency contacts. She trusts him explicitly and he is privy to all her medical concerns. He has our permission to advocate for her health however he sees fit."

"Thank you," Paul said.

"I'll walk with you," Dr. Tripodi said. She shook hands with everyone in the room and she and Paul made their exit.

When they were out of earshot, the family behind them, Paul asked, "Colleague to colleague, Mabel, what's her prognosis? Are we going to lose this baby?"

"Paul, you know better than any of us that I can't answer that with any certainty. Simone has a long recovery ahead of her. This pregnancy isn't going to make that easy. Only God knows for certain what will happen from here.

Friend to friend, I will do everything in my medical power
to help you both see this pregnancy to term. But if I were
you and you believe in a higher power, I'd start praying."

Paul nodded his head slowly. "Praying is the only thing
I've been able to do."

Chapter 17

Hours after surgery ended, Paul was back in his hospital office when the Black brothers came strolling in. It was well after midnight and Paul had been there most of the day. He'd spoken to his brother twice, Oliver promising to be there on the next flight headed out of Atlanta. Simone was resting comfortably in the intensive care unit and they had specific instructions to contact him immediately if there was any change to her condition. Her mother had refused to leave, and the last time Paul had gone down to check on her, they had made Judith comfortable in a reclining chair in the corner of the room.

The brothers all found a seat, making themselves at home. It didn't take rocket science for Paul to figure out they were there about the case and he was eager to hear what they had learned.

"Have you seen the news?" Ellington questioned.

Paul shook his head. "No. Why?"

"You need to," Davis responded. He reached for the remote control on the small television in the corner of the office and turned the device to the local news station.

The evening newscaster was standing on the steps of the hospital, a microphone in hand. The hospital signage was just over his left shoulder, the angle just so to capitalize on the location and put him screen center. The lights from the emergency entrance illuminated the shot.

"This is Wesley Wallace and I am here at Northwestern

Memorial Hospital where a thirty-four-year-old attorney and former state prosecutor is in critical condition, suffering from gunshot wounds and struggling to survive!"

The camera transitioned to a shot of the hospital steps where the offense occurred; multiple police officers stood around assessing the scene. The reporter continued. "Right now, a community is sending up prayers for the daughter of the Chicago police Superintendent, Jerome Black. His daughter, Simone Black, was critically wounded by gunfire in a drive-by shooting this afternoon. Friends and family posted these images of Ms. Black, a local attorney now in private practice, on social media. Her parents and family are by her side in the hospital tonight and are asking for prayers."

The camera spotlighted two nurses, capturing their comments in quick sound bites.

"My heart goes out to the family. I can't begin to imagine what they must be feeling."

"This was such a senseless crime!"

There were more shots of the crime scene and the police as the reporter continued to narrate the story.

"Police say Ms. Black was preparing for a press conference to announce a class-action lawsuit against drug giant Lender Pharmaceuticals and the hospital's decision to pull the drug Halphedrone-B and two other blood-pressure medications pending the results of an FDA investigation into contamination allegations. Right now, police are looking to see if cameras picked up the assault and images of the shooter who is still out there. They are not saying whether or not Ms. Black was targeted."

The camera returned to the reporter. "Witnesses say that a silver Jaguar was seen speeding away from the scene. Chicago police are asking people to come forward and call Crime Stoppers if they have any information. This is Wesley Wallace for ABC 7 Chicago. Back to you, Mark."

The scene shifted to the studio and the news desk.

"Thank you, Wesley. And in related news, John Mitchell Lender, CEO and founder of Lender Pharmaceuticals, was found dead this evening in what is believed to be a self-inflicted gunshot wound. Police are not saying if the two shootings are in any way connected. Lender Pharmaceuticals develops and produces medicines and vaccines for a wide range of medical disciplines and has a net worth in excess of fifty-four billion dollars. We will keep you posted as we learn more information."

Davis turned off the TV, and all the brothers turned back to stare at Paul.

Paul sat back in his chair, not knowing when he'd shifted forward in his seat. Hearing them talk about Simone had made him cringe with hurt, hating that what had happened had been reduced to an assortment of emotionless soundbites. But the revelation that John Mitchell Lender was dead suddenly splayed his curiosity wide open. "Was it a suicide?" he questioned, turning toward Parker.

Parker and Armstrong exchanged a look. "We don't think so," he answered. "It's just too convenient and the initial forensics don't support that story. But someone has gone to great lengths to make it look like one. And conveniently, the gun found beside him was the same caliber as the weapon used to shoot Simone."

"We're still waiting on the ballistics report, but I'm betting it's the same gun," Armstrong said.

"Which would tie the two cases together and put Simone's shooting on him. And attribute his death to guilt," Parker surmised.

"But you don't think that's what happened?" Paul asked again.

There was a loud pause, no one saying anything.

"If it were that neat, it would allow your friend Vivian Lincoln to slide right into the CEO position," Mingus interjected. "She stands to inherit all of his stock, which would give her controlling interest in the business and make her a very wealthy woman."

"So, the bigger question then becomes," Ellington added, "what do you believe, Paul? Do you think Vivian Lincoln's hands are clean in all of this?"

Paul shook his head emphatically. "Hell, no. Not at all," he answered without hesitation.

Parker nodded. "We don't think she's innocent in all of this, either."

"So how do you prove it?" Davis asked.

Silence filled the space a second time. The quiet felt stifling, nothing but the sound of a ticking clock and the scuttle of nurses on their evening rounds outside the door.

"How about a confession?" Paul suddenly asked.

"We always welcome a confession," Parker answered. "How do you propose to make that happen?"

Paul stood. "I have an idea."

The decision to keep Simone sedated in a drug-induced coma had been for her benefit, giving her body time to simply rest and heal. Another two hours had passed before Paul was able to relieve her mother and sit by Simone's side. The matriarch hadn't wanted to move, but Armstrong had insisted, finally convincing his mother that she needed as much rest as her youngest daughter.

Paul anticipated being with her most of the morning until Judith returned, wanting to stay with her baby girl. He fully understood because until Simone opened her eyes and gave him one of her snarky comments, he knew there was little else he'd be able to accomplish. He needed to sleep, but rest avoided him, in case he closed his eyes and missed something. He reached for her medical chart outside the room's door, reading through all the doctors' notes. He had a question or two and he made a few mental notes to follow up with them once the staff changed shifts and they made their new day rounds.

She looked fragile, he thought as he stood staring down at her. Her mother had brushed her daughter's hair, wrapping it with a pretied silk slip-on scarf. He knew Simone would appreciate the gesture. Cords connected her to machines that were monitoring her vital signs. Her blood pressure was still erratic and a cause for concern, but the doctors were still optimistic about her having a full recovery.

Paul blew a soft sigh as he drew the backs of his fingers down the side of her face. She was tough as nails and he trusted that in no time at all she'd be back to herself and giving him a hard time. He didn't have the same trust about their baby but as one of the nurses had pointed out, they'd seen things happen that none of them could ever explain. It would be God's will and he continued to pray that God knew his and Simone's hearts.

He leaned to kiss her cheek then moved back to that recliner. He pushed it closer to the bed so that he could reach out to hold Simone's hand. It was only hours later, when Judith returned and woke him up, that he'd realized he'd been sleeping soundly, his fingers still locked tightly with Simone's.

Paul's decision on calling Vivian Lincoln to offer his condolences on her loss came with its own level of anxiety. After spending time with Simone and her mother, he'd gone back to Simone's house to shower and change. Beginning to feel like himself again, he sat down and ate a bowl of cereal and milk. After calling the hospital to check once again on Simone, he sat down to set things in motion, hoping what he planned wouldn't come back to bite him in the ass.

Vivian had been surprised to hear from him, or she pretended to be. Paul had used that to his advantage because he was pretending. Pretending to be a concerned friend as he spun a web of lies as he talked to her.

"I do have some compassion, Vivian. Mr. Lender was a leader in the drug business. His initial efforts in the game served many people well. I believe in giving credit where credit is due. I was also concerned about you. I know this can't be easy."

"That's kind of you to say. He was dedicated to the business. I hate that he was in so much emotional pain that he would take his own life!"

"I also wanted to apologize," Paul continued. "During your visit the other day we both said some pretty awful things to each other."

"I agree and I want you to know that I was just talking out of frustration. The lawsuit and all..." Her voice trailed off, leaving the comment open for interpretation.

Paul took a breath. "Let's not talk about that. Hopefully, with everything that's happened, we can resolve it privately and make it all go away."

"If it could be that easy," Vivian gushed.

"I understand. I also need to apologize for standing you up when we ran into each other in Detroit. My schedule blew up on me and I just needed to take off."

"I admit, Paul, that did hurt my feelings."

"I would never purposely hurt you. I'm not that kind of man. In fact, if I'm honest, I must admit that I was a little intimidated. You're a beautiful woman and you've dated some very eligible men, if I believe what I've read in the tabloids. I've questioned if I would be able to measure up." Paul was grateful they weren't face-to-face. He pretended to gag, pointing his index finger toward the back of his throat.

Vivian giggled. "Fake news," she said. "Most of it anyway. And if I didn't think you'd make the cut I wouldn't have shown any interest." She giggled again.

Paul rolled his eyes a second time. If he could have reached through the phone line he would have pulled her through the device and wrung her thin neck. He'd never been a violent man, but it was taking everything in him not to rage, wanting to punish her for putting Simone in that hospital bed. He took a deep and held it before he spoke. "Well," he said, another lie rolling off his tongue, "I hope we can still be friends and move forward."

"About that lawsuit…" she started.

Paul interrupted her. "I regret that as well, but what I was seeing frightened me."

"I so wish you had come to me first. I'm sure I could have explained everything so that your concerns would have been alleviated. But not to worry. Our team here is handling things."

"Well, I'm not sure what's going to happen. I don't know if you heard, but the attorney on the case was shot in a drive-by yesterday afternoon. They're not sure she's going to make it."

"Tch, tch, tch!" Vivian exclaimed. "I did hear that and it's such a shame. Have you heard whether or not they have any leads yet?"

"No," Paul responded. "I do know they're questioning whether or not Mr. Lender's death was related. Because of the lawsuit, of course."

"I do know he was very upset about the allegations against him. But I don't want you to blame yourself. You couldn't have known he'd take things so personally."

"No, I couldn't have known that," Paul replied.

There was suddenly an awkward silence and Paul knew he needed to do something to change that. He took a deep breath.

"I don't want to take up any more of your time, Vivian. I'm sure you need to get back to your family. Perhaps we can get together for a drink sometime soon?"

"How about tonight?" she asked.

The question stunned him, coming out of the blue. He didn't know what he had expected, but he hadn't expected her to jump at the bait so quickly. Now he wondered if maybe she had plans for him that he hadn't anticipated.

After agreeing to meet her, he was even more conflicted when she insisted he come to her home. Her excuses as to why she couldn't go out had run the gamut from her not being dressed, to the fact she didn't feel like going out, and each excuse escalated with a hint of sexual innuendo. When they'd settled on a time, he disconnected the call, turning to look at Mingus and Armstrong and feeling like a deer caught in headlights.

"Let's get a mic and camera on you," Armstrong said.

"Are you sure she won't be able to tell that I'm wired?"

"The only way she's going to know is if you take your clothes off to show her."

Mingus laughed. "I wouldn't let that happen if I were you." He jostled his brother's arm. "Can you see him trying to explain that one to Simone?"

Paul shook his head. "Not funny. You both know Simone would kill me!"

"That's putting it mildly. Simone would crush you like

a bug, revive you and do it again just to make sure you suffered!"

"Well, since y'all are putting me up to this, I can't do anything that will get you killed, too. Because she would crush all of us!"

"I know that's right!" Mingus quipped, still chuckling under his breath.

"Just try to relax," Armstrong emphasized. "If you get nervous and start sweating you might short out the system and electrocute yourself."

Paul laughed, the nervous chuckle sounding awkward to his own ear. He was suddenly having second thoughts, questioning if he could do what was needed without showing his hand. Not wanting Simone's brothers to see his discomfort, he deflected. "So, is this how you all get rid of your sister's boyfriends?" he asked, trying to ease the tension that had risen in his heart.

Mingus shook his head. "Nah! I just tell them to go away."

Armstrong nodded. "We all do. We can be very convincing."

There was a moment of pause and then the three burst out laughing. The moment of levity eased the tension, necessary so that they weren't all consumed with rage and sorrow, worrying about what would happen next.

"If you get into trouble and need our help, just say your safe word. We'll be there before you know it."

"Safe word?"

"Something easy that lets us know you're in trouble. A word you won't forget in a pinch," Armstrong added.

Paul nodded, a slight smile pulling at his mouth. "French toast."

Mingus grimaced. "French toast?"

"It's the only thing your sister can cook and cook well."

Laughter filled the room a second time.

The next few minutes were spent taping a microphone and battery pack to his upper torso so that it wouldn't be easily exposed. Armstrong explained how the micro camera hidden in his lapel pin worked. After checking all the connections and testing the volume levels, the two brothers wished him good luck and sent him on his way. They followed behind him in an unmarked van.

The ride to Vivian's was fraught with nervous energy. Paul talked into the microphone the entire time, fighting to dispel the anxiety that had him wanting to turn around and change his mind. The idea of playing on Vivian's romantic interest in him had sounded like a good idea at first, but now he was having second thoughts. Maybe, he mused, she wasn't as enthralled as he sometimes imagined. Perhaps she was wanting to get him before he was able to get her. Maybe they were all wrong and Vivian didn't have anything to do with Simone's shooting. His cell phone rang, lighting up on the car's dashboard. He depressed the answer key, the Bluetooth connection filling the vehicle's audio system.

"Stop talking," Armstrong admonished. "You're driving yourself crazy."

"You're driving us crazy," Mingus yelled.

Paul laughed. "Sorry about that. I was just trying to pass the time."

"Just practice your pick-up lines. This woman is looking to get into your pants. Work that and make it work for you. Show us that romantic side Simone is always bragging about."

"Just don't screw this up," Armstrong chided. "This may be the only opportunity we get to nail this broad."

Paul nodded, even though neither man could see him. "I know what I'm doing," he said. He took a deep breath, thinking of Simone and the baby and what had put them all in this position in the first place. After a quick call to the hospital to make sure nothing had changed with her condition, he stepped out of his car. His jaw tightened and his anger rose tenfold, fueling his objective. "I've got this," he said, signaling he was ready. "You don't have to worry about me."

Vivian's luxurious residence was located in Lakeshore East, in one of Chicago's newest high-rise apartment buildings. Paul was slightly taken aback when Vivian opened the door wearing a sheer red negligee that was super short and cut extremely low. Double D breasts looked like they were about to explode past the expensive lace and the hem barely covered a matching lace thong. He suddenly broke out into a sweat, fighting not to let his disgust show on his face. Armstrong's comment about him electrocuting himself suddenly flooded his thoughts.

"Wow!" he exclaimed, as he stepped through the entrance, his grin like a mask settling in place. "I wasn't expecting…"

Vivian pressed her index finger to his lips to stall his comment. "I thought I'd surprise you."

"Well, I'm definitely surprised," Paul said. "You look incredible."

"You are exactly what I need tonight!" she said as she grabbed his hand and pulled him inside to the living room. "Let me pour you a drink. I make a mean cocktail. Just tell me what your booze of choice is."

"No. Thank you. I don't drink."

"How can you not drink?"

"It's not a habit I ever picked up because I'm usually on call at the hospital."

"The hospital is *why* I drink," she said. "I've always

hated pushing meds at doctors, going from door to door like some snake-oil salesman. And everyone there is always sick with some horrible disease."

"That's why it's a hospital!" Paul chuckled. He bit back the snarky comment at the tip of his tongue, wanting to rail at her about the "snake-oil" she and Lender had been peddling to patients.

She shrugged her narrow shoulders. "Whatever." She moved to the bar and poured herself a tumbler of scotch. "I'm glad you came," she said.

Paul faked another smile as he sat down. "Me, too."

Vivian moved to the sofa and dropped down beside him. "I've had a rough few days."

"I understand. Losing someone you care about is always hard."

She waved a dismissive hand, but she didn't say anything.

Paul spoke instead. "I'm glad I can be here to support you."

"I'm a little confused about that. Every time I tried to hook up with you before, you weren't interested. Why now?"

"I told you. I was intimidated. I've never been a big ladies' man and I don't date much."

"What happened with you and that woman you were dating?" Her brow lifted as she stared at him.

Paul felt the muscles in his face slide into a deep frown, a nervous twitch pulling at his eye. "It didn't work out," he lied.

A look crossed the woman's face. Like she had questions, or maybe knew something he didn't. Instead of commenting, she took another sip of her beverage. When she spoke, her tone had changed. "You disappoint me, Dr. Reilly."

Revelation simmered in Paul's heart. He instinctively knew he had made a mistake as she stood up and moved back to stand in front of the bar. He knew he needed to think fast, still unsure what was going through her head. He took a breath. "Why's that?" he asked.

"Why don't you just tell me why you're really here?"

"You invited me."

"It's more than that. You're here pretending to be interested in me and we both know you're not."

Paul continued to play dumb. "Why would you say that?"

"Why did you lie about your girlfriend? I know you were dating that attorney."

Paul hesitated, meeting her gaze evenly. Something unspoken shifted between them, a battle of wills coming to a head. "Why did you shoot her?" he finally asked.

Vivian stared at him. Her eyes narrowed, the lids hooded as she eyed him. "You really have become a problem," she answered. She reached for her cell phone and began to text someone a message.

Paul went on the offense, his anger painting every word. He snapped, "You don't really think you're going to get away with it, do you?"

Vivian laughed, resting her phone back on the bar as she took another sip of her drink. "I've already gotten away with it and you'll never be able to prove otherwise."

"You believe that?"

"Haven't you heard? My poor, depressed father-in-law shot that woman. Then he killed himself. It's so sad."

"So, you killed him, too?"

"You can't prove that, either."

"I could go to the police."

Vivian laughed a second time, her tone bordering on histrionics. "You could, but I'll never let that happen."

"Why? Why did you do it?"

"Why wouldn't I? I now *own* this company. I can afford to make you and the problems you've caused me just go away just like that." She snapped her fingers to emphasize her statement.

"So, you plan to kill me, too?"

"Of course not, you, silly boy!" she said facetiously. "You showed up on my doorstep, raging about what John Mitchell had done. You became violent and I had to defend myself."

"No one's going to buy that."

"You sure about that?"

"I've never been violent toward a woman a day in my life," Paul retorted.

"Then maybe we were having an affair and I tried to break it off? You didn't know how to take rejection well. You broke in when I wasn't expecting you and I thought you were a burglar! Oops! Wouldn't that be tragic?"

It was only then that Paul saw the gun lying on the polished bar top. He suddenly hoped the camera had picked it up and the police team had seen it, too. He refocused his attention on Vivian, assessing how erratic she was becoming, her behavior fueled by too much drink.

"You're quite the storyteller."

"A girl has to be creative."

"I still don't understand. All of this because I discovered you were selling a contaminated drug?"

Vivian shook her head. "Because I was making the company money and you and your do-good histrionics threaten that almighty dollar. Yes, we sold those drugs. And yes, we knew they were no good, but we needed that financial boost. We'd taken a hit with products that had continually been rejected. Millions of dollars sitting in a warehouse rotting away!"

She took another gulp of scotch before continuing. "And John Mitchell, bless his soul, was ready to retire. I had to prove myself worthy of assuming the helm because he wanted to hand the reins of the company to the current chief operating officer. I couldn't let that happen. So, I did what I had to do."

"Those drugs killed innocent people. Children who trusted us to help them." Paul's voice rose slightly.

"It's a hazard of doing business," she quipped.

"And you had to shoot Simone?"

"I had to stall that information from becoming public knowledge until I could get ahead of it. Shifting the dialogue becomes easy when you toss guns and gun violence into the conversation. Had my guys gotten the two of you the first time, we wouldn't be having this conversation!" She shrugged her shoulders.

"And you pulled the trigger on Simone yourself?"

"Don't be stupid. Why would I get my hands dirty when I can pay people to do that for me? All I did was speed past the hospital after you and I talked. It was a nice distraction, don't you think?"

"And killing Lender?"

"He was a dead man walking. Stage four pancreatic cancer. But I couldn't risk him finding out what I had done. That might have gotten me cut from the will."

Paul suddenly wanted to slap the smirk off her face. He clenched his fists tightly, containing the emotion. "So, what now?"

Vivian moved behind the bar, pouring herself another drink. She gulped it down, then slapped the tumbler against the wood surface. Movement in the doorway caught Paul's eye and he turned to see the two men from the night he and Simone had been shot at standing there with their guns raised. Vivian threw the duo her own look.

"Make it look like an accident," she said, as she moved toward the other door.

"Wait!" Paul exclaimed, holding up his hand as he turned toward her.

She turned back around, eyeing him smugly. "Yes?"

"Doesn't a dying man get one last meal? Because I could really use some French toast right about now!" Then everything went black as pain exploded in the back of his head.

Paul later discovered he'd missed most of the excitement. When he came to, Mingus was staring down at him as EMS checked his vital signs. A dozen or more police officers were milling around the apartment and Vivian was in handcuffs.

"Nice job!" Mingus said, giving him a thumbs-up. "And you didn't have to take your clothes off."

Paul groaned as he sat up, a hand clutching the back of his head.

"Sir, you need to lie still," the paramedic intoned.

"I'm good. I'll be all right," he said. He turned back to Simone's brother. "What happened?"

"You said your safe word and the cavalry came running." Mingus shrugged nonchalantly.

"What about Moe and Larry?" he asked, referring to Vivian's two-man goon squad.

"Moe took a bullet, but he'll live. Larry wasn't feeling quite so froggy. He gave himself up without incident."

Paul nodded. "Did you get everything on tape?"

"Audio and video. It should play out nicely in court. If it even gets that far."

Superintendent Black suddenly entered the room. He shook his son's hand and then gave Paul a look. "We're going to need a statement from you, son, as soon as you're feeling up to it."

"Yes, sir."

"That was some nice police work. You made the family proud. And the city of Chicago is indebted to you."

"Thank you, sir."

The patriarch turned back to Mingus. "What about that confession?"

"Parker has the tape. It was all by the book so you shouldn't have any problems with it. Captain Black made sure he got everything he needed."

Jerome nodded. "I need you to escort Dr. Reilly to the hospital, unless he wants to ride there with EMS?"

Paul shook his head. "That's not necessary. I really am good," he said.

"It's necessary," Jerome answered. "Simone's awake and she's asking for you."

Although everyone kept telling her to relax, Simone was finding that difficult. The monitors kept beeping in response to her anxiety and a nurse hovered over her to scrutinize the spikes in her blood pressure.

"Where's Paul?" she questioned again, unhappy with the previous answers to her question. "Why isn't he here?"

Her mother sighed, frustration furrowing her brow. "Paul is on his way, Simone."

"He was shot, wasn't he? Is he dead? You're not telling me something."

"Baby girl, Paul is fine. He needed some rest and he ran home to take a shower. He's on his way. I promise. Now, you need to relax. Your getting upset is not good for you or the baby!"

Simone closed her eyes, focusing on her breathing. She inhaled slowly through her nose and then exhaled out of her mouth. Comprehending that she'd been shot and was in the hospital recovering felt surreal. Knowing that she and her baby had survived was a blessing and all she wanted was for Paul to be there, holding her hand, so she could believe it wasn't just a dream she couldn't escape from. She took another deep breath.

"That's much better," the nurse said, her head bobbing up and down. "Keep thinking good thoughts and I'll be back in a few minutes to look in on you." The woman made one last check of Simone's IV and then she exited the room.

Judith moved back to her daughter's side, pulling up a chair to the bedside. "You had us worried."

"Do they know who did this?"

Her mother nodded. "Your father said they're following up on a few leads and they have their eye on a suspect. But don't you worry about that. You know your father."

Simone nodded. She shifted against the bed's mattress, trying to make herself comfortable. She ached, but the pain was being dulled nicely by some seriously good meds. "Are you and Daddy good?" she suddenly asked. "With each other, I mean."

Judith smiled. "Why would you ask me something like that, Simone?"

Simone didn't miss the slight twitch in her mother's face, the muscle above her eye constricting. "We've all been worried about you. You two have secrets and that scares us sometimes."

Her mother chuckled, her tone slightly strained. "Your father and I have issues like every other married couple. But we love each other, and we love our family. There is nothing between us that any of you need to be concerned about."

Simone gave her mother a slight nod. "Okay. Tell Vaughan. She and Ellington are scared."

"I will. But you need to rest. We want you home and you can't come home if you don't take care of yourself."

"I want Paul. He should be here."

"Paul's coming, baby. He'll be here very soon."

Simone closed her eyes and seemed to drift off for a split second. She suddenly opened them again, reaching for her mother's hand.

"I think this baby is a boy."

Her mother's smile widened. "What makes you think that?"

"I saw him. I was holding him in my arms, and he was smiling up at me. He said his name is Nino Jerome Reilly."

"Nino?"

"For Nina Simone. Like his mommy!"

"That's a beautiful name."

"He's a beautiful baby!" she muttered as she drifted back off to sleep. "He's so beautiful! Just like his daddy."

The next time Simone opened her eyes Paul was sitting in the chair by her side. She could feel a wide grin spread across her face. He smiled back as they locked gazes, taking each other in. Everything in their small world felt right again, joy rising like a phoenix from the ashes.

"Hey there, sleepyhead!" Paul whispered loudly.

"Hey yourself! I was starting to think that you were dead," Simone replied. "They couldn't find you!"

"I'm not going anywhere, and neither are you. How are you feeling?"

"Like I've been run over by a tractor trailer."

"That's to be expected."

"Tell me the truth—how's our baby? And I want the

doctor answer, not the boyfriend-trying-to-be-protective answer."

Paul nodded. "Tough as nails. He's hanging in here, too. He needs you to be strong for him, though. So, you need to rest and do what the doctors tell you to do." Paul squeezed her hand, entwining their fingers together easily.

"Someone shot me," she said, an air of surprise in her voice.

"I think they were trying to shoot me," he answered.

"It was that witch Vivian, wasn't it?"

He nodded again. "Your father and brothers slapped the handcuffs on her a few hours ago. It's over. We got a full confession about her involvement with the drug scheme, your shooting and the murder of John Mitchell Lender."

"She killed John Mitchell Lender?"

"Sadly, yes she did."

"I told you she was crazy. We are lucky to be alive."

"Yes, we are."

"You need to listen to me more often."

"Yes, dear."

"I mean it, Paul! I am a great judge of character and everything about that woman screamed there was something not right about her."

"I know."

"I saved you. Just imagine what might've happened if I hadn't come back into your life."

Paul smiled. "You are the best thing that has ever happened to me, Simone Black!"

Simone reached for the front of his shirt and pulled him toward her to be kissed. "And don't you ever forget it," she said as she captured his lips with her own.

Chapter 18

Simone spent six weeks recovering from her injuries. All six of those weeks were passed in the hospital to alleviate concerns with her pregnancy. Paul never left her side, every waking moment spent encouraging her to do what the doctors ordered. Simone had proven herself to be a difficult patient at best, wanting only to return to her job to follow the prosecution of Vivian Lincoln and get back to work on their lawsuit.

Lender Pharmaceuticals was still trending in social media. Halphedrone-B had been recalled and surviving patients had been provided with free medication from one of their competitors. Their stock had plummeted and virtually overnight Vivian's gold mine had become completely worthless, overrun with lawsuits and legal entanglements that would eventually shutter its doors.

Overseas, Paul's patients were invigorated, suddenly thriving in ways many had thought unfathomable. Hope was renewed in communities that had lost sight of such months earlier. Vaughan had arranged a week-long media blitz for Paul to tell his story and shed light on the broader problem of health care challenges in the United States and abroad, and the medical community, politicians and social activists were all stepping up to help. Everyone knew the spotlight wouldn't last long before something or someone else took over the front pages, but they were determined to make the most from the moment as they could manage.

The city of Chicago had honored Paul for his help in bringing down Vivian, and the hospital lauded him as a hero for his efforts to expose Lender Pharmaceuticals for their criminal endeavors. He'd taken a short leave of absence from his patients to devote himself exclusively to Simone's recovery. Their time together was golden as they negotiated their future life together and imagined what life would be like when their son was born.

"Simone, I'm not giving up my mission work."

Simone threw up her hands in frustration. "I'm not asking you to give it up, Paul. But I am saying you need to cut back once Nino is born. He needs his father around. Who's going to teach him how to be a man if you're halfway around the world?"

"First, I'll be around to teach my son how to be a man. You can trust that! And secondly, have you met your father and your brothers? Nino will not lack male role models."

"Well, I'm only agreeing to traveling with you on two mission trips per year."

"Well, that's something. But I'm willing to bet that once you do those two, you'll want to do more, and it'll be a great way to teach our son how to look out for others who might not be as blessed as he is."

"You'll have to tell my parents. But I warn you, my father isn't going to be happy about any of it."

Paul laughed. "Your father loves me. He and I are great friends. He will be just fine! Now, are you ready for them to bring the wheelchair so we can get you out of here?"

"I've been ready. I don't know what's been taking you so long."

Paul shook his head. "Good, because we're late for Sunday dinner. I'm sure your mother is ready to send out a search team for us."

"For me maybe. I am carrying the heir to the Black family throne. You just knocked up their daughter!"

Paul laughed. "You are in for such a surprise after that baby gets here and you no longer get any attention!"

Simone rolled her eyes skyward and then she laughed with him, joy resonating warmly through the room.

An hour later Paul held her hand as they entered the Black family home. They called out in greeting as they maneuvered their way toward the family room and the back of the house. Loud cheers greeted them as they stepped into the space. Vaughan, Joanna and Armstrong's wife, Danni, had decorated the room with balloons and streamers and an oversize welcome-home sign hung from the ceiling.

Simone's parents stood together arm in arm, tears streaming from her mother's eyes. The matriarch stepped forward to give them both a hug.

"I can't tell you how happy this day makes me!" Judith said. She swiped at her eyes with her fingers.

"We missed you, kid," Vaughan echoed.

"Yeah, yeah, yeah!" Davis said teasingly. "We missed you like a fungus!"

The room laughed as everyone stepped up to embrace Simone and welcome her back into the fold.

Oliver stepped forward to give her a big bear hug.

"I'm so glad you made it," Simone exclaimed. "I was afraid you were stuck in Atlanta!"

"I wouldn't miss this for anything in the world," he said as he and Paul bumped fists.

Oliver gestured to a man standing behind him. "Let me introduce you to my new friend," he said as he gave her a wink of his eye. "He's a police officer!"

Simone grinned.

"Simone, this is Liam. Liam, this is my brother's fiancée, Simone."

The man named Liam stepped forward to shake her hand."

She shook her head. "We're huggers around here," she said as she wrapped her arms around the man's shoulders. "It's very nice to meet you!"

She gave Oliver a look and a thumbs-up over the man's shoulder.

The brother laughed heartily.

Simone laughed with them as Paul guided her to a seat and insisted that she sit down. "You'd think I haven't seen you people in months, the way you all are acting," she teased.

"Baby girl, we're just glad we don't have to go back up to that hospital to see your pretty face," her father interjected.

Simone blew her father a kiss. "I love you, too, Daddy!"

"Well, I don't know about anyone else," Ellington said, "but now that Simone isn't holding up the meal, I'm hungry!"

They all laughed.

"The food is ready. We can all eat," Judith said.

Laughter was infectious as it spread from one room to the other, everyone filing into the dining room to eat. Simone sat back and took it all in. Her hand rested on her abdomen and she sensed that her little bundle of energy was as excited for the experience as she was. She felt Paul looking at her and when she turned to meet his gaze, there was an overwhelming look of love across his face.

"You good?" he asked, leaning to kiss her cheek.

She nodded. "I'm better than good. And as soon as I get some of my mother's lasagna I'm going to be great!"

"I love you," he said, every ounce of his emotion shimmering through his expression.

Simone lifted her face to his, kissing him gently. "I love you, too!"

Jerome suddenly slammed a palm against the table. "Since there's so much love going around the room, someone tell me when you plan to make an honest woman of my daughter. And Mingus, what the hell are you waiting for? Women like Joanna don't grow on trees, son!"

Mingus choked on the glass of tea he'd been drinking. He shot Joanna a look, amused by the heat that colored her cheeks a vibrant shade of red. "How did I get drawn into this?" he said, laughing.

"Well, someone needs to do something. Your mother's ready for another wedding. And more grandchildren!"

The low murmur in the room rose to a thunderous ruckus as they continued to tease and joke with each other. Another thirty minutes passed as they finished off the vegetable lasagna, Caesar salad and homemade crusty bread. Dessert was peach cobbler topped with vanilla ice cream.

As forks dropped against empty plates Judith cleared her throat for their attention. She and Jerome exchanged a look and as Simone watched them, she sensed the mood had suddenly turned serious. Her siblings sensed it as well, quiet rising through the room like a morning mist.

"What's wrong, Mom?" Davis asked, eyeing both of his parents with concern.

The matriarch shook her head. "I'm very happy," she said softly. "Nothing could bring me greater joy than to be surrounded by my family and our friends."

"Then why so melancholy?" Vaughan questioned, she and Simone exchanging a look.

Jerome stood, moving to stand behind his wife's chair.

He pressed his hands to her shoulders, and you could feel her fall back against his strength for support. "Your mother has something she wants to share with all of you."

Oliver held up his hand. "Judge Black, Liam and I can excuse ourselves if you'd prefer. We wouldn't want to intrude…"

Judith shook her head. "Oliver, you're as much family to us as Paul is. And I have a good feeling about Liam." She gave the two men a smile. "In fact, I imagine we might be planning your wedding before I can get Simone or Mingus to even consider the idea."

Everyone around the table laughed. Neither Mingus nor Simone was amused.

"I've considered it," Mingus muttered as he pulled Joanna into his arms and hugged her warmly.

Judith continued. "I'm being blackmailed," she said, the words falling from her mouth with a loud clatter.

Her children all sat upright, shifting forward in their seats.

"I'm telling you this because I have no intentions of giving in to the demands. Your father and I have reached out to the FBI and they're working on the case, but you all need to be prepared because you're going to hear some things about me."

"What kind of things?" Ellington questioned.

"Things in my past that I had hoped would never come to light."

Jerome gently kneaded her shoulders. He pressed a kiss to the top of her head.

"But Daddy knows, right?" Simone asked.

Jerome nodded his head. "Yes, I do," he said.

Armstrong reached for his mother's hand. "What are we going to hear, Mom? You know you can tell us anything, right?"

A tear rolled over her cheek. "Recently, I asked Mingus to find someone for me. A young man named Fabian Scott. Mingus discovered he lives very near here, in Saint Louis."

"So, who is this Fabian Scott and what does he have to do with you being blackmailed?" Parker asked.

Judith swept the table with her eyes, pausing to give them each a look. "Fabian is my son. My eldest son. I gave birth to him when I was seventeen and I gave him up for adoption."

"Whoa," Davis muttered, everyone else falling silent as shock swept through the space.

"Someone has been threatening to expose that information if your mother doesn't vote favorably on a case that's coming up in her jurisdiction," Jerome said. "Your mother wants to reach out to the boy so that he isn't blindsided by the news."

"I don't know if that's a good idea," Ellington said.

"Me, neither," Simone added. "If the adoption was closed and he's not listed in the mutual consent registry, he may not want to be contacted. That might blow up into an even bigger problem for you. And, if your methods to find him were slightly shady…" She hesitated, shooting her brother a look.

"He's registered," Mingus interjected. "He filed to have his information released to his birth parents ten years ago."

"Who's his father?" Davis suddenly questioned.

Judith shook her head. "That's not important right now."

Her youngest son persisted. "I think we have a right to know."

"I think you better check your tone," Armstrong snapped at his brother.

Jerome gave his youngest son a look that sat him back in his seat.

Contrition washed over the younger man's face and he apologized. "I'm sorry," Davis said softly.

"We'll support whatever you need to do," Vaughan said. She rose from her seat to give her mother a hug.

Judith pressed a cloth napkin to the moisture that dampened her cheeks. "I know you all have questions and I'll answer them for you in due time. I promise. Right now, though," she turned toward Ellington, "I need you to sit down with me and your father so we can decide the best way to approach this."

"Yes, ma'am," Ellington replied.

Judith rose from her seat, turning to wrap her arms around her husband's shoulders. Jerome hugged her tightly before she pulled herself from him. She rounded the table to give each of them a hug.

She paused to whisper in Simone's ear. "No matter what your circumstances, you will always do whatever you need to do to protect your child. Just keep trusting your instincts and you, Paul and Nino will be just fine! I love you!"

Simone nodded, fighting back her own tears. She turned to kiss her mother's cheek. Minutes later her parents and Ellington had disappeared up to her office, the door closed firmly behind them.

Parker directed his attention to Mingus. "How long have you known this?"

"A few weeks. Mom asked me to do a little digging and she swore me not to discuss it with anyone."

"What do you know about him?"

Mingus shrugged. "He's an English teacher and he's written a few books."

Vaughan was suddenly looking up Fabian Scott's name

online. "I don't see anything published by anyone called Fabian Scott."

"I never said he published under his name."

"Is he married?"

"Where did he go to school?"

"Does he have any kids?"

They were all throwing questions at Mingus like wild darts being tossed at a country bar. But it quickly became obvious that he had nothing else left to share. He stood up, extending his hand toward Joanna. "We're out of here. I'll catch up with you all later."

"We're leaving, too," Danni said as she and Armstrong exchanged a look. "I'm working a case tonight, so I have to get to the precinct."

"I'm staying," Parker said. "I want to know what the FBI is doing about mom being blackmailed."

"I have questions, too," Davis said. "And she owes us some answers. How could she just give up her child?"

"Don't do that," Vaughan said. "Until Mom's ready to share the details with us you have no right to judge her!"

"Like hell I don't!" Davis snapped.

"What's wrong with you?" Armstrong questioned, eyeing his baby brother suspiciously.

Mingus was still standing in the doorway, Joanna leaning into his side. "You need to tell them," he said, the comment directed at Davis.

"Shut up, Mingus!" his brother snapped.

"Tell us what?" Vaughan asked.

"Nothing!" Davis said. He grabbed a stack of plates from the table and headed into the kitchen to do the dirty dishes.

Silence descended on the room, everyone looking at each other but no one saying anything. The awkward moment passed as quickly as it had arrived.

Paul nodded, changing the subject. "Well, Simone needs to go get some rest. So, we're headed home, too."

"We'll catch a ride back to the hotel with you, if you don't mind," Oliver added.

"I don't recall anyone asking Simone what she wanted," Simone quipped.

Paul met the look she was giving him. "You can't stress yourself out, Simone. You haven't been out of the hospital a full day yet."

"I still want me another piece of cobbler and ice cream," she said.

Vaughan laughed. "She is eating for two now!"

"Simone has always eaten for two," Parker said. "Now she's eating for an army!"

"Whatever! One of you just put me some more dessert into a container, please!"

The ride home was relatively quiet. No one mentioned Simone's mother or the bomb she'd tossed into the room leaving everyone reeling from the fallout. Instead, Simone peppered Liam with questions and by the time they reached their hotel destination, she too was convinced that Liam was a keeper. She liked the man and it was obvious he cared about Oliver.

After saying good-night to the two men, Paul turned the car toward home. He'd just exited off the interstate when Simone grabbed his arm, startling him out of the calm that had surrounded them.

"What's wrong?"

"Nothing. I feel fine. But I don't want to go home."

"Excuse me? Simone, you need to rest."

"I need to be married. How far are we from Vegas?"

Paul laughed. "We are not driving to Vegas!"

"Why not? Don't you want to marry me?"

"You know I want you to be my wife more than any-thing else in this world. You don't need to even ask that question."

"Then let's just do it. Let's elope! Make an honest woman out of me!"

"Is that even possible?" Paul asked, chuckling softly.

"Your father said that," Simone replied, speaking at her stomach. "Never let him forget it, Nino!"

Paul reached a warm palm out and placed it against her tummy. She still wasn't showing but both were acutely aware that their future lay snugly beneath the palm of his hand. Simone was typing into her cell phone, waiting for a page to load. She suddenly waved the device excitedly.

"Okay, so a road trip might be a bit much but there's a nonstop flight leaving at seven tonight. We can be there in four hours and married in five!"

"You're serious?"

"I'm very serious. If I'm going to be divvying up my time going around the world with you, we might as well start now."

"You don't want your family there?"

"They'll be there with us in spirit and we can always Skype them in."

"What about your mother?"

"What about her? My mom has everything handled. You can bet that telling us tonight was only a formality. She already knew what she was going to do and how all of this is going to play out. I'm sure we'll meet my new brother in due time."

Paul hesitated. "I don't know, Simone…"

"Paul Reilly, I love you. I want to be your wife. Will you marry me?"

"I love you too and yes, I will definitely marry you."

"Then you better do it now before I change my mind," Simone said definitively.

Laughter rumbled from Paul's midsection. "Okay, but I'll do all the packing. Let's go to the house—you need to put your feet up, and I'll throw some things into a bag for us."

Simone began to type again into her device. "Good! That's settled. Tickets have been purchased. We can pick them up at the gate."

"And I have one more condition."

"Really, Paul? These tickets are nonrefundable."

"Send a message to your family, and my brother, please. If anyone wants to join us, I'll pick up the tab for their plane tickets, too. We might as well make this a party!"

Simone grinned widely, her smile spreading like a canyon across her face. "I do like how you think, Dr. Reilly!"

Shortly before midnight on the fourteenth of the month, Paul Reilly married Simone Black at The Little White Church in Las Vegas, Nevada. She wore a champagne-colored satin gown borrowed from her mother's closet and courtesy of the hotel's concierge and a talented tailor named Alberto, it fit her to perfection. She carried a bouquet of classic red roses to match her red-bottomed high heels and her mother had finger-waved the short length of her hair into a style reminiscent of the 1920s flapper era. She was stunning and Paul proclaimed her the most beautiful bride he had ever seen in his lifetime.

Paul looked dashing in the one black tuxedo he had owned since forever. As he stood at the chapel altar, waiting for her to descend the aisle, he knew beyond any doubt that he was the luckiest man in the whole wide world. His brother Oliver stood beside him as his best man. Simone's sister Vaughan was her maid of honor.

Her parents had been the first to accept the invitation and they had flown back immediately after the ceremony. Simone's brother Armstrong and his wife were the only ones unable to make it to Vegas, their responsibilities to the Chicago Police Department claiming their time. But they watched the ceremony on their iPads in Armstrong's office at the police station as Davis streamed it to them live.

It was everything any of them could have ever imagined and Jerome giving Paul his blessing just minutes before the ceremony was icing on some very sweet cake. Hours later they lay side by side in the Piazza suite at The Venetian Resort. The luxury accommodations, with marbled floors, oversize king bed and jetted tubs, were the epitome of grace and elegance and afforded them the highest level of comfort. Simone had already decided they wouldn't leave that bed for at least a week.

"You have to be exhausted," Paul said, as he lifted himself up on his elbow, resting his head in his hand as he stared down at her.

"I'm tired, but I feel amazing."

Paul leaned to kiss her lips. "I'm glad we did this. It was the most perfect wedding and I'm happy our family could be here to celebrate with us."

"I love my people and I'm glad they're now your people, too!"

Paul kissed her again, leaning over her gently as she pulled him down against her.

Outside, a partial moon was beginning to disappear behind a cluster of clouds. The evening air was warm, and a gentle breeze blew through the opened balcony door.

Breaking the kiss Paul rolled from her, lowering himself against her side. He wrapped his arm around her torso and hugged her to him. His hands danced lightly against her back and waist, his fingers teasing like the easy caress of a down feather. Simone's eyes closed and then opened and closed again. She turned, pressing herself tightly to him as she tossed her leg over his hip, her naked body kissing his sweetly. Heat billowed between them feeling like someone had lit a match to the furnace.

A few short minutes passed before she was sleeping soundly, whispery snores blowing past her parted lips. Paul took a deep breath as he watched her, feeling his own body beginning to slide into a gentle state of warmth and calm. His own eyes fluttered back and forth, open and then closed. Like every night prior, he lifted her in prayer and thanked God for the blessings that had been bestowed on them. He was grateful. Love had torn them apart and love had reunited them. Life just didn't get any better.

* * * * *

LET'S TALK
Romance

For exclusive extracts, competitions
and special offers, find us online:

 facebook.com/millsandboon

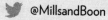 @MillsandBoon

@MillsandBoonUK

Get in touch on 01413 063232

For all the latest titles coming soon, visit
millsandboon.co.uk/nextmonth

MILLS & BOON

THE HEART OF ROMANCE

A ROMANCE FOR EVERY READER

MODERN

Prepare to be swept off your feet by sophisticated, sexy and seductive heroes, in some of the world's most glamourous and romantic locations, where power and passion collide.

HISTORICAL

Escape with historical heroes from time gone by. Whether your passion is for wicked Regency Rakes, muscled Vikings or rugged Highlanders, awaken the romance of the past.

MEDICAL

Set your pulse racing with dedicated, delectable doctors in the high-pressure world of medicine, where emotions run high and passion, comfort and love are the best medicine.

True Love

Celebrate true love with tender stories of heartfelt romance, from the rush of falling in love to the joy a new baby can bring, and a focus on the emotional heart of a relationship.

Desire

Indulge in secrets and scandal, intense drama and plenty of sizzling hot action with powerful and passionate heroes who have it all: wealth, status, good looks…everything but the right woman.

HEROES

Experience all the excitement of a gripping thriller, with an intense romance at its heart. Resourceful, true-to-life women and strong, fearless men face danger and desire - a killer combination!

To see which titles are coming soon, please visit

millsandboon.co.uk/nextmonth

JOIN US ON SOCIAL MEDIA!

Stay up to date with our latest releases, author news and gossip, special offers and discounts, and all the behind-the-scenes action from Mills & Boon...

 millsandboon

 millsandboonuk

 millsandboon

It might just be true love...